A Great New Nation Is Born!

The scene was Yorktown in 1781. General George Washington and his aides were riding to accept the British surrender. Suddenly Washington looked skyward. "What kind of bird is that?" asked a French officer on Washington's staff.

"He is an eagle, suh," called a Virginian. "He is what we call a bald eagle."

"Gentlemen, look upwards, and behold that eagle in the sky," cried the Frenchman, "an American eagle and free as the air in which he flies! Today, my friends, a new nation soars to take a sure place in God's world!"

F. van Wyck Mason
EAGLE IN THE SKY

A BERKLEY MEDALLION BOOK
published by
BERKLEY PUBLISHING CORPORATION

Harold Matson Co., Inc.
22 East 40th Street
New York, N. Y. 10016

SBN 425–02993–X

*BERKLEY MEDALLION BOOKS are published
by
Berkley Publishing Corporation
200 Madison Avenue
New York, N. Y. 10016*

BERKLEY MEDALLION BOOK® TM 757,375

Printed in the United States of America

Berkley Medallion Edition, NOVEMBER, 1975
SECOND PRINTING

TO MY UNCLE
ROCKWELL A. COFFIN, M.D.
A VERY GIFTED PHYSICIAN

AND TO THE MEMORY OF
THOSE PHYSICIANS AND SURGEONS
WHO SERVED AS BEST THEY MIGHT
IN THE
MEDICAL DEPARTMENT OF
THE
CONTINENTAL ARMY
OF
THE UNITED STATES

FOREWORD

IN ATTEMPTING to depict medical men of various sorts as they practiced during the years 1780–81, I have drawn largely on contemporary diaries and letters—a rich but confusing source. Because the same disease was known under various names and the treatments or remedies for it varied so widely, it proved difficult to select ailments recognizable to a modern reader and to select the most interesting of the several treatments. Doctor James Thatcher's invaluable and wonderfully detailed diary of his career, as a physician with the Continental Army, served as the backbone of the medical elements in this tale. My obligations to his memory are as profound as they are numerous.

Certain of my readers may question the small size of the *Grand Turk III* in view of the huge crew she carried on departure from Boston. Yet her dimensions and armament are almost exactly those of the *Rattlesnake,* an American privateer out of Salem, which shipped an even more numerous crew in the same year.

Research conducted at the British Museum, subsequent to the completion of this volume, reveals that Captain David Graves, in command of the flagship H.B.M.S. *London* at the Battle of the Capes, was directly responsible for the flying of contradictory signals: an error which had momentous effects upon American history. Probably the fact that Captain Graves was the commanding Admiral's son diverted from him the just wrath of Vice-Admiral Sir Samuel Hood and Rear-Admiral Sir Francis Drake.

My deep appreciation for invaluable assistance goes once more to Mr. Robert H. Haynes of the Library of Harvard College and to his assistants. To the Enoch Pratt Library of Baltimore and to Mr. Emerson Greenaway, its librarian, I owe a very considerable debt of gratitude, while Doctors Merrel L. Stout and Benjamin Tappan of

Baltimore are heartily to be thanked for their advice on various medical aspects of this story.

My secretary, Miss Justine Gilkey, must be credited with many valuable suggestions and an unfailing enthusiasm which went far towards making the preparation of this book a pleasant task.

F. VAN WYCK MASON

Gunner's Hill
Riderwood, Maryland

EAGLE IN THE SKY

GLOSSARY OF MEDICAL TERMS

**LATE
EIGHTEENTH CENTURY   TWENTIETH CENTURY**

Animal Economy	Bowel Movements
Corruption	Infection
Commotion	Concussion
Costiveness	Constipation
Canine Madness	Hydrophobia
Cramp Colic	Appendicitis, also Typhlitis
Clyster (Glyster)	Enema
Extravasated Blood	Rupture of Blood Vessel
Falling Sickness	Epilepsy
Flux of Humour	Circulation
French Pox	Venereal Disease, Syphilis and/or Gonorrhea
Green Sickness	Anemia
Hip Gout	Osteomylitis
Hallucination	Delirium
King's Evil	Scrofula
Long Sickness	Tuberculosis
Lues Venera	Venereal Disease, Syphilis and/or Gonorrhea
Lung Fever	Pneumonia
Mania	Insanity
Mortification	Infection
Nostalgia	Homesickness
Putrid Fever	Diphtheria
Remitting Fever	Malaria
Sanguinous Crust	Scab
Screws	Rheumatism
Ship's Fever (Jail Fever or Camp Fever)	Typhus
Sore Throat Distemper	Quinsy
Strangery	Rupture or Stricture
Venesection	Bleeding

CONTENTS

CONTENTS

Book One—The Port

PART I—THE NEOPHYTES

PART II—DIVERGENT COURSES

CONTENTS

Book Two—The Sea

PART I—THE BRIG
GRAND TURK III—TWELVE GUNS

PART II—ANNABERG

CONTENTS

PART III—THE HUDSON

Book Three—The River

PART I—EASTERN DISTRICT

PART II—WATERS OF DESTINY

Contents

Book One ★ *The Port*

PART I—THE NEOPHYTES

1. EVE OF THE NEW YEAR, 1780

SABRA STANTON extended slim hands to the fire and over her shoulder watched her uncle's goose-quill pen drive deliberately, precisely, over a new sheet of foolscap on his desk. Doctor William Townsend's students could tell anyone who might be interested that he never permitted himself to become hurried; even during the more critical moments of an amputation he took enough time to work surely and steadily.

The clear, yellow-red flame of a single whale-oil lamp projected her uncle's aquiline profile and neat club wig in faithful silhouette against the study's furthest wall.

That wind, roaring in from the sea and over Boston Harbor, was so cruelly edged that Sabra wished she had selected a thicker cloak to bring Uncle Will Mamma's invitation to New Year's dinner. She wouldn't be a mite surprised if at any minute snow began to fall.

Br-r-r. Seated silent in her chair, Sabra Stanton could see her breath escaping in a series of faint cloudlets. Sophie, the doctor's huge black housekeeper, really should have kindled the consultation room grate hours ago, for, despite this cheery new blaze, the air remained chilly and crept up beneath Sabra's five petticoats to raise goose-pimples on her calves.

As, gradually, the study grew warmer, Sabra commenced to recognize that familiar, and inexplicably stimulating, odor which she knew emanated from row upon row of calfskin-bound volumes ranged across shelves built opposite the mantelpiece. Soon she became aware of other smells—the sharp scents of those herbs and spices she knew to be stored in a fascinating variety of odd-shaped jars and bottles.

Sabra's wide gray eyes wandered upwards and came to rest upon a small plaster bust of Galen glaring down from its pedestal above the study's entrance. Poor Galen! He sadly needed dusting again. Mamma was right; black Sophie would never make better than a tolerable

3

housekeeper. Still, old Sophie's lack of gumption was
fortunate—else she might not have chanced in to witness
what was promising to become a significant little ceremony.

Lord. Uncle Will and his three apprentices were looking solemn as so many stuffed owls—and about as talka-
tive. Quietly, Sabra eased her slippered feet out of those
damp, white pine pattens on which she had crossed the
treacherous ice and mud of Bennett Street and made a little scuffling noise, but nobody cast her a look. Why, a
body could easily delude herself into believing a coro-
ner's inquest to be in progress. Not once during the past
two years could she recall having seen Lucius Devoe sit
so very still.

Again her gaze came to rest upon her uncle's thin and
slightly stooped shoulders. She realized, all at once, that
he was wearing his Sunday coat of mulberry velvet
adorned by dark blue cuffs and a double row of gilt lead
buttons. Glory! This must be more of an occasion than
she'd realized. Like most Boston physicians, William
Townsend customarily attended to his practice in a suit
of unrelieved black. On reflection, Sabra decided that
Uncle Will had not spruced up in honor of his apprentices, but in order to celebrate this eve of the New Year
in the company of his fellow surgeons on duty at that
army hospital away out in Jamaica Plain.

La! How uncommon dashing Lucius Devoe was looking this evening. Hastily Sabra dropped her eyes, aware
that a warm current had commenced to mount, tingling
towards the rim of her bodice. It was irritating, thought
Sabra, to realize that not once in many minutes had the
lean young Jamaican's intense, brightly sombre eyes become fixed upon her. Instead, they were following every
movement of Doctor Townsend's softly scratching goose
quill.

A bold impulse offered itself. Dared she, on such short
notice, invite a comparative stranger into Papa's house?
Why not? Hadn't Papa bade her bring in whomever she
chose, to sample a goblet or two of prime Madeira? As a
rule Papa was most strict but, judging from the jovial
manner in which he had been holding forth when she had
left for Uncle Will's, he wouldn't object. Maybe he'd retire early? Mamma invariably accompanied her spouse
up to bed, so she and Lucius—or Asa Peabody, perhaps,

since Lucius was proving so provokingly inattentive—
might find an opportunity to sit by themselves for a
while.

Deliberately, William Townsend, M.D., thrust his quill
deep into a glass filled with bird shot and with his one
good eye considered the writing he had just completed.
At length he nodded absently, redipped his pen and then
with a bold flourish signed his name.

Now at long last, Lucius Devoe turned to smile at Sabra in her large wing chair beside the fireplace, but she
pretended not to notice, appeared completely absorbed
in watching her uncle place before him a second sheet of
foolscap.

In his usual leisurely fashion Doctor Townsend wrote
the word "Certificate" in large letters across its top;
then, for an instant, the old physician's gaze flickered
over to consider Peter Burnham, a broad-shouldered and
solid young fellow of near twenty-five years. Townsend
saw dark red hair clubbed by a smart tie of dark green
grosgrain ribbon framing a squarish face dominated by
wide-set, dark blue eyes, a short nose and a jaw so strong
as to verge on the pugnacious.

Doctor Townsend felt confident of one thing—Peter
Burnham would fight for whatever he held to be right;
God grant that also he might acquire a greater measure of
patience. Unless all signs failed he should rise high in his
chosen field—that unfashionable and sadly neglected
branch of medicine described as male midwifery.

Sabra, bored, looked out of the window. Sure enough,
it was snowing. Good. On New Year's Day the offal and
trash piled high in the streets of Boston would be hidden
beneath a clean white counterpane.

The old physician's massively modelled countenance,
now blotched with the brown flecks of advancing years,
relaxed. What a deep satisfaction it was to prepare this
third and last certificate Of these three students only Asa
Peabody possessed the emotionally level, but endlessly
inquiring mind of a possibly great physician; trust young
Peabody to pounce upon illogical elements in even the
most approved treatments. The Lord, and Doctor Townsend, knew how willing Asa Peabody was to work. The
young fellow had nigh ruined his eyes from studying too
late by the feeble light cast by cheap and malodorous
beef-tallow candles.

On this third certificate, William Townsend altered his text a trifle to read;

CERTIFICATE
TO ALL WHO SHALL SEE THESE
PRESENTS GREETINGS:

Asa Peabody hath serv'd Apprenticeship under me for two Years, two Months, in Ye Studie and Pracktice of Physicks and Surgery, during which Time he hath prov'd himself Uncommon Studious, Able and Gift'd. Therefore, I can, with full Confidence, Recommend him to Ye Publick as a Bachelor of Medicine excellently Qualified in Ye above Branches.

Wm. Townsend, M.D.

Boston, Massachusetts
1st January 1780.

Doctor Townsend reached into the tail of his best coat and, producing a yellow silk kerchief, wiped from the chill-reddened end of his sharp nose a pellucid drop. Weatherbeaten countenance creased in a smile, he got to his feet, remained absently rubbing together large and deceptively clumsy-appearing hands.

"Sabra, my dear, pray summon Sophie and instruct her to fetch four of the small glasses and a decanter she will find in the corner cupboard."

Asa Peabody's clear brown eyes watched Sabra Stanton's quick and graceful progress across the study. To his eyes, dry and aching after a long day spent in translating the Latin text of Giovanni Morgagni's *De Sedibus et Causis Morborum*, the sight of her nearly matured beauty came as a soothing balm. Right now her carefully coiffed dark brown hair displayed unsuspected copper-red tints by the firelight.

When Sabra returned, followed by black Sophie, she flashed him a vivid, red-lipped smile. Nonetheless he guessed that her attention really was centered upon Lucius Devoe. The old Negress displayed her few remaining teeth in a wide and anticipatory smile when she set down the salver before Doctor Townsend.

Straightening a plain white stock, Asa wished that his black coat—he owned no other—had not become so marked by medicines, ink and certain red-brown splashes of grimmer origin; although he'd scrubbed and scrubbed at them they had proved quite indelible.

"Ahem." Doctor Townsend cleared his throat, peered about in rare amiability. "Young gentlemen, pray I trust you will join me in a tot of Spanish brandy? 'Twas taken by the *Prudence*, privateer, and came as a gift from a grateful patient, one Captain Thomas Park. He hails from Groton in Connecticut, but is nonetheless a most able sea captain. I—ahem—suggest that we toast your future? God knows uncommon resolution is required to even contemplate the possibilities of this coming year." Gravely, all four men lifted their glasses and drank.

Doctor Townsend's blind left eye gleamed white as that of Galen's plaster bust as he raised his glass in Sabra's direction. "My winsome niece, I am pleased you chanced by." Townsend put down his glass and adopted a grave mien. "Gentlemen and fellow physicians; now that you have joined the ancient, honorable and merciful company of physicians and chirurgeons I bid you welcome."

The old man's single pale blue eye studied his ex-apprentices for the last time. Tallest by half a head, Asa Peabody revealed his country origins in clumsy, homemade brogues, white cotton-thread hose and the old-fashioned cut of a homespun coat. His waistcoat was secured by cherry-wood buttons—probably whittled by his own hand. To some people Peabody's features might have seemed a little long his mouth too wide, but the eyes peering steadily from beneath straight and rather heavy brows were large and set well apart.

Probably because Peter Brunham's body was thick and his legs and arms powerfully constructed he appeared bigger than Peabody; yet he wasn't. Such copper-red hair and bold blue eyes were distinctive enough, but Burnham's features were so handsomely proportioned that, in later years, they would inspire Mr. Rembrandt Peale to reproduce them on canvas. Burnham's costume suggested him to be exactly what he was—the son of a prosperous hardware merchant. He wore a dove-gray coat of fine French gabardine, equipped with flat pewter buttons bearing his monogram; black thread hose, black knee breeches. His vest was a gay, sky-blue satin affair lavishly embroidered with yellow flowers of some unidentifiable variety.

Nearest to the fireplace stood Lucius Devoe, looking miserably poor in his only suit of threadbare black serge. Today, in honor of the occasion, he wore at his throat a pathetic scrap of torn and mended lace. The young Jamaican's extreme poverty further could be read in frayed shirt cuffs, patched shoes and the shiny state of his coat collar. Lucius Devoe's features, a shade less dark than olive, were almost never in repose. His forehead, nose and cheekbones were cleanly modelled and well proportioned. But what one noticed first about him was the alertness of his very dark blue eyes.

Mechlin lace at Doctor Townsend's wrists gleamed briefly when he picked up a certificate. "In the past you have heard me speak many times—doubtless at too great a length on occasion—therefore my final remarks will be brief."

He went stalking across the study and the gilt buttons of his waistcoat flashed as his big, heavily freckled hand closed on Asa's. "Doctor Peabody," said he gravely, "in your regard I entertain the fondest expectations. May your admirable concentration on anatomy reward both you and mankind."

"You—you are very kind, sir," was all Asa could find to say; Lord, how he yearned for the gift of eloquence.

"Godfreys! I've made out!" he thought. "Why, why I'm a full-fledged physician. Oh, if only Pa could know about it."

The texture of this certificate between his fingers was sure-enough evidence that this long-hoped-for hour indeed had arrived. Yes, behind him stretched the years of toil at net, handline, and trawl; why, even yet, he retained remnants of calluses at those points where his thumbs would close over a dory's oars. Well, he was now a Bachelor of Medicine. So far so good. He intended some day to add the venerated initials, M. D., to his name. Right now, not twenty medical men in all Massachusetts held that coveted degree.

Asa's cheeks went dark red when Sabra raised heavily lashed lids and, looking him full in the eyes, curved her lovely mouth into a warm, slow smile. How suddenly mature, how grown-up she seemed in her blue, rose and white brocade. The hood of her Capuchin cloak had disarranged her hair causing a stray chestnut curl to oscillate over her forehead.

As from afar, he heard Doctor Townsend's dry precise

voice saying, "Doctor Burnham, my best wishes will accompany you wherever you fare." The old physician's one eye twinkled. "I'm thinking that red hair and those blue eyes will carry you a long way—in more than one fashion."

Peter Burnham's hand closed over his certificate. "Thank you, sir. Always I shall endeavor to remain a credit to you, your skill, and your principles." Then he grinned a grin which, like oil on water, spread all over his ruddy features and became reflected in merry blue eyes.

"Doctor Devoe." Sabra looked up expectantly in time to see her uncle draw himself to full height. He spoke less lightly. "You have labored industriously and under great handicaps; though a stranger to our land and to this city you have made friends and won respect. For you I have one final word of counsel. Weigh your every decision with care—and probity."

Alone of the three Devoe bowed, and without affectation. "Doctor Townsend, as long as I live I shall cherish your precepts."

Somewhere in Bennett Street a reveler discharged a musketoon, sent its report banging along that narrow thoroughfare, then uttered a series of drunken war whoops. "*He-e-e! Yah-yip! Yah! Yip! Yip!*" Windows commenced to bang up. Though Sabra started, glanced anxiously towards the leaded and diapered windows, none of the men paid any heed to this outburst of holiday spirit. Again, Doctor Townsend raised his little, thin-stemmed glass.

"Gentlemen," his gaze included all three of the oddly contrasting figures before him. "To our beloved and sorely beset Country! I adjure you to remain constant to her cause. Too many brave men already have given it their lives." A wry smile wrinkled the old surgeon's parchment-hued features. "I feel confident that you will serve our Country second only to Humanity."

Doctor Townsend put down his glass, seized a fob decorated with three great seals and pulled out a tremendous gold watch to squint short-sightedly at its dial. "Um. Still four hours until midnight. Will one of you gentlemen see my niece across the street? I must be off—" He went out into the hallway, yelled in a surprisingly vigorous voice, "Sophie! Tell Socrates to fetch my chaise around front."

"Ahem, Doctor," Burnham's hand closed on Asa's

shoulder. " 'Twould seem that just about a tot apiece remains in yonder decanter. What d'you say?''

The solemn expression vanished from Asa Peabody's face as suddenly as a chalked word under the stroke of a sponge. "Um. Why not? Spanish brandy's fine as milkweed—it's got Demerara or Jamaica rum beat all to hollow. What say, Lucius?''

"Let's not be greedy," Devoe suggested. "Shall we invite Mistress Stanton to toast our future?''

"Why, why yes. But ain't brandy a mite heady for—for—'' Asa stammered, then went red to the ears.

Sabra Stanton caught up a furry little black kitten and treated him to an amused look. "I will thank you, Doctor,'' she emphasized the title, "not to prescribe for me until consulted.'' Lips the color of ox-blood cherries curved. "Also pray recall that I am a spinster of eighteen, and fully capable of coping with a trifle—just a trifle—of Uncle William's Spanish brandy.''

Judas Maccabaeus! There, bright and fresh beside the shining brass of the fireplace, she reminded Asa of a summer sunrise over Englishman's Bay—all sparkle and clear colors. Yes, sir, right now he'd give a pretty penny to be possessed of a gift of gab approaching Lucius Devoe's. Every time he contrived to turn Mistress Stanton a compliment, why he'd get all tangled up with himself, like Wallace Fenlason handling a trawl tub.

After these two years odd in Boston he'd noticed a fellow never got ahead by being too quiet—nor by flapping his fins too much, either.

The three new physicians were lifting their glasses to Sabra when the clock in the New Brick Church over on Hanover Street sounded eight ponderous, self-important notes.

"Mercy!" Sabra quickly put down first her glass, then the kitten and hurried into pattens and muffler. "I'd no notion it was so late. Papa will be terribly vexed. Doctor Devoe?'' She enjoyed the moment immensely. "Will you escort me across the street?''

While Peter looked on, vastly amused, Asa hurried to drape a gray, blue-lined camlet cloak about Sabra's shoulders, then muttered, "You'd best not let your pa sniff the brandy, had you?''

Sabra's gray eyes flew wide open. "Mercy no! He—he'd have conniption cat fits!''

"I do declare you think of everything, Asa," Devoe laughed; then, after fumbling in his rusty black coat, produced a pair of cloves. "My very first prescription is for you, Mistress Stanton. If you'll chew on these I'll defy anybody to suspect."

Asa swallowed hard on his chagrin; if only she'd included him in the invitation to see her home. On opening the door he noticed again a tantalizing fragrance of allspice, that the hall light drew brief, but lovely, auburn tints from those brown curls just visible beneath Sabra's hood.

"Good night Doctor Peabody, Doctor Burnham," Sabra called over her shoulder. "God send you both a prosperous New Year and many more."

In leaving Devoe grinned. "Won't you fellows join me at the Noah's Ark later on? Might wet our certificates, eh what?"

Burnham nudged Asa, said they'd other plans, whereupon Devoe nodded, then offered Sabra an arm down steps powdered by a light snow which already had sharply outlined a series of frozen black ruts marking the length of Bennett Street. From the doorway Asa and his companion watched the girl and her escort cross to a large red brick dwelling situated almost directly opposite Doctor Townsend's much smaller one. Asa noticed that the two figures appeared to be standing unnecessarily close together beneath a handsome portico before Samuel Stanton's mansion. A flood of yellow light suddenly sprang out briefly to silhouette the waiting couple, then vanished almost at once.

Burnham laughed quietly, began pulling on a pair of red worsted mittens. "Mark Lucius' little gesture to impress Sabra? Poor devil. If any of us know the Ark's prices are beyond our means, it's he. A plague out of Egypt on him, anyhow." In a quick gesture Peter flung a black triple cape across his powerful shoulders. "Let's go see what deviltry Cross Street offers. There's sure to be something afoot."

Arm in arm because of the treacherous footing, the new physicians swung off down the street. Asa nodded mechanically, tried to dismiss Sabra from his mind; as Pa used to say, there was no use in trying to drown a sorrow that could swim.

"Who knows," Peter chuckled, "but some pretty

wench may become tempted to greet the New Year by
bestowing her affections on us for love's own sweet
sake?''

"That's the smartest notion you've taken in a year,
Peter. Aye, let's heave ahead for the primrose path.''
When the feather-gentle flakes commenced to fly harder,
Asa halted to rearrange his two-yard-long homespun
muffler. "Oh, one thing don't forget. The execution takes
place tomorrow morning and we won't get that cadaver if
we're not on hand to cut it down. As you know, corpses
are all-fired hard to come by. Why, I had to argue near
three hours before that boozy old sot of a regimental surgeon would sign a permit.''

"Aye, I won't forget, and Heaven comfort the poor
dog who's going to hang. Thank God it's not me!''

Peter stooped, fashioned a snow ball and hurled it at
the nearest window; then flung another at the night-
capped and irate citizen who looked out to learn what
was amiss.

"Damn it, Asa, forget that giddy girl and cheer up. After all 'tis the eve of a New Year and we hold certificates
signed by the best damn' surgeon-physician in New England. Can't you get that through your head?''

II. THE RED LION

PETER BURNHAM and Asa Peabody descended the long
slope of Hanover Street with care. Footwalks did parallel
that thoroughfare but their surfaces were so irregular, so
dotted by frozen puddles veiled beneath new snow that
footing was treacherous. Ear tips a-tingle, the two men
bent their bodies against a wind driving flurries of fine dry
snow in from Massachusetts Bay. These flakes had such
sharp edges that they cruelly stung a wayfarer's face and
created a distinct singing noise high in the sky.

Tonight lights glowed in unusually many houses. A
stray, rough-coated cur crept out from under a door-
stoop, sniffed discouragedly at Peter's heels, then scur-
ried off into the driving snow.

In this part of Boston stood a few new houses constructed to replace habitations torn down to warm General Gage's British troops during that dreadful, never-to-
be-forgotten winter of 1775–1776. Even now, five years

later, only the trunks of very young saplings could be seen about town for, in their desperate efforts to find fuel, the Redcoats had hacked down every sizeable tree in Boston and the vicinity.

"Godfreys! How'd you like to be at sea tonight?" Asa panted over the roaring wind.

"Fine, if I look as addled as you talk," Peter yelled back. " 'Tis certain-sure three 'B' weather."

"Three 'B'?" Asa had to cup his hands.

"Aye!" Peter roared in deep-throated merriment. " 'Bed, blonde and bottle weather,' as we call it down in Connecticut."

At the intersection of Hanover and Bennett Streets there was animation. Two, three chairs, screened with brocade curtains, jolted by. All were preceded by link boys, bearing torches at which the wind tore so furiously that they shed very little light and caused the panting, purple-faced porters to slip and stumble beneath their shoulder straps. A handful of horsemen came clop-clopping along, muffled heads bent to the wind and hugging their riding capes about them. The saddle horses moved slowly, blowing clouds of steam and setting their feet down with care.

Before a mean-looking ordinary a group of leather-clad apprentices were engaged in a hilarious snow fight. Semi-drunken, they yelled and pushed each other about in a rough, but good-natured frolic. A burly, scarlet-faced roundsman, complete with hooded lantern, oaken staff and klopper, remained to one side sublimely—and un-doubtedly wisely—indifferent to this uproar.

Long before his companion, Asa Peabody recognized the distant booming crash of breakers hurling themselves against the Barricado—a defense long since constructed to protect Boston's inner harbor and wharves from the threat of fire ships. All along Hanover Street swing-boards of many sizes and designs were swaying wildly, creaking under the force of the wind. They advertised a wide variety of trades and occupations: "S. Talbot, Cordwainer," "Lot Smith & Sons, Tailors."

Asa paused before B. Edes' book shop, rubbed fine snow from a windowpane and squinted in to learn wheth-er that yearned-for copy of *Plain, Concise, Practical Remarks of the Treatment of Wounds and Fractures* by one John Jones, M.D., of Edinburgh in Scotland, had yet been sold. For six weeks now, that fat brown tome forcibly had reminded Asa of his near-to-penniless state. It was, in Doctor Townsend's opinion, an excellent volume and cost but fifteen shillings. Yet, for all that it mattered to Asa Peabody, its price might have been fifteen pounds sterling.

From Prince Street appeared a dark tangle of sailors; privateersmen, if one were to judge by their long black pigtails, heavy, brass-hilted cutlasses, blue or red stocking caps and brass-buttoned sea jackets. The roisterers had locked arms with a bevy of frowsy girls who skipped along between their escorts screaming with laughter and joining shrilly in the chorus of an obscene ballad concerning Molly Packett and the manner in which she'd torn her placket.

"Hi, lads!" A great, bandy-legged fellow whose collar kept blowing up over his head, hailed the two doctors in boisterous good fellowship.

"C'mon wi' us, and if yer as smart as ye look ye'll sign on aboard the *Grand Turk III,* Capt'n Robert Ashton, best damn' privateersman afloat! Ain't he, lads?"

"Aye!" they roared. "Sign of for fun, frolic an' the pick o' the West Indy girls! Goo' ol' *Grand Turk.* Huzzah! Huzzah! Pass the bottle, mates!"

One of the celebrants pranced ahead playing a shrill tune on a penny whistle. The gang yelped with laughter when he tripped on the frozen mud, went sprawling, but kept on playing "Moll Tearsheet's Lament."

All the inns and taverns were jam-packed and their stableyards crowded with waiting snow-flecked saddle or coach horses. These poor beasts stood huddled miserably together, heads down and shivering.

Hugging their cloaks to them, the two friends turned at last into the whirling snow of Prince Street where they found the crowd thicker and lights glowing in almost every window. Before one window a small crowd had collected to admire a number of elaborate designs cut out of black paper and illumined by candles placed behind them.

"Beats the Dutch, this craze for papyrotamia," remarked Burnham, flailing his arms. "Of course, a handsomely cut silhouette is a different matter. Well, doctor," he grinned and threw back his red head, "where away? The Red Lion?"

Asa shook snow from his muffler, looked curiously

about. It wasn't often he found himself in this part of town. "Anywhere the beer is cheap, Peter."

Burnham laughed, thrust an arm through his companion's. "Aside from our cadaver money I possess twelve shillings, six pence, hard money! So on to the Red Lion!" To a sudden clamor he swung about. "What's up?"

Before a candle-maker's shop lay a saddle horse. Having slipped and fallen, the gaunt beast was now snorting in terror and struggling ineffectually to regain its footing. The owner, hatless and far gone in rum, was staggering about, alternately yanking at his mount's bridle or dealing it vicious kicks in the belly.

Burnham shouldered his way through a gathering crowd. "Better let the poor critter alone a bit; it's too scared to rise."

"Min' yer own bloody business!" bellowed the drunkard who looked like a printer. "'S my hoss and I'll kick him all I've a mind to."

Peter's hand closed on the other's collar, then, without apparent effort, heaved him clear of the snow and held him struggling and cursing at arm's length. "Now hark you, friend," he announced in perfect good-humor, "I really don't fancy people who belabor helpless dumb beasts." He cocked back his left fist. "Do you wish me to go on disliking you?"

The crowd roared with amusement. The rider was a small man, and dangled from Burnham's fist as helpless as a kitten from a mother cat's mouth.

The rider struggled and lashed out with his booted feet an instant; then, yielding to a twist of alcoholic humor, he suddenly began to roar with laughter. "N-no. If m' danged horse won' get up—suppose you carry me home? I surely despise walking."

Peter Burnham grinned like a huge small boy and set the ruffled little man on his feet—even brushed the snow from his shoulder. "So do I."

Asa, meanwhile, held down the head of the prostrate animal until it ceased struggling. Experienced in such homely matters, he directed, "Fetch some ashes out of yonder barrel, somebody."

"That's right," a tipsy tanner's apprentice agreed, "'s all ice here—o' course critter can't stand up. I'd fall flat on my arse meself." And, to the enjoyment of the crowd, he did just that.

Once ashes were spread, Asa found no trouble in aid-ing the fallen animal to its feet; under his knowledgeable hand, it forgot its fright, quit trembling.

"I'm vastly obleeged, damned if I ain't," the rider declared, while employing an elbow to remove a coating of snow and manure from his shabby, low-crowned castor hat. "What say you gents join me in a tumbler of sperrit?"

The two new doctors exchanged silent opinions. "Alack, we've not the time, friend," Peter said; then the two resumed their progress through suddenly thinning snow.

There was trouble of a different sort before the Mermaid Tavern. Some countryman most unconcernedly had unyoked his span of oxen from a ponderous, roughly built chebbobin charged with a load of heavy timbers destined for some nearby shipyard. The oxen could only recently have been removed, since some droppings before the sledge were still giving off spirals of steam.

A beefy watchman was stamping about, waving his lantern and bawling loud enough to wake the dead. "Hi! Git this 'bobin off'n the street. Who in tarnation's left this ratted lumber yard on a public thoroughfare? 'Tis dead agin ordinances, it is."

"Where is this Red Lion?" Asa demanded. "I'm colder'n a cod line in February and so peckish I could gnaw the bones out of my landlady's Sunday stays."

"It ain't far now," Peter encouraged. "Besides we both felt colder waiting for old Doc Townsend to sign those certificates."

All the grog shops and quasi-brothels situated nearest the waterfront were roaring, crowded to capacity. From them pipe music or the twanging of Spanish guitars beat out into the street. The out-and-out bordelloes, Peter explained, were less brilliantly lighted, but from them the scraping of fiddles sounded louder and one could catch the thump of feet mingled with a deal of high-pitched laughter and an occasional scream.

Presently a swing-board adorned with a prancing red lion loomed ahead.

"Hold your hat and look alive," Peter cautioned. "We'll find no prayer meeting going on in there."

In the wake of six or eight soldiers clad in a weird miscellany of blue, brown and even gray uniforms, they bore down on a wide doorway through which were rushing blasts of hot air reeking of tobacco smoke and pungent with odors of sweat, lemon peel, cloves and rum.

Asa blinked and Burnham gasped. "Whew! That's a genuine six-cornered stink!"

To describe the Red Lion as packed to overflowing would have constituted a stark understatement; seated at long hurdle tables ranged at right angles to the entrance were mahogany-faced Spaniards, nervous, feverishly gay Frenchmen, stolid half-breed Indians and Dutchmen. There were even a few Negroes. Riggers, shipwrights, armorers, rope spinners, chandlers, and a swarm of heavily sweating laborers crowded each other and drank deep draughts of ale from wooden noggins or jacks of copper-bound waxed leather.

Peter jerked a nod to a far corner. "Look, a riffler! Thought the brutes had all gone home."

Sure enough yonder lounged a brutal, Indian-like rifleman clad in greasy buckskins adorned at forearm and chest by green-dyed thrums easily a foot long.

A few farmers looking self-conscious and uneasy in their rabbit skin caps, horsehide or deerskin jerkins and clumsy, home-pegged boots, were drinking applejack and getting mighty high on it, too.

But the vast majority of the Red Lion's patrons were seafaring men; fishermen, West Indian traders and, of course, seamen out of the half-dozen privateers in port.

Peter, casting about for a place, left Asa considering a notice board, literally choked with vari-colored handbills, which displayed the usual sailing warnings, offers of exchange, recruiting notices and such:

To be SOLD: Wednesday, likely young NEGRO WOMAN. understands House work. Common looking and has had the Small Pox. M. Brunnes at Store No. 25 on Long Wharf.

Notice is hereby giv'n that I, Lobiel Harron, being Employed by a number of Gentlemen, intend to ride as a Messenger between Boston Town in Massachusetts and Newport in Rhode Island, once a Fortnight in Winter and once a Week in Summer. Any Gentlemen having letters to send, by leaving them at the Red Lion, may Depend they shall be called for by their humble servant.

Peter Burnham now was seeking places in a second

room beyond the bar, though out there smoke and cooking fumes from the kitchens blued the air.

A sudden uproar at the entrance prompted Asa to turn in time to see the *Grand Turk's* leave party come swaggering in amid a blast of most welcome cold air.

"Step up, one and all!" called the leader of the *Grand Turk's* men. A vast, hairy-handed fellow, he affected a blue and white striped jersey, canary silk scarf and a dull red jacket of kerseymere. He wore, Asa noted, not brass earrings but hoops of rich red gold in both his ears. On the speaker's shoulder balanced a small black and white monkey in a green jacket and kilt. When its poise was threatened the pet put out a tiny black paw and gripped one of the privateersman's earrings.

"Who'll join Luke Tarbell and his bully boys fer a swig of old Mother's ruin? Don't hold back, lads, there's yer guarantee of earnest." The bar rang when onto its dripping surface he tossed a pair of broad gold Spanish pieces.

Just as an enthusiastic rush of guests subsided, a fresh excitement attracted the attention of the Red Lion's patrons.

"What's this? What's this?" Mr. Perkins, fat features fiery, was flinging a sheaf of clean white Continental bank notes onto the beer-marked table before a thin, red-nosed soldier—a sergeant by the green worsted knot on his right shoulder.

"That's money, Mister," he growled. "Take it and like it."

"I'll do neither and damn yer eyes fer a bold rogue. Expecting to pass such trash."

"'Tain't trash. Law says it's legal currency," rasped a big private in a faded brown uniform. He coughed heavily and Asa noted that his eyes were hollow, that the gray-pink tinge of recent sickness stained his cheeks.

"Legal fiddlesticks," snorted the publican breathing hard through a bulbous and red-veined nose. He dropped his voice. "Ain't you fellers got just a leetle hard money?"

"No. We ain't out o' no hole-in-the-wall privateer." The sergeant got up, his hands nervously opening and shutting. His companions followed suit, scowling and closing in, shoulder to shoulder.

The innkeeper hesitated, decided to temporize, spoke

less belligerently. "Now, boys, ain't no one can rightly say Joel Perkins is hard on the defenders o' this fair land of ours." His little blue eyes narrowed. "Being as this is the eve o' the New Year, I'll accept Noo York or Connetycut notes at fifty per cent discount."

"Look, Mister, we ain't no cheats," the thin soldier said bitterly. "Honest, we got nawthin' but what we're paid in—Continental notes."

Mr. Perkins aimed a slap at a passing and quite inoffensive pot boy, then levelled a hairy sausage of a finger at the doorway. "Get out! The pack of ye! Them notes ain't worth a thin damn. Next time you want charity go seek an almshouse."

The soldiers glowered, hesitated, then a corporal in a dirty gray uniform pulled a sheaf of notes from each of his side pockets. "Here, you goddam' fat-bellied patriots. Help yerselves to this bum wad!" The corporal flung the double handful of Continental notes up against the smoke-browned and fly-specked plaster above his head. The white bits of paper fluttered, scaled briefly about like a flock of miniature gulls. The only man who bothered to pick up a note used it as a spill to light his pipe.

The sergeant paused on his way to the door, shook his fist at the smoke-veiled room. "That was my first pay in six months. I pray God some day soon the Lobsterbacks will come back and burn down this goddam' rat trap called Boston over yer ears, you goddam' ungrateful crotch-festered civilians!"

The corporal spat resoundingly on his way out, snarled, "Damn me to Tophet ef I don't sign aboard a letter-of-marque come sunup."

The soldiers stormed out into the street. Nobody paid them much heed.

Peter, having secured a small table, ordered applejack toddies. He winked. "That's a tipple will bring us to action quicker'n you can clamp a bloodvessel.

"Gentle stuff, eh?" Peter demanded, his somewhat pallid features gone scarlet. "A veritable anodyne."

"Aye, for Lucifer!" choked Asa, using the heel of his hand to wipe great tears from his eyes. "Judas Maccabaeus! Why didn't you warn me this stuff would raise blisters on a capstanhead?"

A big broken-nosed marine out of some privateer leaned back on his bench, used a piggin to beat time as he

raised a chanty concerning the pleasures and perils of
"Teachin' School Down on the Cape." Immediately the
crowd joined lustily in on the choruses, set the roof
beams to reverberating. Perspiring serving wenches
switched hips, giggled incessantly as they hustled about
refilling beakers, jacks and mugs, and bestowing moist
kisses on favored patrons.

III. A Ballad New-Come from Ireland

A COMMOTION in the kitchen caused near-by patrons to
witness the abrupt entrance of a scrawny, gray-faced
man. Nearing middle age, he wore a soiled, bottle-green
waistcoat, greasy durant breeches and ragged worsted
stockings. Scant, ginger-colored hair straggled untidily
downwards as if attempting to conceal the grime on his
neck and a very dirty stock of brown leather.

"Wot have we here?" demanded a pimply merchant's
clerk. "A musicker, I'll be bound! Well, old gaffer, do
you aim to play us the minooet?"

The dirty old man made but slow progress between the
tables because in one hand he was carrying a flageolet
while with the other he tried to manage a crude crutch.
The musician's left leg, Asa noted, was shrunken and
several inches shorter than its companion.

"If ye'll only make way, kind friends," he was pleading in a whining, high-pitched voice, "ye'll greet the New
Year on the wings o' the sweetest music. I vow ye've a
rare treat in store, gentlemen."

"Go ahead, Gimpey—let's hear what ye can do."

In rough good humor the revellers drew aside, permitting the cripple to thump along towards a small clear
space formed by the junction of taproom and bar. The
musician held the crowd's attention just long enough to
permit the comparatively unobserved appearance of a
black-haired girl wearing a dingy, striped red and white
skirt and a Robinson vest of faded blue. Over this last she
had crossed a ragged yellow shawl. At a quick estimate
Asa guessed this small, ghastly pale creature could not
yet have attained eighteen years. A double row of small
metal discs jingled softly along the rim of the curious little hand drum she carried at her side.

"So this is old Gimpey's treat?" Peter commented

over his toddy. "What a dirty little vixen it is! Stab me," he added suddenly. "What remarkable eyes!"

He was right Asa decided; the girl's large and very black eyes were heavily lashed and lifted, ever so faintly, at their outer corners. Lips compressed, the girl struck as hard as she could at hands reaching out in attempt to pinch her buttocks or to snatch off her garters.

"Quite the little hellcat, eh?"

"Can you blame her?" Asa felt mad clear through to see the way these revellers, now far gone in liquor, made a game of this luckless waif and, quite without shame, offered incredibly obscene invitations.

When she brushed by Peter's table he could tell that her petticoat must have been cut for some woman considerably taller than this girl; its spotted fabric trailed a path through the spit and sawdust on the floor. This pallid little creature had made an effort to secure abundant black hair with a band of faded yellow silk ribbon; but the knot must have been badly tied for in a minute it would fall away.

She had almost succeeded in joining the musician when an unshaven young teamster in a brown and white calfskin waistcoat dexterously flipped up the girl's ragged petticoat and venting a raucous guffaw, jerked undone a pathetic rag garter. The would-be entertainer's lumpy black stocking slipped and fell, gathering in ungainly wrinkles about her slim ankle.

Small pointed teeth bared, she whirled and used her hand drum to slash at the teamster's head. "Satan trample your beastly guts!"

"Ho! Kitty's got claws!" roared Peter in huge delight because those metal discs on the drum had sketched three bloody lines across the fellow's cheek.

"You—you goddam' viper!" Still clutching the garter, the teamster surged up, but was pulled back to a sitting position by his companions.

"Let be, Abner! Ye won yer prize, ain't yer? Even if ye've had to pay for the doxy's garter, ye can brag all over Essex County on it."

"A spirited piece," Peter chuckled raising a second toddy. "Notice her leg? 'Twas shapely, my lad, shapely. Were a man to scrub hard enough, I'll wager he might find real looks under all that dirt."

In the clear space the cripple had rested his crutch

against a table and was wetting blue, pinched-looking lips before sounding a few experimental notes on his flageolet.

Though mightily embarrassed, Asa kept his attention on the girl, watched her swiftly rip a strip from the hem of her petticoat and with it resecure her fallen stocking.

The buzz of conversation slackened. "For yer pleasure, kind friends," the musician whined, "Mistress Hilde will now sing—"

"Mistress Hilde's a bloody whore!" came a raucous call from the depths of the bar. "Three pennies weekdays, six pence Saturdays—"

"—Nonetheless," the cripple insisted hurriedly, "Mistress Hilde now will entertain you. For God's sake sing out, lass."

Once her companion had struck up a lively air, Mistress Hilde forced onto her pallid lips such a pitiful caricature of a smile that her expression reminded Asa of an occasion up in Machias, when some children had cornered a half-grown cat. They were pelting the unhappy creature with clods until he'd put an end to their sport.

Thin hands violently a-tremble, the girl called Hilde nodded to her companion and commenced an accompaniment on her little hand drum. Presently she tilted back her head and began a lively Irish ballad in a stronger voice than her fragility suggested to be possible. The quality of her notes was fairly true, Peter decided, settling back. Hands plunged in pockets he listened carefully though his blue eyes were becoming heavily lidded with the heat and liquor. "Well, Asa, what do you think?"

"She has pretty hands," Asa commented. "But, if ever I've beheld a person fairly primed to take the long sickness—"

"Pox for a blue-nosed sobersides!" Peter grinned and, once the girl had ceased singing, called, "Catch!" and spun her a silver sixpenny bit. Dexterously she caught the coin in her little hand drum, then curtsied at the same time flashing an uncertain smile.

Suddenly Asa's hand closed on his companion's wrist. "Of all things—see that symbol painted on the drumhead?"

"That blue thing?" the red-haired doctor demanded. "What of it?"

"Yonder's a Mic-Mac totem!—that of the Turtle clan. Strange. How d' you suppose it got so far south as Boston?"

"Sing again, lass!"

"Good enough. Let's have some more."

Patrons tossed out into the sawdust of the clear space coppers or creased and dirty paper notes of varied origin. The cripple hopped about paying small attention to the paper, but carefully retrieving any hard money from the thick sawdust. The girl, however, remained where she was, uninterested, erect, and somehow infinitely aloof from the smoke and stenches of the taproom.

Eventually the musician picked up his pipe and prepared to play. "Mistress Hilde will now regale ye one and all wi' a sad love song—by Mr. Henry Carey. She does real good by it."

His reed sounded an introductory flourish, then the black-haired girl commenced to sing.

> "Of all the girls that are so smart
> There's none like pretty Sally;
> She is the darling of my heart
> And she lives in our alley.
> There is no lady in the land
> Is half so sweet as—"

She faltered, then continued, despite the fact that, out in Cross Street, was sounding a distinctive, shivering clash recognized by more than a few of the seamen present, as that of Moorish cymbals. The clangor sounded louder. More heads swung expectantly towards the door; the crowd lost interest in raven-haired Hilde and her sad love song.

IV. DOCTOR ALEXANDER SAXNAY

AT THE RED LION'S entrance the cymbal player struck a final, great shivering note, leaving only the clamor raised by many excited dogs to penetrate within. The *Grand Turk's* leave party fell silent, turned rough, wind-reddened faces to regard a stalwart Negro standing framed in that black rectangle formed by the doorway.

Quite unlike any other black the guests had ever seen,

this apparition's skin shone, not brown-black like those of the slaves and freedmen around Boston Town, but a glossy blue-black. Little scars arranged in curious patterns, such as chevrons and semicircles, decorated his forehead, cheeks, chin. The white surrounding his restless little black eyes glowed yellow as strips of lemon peel. No less bizarre was this black man's outer costume, consisting as it did of a scarlet cloak heavily embroidered with all manner of outlandish characters done in tinsel and sequins. Secured to his green and gold turban by a glowing red stone, nodded a graceful white egret plume tall enough to touch the lintel when the blackamoor entered to salaam profoundly once, twice—three times.

Feeling a little drunk on his third toddy, Asa gaped like a country bumpkin at a conjurer, and stood up the better to see, just as Hilde broke off singing. Absently the singer puffed a disordered black mane with her fingers; stood peering—half resentfully, half curiously—at this unlucky and successful counter-attraction.

Twice more the blue-black Negro struck his great brass cymbals, then, looking glassy-eyed straight before him, chanted. "Mek way! Mek way, my marsters! Mek way fo' Doctuh Saxnay, de mos' mirac'lous, de mos' magnificent, de mos' omnipotent, de gre'test physicker ob all de ages!"

Reluctantly, but definitely impressed, occupants of near-by tables drew back to let the blackamoor pass.

"What in the Tophet is he up to?" Asa muttered.

Peter winked a smoke-reddened eye. "Just listen!"

"Mek way fo' de gre't Doctuh Saxnay, Physicker Extra-ordinary to His Mos' Royal Highness, de Prince ob Thurn an' Taxis; Lord High Chirungeon to de pu'ssant Bashaw ob Tripoli; Learned Chamberlain to de Sacred Medical College ob Szged in de Kingdom ob Hungary!"

Because of his stature Asa had no trouble in witnessing the appearance of one of the most remarkable figures he had ever beheld. Lean and saturnine as pickled alewife, Doctor Saxnay's face was rendered memorable by narrow and sharply up-sweeping brows, a long, jutting blue chin, and a livid birthmark covering one whole side of his features. With nonchalance bordering on disdain the newcomer lingered in the doorway brushing snow flakes from a glossy fur coat of foreign cut and secured at his throat by a pair of enormous, diamond-studded clasps.

In one fleshless, but liberally be-ringed, hand Doctor Saxnay held an ebony walking stick, the golden head of which was shaped like that of a bulldog. Tear-shaped pearls, dangling from long and yellowish ear lobes, added to this personage's exotic appearance. Although of average height, the new arrival appeared to be taller because his peruke was dressed by some outlandish mode into what appeared to be a pair of well-curled but woolly horns.

Attracted by this clangor of cymbals, Mr. Perkins' kitchen staff made bold to come shuffling in all red and sweating. Even the pinch-faced turnspit boy had deserted his post, venturing a box on the ear, in order to gaze on this glittering pair.

Luke Tarbell of the *Grand Turk's* company chuckled and started forward, yellowish teeth a-glint. "Prick my vitals if here ain't a pretty popinjay ripe fer pluckin'! What say, lads, shall us teach this furrin bugger a new hornpipe?"

Doctor Saxnay's chest inflated itself like that of an amorous bullfrog and, in one of the biggest voices Asa had ever heard he roared, "Silence! Thou poxy purblind specimen of *sus domesticus!*" At the same time Doctor Saxnay blew out his cheeks and fixed upon the privateersman an enormous and protuberant pair of eyes. Their irises were of a clear bright green which reminded Asa of grass sprouting on a manure hill. Doctor Saxnay, moreover, proved able to dilate and contract those unearthly pupils at will. When he did so the privateersman stepped quickly back among his fellows.

"Nay, friend, do not flinch. I quite forgive you!" boomed he in the fur coat. "Even before tonight I have cast pearls before swine." He raised both arms in a wide gesture. "Harken, people of Boston, and rejoice! I, Alexander Saxnay, the great Healer, the Master Physician, have journeyed from far lands to offer you—one and all—health, wealth and happiness!"

His round chin raised a little, the massive figure looked levelly about, then treated the company to a curiously winning smile. "Eastern sages have proclaimed that time is precious and of the essence; therefore, my friends, I will to the point."

Advancing further into the tavern, Doctor Saxnay permitted his black servant to assist him out of the fur coat and presently stood revealed in a suit of Chinese yellow, scarlet waistcoat and stockings. Many precious-looking stones glittered on his buttons and shoe buckles, but they appeared no more brilliant than this foreigner's restless eyes.

"You behold me newly arrived on your hospitable shores as a Messiah of hope, on an embassy of mercy to heal the sick, the halt and the blind among you." Doctor Saxnay raised his already tremendous voice until it drowned out all other sounds. "Mark you well, my friends, within me lies the power to heal the afflicted, to make the blind see, to cut for the stone, to make fruitful the barren, to lend fresh vigor to withered loins—"

"Hurray!" a voice shouted from the background. "Old Capt'n Hazard will be 'round fust thing in the morning."

Doctor Saxnay smiled tolerantly, produced a very elegant tortoise-shell and gold snuff box and, employing none-too-clean fingers, dipped himself a generous pinch of the brown powder.

Asa swallowed the last of his toddy, nodded owlishly. "Must study with him, musn' we, Peter? Been missing a great deal."

"Aye, can you believe your ears?" Peter seemed vastly amused.

Doctor Saxnay recommenced his oration by indicating an ornate leather purse dangling from his belt. "Within this wallet lie a few magical golden beads fetched, at vast hazard and great expense, from the Cyclades—the Isles of the Blest. Believe me, friends, there is no describing the occult powers of these Golden Beads. Dissolved into Saxnay's Golden Elixir—a secret of my own discovery— they will restore addled wits, cure the itch and, among other benefits, avert the Evil Eye! Wear but a single one of these beads about your neck and ye'll remain forever proof against the dread ravages of camp fever, the ague, the plague, the dropsy, or the festering gout, and—" he lowered his voice, looked slyly about, " 'twill cure the most stubborn cases of the *lues venera.*"

Conscious that now his words were creating a deep impression, Doctor Saxnay paused to draw a deep breath. "A word of warning, my worthy friends, ere I depart. You must hasten to avail yourselves of the priceless opportunity I offer. Alas, soon I quit these hospitable shores—the Viceroy of New Granada has pled for my attendance, offering a rajah's ransom for my advice. Until I sail for the Spanish Main I have, ahem, taken up lodgings at Number Ten in Hillier's Lane. Bahram! My surtout!" In a gesture of magnificent negligence he slid his arms into the fur coat his assistant held up.

"Doctor! Doctor! Don't go!" It was the crippled flageolet player who cried out. He snatched up his crutch and struggled forward, eagerness lighting his waxen features. "Pray, kind sir, could you—can you restore the use of this limb?"

Doctor Saxnay frowned; then, narrowing his curious green eyes, he bent, made a pretense of examining the rigid and shortened limb. Presently he clapped the crippled man heartily on the shoulder. "You are in luck, my good man. Come to my lodgings tomorrow, Number Ten Hillier's Lane—" he emphasized the address—"and, for a modest fee, I will supply you with a rare Arabian unguent which, when applied according to my directions, will unlock those twisted bones and sinews."

"'Fore God, Doctor, you ain't a-funnin' me?"

"Nay. Within a week you shall walk as free and easy as you did in boyhood; mine, sir, is the wisdom of the ancients and the secrets of the most modern teachers in the great schools of Leyden, Edinburgh, and Vienna. Good people, I bid you good night and adieu."

Twice Doctor Saxnay flourished his ebony walking stick and each time a small whitish cloud of spice-scented powder sprang from its head. Grandly he stalked back out into the whirling snow.

Peter Burnham made a flatulent noise with his lips before drinking deep. "It's ten to one that catchpenny quack will touch more hard money in one day than do Doctor Aspinwall or Doctor Townsend in a month! Verily, how does the saying go? 'Earth has her limits but human stupidity reaches to the stars themselves.'"

"Eh?"

"I'll prove it to you."

Peter arose and intercepted the crippled musician who was dragging by with a transported expression lighting his gaunt features.

"My friend, I, too, am a physician and a surgeon," Peter announced, flushing at this first use of his new title. "Pray permit me to examine your leg."

Suspicion entered the cripple's manner. "What fur? No doctor this side o' the sea knows anythin'."

"Indeed? I take it you prefer a foreigner's, any foreigner's verdict?"

"Why not? I've gone everywhere, tried everything, even *aqua animalis* and that was fearful expensive. Well, go ahead take a look—'tis been like that ever since I took my wound up to Bennington."

While the girl Hilde looked on, sullen and expressionless, her companion dropped heavily onto a bench between the two doctors. Peter's fingers gently exploring the cripple's knee quickly determined that the patella or kneecap had been fractured, that his quadriceps and gastrocnemius tendons had atrophied and now were as hard and inflexible as lignum vitae.

"Took a Hessian baynit through that knee," the man explained wearily. "Ain't had no use of it since."

Peter straightened, found himself wretched at the necessity of banishing that hope written so large across the tired face peering up into his.

"In God's name, sir," quavered the cripple, "say that ye can cure me and can make me walk again?"

"I wish I could," Peter replied quietly, "but I can't. No more can that gaudy charlatan who has just gone out."

The flageolet player recoiled, grabbing up his crutch. "Yer lyin', that's what ye are! Doctor Saxnay knows more'n you. He ain't no country hoss doctor. He's studied in Yerrup, he has. Didn't you hear him say he's learned the secrets of the East? That unguent he told of 'll loosen this joint."

"Believe what you please," Asa put in, "but I'm a surgeon, too, and I'm ready to vow, on a stack of Bibles as tall as you want, that no ointment in this world can fashion you a new kneecap."

V. DONNYBROOK FAIR

A FEW MINUTES short of midnight a second group of privateersmen came stamping into the Red Lion. A single glance betrayed the fact that they had been patronizing an imposing number of waterfront grog shops. Their leader was a black-browed, bandy-legged fellow wearing an elaborate green uniform adorned with sergeant's stripes done in white. Followed by a roistering gang of deckhands in knitted stocking caps, wide leather belts, brass-buckled brogues and stained petticoat breeches, he swaggered in and, swaying slightly, surveyed the taproom in insolent self-assurance.

Like hounds on finding their yard is invaded by a strange pack the *Grand Turk's* men stiffened, gathered their feet under them and closed in together. As Luke Tarbell had done, the marine sergeant tossed a handful of small gold and silver coins ringing onto the bar and bellowed.

"Name yer tipple! The drinks are on me. Everybody's a-got to drink to the *Dauntless*—best damn' privateer afloat!" Belligerently, he added, "An' I won't take 'no' for an answer!"

"'Twas the *Dauntless* prized one o' Gen'ral Henry Clinton's store ships last month and her with nigh ten thousand golden guineas aboard!" someone muttered at a table near by Asa's.

"To hell with you and yer drinks," Tarbell rasped. "We don't drink with no puddle-rakers. Go fry yer fat butt somewheres else!"

Asa, reading the omens, roused himself, muttered, "Rig for a squall, Peter," and, after pushing his table further away from the wall, seized a Madeira bottle by its neck.

"What hulk-scrapin' say dat? Mebbe it was you, little boy?" A big, yellow-skinned mulatto wearing a tarred round straw hat drove an elbow viciously hard into the ribs of one of the *Grand Turk's* crew. "Make room for a real fightin' man!" he roared waving an enormous fist. "Ah's got me one powahful thirst!"

"Stow it, you sassy half-baked 'coon!" snarled the *Grand Turk's* man and swung his tankard at the mulatto so quickly the other couldn't duck and so caught the heavy stone mug full on the chin. Half dazed, the mulatto reeled into the arms of a shipmate.

"Faith and 'twill be ould Donnybrook Fair all over again!" exulted an Irish teamster joyfully balling his fists.

Before Asa could even bat his eyes the taproom had become a battleground. The rival privateersmen caught up chairs, platters, bottles, anything handy and, howling obscenities, strove earnestly to bash in each other's heads.

Babbling futile curses, Mr. Perkins struggled towards

the door. "Watch! Watch ho!" he yelled. "Come quick, for God's sake!"

"Ahh-h. Let the lads have their frolic." A wooden piggin sailed through the air, narrowly missed the publican's brown scratch wig, but splashed him with ale.

Inevitably the fight involved by-standers; many mechanics, drovers, and apprentices joined in for the pure joy of brawling.

Fists flashed, tableware and bottles arched through the smoke, chairs came crashing down; sounded panting grunts and the smack of flesh against flesh, but above all arose the thin and frightened squalling of serving girls struggling to reach comparative safety in the kitchen.

Asa and Peter tipped their table on edge, legs outwards, and, in a fine impartial spirit, hurled whatever missiles came to hand at the heaving, flailing combatants.

Once the tide of battle surged up to him, the cripple, swearing frightful oaths, took his crutch by its toe and laid about him with surprising effectiveness. Flattened against the wall behind her companion the black-haired girl stood flinching, one grimy arm raised to shield her pointed little face.

Finally a billow of hot grimacing faces—all yelling mouths and furious eyes and a tangle of bodies fringed by flailing arms and kicking legs—crashed against the table sheltering the two physicians. Aroused to the necessity of defending himself, Asa caught up a broken chair leg in time to parry the wild swinging of a broom handle in the hands of an enraged mechanic.

One of the *Dauntless'* crew unwisely fetched Peter a shrewd clip on the jaw, whereupon that red-haired individual ripped off coat and waistcoat and plunged very effectively into the battle. His attack took the trouble-making privateersmen on their flank which unexpected assault turned the course of the brawl in the favor of the *Grand Turk's* sadly battered and outnumbered crew.

"Watch! 'Ware the watch!" Somebody began shouting and, sure enough, the distinctive staccato rattle of several wooden kloppers could be heard in Cross Street.

"The watch! Out o' my way! One side!" Such of the combatants as were able snatched what possessions they could and went leaping, crashing through the kitchens and so out the back door leaving in their wake a hurrah's nest of overturned tables, chairs, and benches. Non-combatants, proceeding with caution, emerged from their refuges to stand anxiously watching the captain of the watch glare about.

"Take 'em!" he snapped to his hot and breathless roundsmen. At once they commenced to uncoil short lengths of cord.

Three privateersmen, apparently badly hurt, lay groaning; and, sitting on the floor among the wreckage was a young apprentice dazedly attempting to staunch a deep knife slash in his forearm. Blood kept spurting from between his hairy fingers.

"Help! It—it won't stop!" the apprentice began to cry. Asa started forward, but one of the watchmen thrust a heavy oaken staff to bar his path.

"Stand where ye are."

"That man's radial artery has been severed—I—I'm a physician."

"That true, Mr. Perkins?"

The landlord overheard and, setting his wig straight, hurried over. "Leave him be, Tom. He's a physicker, sure enough. He took no part in it. I saw him stand aside," the inn-keeper lied, then he caught Asa by an arm. "For God's sake sew the clumsy bastard up; he's bleeding all over my place. Lord's mercy! And I try to run a respectable ordinary."

"I will—if you'll let be my friend Doctor Burnham. He was provoked into this brawl."

Peter was not a lovely sight as he stood there, panting, red hair loose, shirt minus a sleeve and splashed with blood drops from a split lip. At Mr. Perkins' nod the watchmen turned away in search of likelier quarry.

"Gorry! the cranium of *homo sapiens* is a plagued hard affair," Peter observed, rubbing swollen knuckles. Asa had been fashioning a tourniquet from a billet of wood and length of cod line. Once he applied pressure, the hemorrhage ceased. "What have we here?" Peter shook the hair out of his eyes to bend over the wounded apprentice. He used a pen knife to cut away the sodden woolen sleeve.

"Thank'e, sir," babbled the youth. "I couldn't stop it no how. Is—is any muscles cut?"

A maidservant ran up to Mr. Perkins, muttered something in his ear which prompted him to rip a curse and come back over to where the two physicians were working.

"One o' my doxies got hurt," he growled. "Will one o'

you gents attend her? But mind, I ain't payin' no fees—''

"You go, Asa, I'll sew this lad up in jig time. Hey! You with the pot belly, fetch me a needle and some linen thread.''

Asa entered the kitchen to discover a group of scullery maids, cooks and spit boys collected in one corner. They were chattering like so many jays, but doing nothing whatever about a figure lying limp at their feet.

Against the dirty sawdust the girl Hilde's quaint, finely featured face was now completely colorless, her scrawny arms and legs were wide flung and her jet hair powdered with bits and chips of wood. In her garish blue and red costume she suggested nothing so much as a rather soiled puppet tossed carelessly away.

"Jest my brimstone luck!" the crippled musician was complaining. He had just doused the unconscious girl with a gourd of water. "Here 'tis New Year's Eve and this little no-good bitch won't be fitten' to sing another note." The fellow's tired, rather frightened brown eyes roved in search of sympathy. "Dunno why I took her on. Wherever that damned Hilde goes, bad luck follers a-horseback.''

Not much time was required to decide that her wound was of minor importance. Asa deduced that some missle had struck the singer just above her left ear hard enough to cut the scalp and to render her unconscious.

"She needs fresh air and quiet," he told the circle of the hot and excited faces above him. "Where can she come by it?''

"There's a cubby off the wine cellar," some one volunteered. "Mebbe that would serve?''

When Asa collected the inert figure in his arms he was not much surprised to discover that she proved a very slight burden, so treading easily, he followed a paunchy little man down some creaky stairs into the chill dark of a cellar. A wavering Betty lamp presently lit a small nook in which the discarded straw packing of wine bottles offered soft, if mouldy-smelling, bedding.

"Mr. Perkins will be hollerin' fer me," the guide explained, placing the lamp on the floor. "I got to hurry above else he'll dock me. He's a main hard master is Joel Perkins—God rot his greedy bones!''

By the Betty lamp's wavering and uncertain light Asa made a more careful examination of the cut, was relieved to discover that the bleeding had ceased. Invisible damage, however, might have been caused to the os temporal by the impact. Once a basin of warm water was fetched by a sympathetic kitchen wench, he commenced an exploration by first washing away dirt accumulated in the vicinity of the wound; then succumbed to a sudden temptation to cleanse the balance of the singer's features.

The kitchen girl shook her head in envy, spoke more to herself than to the big young physician, "My, ain't she the pretty one?"

To Asa's mounting surprise the singer's skin proved to be a clear, almost translucent white and of a very fine texture. Even by this uncertain light he could tell that her brows were slender, gently arched and so fine they might have been cut from moleskin. Her eyes were distinguished by a faint bluish pattern of veining in their upper lids. He searched for her pulse. He'd never been able to afford a watch; consequently he'd learned to toll off the seconds pretty accurately. Um. Normal but soft.

Once the contusion had been thoroughly cleaned, Asa contrived a pledget of his last good handkerchief and secured it into place with a strip torn from the bedraggled red petticoat. Characteristically, he was unaware that this last operation had exposed the singer's straight, very thin legs until flesh showed above the tops of her often-darned black cotton stockings.

His next step must be to restore the girl's consciousness. "Find Doctor Burnham and request him to fetch down a dram of spirit," he instructed the wide-eyed scullery maid.

Then, awkwardly, he set about easing those tie strings securing Hilde's skirt and petticoats but confining her diaphragm. Soon he perceived his patient's respiration was even more seriously hampered by her tight-laced stays. To find the knot securing the coarse spun yarn doing duty as laces was difficult, but Asa persisted and was rewarded by an immediate improvement in his patient's breathing. All at once he heard the tap-tapping of a crutch advancing across the floor and straightened hurriedly.

"By God, Doc," sniggered the cripple, "yer a sight slicker'n I figgered; never did see a female's underpinnin' cast adrift quicker." Leering, he hobbled forward extending a tremblingly eager hand. "I'll thank ye fer two

shillin's, Doc, then old Jabez will give yer leave to indulge yer every fancy.''

Asa stood so erect that his unruly dark hair brushed
cobwebs festooning the beams. He wasn't angry yet; but
he spoke sharply. ''For a former soldier you certainly
have fallen a far piece, Jabez.''

The cripple's fawning manner departed and his ragged
teeth shone as he snarled, ''I ain't askin' fer preachin',
only whut's justly owin'. Me, I didn't take up pimpin' fer
choice, only there's no care, pay or pension fer soldiers
crippled in the public defense. They can starve just as
easy as can be.''

''Rather than my owing you, you are in my debt for
dressing this poor bawd's hurt. But I'm not asking even a
Continental.''

''You ain't?''

''No. For your information, this girl is exhausted and
half-starved to boot. First sickness she takes will be the
end of her.''

'' 'Twill be a mercy.'' Jabez seated himself on an empty rum barrel. ''It's a pity she's so danged stubborn—so
set above herself. Old Lizzie's taken a strap to her
more'n once, but it ain't done no good.''

Asa's eyes considered the dingy figure sprawled across
the straw at his feet. ''You don't mean a body'd beat a
poor little thing like this?''

''It's a hard world, Doc,'' sighed the cripple; he blew a
thin and reddish nose between his fingers and absently
wiped them on his breeches. ''One way or another, we all
got to earn our keep. Besides, Hilde ain't the child she
looks; she must be goin' on nineteen. She's a queer one,
an' no mistake; too high in her stomach for her condition,
I'd say.''

Concerned, but not overly moved, Asa considered the
short oval of the singer's features at the moment silhou-
etted against the sable tangle of her hair. To her quicken-
ing breathing, breasts, almost childishly small and immature, barely stirred beneath her sweat-stained shift. What
the devil had become of the spirit he'd sent for? Peter
must still be engaged in tying off the apprentice's severed
artery.

''Where does this Hilde hail from?'' More to make
conversation than out of any curiosity, Asa put the question.

"Hilde says she's from New Scotland but she claims she don't know just where. Only one thing is sure; old Lizzie Wright bought her bond off'n a Scotch Papist from up Canady way. Swore she'd made a prime doxy, he did; then took his money and walked off." Jabez spat untidily. "He lied like Lucifer—Lizzie claims she's never been given more trouble by any wench in her whole life and, mark you, old Lizzie ain't noways unreasonable, neither."

"How'd you come to have this Hilde along with you tonight?"

"Sometimes I rents her off Lizzie to sing for me in the taverns." Jabez sniffed. "Stand to lose three shillings on this night's work; main hard luck on a poor old soldier, it is."

After a brief silence Asa said, "I sent up for some grog quite a while back. Be a good fellow and go see what's happened to it, will you? And there's no need to look at me like that."

"Fancy yer to be trusted, Doctor," Jabez admitted grudgingly, "even if you did try to cozen me about Doctor Saxnay's ointment. I know 'twill limber my leg," he added in a sort of desperate conviction.

"If it does," the young doctor promised, "you're free to kick my bottom across Boston Common and back again."

The veteran still was clumping up to the kitchen when a sharp sigh drew Asa's attention. The girl's long, blue-black lashes were stirring a trifle, her spidery thin fingers began uncertainly to flex themselves.

"Can you hear me?" he inquired gently.

The violet-blue lips moved several instants before any sound was emitted.

"Eh?"

"*We-la-boog-we.*" The girl called Hilde sighed, then added something like, "*We-loo-lin.*"

Asa started, bent closer, thought, "Godfreys, it's Mic-Mac she's talking!" In Passamaquoddy—a related dialect of Algonquin—the speech of nearly all the Indians in the vicinity of Machias, he inquired her name.

"*Kwee-a-lin,*" she whispered.

"Little Dove? Is that it?"

The girl's eyes still unseeing opened just a little. "*Kway!*" She gave the word of greeting.

"*Kway!*"

"Why—why—" She struggled to rise but he placed a restraining hand on her forehead. "You'd best lie quiet. You've been hurt." She lay back breathing faster and faster, staring up in wonderment at the broad and friendly face above.

"You—you are a physician?"

"Aye. You are not badly harmed. There is nothing to fear."

"You'd better go away—" she faltered. "I—I can't pay you."

"A matter of no importance," he reassured. "You'll need care though, lest a commotion arise."

She turned her head aside then, in an odd gesture briefly pressed both hands hard over her lips. "Where do you live? I will go there. Indeed I will."

He soothed her, became so much absorbed in a consideration of her frail state that he quite missed the implication of her promise. "I lodge at the Widow Southeby's in Sudbury Street. It's Number Fifty-one; I'm generally in after supper. That cut should be examined, certainly within two days' time. But if you experience any dizzy spells you must send for me."

Judas Maccabaeus! A realization came over Asa; he was actually prescribing! It'd be something to receive his first patient—even a non-paying one—in what he chose to call his consulting room, though, for a fact, it was no more than an unused storeroom of Mrs. Southeby's.

He stared happily into space. Tomorrow he'd hang that little sign he'd whittled during early winter evenings and the world would know that "Doctor Peabody" had set up practice for himself. It was a fine sign. Even back in Machias, where clever carvers were the rule, everyone admitted that Morgan Peabody's third son was extra clever with his jackknife. In fact, while studying with Doctor Townsend, Asa owed a good part of his living to the skill and industry with which he fashioned butter stamps, lard paddles and all manner of piggins, noggins and other wooden tableware.

On glancing at his patient he was disconcerted to watch two small tears well from under the singer's tight shut eyelids and go slipping down over her cheeks. "Does your head hurt?"

"Where is Jabez?" she inquired. "I—I'll get a beating for this."

Suddenly outraged, he burst out, "If either he, or anybody else, lays a finger on you just you tell me and I—well, I'll have the law on 'em."

"You have been—good, Doctor, too good. Please, what are you called?"

Asa told her.

"You spoke Algonquin?" the girl inquired timidly. "Or was I dreaming?"

"Always each spring a few Mic-Macs visit a 'Quoddy camp across the river from my home."

"Home?" Hilde lingered on the word.

"Machias, in the Eastern District of Massachusetts." He smiled. "It's away beyond Frenchman's Bay near to Nova Scotia. Where do you come from?"

The girl called Hilde closed her eyes as if infinitely weary. "I wish I knew."

VI. A SMALL, CONVIVIAL GATHERING

THAT THE SAMUEL STANTONS had been, and were, entertaining on a scale far more elaborate than Sabra's casual invitation had suggested, Lucius Devoe surmised the instant he set foot beyond the great, white-painted front door and its brass dolphin knocker. A black manservant in a powdered wig and chocolate livery was gravely trimming candles in graceful candelabra and girandoles while a younger slave rearranged silver cups and some glasses about a punch stand decorated with holly and evergreens of varying kinds.

Mrs. Stanton, long crippled by rheumatism, was seated in a big wing chair but received her daughter's guest pleasantly enough. Her spacious white-painted drawing room was empty, temporarily deserted by her guests.

To the Jamaican, Sabra's tiny mother represented something new in his experience—an American lady of quality. On the lady's carefully coiffed and powdered hair had been placed a precisely pleated palisade cape of muslin adorned with a rose-colored ribbon. Mrs. Stanton's party gown of brocade and rose-colored silk lace was a handsome affair festooned in flounces and bound with silver gimp. All in all Mrs. Stanton appeared so delicately diminutive that, perched in her big chair, she suggested a huge French doll. Her voice, when she acknowledged Lucius' presentation and careful bow, was deeper and more compelling than he would have expected.

"Pray make yourself at home, Doctor, and assist us in giving the New Year a hearty welcome."

Sabra, as Lucius had learned long since, was the second of Samuel Stanton's three daughters. That must be Phoebe, the eldest, so much taller and darker than Sabra and still wearing the widow's weeds and mourning ring she had donned the day after the *Gazette* had published a casualty list following General George Washington's nearly disastrous retreat from Long Island.

Phoebe, it was commonly assumed, never would get over the loss of her husband, Cornet Nathaniel Hitchcock, gallantly fallen while covering the defeated army's embarkation. But Lucius, noting the young widow's dancing eye, light step and ready smile, was not at all certain about the enduring quality of her grief.

Theodosia, a merry, seemingly empty-headed, blonde, blue-eyed girl was, by a scant year, Sabra's junior, but in her gown of celestial blue silk, white satin petticoat and Italian gauze neckerchief she appeared much older than her sixteen summers. Endowed with what her mother called "man-trap" dimples, she displayed them constantly.

"Already," Sabra whispered, "Theodosia has broken more than one callow heart. Think of it! And the minx has only begun to understand the use of her charms."

"Wallace Blanchard's been courting Phoebe for over a year," Sabra went on. "Everyone knows he's worshipped her since long before she decided to become Mrs. Hitchcock."

Lucius deduced that Blanchard must be well along the road to success—if a body were to judge from the way that young widow kept an eye on the front door. Why, right now, she was making the most transparent pretense of rearranging the drawing room's yellow brocade curtains in order to steal a look through the prettily frost-rimmed windowpanes.

During his first few minutes inside the old merchant's imposing mansion Lucius Devoe had suffered acutely; he felt hopelessly out of place. His plain, poorly cut and threadbare suit, his darned gray wool hose and well-patched shoes he knew had been covertly, but thoroughly, noted by little Mrs. Stanton's sharp black eyes.

Flushing red as a turkey gobbler's neck, he adopted a fresh attitude. Since there was nothing immediately to be done about his sorry appearance, Lucius at once employed a familiar private tactic; he pretended that he stood clad in the most elegant of London-cut Lincoln green velvet; that his stockings were of Italian silk, brave with scarlet clocks; that Valenciennes lace glistened at his wrists and throat. Why not? They'd be there some day, sure enough.

To Sabra's surprise and partial pique, he seated himself beside Mrs. Stanton and set about to entertain her with cleverly told tales about Jamaica and his life there. When he had obtained her complete attention, he described, in detail, a fine, if purely imaginary, cattle penn near Constant Spring, once owned by the Devoe family. Lucius took care, though, not to paint the former Devoe property as too imposing.

"'Twas an ill day, Ma'am," he declared soberly, "when Papa fell in an affair of honor; 'twas with an officer of the Port Royal garrison. Poor Mamma had no head for business and, alack, her intendant was a glib rascal. The villain not only embezzled her profits, but cozened my mother about the true situation of our estate until, all at once, he declared us to be quite ruined."

The delicate lines of Mrs. Stanton's pink and white features softened. She fetched a little sigh. "Poor, deceived creature. I declare, women should be allowed more education in matters of business, so often do widows lie at the mercy of the first unprincipled rogue. Tell me, Doctor Devoe, did you have brothers and sisters?"

"Three, Ma'am," Lucius told her, truthfully enough. "They and my dear Mamma all perished of the *coup-de-bar* fever which desolated Port Royal in 'seventy-three. I," sadly, he dropped his gaze, "was left friendless, penniless and alone."

During his discourse Lucius' gaze roved over this splendid room, noted that its chandeliers, small, but beautifully fashioned, were of real cut glass. Steel engravings from London and Paris adorned the pale yellow walls, together with an extensive collection of family portraits.

Hung directly above the fireplace was the portrait of a bold-looking young man whose luxuriant brown curls fell all the way to the shoulder pieces of a gold-mounted steel cuirass. His name, Sampson Stanton, Gent., and the dates 1605-1683 had been inscribed in flowing gold script on a small black tablet let into a frame of tarnished gilt wood. He, Lucius deduced, would be Sabra's original ancestor in America.

About the walls hung perhaps a dozen other portraits of men with strong features and cold blue eyes.

No rag rugs, but a deep and soft Turkey carpet, graced Stanton's polished hardwood floor. Brass fire tools, andirons and an ornate fender protecting the wide fireplace showed hours of polishing; they glowed as if fashioned of yellow gold.

He hated to estimate the cost of the spermaceti candles lighting this gracious room. They gave off no pungent, smoky reek of beef tallow, only a deliciously clear yellow light.

A number of men's voices maintained an uneven obbligato in the dining room where, as Mrs. Stanton stated, Mr. Stanton and his guests were lingering over port and churchwarden pipes. Every now and then a deep, and hastily muffled, burst of laughter would break in on the Jamaican's discourse.

This house, he was silently resolving, set a pattern for the quietly opulent manner in which Lucius Devoe, M.D., intended to live—before not very long, too. It was to make possible such luxuries that he'd quit Port Royal and the dubious security of his father's squalid little house, which might be well enough for a carpenter's mate employed at His Majesty's dockyard—but not for that man's son.

On his way to fetch Mrs. Stanton a glass of Oporto, Lucius moved slowly. Well, so far, he hadn't accumulated much of this world's goods, yet it was certain he'd taken more than a few steps up that bewildering, often treacherous, path leading to fame, power and property.

His decision to run away from His Majesty's dockyard in Jamaica and to sign as cabin boy aboard the *Active* had constituted an initial turning point in his life. A superannuated brig out of Boston, the *Active* was, all the same, engaged in an incredibly lucrative business—the triangle trade. Like other merchantmen in this commerce, she would transport manufactured goods, lumber, salt fish, hides and rum from New England to the West Coast of Africa and there trade for spices, ivory, gold dust—and slaves—for transport to the West Indies. At one of those hot and hazy ports down in the Antilles the old ship would sell her African goods, then make sail back to New England, deep laden with rum, sugar and milled money. Two cruises aboard the *Active* had earned him a sum sizeable enough to warrant his request for a proper discharge.

For a while Lucius had toyed with the notion of setting himself up as a ship owner, but he'd been astute enough to realize that even the normal hazards of the trade were many. Wise beyond his years, he had foreseen the inevitability of a clash between the American Colonies and their Mother Country. A study of medicine seemed to offer wider and less hazardous opportunities.

While Lucius was pouring the Oporto, he perceived that, on this date, he had reached the second great milestone along the route to success. Yes, by the grace of God and his own diligent efforts, he had, at long last, entered well-equipped on a highly respected profession. Physicians the world over had, of late, become eligible to frequent the most exclusive of drawing rooms. Stepping softly and quickly, he reentered the salon, thinking, "What I need most pressingly right now is enough money to put up a respectable front. I can't go anywhere in these damned apprentice's rags."

From the direction of the dining room sounded a scraping of chairs, then doors banged back and the voices swelled louder. Evidently, a majority of the gentlemen had decided to patronize a pair of comfortably warmed brick privies standing amid a little orchard in Samuel Stanton's backyard.

Sabra's father appeared, him pumpkin-round red face a-gleam with perspiration. He'd a splash of cranberry sauce on his waistcoat of pale blue satin and specks of snuff speckled his lace.

"Well, well," he cried on spying Lucius Devoe. "Who have we here? Eh? Who is he, my dear?" On heavy but still muscular legs, the merchant traversed his salon, keen gray eyes busy with his daughter's guest. He reminded Lucius of a rich East Indiaman entering port.

"Mr. Stanton," Mrs. Stanton informed him evenly and

at the same time signalled her spouse to remove the snuff specks, "this is Lucius Devoe, an acquaintance of Sabra's, or should I say Doctor Devoe?"

"You're one of Billy Townsend's students, eh? How is the old rascal—still pickling cats and rats?"

"Papa, please! Doctor Devoe is a student no longer," Sabra broke in. "Uncle Will certificated Doctor Devoe, Asa Peabody, and Peter Burnham tonight. I—I chanced to be there."

"Young man, pray accept my hearty best wishes," Mr. Stanton offered a pudgy pink fist. "My brother-in-law ain't easy to satisfy—none of that family is."

Lucius bowed deeply, gracefully. "Your humble obedient servant, sir."

Over his shoulder Mr. Stanton called to a gentleman just entering the salon, "You'd best look lively, Aspinwall; you've fresh competition in town."

The Jamaican's second bow was the essence of deference; his heart was hammering wildly. To think that he was being presented to the great Doctor Aspinwall! Why, Aspinwall stood nigh to the very top of the medical profession in Massachusetts. Doctor Townsend was only an assistant surgeon at the army hospital in Jamaica Plain. Doctor Aspinwall was its chief.

"You have elected an exacting profession, young man." William Aspinwall's craggy ivory-tinted features relaxed a trifle. It was only then that Lucius perceived that he, like Doctor Townsend, had lost the sight of an eye. "Not for many a moon will you appreciate its manifold demands upon your existence. Allow me to assure you that the digging of ditches is, by comparison, far less arduous."

One by one, other gentlemen appeared, surreptitiously picking their teeth with small gold picks kept in their vest pockets. Lucius too took care to catch each and every name, to memorize them. Long since, he had perceived how ridiculously flattered most men are to be recognized by name.

The first was Mr. John Langdon, of Portsmouth in New Hampshire; a tall, solid individual in a sober brown coat bound in black. Only a profusion of jewelled seals dangled from his watch pocket suggested him to be a man of considerable means.

"Mr. Langdon is growing very rich. He owns seven privateers," Sabra informed in undertone.

"Phoebe, pray offer the oranges," Mrs. Stanton directed as carelessly as if, in these days of interrupted trade with the West Indies, oranges were not almost of a value with rubies and emeralds.

The man with a fat, larval face was Briggs Hallowell—Lucius recognized the name immediately. It appeared regularly in the *Boston Gazette* as auctioneer over many a prize vessel. Hallowell appeared in company with a sunburnt, broad-shouldered individual who walked with the peculiar, swinging gait of a seafaring man. The stranger presented a striking figure in a truly magnificent coat of sky-blue velvet adorned by silvered vellum lapels and ornamented with a profusion of silver lace. Lucius' fingertips began to tingle. Jupiter! Those looked like solid gold buckles secured to the stranger's yellow morocco pumps. Yellow bristles faintly blurring the point of his jaw indicated that Mr. Hallowell's friend might be blond, though there was no being sure; his carefully curled chop wig was white as any snow field.

"Mrs. Stanton," Hallowell bowed awkwardly. "This is Mounseer Fougère, master of His Most Christian Majesty's sloop-of-war, *Ecureuil*."

The Frenchman made a very elegant bow, then bent to brush Mrs. Stanton's fingers with his lips. His vivid blue hair-ribbon—its ends were nocked into neat swallow's tails—fluttered so bravely that Theodosia gave a little ecstatic sigh and bit her lips cruelly hard behind her fan to give them color.

"*Cette honneur m'accomble,*" declared the French naval officer in deep and very resonant tones. "Consider me your most devoted slave, Madame."

Lucius couldn't have been more surprised. Such Frenchmen as he had met while serving aboard the *Active* had been almost without exception dark, hairy and small-sized fellows, quick and nervous as race horses at the barrier. This solid young wind-beaten giant was something new. From hard blue eyes to powerful legs, he could not have differed more from the common concept of a Frenchman.

Mrs. Stanton considered M. Fougère with sharp attention. So this chap commanded one of the French King's vessels-of-war, did he? If he was typical of the officers commanding the vessels of Admiral de Ternay's squadron, Messrs. Arbuthnot, Graves and Hood were due for some surprises.

Lucius realized suddenly that not only Sabra but both of her sisters were lost in a shameless admiration of M. Fougère's apparel. In open envy they studied his exquisitely fine Alençon laces, the sheerness of his white silk stockings and the elegant shape of yellow morocco pumps supported by high heels of a brilliant scarlet.

The slender young Jamaican was taking care not to address too much attention to Sabra, although, whenever she dared, she cast him a slow and lovely smile. Jupiter! How very sweet and warm-looking she appeared in her blue and rose dress. Only once did he seize an opportunity of addressing her privately. When Mrs. Stanton demanded birch logs to brighten the fire he'd sped to fetch them, found Sabra a step behind. Intoxicated with the trend of the evening, he had made bold to give her slim fingers a quick squeeze.

"When shall I see you again?"

"Possibly day after tomorrow. I intend to fetch some comforts to Doctor Blanchard's marine hospital for Mamma."

"When?"

"Oh, about three of the afternoon."

"Capital." Her acumen delighted him. As a rendezvous the hospital presented the most natural place imaginable.

When, unobtrusively, he reappeared, liquor-warmed conversation was causing the Stantons' salon to reverberate.

"Plague take it, Doctor," a big, heavily pockmarked lawyer was demanding of Aspinwall, "why not admit that we in America have bit off more than we can chew? I say, let's make peace, even if it means losing territory south of Chesapeake Bay. 'Tis said the British are as weary of this contest as ourselves and are fearful of the French threat to their West Indies."

"No, Greenslett. We can't let the southern states go British." Doctor Aspinwall shook his white-wigged head so vigorously that its black tie ribbon fluttered like a blackbird caught in a squall of wind.

"But Savannah is already lost and the betting's five to one Charleston will fall to Clinton and Graves within a matter of weeks. The Carolinas are British already to all intents and purposes."

"I don't agree. Ben Lincoln's down there with near five thousand men—and they claim he's a damned able general."

"Fiddlesticks!" snapped Greenslett. "Old Granny Lincoln's not another Greene or even a Wayne. Even that Frenchy boy, Lafayette, is more able. No, Will, I fear we must abandon the southern colonies. Come now, is it not wiser by far to reach a compromise with Parliament? Once we have assured our own independence here in the north we must build up our strength, create a strong army and navy. Then, and only then, can we sensibly attempt to include the southern states." The speaker took an agitated pinch of snuff. "Gad, Doctor, if you haven't seen Georgia and the Carolinas you've no concept of how poor and under-populated they are—"

"Never, sir, never!" Doctor Aspinwall's tone was incisive as one of his own scalpels. "Our southern neighbors should, and must, be considered an integral part of our Union—quite as much as Massachusetts or New York!"

Mrs. Stanton, alert to the rising pitch of voices, inquired of her husband in her clear, slightly nasal tones, "Mr. Stanton, pray inquire of Monsieur Fougère whether he in any way credits an unhappy rumor we have encountered so persistently of late?"

"Ma'am?" Mr. Stanton demanded, a glowing coal poised in small brass tongs held over his pipe bowl. "Rumor? What rumor?"

Methodically, Mrs. Stanton smoothed the brocade of her skirt. "Why," said she primly, " 'tis being bruited about Boston that the kings of England and France are prepared to effect first a truce and then a reconciliation."

"Eh?" was Mr. Hallowell's abrupt ejaculation. "What's that about a reconciliation?"

Lucius listened hard. He began to conjecture rapidly. A truce or a peace between England and France? How would such an event affect the future? He'd discovered long since that the people who most frequently got ahead in the world were the ones who figured on what not a week, nor yet a month, but what a year or more might bring.

After Mr. Greenslett, the black-haired lawyer, had made a quick translation, the Frenchman looked first confused, then offended and ended by waving big brown hands in violent negation.

"Monsieur Fougère has heard of no truce in prospect," Greenslett explained. "He desires to hear further concerning this rumor."

Sabra's mother nodded quickly, "Pray tell him, sir, that the gossip runs thus: The French King is to abandon his alliance with America because King George's Parliament has agreed to return all Canada to French sovereignty. The French forces are then to assist the British in subduing us. I trust there is no truth to it?"

Everyone looked at the big blue-clad Frenchman. *"Impossible! C'est impossible! Jamais, mes amis! L'idée est ridicule!"*

"Perhaps. I hope so. Have you heard this tale before, William?" Stanton demanded of Doctor Aspinwall.

The doctor nodded. "Aye! In my opinion 'tis but some Tory's trouble-mongering. Eh, M'sieu Fougère?"

The naval officer's assent was vehement. Never would Louis XVI break his pledged word, or abandon his obligations to the Congress. The present alliance with America was presenting what His Most Christian Majesty and his ministers most earnestly desired—an opportunity to humble England's arrogance and boastful pride.

Color tinging his bronzed cheeks the big Frenchman looked about, blue eyes gleaming. Were mesdames, and these gentlemen, aware that the Dutch were on the verge of joining Spain, France and America in their coalition against George III?

Only Mr. Langdon had heard the good news. A small cheer arose and the girls clapped softly.

"Let's drink to that," Mr. Stanton suggested. "I say, what the deuce *is* the Dutch king's name?"

Nobody seemed to know so Lucius Devoe spoke for the first time. "I believe, sir, the Dutch have no king but a Stadtholder. He is William the Fifth and rules through a body called the States-General."

"Stateholder or king makes no mind," called Hallowell. "Let's toast something in a hurry; my whistle's drier than a charity sermon!"

VII. HOME FROM THE WARS

"PHOEBE, my dear, it lacks but a few minutes of twelve," Mrs. Stanton observed. "Pray instruct Eben to fetch in the toddy."

Presently, an elderly Negro shuffled in proudly bearing a huge Sheffield punch bowl on a salver; from that great, gleaming receptacle rose fragrant spirals of vapor redolent of mulled Oporto, oranges, cloves, cinnamon, and roasted apples.

Teeth gleaming and brass earrings a-glint, Eben deposited his burden on the sideboard amid a veritable squadron of dishes filled with raisins, nuts, popped corn and cookies of half a dozen sorts. The gentlemen crowded about without delay, dipping up the savory liquid in silver goblets and mugs. Sabra, dark eyes alight, pressed an extra large goblet upon Lucius.

"It smells divine," she begged softly. "Save me a sip. Papa's Canary wine is feckless—fit only for children like Theodosia and invalids."

Lovelier than ever, Theodosia devoted her attention and dimples to M. Fougère and struggled stubbornly to converse in her painfully inadequate school-taught French. More than a little charmed, the Frenchman brought her food and a small green wine glass of that Canary so despised by Sabra.

"Ten minutes till the New Year," boomed Hallowell. "I say, Sam—I don't remember that clock."

"You wouldn't, though you sold it to me at the *Mermaid's* prize sale."

"She the same *Mermaid* who was taken off Sandy Hook by a privateer?"

"Aye, by the *Grand Turk*. 'Twas a handsome affair, they say, with her skipper—name of Ashton—Robert Ashton, I think—decoying this merchantman right out from under the guns of two frigates guarding the Jamaica convoy. He's quite a fortunate skipper is Captain Ashton. I'm told he's grown almighty well-to-do through his privateering, for all he's just a Virginian and no real seaman."

The handsome brass knocker on the front door fell twice very softly, but Cornet Hitchcock's widow heard it.

"I'll go see who it is, Mamma," Phoebe announced

quickly, and all but ran from the drawing room, black skirts and petticoat a-rustling.

Smiling the brightest of smiles, Phoebe entered the hallway in time to see Eben's chocolate back and canary-colored waistcoat bowing low.

In the warm yellow light cast by a leaded fanlight, the caller, a tall man of early middle age, was brushing a sprinkling of snow from a bottle-green riding cape and, at the same time, gently kicking one black riding boot against the other to rid them of a white crust.

When he saw Phoebe the caller's heavy brows went up and his strong red-brown features lit; immediately, they lost their natural gravity of expression.

"Your servant, Mrs. Hitchcock." He spoke formally for Eben's benefit. Like most good servants Eben was a snob, and a stickler for the niceties. "Am I in time to greet the New Year?" Doctor Wallace Blanchard made the widow a leg; while not exactly graceful it was nonetheless easy. She returned his salutation with a mock formal curtsey which set her wide black skirts to describing fetching semi-circles on the well-polished floor. Her handsome dark eyes never for a moment left his clear gray ones.

Once Eben had disappeared with Blanchard's beaver hat and riding cape, Phoebe caught her breath, swayed forward and cried softly, "Oh, Wallace, where ever have you been? I—I've been so exercised—it, it's not good—all that ship fever being in port. Besides I—I've wanted you with me."

"Dear Phoebe," Wallace Blanchard took her hand in both of his—he must have ridden quite a long way, they were quite cold. "Bless you for worrying—a doctor's family soon learns not to." He sniffed and good-natured lines crinkled at the corners of his eyes. "One judges that the spirit of the New Year is already strong. Who are your guests?"

"Just a small, convivial gathering; Doctor Aspinwall and some others of Papa's friends—and a queer, shy friend of Sabra's. He's from the West Indies."

"Lucius Devoe?"

She looked startled. "Where did you know him? What is he really like when he's not wearing company manners?"

"He's a promising young man—very. A hard worker and very clever in his operating."

"Then you've seen him at work?"

"Often. He and your Uncle William's other students assist me at my hospital—the Drydock, you know. I hope they still will—"

"Oh—ho! So *that's* where Sabra met him."

"It's quite likely—where are the guests?"

"At the punch bowl, I suspect."

"Um. That's sensible. I—well, shall we join 'em?"

She hesitated, her steady dark eyes peering curiously up into his steel gray ones. "Wallace, are you keeping something?"

"Possibly," he smiled. "The holiday season is made for small mysteries." Laughing, Blanchard offered his arm and led her back into the warmth and cheer of the salon. Once he had made his respects to his host, Mrs. Stanton and to their daughters, he looked about. Ah. Yonder was Devoe, the West Indian chap. Blanchard, noting that the small, alert, black-clad figure was lingering, not quite easily, in the background, cast him a friendly smile and greeting.

"Wallace, my dear boy! Welcome home," Doctor Aspinwall's grip was hearty. In an anxious undertone he queried, "You secured the instruments?"

The joviality faded from Blanchard's manner. "A few, sir."

"How many?"

"Two chests of surgeon's tools—and three trepanning sets."

"If that's all they'll furnish, God help us!"

"I argued and argued, sir, till Doctor Shippen came near to having me pitched out of his office, neck and crop."

"I'm sure you did your level best, Blanchard," Doctor Aspinwall's long face fell into gloomy lines, "but we never can make out with so few. You're certain that's all the Director-General would give you?"

"'Twas not Doctor Shippen's choice, sir. There can be no doubt that the Medical Department's stocks are next to exhausted." Doctor Blanchard held reddened hands out to the blazing birch logs. "Following your suggestion I then sought Jonathan Potts, Purveyor-General, but neither he nor Doctor Craik, General Washington's own physician, could help the Northern Department by so much as a single medicine chest. Potts, did, however, requisition for our benefit ten each of glysters, syringes, probes, spatulas; also three hundred captured blankets, two dozen bullet forceps, a bale of lint, and six chests of ordinary physicks. They are already on the way—"

"Dear Doctor Blanchard it is *so* nice to have you back," Theodosia burst in on the conversation. "Tell me what do the ladies wear these days in New York?"

"Since I wasn't fortunate enough to get captured," Blanchard replied lightly, "I'm in no position to describe the prevailing modes from London. But, Theo, you shall receive a present come midnight."

Theodosia twined a pale arm about his dark green one. "A present! What is it? An import from France? A French merchantman made port the other day—M. Fougère, yonder, convoyed him in." Hopefully, she peered up at him. "*Please* say it's a bottle of scent. I declare I'd sell my soul for a vial of Essence of Bergamot."

"Theodosia!" Mrs. Stanton's disapproval was instant and emphatic. "You forget yourself."

Fortunately a contretemps was dispelled by Sabra, who, eyes a-light, was leading forward the slender Jamaican. "Doctor Blanchard, do you remember Doctor Devoe?"

"We have met many times." Blanchard flashed a wholly friendly smile. "So it's 'Doctor' now! My best wishes, sir, and congratulations. Doctor Townsend is not ready to certificate anyone or everyone. You've had capital instruction."

"The best in New England," Aspinwall agreed unexpectedly.

"I am deeply sensible, sir, of your kind opinion," Devoe murmured. This was praise from a direction that really counted. For a long time—nearly a year to be exact—he had been seized with admiration for Wallace Blanchard's long, and almost unaided, struggle to establish a hospital for the care of sick and wounded seamen. As the war progressed the disabled, in ever-increasing numbers, were being fetched into Boston, there to be brought ashore and as quickly abandoned by privateer captains and owners who concerned themselves chiefly with the prospects of prize money and its division into as few shares as possible.

"Ah, thank you, Mrs. Hitchcock." Blanchard turned aside to accept a silver goblet of toddy.

Sabra must have contrived to steal a few sips of toddy,

Lucius judged, from the unusually easy way her tongue ran on. Jupiter! She was a challenge to the imagination—and an inspiration. Of course, eventually, she would have to be controlled. A man couldn't tolerate his wife sneaking drinks even if they did render her wondrously cheerful and lovely in soft autumnal tints.

The toddy was affecting him too; since Doctor Blanchard had recognized him he'd experienced an increasing self-confidence. Threadbare or not, it was quite something to be entertained at the home of Samuel Stanton, gentleman, owner or part owner of a dozen merchant vessels. Jupiter in Olympus! As the liquid warmed, tugged at his stomach, Lucius felt increasingly convinced that this was the level of society to which he really belonged. The room rocked just a trifle but he righted it; Sabra's skirts were whispering in his direction. She was carrying an orange and, to·his flaming embarrassment, slipped it none too slyly into his coat pocket. He hoped Mrs. Stanton wouldn't notice the bulge; she might imagine that he had purloined the precious bit of fruit.

Screened behind a chair back, her hand caught his, exerted on it a timid pressure.

"Oh, Lucius, before long these people will feel honored to come to you." Her melodious voice rang with conviction. "As if it had already happened, I am sure that you will go far—that you will rise to the zenith of your profession. Doctor Townsend has told Papa and Doctor Blanchard so. You are ever so clever."

"Did he? Did he indeed?" Devoe felt a sparkling current surge through him.

"La! What can you two be gabbing so mighty solemn about?" Theodosia, blue skirt a-flutter, came sailing up. "Come fill your goblets. Mr. Hallowell declares 'tis but a minute to midnight."

Phoebe Hitchcock took Doctor Blanchard's arm, demanded softly, "Wallace, now that we mark the last gasp of 1779—what is your surprise?"

"'Tis not yet midnight," Blanchard reminded. Turning away, he parted the glass curtains and peered briefly out into Bennett Street. He must have seen something, for immediately he crossed to address his hosts.

"Mrs. Stanton, Madame, and you, sir. On the last stroke of twelve I beg you to address your attention yonder." His hand indicated the front hall. Out there a pair of fragrant gray-green bayberry candles were burning on a card table.

"God bless my soul, Blanchard, what kind of prank are you up to?" Mr. Stanton was redder of countenance than ever, and he spoke a bit thickly. Everyone fell silent because, near the waterfront, a cannon boomed; then another set the snow-covered hills about Boston to reverberating.

"To the New Year!" called Hallowell.

Fougère cried, "*Heureuse année!*"

Down the street a church bell commenced to clang and bong; another bell increased the clangor. Then, like a soprano joining in a deep male chorus, the hall clock added its silvery tones to announce the moment of midnight.

The company faced about as the front door opened suddenly to admit a tall officer who whipped off a cockaded tricorne but never paused. His long stride into the salon caused his riding coat to fly apart, disclosing travel-stained doeskin breeches, blue tunic, deep red lapels and several gilded but tarnished buttons.

"Oh, Joshua!" Theodosia screamed and ran forward but Sabra checked her impetuous rush. Blanchard smiled.

Mrs. Stanton half rose, perforce fell back and in a choked voice faltered as young Captain Stanton knelt to kiss her hand, "My son, oh, Joshua, Joshua, my son!"

There was a distinctive Stanton set to this young officer's wind-reddened features; his eyes were bright and piercing as his mother's.

"Praise God, it's my boy!" old Mr. Stanton cried. "Home and safe. Welcome, lad. Welcome home from the wars. Don't cry, you silly girls, just because your brother's home."

VIII. GALLOWS TREE

SNOW, fallen during the night, had spread a dazzling new blue-white covering not only over the farmers' fields, but veiled also those old entrenchments and redoubts scarring Boston Neck. Sometimes formidable drifts over the road to Dorchester Heights had barred Asa Peabody's way and delayed his progress. In addition the hired horse had proved to be ill-shod and so aged that its lower lip hung loose.

After sunup the temperature unexpectedly had dropped and now a brisk breeze out of the west was nipping savagely at Asa's nose and so much of his ears as showed above the rough gray muffler. This being of a Sunday's morning, the rented two-wheeled cart encountered little traffic, beyond a scattering of citizens tramping into Boston to attend Divine Services.

Godfreys! but this wind was keen. Even at this late hour the cattle still stood close to their barns or nosed dispiritedly at snow-capped straw stacks in the stableyards. Once the physician's cart turned to traverse a wide cornfield, a flock of crows reluctantly rose from among the shocks of sere, wind-whipped stalks. More already were winging in from the slate-gray, mud flats along Back Bay where a rising tide had halted their restless quest for offal, clams and stranded fishes. In ragged formation the sable column joined, headed for a woods beyond the outskirts of Dorchester; their cawing sounded sharp and clear in the blue winter sky.

Presently the horse panted around a turn in the deeply rutted road. Asa raised his gaze from the beast's steaming and furry rump to behold his goal. Stark, lonely and black against the sky, the gallows tree stood on the summit of a little knoll rising from the midst of a broad field. The tree, a gale-twisted red oak, had been struck by lightning a few years back and half killed. Asa shielded his gaze against the glare, was not particularly surprised to discern quite a small crowd gathered about that lonely oak.

Over his shoulder he cast a glance at Peter Burnham's figure lying huddled under a horse blanket on a pile of straw at the bottom of the cart. He was, at the moment, snoring manfully and clutching his cloak about him. Phew! What a head he'd have when he came to. Asa himself wasn't feeling any too spry this morning, thanks to three of Mr. Perkins' hot rum toddies. He drew several deep breaths of the crisp and invigorating morning air.

Because of increased desertions and other crimes committed by troops garrisoned in Boston, executions had become frequent. This would explain the small size of the crowd waiting, in a loose circle, about the gallows tree.

To the left of the oak a half-platoon of blue-faced soldiers in white cross belts and un-matched brown uniforms waited, stamping their feet and blowing on their hands. To a man, they were cursing the necessity of marching a long half-mile out from those ramshackle barracks originally constructed to shelter the Patriot Army during its siege of Boston back in 1775 and 1776.

Once Asa's rented cart jolted nearer, he became aware that of the handful of civilians in attendance nearly two thirds were women and girls. How curious a fact. What in the world would bring them 'way out here on such a bitter Sunday morning? Most of the spectators were seated on a fallen log and had drawn their clogged feet up under their skirts, suggesting a row of gray and dun-colored birds perched on a limb.

"Whoa!" Asa drew hard on his reins of frayed rope. The horse sighed, halted immediately knee-deep in snow and drooped its heavy head.

The beast seeming entirely content to remain where it was, Asa wound his reins about the whipstock, then vaulted to the ground and, spraying snow before him, waded over to the officer in command. The lieutenant, standing somewhat to one side in company with a little drummer boy, wore a rusty black tricorne askew and fidgetted irritably at his sword knot. For all that this was Sunday, his uniform was anything but smart. Asa saw that tears in the dark blue revers of this officer's overcoat had been but clumsily mended with black thread; moreover, his buttons were dull as ditch water.

"Beg pardon, sir; I seek Captain Morgan," Asa began politely.

"Oh, you do, do you now?" The officer cast Asa's black-clad figure a glance devoid of interest.

"Yes."

"Well, he ain't here," the lieutenant grunted. "Lucky bugger's sleeping off last night's jollification. What the Devil d'you want?"

Asa bent suddenly, sombre brown eyes on the speaker. "Civility, sir, is common property. Why not avail yourself of your share?"

The lieutenant stared, then snorted, "You can stow the preaching. I've asked you already, what d'you want?"

"Here." Asa bit back his resentment, thrust out the order prepared by Captain Morgan.

Frowning in a glare off the snow the lieutenant scanned Asa's paper; his unshaven mouth tightened in a contemptuous grin. "So you've come a-body-snatching, eh?"

Asa's wide brown features went a darker hue, but he hung onto his temper. After all, if he were to study the effect of a sudden interruption of the flow of blood to the liver, spleen and lungs, he badly needed this cadaver.

The unshaven lieutenant's nod was brusque as he returned the permit. "Seems in order. But mind, you'll have to cut the rogue down yourself. Damned if I'll have my men do it."

He jerked his head to the left. Up a little gully there was a dark movement obscured somewhat by steam in the intense cold. By twos and threes the soldiers craned their necks to watch the deliberate appearance of a sledge drawn by a pair of solemn liver-and-white-colored oxen. They were toiling upwards and, at each stride, the snow spurted ahead of the oxens' knobby knees. The effect reminded Asa of spray flying to either side of a fast-sailing vessel's cutwater.

"Well, Doctor, here comes your gallows' fruit," the lieutenant grunted in a half-hearted effort to atone for his previous churlishness. "Red Tom Duneen ought to keep you busy whittling for a good spell; he's a powerful big bruiser." He turned to the drummer boy. "Well, let's get on with it. Get ready to beat the 'Rogue's March.'"

"Yes, sir." The drummer boy nodded, tried by blowing on his chilled fingers to warm them.

The officer caught his breath, then bellowed, "Platoon, at-ten-shun!" Next he gave a series of orders which ranged his men in a hollow square about the oak. Meantime the civilian spectators, perhaps twenty-five in number, hurriedly put away food baskets, readjusted their scarves and footgear; then, still chewing, scrambled up onto various boulders and the log to obtain a clearer view of the impending execution.

No scaffold had been built beneath the oak, so the only indication of what impended was the presence of a noose dangling from a powerful lower limb. Starkly yellow, it swayed against the brilliant winter sky.

Asa debated waking Peter Burnham; still, despite a swollen jaw and slightly blackened eye the Connecticuter looked so comfortable he allowed him to sleep on.

Again Asa directed his attention to the nearing hay sledge and its human freight. In a matter of minutes now one of its two passengers would be dead; how pitiful to perish on so lovely and sunshiny a morning. Although

Asa had witnessed death many times and in varied guises, never before had he experienced so powerful a sense of revulsion. Here, a vigorous man in the prime of his life was about to suffer death; a period put to his hopes, hates, loves and ambitions.

Now the oxen were wading much closer, heads bent against the slope, their breathing creating silvery billows about their horns. To either side of the hay sledge three purple-faced infantrymen marched knee deep in the snow; every now and then the early morning sunlight would draw a blinding reflection from their needle-sharp bayonets. The ox drover, a bearded old farmer, walked close enough to his sledge to grip the hickory rail and yet manage his span.

The prisoner's seat—an empty powder keg—was not so low but that one could fail to witness his blank despairing expression; that his hands, pinioned tightly behind his back, were clenched. The condemned man, the onlookers perceived, was wearing a ragged brown uniform jacket—from which all buttons had been cut away—ragged black breeches and white woolen hose. One of his stockings had slipped, exposing the sinewy, hair-covered calf of his leg.

The other passenger was a spectacled little priest in clerical black. Adjusting his balance, he swayed awkwardly to the motion of the sledge, all the time reciting prayers.

The infantry forming the square momentarily moved apart to permit the sledge passage. It was at that precise instant that the prisoner, a hulking red-haired fellow, sprang suddenly to his feet and, with a thrust of his shoulders, knocked the priest out of the sledge so violently that the ministrant's shovel hat and prayerbook flew far out over the snow.

Though hampered by bound arms, Duneen, screaming in hoarse insensate defiance, cleared the hay sledge's low rail, but on landing lost his footing and went floundering, rolling, over and over in the snow.

Snow-covered from head to foot, Tom Duneen regained his feet, thought to detect a gap and charged towards it, still screeching his terror, his revolt at what was about to be done to him. Someone tripped him whereat a trio of guards dropped their muskets and, like hounds on a deer, flung themselves upon him.

Duneen's foot lashed out desperately, caught one soldier such a kick in the crotch that he doubled up screaming out his agony. With a desperate thrust of massive shoulders the prisoner bowled another clean off his feet, but still remained hemmed in.

"Ah-h-h! Ah-h-h!" Duneen kept roaring, blue eyes rolling wildly in the scarlet area of his face.

"Here's fer ye, yer murdering Papist dog!" rasped a sergeant and brought the heavy ash staff of his spear-like espantoon crashing down on Duneen's red hair. The prisoner uttered a grunt, audible even where Asa stood twenty yards away; then cross-eyed under the blow he sank to his knees, sobbing something quite incoherent. There he remained because infantrymen had leveled bayonet points at the huge Irishman's chest on which an orange-hued mat of hair had burst through his soiled brown tunic.

"Ah, no, lads! Mercy!" the prisoner was gibbering. "Don't hang poor Tom Duneen. I can't, I—I won't die. Mercy, for the love of Mary. Help! Please, please, Lieut'nt Anson, don't let 'em kill me. Crogan! Ye'll help me? Don't we come from the same village?"

"Be still, ye treacherous murdering dog," snarled the sergeant. "'Tis spoiling a very pretty hangin' yez are."

"Hang him! Hang him!" shrilled one of the women gazing in wide-eyed fascination upon Duneen's struggles.

Duneen must always have been a powerful man but, strengthened by his mortal terror, he raged like a bound Titan and several minutes elapsed before the guards succeeded in applying additional bonds and were able to lug the condemned man, still struggling and screaming back onto the hay sledge. Asa realized that no less than four stalwart and lustily cursing privates were required to hold him down.

The priest had found his spectacles and now was engaged in wiping snow from his prayerbook. But when he commenced to pray again he did not climb back onto the hay sledge.

The execution detail shifted nervously in their ranks and breathed mighty hard because the doomed man kept up his inhuman screaming. It was so poignant of a searing, tearing fear that Asa felt hairs on the back of his neck stir and rise.

"Gag him, you God-damned fools!" the lieutenant

yelled. "Crogan, if you don't shut that bastard up in two minutes, I'll break you back to ranks."

Once the prisoner's dreadful sobbing cries had been stifled by a scarf twisted about his mouth, the lieutenant hawked, spat and then drew from his belt a scroll of blue paper. He glanced at the civilian group. Evidently in the grip of a macabre awe, a few women had turned aside, but most of them looked on, open-mouthed, in delicious horror.

"Hear ye, hear ye, one and all!" Lieutenant Anson intoned. "Having been duly tried by a competent Court-Martial, former Corporal Thomas Duneen, B Company, Second Massachusetts Infantry, has been found guilty on two counts of murder, three of desertion, and one of counterfeiting the currency of the Sovereign State of Massachusetts. The Court-Martial therefore has ordered this prisoner, the said Thomas Duneen, to be conducted to this place of execution"—

Lieutenant Anson paused to catch his breath,—"and on the morning of January the First, in the year of our Lord 1780, the said Thomas Duneen shall be hanged by the neck until dead, dead, dead. May God take mercy on his soul." Using absurd care, Lieutenant Anson folded the scroll and tucked it back into his sword belt. He then drew a sword, a slight dress weapon equipped with a slender, useless curved blade. In a low voice he called, "Drummer, sound off!"

Once the complicated cadence of the "Rogue's March" began to beat through the clear winter air, the hay sledge slid forward. Squarely under that noose swaying against the sky the driver halted his oxen and in almost shocking abruptness the drum ceased to rattle. A woman commenced unmirthfully to giggle.

The priest held a crucifix high before the doomed man's eyes, made the sign of the cross, then closed his prayerbook and turned uncertainly aside, pallid lips fluttering in silent prayer.

The prisoner's struggles slowed, then ceased altogether when Sergeant Crogan climbed onto the sledge, bent and replaced the powder keg on its end. Two infantrymen raised Duneen to his feet; they had to support him by his elbows because the murderer's knees wavered like those of a man far gone in liquor.

"Will yez behave?" the sergeant demanded while adjusting the noose. "Ye can make a speech, then."

Duneen nodded and had his gagging scarf removed. Asa could tell that the prisoner had calmed and, though his bloodshot eyes still rolled, he stood straight and still; handsome in a bold, brutal fashion.

"'Tis steady I am again, bhoys," he called in a loud, clear voice. "Forgive me for the trouble I've given yez for 'tis a Judas-guilty sinner that I am." Blinking from the glare off the dazzling snow fields he looked about. "Father, will yez pray the Blessed Virgin, in her great mercy, to overlook my crimes?" The priest nodded. "Then, Sergeant, dear, let's get on wi' this business; ye'll be terrible dry 'fore 'tis done."

Sergeant Crogan smiled for the first time, patted Duneen on the shoulder. "Sure and I will, Tom, and never a word will I tell yer mother how ye died." Even while speaking the sergeant pulled out a blue India handkerchief and bound it over the condemned's eyes.

"Speech!" "Hi! None of that!" the crowd began to yell. "Let him talk. We've walked four miles to hear him."

"Silence!" the lieutenant snapped. He had gone pale and continued to swallow nothing very hard.

"Climb up on the keg, Tom. 'Twill give a farther fall and break yer neck, an' yer lucky." The sergeant put a hand under Duneen's elbow, guided him to the powder barrel now placed at the cart's tail and helped him up on it.

"Ye always were a foine chum, Dan," choked the prisoner, then in a husky whisper added, "but, oh Dan, I'm mortal feared."

The lieutenant's sword glistened in an upward movement, remained up, shone blue-white like an icicle in the wintry light. The drum commenced to roll, slowly at first, then fast, faster, and yet faster. Asa felt his throat close, sweat break out on his mittened hands.

The ox drover shifted his chew of tobacco and kept one eye on the sword as, expectantly, he lifted his ox goad. The sergeant and his fellows retreated to the front of the sledge leaving Duneen precariously balanced on the keg.

In a glittering arc the lieutenant's sword swept downwards and, almost simultaneously, the drover jabbed his near ox. "Hup, you Judy!" he sang out. "Hup, you Jack!" Obedient, the great creatures bent their heads and settled into the oaken oxbows, steam clouding their heads. The sledge's runners creaked in the snow.

A pang akin to nausea made Asa's stomach tighten, his bowels contract, when he watched Duneen's brown-clad figure topple awkwardly off the keg. Under the sudden drag the big oak branch bent, but snapped back and bits of dark brown bark rained down to speckle the snow.

Tom Duneen's fall was a scant three feet; he suffered no broken neck.

Impressions of what followed remained engraved in Asa's memory as long as he lived; a burly figure revolving slowly at the end of the rope, twisting, bucking in powerful but futile contortions which endured for nearly five minutes. All this while the green-faced drummer boy kept beating the long roll; horrified and keeping eyes fixed on his officer.

When, at long last, Tom Duneen's body hung motionless, a dark outline against the raw blue of the sky, Lieutenant Anson lowered his sword and rasped, "Sergeant, take over."

There followed a considerable flashing of bayonets and clatter of accoutrements; then, presently, the drummer boy fell in at the head of the platoon and, on command, struck up the "Bataille." In unaccustomed smartness, the infantry shouldered their pieces and marched off.

The civilians meantime had picked up their baskets and, in gabbing groups, strayed back along the cart track towards Boston. The lieutenant fished in the pocket of his coattail, brought out a small stone bottle from which he took a long, long drink. "Have a drink, Doctor?"

Still numbed and shaken to the depth of his being, Asa shook his head. How easy it was to take life, he was thinking, and how very difficult it was to save.

"Drink?" Peter Burnham's dishevelled red head appeared over the edge of the cart. Straw stalks clung to his tangled ruddy hair and lent him a comical appearance. "For God's sake, give me a swallow. My mouth's drier'n a damn' chalk pit."

The lieutenant gaped at this sudden apparition; then laughed and passed over his bottle. "Yer main lucky to have missed this bad business. Help yourself." Sword tucked under arm and threadbare gray cape a-swing, Lieutenant Anson ran after the ox sledge and jumped aboard.

Soon only the two young physicians remained below the gallows tree.

IX. IN A DARK CELLAR

FRAYED AND GREASY, the rope tautened until the tackle block creaked and its roller commenced slowly to revolve. Presently, rapid dripping sounds filled a damp stillness pervading the cellar and drowned out the soft panting of three men heaving on the line.

"Sway away! Smartly now," Asa gasped, keeping an eye on the brim of a brine tun. Slowly, smoothly was appearing the sodden head and pallid shoulders of ex-Corporal Tom Duneen's cadaver. Lank red hair dangled stringily, hid the dead man's features and all but concealed a sharp steel hook lifting the corpse by its chin. Briny odors, reminiscent of a fish-pickling works, grew stronger.

"By God, he must be made of lead," grunted Peter Burnham.

More and more of the torso became visible, climbed steadily towards the cobwebbed beams overhead.

At last the cadaver dangled nearly up to the beams and spattered brine back into the old rum barrel. Hunching his slight shoulders, the Jamaican trundled forward a heavy kitchen table.

"Lower away—handsomely now!" Asa directed. "Grab the bastard's ankles, Lucius, and steady him down."

A soft *bump!* marked the impact of the cadaver's heels; by easing on the hoist line the ghastly figure was permitted to collapse gradually. Because the skin of the dead man's legs already had been removed clear up to his thighs, their musculature now was revealed, blue-black, in a sharp and fascinating relief.

"Pretty, ain't he?" Peter demanded admiringly, then using the back of a powerful hand he wiped sweat from his chin. "Look at the rascal's biceps and rhomboid muscles! The late-lamented Corporal Duneen must have sweated plenty with a pick and shovel to develop such a back and arms.''

Lucius crossed the cellar to trim one of their two whale-oil lamps into greater efficiency. ''If you two butchers are about ready to begin your hacking, I'll get after my own work.''

From a shallow pickling tub the Jamaican removed an old market basket containing the executed criminal's vital organs. This he deposited, leaking copiously, upon a small table after hurriedly pushing to safety, sheets of sketching paper, pencils and a number of water colors. Sighing softly, Lucius selected the bloody, purplish spleen and, after testing the edge of his knife, commenced to section it—hard work because the yellow-red lamplight was abominably inadequate. Due to a violent popular prejudice against dissections, they hadn't dared take advantage of two carefully boarded-up windows which might have admitted considerable daylight into Widow Southeby's cellar.

Only because faded old Amanda Southeby was a physician's relict had she consented, most reluctantly, to the use of her cellar for so nefarious a purpose. These days she was existing in a perpetual twitter of anxiety.

While thoughtfully considering the cadaver, Asa dried his hands on a gruesomely stained canvas apron protecting his clothes. Frowning, he opened a worn black leather bag, selected a heavy-bladed dissection knife, then refreshed his memory by making a close inspection of the muscle patterns revealed in purplish red and occasionally black tones. What a miraculous and incredibly complicated piece of engineering the human body represented! Would Medicine ever come to understand the last of its discoveries? Certainly not in his lifetime, nor in that of his children.

''Have you any special desire to work on poor Tom's murderous heart?''

''No, I'm for a knee joint today,'' Peter replied slowly. ''Quite an improvement, this, on attempting conclusions from old Fothergill's anatomical charts, eh what?''

''Good old Tom Duneen,'' Asa mumbled and bent over the great jelly-like clot of the heart.

''Fothergill, I'm sure, is wrong about the extent and use of the quadriceps tendon of the knee.'' Peter's lips, still swollen from the impact of someone's fist—events at the Red Lion remained cloudy—compressed themselves. "God's truth, Asa, why should people object to the dissection of a human body? How're we to learn what's wrong with 'em if we don't know what's right? Steady all!" His hand commenced covertly to creep out towards an oaken wedge used to steady the cadaver's limbs. He seized the bit of wood and flung it violently at a far corner, inducing thereby a shrill cry and a small, frantic commotion.

"Got him!" Peter cried, "a real sachem, too—" He ran over to hold up by its tail a fat and still squirming, brown rat.

"Oh, for God's sake—" Lucius glanced up irritatedly—"can't you grow up? I'm trying to work. Look, Asa, what do you think? I maintain Boerhaave is entirely wrong in his assumption that the various humours are distributed about the body by the blood stream. How could yellow or black bile become introduced into the blood stream? There's no known inlet." He put down his water-color brush to wave an impassioned hand. "Look for yourselves. The liver and the pancreas are separate organisms." He spoke deliberately, black brows almost united. "Yes, I am convinced Doctor Boerhaave's theory of morbid acrimonies in the blood are—well, untenable—for all he's a great man."

The sound of Widow Southeby's stout, home-pegged shoes moving about the kitchen floor just overhead sounded quite distinctly in the silence that followed.

Somewhere down the street a dog began yapping persistently at a passer-by. Peter tossed the dead rat into a trash box and returned to his work.

Presently he observed, "Old Townsend was thorough, granted; but d'you know, Asa, he's omitted a cardinal item in our training?"

"Eh?" Asa glanced up.

"Hardly a word has he imparted concerning female anatomy, let alone afford us opportunity for dissection."

"Of course not," Lucius snapped over his shoulder. "Willie Townsend's an eminently respectable old fogey. Chance a scandal? Not he."

"Yes," Peter continued as if he had heard nothing, "females are structurally very different from men—as we have had the pleasure of discovering on occasion. For instance, a woman's femur sets into her pelvis at an angle very different from that of a male. It follows, therefore, that there must be no end of important variations in the structure of other joints—particularly in the pelvic region.'' He continued cutting, bending low in the uncertain red-yellow glare of the lantern. Abruptly he straightened, faced his companions, ''I mean to dissect a female before the winter's out, come what may.''

''Avast there,'' warned Asa, a grim set to his features. ''The time for that lies somewhere in the future. Don't risk ruining your career at its start by treading such all-fired dangerous ground.''

''Your hardihood and curiosity exceed your discretion, my lad,'' Devoe told him earnestly. ''Jupiter! The Boston public is dead-set enough even against the dissection of criminals. Were you ever detected exploring the tender mysteries of the female form divine you could count yourself lucky to escape with a suit of tar and feathers and a term in prison.''

''Aye, Lucius, you're quite right. Possibly researches of such a nature might be tolerated in Philadelphia, but not in Boston. Odds fish! By all accounts the Pennsylvanians have attained an almost Continental quality in their instruction of Medicine.''

Peter's voice assumed a quietly serious quality which Asa recognized and respected. ''Then I claim it's high time Boston was brought up to date! Who dares deny that women and their anatomy and diseases are no less deserving of study than those of their husbands and sons? What intelligent person dares claim it's God's law that one woman in five should die in childbed?'' His voice deepened with his earnestness. ''What do we understand of the decay of breast? Nothing! Absolutely nothing. Or of the sanguinous flux? Again nothing. If no one else will undertake this study of female anatomy I intend to, that's all.''

Asa nodded. No wonder Peter felt so strongly. Down in New London he had suffered a lonely, loveless childhood as the sole survivor of Daniel Burnham's five children; moreover his mother had perished of the dreaded and all-too-prevalent childbed fever.

The big, redheaded young doctor lowered his voice and looked up, one hand still grasping the great aductor tendon. ''In fact, my friends—I—'' He hesitated, blinked, then continued in tones of scarcely suppressed excitement, "I have—we—you may, if you wish, have an opportunity of—"

Asa's broad figure straightened; the expression of his dark brown eyes was intense. "Peter—you *haven't?* You haven't gone hunting female cadavers."

"Yes." His tone was a trifle defiant. "I entered conversation with a certain carter last night; for the modest sum of five pounds, hard money, this fellow vows he can procure the corpse of a young woman."

"Impossible!" Lucius stared over his half-completed water-color sketch. "He'd not dare rob a graveyard for such a sum!"

Peter grinned. "For him there is no need. The rascal's brother is an undertaker. I tell you it's safe—a golden opp—"

He broke off short and all three men started. By the lantern light the whites of their eyes shone yellow when a sudden and impatient knocking sounded upstairs.

"My God, it's the watch!" Peter breathed; then all three commenced hurriedly to hide valuable instruments. They, at least, must be preserved in the event of an arrest.

"Open up," a deep voice called. "God's life! 'Tis cold out here."

"Patience, kind sirs—" They heard the widow's reedy voice quavering; her steps came pattering to the head of a set of ladder steps communicating with the cellar. "Don't make a sound, sirs," she whispered hoarsely, "not a sound, mind, 'til I knock the safety signal."

Blood began surging in Asa's ears. Judas Maccabaeus! Why should three reputable physicians thus be made to feel like so many rogues surprised at counterfeiting? Their possession of this executed criminal's remains was entirely legal. And yet, and yet—the public was just as dangerous as it was stupid about dissections.

In the deathly stillness of the cellar they could hear Mrs. Southeby fumbling at her door chain.

"Lord send she staves them off." Then, softly, Peter repeated a grim jingle circulated among the low taverns and pot houses of Boston,

> "Them body-snatchers they have come
> And made a snatch at me
> It's very hard, them kind of men
> As won't let a body be."

"Oh, do be quiet. This is no matter for jest." Lucius was standing tense, ready to blow out the second lantern, his dark eyes looking enormous. Sharp in his mind dwelt the fate of one Doctor Phineas Jackson. He'd been stoned to death up in the Hampshire grants because his neighbors found concealed in his woodshed the half-dissected corpse of a suicide. Yes, they'd murdered him, in their superstitious savagery, for all that the cadavers of suicides and executed criminals constituted legal subjects for studies by the medical profession.

"Your indulgence, sirs," they could hear Mrs. Southeby beg, cautiously opening her door. "I could not come more quickly—I—I was not fully attired. Do you look for lodgings?"

Standing on her stoop and ringed about by the yapping curs of the neighborhood stood no hard-faced roundsmen in coarse brown cloaks, but two well-dressed gentlemen; one of them was wearing regimentals of some sort. For the life of her Amanda Southeby had never learned to distinguish between the uniforms of the Continental Service, and those of the Connecticut or Massachusetts Army. The significance of that bright yellow binding on his weather-beaten black tricorne quite escaped her.

Politely, the civilian lifted a silver-buckled beaver hat. "I am Doctor Blanchard," he announced, "and this is Captain Stanton of the Continental Artillery. We are seeking one Doctor Asa Peabody. That is his shingle, I presume?"

Mrs. Southeby sighed, smiled in relief. "Yes, carved it himself. He's mighty clever with his knife."

"In more ways than one, let's hope," smiled Blanchard. He eyed young Peaboldy's landlady with curiosity, saw a very short and faded-looking old woman with an intelligent face. Though obviously poverty-poor, she was neat to admiration in her well-mended gown, apron and crisp mob cap.

"Doctor Peabody is at home?"

"Why, why—yes, sir. Pray to enter." She stepped back and smiled a trifle embarrassedly as she indicated a door to her right. "Yonder is the doctor's, er—consultation room. I'm afeared it ain't much—yet. Doctor Asa's able, but he's just commenced to practice—hereabouts." She added the last hastily lest she lose these prospective patients for her favorite lodger.

Nerves still a-twitter, Mrs. Southeby opened the door to a chamber so very small and narrow that Stanton guessed it must once have served as a powdering room. Three persons would find difficulty in seating themselves therein.

If anything was in the least impressive about Asa Peabody's consultation room it was the expert, if plain, carpentering evident in a pair of home-made chairs, a table and a desk. On entering Blanchard glanced at a shelf supporting a mere handful of books on surgery, physick and pharmacy. He approved this selection since it included such standard works as John Hunter's *Natural History of ye Human Teeth,* Northcotes' *Marine Chirurgeon,* and William Cullen's celebrated *Lectures on Materia Medica.*

There wasn't much of a stock of herbs, drugs and medicines in evidence on the only other shelf, but Wallace Blanchard was pleased to note that Doctor Townsend's ex-apprentice favored no elaborately named nostrums or pills; the supply consisted of drugs of proven value such as antimony, mercury, chinchona, jalop, and paregoric—all neatly labelled in a strong and legible script.

Suggestive of an excited brown bantam hen, Mrs. Southeby fluttered back into the hallway. "Pray seat yourselves, gentlemen, and I'll go fetch Doctor Peabody."

x. THE INTERVIEW

ASA APPEARED, hurriedly buttoning his coat. What in Tophet could Doctor Blanchard be wanting so much as to justify his coming to this mean part of town?

"Captain Joshua Stanton—Doctor Peabody," Doctor Blanchard smiled a singularly winning smile and drew his hand out of the small rabbit skin muff he wore slung about his neck. "I, ahem, believe you are acquainted with Captain Stanton's sister."

The tall young officer grinned, offered his hand. "Since my return from the war my sister has spoken well of you, Doctor, and often."

"She—she did?" Color raced out along Asa's wide cheek bones. So Sabra Stanton *had* thought of him, and favorably, for all her cavalier refusal of his company a

few nights ago? What a sweet enigma she presented.
"Th-thank you, Captain. Won't you please be seated,
though I fear you will find it a trifle chilly in here."

Captain Stanton kicked his military riding boots, heavy
black affairs adorned with bright brass spurs, to rid them
of melting snow. "It seems like summer here after the
cold wildernesses of New Jersey." He pulled aside his
light blue riding cloak revealing a dark blue tunic turned
up in scarlet and bearing bright yellow buttons.

"You are evidently occupied, so we will be brief,"
Blanchard announced, steel-gray eyes searching Asa's
brown ones. "On my recent travels I had the honor of
tarrying for a few days at General Washington's headquarters near Morristown. There, Doctor John Cochran,
Surgeon-General for the Central Medical Department of
the Army, requested that I nominate a capable young
physician to be commissioned as surgeon's mate on his
staff. Indeed a rare opportunity—"

Asa nodded. "A golden opportunity, sir."

"The marine hospital here has first call on whatever
slight ability I possess, but I would cheerfully surrender a
finger for the experience to be gained from such a post
with Doctor Cochran."

"An ear perhaps, but not a finger, Wallace," Stanton
laughed. "A surgeon's fingers speak his skill, or so I'm
told."

Asa regarded first one then the other of his callers.
"What has all this to do with me?"

"Considerable." Doctor Blanchard slid his hands back
into the muff. "Doctor Townsend has suggested that
Captain Stanton and I discuss this proposal with you."

"Me?" A post on the staff of the Surgeon-General?
Godfreys! If there was any place in North America
where a new physician might observe evidences of excellent medical skill and thinking, it would be on Cochran's
staff. Infinite varieties of wounds, sicknesses and plagues
must inevitably offer themselves for treatment, diagnosis
and study.

Asa's breath went out slowly. Could he, were he selected, satisfactorily discharge his duties? Conscience's
sharp spurs began to rowel ambition. Could a fisherman's
son, but three years out of Machias and the dark forests
of the Maine District of Massachusetts, possess the clev-

erness and capacity for demands so great? Lord knew he spelled reasonably well, but his Latin surely would disgrace him among the scholarly, and sometimes supercilious, graduates of Edinburgh, Padua and Leyden. The deficiencies in his education—as he had known all along—were many, though no better instructor than William Townsend existed in New England.

Doctor Blanchard's gaze wandering out of the window, came to rest upon the spire of the Old North Church. "What Doctor Cochran especially desires is a surgeon more than commonly competent in anatomy. Both Doctor Shippen, the Director-General, and Doctor Gibbs, his deputy, feel that far too many amputations are being performed."

"You're damned right in that! The heft of the regimental surgeons are ignorant, venal butchers," young Stanton broke in. "They're scamps and cheats, almost without exception. His Excellency says so all the time!"

Blanchard produced a tortoise-shell snuff box, helped himself when the others refused. Once he had produced a hearty sneeze he opened a writing case and produced a document.

"Here, Peabody, better read it."

The rank offered, Asa found, was that of surgeon's-mate—it being held fitting that a candidate should commence in the lowest grade. However, Doctor Cochran promised swift promotion to the rank of junior surgeon should the newcomer prove qualified.

"The pay, I might add, Peabody, is scarcely munificent." Doctor Blanchard looked embarrassed. "A surgeon's-mate with our Army will—if funds are available, which is seldom—draw one dollar and a half per diem, plus two rations; a junior-surgeon is entitled to two dollars the day and four rations."

Although he suspected all too well the answer, Asa queried, "This salary will be paid in hard money or in paper?"

Stanton slapped his thigh, roared with bitter laughter. "Hard money? You civilians are the essence of comedy. Hard money for pay? Stab me, that's rare!" He sobered. "I'll not attempt to deceive you. You'll be paid in Continental currency, but there is a ray of comfort in that. Continentals are so damned depreciated something will

have to be done; some of our best line regiments hover
on the verge of mutiny. Old Bob Morris talked confidently of a loan of gold from the French or maybe the Dutch.
Alex Hamilton, the general's aide, swore 'tis likely."

"You said the line regiments are on the brink of mutiny?"

"Yes," Stanton admitted. "Can't blame them, though.
They fight, suffer, and starve—and watch the fat-cat merchants in Philadelphia, Boston, New London, Portsmouth and a half-dozen other prosperous ports eat their
heads off and pile up fortunes."

Doctor Blanchard stirred, frowned a little. "Possibly,
Captain, you are becoming unduly discouraging before it
becomes necessary. You see, Doctor Peabody, certain
qualifications are to be fulfilled before—er—the matter of
a stipend becomes cogent."

Without further delay Doctor Blanchard propounded a
series of questions on the diagnosis of various maladies;
the majority were so elementary that, as a rule, Asa had
an answer before the query could be completed.

"Possibly, Doctor Peabody, you are familiar with a
certain Doctor Ball of Northborough's remedy for the
scratches? Yes? Of what does it compose?"

Asa smiled. "Take one quart of fishworms and wash
clean. Stew them together with one pound of hog's lard,
then filter through a strainer. To this add a half-pint of
turpentine, a half-pint of good brandy, then simmer the
whole together—"

"—Your opinion of the remedy's value?" Blanchard
cut in.

"It's a spoiling of good brandy, nothing else."

"Agreed." Blanchard smiled. "What would you prescribe as a tonic for a general debilitation?"

Asa viewed a crack in the opposite wall; then, without
hesitation, replied, "Triturated mercury rubbed well into
the patient's arms and thighs. Twenty to forty grains of
the same administered by glister; sixty-four grains by
mouth, a total of 5,704 grains. There are, of course, other
excellent tonics such as those recommended by Doctor
Murray of the University of Edinburgh."

"—And they are?"

"Iron, copper, arsenic, nitric acid, quinine, gentian,
limes, and mahogany; I don't hold with that last; can't
perceive any reason for it."

Mechanically the visitor nodded, considered his notes. "And as stimulants?"

"Camphor, opium, musk ammonia, alcohol, and strychnine," came the prompt reply.

Blanchard shot a sidewise glance at Captain Stanton who had yet to write a zero on the tally he was keeping.

"What do you hold to be good disinfectants?"

For the first time Asa hesitated, lifted a broad hand to finger his chin. "I'm afraid, sir, there ain't any I know of as yet. Hot wine, charcoal and quick lime are helpful, but they don't really accomplish much. Mind if I mention a private theory?"

Doctor Blanchard did not.

"Don't know why, but the use of heat is beneficial. 'Pears to me that amputations and wounds heal quicker and cleaner if a surgeon's instruments have been warmed before use. I'm wondering if maybe heat soothes severed nerves and fibres?"

"It may be—though I've not noticed it," Doctor Blanchard's interest was merely transitory. "Now a few inquiries concerning human anatomy. Where are you going?"

Asa had started towards the door. "A moment, sir. The best answer may be a simple demonstration."

Almost immediately Asa Peabody's angular figure refilled the door frame; he was carrying a linen sack in one hand and in the other a short length of bandage. When placed on the table before Doctor Blanchard, the sack gave off a curious, dry rustling noise. Puzzled, the older physician glanced into it.

"Why, it's full of human bones!"

"Pray, accord me your indulgence." Asa placed the bandage in Captain Stanton's hands. "Will you blindfold me, sir? Securely, that I may see nothing whatsoever."

Captain Stanton accepted the bandage and stood up. Asa felt envious of his wind-reddened complexion, his sturdy figure in blue and scarlet, his handsome countenance and crisp blond hair. Captain Stanton fairly radiated a subtle animal vigor and virility and an aura like a clean, strong wind enveloped him.

When the staff officer had completed his task, Asa groped to a seat beside his examiner. "Now, sir, pray select any of the bones, at random, please. I will endeavor to describe it."

Incredulity swept Blanchard's pointed features. "Really, Peabody, you cannot be serious!"

Exhibiting a touch of impatience, Asa held out his hand. Blanchard fumbled in the sack, selected a long thin bone.

"That, sir, is a fibula of the right leg, I believe. This," he stated when another specimen was thrust into his hand, "is the left clavicula."

"And this?"

"The os capitulum radii."

At once incredulous and fascinated, Blanchard continued his catechism until the desk was piled high with glistening, yellow-white bones.

Only once during what became a long recital did Asa fall into error—in confusing certain of the ribs. "Please excuse me, sir, I have not gone through this exercise of late."

"Excuse you? Man alive, you are unique!" Blanchard sprang up and offered his hand as Asa slipped off his blindfold. "I'll wager not five men in North America could approximate your performance. 'Pon my word, why didn't you disclose your knowledge to me at the Drydock? Have you ever demonstrated your proficiency to Doctor Townsend?"

"No," Asa replied simply. "You are both busy men. Besides, I feared you might deem me forward."

"Forward! 'Fore God, Doctor, you're a genius." Beaming, Blanchard turned on his companion. "Well, Captain, I'll certify as to his medical abilities. What's more we've discovered a genius."

Though he understood little of the moment's significance, Captain Stanton nodded, sniffed a drop from the end of his nose. "With regard to my province—that of intelligence, bodily health and, er—appearance, Doctor Peabody appears more than satisfactory. Shall we proceed?"

Once he had shoved aside the bones far enough to afford space in which to write, the artillery officer produced a quill case and a printed form. Next he blew hard on his fingers.

"Age?"

"Twenty-six."

"Native of—?"

"Machias, in the Maine District of Massachusetts."

He filled in other parts. "Parents living?"

"Ma's dead. Pa was still alive the last I heard—nigh on two years ago."

"Single?"

Asa nodded.

"Can you leave for New Jersey in three days' time?"

Three days, Asa calculated rapidly, was mighty short notice but, by working extra hard, he should be able to complete this hard-earned dissection of the heart and maybe write up a few notes. Stanton misunderstood his preoccupation, felt an inexplicable interest and warm sympathy for this tall young fellow of his own age.

"I wish you to accompany me on the southward journey, so, if your affairs do not admit of such a rapid settlement, I will be glad to delay departure another day." He tested his pocket. After five years of war Joshua Stanton had learned that but three major elements shaped most considerations—self-preservation, love and, last but far from least—money.

The simplicity of Doctor Peabody's attire, the stark bareness of this chilly room indicated certain lacks. "Since an officer joining our staff must necessarily acquire some er—equipment, I have been authorized by the paymaster to advance you the sum of thirty Spanish dollars."

Of course the paymaster had done no such thing, but, Stanton reckoned, after what he had just seen, that it would be a fine thing to advance such a sum. He produced not hard money, nor paper notes of uncertain value, but a draft for so much silver on Mr. Robert Morris' bank in Philadelphia.

"You'll find this draft will be honored in full value at any counting house in Massachusetts," Stanton predicted quietly.

"Thank you, sir." Asa experienced a sudden awe of Sabra's brother.

Captain Stanton then handed Asa a much-stamped and counter-signed document. "Please preserve this with care, Doctor; it is your travelling orders to General Headquarters."

"Why not swear him in?" Blanchard demanded. "No time like the present."

"Can't. Only some soft-bottomed chair-warmer out of the Adjutant-General's Corps is qualified."

"Then tend to it with all speed. I fear you can't appreciate what an amazing feat Doctor Peabody has just performed." Doctor Blanchard was pleased to see how young Peabody reddened under the praise. "You must have toiled like a Moorish slave to achieve such proficiency."

Captain Stanton's stubby fingers struggled to hook the clasp of the light blue riding cloak.

"Doctor Peabody won't run out on us, Wallace; oath or no oath." His broad brown hand closed like a deadfall on Asa's. "Earnest congratulations on your appointment, sir, and to the poor freezing wretches, rotting at Yellow Springs Hospital." He checked himself on his way to the door. "Your grade of surgeon's-mate equals the rank of a captain in a line regiment, so we shall be equals on our travels southward—a journey I commence to anticipate. Your servant, sir."

Once Asa's callers had departed he remained motionless in his chair, so great was the multitude of emotions churning within him. He smiled happily on those travelling orders instructing him, with all speed, to report himself to the post adjutant on duty at West Point.

Judas Maccabaeus! This luck was all but overwhelming. Only with difficulty could he deny an impulse to yell his delight and rush down cellar to tell the others. Just think of it. Once he took his oath to serve for the duration of this war, he likely would become appointed to the Commander-in-Chief's official family.

What a priceless opportunity to observe theories and methods advanced by such colossi of the American medical world as Doctor William Shippen, Director-General of the Medical Service; Doctor Bodo Otto, the great Pennsylvanian German; Doctor John Morgan, and that amazing Doctor Benjamin Rush who had been Physician-General until '78 and now had become Shippen's mortal enemy. Truly, his career was setting sail to an uncommon fair breeze.

Come to think on it, Sabra Stanton now was no longer quite so hopelessly out of reach; a captain's pay, while not munificent, was a sight more than a lot of young couples began with. But would she prove willing to surrender the comfortable life in which she had been reared? Again, could Sabra ever return his tender sentiments, or would her emotions limit themselves to mere friendliness? The fact that she had spoken favorably to her brother *did* seem encouraging.

Um, when the war ended, he hoped he might find opportunity to continue his studies at the new School of Medicine in Philadelphia. Later, he might even travel abroad to Edinburgh and there, at the very fountainhead of all modern surgery and physick, earn his degree as Doctor of Medicine. How earnestly, how hard he intended to labor during the months to come. Yes sir, he was going to make Pa feel all-fired proud of his third son.

In that connection came a sobering thought. How was Pa getting on these days? He was growing old and that wound he'd taken in front of Louisburg during the old French War always had given him trouble. Of course, Charity, Pa's second wife, was still young and should be able to care for him; on the other hand, she thrice had been blessed with issue—as the phrase went.

Seemed odd to think of young children scampering once more about Pa's old double cabin. If anything happened to Pa who would look out for these youngsters? It would never do to allow any member of the Peabody family to become a public charge.

His mind ran on. Brother Ahab *might* have returned with a fortune won at privateering. Every day one heard of such men returning to their home village bent under a sea chest crammed with spoils; more still, never returned at all.

It wouldn't do to crow over his good fortune, Asa reflected; he'd take care to appear modest before Peter and Lucius and to set small store by his appointment. Abruptly, he became aware of those holes in his coarse gray woollen stockings; they were admitting cold air.

Still considering steps incident to his adopting the Army Asa arose—someone had knocked. Mrs. Southeby bustled by and presently thrust her winter's apple of a face around the doorway. On it was written a curious blend of pride, excitement and disapproval.

"Doctor Peabody!" she cried. "I—well, gracious me—I expect your very first patient is a-waiting outside."

"A patient? A patient *asking for me?*" Asa started. Some passer-by must have noticed his shingle. "Well," he said and attempted to reproduce Doctor Townsend's grave manner. "Well, pray show him in, Mrs. Southeby."

" 'Tain't a him," Mrs. Southeby said and her lips tightened. "It's a her. This is your office, Doctor, but the sooner she's out of it, the better I'll be satisfied."

xi. Doctor Peabody's Patient

LIZZIE WRIGHT splashed another—and final—bucket of hot water into her establishment's one hip bath; then, panting, pushed a strand of sand-colored hair from before small and piggy blue eyes. Though battered and much dented, the bath was her pride and joy. Of real copper, it certainly was the only such convenience in all the neighborhood—a fact which put firm ground under Lizzie's oft-repeated contention that her wenches were the cleanest to be found anywhere in Battery Street. Actually, the bath gathered dust thirteen days a fortnight.

"The good Lord alone knows why I toil like a black slave to accommodate such a worthless, finicky, la-de-dah baggage like you, Hilde. Yer a lucky girl, but too addled in the head to know it."

The madam used her chapped and black-nailed forefinger to scrape from her brow a thin film of sweat. Resentfully, she regarded her doxy's slight figure seated, shivering violently, on the bed's edge. "Just you understand me well, Hilde. Now that ye'll be fresh-washed as any nabob's fancy-girl, yer to demand *and get* ten shilling, else ye'll taste the strap again, and twice as hard."

"Yes'm." Hilde Mention kept miserable black eyes fixed on her own dirty bare toes curling against the chill of the floor. "I'll do the best I can, indeed I will. I—I'll give this one a real first-class tumble. I really will."

For all she'd been asleep near fourteen hours Hilde still felt uncommon sleepy and weary; incapable of further revolt. She sighed and shivered when warm air from the bath fanned the black hair hanging so limp and greasy over her forehead.

"You'll not regret this kindness, Mrs. Wright. The—this doctor's queer about soap and water. Why, he—he washed me himself."

"I'll wager he did and had ye, too, ye cheating little vixen."

Hilde paid the bawd mistress no heed. In her mind's eye she was visualizing Doctor Peabody's grave young face bending above her in the cellar of the Red Lion.

"He'll pay well, Ma'am. I'm sure on it," Hilde insisted; then fell silent because she guessed she mustn't promise too much. For the first time during her varied and bewildering ill-fortunes she had brought herself to utter a deliberate falsehood.

Doctor Peabody had been so kind, honest-spoken and steady. The only other such person she'd known had been Mooinaskw; she'd dearly loved her Mic-Mac foster mother, for all that the old woman smelt much like the she-bear for which she was named.

"He'd better pay well—hard money too. Mind ye git back here by five. There's a nice sea capt'n been taken by yer looks, though God knows why he'd want a bag o' bones like you."

Lizzie Wright wiped her hands on a dull blue apron. "Ye've been livin' here on the fat o' the land these past three months and 'ave yet to earn me a pound. Declare, I can't figger what ails ye."

The madam paused, hands on hips, blotchy features set in an expression of frank bewilderment. "You get my fanciest gent customers fair slobberin' fer you and yet ye freezes 'em. Why, they'd buy ye laces an' farthingales an' rings an' mebbe furs if ye'd only study to please 'em. What for do ye want 'em to swear they loves ye? Pah!" Mrs. Wright spat resoundingly. "That's fer love! Fer all their silly tales men an' boys don't come to Battery Street lookin' fer love—only to glut their lust and try the fancy games they dassent to at home. And you, you silly ninny, keep on moonin' of a knight in shinin' silver armor who'll come a-ridin' to carry you off ter everlastin' bliss."

Overcome by the girl's unreasonableness Ma Wright caught up a stick of kindling and fetched Hilde such a resounding whack on her thigh that she gasped and cringed. "Mebbe that'll warn ye to get such notions out o' yer head. Just you come back empty-handed and I'll have Jack give you such a hidin' yer won't walk fer a week!"

The perfect answer occurred to Hilde as, slowly, she rubbed the smarting spot. A slow, wise smile curved her lips, thin and blue, but still subtly lovely.

"I—I guess you're right, Ma'am. There are no longer any knights. From now on I—I shall cease to look for one."

Ma Wright snorted, tossed her stick onto the tiny fire beyond the hip bath. "Now ye talk like a wench with wits in her head. Ye can make yer fancy airs and graces tickle my gents. Why, ye could even pass yerself fer a virgin and earn a real pretty penny from 'em. Now get in there afore it gets cold." Ma Wright jerked a thumb at the hip bath. "A bath in mid-winter—why I humor such a worthless trollop's crazy notions, I'll never know. I'll warrant the water kills ye."

The air rose glacially cold beneath Hilde's coarse linen shift when she began to loosen the tie strings of her three soiled and often mended petticoats. Was it necessary really to wash all over? Even the well-to-do bathed but once a week in summer and less than once a month during the cold months. Dimly, from that evening at the Red Lion, she remembered something the doctor had remarked about her uncleanliness. Why? Men were such curious creatures concerning their pleasures. Maybe he derived a sensuous pleasure in caressing a clean skin?

A sharp west wind, beating through the garret's floor, lifted little puffs of dust and sent chills climbing up Hilde's thin legs as Lizzie Wright waddled out, enormous buttocks rolling under her faded callimanco skirt like ground swells across a sand bar. Said she over a huge and flabby shoulder, "Mind ye, Miss, yer bound in my employ fer two more years. God help ye if yer minded to run off and try to bilk me."

Muttering, the bawd mistress clumped off downstairs. Pretty soon Hilde heard her scolding Minnie, a big-breasted blonde girl from the Hampshire grants; most everybody thought her pretty in a heavy, cow-like way, but not quite bright. She was crying now because patrons were beginning to notice her pregnancy and so fight shy of her.

Defiantly, Hilde placed the last remaining slivers of wood upon her tiny, heatless fire; then, amazed at her own temerity, she pulled three hickory slats from under her straw mattress and added them to the blaze. For once she intended to be warm. The hickory blazed, then began to snap and crackle so loudly Hilde feared Ma Wright would surely hear.

Locking her teeth, Hilde pulled the shift over her head, and immediately felt the chill air bite so savagely that her skin, pale and thin as new vellum, became pebbly while her thin breasts shrunk in on themselves until they presented hardly any contours at all.

Toes recoiling from contact with the gritty floor, she crossed to the hip bath and eased herself into the four inches of steaming water. Due to the displacement of her slim body the water rose a little and warmed her lean stomach, but stung that dull red welt raised by Lizzie Wright's faggot. A shapeless blob of yellowish gray soft soap lay ready on the floor.

The hot water created a wonderful and unfamiliar languor while the back of the copper bath caught and magnified the heat generated by the burning slats. Gradually, warmth flooded Hilde's body, inducing a blessed lassitude in a mind too long subjected to desperate discomfort and fear. Relaxing, her next moves seemed wise and clear. She must refuse the loan of brown Jennie's new petticoat; it wouldn't be fair, under the circumstances, to borrow it.

Magically, the warm air and water appeared to dispel that fatigue which, for some time now, had gripped her. Why, it had required tremendous exertions to climb more than a few steps at a time.

At length Hilde sighed, commenced methodically to scrub herself. She felt only mildly repelled by grayish curds forming a circle about the inside of the bath—perhaps for the reason that Wejek and Mooinaskw never had minded dirt; few Indians did. Yielding to a sudden temptation, she soaped her hair and as promptly repented the move because the harsh stuff stung her eyes and the cut on her head.

"Ca-a-a!" she choked, just as she had in childhood, while groping for a strip of rag doing duty as a towel. All the same it felt good, a little later, to notice a new and lustrous softness in her blue-black mane.

Once she had dried herself, Hilde lingered a moment to let the unaccustomed warmth play over her back, thin little buttocks and legs; thank goodness, the welt was fading. What, she wondered, could be causing this faintest imaginable greenish tinge in her skin?

First, she was going to discharge her debt to Doctor Peabody—or attempt to. How amazing; she was almost glad at the prospect of going to a man. Surely, he would be gentle and tender? If only she had met Doctor Peabody when first she'd reached Boston: of course now it was too late—much too late.

Hurrying into her only other shift she was surprised to feel hungry, ravenously so. Of late she had become quite accustomed to enduring the pangs caused by an empty belly. There being nothing to eat, Hilde swallowed several deep gulps from a lead-mended jug standing beside her bed. Sure enough, the water took an edge off her appetite.

While tying on her petticoats, Hilde wondered yet again what it was that restrained her from complying with her mistress' urgings. True, on a few rare occasions, it might have been easy to show the way up those well-worn stairs to some of the ruddy young mariners who came rolling into Battery Street with the salt freshness of the sea wind still strong about their hair and clothes. All along, her instinctive revulsion against this life had been perplexing. It wasn't that she held herself above the customers—no matter what Ma Wright and the other girls believed. During her brief life she'd lived among none but plain, ignorant and very ordinary folk—had never so much as put foot inside a mansion.

Other country-bred girls, too, had proved restive for a while—had revolted at the contact of too eager hands, at the odors of stale sweat, rum and tobacco no less than at the incredibly obscene conversation of most patrons. Yet, sooner or later, they'd quite successfully overcome this disgust and had come to enjoy their new profession. Why had she, alone of them all, never given in—aside from those very few occasions on which she had become too utterly exhausted to struggle any longer?

Hilde dressed her hair with unusual care into a jet aureole, decorated it with a small bow of clean, bright blue ribbon, which, for no particular reason, she had preserved for some great occasion. A mirthless chuckle escaped her. What would the skates and sculpins swimming around Mr. Clarke's wharf make of such gay nonsense?

In a hurry now, Hilde laced up a brown velvet bodice, adjusted the set of her green and brown striped kersey skirt, then flung a frayed gray shawl about her shoulders. What a pity there was no mirror; she would like to have

learned whether this heat she felt burning in her cheeks
had relieved the customary dead-white of her complexion.

For a last time Hilde's hands crept out to the dying
coals. She felt fine as satin at the prospect of quitting this
wretched, icy box of a room, those sordid rags of under-
clothes dangling so uglily from wooden pegs driven into
beams gray with cobwebs and dust. God pity the next
poor female who must inhabit these dreary surroundings.
One would probably be moved in tomorrow; what with
the hard times, the war, and the ever-lengthening casualty lists, girls and young women a-plenty came drifting
from up and down the coast into Boston, a thriving metropolis where twelve thousand souls made their homes.

The January air was cold enough in itself, but, driven
by the westerly breeze that was blowing, it stung Hilde's
body through the scant protection of her petticoats,
shawl and skirt like the bite of a wasp, and nipped cruelly
at her uncovered and still damp head and ears. Luckily, a
brief winter sun was shining, drawing pale yellow reflections from windows of the fine new houses dotting Bea-
con Hill.

Hilde knew that the distance to Sudbury Street was not
very great, but her legs were feeling so queerly uncertain
she wondered how much time would be consumed in
reaching Doctor Peabody's address.

Presently, the narrow and muddy street she was following began to slope upwards; at once her breath grew
very short. But by clutching at fence palings, whenever
the going became icy, she made fair progress up Middle
Street. She guessed she had applied too much lip rouge;
well-dressed males on their way to and from the various
business establishments located along Princes' Street,
were casting speculative, side-long glances her way.

Hilde soon was forced to halt every few hundred feet
in order to catch her wind. Once as she paused, trying to
warm thin red-blue hands under her armpits, she thought,
"Wonder why I've been thinking just now not in English,
nor in German, but in Mic-Mac? And why should an occasional French word or phrase come back to me? Odd,
now I'll never know when, or where, I was born; in
another few hours it won't matter at all."

Although breathing painfully hard, Hilde started upwards again, the dirty snow crunching under her square-toed shoes; many of the oaken pegs securing their soles had dropped out and now admitted cold and slush.

It is an odd thing to have gone through life lacking any idea of who one really is, she mused as she struggled along. The last name seemed right for some reason—Mention. Plenty of people had commented on her oval features, slender hands and narrow feet—and on the very faint slant of her eyes.

Where her name of Hildegard came from, Hilde knew well enough; Frau Schroeder had called her that, piously declaring it shameful that a white and presumably Christian girl should be known by the outlandish Indian name of *Kwee-a-lin*.

Outlandish or not, Hilde reflected, those savages, the Mic-Macs, were the kindest people she'd ever met. How she had loved their lazy good nature and their simple sense of honor and justice.

She had to rest again and found a seat on someone's dust bin. More rapidly, now, flowed the stream of her thoughts.

Sometimes, when she was little she used to dream of a great vessel struggling in a furious storm, of men shouting, of whirling torrents of white water. Why? There must be something to it, because she'd had that vision many times.

If only the Reverend Neidiger had left her alone. She was completely happy that day playing, dirty and half-naked, among those dark-complexioned children in the bark wigwam of Wejek, sub-chief of the Mic-Macs. A stiff smile curved Hilde's lips. Wejek and dear old Mooinaskw could be stern, but generally were most indulgent with her. It being the Algonquin custom for children to adopt their mother's clan, Mooinaskw had her inducted into her Turtle Clan. How proud and happy she had been.

Oh why, of all the Indian villages in Nova Scotia, had the Reverend Hugo Neidiger to wander, lost and on the point of starvation, into their village? But for that her life might have continued a happy one. Unluckily the pastor noticed her, a pale-skinned little savage girl, packing dried blueberries in birch bark cones.

Br-r-r-r. The wind roaring down Sudbury Street tore anew at Hilde's shawl and gnawed her cheeks. She sighed and started on.

She wondered what arguments the Reverend Doctor Neidiger used on Wejek and what price he paid for her ransom. Wejek wasn't one to give things away—except to friends. How she had kicked, clawed and squalled at being parted from Mooinaskw. She remembered scratching four scarlet furrows across the Reverend Doctor Neidiger's cheek before he gave her a box on the ear and tossed her frightened half to death onto the bottom of the old canoe Wejek gave him.

She could not recall how many days passed before they reached the mouth of a big river and saw the cold, dark blue ocean glimmering in the distance; but she knew that exactly two days later, they arrived in Lunenberg and saw many of the white men's lodges standing about a little bay.

Hilde supposed Minna Schroeder and Helmuth, her huge stupid-looking husband, meant to do their Hanoverian best by her, but from the start they were over-ready to whip her for even the least disobedience of rules she couldn't understand. And that wasn't all that made her miserable; the little Schroeders, all ten of them, hated her for being so different. How they had tormented her every waking moment in a hundred ways, how they had mocked and ridiculed her poor efforts to learn their ugly language.

Eventually, of course, she learned to live, to dress and to conduct herself somewhat like a white girl. After a year or two, things got a little better because she became more useful and excelled in the household arts, especially needlework. And Frau Schroeder had insisted that she not neglect her ABC's, simple arithmetic and the Bible. They instructed her, too, how to make her prayers to that severe and quite colorless Lutheran God of theirs.

It came to the slowly walking girl all of a sudden that her sense of aloneness, more than any single factor, was the force which, before very long, would guide her feet out to the end of Mr. Clarke's wharf.

An errand boy, bent under a wicker basket from which dangled the pathetic head and ears of a big rabbit, cocked an impudent eye as Hilde rested yet again, breast heaving, against the porch pillar of a tidy, red brick house.

According to Minna Schroeder's reckoning, she must have been about sixteen when olive-skinned and broad-chested young Amadée Rossignol appeared in Lunenburg. Amadée was gay, indeed, and loved to flash his even white teeth at the giggling village girls, but above all, he loved to sing. Everyone, even Helmuth Shroeder, admitted that this *coureur de bois* sang sweeter than any warbler, sweeter even than the nightingale for which he was named.

Schroeder could find only one thing against Amadée; beyond a doubt there was Huron blood in his veins. The fathers of the village therefore kept him at arm's length from their daughters—as if his mixed blood made him unclean.

When the *coureur de bois* chanced on Hilde, plucking a chicken behind the Schroeder's barn, she addressed him in Mic-Mac. He replied in the same tongue and, unbidden, dropped onto his heels beside her.

"*Okwotu, Kwee-a-lin, nuguwa kulokuwech*—Kwee-a-lin is beautiful as the North Star," he had told her lightly.

It was two days after her conversation with Amadée that Frau Schroeder sent her to the hill pasture to fetch in Lorelei, the milch cow. She was well out of sight and nearly out of earshot of Helmuth Schroeder's farm when, silent and sudden as an owl swooping out of thicket, Amadée Rossignol seized her and clapped a hand over her mouth.

"Do not fear, little Dove. They will not come. All day I have watched and waited."

Then, alternately walking and dog trotting, the *coureur de bois* led his terrified but dry-eyed prisoner deeper into the tall forest.

All during their week's journey into the interior Amadée remained cheerful and solicitous of Hilde's comfort. But he made no love to her, other than by voice, until they reached his hunting cabin beside a pretty little stone-filled lake.

She'd owed her living to Amadée since coming to Boston; 'twas he who had taught her how to control her voice and how to sing the words and melodies of near half-a-hundred French, English and Scottish songs.

When she was about halfway up the long incline presented by Sudbury Street, Hilde's knees began quivering so violently that presently she had to pause; to encourage herself, she looked back down the hill to see how far she already had come.

Everything might have turned out very differently, she assured herself, if Amadée had only been able to make her love him. He was so handsome, so brave and woodswise she'd have been content to dress his furs and rear his children.

Probably it was rum and that Huron streak in Amadée's nature which made such a demon of him.

The approach of spring made Amadée unbearable; unfortunately he took to drinking up the liquor he had hoarded for late winter trading.

Twice she had tied on her bear paw snowshoes and started out into the forest with a little bag of food. But always the fierce cold and eerie howling of wolves were too frightening and she returned quaking to the cabin.

The ice in the stream had already broken when Adam Farquhar appeared, silent as a drifting shadow, down a slope to the westward.

Later, she learned that he had been once, long, long ago, a Highland Scot. Luckily, Amadée was away tending his trap line, so she made Adam welcome and gave him food—which he ate like the starving man he was— and enough rum to loosen his tongue. He claimed to be travelling in bad luck—some wandering Malichetes had surprised his camp three days earlier and had appropriated his whole winter's take of pelts. "I slew one o' their sentries and cleared out," Adam said, his bold blue eyes busy with her. She realized then he was puzzled by the bruises showing on her arms and the swelling on her chin—Amadée had never been more devilish than on the night before.

Perhaps it was because this gaunt, florid-faced Scot spoke Ambenaki—she could understand it—and was so quiet and unemotional that an hour after Adam's appearance, they shouldered two pack loads of food, some of Amadée's choicest furs and started to the southeast.

She lived nearly a year with Adam in a smoky, smelly lodge in the forest beyond a little palisaded fort which protected Port Mouton from Yankee raiders. Besides, she found occupation and profit sewing for the garrison, supplementing the living Adam made by hunting meat for the officers.

Then, one day, Adam told her to collect her possessions.

"I am taking some furs down Boston-way for Mr. Mitchell, the factor here," was all he'd offered by way of explanation.

The beating of Hilde's heart having slowed, she put foot once more to the icy cobbles and re-commenced her journey towards Doctor Peabody's.

Why had she believed Adam when he vowed it wiser for her to stay and try her fortune in this great, heartless city? He told her all had been arranged to assure her future, he having bound her to serve two years as chambermaid to a kind and respectable woman, a Mrs. Wright.

Six months had passed since that day, but the perfection of Adam's betrayal she appreciated almost at once. Under Massachusetts law, no girl could be bound against her will into service in a brothel—*except* a waif, orphan, or girl, lacking family or means, who might become a public charge!

At last Number Fifty-one Sudbury Street loomed before Hilde's eyes. There could be no doubt that this was the correct address; a new, hand-carved sign read: "A. Peabody, B.M."

Praying that the doctor might not be out, Hilde drew a deep breath, climbed three steps and reached for a tarnished brass knocker and rapped timidly. She listened, but heard only her heart. It was pounding like the hoofs of a runaway horse.

She was rearranging her shawl when the door to Number Fifty-one creaked open and a wrinkle-faced little woman stuck her head out. When she noticed the caller's lip rouge she drew back a little before demanding sharply, "Well? What do you want here?"

"I—I seek Doctor Peabody," Hilde faltered. "He told me I was to come here for—for treatment."

XII. GREEN SICKNESS

DOCTOR ASA PEABODY warned himself that he must appear at once calm, dignified and confident in manner and mien. Godfreys, he hadn't felt half so excited since that time he'd sailed a battered old dory—he'd worked and saved mighty hard to buy it—out past the Point on his way to set trawls of his own. That hadn't been a mean achievement for a boy of twelve. Pa claimed it showed he'd a sound bottom to his nature and that, most likely, in later life he might accomplish what he set out to do—provided he didn't set his sights too high.

Fingers annoyingly a-quiver, Asa pushed his travel orders into a drawer, rose and mechanically set straight his stock as a timid tap sounded at his door. It was so faint that only a child or a very old person could have made it.

Asa faced the door, called briskly, "Please to enter."

At first he failed in recognizing this small, black-haired young woman hesitating on his threshold; details of that brawl at the Red Lion already had faded from his memory. All the same he saw at a glance that this girl was deathly pale and thin as any bittern.

"Good afternoon, Doctor Peabody, I—I see that you do not remember?" His caller sounded surprised and regretful.

A wide and friendly smile dispersed the uncertainty on his broad features. "Why, as God's my life, 'tis Mistress Hilde. So you obeyed my instructions? Do come in. I am very glad to see you."

"Are you?" she demanded, her great dark eyes flying wide open. "Are you really, Doctor?"

"Of course. Please be seated," he urged, at the same time trying to conceal his lively disappointment. Here was no bona fide patient; just another charity case such as he had already treated by the dozen. Still, perhaps, it was fitting that this pitiful creature should be the first to enter his consulting room—a physician's mission, he held, was not essentially to make money.

"You've been resting? Eating as I advised?" he demanded, noting her labored breathing and the complete lack of color in her meager cheeks—they should have been glowing on a day cold as this. Those pale brown demi-lunes beneath her eyes, though oddly attractive, should not have existed at all. Um—and what of that very faint, but still noticeable, greenish tinge to the skin about her neck and near her temples?

At the same time he was aware that her intense black eyes were taking him in from scuffed shoes to carelessly combed brown hair. A wavering smile crossed lips which, beneath their trace of paint, were lavender-hued.

The afternoon sun lit the chill small chamber so effec-

tively that, for the first time, he saw his patient clearly
and was struck by the evanescent beauty of this thin,
anxious-appearing little thing. To Asa's great surprise her
garments today were irreproachably clean and not a trace
of grime lingered about her neck or the roots of her hair.
Right now it shone as glossily blue-black as a sea scoter's
breast. Perched restlessly on her chair she locked hands
before her knees; her eyes never left his face.

His hand went out towards her head. "So long as you
are here, Hilde, let me examine that cut."

A single glance reassured him that the contusion was
just as insignificant as he had remembered; moreover it
was healing well. Why then had this young female come
to him? Surely she had not walked so far—weak as she
most evidently was—just to invite examination of this
trivial hurt?

"Is—is it mending, sir?"

"Aye, a firm sanguineous crust has formed," he reassured. "But you must be careful with your comb not to
dislodge it."

By this clear light he could distinguish very distinctly
the blue veins in Hilde's eyelids. What the Devil? Her
eyes kept narrowing as if she were very weary. Prompted
by a sudden curiosity he took her hand and tested her
pulse; his misgivings multiplied at finding it so very slow
and weak.

"You are most kind, Doctor," she faltered. What
should she do next? She felt an overwhelming desire to
rest—to cling, secure and untroubled, to Doctor Peabody's sturdy shoulders for a long, a very long, time.
"You must smile," she prompted herself, "you must
please Doctor Peabody—he dressed your hurt and was
good to you—the least you can offer in return is a smiling
face." Mrs. Wright always reminded her girls that most
men despised long faces and sad stories.

"Tell me," he inquired once more, "have you been reposing as I instructed you?"

"Oh, yes, Doctor. I—well—Mrs. Wright let me lie
abed yesterday all day long"

"You have had plenty to eat?"

Not being a practiced liar she only dropped her eyes to
regard her wrist still imprisoned between his strong stubby fingers.

"Look at me, Hilde," he directed very gently, "and

tell me the exact truth. Have you had enough to eat these last few days?''

A long sigh escaped her. ''Well, not exactly. You see, Doctor, I—I haven't been earning much, and—''

''When did you last eat?''

''Yesterday at noon.''

''Of what did that meal consist?''

''Bread.''

''Is that all?''

''Yes, sir. Mrs. Wright said 'twas all I deserved.''

''Lucifer take such a woman!'' Indignation boiled within him. How far more cruel people could be to one another than the beasts of the forest.

By now he was fairly certain of what ailed his patient. Too many poor girls between the ages of sixteen and eighteen were prone to become afflicted with the mysterious green sickness. A majority died, drained of vitality like drought-stricken lilies withering on their stalks.

''Doctor Peabody, I—I didn't come here for sympathy. You were so good, so very kind I—I—'' She was smiling now and took his hand in hers then, caressing it shyly, tried to rest her head on his shoulder; but abruptly he stood up.

''Wait here,'' he directed shortly, ''I will return in a moment.''

When she heard his footsteps retreating down the hallway, tears slowly filled Hilde's eyes, stung at their heavy lids. So, he would not have her? He had refused the one recompense it remained in her power to bestow? At the same time Hilde sensed that that wasn't, couldn't be, the reason for his hurrying off; he had not even perceived what she intended.

Before Asa could get to Mrs. Southeby's kitchen Peter Burnham, grinning widely, appeared at the head of the cellar steps and flung both arms about him in a bear hug. ''Justice triumphs. Congratulations, my bold new surgeon's mate!''

Asa flushed crimson. ''Why, why, who told you? How the Devil d'you know?''

''Oh, come off it! You know a mouse can't scratch its bottom in this house but everyone hears it.''

Lucius Devoe's slight figure now appeared in the dark rectangle leading below. He offered his hand, beat Asa's shoulder blades.

"God love you, man!" Peter burst out. "We heard every syllable you, Blanchard and his military friend uttered. You'll go far—damned far. Eh, Lucius?"

"A fine post for a competent surgeon," the Jamaican smiled. "I'll confess I'd give a little finger to meet with such an opportunity. Indeed, I envy you with all my heart."

And this was no less than the truth. Why? Why, in God's name couldn't he, Lucius Devoe, have been nominated by Doctor Townsend? Imagine becoming a member of the Commander-in-Chief's military family, finding oneself in the center of great events. Aye, 'twas a priceless opportunity!—worthy of a man able to capitalize fully upon it.

Lucius sucked the linings of his cheeks between his teeth to keep from blurting out his disappointment. He should have expected such a decision, of course. What else could a Jamaican, a semi-foreigner expect? 'Fore God, he knew he possessed ability equal to Peabody's—aye, greater. He foresaw that Peabody would go plodding along, like the country oaf he was, doing well enough, no doubt, but accomplishing nothing either brilliant or original. Asa, that transplanted son of a Maine fisherman, possessed no more social sense than an ox! Why, he didn't know even the first thing about clothes, cards, or dancing; and he sat a saddle horse like a sack of meal. Such a fellow would be laughed right out of such smart society as surrounded General Washington.

Peter chuckled. "Tonight we'll start you right on your military career—get royally pickled. At the Red Lion, eh? For old times' sake. You'll join us, Lucius?"

"With pleasure. My sincere best wishes to you again, Asa. You certainly are Fortune's foster child." Devoe laughed then swung off down Sudbury Street after Peter Burnham's solid, blue-clad figure.

Asa called for Mrs. Southeby, but she had stepped out, most likely to borrow some item from a neighbor.

The kitchen cupboard yielded half a smoked herring, a lump of cheese, some skimmed milk and the very stale heel of a loaf. If only he could come across a bit of real tea; right now something hot and mildly stimulating would restore his patient better than anything else. All he found in the canister was a miserable substitute called "liberty tea"—dried raspberry leaves in reality.

As usual, a tea kettle sat on the back of the stove sending up wandering feathers of steam, so he flung some leaves into the cup and stirred it until the brew took on an amber color. Then, loading the food onto a wooden trencher, he retraced his steps.

To Asa's surprised annoyance his consultation room was empty, but a soft noise from upstairs prompted him to call out, "I say, Mistress Hilde, where are you?"

"Up here," her voice sounded low and quivering. "Please come—"

What the Devil? She'd no business up there. Leaving plate and cup on his desk, he took the stairs two at a time and found the door to his room just a trifle ajar. On pushing it wider he emitted an incredulous gasp. There, standing beside his bed was his patient, her garments forming a white and green puddle at her feet. Save for white stockings and yellow ribbon garters supporting them Hilde was quite nude, though she yet held her petticoat dangling from one hand. Further, she had loosened her abundant black hair, permitting it to tumble in a sable cascade over one shoulder. It was so long it reached almost as low as the red marks her petticoat ties had sketched about her waist.

Straight, thin and white as some medieval craftsman's carved ivory representation of Eve, Hilde stood waiting, her immature, pale pink-tipped breasts lifting very rapidly to her respiration.

Every detail of her rib structure was recognizable, also the planes of her pelvis and shoulder bones. Scarlet to the brows, Asa remained rooted, will power momentarily atrophied. For all his medical training, never, until this moment, had he beheld a mature female completely nude.

"Wh—what—" he choked. "Have you gone mad?"

"Oh, no." Her eyes wavered, fell. "You see, I—I haven't any money and since you were so—so very good and kind to me the other night—I—"

Suddenly he collected himself, turned aside his head. He was sweating like a stevedore and about as clever. "For Heaven's sake put your things on again."

She covered her face with both hands, commenced to sob. "I had not deemed myself to be so very undesirable. Please forgive me." Then in a muffled voice, "*Mon Dieu, c'est bien le fin—je ne peux plus—*"

At the sound of a faint thud Asa spun about to find that Hilde Mention had lost consciousness. Thin limbs awkwardly outflung, she lay inert on the bare pine floorboards with her jet hair streaming in all directions like spilled ink.

Conscience-stricken, he hurried to pick up the frail figure and was about to place the senseless girl on his bed when a voice, shrill with outrage, demanded:

"Well, sir! What sort of scandalous conduct is this?" A cone of sugar still in one hand, Mrs. Southeby was glaring from the doorway. "Never in my born days have I seen the like of it!"

"Mrs. Southeby! Please pull back the coverlet when I lift her." Right now, Asa Peabody was far from suggesting a grave young physician, capable of dealing with any and all crises. "My arms are full."

"So I see," she snapped in icy tones. "Here's a pretty howd'y'do. The idee your carrying on like this in my decent house when my back's turned."

"But Mrs. Southeby—" Asa stood helpless, more and more aware of the pale figure lying limp in his arms.

"Don't you dare 'but' me, young man! I'm a respectable widow, poor as Job's turkey though I be. I've never been so 'shamed in my life." Mrs. Southeby swelled like an angry mother hen. "Get out of here—you and your shameless—" she sputtered, "else I'll have the watch on you. There's laws against such immodest conduct. Come on, you and your alley cat can get out of my house right now!"

Correctly, he realized that his landlady was beyond reasoning, so he almost flung Hilde onto his bed, took the widow by both shoulders and shook her gently. "Just you listen to me, Mrs. Southeby; listen, and stop this witless ranting."

"Ranting! How dare you!"

"You deem yourself a real Christian, don't you?" he demanded, dark eyes glowing. "Answer me, Mrs. Southeby. Answer me!"

"A fine one, you, to put such a question even while your—your leman defiles this house."

"You do neither yourself nor me much credit by such talk," Asa grimly informed her. "Now listen. This is God's truth. This young woman came here very ill—"

"Why'd she strip herself nekkid as an egg?"

"She was out of her senses with fever and fainted as you came in."

"A likely tale!" sniffed the landlady, but ceased trying to break away. "Just you take your hands off me, Asa Peabody. You know right well if I hadn't come home the minute I did you'd be with her in that bed. I—I hate you!"

"Have I ever before given you cause for complaint, Ma'am?"

Fluttering, smoothing her sleeves back into place, she evaded his look. "Not exactly, but this—"

"Then, please—I need your help."

He turned, drew a patched and faded crazy quilt over the motionless, marble-pale figure.

"Please see if you can't rouse her. You, as a doctor's widow, ought to know how. I'll go fetch some stimulants."

"I'll wager she's shamming." Breathing heavily, Mrs. Southeby bent, took the girl by one emaciated bare shoulder and shrilled right in Hilde's ear, "Wake up! Get your clothes on and get out of here!"

"Oh, for Heaven's sake, Ma'am, stop such nonsense. The girl's ill, I tell you. Look at that green tint to her skin."

He was right, she saw. This strange girl with the Devil's brand on her lips lay motionless, an almost shadowy figure so colorless against pillowcase and counterpane. Her narrow chest remained quite motionless.

At that Mrs. Southeby straightened her mob cap and stood erect.

"Forgive me, Doctor," she held out a pleading, work-wrinkled hand. "I—I don't rightly know why I've been acting like I did. I ought to have known you would never cause me shame." Her pointed features gradually softened in their expression. "Poor little body. Why, she's thin nor any rail. What ails her?" Then anxiety crept into the widow's manner. "You—you don't figger she's taken the ship's fever?"

"I'm not sure what's wrong, but at any rate it ain't the pox nor the ship's fever, either. Looks more like the green sickness," Asa replied.

With that he descended to his consultation room to make a selection of those self-same stimulants he had so recently described to Doctor Blanchard.

XIII. THE DRYDOCK

ONLY WHEN ONE learned that Doctor Blanchard's marine hospital had been constructed as a sail loft did one appreciate that its interior was warmer than might have been expected. As it was, water standing in the wooden pails between the cots froze only towards dawn. Yes, other physicians fresh returned from service with the military commented enviously upon the two large stoves which stood, one at either end of the long corridor, and removed the worst of the chill from the four big subdivisions of the original loft.

Doctor Blanchard was proud, though modestly so, of his institution, and well he might be, Peter Burnham reflected. Almost single-handed, he had painfully, persistently collected scarce surgical instruments and medical supplies and had solicited successfully—few could resist his well-bred charm—gifts of bedclothes, food and bandages. Few in Boston were aware that the bulk of his own modest fortune had been devoted to establishing what he facetiously termed his "drydock"—a human repair yard for the battered, broken, and decaying hulks of seafaring men heartlessly abandoned on the waterfront by greedy privateer masters and equally callous Continental naval captains.

"Our main difficulty," Doctor Blanchard was repeating for the hundredth time, "is an insufficiency of light and air. The longer I practice, Burnham, the more positive I am that, for some reason, sunlight and good ventilation speed the recovery of my patients."

"Could it be," Peter Burnham suggested thoughtfully, "that, since sunlight encourages the growth of healthy vegetable fibre, it also stimulates the restoration of healthy body fibres?"

"I wonder. I wonder," Blanchard muttered. "On the other hand, does not sunlight also hasten putrefaction in those same fibres?"

Lucius Devoe thought a moment then ventured, "Burnham speaks of healthy, live tissue—or fibre as he calls it. You speak, perhaps, of damaged ones. It's indeed a matter for reflection."

Walking slowly, the three doctors proceeded along the corridor trying to ignore the dreary, monotonous moaning of a stalwart Swede whose foot Lucius had but recently removed. Lucius was saying, "'Tis a valuable theorem ye've proved here, sir, that of placing the wounded apart from the diseased. For all that, in military hospitals, the doctors count a disabled man a disabled man, no matter what the cause."

"Well may you say so," Blanchard smiled. "Many's the time I've found a patient suffering no more than a broken leg bedded side by side with a fever patient or some poor dog rotten with the *lues venera*. In some field hospitals I've beheld as many as four patients under the same blanket and each suffering from a different disability. Hold your breath, now."

Doctor Blanchard checked his stride, quickly opened the door to a room marked crudely in red lead: "Pesteriferous Patients."

"I forget. You are both proof of the pox?" he inquired.

"Aye, we inoculated each other a year ago," Peter told him and tried quite unsuccessfully to ignore a dreadful stench pouring out into the passage.

Doctor Blanchard lifted his silver-headed walking stick—it almost never left his hand—and, by pressing a button, flipped open a cap on its richly chased knob. This knob contained a cavity charged with powdered allspice; beneath the cap it was further protected by a perforated cover.

A quick flick or two of Blanchard's wrist scattered a cloud of fragrant white particles into the air. When he advanced into the ward he held the knob directly under his nostrils.

Peter, meanwhile, offered Lucius snuff from a battered pewter box, then sniffed a pinch himself. Snuff was held to be a prime preventive against contagion.

For all his precautions, Peter gagged just the same, once he had progressed well into this dim, bare room. Beds, pallets and cots of all descriptions lined the walls; but no less than two patients occupied any of them—they needed each other for warmth, Blanchard explained.

Lucius thought. "Lucky it's so deathly cold in here; the stink otherwise, would be intolerable."

Why, Peter asked himself, did the pox and ship fever—otherwise "camp" or "jail" fever, all of which were one and the same disease, by Peter's observation—become so prevalent during the *cold* months of the year? Indiscriminate crowding of men together in barracks and ships certainly did appear to encourage the contagion.

On various beds shadowy figures commenced to rear themselves to a sitting position, the weaker ones held up hands tipped with writhing fingers. Hoarse voices croaked, demanded help.

"Oh, God, Doctor, *can't* I leave yet?" "My bed's fouled—couldn't help it." "Me, I've a turrible fever, Doc—can't you give me sumptin'?" "My arms swoll so's the skin's splittin'." Though the chorus of complaint swelled and swelled, Blanchard appeared to pay no heed.

"Job! Job! Where the Devil have you got to?"

Out of an alcove a stooped, gray-haired old Negro came shuffling; he carried a pair of overflowing wooden slop pails. "Heah Ah is, suh. One ob dem fellahs in Baid Seben look lak he 'bout tuh die, suh."

"I was afraid of that," Blanchard muttered. "Surely, some better means of securing immunity from the pox must be devised." Louder he said, "All the patients in this ward are inoculation cases; this year I've had uncommon bad luck with them. Maybe it's this cold winter—as a rule I don't lose more than three inoculation patients out of one hundred."

Burnham, his face shadowy, fingered his chin in thought. "Pray God some day we will devise some other means of producing immunity. The pox is such a loathsome disease."

"Tell me, Mr. Devoe, and you, Mr. Burnham"—within the medical profession only M.D.'s could correctly be called "Doctor"—"have you ever wondered why cows suffer from a pox on their udders; it appears a very similar disease and yet they don't die. Now if the two diseases were in some way related—I wonder—"

While Blanchard talked, Peter considered the ward, which consisted of perhaps fifteen beds, mostly crude corded wooden frames; sacks stuffed with straw were substituted for mattresses. Old packing cases or arms chests did duty as tables, and crude shelves nailed to the peeling, whitewashed walls were stacked high with the possessions of the sick. Air was admitted by a pair of panes purposely left glassless and far from dissipated the reek of grimy clothes, unwashed bodies, excreta, vomit and those unusually dreadful smells peculiar to the small pox.

Once the inoculation ward's door closed on the piteous clamor of its inmates Blanchard paused before another door marked: "Chirurgical Ward."

Said he, "When we enter, I wish Mr. Burnham to inspect those patients on the even-numbered beds. No doubt some pledgets will require changing. Oh yes, pray test the ligatures on the patient in Bed Six—they should be ready to come away. Mr. Devoe, will you be good enough to treat the patients on the odd-numbered beds while I prepare some medicines?"

The light was so wretched that Peter found it all but impossible to determine exactly the state of an ulcer he found on the leg of a gaunt, bearded scarecrow who had once been a gunner's mate. "This dressing needs a change."

"Fer Gawd's sake, mate, go easy," he begged. "Wait a moment." The patient pulled from beneath his pillow a thick piece of leather and thrust it between his teeth. Then he locked his hands around the bedstead before Peter produced a scalpel from his pocket and commenced, as delicately as he might, to cut away the matted fabric. For all his care, the gaunt giant whimpered like a puppy.

Two Negroes were employed in this ward; they appeared to be decent and wore dark green aprons; their liquid kindly eyes watched the new doctors' every move. For all their stupidity and slowness, they constituted a vast improvement on the drunken, utterly irresponsible harridans, "wasters" and hard characters, who usually performed—or failed to perform—orderly duties about most military hospitals.

Absorbed in his work, Peter soon forgot the incredible, all-permeating stench. While knotting a fresh bandage about the patient's hairy, still quivering thigh his mind ran on the future.

Some day, Peter determined, he'd have a hospital of his own, one devoted to the care of females. One of its principal departments would be devoted to the science of midwifery. Together with his ever-widening field of observations, grew a conviction that medical ignorance on the subject of feminine ailments and anatomy was all but complete. Why, he asked himself while inspecting the next bed, was it not logical for special studies to be made concerning those physical processes which attended pregnancy and child bearing? As it was, male midwives,

for no sensible reason, were considered the very scum of
the medical profession—hardly a cut above those under-
takers waiting at the other end of life's cycle.

Why? Every year, men, in every station of society,
lost cherished wives, infants, sorely needed mothers—
why? If there was any explanation it lay in prudery and a
mistaken, misinterpreted passage from Genesis 3:16
which set forth:

> Unto the woman He said, I will greatly multiply thy sor-
> row and thy conception; in sorrow thou shalt bring forth
> children; and thy desire shall be to thy husband, and he
> shall rule over thee.

What cruel, stupid nonsense! Surely, God in His infinite mercy, had not intended that countless thousands of
innocent babes should perish in the very act of entering
upon life? It wasn't sensible. After all, one could, if one
knew one's Bible well enough, find in it authority for almost any act—including homicide.

It seemed difficult to credit that, since the dawn of medical history, no special instruments had been designed
to assist labor—provided one expected certain forcep ex-
tractors which for nigh on a hundred years had been a
jealously guarded secret of the Chamberlen family in
England.

To think that only one school of midwifery existed in
all Christendom. Sir Fielding Ould, defying church and
layman alike, was reported to be making sound, if unspectacular, researches into the mechanics of childbirth.

How many times he had read and re-read Doctor William Smellie's treatise on midwifery Peter couldn't imagine, but even now he could quote whole passages from it,
verbatim. Alas, that single, small volume explained little
beyond outlining, in rudimentary fashion, the mech-
anisms of labor and delivering a warning against an indiscriminate use of forceps.

When at length, Peter and Lucius finished their inspection and treatments they sought the hallway. Blanchard
met them. Singlehanded he had coped with the surgical
ward opposite; he must have met with trouble for his
black wool cuffs had been turned back and splashes of
bright arterial blood were spotting his forearms.

Said he, "That will be all for now. I thank you, gentlemen, indeed—and so do my patients." He gazed fixedly at the floor, then continued with a trace of embarrassment. "I have just now received intelligence that the privateer *Success* has signalled Castle William and is reported standing towards the Inner Harbor under jury rigging. If, as it would appear, she has fought a heavy engagement, there'll be a barge full of wounded rowed ashore tomorrow. May I count on your assistance?" He turned a tired face, added, "I wish I could pay you in other than experience."

Blanchard was pleased that they agreed without hesitation. God knew, as brand-new practitioners, they had no more important claims on their time than ex-Corporal Duneen's half-dissected corpse.

"Good afternoon, sir," Peter said at the head of the stairs leading below, "See you at the Red Lion come suppertime, Lucius," and went tramping off downstairs.

From the purposeful manner in which Burnham made for the street Lucius Devoe deduced that he'd something on is mind. What? That female cadaver? Very likely. Why else, when he and Peter had been approaching the Drydock, should a low-appearing rogue, a carter—which fitted in with Peter's previous remarks on the subject—have sidled up to mutter a few earnest sentences into Burnham's ear.

Jupiter! That must be what was up.

Well, if Peter *did* manage to come undetected by a female corpse, then Lucius Devoe certainly would seize this opportunity to increase his experience to the fullest. Doctor Townsend was entirely right. No medical man could ever learn too much about anatomy, whether he intended to practice as a physician or as a surgeon.

"Young gentlemen," old Townsend had reiterated time and again, "I counsel you to familiarize yourselves with the structure and parts of the human body as thoroughly as a shipwright studies the plans for a vessel he contemplates."

Lucius remained undecided at the top of the worn staircase. Slowly, he rubbed chilled hands together. Why should Peter Burnham be so daft on the subject of female ailments and childbirth? Could it be that the Connecticuter was shrewder than he appeared on the surface? Um—maybe so. Women, Lucius long since had decided, were considerably more scary and fearful of disease than men;

consequently, they were readier to expend money on medical advice.

Lucius cocked an ear. Had the Drydock's front door been opened? He was almost certain he heard a girl's voice addressing the porter. "Stab me," he thought. "She's come after all. Well, well! Lord love a duck if old Sam Stanton's pretty daughter hasn't come a-running after a penniless young physician!"

Sure enough, it was Sabra Stanton below and looking pretty as a painting in her French gray cloak and black calash hat. Feet drawn primly together, she sat on a bench in the hospital's bleak receiving room; a big, cloth-covered basket reposed on the red-tiled floor at her feet. It warmed his hungry heart to see the radiant smile formed by her full, dark red lips when he advanced—not too quickly—in her direction.

"Why, Doctor Devoe!" she cried, utterly at ease, "What an uncommon pleasant surprise."

"Your humble obleeged servant, Mistress—" To Lucius' intense annoyance the bow he made her proved none too graceful. Flushing, he continued, "I vow, Mistress Stanton, you look every bit the true Angel of Mercy."

"You are overly kind, sir. Pray fetch my basket to the porter's wicket." Sabra arose and, skirts demurely a-sway, crossed to a small window and rang the little bell there.

In response to her ringing the porter presently appeared and relieved Lucius of the charity basket. When he had gone the two stood gazing at each other in an awkward silence.

"Damn! She's met me on her own initiative," Lucius was thinking, "I must suggest something to do; she may never come here another time. Oh, I must make the most of this afternoon. But how?" Two shillings cash were every farthing he owned in all the world. He thought frantically. Recollections of Peter's well-filled purse and of Asa's sudden affluence on adopting the army set a dull resentment to burning in his mind.

Unexpectedly, Sabra solved the problem for him. "Jennie Fletcher, my cousin, lives in the next street," she informed him. "She has bid us to sip chocolate with her. Do you care to accept?"

"If the idea pleases you." His reply was the essence of

genteel carelessness. "If your cousin possesses but a particle of your loveliness it will be a real treat." Here was luck indeed and another short step towards reducing the citadel of smart society.

"Then shall we leave? It's cold in here." Seen like this, in her hooded, gray cape gaily lined in scarlet, Sabra appeared more than pretty—a spirited young girl who promised before long to develop into a truly beautiful young woman.

A-quiver with anticipation, Lucius smoothed the thinning nap of his black tricorne hat, then twisted higher an enormous muffler—that make-do for an overcoat adopted by the lower middle class. Once they had reached the street Sabra paused, regarded him steadily.

"Mamma was pleased by your courtesy in making a dinner call. She bade me explain that only her infirmity made it impossible for her to receive you."

"The loss was mine, Ma'am." Lucius was feeling infinitely relieved. Of course, he hadn't been really bidden to dinner on the eve of the New Year and it might have been considered impertinent to call as he had. On the other hand he'd calculated it might have been a shrewd move to make his call at an hour when Mistress Sabra might not be expected to be at home.

"I presume you have heard of our friend Peabody's good fortune?"

"To be sure. I assured Joshua, er—Captain Stanton, that, in my opinion, you were best suited for such an appointment; but Joshua said he felt bound to abide by Doctor Townsend's recommendation. It isn't that Asa Peabody ain't capable, but he's so unimaginative, so—so heavy. I'm certain you could make so—so much more of the post."

Impulsively, the Jamaican raised the girl's blue-mittened hand from its position on his arm and brushed his lips across the soft, close-knitted wool. "God bless you, dear lady. Chance, they say, is an enigmatic goddess; who knows but that she may yet afford me the opportunity of proving your—your flattering estimate of my poor abilities?"

They walked along Tremont Street until that thoroughfare merged with the travel-stained snow covering Common Street. Here, quadruple rows of young fountain elms sketched a fine black tracery against the clouds. Before long they halted before a small, but handsomely designed, brick house trimmed in white.

"Jennie is a dear poppet," Sabra stated while they waited on the stoop, "but her mamma is—well—what Papa calls something of a dragon. No wonder, the poor lady suffers terribly from recurrent megrims; half the physicians in Massachusetts, Uncle Will included, have failed to relieve 'em." Then Sabra added softly, "I expect Mrs. Fletcher would pay a pretty penny to be rid of her trouble."

So ho? It seemed that Mistress Sabra, like Peter, was possessed of unsuspected subtlety. He must learn not to snap-judge people so readily.

An Irish maid, pretty though suffering from a bad cold, ushered the callers into a small library walled by shelf on shelf of expensively bound volumes.

"Mistress begs yer indulgence, sir and Ma'am," the maid explained. " 'Tis that the hairdresser has just now left."

Sir! Lucius fairly glowed at the maid's quick curtsey and respectful manner. How very snug it was in here before a birchlog fire snapping behind glistening brass andirons fashioned like scallop shells; snug, secure and established. graceful silver and cut-glass decanter of sherry, together with three glasses, extended an unspoken invitation from a mahogany end table flanking a long settee upholstered in green and pink silk.

"Quickly, quickly, pour me a glass," Sabra begged.

Lucius jumped to obey, for all the command was, to him, disconcerting in the extreme. She stood before the blaze with her cheeks bright as winter apples; a strong, well-formed figure. She'd a will of her own, Lucius guessed, and wasn't too afraid of conventions.

"I vow, Mr. Devoe," Sabra used the correct, but less flattering title, "I'm chilled through and through. Doctor Blanchard's waiting room boasts more draughts than John Hancock has shillings."

Just as she had seen Mamma's friends do it, Sabra held out her wine glass; the goblets struck a brief, shivering musical note as their eyes met and clung, then her small chin rose a trifle as if in challenge.

"To your prospering practice, Lucius. I have every confidence in it." Even while replacing his glass on the table Lucius had, for the third time, reached a momentous decision regarding his career.

Come what might Sabra Stanton was going to become his wife. Yes, she would make an ideal mate for an ambitious man. The very fact that she'd brought him here to try his skill on Mrs. Fletcher's megrims proved that. Aye, Sabra Stanton possessed wit, charm, beauty and, for her, no social barriers existed in North America.

Hold on. Was America a large enough field? Yes. He was sure of it. With her independence once assured, there was no telling how great, how rich the new nation might grow. What a wife to assist his climb to the pinnacle of fame! Under that rich, chestnut hair dwelt an untapped wealth of intelligence and will power. Long since, he'd noticed how certain, otherwise brilliant, physicians lost practice through the tactlessness and unimaginativeness of their wives.

"My sweet! Alas, that I am so ignorant of clever words!" he cried very softly. "I would I could declare my sentiments—" Failing to find suitable words Lucius broke off and, dark eyes glowing, risked putting an arm about Sabra's waist. He braced himself for a slap and was prepared to counter her affronted protests. Jupiter! Why, Sabra's mouth, fragrant and shiny-lipped, was rising unsteadily and quivering a little, to meet his lips. What lovely pink and white tints shone once her head was tilted back.

For once Lucius' self-possession deserted him. His lean arms trembled as they went about the yielding softness of her body. Fiercely he pressed his mouth against hers.

Swaying, the two figures clung to one another a long moment; then Sabra stepped back, deliciously flushed, and pushed him away.

"Why—what can have possessed me?" Subconsciously she pressed a hand to the unusually full contours of her bodice. "Whatever will you think of me, Lucius?"

"Only that you are loveliness personified. Oh, Sabra, my sweet, my adored one, have mercy on me." He drew her to him again, but by this time he had regained his self-control and contented himself by employing his lips only to caress her eyelids and narrow, gently sweeping brows.

"My future stretches before me like a dark and uncertain path," he whispered. "I offer you only myself, and my fixed determination to become a physician of world renown. How dare I confess that I *must* have you, nay that I crave your love?"

"You will go far, Lucius," Sabra murmured, "I feel it in my very soul."

"Oh, darling dear," Lucius held her at arm's length, peered steadily into her great gray eyes. "Sabra, have you the love, the confidence, the amazing courage to become my wife?"

For answer she swayed near, memorizing every detail of his strong and well-proportioned features, then her arms slipped up about his neck, quite easily, since they were almost of equal height. "Oh yes, Lucius—yes, yes, yes! You are clever and industrious, that I already know. Handsome, too—and if, as you declare, you truly and sweetly love me, that will suffice."

Aware of the violent beating of a pulse in his temple, Lucius whispered hurriedly into her ear. "Truly, my heart, with you at my shoulder lending courage, strength and understanding, no obstacle can long obstruct my path." He sobered, gave a short laugh. "I will not have you think our task will be easy—some in this country mistrust me because of my Jamaican speech, saying I am no true American; others envy my ability to learn so readily."

Sabra shook her head violently. "We will prove them wrong. Yes, darling, we will build your career together, and earn you such a name in your profession that it will shine across the ocean like a bright new sun, challenging the weary moons of the Old World."

They stood quite still a few feet apart, gazing hungrily and a little frightened upon each other. Above a soft snapping of the birch logs sounded the weak, insistent whining of a spaniel puppy pleading to be let in from the hall.

"But your family?"

"Do not concern yourself on that score, my sweet Lucius; that will be my task. Papa, Mamma, Joshua all will be proud to welcome you into our family. Come, kiss me again before Jennie comes down."

xiv. The First Patient of Doctor Burnham

"God love me, 'tis wonderful to be ashore and home again." Captain Robert Ashton, master-owner of the twelve-gun privateer brig, *Grand Turk III*, sighed comfortably while brushing a scattering of yellow johnny-cake crumbs from his Sunday best waistcoat of Turkey red silk. Once he had pushed his chair back from the dining table, Harriett, darker-haired of the Ashton's twin girls, instantly scuttled from her seat with the speed of a small white rabbit to return from the living room clutching a pipe, tobacco canister and tinder pistol. After smiling sweetly on her father, Harriett turned and, in triumph, stuck out the tip of a pink tongue at Susan, her twin.

"Smarty!" Susan shrilled and felt called upon to pursue her sister from the long, low-ceilinged dining room. It was a chamber in which Captain Ashton found a deal of satisfaction; did not yonder glisten a handsome sideboard of the finest Honduran mahogany? He'd captured it, and a set of dining room chairs, three years back in His British Majesty's transport *Staghound.* Bound for Jamaica, she had been deep with the household goods of certain high and mighty officers on duty at Spanish Town. Following a small belch induced by the excellent mutton, fowl and beef he had just consumed, the captain smiled reflectively on a pair of elaborate sterling silver candelabra and a huge salver of Sheffield plate between them. "Let's see, where did I acquire those?" he mused. "Oh yes, 'twas from that privateer we took off Lunenburg in Nova Scotia."

Ashton neglected Harriett's tinder pistol, instead lit his pipe with a spill of paper from a supply standing in a brass jar near the fireplace.

"This genteel comfort," he went on to himself, "is a far cry from the early days of the war. Come to think on it, I've been uncommon fortunate." He had been shrewd—and able, too. So much so that his brig seldom made port with less than a pair of prizes sailing under her guns. he reckoned 'twas because of his record that he could ship the pick of seamen who sought, by the dozen, to sign articles for a cruise aboard the *Grand Turk III.*

Aware of a necessity for settling his truly prodigious

Sunday dinner, he took a short turn down the room, then paused and looked out into the street. 'Twas Sunday again, damn it! Though he felt fine to be with his family, Rob Ashton hated this dreary, Dissenter-enforced, inactivity consequent to attendance at Divine Services.

He, his wife and the twins invariably proceeded in a sedate little procession over to Christ Church in Salem Street for, as a Virginian, born of a good family, he adhered to the Church of England. Down in Norfolk where he hailed from, you'd find no evidence of this dismal Sabbatarianism—one could go calling, school a promising hunter, or even pit a pair of stags—young fighting cocks—but in muffs, to be sure.

"Come, ducky—another spoonful and not onto your bib, young man." His wife's clipped, English voice sounded serene and clear from the pantry where small David, aged two, was hungrily and audibly, partaking of his victuals.

Presently Andrea Ashton appeared, smiling from her clear, gold-splintered hazel eyes as well as with her lips. "Captain Ashton, your elder son enjoys an Ashton appetite. I thought he'd never have done."

Rob Ashton chuckled, placed an arm about his wife's waist—still a slender one for all that she had borne him four children in as many years—and brushed her cheek with his lips.

Playfully she tapped the captain's hand. "La, sir, 'tis ever the gallant gentleman you remain. Those French and Spanish hussies keep you in practice, I'll warrant."

His squarish, weatherbeaten features relaxed. "Of course, my pet, of course; every evening and twice of a Saturday. You'll join me in a glass of Madeira?"

Andrea Grenville Ashton hesitated, glanced through the open door into the hallway, and shook a handsomely modelled head. Oh, bother! The grandmother clock, in its niche on the staircase landing, warned that very soon now Robert junior, would awake and demand nursing.

A little wearily, Andrea patted free her husband's deeply tanned hand. "Between feeding the both of you Roberts, I've not time to sip Madeira. Why must all of you Ashtons dine so heartily?" She smiled. "For a baby of six months, yonder Robbie is a most notable trencherman. I do protest he sucks near twice as long as Davey ever did."

"Nonsense. Come, my dear, let us have a glass together; Robbie will let you know when he's awake." In firm gentleness Rob led his wife back to the table and there poured a glass of clear, mellow Madeira.

He raised his glass, a sturdy brown-haired man looking a little older than his actual thirty-two years. "Your health, my love; you shine as a mother, and as a wife."

Andrea turned quickly, tenderness bright in her expression. "Thank you, sweeting," she whispered. "And to you, sir; 'tis wond'rous fun being married to you, Captain Ashton. Let us proceed to the living room. I'd sit on your lap if the girls weren't about."

"They've gone aloft—"

"'Upstairs,' you incorrigible sea dog."

Smiling, Andrea settled onto his knees, permitting him to caress, almost shyly, the smooth texture of her light blond tresses. Andrea thought, "Truly life has been kind; it has granted Rob and me children, health, happiness and a more than modest fortune. If only we could continue just like this. Oh, a pox on this damned, confounded war! Can it be that we've reached the sum of our luck?"

An indefinable uneasiness gripped her but she shook it off and ran her fingers through Rob's neatly clubbed hair. After many smokeless months she found the fumes of his pipe delightful.

Pray God that the infant would not awaken straight away; Robbie was gifted with what Rob called a "mighty telling quarterdeck bellow." What a fine, healthy baby he was; sturdier even than David. The little girls, of course, were vastly intrigued by him and loved to watch Robbie blow bubbles and threaten the air violently with tiny pink fists.

Yes. What with various plagues breaking out—as they always did in a busy port like Boston—she and Rob had been uncommon lucky to keep all their children alive and well. It was the rule for almost every couple to expect the loss of one child in three; a person had only to inspect the burying grounds around Boston to credit that.

During the past three and a half years Susan and Harriett had thrived. Though twins, they certainly were not identical—a fact for which Andrea was deeply grateful. Blonde Susan, so Rob gravely maintained, favored her and promised to develop a tall and slender carriage, high-bridged nose and clear hazel eyes. Harriett, on the other hand, favored the Ashton clan by being chunkily built, having a round head and lively brown eyes and hair. Her skin, too, was perceptibly darker than Susan's.

David's hair had come in reddish and Andrea suffered a good bit of quiet teasing from Rob because of it. So far, their oldest lad resembled nobody but his small, plump and serious self. It was still much too early to predict whom Robert, Jr., might or might not resemble; in fact, her husband in a rum-truthful moment had maintained that their newest baby suggested nothing so much as a poorly coddled egg.

Presently Andrea arose, covertly eased her stays at their top, then sought her sewing basket before settling again on a chair across the fireplace from Rob.

Muffling another comfortable little belch, he crossed to select a coal from the hearth and, in a pair of brass tongs, held it to his pipe bowl. Only then did he notice his wife's abstraction. Patricianly handsome in her flowered gown of yellow damask, Andrea was sitting as erect as usual, but considering with unseeing eyes the wonderfully delicate ivory and bone model of a French bugalet—an odd, outlandish rig calling for two masts—which he'd discovered years ago, aboard a prize. Rob possessed such passion for fine and accurate ship models that quite a collection of them decorated his office at the rear of the house. Probably this hobby stemmed from the fact that he'd patterned the *Grand Turk*—the first ship he'd built—after a French toy very much resembling this in craftsmanship.

"Wherefore the brown study, my love?"

Andrea looked up quickly, hazel eyes earnestly questioning. "Rob, dearest one—do you plan to go to sea again soon?"

All through Sunday dinner Rob had dreaded her asking just that question. The Devil fly away with his brig's first officer! Why had Gideon Pickering, that lanky and taciturn Connecticuter out of Groton, felt it incumbent upon him to stop by and raise the question of a sailing date?

Rob's sturdy legs, well outlined in white Italian silk stockings, took him to the far end of the living room and halfway back. By the mantelpiece he paused, a solid, dependable sort of man. Above his best jabot of sparkling Valenciennes lace a frown creased his features.

"You may as well learn now," he told Andrea evenly, "that we shall sail soon because I have serving aboard the *Turk* at present, the best trained crew I have ever signed. Should I delay too long in port, I'll likely lose most of my best hands—and I can't afford to part with a single gunner. The *Dauntless'* skipper, for instance, is offering top pay.''

Rob always had set great store on the accuracy of the *Grand Turk*'s broadsides. Long ago, he had reasoned that accurate gunnery paid well in several directions—it caused an enemy to strike his colors quicker, thereby reducing casualties and damage to his ship.

Andrea bit her lip. ''Oh, Rob—must you go again so soon? Why, we've hardly had you with us a fortnight.''

''I fear so. I have received intelligence that Sir Henry Clinton, down in New York, is expecting the arrival of a convoy from Cork.''

Joyous cries raised by the twins, now romping upstairs, filled an uncomfortable silence. Rob put down his cold pipe, commenced to drum absently upon the mantel of gleaming yellow pine.

''Pray believe that I lament this necessity of putting to sea so soon, sweeting; 'fore God I do.''

''Why continue privateering at all?'' Andrea demanded tensely. ''You hate fighting, you know, quite as much as you enjoy trading. You have amassed for us a very sizeable fortune—you own three vessels outright and a warehouse filled with Sheffield and West Indies goods. Here in Boston you are extremely well regarded and have connections with all the best merchants.'' She reached out, took his hands. ''And, Rob, need I remind you that now you have quite a family to look after?''

A faint smile lit his weathered features. ''No. We seem to have done extra well in that respect, too.''

''Rob, for our sakes, won't you give over privateering? For near five years you have been monstrous fortunate; stop now, whilst you may. Oh, darling, some day one of those fast new British frigates they speak of will come up with the *Grand Turk* and then—and then you'll be killed or captured—and the Admiralty won't exchange seamen any longer.

''Won't you take up trading abroad again? Mr. Phillips, Mr. Leverett—oh, everybody—vows that now that the French and Spanish are at war against England, trade over here will become ever so brisk.''

The captain's stubby fingers continued their drumming. "Everything you say is true," Rob admitted, "except that last. To be sure trade may flourish, but it will be a chancy traffic. Neither the Dons nor the Frenchies will send their prizes here for sale because there's no hard money to be had. Deprived of the goods we fetch to prize auctions in our privateers, Boston trade would stagnate." He spoke carefully, selecting his words, "You speak of trading abroad. Tell me, my dear, what chance has an unarmed merchant vessel of reaching her destination these days?"

Andrea sighed, made a small helpless motion with one hand.

"Again, what would I use for money? Real goods are the only worthwhile currency at present. No standard currency exists in all North America, unless you count an occasional piece-of-eight, or Spanish dollar." He stared out into the street. "To top everything, I heard Lem Abbott swear at the coffee house yesterday that the Congress is about to declare all Continental notes invalid. Tell me, sweeting, how I can do business deprived of currency and credit?"

Rob seated himself again after patting his wife's hand. "You are entirely correct in that I abominate privateering and the undoubted risks such a career entails, but the time is not yet ripe to quit." Andrea looked so melancholy, he added cheerily. "Perhaps this cruise will be my last. Who knows that, ere long, this accursed war will have taken a decisive turn; enough, at least, to let a man foresee what's likely to chance come six months or a year."

"Decisive, why?"

"Haven't you heard that the French king's preparing two great armies to serve in America this spring?"

"So I've heard; but I don't count on it. The French king's a fool and his ministers are foxes," Andrea said, then attempted a new tack. "If you feel the *Grand Turk* must go to sea again why not put Mr. Pickering in command for this cruise? You've always thought so highly of him."

"Gideon's a good and able officer," Ashton admitted, frowning at the brass fender by his feet. "But there's a vast difference between a good first officer and a satisfactory skipper. Gideon's a born pessimist and over-severe in the matter of discipline."

Plague take it, such a suggestion wasn't at all like Andrea; she'd never before protested his going to sea, not even when the twins were infants and she large with David.

Rob felt he was making a wise decision; though he failed to mention a further reason. Slowly but surely, Yankee private ships-of-war, swarming out from dozens of little bays and river mouths, were whittling away at the enemy's supply routes, costing the merchants of the United Kingdom millions of pounds each year. The British ministry's antidote, as every ship's boy in America knew, was to furnish naval convoy for helpless cargo carriers; that entailed great loss of time for the merchants while also forcing the Royal Navy to divert its vessels from military operations.

It was well that the privateers carried on with this raiding—now that the Continental Navy had been all but crushed, blotted out of existence. No one could deny that privately owned men-of-war were, to a serious degree, interfering with the supplies and reinforcements dispatched to Sir Henry Clinton in New York and to British garrisons in Savannah.

Because Rob always had known what he was doing, Andrea silently admitted her defeat and returned to the dining room in order to lock the sugar box.

Ah—Master Robbie at last. From above sounded faint and sleepy whimperings. Instinctively Andrea's fingers commenced to untie her bodice laces. She'd better hurry upstairs before the baby really got to howling and upsetting the other children. Oh bother! The twins now were racing around like a pair of squirrels.

She paused in the living room doorway, the strings of her bodice hanging loose and her breasts swelling ripe and round against the sheer lawn of her undershift. "I'm sure you know best, Rob," she told him, smiling. "Still, I wish you'd mull over my suggestion about sending Pickering in your stead."

Captain Ashton got up, moved towards his wife. "My darling, because you never have spoken in this strain before," he began in his soft Virginian voice, "I will give the matter my deepest—"

The words died on his lips, banished by a thin scream and a gasp, followed by something bumping and thumping down the stairs. Andrea stifled a cry and whirled about. "Rob! Come quick!"

"Oh, God have mercy!" she gasped, swooping down

on Susan. The child lay motionless at the foot of the staircase, her left arm thrust from under her at a shocking and unnatural angle.

A single terrified glance apprised Rob that from his daughter's elbow was protruding a slim splinter of bone. White and sharp-looking as a small bayonet, it had pierced the child's pale blue muslin sleeve; already a bright red stain was soaking the fabric.

Rob picked up Susan's limp, diminutive form and placed the white-faced little thing on the living room divan. It was entirely characteristic of Andrea Ashton that she indulged in no hysterics, broke into no useless lamentations—only her eyes betrayed her anguish.

"What shall I do, Rob? Shall I try to restore her?"

"No. Poor child's insensible, and so can't suffer."

He started for the door. "Whom do you employ as physician?"

"Doctor Chase," she called at the same time slipping a cushion under her daughter's dark head. "Oh dear! It's a long way to his house."

"Is no doctor any nearer?" The captain's voice had assumed a metallic quality any of his officers would have recognized.

"No. Wait! Hester said a new doctor has set up practice just around the corner in Charter Street."

"His name?"

"I don't know, but—oh Rob, fetch him. Quickly! *Quickly!*"

Without delaying for hat, coat or cape, Rob Ashton went pelting out down Snow Street. A moment later he was rounding the corner into Charter Street searching for a physician's name on one of the house fronts.

He saw it almost at once, a modest shingle bearing the name "P. Burnham, B.M." nailed below a ground floor window. Captain Ashton was pounding up a short ash-strewn walk when a young fellow appeared at the door.

"Your pardon," Rob panted. "There has been an accident. I seek a Doctor Burnham."

"I am he, sir, and at your service."

"Please to follow me at once, please. My daughter has fallen the length of the stairs and has broken her arm and God alone knows what else."

"In an instant, sir, I will accompany you."

Peter ran back into the house and reappeared carrying

a scarred old saddle bag containing his instrument case, bandages and a small stock of medicines.

Once in the privateersman's living room, Peter ran to the divan, slit the child's sleeve and, watched in miserable silence by the Ashtons, made a rapid examination. As he feared, his first patient had suffered a compound fracture; unluckily both the radius and the ulnar bones had been broken. What made the fracture dangerous was that the ulna protruded, jaggedly, a full two inches through the flesh and that the puncture was bleeding freely.

Captain Ashton cleared his throat gruffly, then announced, "I am conducting Mrs. Ashton outside. I will return immediately."

"No, no! I don't wish to go," Andrea protested. "Susan is my child, too. You know I am no coward."

"That I know—and well. But believe me, this is a different matter."

To break the news to his wife that an amputation of Susan's arm necessarily must take place, would require tact and preparation. Rob stared on his daughter from miserable eyes. It revolted his soul to realize that this bright, merry little creature was doomed to go through life maimed, a spinster, and an object of pity, but if Susan were to survive, no other course was open. On shipboard, as everywhere else, a compound fracture resulted in gangrene and dreadful death—failing immediate amputation. Such a wound became turgid and filled with malignant pus.

Rob swallowed hard, he felt all green and gray inside as he led Andrea stony-faced and walking stiffly back to his office. There he placed both hands on shoulders quivering beneath his touch.

"We have weathered many trials together, dear," he reminded her, the pain he was suffering written across his bronzed face in harsh and ageing lines. "This is the greatest; let us meet it courageously."

"Yes, but Rob, Rob—she's so little, so soft, so—so innocent."

"Her life, at least, will be assured," Rob reminded; he was trying to be soothing, but his fingertips left reddish marks on his wife's arms.

"Oh, Rob, Rob!" Her hazel eyes were terrible in their fear. "She's such a b-baby. He c-can't—he must not c-cut her."

He gave his wife a heart-broken look. "Then you—you understand?"

Andrea's eyes closed and she swallowed spasmodically. "Quite. Only last month the Hartwell boy broke his leg the same way. Doctor Appleby was forced to—to cut it off. It being a pierced break he had no choice—so Doctor Appleby declared."

"Captain Ashton?" Doctor Burnham's voice reverberated from beyond the gray-white painted panels of the living room door. "Please to come here, sir, at once."

Rob drew himself stiffly erect, his hands came away from Andrea's trembling shoulders. "Pray attend the other children, my dear." By now small Harriett's frightened wails and little Robbie's hungry yells were making the whole house resound.

A taut expression—the captain's older seamen would have recognized it—immobilized Robert Ashton's features when he put hand to the cold brass knob of the living room door.

Susan was still unconscious. Young Doctor Burnham, a bit pale and very serious of mien, had removed his coat and was rolling up the sleeves of a worn linen shirt. On a chair beside the sofa reposed the open instrument case. The glitter of steel shining within it made Rob flinch.

He swallowed hard. "Well, Doctor?"

"Your daughter, sir," Peter explained, blue eyes intent on the sea captain's deep-set brown ones, "has either swooned from alarm and anguish or has suffered a commotion. However, I can assure you that no other bones have been fractured."

"Please proceed—what—what of my child's arm?"

Peter drew a long slow breath. "As a privateer captain you must have beheld many fractured limbs; you are aware, therefore, of the usual treatment for such injuries?"

"Aye."

"Few such fractures, even if expertly set, escape with a mere discharge of laudable pus. Therefore amputation is resorted to."

Burnham passed a hand over his curling red hair. He was debating fiercely within himself. Here lay his first patient—he must not lose her! And yet, and yet, was it not worse certainly to maim this poor child for life? "In a child so young," he observed, "once corruption takes hold there remains but small hope of recovery."

Ashton fixed unseeing eyes upon a shaft of sunlight sketching a brilliant rectangle on the white marble of his hearth-stone.

"Are you inclined, Captain, to accept a risk?"

"What risk?"

"That I attempt to preserve your daughter's arm—"

"Of course!"

"Wait. I'll not disguise that such an effort will be made at the risk of her life."

Rob's hand closed hard on the doctor's shoulder. "What are you sayin'? Speak plainly, suh." His Virginian accent was, all at once, very noticeable.

"That I may be able to save your daughter's arm— provided you and Mrs. Ashton understand that she may perish in the attempt. I—well, I feel confident of success, else I would not mention it."

Ashton hesitated, slowly beat one fist against the other. At length he looked up. "Suh, I believe I would rather see Susan dead than—than an unhappy cripple."

Why in Tophet had his first case to be like this? What a damned fine start for his practice.

Peter turned to face the captain standing very straight before his living room fireplace. "Captain Ashton, I believe I am justified in attempting to set this fracture."

"Very well." A shadow of a smile curved Rob's lips; he recognized courage when he saw it. "How may I assist you, suh?"

"Pray heat a gill of the purest French brandy you have."

Once the privateer captain had stumped out, Peter began rigging the cloth windlass with which he intended to extend the arm; next he laid out pledgets of lamb's wool and a bottle of neat's-foot oil.

Um. He felt pleased to see that the skin of the child's arm was uncommonly clean—again, it was fortunate that Captain Ashton's daughter was remaining so blissfully unconscious.

Presently, Ashton returned carrying a little pewter mug. His black brows put an unspoken query.

"Oh, you are curious about my use of this brandy?"

"Aye."

"Most of Boston's well water is more or less polluted," Peter explained. "Therefore I prefer to wash a protruding bone with brandy. One Doctor Dasturge, a renowned French surgeon, has met considerable success with this procedure."

Peter worked rapidly, but was concerned to note how very red grew the lacerated tissues under the raw spirit. Another time, perhaps, he'd employ claret or Madeira. They might prove less inflaming. "Captain, will you please throw a clove hitch about the child's arm with this length of bandage?" Great blisters of perspiration were breaking, trickling down into Captain Ashton's heavy brows. "Please grasp the patient under her armpits and steady her when I pull. Ready? Now!"

Peter applied his full weight to the bandage and little by little the bone splinter disappeared into the wound. Maintaining the pull with his left hand he manipulated the supple young bones back into position.

"Now, Captain, steady does it," he panted just as he'd heard Doctor Townsend. "The bones are in line—ease off gently, gently."

Binding the splints into place, Peter felt encouraged, momentarily at least. Now Susan's bandaged arm lay secure, yet comfortable in its bed of bran within the splint.

Peter said while pulling on his coat, "Her breathing quickens so she will soon regain her senses. Pray inform Mrs. Ashton that she must expect this child to become feverish. At seven of this evening I shall return."

"For God's sake do!" urged poor Rob. "I, suh, am fair undone."

xv. DOCTOR SAXNAY'S GOLDEN ELIXIR

BAHRAM CURSED SOFTLY in Fulah, his native dialect. That he was beginning to forget it was not surprising inasmuch as Bahram must have been nearing ten years of age when, naked as a fish, he had been driven exhausted and utterly terror-stricken into Senhor Campão's slave kaffle at Whydah on the West Coast of Africa.

Since then, Bahram's experiences had been many and varied. For instance, he had committed murder in escaping from unendurable toil in certain steamy and sour-smelling indigo fields below Charles Town, South Carolina. Posing as a freedman, the big black had found refuge aboard a lugger, the hard-bitten crew of which were setting out to hunt certain islands for wild cattle. Out of these beasts they manufactured the tasteless yet nourishing *boucan,* sold as slave food in Hispaniola and Saint Domingue.

Should such a lugger, by chance of course, intercept a weaker craft and there were present no witnesses saving the sun and the sea, events were likely to follow a short and bloody course. Small wonder such *boucaniers* earned the hearty dread of small vessels cruising the Greater and Lesser Antilles.

Laws! Bahram shivered. Dis heah Boston Town was de coldes' dampes' place he *ever* put foot in. Right now jist a touch o' hot Jamaica sun on his back would feel fine! Why free folks ever figgered to live in a perishin' col' climate like dis waren't for no black boy to understan'. Bahram's fingernails scratched softly when, bending, he attempted to scrape hoar frost from a windowpane. Presently he could see into the street below.

A long line of patients was stamping and swinging their arms while waiting. "Stoopid ijits," Bahram rumbled, then a sound of voices and footsteps from above prompted him to straighten up and adjust his enormous red and yellow striped turban.

He donned his obsequious, meaningless grin. Pshew! Only a door at the head of the stairs had blown open permitting Doctor Saxnay's unctuous voice to be heard, "What you have suffered, most respected Madame, is the merest touch of the falling evil. 'Tis readily corrected by my arts."

"But, Doctor, my seizures have grown worse of late," came a plaintive voice. "Oh, noble sir, do give me hope—even a trifling one. My husband's affections cool, my children dread and fear me in my fits. Can you accomplish something?"

"Ahem," boomed Saxnay's bass accents. "Surely, Madame, you must have possessed some confidence ere you came to seek me out? Um-m. Let me see, the falling sickness, eh? Aggravating, eh?" Came a sound of bottles clinking against one another and the snap of a lock being undone.

"Here, most respected Madame, is a vial of my rare

and most precious Golden Elixir. 'Tis a sovereign remedy 'gainst the falling evil.''

"You—you are convinced it will restore me?"

"You shame me, Madame, by such a doubt. Why, but six months gone this Elixir restored to full and blooming health the gracious Princess Elnora, daughter of His Mighty Excellency Don Orlando Gomez, Viceroy of all the Brazils.'' Then he added smoothly, ''Though this decoction be powerful, you must be patient; time is required to benefit from its beneficial power.''

"Oh, God bless you, Doctor." The patient's voice swelled with hope, like an organ note when the *fortissimo* stop is pulled out. "Yes, of course, I shall be patient, patient as Job himself. Give it me! Oh, give it me quickly!"

Bahram sighed. Why in Sheol didn't the Master send this silly woman on her way? Probably because Doctor Saxnay hadn't yet estimated how much the patient upstairs would, and could, pay for a worthless mixture of alcohol, water, and Jesuit's bark; minute particles of pure gold leaf afloat in it seemed to hypnotize cleverer persons than this distracted housewife.

"Oh, Doctor, surely you are an angel sent from Heaven! How can I thank you? My last fit was so fearful—I foamed all over the floor.'' The patient caught her breath. "And what—what is your fee?''

"Um," Saxnay mumbled, "as to the fee—ahem—I hardly know what to say, loathing such sordid considerations as I do. Heretofore my patients have included only the princely, the noble and the very rich—''

"Oh, please, noble sir, be generous. I *must* have your Elixir.''

"To you, dear lady, 'twill cost but two pounds, hard money, for this half-ounce vial. 'Tis practically a gift, Madame, my usual price is six pounds, gold, for this boon to humanity.''

"T—two pounds? Oh, but that is a great deal of money, especially in Boston.''

"Pray don't excite yourself, Madame," came Doctor Saxnay's brisk voice. "If you deem my Golden Elixir over-dear, why, allow me to present this vial, gratis—'' Downstairs Bahram chuckled. "De ole Doctuh, he one clever debbil. He understan' dese queer Yankee people a'ready.''

Instantly, the patient changed her tune. "Why, Doctor! I'm no charity patient—Jedediah's new saddle horse simply will have to wait."

Bahram sighed, and to think he'd figgered dis lady had real wits; now look at her come flyin' down de stairs smilin' lak she done seen de Lawd Jesus Himse'f. Clutching the vial, now done up in purple paper, the patient hurried by without even noticing Bahram's profound salaam.

B-r-r-r. The big Fulah braced himself against that penetrating blast which came rushing through the door whenever he opened it to beckon in the next patient. This one proved to be an obviously feeble-minded, half-grown boy guided by anxious, round-eyed parents.

Grinning, Bahram admitted the trio and, according to his training, gobbled directions at them in Fulah. While they yet stared in bewilderment he conducted the little group to the stairs where he salaamed thrice, so low that a white egret's plume in his turban all but brushed the floor.

"We are to go up?" the man inquired. Bahram nodded, stared not without sympathy on the mewing, gurgling idiot boy who kept lurching off balance and every now and then burst into peals of nonsensical laughter.

In a magnificent banyan of electric blue embroidered in gold thread with all manner of mysterious symbols, Doctor Saxnay greeted his clients at the head of the stairs. While climbing, the callers became aware that this magnificent personage wore a canary brocade waistcoat, chocolate-hued satin breeches, scarlet silk stockings and vivid green Turkish slippers—the points of which curled upwards in a most engaging fashion. From under a magnificent white peruke of slightly old-fashioned mode those clear-green eyes peered out, calm and reassuring in their expression.

Doctor Saxnay offered the father a hand heavy with rings adorned by huge emeralds and rubies—at least they purported to be such. Graciousness incarnate, he assisted the idiot onto the landing.

"Ah, the poor, afflicted little fellow. I am pleased, nay honored, sir, you have brought him to my attention." He rolled his eyes towards the fly-brown plaster ceiling. "Indeed, my friends, 'tis moments like these which prompt me to feel that, this, my healing mission is but a direct manifestation of our Lord's eternal and boundless mercy."

In Doctor Saxnay's consulting room the patient's parents peered, goggle-eyed and uneasy, at a stuffed alligator swinging from a hook let into the ceiling above Doctor Saxnay's desk. To their right stood a group consisting of a skeletonic cat carrying a fish-like skeleton in its yellow teeth and blankly regarding a skeletonic bird. Attached to the walls, colored anatomical charts blazed at the visitors while across the bureau was arranged an imposing array of urns and vats containing everything from pickled kittens to live hop-toads and a great, emerald-eyed snake.

"Your name, sir?"

"Anthony Huston, Esquire, of Framingham. This lady is my wife, and this unhappy child our only offspring."

"He's been witless since birth, eh?" Doctor Saxnay settled back in a chair so elaborately gilded and carved it suggested a throne. Deliberately, he then joined forefingers, steeple-like, under the brownish birthmark disfiguring his long jaw.

"Poor Frederick never has been right," the mother admitted heavily. It was clear she was not entertaining much hope, that only her husband's urgings had prompted this visit.

"Hm, just so, just so."

Mr. Huston stated anxiously, "He is our only child, and—and—Doctor Townsend declares Amanda, here, can conceive no others. Can nothing be done?" Doctor Saxnay looked up, scowled at the alligator and pretended to deliberate.

"Um-m. Let us see—and 'twill cost you not a penny, sir, for diagnosis—my skill is for humanity's sake," he added.

Following a planned pause the glittering figure arose, raised one hand as if in benediction, then brought it to rest upon the idiot's head. Swiftly, his long, grimy fingers explored the boy's cranium. Doctor Saxnay stepped back, his yellow-tinted features alight.

"*Magnifique! Wunderbar!* Wonderful! Prepare to rejoice. Madame, you should, like the infidels cry, '*Allabu Akbar!*' and praise an All-Merciful God!"

The couple started, glanced uncertainly at each other. Tears filled Mrs. Huston's eyes. "There is room for hope?"

Saxnay considered the group of skeletons. "Assuredly hope is yours, but—"

"—But what?"

"I shall have to perform an operation."

"Oh, Doctor, would you have to hurt poor Freddie?"

"The merest trifle, dear Madame," boomed Doctor Saxnay, "thanks to my skill. 'Tis a treatment requires the greatest art and delicacy and knowledge. I learned of this remedy from an infidel *tabit* whilst I lay captive to the heathen Bey of Tunis." Saxnay now spoke softly, as if loath to bring up a distasteful subject. "Er—Mr. Huston, just what premium do you place upon the return of your son's sanity?"

The merchant turned brick-red, looked miserably at his wife. "M—maybe I could bring together ten pounds— gold. Will that suffice?" Fearfully, his wide eyes clung to Saxnay's birthmark-blotched yellow features.

Doctor Saxnay hesitated, considered a row of bottles to his left, then looked out of the window before shrugging. "Evidently, my good sir, you are abysmally ignorant of the supreme skill required in such an operation? But two years gone I was, for a similar operation, fee'd one hundred golden ducats by His Serene Highness the Margrave of Thurn and Taxis."

"He, he, he!" gurgled the idiot and, escaping his parents' hands, collapsed onto the floor, there to lie kicking and waving his limbs like an infant of six months.

The florid little merchant cast his wife an anguished look before stooping to raise his child. Saliva was drooling down the idiot's fresh, pink cheeks and his vacant brown eyes rolled uncontrollably.

"Oh John, we could sell my pearl and topaz earrings," cried Mrs. Huston. "Doctor Saxnay, I would sell anything, everything to see poor Freddie become reasonable."

Doctor Saxnay prompted softly, "The earrings might fetch?"

"Five pounds hard money at the least," Huston grunted. "Paid seven for 'em afore the war."

Doctor Saxnay turned, a benign expression adorning his unwashed face. "*Ave Maria!* Such tender and unselfish parental devotion shall not go unrewarded. To refuse you an operation—even for such a pittance—would be less than Christian."

"You'll perform it? And for only fifteen pounds? Oh, learned sir, my God reward your noble nature." Mrs.

Huston bent quickly and kissed Doctor Saxnay's well be-ringed fingers.

"You have permission to mention me in your prayers. Bahram! Come up here."

The Negro knew perfectly well what was expected, halted just inside the consulting room door, and so wait-ed with head bowed and sable hands crossed above his chest.

Saxnay made a lordly and slightly weary gesture. "Fetch my golden scalpel, Bahram, the curved silver needles and pure silk ligatures."

"Yas, yo' Nobility. Yassuh, Doctuh Saxnay. Direc'-ly." Salaaming, Bahram shuffled backwards out of the room and into Saxnay's bedroom where he looked about until he came upon a bottle of Spanish brandy hidden in-side a chamberpot. After taking a deep swallow he select-ed four small, translucent smooth stones veined by some dark red mineral, from a collection in the washstand's drawer. These Bahram secreted in a false bottom to the quack's scalpel case.

Egret plume nodding above his turban, the big Negro brought in a case of operating instruments and solemnly knelt to offer them on a brilliantly polished brass salver. Doctor Saxnay meanwhile threaded a length of linen into a curved needle which, with two similar ones, he thrust into the none-too-clean lapel of his electric blue ban-yan.

"Bahram," he directed, rolling up the dingy lace at his cuffs, "this poor lad is deprived of reason; take care to hold him steady. Sir and Madame, during the operation you will seat yourselves on yonder couch and under no circumstance move or make an outcry. Should my hand slip but the merest trifle, certain death will result."

Doctor Saxnay made a convincing pretense of search-ing through the child's hair, nodded to himself two or three times and at the same time deftly palmed the stones.

"Hum! Yes, 'tis as I expected. The cause of the pa-tient's witlessness is inescapable. What we of the medi-cal aristocracy call 'stones of Jupiter' are pressed against his poor little brain. Once my skill relieves said pressure your son will become as reasonable and clever as any lad of this great and prosperous metropolis."

Very softly Mrs. Huston commenced to sob. "Pray be

gentle, noble sir. You'll not hurt my Freddie, will you? He is so—so very helpless."

The merchant put an arm about his wife's shoulders. "Of course he won't hurt the boy. Doctor Saxnay has been chirurgeon extraordinary to kings, princes and—and—"

"Emirs and Bashaws," Saxnay supplied over his shoulder.

Employing a linen band Bahram none too gently secured the babbling imbecile into a rough wooden chair but was forced to steady the child's constantly twitching head between huge, blue-black hands.

"Let me see, how do the instructions go?" Doctor Saxnay half closed his curious pale green eyes then, staring hard at the floor, commenced to recite in Latin nothing more nor less than a particularly lewd verse from the *Satyricon*.

At first the child only whimpered softly, but when Doctor Saxnay parted his soft blond curls and made a shallow incision some two inches in length, the idiot commenced to squall shrilly; under Bahram's massive hands the lad squirmed and twisted, but to no avail.

"Ha!" A stone seemed to pop out through the blood flowing freely from the incision and, in a triumphant gesture, Doctor Saxnay flung it clattering onto the brass tray at his elbow.

"There, there, my unhappy little man," Saxnay soothed. "No longer will you suffer for want of a chirurgeon's skill. Steady him, Bahram. I said *steady him*, you black ape."

Presently a second stone tinkled onto the tray, a third, then, after an elaborately timed delay, a fourth. By now Bahram was forced to throw a gorilla-like arm about the child's neck and so restrain the shrieking idiot.

"Patience—'tis nigh over." Whipping one of the curved needles from his lapel Doctor Saxnay's knotty fingers made a dozen quite expert stitches in the scalp, gradually closing the readily bleeding incision. By now bright streaks of blood were marking the boy's neck and staining his prettily embroidered shirt. Next Saxnay applied a pledget of lamb's wool to the horribly matted hair and bandaged it into place.

"Ha! 'Tis done. But take care he does not tear loose the bandage."

Yellow and black teeth exposed in a patronizing smirk, Doctor Saxnay, using a bloodstained forefinger, motioned the pallid and trembling parents to rise and approach.

"Uncommonly blessed people!" he boomed. "I give you back your son. Now that the pressure exerted by the stones of Jupiter has been relieved, Master Frederick will commence his recovery. However, I counsel patience, patience and more patience, my friends; for Dame Nature to dispel fogs accumulated by the years is no rapid matter."

"Oh, Doctor. How long will it be?"

"Not more than a month, Madame, and ere the snow is melted you will find in your fine young lad a source of pride and joy—a vast credit to his charming and intelligent parents." Doctor Saxnay's smile faded as he extended a hairy, blood-marked hand. "Fifteen pounds I believe we agreed?"

"Yes, that was agreed." From a knotted handkerchief Mr. Huston commenced to sort a strange collection of gold coins. Bahram recognized fat English sovereigns, ornate Spanish doubloons, Portuguese escudos, and a few very old French coins bearing the effigy of Louis the Fourteenth of France.

"Nine pound, seven and six," Mr. Huston announced.

"Very good, and now Madame, your earrings?" Saxnay need not have spoken. Mrs. Huston was almost tearing free the ornaments.

"Oh, God bless and prosper you, dear noble surgeon!" Mrs. Huston was sobbing. "You have granted us all a new life. Come, my poor poppet." Gray skirts rustling, she gathered up the pale, blood-streaked child and, a moment later, the little family was clumping down the stairs.

XVI. SHARE AND SHARE

A SARDONIC GRIN on his thick, liver-colored lips, Bahram admitted the next patient—one who immediately puzzled and vaguely disquieted him. He reckon de Doctuh couldn't take many shillin's out 'er dis feller. Look at dem scuffed shoes and dat frayed and mended stock.

"Yo' name, suh?"

Said he crisply, "It's Devoe, Mr. Lucius Devoe."

"Yo' wants to see de Doctuh?"

"Say 'sir' when you address me," snapped the black-clad figure, "and don't be an ass. Why else have I been shivering outside this door the last hour?"

Once in Doctor Saxnay's exotic consulting room, the new patient's dark eyes ran over his surroundings missing no detail. What considerations prompted this weird display? The stuffed alligator, the skeletonic group, that monkey's skull grinning from its shelf must in some way forward Doctor Saxnay's purposes. The charts, Lucius saw at a glance, were of no medical value, just gaudy gibberish.

He was aware of undergoing a sharp estimate by the quack's greenish eyes.

"Well, young sir, and why have you come to me?"

Lucius fetched a convincingly racking cough, sputtered, "Alas, I fear I am afflicted with the long sickness."

"Ah, so?" Doctor Saxnay settled back, unlcean fingers working slowly on his chair's arms. "That is what, in Scotland, we call an inflammation of the lungs."

"I had hoped, perchance, your famous Golden Elixir might speed my return to health," Lucius stated, steadily regarding Doctor Saxnay's face. "Friends of mine were present some nights ago at an inn called the Red Lion."

"Were they indeed?" Doctor Saxnay arose, followed the points of his green slippers the length of the floor, then paused before a generous fire of sea coal. "You mentioned my world-renowned Golden Elixir?"

"Yes, learned sir," came the humble assent. "But I fear I have not sufficient money to—"

"Courage, my friend, but a single drop will speed you months on your route towards a recovery of the full bloom of health." That Saxnay wished to rid himself of this evidently penurious young man with the penetrating stare was very evident. "What can you pay?"

"Alas, Doctor, I possess in hard money but a single shilling." Lucius experienced both disappointment and contempt when Doctor Saxnay crossed to an urn filled with some shining yellow liquid and measured half a tea-spoonful into a tiny glass vial.

"Here you are my young friend. You may well thank your lucky planets for sending you to so generous a practitioner."

Saxnay halted, vial in hand. His patient was grinning a most impudent grin.

So, Lucius thought, this mountebank is ready to clutch

at every penny? He recalled a jingle from the old country:

> From the poor man's pay
> The nostrum takes no trifling part away.

A plan which had been forming since early the night before, now appeared entirely feasible. Lucius produced a very worn silver shilling piece.

"That won't do—it's too light," Doctor Saxnay pointed out sharply.

"There's no doubt of that," Lucius admitted, his face thrust a few inches from Doctor Saxnay's. "However, certainly it gives full value for whatever benefit I may derive from yonder bilge water."

"Sirrah!" Doctor Saxnay's voice swelled, made the room resound. "How dare you insult the Physician Extraordinary to His Serene Highness the Sultan of Kurdistan?"

"Suppose you drop that nonsense?" Lucius suggested quite calmly. "It impresses me not in the least. I have come to—"

"Get out! Get out of here," snarled Saxnay, his peruke's yellowish curls a-tremble. "Begone, you—you ignorant ungrateful dog. Begone! ere, my patience exhausted, I summon my slave."

The slight figure in rusty black arose, but made no motion to depart. "As you wish, but tell me, would your patience remain exhausted were I to put you in the path of touching—say one hundred pounds of hard money?"

"Eh?" Doctor Saxnay's gaudy figure halted in midmotion towards the door. "Did you mention one hundred pounds?"

Uninvited, Lucius seated himself, thrust thin and sodden shoe soles so close to the fire that immediately they commenced to give off twisting feathers of steam.

"Speak up, sirrah!" Saxnay snapped, yellow features taut and intent. "And do not attempt to cozen me."

Lucius only grinned for a long moment, then said briskly, "From this ridiculous offer of the elixir, Your Unwashed Excellency, 'tis obvious you're a shilling-crazy fellow. As for myself, I *must* have money at once."

Doctor Saxnay resumed his throne, pale eyes narrowed. "Here," he was thinking, "is a cold fish—and a damned shrewd one."

"The first part of your observation, young sir, is both astute and true. So you propose to make us considerable money? Well, well."

The Jamaican leaned forward, his light voice quick and intent. "As a physician of this town I have a few wealthy friends and access to a certain number of the great houses."

Doctor Saxnay left off picking his nose, emitted an incredulous snort. "Have you indeed? I must say you look the part in your threadbare rags and shoes so patched they're ready to fall off."

Lucius' equanimity remained undisturbed. "I have only just set up practice, and in Boston a new physician don't grow fat in a hurry. Let us come to the point."

"Well?"

"I have been summoned to treat a wealthy and none-too-intelligent widow. Since her ailments are largely figments of her own idle imagination, I don't fancy you could do her any harm." Surprising even himself, Lucius found he was in complete control of this situation.

"I shall not listen to such insulting nonsense," snapped Saxnay.

In monumental dignity Lucius arose. "So be it, Your Griminess. I bow in respect to a man whose integrity soars above the consideration of one hundred pounds in exchange for perhaps a half-hour of mumbo-jumbo, cabalistic theatrics and such rot."

"Hold hard there." Doctor Saxnay jumped up, barred the way to his door. "Wait a moment. Exactly what's your idea of a split?"

"Your fee," the Jamaican informed him evenly, "will be one hundred pounds. I am convinced you're practiced enough in your shams to be convincing—"

"Yer bloody kind," grunted Doctor Saxnay, greed glittering in his pale eyes. "Who is this widow?"

Lucius winked. "Tut! Tut! my dear Doctor, you shall learn that only when I present you to her. Oh, yes, there's one more point: you must deputize me to take up our fee."

A sneer twisted the other's lavender-hued lips. "Oh, come off it—do you take me for a simpleton?"

"No, not a simpleton. That's why I'm here. I would

not cheat you of a single ha'penny. I intend to build a great practice here in Boston.''

"What's the split?"

"Share and share alike. Take it or leave it.''

The garish figure beside the fireplace commenced to laugh heartily. But a touch of respect now entered his manner. "Stab me, if you ain't a smart young tyke. Well, chum, then 'tis a go. When shall we call on the charming Madame—?'' Doctor Saxnay left the sentence dangling.

''—Mrs. Whoknows?'' Lucius chuckled. ''Tomorrow at three of the afternoon. I will come here. See that you hire the best possible carriage. 'Twouldn't do for the Chirurgeon Extraordinary of the King of—of—''

"Saxony and to the Margrave of Brandenburg," Saxnay supplied.

''—To arrive in any mean conveyance.''

Doctor Lucius Devoe recaptured his battered black tricorner hat—also the worn shilling Doctor Saxnay had, in a careless moment, left on the table.

Grudging admiration manifested itself in the charlatan's attitude when he predicted, "Ye'll go far, Mister Devoe, mark my words. 'Specially if ye've any real knowledge of medicine, which, o' course,'' he bared his bad teeth in a wide grin, "I ain't.''

Whistling, Lucius departed along a street leading towards Mrs. Fletcher's comfortable residence.

XVII. ADIEUX

IN SOLID SATISFACTION Asa Peabody, B.M., surveyed the new travelling chest, admired his initials sketched in bright, brass-headed nails ornamenting its wooden lid. Part of his satisfaction stemmed from the fact that he had come by this fine chest so cheaply. Till recently, it had been the property of a carpenter who, unluckily for him, had signed articles aboard the privateer schooner *Freedom*, eight guns, out of Chatham. Barely at sea, she'd been taken by H.B.M.S. *Iris*, formerly the U.S. frigate *John Hancock*. During a brief running engagement the carpenter had lost his head in more senses than one, or so the auctioneer had pointed out in macabre waggishness.

The most treasured of its contents was Doctor Townsend's unexpected gift of a not new, but very handsome, set of French surgical and trepanning instruments.

"You'll need these, lad," the old doctor had said in his gruff way. "Full well I know good knives and such are scarcer than scarce with the Army." He'd brushed aside all thanks, though such elegant instruments must have cost him a very pretty penny.

Asa smiled happily to himself and his whole being thrilled. Tomorrow, Asa Peabody of Machias, would commence his long journey southwards, into a strange country and towards a most unpredictable future. Judas Maccabaeus! Ever since he'd been a little tacker in homespun dresses he'd yearned to journey far and wide. He allowed he'd have to do some tall riding before he fetched up to Fort Arnold at West Point. All he knew about the Fort was that 'twas situated on a great and historic river, the Hudson. Folks claimed the Hudson was near thrice as wide as the frozen Charles out yonder— even at its broadest point.

First, he and Joshua Stanton would cross into Rhode Island from whence the British Army had finally been driven. The Royal Navy, though, still kept blockade ships prowling about the entrance to Narragansett Bay. Next they'd ride across Connecticut where Peter Burnham hailed from; he planned to look in for a day or so on Peter's pa in New London. Captain Stanton had explained they must circle wide around New York Town because General Sir Henry Clinton and some seven thousand British regulars were holding hard onto it.

At the door to his consulting room sounded a light knock, then Mrs. Southeby appeared to stand with hands held behind her.

She fetched a deep sigh. "I'm real grieved to see you leave, Doctor Peabody. You've been a fine good lodger, you have—and—and nobody ever whittled a prettier cracker stamp than you. I—I—" From behind her she produced a pair of bright red mittens. "I hope you'll not think me bold, but I—I've made these for you. I hope they will prove useful."

"Why, Mrs. Southeby!" Asa felt his throat thicken. "They're fine—really beautiful mittens, full-pegged and everything."

"Finest wool I could come across in Boston," Mrs.

Southeby avowed simply. "Mind you don't dry 'em by a hot fire, else they'll shrink down to fit a cat. Take care of 'em, Doctor, and they'll keep your fingers warm for your work, even if you get soaked through. When do you leave on your travels?"

"Tomorrow, Ma'am. I lodge tonight at Captain Stanton's. Barring accidents, we leave for Providence by post sleigh first thing in the morning." He took her small and wrinkled hands. "You have been mighty kind to me, Mistress Southeby, and patient with my poverty and queer hours and—and, what's been going on in your cellar. I'll endeavor to justify your good opinion of me."

"You will, Doctor, I'm certain-sure of it."

"Did Doctor Burnham—?"

"Yes, this morning he fetched the last of that miscreant away."

"And my humble thanks again in the matter of—of my first patient."

"Rubbish. It was only Christian to take in the poor creature."

The widow folded her hands across her lean belly. "I'll miss you sore, lad. 'Twill be turrible quiet hereabouts when you've gone. Oh dear, for me it's been 'most like havin' a family once again. Do you—do you mind?" Before he could answer she'd pulled down his head and kissed him hard, first as one cheek and then the other. "God bless and prosper you, Asa Peabody, and don't you forget, whatever chances—success or failure—you'll always find a home here."

"I won't, Ma'am," he murmured softly. "Indeed I won't."

Mrs. Southeby sniffed, squared her frail shoulders. "Now then, no more nonsense. Don't forget what that Doctor Townsend's taught you and, above all, stand up to them regimental surgeons. My Henry always named them a pack of unprincipled villains—the most of them, that is."

Fluttering much like a small brown hen surprised by a wind squall, Mrs. Southeby retreated toward the kitchen.

Asa was on the point of locking his clothes chest when, on the staircase, light steps sounded. It was Hilde, her hair brushed and glossy and her green shawl stitched neatly in place—pins were far too expensive for such a purpose. Spots of color glowed in the pale smooth sheen of her cheeks.

"What in Tophet are you doing out of bed?" Asa demanded in rough kindness.

"I—well, I heard of your impending departure." The girl paused on the second step from the bottom; even so she remained just a bit below the level of his eyes. "Anyway, I feel ever so much stronger now."

He shook his head. "Shouldn't have got up, you know. Three days ago you would have lost a wrassle with a mouse and you still ain't over-spry. So, Mistress Mention, you'd best return to your room. I'll look in for a final examination. Really, I will."

Hilde's huge black eyes probed his features. "I am most profoundly grateful," she stated, clinging to the banister with a slender blue-veined hand, "but I am leaving now."

"Leaving? Why?"

Her gaze fell away. "I-I must, really I must. Please don't press me, Doctor. I—I wish there was some way I could prove my gratitude for—for all you've done."

"No call to fret yourself on that score," he assured her awkwardly. "Most of what ailed you, Hilde, was hunger. I will be frank—you have a touch of green sickness, especially dangerous to a girl of your tender years. Whatever chances, you must eat heartily."

"Oh, yes, Doctor." During these past three days and blissfully warm and comfortable nights Hilde had pondered her future, and, with a return of strength, she had arrived at a firm decision. Rough though her life among the Mic-Macs had been, it yet remained her only experience with happiness and security. Something deep within her nature craved the empty serenity of the woods, reassociation with those smells and sounds loved of her early childhood. By now, Hilde felt sure she would never feel truly at home among white people because her sense of values, her judgment seemed always at fault regarding her own race.

Therefore, she was determined, by hook or crook, to win her way back to Nova Scotia, back to the lodge of Mooinaskw and Wejek.

Yesterday evening, as she lay luxuriously drowsing in Mrs. Southeby's second-best bed, it had come over her that she must not linger in Boston, not even a day. Lizzie Wright owned her bond and undoubtedly must have advertised her disappearance. Why, the madam could, and undoubtedly would, cause her to be cast into jail.

Jail? The very thought of bars and confinement sent shivers a-running up Hilde's thin legs and set goosepimples to breaking out on her shoulder blades. All too vividly Hilde could recall bringing comforts to Belle and Fanny, a pair of Mrs. Wright's girls who'd been jailed for stabbing and robbing a selectman from Ipswich. The fearful squalor, the appalling filthiness and the blank, despairing aspect of the inmates she would never forget.

"Yes, Doctor, please be assured I have decided on a wise course," she informed him—just as if she knew when, and how, she was going to regain Wejek's village.

"May *le bon Dieu* bless your generous clean soul!" Hilde Mention suddenly descended the last step and, in an unconsciously graceful movement, knelt on one knee in front of the ungainly but commanding figure in black. Before Asa divined her purpose her soft lips were pressed to the back of his hand.

Red to his hair line, Asa lifted Hilde to her feet, attempted rough good humor. "Come now, Hilde, up to Machias we'd say that's no way for a pretty girl to kiss a man."

Her soul soaring into wide black eyes, Hilde looked up at him. "You don't really want me to kiss you—on the mouth?"

Spurred by some unfathomable impulse, Asa caught her in his arms, planted a hard kiss on her parted lips. He grinned sheepishly after that and, as he put her down, said, "Whatever's happened to you, Hilde Mention, and I allow it's been a-plenty, it ain't mucked you. Why, I hold you no more of a real harlot than," the name came tumbling out, "than Sabra Stanton."

Hilde's pointed, somberly lovely features became transfigured. "You really believe that? *Really?*"

"As I live and breathe, Hilde. We can't all rule our destinies." Confused and embarrassed he turned into his consulting room. "Look, I'm going to write you a letter to a friend of Doctor Townsend, my instructor. 'Tis a female who maintains a most respectable lodging house."

Asa re-opened his travelling desk, and scrawled a recommendation. If he understood William Townsend as he thought he did, the old surgeon would do whatever possible for this delicate, shy little creature. In folding the sheet Asa enclosed a Rhode Island ten shilling note which ought to fetch six almost anywhere in Massachusetts.

Hilde's shadowed eyes came to rest upon the new chest. "Why are you leaving Boston?"

He methodically packed his quill. "I have accepted a surgeon-mate's commission with the army."

The light faded from Hilde's expression. "May I wish you all the fortune in the world?" Somewhere, from amid the recesses of her memory appeared an inspiration, and though such a gesture might appear akin to effrontery, she pulled from her hair the little length of clean yellow ribbon. Swiftly, she tied it into a perky rosette. "Please, Doctor Asa, promise to keep this with you—a little while at least—to remind you of my gratitude," her voice then grew stronger, richer, "and—and my true love."

She shoved the token into Asa's hand and was out of the door into the street before he could recover.

"Hilde! Hilde! come back!" But she kept on hurrying along Sudbury Street and did not even turn her head.

XVIII. MESSENGER FROM MACHIAS

TO ASA PEABODY'S DISMAY, the unexpected visit of a numerous family of cousins, the David Pages from Newburyport, had filled every bed and room in Samuel Stanton's big residence. Captain Joshua Stanton, however, had procured lodgings for the new surgeon's mate at a near-by ordinary and to it Asa intended to repair soon after enjoying an abundant supper at the Stanton Home. A long and cold ride was in prospect for the morrow.

Joshua Stanton, his yellow hair clubbed by a dark blue grosgrain ribbon, started to speak but, noting Asa's preoccupation with Sabra, merely puffed on a long churchwarden pipe and, legs outstretched, stared into the leaping flames of the living room fire.

God in Heaven! How much time would pass before he might again enjoy such ease? Wasn't much comfort to be

found in General Knox's winter encampment outside of
Morristown. New Jersey might be quite a bit further
south, but it seemed every bit as cold as here. He wondered whether his promised promotion had been published. As a major, he'd rate considerably more comfortable quarters. He dozed.

Never, thought Asa Peabody, had Sabra appeared so
warmly, softly feminine, so animated and so gracious towards him. In his ears still was ringing the music of her
good wishes on his appointment.

"Papa declares that half the physician-surgeons in
Boston would yield their eye teeth for such an appointment," Sabra murmured. "Imagine! Soon you'll be one
of General Washington's own family. I thrill to my fingertips at the prospect, Doctor."

"For a fact, Mistress Stanton, I yet can't understand
why they selected me," Asa admitted, quite without
affectation. "I'm not half so clever as Peter Burnham."

"Evidently Uncle Will don't agree." Sabra's dark red
lips curved as, successfully, she stifled a sensation of resentment. It was Lucius, of course, who should have received the appointment. Who could deny the lithe young
Jamaican's alertness and ability? And yet—Sabra was
determined to be fair in the matter—Josh, a veritable
fount of wisdom, evidently was setting great store by this
big ex-fisherman—liked him vastly.

Asa was thinking he could never in his life recall a
more agreeable evening. Mr. and Mrs. Stanton had been
graciousness personified but, at supper, Sabra directed
some gay sallies in his direction which had set him to
flushing like a schoolboy. In a year or so, Asa reckoned,
some of her girlish giddiness would wear off and she
would develop into a rare fine woman.

It was only towards the end of the evening that, in Mr.
Stanton's library, Asa contrived a few private words with
Sabra.

"I hope, Mistress Stanton," he said, powerful hands
locked on the back of a chair, "I shall justify the flattering sentiments expressed by your brother and Doctor
Townsend." He went red in the face, picked his words in
painful care. "Dare I hope that—that you will think of
me on occasion?"

Sabra's teeth glistened to an instant smile, her hand
came to rest briefly on his. "I shall, Asa, indeed I shall."

For all that they first had met over a year earlier, this was her first use of his Christian name.

After all, Sabra was deciding, kind words constituted no disloyalty to Lucius—and Asa might be able to help along her true love. As Papa frequently stated, and had caused her to cross-stitch on a sampler, "He who has a thousand friends has not a friend to spare—but he who has an enemy shall meet him everywhere." Her gaze came to rest in genuine admiration on Asa's red-brown countenance. "I shall tell Josh that I count on him to fetch you back when next he comes home on leave."

Perspiring all at once, Asa attempted to contrive a reply at once clever, forthright and tender, but for the life of him he couldn't; merely gagged, towering before the mantelpiece with muscular wrists protruding from the too short sleeves of a new, dark blue jacket. His hands moved restlessly, as if they were uncertain as to what to do with themselves.

"You are sweeter'n wild honey to say that—and I—I shall make bold to write, Sabra." Judas Maccabaeus! He'd called Sabra by her Christian name!

"And I—I shall certainly make reply," Sabra smiled and turned to the bookcases. Following a momentary hesitation, she selected a slim volume bound in brown calfskin and very liberally adorned with gold leaf.

"Here, Asa, is a romance," Sabra told him, the book momentarily pressed against the gentle curves of her bosom. "It is tender and true and, oh, so romantic. *Evelina* is my favorite book. Pray, take this to the wars with you."

As Sabra handed him the little book her serene gray eyes met and looked steadily up into his dark brown ones. His fingers tingled and he flushed to his ear tips. Sabra Stanton was presenting him something of her very own.

"Why, why, Sabra, I scarce know how to thank you," he stammered. "I shall treasure this volume always; it will bring you nearer. Sabra—will you—would you wait till I return? That is—not promise your hand?"

Something in his tone touched a deep chord in her being. She raised her eyes. "Yes—dear. I—I promise."

All at once she realized what she had said. Was this being fair to Lucius? Definitely not. Then it came to her that Lucius' fascination for her was an odd thing. When he

was present he seemed to fill the whole world, to domi-
nate it and her—seemed to create one of those spells described in the old fairy tales.

Away from him everything appeared in a slightly different light. Asa for instance. Side by side Asa appeared
crude and stupid by comparison to Lucius—yet her deep-
rooted common sense warned her that this was not so. If
only Lucius weren't so utterly romantic, good-looking,
and ambitious.

Maybe she'd been indiscreet that afternoon at Jennie
Fletcher's? Come to think of it, how could she have acted so? Allowing Lucius to kiss her! She had been precipitate and no mistake about it. Mercy! Asa must be very
like Papa had been in his younger days, when first he'd
ventured up to Boston from Falmouth on Cape Cod.

"You will write to me?" she reminded.

"At every opportunity. You see, when I have established my position in the Medical Department I shall
want an answer to a—a most serious question."

"Certainly you shall have opportunity to ask it—"

Joshua Stanton came clumping tactfully loud, to the library door. "Crimanently! Sabra, can't you let poor Asa
be? He's yet to pack at the inn and we've a long, long ride
in store tomorrow." The young artillery officer stood
grinning at them, his pipe held in one hand, quite a brave
figure in his blue and scarlet regimentals—having been
mended, pressed and adorned with a new set of flat yellow buttons they looked like new.

"You old growly-grub. It's yourself that wants to go to
bed." Sabra in wrinkling a short pink nose at him tried to
ignore the blush staining her smooth cheeks.

A few minutes later Asa was striding off towards the
Blue Turkey Tavern, at which Joshua had lodged him.
Under his cloak he was holding Sabra's gift in a death
grip while breathing the rarefied atmosphere of un-
dreamed of happiness. Sabra had called him "Asa," had
given him a token, had promised to correspond. Godfreys! She had seemed to promise even more.

Smiling happily in the chill darkness he swung briskly
along towards the narrow length off Orange Street.
Plague take it! If women weren't just as unpredictable as
a black duck's flighting. Here all along he'd been figuring
that Lucius was steering a windward course and all-fired
close to Sabra's affections.

He commenced to whistle "The White Cockade." No

girl—like Sabra Stanton—who had given her heart to another, could have been so almighty sweet and tender as she had been to him. *Er-r-ou-ow-ou!* Danged if he could help raising such a 'Quoddy war whoop that windows banged up in all directions and curses came ringing down at him. He didn't care. For sure now, he'd labor mightily to make Sabra, Joshua and Doctor Townsend proud of their confidence.

His long legs carried him so rapidly along Orange Street that, pretty soon, he saw the feeble lights of the Blue Turkey sketching a set of yellow bars across the frozen dirt of the street.

The hour being late, it was all of half after nine, he found the taproom occupied only by a sleepy-eyed drawer, a pair of semi-drunken clerks involved in a political argument and a lad drowsing in a far corner. Asa was unhooking his cloak when the boy roused, stared an instant, then ran over to him, a look of gladness mingled with inexpressible relief on his small and badly chapped red face.

"Asey! Praise the Lord! Oh, Asey, I've searched everywhere for ye."

The young doctor flung his arms about this lad who spoke with the twangless accent of the Eastern District. "Morgan! I hardly knew ye. My, you've grown like a burdock."

Watched in dull curiosity by the drawer, Asa held his brother at admiring arm's length. He saw a gangling lad in coarse duroys and the kind of thick gray woollen stockings Ma used to knit of a winter's evening. In one big, rawboned hand he clutched a fisherman's coarse, blue woollen stocking cap. Morgan, junior, certain-sure favored Pa; had the same broad forehead; same straight nose; same square shoulders that, sometime, would fill out and become uncommon broad. Young Morgan's fair hair was shaggy as a colt's tail and he'd a mouth wide as Sanborn's Cove.

"Asey," Morgan blinked a little. "I have searched this great town high and low fer ye these past two days."

"Stuck to it, didn't you? Now let's celebrate." He slapped the table, drew the drawer's attention. "Two mugs of—" he was going to say applejack but changed it to, "a brown ale and birch beer." Morgan couldn't be more than fifteen, or was it fourteen years, of age?

Feeling so extra good already, it was simply elegant to

find one of his family like this and to tell him about his wonderful appointment. Before Morgan, he guessed he could let himself go and maybe crow a little.

"Sit down, lad. This is finer'n eel hair. You've arrived in a happy hour." Morgan looked embarrassed and tried to interrupt, but ended by grinning all over as Asa rushed on. "What d'you guess? Tomorrow I'm to be sworn in to be an officer on the highest staff in our Army. Why, I'm to serve under General Washington's own self. Ain't that something?"

"Why, it sure is. I guess."

To Asa's profound astonishment Morgan's round red features failed to light up.

"What ails you?" Something in the boy's expression extinguished Asa's exuberance as effectively as a bucket of cold water. "Ain't anything wrong to home is there?"

"Dunno, Asey. Maybe ye'd better read this."

The boy fumbled into the depth of his coarse Osnabruck shirt till he produced a fold of paper; it was sweat-marked, wrinkled and frayed around its edges. "Pa sent it."

A chill flood of misgivings extinguished the last of those lovely sparks kindled during the past few hours.

Asa found considerable difficulty in deciphering his father's crabbed handwriting; nor was the shaky manner in which Pa's pen had formed the letters at all reassuring. He wrote:

Machias, ye 26th day of December, 1779

Asa, my Son:

Greetings. Only direst Necessity prompts me to put Pen to paper in this Fashun. Never have we hear in Machias suffer'd so unchancy a yere as this just passed. Three Vessels of this Village, among them that of y'r Bro. Uzziel were lost with all hands during the High Courses and Tempests of Septembre—a woundy Blow to our Community. From Ahab I have rec'd no Word in above a Year. I guess he must have been killed or made prisoner at sea. To make matters yet more hard the cursed British, since their rade of two Yeres ago, have blockaded ye Coast. Now not a fisherman or coaster dares putt to see. You know full well I would not Burthen you with my cares, my Son, but in Truth, my affairs are in Desperate straits. As to our Family, ye only able-bodied male of our name is Morgan buy whose Hand I trust you will receive this. Lionel is—

"—How old is Lionel? I forget."

"Nine, Asey, goin' on ten," the boy replied. "Li tries to be handy, but he's awful puny, still."

Asa resumed reading:

—Lionel is too small to lift a trawl reel. Now to the Nub of ye matter. Mrs. Peabody, y're stepmother suffers greatly from what Doctor Falconer declares to be a Decay of ye Breast and I fear is not long for this world, and Purity y'r half-sister is very ill of a Distemper of ye throat.

Therefore, my only remaining groan son, I do beseach you to Return at once to Machias. Alas, I am groan so olde I am no longer Equal to ye Burthen of our Household. Pray believe 'tis only in greatest Reluctance that I do charge You to come to our Family's succor. God speed y'r Return and keep You safe.

Y'r ever affect'n'te Father.

M. Peabody.

P.S. Jerusha, our last milch cow died this morning, a sad blow to us all.

Asa Peabody's long black-clad figure sagged upon the greasy wood of the bench. All the while watched by his younger brother, he deciphered the letter again.

Eagerly Morgan Peabody drank of the bitter birch beer, then wiped his lips on the chapped back of a hand that always looked grayish red nowadays. He felt bone-tired, as a boy would who had spent two full days roaming about the streets of Boston. Gorry, it was late; all of ten o'clock. The warmth of the taproom and effect of the birch beer began dragging hard at his eyelids, but he felt less unhappy now. He'd come up with Asey and just in time, too. Now Asey could do the lion's share of worrying.

His older brother's voice intruded on Morgan's drowsiness. "Pa don't mention himself."

"He ain't so spry," Morgan replied smothering a yawn, "and that's a fact. Remember that old baynit wound he took up to the in-taking of Louisburg?. Well, it's opened again so's he can't walk any more, nor do any heavy chores."

The lad then went on to describe in full detail how two Machias men had escaped from the naval prison at Halifax and, become but emaciated wrecks of human beings, had made their way home in a smuggler so quickly that with them they brought along the ever-dreaded jail fever. Doctor Parker, the other local doctor, who'd never been much account anyhow, had taken to drinking and was even less use now that the churchyards of Machias were growing hump-backed with new graves.

Asa passed a hand over his face, stared a while at his untasted ale. At last, fetching a deep breath, he said, "Morgan, my room's the first to the right of the landing; go turn in—we'll share the bed."

"Ain't you comin' up?"

"No. I've some letters to write. By the bye, the ship you came in. She's still in port?"

"Aye, but we'll have to be aboard the *Sally* by six o' the morning or get left behind. Skipper warned me," the lad said, then stumbled off, casting loose his jacket buttons as he scuffed along.

Long after the two clerks had concluded their political discussion—with each still more firmly set in his convictions—Asa's pen travelled on and on over pages of foolscap tinted yellow-orange by a tallow dip candle which gave off smoke that smelt like scorched beef.

What sheer misery it was, having to compose long explanatory letters to Doctor Townsend and Doctor Blanchard. It proved a little easier to prepare a shorter missive to Captain Stanton returning the draft for thirty dollars—he would more readily understand the demands of Duty.

These, he followed by a brief note of farewell to Peter Burnham, suggesting that he apply for the appointment; he felt confident Doctor Townsend and Doctor Blanchard would endorse his application. To Lucius he wrote instructing him to seek the Blue Turkey. He was leaving behind a book on physick which he knew the Jamaican wanted, but could not afford.

Each sentence, painstakingly formed by his goose-quill pen, loomed a funereal black, eclipsing, word by word, all those once-glittering hopes and ambitions. To follow any other course than that which he was adopting never even occurred to him.

At the very last Asa wrote a few falsely cheerful lines to Sabra—he'd be back soon and take up his surgeon's-mate commission. Fiddle-faddle! He knew well enough that once he reached Machias he'd be bound by bonds tighter than ever had been that old Pagan Titan called Prometheus.

This was the hardest of all the letters to write—and the most inept. The bright image of Sabra burned so newly bright, so infinitely desirable in his brain. On the envelope he wrote instructions for Lucius to deliver the same to Sabra's own hand. Lord, how he hoped she'd understand what had chanced to wrech his hopes—and be patient—for if half of what Pa had written was true, it'd be a dreary long while before he sailed again into Boston Harbor.

PART II—DIVERGENT COURSES

XIX. NEW PROSPECTS

IN AN OBSCURE corner of the Golden Ox Yoke, an ordinary particularly favored of teamsters, horse dealers and the like, Doctor Peter Burnham leaned well over his beer-stained table and considered, with shrewd attention, the blunt and battered features of Murdo Moore, his companion. That worthy represented himself as driver to a busy, but none-too-sober, undertaker of the town.

Beneath black and bushy brows which merged into a single line, Murdo Moore narrowed red-veined blue eyes and spoke in a hoarse whisper reeking of rum and chewing tobacco. "Aye, yer Honor, I offer ye as choice a young female corpse as ye'll behold in yer lifetime! 'Tis a chancy business, but I'll manage it an' ye meet my price."

Peter glanced over his shoulder to reassure himself that all present were quite uninterested in his affairs. Wouldn't do to tolerate eavesdropping—not in so desperately risky a matter as this. "Of what did she die?"

The other blew his nose between his fingers, then wiped them on leather breeches shiny with use and dirt. "Why, yer Honor, 'twas of love, ye might say—er—she was what ye'd call a doxy." Moore's red-lidded eyes shifted. "That's the only reason I'd risk snatching a female body."

"I don't follow you."

"There'll be none to worry, or ask questions, over what becomes o' such a pore and friendless baggage's mortal remains."

Peter put down his beer pot and studied his ill-favored companion with sudden suspicion. "When you say she died of 'love,' you don't mean the *lues venera?*"

"Lor' love ye no, sir," the ill-smelling rogue's gaze examined their surroundings before he muttered. "The bawd keeper claimed 'twas from some seizure o' her vital organs. The poor wench suddenly and without no warning at all fell dead. 'Tis a fine-lookin' healthy corpse, purty, too—only a day old."

Peter's elation grew with the realization that, indeed, a rare opportunity was presenting itself. Um. This girl most likely had died of some heart ailment, which was all to the good. The heart presented so many mysterious and delicate problems.

"Now look you, Moore, you'll swear you've come by this body honestly?"

Without checking his gulping, the teamster nodded several times. "Aye, the bawd keeper wants three pounds, ten sterling. Fer that he'll even write a bill of sale."

"Surprising, considering dangers involved; still, I'll accept your word on it." But for all that, doubts lingered in Peter's mind concerning the legality of such a transaction. God in Heaven, what an opportunity to push aside, even just a little, the thick veil of ignorance concerning the physiology of the human female.

"The corpse—where is it?"

Murdo Moore frowned, considered a spot of mutton grease gleaming on the shiny planks on the table. "That's as may be, Yer Honor. First, suppose ye tells what will ye pay—hard money?"

"Five pounds, or nothing—I'm no haggler." That was a great deal of money, more than he could afford, still it wouldn't do to have this ill-favored rogue wagging a dissatisfied tongue.

"Ye mean that?"

"Five pounds is what I said."

"Why then—'tis a bargain."

Peter swallowed a short gulp of bitter ale, thought hard. "Two things provided. First, you are quite certain that no one other than the bawd keeper knows of this business?"

"None, Yer Honor."

"Second. Ye'll never breathe a word, drunk or sober?"

Moore belched loudly. "You can lay to that too, Yer Honor. I've no hankerin' to be strung to a tree." Moore's reddish eyes briefly met the doctor's. "They've a long docket agin me already at the Court House."

Slowly, Peter passed a hand over his dull red hair, sighed and took his decision. "Where shall I find you, and when?"

"Ten of this night, Yer Honor. At the river end o'

Green Lane ye'll find an old disused stable—'tis called Bramwell's barn. I'll fetch the body there, and no further.''

"So far so good, but how am I to get the cadaver to my—my study?''

"That's fer Yer Honor to figger out," growled Moore and no amount of persuasion or bribery would shake the teamster from his determination.

Peter's sense of elation vanished. Damn! The task of transferring the illegal remains from a cart into the Widow Southeby's cellar would require the efforts of at least two men. On whom dared he call? The obvious solution was Lucius Devoe. That ambitious student would be eager to participate in subsequent dissection.

"I'll take a half o' that oof now," Murdo Moore growled, bushy brows again a single mark across his forehead.

Peter's light blue eyes took on a hard glint. "You'll get the bawd keeper's fee now, your own share you'll handle when I receive the cadaver.''

"Cooney, ain't yer? Well, I allow you won't try to cozen me." The other spat into the foul sawdust at his feet, then bent forward and spoke in a hurried undertone. "Though, 'twill be blacker than Satan's pocket, don't show nary a glim. When ye reach Bramwell's barn ye'll hum a stave o' 'The World Turned Upside Down.' Understand? Then I'll show you to the cart; ye can return it to Tim O'Brien's stable.''

Great was Peter's astonishment to find a letter awaiting him at his lodgings. Increasingly dismayed, he read:

Respected Friend Peter:
   Word hath just reached me that my Family in Machias is in dire Straits. Filial Duty leaves me no choice but to Repair thither at once and I shall have sailed ere you Receive this. Since now there can be no Army Career for me I have writ Doctor Townsend suggesting you in my Place with Gen'l Washington's Staff so pray seek him at once. Am confident you will receive ye appointment. May good luck attend you always. Vale!
                    Y'r humble and obed't Servant,
                              A. Peabody, B.M.

For many moments Peter sat staring unseeingly at the note. Poor Asa! What a terrible, bitter blow to hopes and ambitions shaped in so painstaking a fashion. Poor old Asa. Only at this moment did Peter appreciate the real depth of his respect and affection for the big gangling Down Easter with his dry humor, deliberate speech and forthright honesty. How characteristic that Asa in his letter hadn't pitied himself or bemoaned his fate; he'd just accepted the fact that he must turn his back on a radiant future and return to a little fishing and lumbering village crowded between sea and wilderness.

For some moments Peter gloomed, then, being young, he ceased to lament Asa's disappointment to rejoice in his own good fortune. Glory hallelujah! To think it would be he, after all, who'd travel to West Point, who'd rub elbows with the great, who'd learn the latest and best methods in physick and surgery. Hallelujah! In his comfortable lodgings, the Connecticuter leaped up and cracked his heels in the air like any schoolboy on the final day of a term. Why, why this was too good to be true. Hold on though. Captain Stanton and Doctor Townsend might entertain other ideas.

Impulsively, Peter clapped on a buckled gray hat and fairly sprinted down to a livery on the corner to rent a saddle horse. By continually kicking his mount, a short-legged cob, he kept up a jolting trot which fetched him into Bennett Street and before Doctor Townsend's doorway within twenty minutes.

An hour later Peter Burnham emerged from his former instructor's familiar brick house. Remounting, he grinned on passers-by, whistled cheerily and fair rode on feather-beds. Tomorrow, come hell or high water he'd become Surgeon's-Mate Burnham.

Papa would be mightily pleased; it would mean something for that old gentleman to stroll into his club in New London and remark ever so off-handedly, "My boy, Peter, is off the wars. Yes, he's to serve on the Commander-in-Chief's own staff." Peter sobered a bit when it dawned that this appointment involved a sharp, if temporary change in plan. What of the Ashton child? She seemed on the way towards proving his warm brandy thesis. Again, he'd find precious little opportunity in the army to study the diseases of females. Holy Moses! Speaking of females—what about that cadaver he'd bought?

Damn! If he knew where to find Murdo Moore he'd

cancel the whole affair, but he didn't. No more could he fail to appear at the rendezvous. To leave the poor rogue waiting indefinitely at the barn, risking discovery and probably lynching, wouldn't be fair. The Burnhams were famous for keeping their commitments. The Devil take that poor girl's cadaver! Was it time yet to look in on Captain Ashton's daughter? No. He'd better locate Lucius first.

For a second time that day, Peter encountered the unexpected. When he did come up with Lucius, it was to discover the Jamaican emerging from a Mr. Levin's haberdasher's shop on Hanover Street.

What a transformation. In place of the familiar rusty black coat and patched shoes, Lucius created the impression of a modish young gentleman of the town. He was garbed in a fine coat under which showed a snuff-colored suit; a jabot of good, but inexpensive, Flemish lace glistened at his throat, and black thread stockings outlined his lean legs. There was an unfamiliar assurance to the way Lucius' well-built shoes—they boasted new bathmetal buckles—pressed the grimy snow of Hanover Street.

"Lucius! Is it indeed you?"

The Jamaican treated his friend to a quick, singularly engaging smile. "Aye, Peter, the Goddess of Chance at last has smiled on me. Right royally, I might add. Last night I could not seem to lose."

There was, Lucius felt, no call to amplify his explanation—which, in a way, was entirely truthful. Had it not been due entirely to chance that, through Sabra Stanton, he had come to know Mrs. Fletcher and so to learn of her imaginary ailments? Chance, too, had decreed that that preposterous and outrageous quack, Doctor Saxnay, should have been victimizing Boston at this particular time. After all, he, Lucius, had but encouraged Chance to serve his necessity.

Peter led the way into a tobacconist's and there disclosed the news of Asa's abrupt change of fortune.

Lucius frowned, bit his lip. "Poor devil. Really, Asa deserved better than banishment to a backwoods hamlet." Then he gave Peter a sharp glance. "Who's to fill his appointment?"

"Doctor Townsend wishes me to take Asa's place. Blanchard and Captain Stanton also approve. Naturally, I accepted."

Lucius offered his hand. "Congratulations, old friend. For a second time they have chosen well." It stung, though, that Doctor Townsend twice should have passed him over. Some day, and before very long, Doctor Townsend and the rest would be constrained to admit their blindness.

"Yes," Lucius thought, "I've made a fair start; but I don't intend to be a hasty and greedy fool. For all Doctor Saxnay's invitation for further association I'll not do it— quick lucre or no. I'll temporize, put off the scandalous old bastard without antagonizing him. I'll let well enough be; I've still thirty pounds and that's a sight more than I've ever had since I sailed aboard the *Active*. A man of Saxnay's kidney can't last long over here, though in Europe a clever rogue can lose himself in the great cities. As I know too damn' well, strangers in America are not less noticeable than a hog on a ballroom floor."

Yes, unless Doctor Saxnay was far smarter than Lucius reckoned, that charlatan had some rude surprises in store. Americans hated to be bilked out of hard-come-by money—especially the gold and silver Saxnay inevitably demanded. Besides, the fellow knew less than nothing about Medicine, a point on which Lucius Devoe's conscience balked more than at any other. Under no circumstances, starve though he might, would he countenance, or be privy to, mal-practice of any sort. Mrs. Fletcher was different—just a silly, rich old woman who wasn't ill save in her idle imagination. Saxnay's foufe-raws hadn't harmed her in the least—for a fact, they had rendered her quite content.

"Come along to my lodgings," Peter was inviting. "I've more news of interest to you."

"Indeed? And what, pray?"

The taller of the two grinned. "I am about to make you a most expensive gift—also a rare opportunity. I'll tell you when we get to my quarters."

Before a fire in Peter's lodging the matter of Murdo Moore's cadaver came out. Lucius looked at once fascinated and a little frightened. "Jupiter! You're running a fearful risk. Why go through with it?"

"I don't want to, but I can't find Moore."

"Um. I see." Lucius gnawed his lip in thought and swift calculation. "Let me understand correctly. My part is merely to wait at Mrs. Southeby's, to help you unload and then drive the empty cart back to O'Brien's stable?"

"Yes. Wish I could stay to work on that dissection! It'll be years, most likely, before I'll come across another such chance. What's wrong? Ain't you pleased?"

"Oh, yes. But for all you're so easy about it, more than one physician has been stoned to death for a similar attempt."

"Each profession has its hazards; any physician worth half his salt must expect to run risks, time and again."

"True enough," Lucius admitted, fingers rubbing up and down his port glass. "I presume you have decided on your route to Mrs. Southeby's? Wouldn't do to make any mistakes."

"From Bramwell's barn I figure I'll follow Green Street to Unity then descend Sudbury Lane; by that time of night that whole neighborhood will be sound asleep."

"Sounds reasonable," the Jamaican agreed. "Very well. You can count on me to be waiting at half after ten in Mrs. Southeby's woodshed."

"Take heed how you unbar the backyard gate," Peter warned. "Damned hinges on it screech like a pair of banshees."

Lucius nodded soberly, then offered his hand. "Best wishes on your appointment."

Beaming, Peter clapped him on the shoulder. "I'll find a post for you, too, soon's I get settled down there. You can count on it."

Count on it? Not much. What ambitious young officer in his right mind would introduce his staff to a man who could, and would, constitute a dangerous rival? Again, the underfed, unpaid and semimutinous Continental Army had become so diminished in numbers it wasn't reasonable to suppose there would be many new posts open; not for a good long while.

Once they had parted Peter sought Captain Robert Ashton's handsome residence, his regrets mounting that he must transfer Susan Ashton—his first patient—to another practitioner. In that connection it came over him that he'd been stupid not to have fetched along Lucius in order to introduce him to the privateer captain and his stately English wife. Lucius, of course, must take over the case. Anybody else would be determined to amputate. Well, he'd 'tend to a presentation first thing tomorrow.

Beyond suffering a slight fever, natural enough under

the circumstances, little Susan appeared to be progressing satisfactorily. It was disturbing, however, to note a deep discoloration and a not inconsiderable swelling in the vicinity of the fracture. Still, the puncture looked healthy and there seemed no definite indication of a formation of pus, laudable or otherwise—quite a pleasant surprise. To reduce the swelling it seemed logical to order continued application of snow or cold water compresses.

Normally, suppuration should have set in by this time. Why hadn't it? Had the hot brandy been responsible? Or had the application of cold compresses merely retarded a formation of pus? Again, it seemed logical that his very prompt reduction of the fracture had some bearing on this promising technique. Perhaps severed tissues and muscles were prone to knit more readily when quickly reunited? Could it be that heat itself encouraged healing? On the other hand cold also appeared beneficial. Where, oh, where did the truth lie? Maybe in the army, where a multitude of such cases would of necessity present themselves, he could arrive at a conclusion.

Another two days, he felt, should decide the matter of Susan. He must get Lucius to record this case history in the greatest detail and post it to him. Gorry! To save such a pretty little girl's arm would prove a capital achievement.

xx. The Body of Jennie McLaren

DOCTOR PETER BURNHAM sat hunched on the seat of the rented two-wheeled cart and bent his head towards a fitful southeast wind. So far all had progressed to plan—with never a hitch to rouse his alarm. To all intents and purposes, his cart conveyed nothing more worthy of note than a load of wheat straw.

Timothy O'Brien's unexpectedly spirited livery stable horse moved smartly along, iron-shod hoofs ringing disconcertingly loud on the cobbles of Green Street. In Unity Street, that older part of town, the houses had been built very close together along a narrow thoroughfare. Here the street presented a confusing pattern of silverblacks, dark grays and jet shadows, lanced here and there by an occasional gleam of candlelight. Near the intersection of Sudbury Street it was black as the Old Nick's heart, but, at half after ten, there was little or no pedestrian traffic.

All the same Peter wondered at a persistent sense of uneasiness. To be sure Murdo Moore's manner had been furtive, but that would be only natural under the circumstances. But need the teamster have grabbed his fee and bolted out of the barn immediately to become lost in the darkness?

What a crying shame he might not profit by this purchase. Vividly he could recall unhooding a dark lantern to make sure he had not been bilked. He hadn't been. The light had disclosed the colorless, placid features of a rather plain young woman whose dead eyes peered up at him almost reproachfully through their half-closed lids.

One recollection, and a disturbing one, came as, nervously, he slapped the reins across the cart horse's broad rump. For those of a trollop, the dead girl's garments had appeared sedate and of exceptionally fine quality. How come? Whores generally were poor and improvident.

Cape tossing in the raw wind, Peter shivered, made an effort to rally his wits. The heavy darkness, tension and imagination were combining to create chimerical dangers. Of course everything would continue to proceed smoothly; no reason to doubt it. Within another ten minutes he'd be driving into Mrs. Southeby's backyard. Pray God, Lucius would be punctual, ready and waiting.

Peter guided the horse around a frozen pool, expertly steadied the animal when, a few rods further along, it slipped on ice hidden in a deep rut. Gorry! He'd never imagined Unity Street to be so long. Peter took a firmer grip on the reins and braced his knees against the heavy jolting of the cart. Lord! How loud those iron tires rasped in this empty blackness. Steady now. Within five minutes he'd have accomplished the trickiest part of this expedition. Beyond Charter Street he would regain a quiet residential district.

A roundsman clumping along with staff and lantern cast the two-wheeled cart an incurious glance, then a pair of patrons staggering out of an inn yelled something to which Peter called a gruff "Good night, to you!" When they shouted some further question he urged the livery horse into a jolting trot.

After another hundred yards Peter realized he could

turn into the comparatively idle length of Snow Street—
in fact he could have turned off this tavern- and inn-lined
thoroughfare sooner—though it would have prolonged
his journey. Come to think of it, he didn't much resemble
a teamster in his triple cape. Sweat broke out on his
palms and along the lining of his stylish buckled beaver
hat.

His breath entered with a soft gasp when, at the entrance to Middle Street, he noted a small knot of roisterers collected under the sign-board of the Eagle Tavern,
or were they just rum-warmed citizens leaving for home?
Something about their stance and the quick way they
swung to face his cart set Peter's nerves to crisping.
Though desperately he yearned to turn aside, he had no
choice but to keep on. Any other course would certainly
invite suspicion. A tall watchman strode out into the middle of the street, raised his staff in one hand and lantern
in the other.

"Halt!" he commanded. "Pull up there. State yer
name and business abroad at this hour."

As the peace officer swung his thick hickory staff
crosswise, barring further progress, certain of the by-
standers drifted off the sidewalk to assist in blocking the
street. Keen barbs of apprehension stabbed at Peter's
brain as he reined in, but he assumed a bold attitude.

"I'm minding my business, sir, and am molesting no
one. Pray allow me to pass."

"I demand yer name and business," growled the
watchman and strode forward in the obvious intention of
seizing the cart horse's bridle. The yellow-red rays of his
whale-oil lantern disclosed narrow unshaven cheeks and
hard eyes peering belligerently from beneath his tricorne
hat.

"I am Paul Bradstreet," Peter replied in as easy a tone
as he could manage. "I have here a load of straw from
Roxbury. My horse fell and I've been delayed."

"Stuff! Yer nag's as fresh as a daisy. Dismount, Mr.
Bradstreet, whilst I take a look." To the gathering crowd
he snapped, "I'll lay long odds he's got more than straw
in that cart. Smuggling's profitable, I hear."

"Git down thar!" "Pull up!" "What's he got in that
there waggin?"

Attracted by the watchman's loud summons, door after door opened, disgorged groups of curious onlookers.

The watchman's lantern now was lighting many faces, gilding them, making eyes appear extra large. Frightened by the hands reaching for its bridle the horse commenced to snort and back up despite Peter's efforts to control it.

Peter insisted, "You've no right to halt me. This is my horse and load of straw. I'm breaking no law, so you've no call to stop me like this."

The minute the words left his lips Peter knew he'd made a terrible mistake.

"He's lying," a voice called. "Yonder *ain't his horse!* That there rig's hired from Tim O'Brien's stable. Used it myself two days back."

The watchman made a snatch at the nag's bit and so startled the creature that it shied violently but the peace officer made good his hold all the same.

"Git down, I tell ye. Git down in the name o' the law!"

"Yep—he's a smuggler all right. Dismount, you!"

The crowd yelled and closed in, an ominous and rapidly shifting black pattern.

"What've ye caught, Caleb?"

"Wager 'tis a horse thief?"

A drunken black-bearded fellow began to bellow, "Come join the fun. We've took a horse thief!"

"Mister Bradstreet," roared the watchman, "will ye git down or must I drag you out o' that waggin?"

A swift estimate of the situation advised against violence. The watchman was big and beefy and stood poised ready for overt motion. Although arguing furiously all the time, Peter obeyed. Of all the outrageous mischances! His only hope now lay in the exercise of brazen effrontery.

"Keep your filthy hands off me," he warned a pair of pot-valiant fellows who came closing in. "Else you'll answer to a magistrate."

"Very likely, very likely," growled the watchman. "That's what all rogues say." He bent over the tail of the cart and plunging an arm into the straw clear up to his elbow he began feeling about. Almost instantly he emitted a triumphant "Ha!"

"What's he got there? What's he got?"

The crowd thickened until Unity Street was filled from one gutter to the other, more shutters commenced to bang back allowing sudden beams of light to fall into the street.

" 'Tis something heavy wrapped in sail cloth," the watchman announced. "Knew he was a bloody smuggler."

"What is it? Sugar? Coffee? Metal goods?"

"Somebody hold up my lantern." Once the flame could illumine the floor of Tim O'Brien's cart the peace officer flinched back uttering a stifled cry of horror.

"Why! Why—he's got a dead body! A woman's body—a young woman's body, by God!"

A terrible clamor broke from the nearest of the spectators. "Body-snatcher!" Infinitely menacing, the cry swelled louder and louder. "The villain's stole some poor female's corpse."

Aware of his deadly peril, Peter unhooked the clasp of his cloak, swung it from his shoulders and in the same motion moved to back up against the high wheel of the cart.

"It was not stolen," he shouted at the scowling roundsman. "I've a bill of sale for proof. Look here—"

Peter might as well have attempted to argue back the onrush of a storm wave charging up a beach. When three or four burly citizens flung themselves forward, Peter, by no means ignorant of the art of rough and tumble, ducked under their wildly flashing arms. Fists flying, he charged, suddenly and effectively employing his weight.

His nearest assailants he sent reeling, tripping over each other. At the same time a savage and unfamiliar exhilaration kindled fires in his brain. The mob ringed him around. Those behind sounded very brave indeed and already were clamoring for his life; those in front recoiled mindful of the two fallen figures, but only for an instant.

"String him up, the dirty defiler of womankind!" "Hanging's too good for a body-snatcher." There was a dreadful, menacing quality to the crowd's outcry. By the dim light of a few lanterns and a pine-knot torch or two, Peter glimpsed clawing hands, clenched fists, open yowling mouths and furious eyes.

He rained blows at this wall of flesh converging upon him, and with such effect that again it retreated. He might then have won free had not a clod of frozen mud come whizzing out of the dark to strike him on the forehead and send him reeling aside, conscious only of innumerable vivid meteors whirling about his his eyeballs.

They'd have killed him had not O'Brien's horse become so maddened that it reared, plunged and struck at the crowd with its front feet. The cart wheels crushed more than one foot and evoked sudden howls of agony. The roundsman who still stood in the cart, was forced to hang on for dear life as loose straw commenced to fall out into the street. Then, in seeming reluctance, the girl's corpse slipped over the tail board and fell out onto the street, garments indecently awry. It lay rigid with hands clenched and teeth faintly a-gleam in the wavering torch-light.

The glassy eyes and tumbled hair were so sharply etched against the trampled snow that the mob froze into a stunned immobility.

"Cover her for God's sake! It's shameful to leave her like that."

Then a well-dressed citizen cried out, "Why! Why, that's Jennie McLaren's body!"

"Are you sure?"

"Aye, she been a neighbor of mine for years. Died day before yesterday."

Their sense of outrage redoubled, the onlookers turned to wreak their will on the offender.

Because quantities of stones, faggots and more clods were whizzing quite indiscriminately through the air, several of the rioters were dropped senseless, and the men pinioning Peter ducked and loosened their grip. Instinct warned him that he'd not be offered a second chance to break free. Though his head still spun, Peter drew a great breath, set his shoulders and surged towards that point where the throng seemed thinnest. Strengthened by terror of impending death, the young doctor drove a path through the mob and though hands grabbed, wrenched and tore at his clothing, he was able to maintain momentum.

The very numbers of his enemies began to react in his favor; most of them couldn't recognize him. By stooping suddenly amid a flurry of flying fists, he tricked his persecutors into striking at each other; at once, a series of helpful free-for-alls commenced. But, inevitably, somebody recognized and tripped him and, before Peter could rise, a very heavy fellow dove upon him, driving every bit of wind from his lungs.

"Here he is!"

In terror-stricken helplessness the doctor squirmed un-

der a torrent of kicks and blows; boots crushed his
fingers and smashed against his ribs. Yielding blindly to
the instinct of self-preservation he continued to struggle
until a kick caught him in the jaw and dazed him. Into his
mouth surged a gust of salty hot blood; it burst in a fine
spray from his writhing lips and spattered the filthy snow.

"We'll preserve decency in this town." "Hang the
bastard!" "String him up!" "A rope!" "Somebody fetch
a rope."

"There's a dandy one in my stable younder," an aged
voice cackled. "Wait till I fetch it."

A pair of scowling teamsters heaved Peter to his feet;
they had to hold him erect since his legs were wavering
like saplings in a breeze.

"Look at him, the foul, body-snatching dog!" yelled
one of them. "Look at him, the indecent wretch."

Spittle splashed into the young physician's eyes and
fingers tore out strands of his long red hair. A primordial
fear of death sickened him as they hauled him, sagging
and stumbling, down the street to a place where some
blacksmith's swing sign was dangling from its heavy,
wrought-iron bracket.

Feigning even, greater weakness than he felt, Peter
struggled, despite the continual impact of blows and
offal, to clear his senses. They made little progress, probably because his guards were bellowing protests at being
pelted so indiscriminately with their prisoner.

A youth, horsed high on the crowd's shoulders, quickly unhooked and brought down the blacksmith's sign.
Menacingly, the stark iron bar stuck out over the street.

"Ah-h, that's it—that's the right idea!"

Exerting a final supreme effort of the will, Peter slowed
before his eyes this mad whirling scene, relaxed every
muscle to simulate a swoon. His knees buckled and his
battered head sagged forward, dripping streams of blood
onto the frozen snow. The infernal uproar swelled, continued.

"Rouse the villain! Let's see him hang higher'n Ha-
man!"

"Here's yer rope! 'Tis a fine new one and I want it
back after," piped the old man from the stoop of his
house. Everybody glanced in his direction; and the
crowd fell back to give the aged man passage.

Endowed with that desperate strength which comes to

those in mortal peril Peter gave a sudden violent twist that broke the relaxed grip of his unwary captors and charged along the path being opened for his would-be hangman. Peter's recovery and subsequent tactics consumed so little time that, for a few priceless instants, the mob remained unaware, barely long enough to permit him to butt, whirl and plunge his way a short distance to the entrance of an alley.

Always a fine runner, Peter hurtled blindly along a winding passage at once both lightless and treacherous. His feet slipped on garbage; he stumbled over firewood and once a bucket sent him reeling breathless and terrified into a wall.

"Stop him!" "Stop thief!" The blood-hungry yelping of his pursuers was fearfully close behind.

Head swimming, Peter sensed, rather than perceived, an opening to his right; for better or for worse, he plunged through it because the foremost of his enemies was running not twenty yards in his rear.

"Oh God, help me!" he wheezed. A tall wooden fence barred his course. Rallying rapidly failing strength, Peter flung himself over the palings, only half heard a sharp snarl of tearing cloth. The skill with which he negotiated this hazard lent him confidence—and perhaps an additional fifty feet of lead. Now his breath was only drawn in agonizing, sucking little gasps. Where he ran, he had not the least notion, but whenever he glimpsed empty blackness ahead he ran for it. Such blackness meant space, precious, life-giving space.

With strength rapidly abandoning him, Peter blundered around the corner of a shabby brick dwelling, fearfully conscious that he was not shaking off the hue and cry. This time he found himself in a dead-end alley—a short *cul-de-sac* ending in a high brick wall. Aware that his vaulting ability was a precious asset, Peter charged straight for the six-foot barrier. God help him! Too late he realized that this wall was crowned by a thick cap of broken glass set in cement!

No turning back was possible, so he grabbed for the top, felt immediately the searing bite of glass slashing deep, deep into his hands. Then, when he heaved over the top, the sharps gouged savagely at his knees. Blood was spurting from his hands, and pouring down his legs— Christ! He had been cut to ribbons.

"There he goes!" "I saw him." "Yes, over the wall!" "Run around and cut him off."

Cruelly hurt and spattering gore as he ran, Peter lurched across some citizen's backyard in which bare fruit trees loomed dimly stark. A watch-dog, rousing from its kennel, emitted a rasping snarl and flew at him. Only by the sheerest luck did the fugitive land a kick which altered the brute's threats to a pained and high-pitched yelping.

Sobbing for breath and sweating at every pore, Peter tried a door giving onto the orchard. Though latched, it gave under his weight and flew inwards permitting the fugitive to struggle along a corridor and into a room. Here he tripped over some half-seen furniture.

Upstairs, frightened outcries arose, but now Peter managed to locate the front door; so slippery with blood were his fingers that they failed in their first attempt to release the bolt. Ha. Now he could peer out into the street. Praise God, it looked empty and, better still, a lane opened directly opposite. The householders upstairs now were summoning the watch at the top of their lungs.

Although Peter thought he had traversed the street quite unseen, he was wrong. Inexorably, the hue and cry arose again, swelling even louder. How hard it was to breathe; blood kept welling into his wounded mouth and, falling down his throat, half choked him.

Thanks to easier going in the lane, he lengthened his lead. Ah, a large square appeared before him, offering the choice of a lumber yard opening to his left and a tannery to his right. Both should afford likely hiding places—providing he didn't leave too broad a blood trail.

The tanner's yard presented the less inviting shelter, yet he decided upon it for just that reason. He could hope that his pursuers might tire themselves out in rummaging about the many stacks of lumber, yonder. Too utterly spent to continue, Peter ran to take refuge in one of perhaps a dozen great casks and vats occupying the tannery yard.

Thank God, the snow about them had been so heavily trampled it might not betray his course. Exerting his last ounce of strength, he pushed aside the wooden cover of a vat and tumbled inside to find himself standing knee-deep in icy cold tanning fluid and wheezing like an overworked draft horse. All the same he took care gently to ease the heavy lid back into place.

XXI. RUINS

FOR A LONG TIME Peter was unable to do anything more than stand in the blessed darkness of the vat and attempt to recapture wits and breath. For the moment an overwhelming numbness, mercifully, blunted his pain. Gradually, his breathing leveled until, at length, he felt able to attempt an estimate of his situation and condition.

Several facts appeared self-evident; he was yet far from safe. As a physician, he could tell that, in his flight, he had suffered very serious hurts and wounds. His left hand, for instance, was frightening in its continued disobedience: his mouth was swollen all out of shape; several of his teeth had been loosened and two were missing. In addition, a couple of his ribs certainly had been fractured—nothing else would explain such blinding flashes of pain whenever he drew breath.

Thrice his pursuers had explored the tannery yard, cursing and poking about the uncovered barrels. Luckily, they were by now too much fatigued and discouraged to lift the vat lids, and eventually had tramped off.

By degrees cold generated by the tanning fluid crept upwards until a paralyzing chill was groping beyond his knees. Once the immediate peril had faded, a reaction set in, so robbing him of his strength that he floundered onto all fours in the bitter-smelling fluid. The acid's stinging at his lacerated hands and knees drove him back to a crouching position.

Had he in reality shaken off his enemies? One thing was certain—he couldn't remain where he was. But what to do? Granting that the hue and cry had subsided, what would be his wisest course? Tomorrow, of course, his true identity would become known—after all, Boston had been his home for nigh on three years and plenty of people knew him and could identify a man with auburn hair. Demands for his arrest and conviction would be screamed from the housetops of the unco'-gude.

No. Most certainly he must not return to his lodgings, especially since his landlord viewed all physicians with an abiding suspicion and had only tolerated such a person because Daniel Burnham's son paid regularly and well. A mean-souled and unimaginative little tailor, he was forever quoting, "He that sinneth before his Maker, let Him fall into the Hands of the Physician."

No more could Peter, in his present condition, seek refuge in any ordinary or inn of the town, no matter how mean. It was in such places that superstition flourished like the green bay tree; above all others, the ignorant and vicious were superstitious concerning the sanctity of the female body.

Stiffly, Peter heaved the lid aside, then, remained for several minutes listening to the tanning fluid dripping from the tatters of his clothes.

If only Asa Peabody had not gone away; he'd have solved such a dilemma. What about taking refuge with Lucius? A good idea, but the Jamaican had said he was moving to more pretentious lodgings. Mrs. Southeby? No. Were he to be discovered refuging on her premises, things might go hard with the widow.

Quite without warning, a wonderful and logical solution presented itself. In his anguish and relief he wept a little.

Peter emerged from his sanctuary just as the clock in the Old North Church boomed three sonorous and reverberating notes. Now, if ever, Boston Town would be still. Three o'clock. Great God! What eons had not passed since he had guided Tim O'Brien's cart into Unity Street?

By slinking, limping from shadow to shadow and doorway to doorway, towards dawn he found himself, weak and still bleeding, crouched behind a pile of firewood stacked in a shed at the rear of Captain Robert Ashton's residence.

Apparently this shed had been designed not only to preserve firewood from rain, but also to ward wintry blasts from the kitchen door. No little will power was required on Peter's part to pause and, nursing his agonizing left hand in the bosom of his shirt, to look backwards. Wouldn't do to expose the Ashtons to questioning. As near as he could tell, he'd left no blood stains on the snow of Captain Ashton's backyard.

He locked his teeth to silence moans that almost broke from his lacerated lips. At first he rapped softly, then, receiving no reply, louder and louder. Pains now were shooting like red hot arrows up his left forearm. Maybe it had been fractured; its hand refused to answer his least command.

At length a small dog roused itself indoors, set up a shrill alarm which continued until a ray of light appeared, shifted, crept out from under the door.

"Quiet, Growler." A bolt slid back, Peter recognized Captain Ashton's deep voice demanding, "What the Devil d'ye want at this ungodly hour?"

"Doctor Burnham," Peter was able to gasp. "Help me."

"Burnham? What's amiss?"

"Help, for God's sake. I—I'm in bad case."

Immediately the kitchen door swung open, releasing a rush of wonderfully warm air.

"Here, let me assist you." The privateer captain lowered a huge, brass-bound boarding pistol and gripped Peter's elbow.

The Virginian helped him to a rush-bottomed kitchen chair; then, by the light of his candle, cast a single intent look at this apparition. Lank red hair was dangling in sodden strands over the young physician's purplish and grotesquely swollen features. Already a small, bright scarlet pool was forming below his lax left arm.

"Good God, man, you're cut to ribbons." Captain Ashton ran out, reappeared with a bottle of Jamaica rum. "Take a big swig, and ye needn't talk lest you've a mind."

Somehow Peter raised his head, summoned a twisted smile. "I'd better tell you—you may not want to harbor me."

"Stuff."

"No. I beg you to listen."

Captain Ashton, gathering a yellow and red banyan about him, hooked bare toes over the rungs of his chair to keep them above the draught.

Peter told his tale, excused his conduct not at all. The captain never once interrupted, only passed the rum bottle from time to time.

When Peter fell silent, he said, "I reckon I understand what roused the people; but I know ye meant nothing evil, only the contrary."

Peter's hallowed eyes focussed themselves. "Susan? How is she?"

Ashton frowned. "Her arm still swells and this evening she appears to becoming more feverish."

"Fever usually mounts at night," Peter mumbled, then fainted dead away.

XXII. SANCTUARY

CAPTAIN ASHTON HELD a flaming spill to his study lamp, which, being filled with pure winter-pressed whale oil, cast a fine clear light. When Peter regained semi-consciousness, he discovered that his right eye wouldn't open. For all that, he could see well enough to tell that he'd never lack cause to remember what had happened tonight.

"Ha. Thought you'd be coming to, pretty soon. Sit steady now."

He was lying lax on an easy chair and Robert Ashton was washing the mud, blood, and slime from his injured left hand—and was hurting him abominably.

The rum strengthened Peter, cleared his head enough for him to realize that while his right hand had suffered two long, deep, and very painful gashes across its palm, no tendons or nerves had been severed. But God in Heaven! How terribly his left hand and wrist had been mangled and slashed by that broken glass. His third, fourth and little finger utterly refused to respond to his most earnest efforts to move them. No use. He could even see the ends of severed muscles in the depths of a hideous gash across the heel of that hand. Successive waves of despair set Peter to trembling. Could he ever operate again?

His broad bronzed face intent, Rob Ashton was, at Peter's insistence, pouring brandy over the gasping physician's mutilated flesh when, her gray eyes wide and questioning, Mrs. Ashton appeared carrying a Betty lamp.

"Mercy save us, it's Doctor Burnahm!"

Andrea did not tarry to ask questions; she flew back upstairs and presently returned, a number of linen strips a-flutter in her hand. Following the patient's directions, she contrived pledgets to staunch a slow, persistent hemorrhage from the wounded hands, then bound them deftly into place. Next she treated vicious cuts on the fugitive's knees, and ended by bathing with hazel water the many little cuts and contusions disfiguring his features.

"I've a vial of laudanum," she announced. "Will you take some?"

Peter's distorted mouth made a grotesque effort to form a smile. "It's as you prescribe, Doctor Ashton," he mumbled. No use to mention his hurt side. Maybe the ribs were only cracked. No telling just yet. Every deep breath lanced his side with devilish sharp bodkins.

The Ashtons helped him, one on each side and murmuring encouragements, to a small warm bedroom on the second floor. Then, casting him a compassionate look, Andrea Ashton withdrew leaving her husband to help Peter out of the foul wreckage of his clothing.

The clocks of Boston were disputing the exact moment of five when Andrea Ashton reappeared carrying a tumbler of laudanum and water. Obedient as any six-year-old, Peter swallowed it, every drop.

"How is Susan faring?" Become a little light-headed, Peter wanted to rise, to examine the child's broken arm. "Need to see for m'self—mustn' lose—arm. Mus' really go—see."

"Certainly—in a moment or two. Just settle back for a little, first," Andrea soothed.

The soporific took almost instant effect whereupon Peter lapsed into a deep slumber.

"Poor man," sighed Andrea, picking up the rags staining her floor. "Why can people, supposedly civilized, Christian people, be so vastly cruel to one another? I wonder what's happened."

Rob Ashton told her what Peter had insisted on reporting, then, casting a thoughtful look at the unconscious physician, remarked, "Let us not deceive ourselves, he is in trouble, my dear, serious trouble. How grave is his danger we will not learn at once."

It was only late of the next afternoon that the privateer captain came to appreciate that he was harboring what appeared to be a felon. Everywhere, broadsides, notices and public criers were offering a handsome reward—fifty pounds no less—for the apprehension of one Peter Burnham, a physician of the town. He stood near five feet, eight inches in height, had blue eyes and red hair.

The crimes of which he stood accused were the theft

and illegal possession of the corpse of one Jennie McLaren, stolen from the residence of Zebediah McLaren, the deceased's father and a thoroughly respectable chandler. There was no doubt over one thing; Boston was fairly boiling with a righteous indignation over this scandalous affair. Not for many a long year would Doctor Peter Burnham dare to walk Boston's streets without fear of arrest.

XXIII. FAREWELL—A LONG FAREWELL

THE MAIL COACH for Providence was no thing of beauty, Captain Stanton decided; its once-elaborate upholstery was ripped and the yellow and black paint of its body had begun to crack and fade. Steel tires rasping, it nonetheless rumbled out of the post house yard behind four sturdy-looking nags and set off southwards for what once had been called the Providence Plantations. Because in wintertime the mail coach left but twice a week quite a small crowd had gathered to witness its departure.

Moodily, Captain Joshua Stanton turned back into the post house to claim a refund on the passages neither he, nor Peter Burnham, would be using. Damnation! Now, he'd for sure have to make the trip back to New Jersey all the way a-horseback.

A little later he was leaving his gloves and riding crop in Doctor Townsend's hall and entering the old physician's study.

"Then you are convinced, sir, that we will hear nothing from Doctor Burnham?" Doctor Blanchard was demanding.

"Under the present conditions? Never. If Burnham's still alive he'll be fleeing as fast and far as he can."

"He's wise in that," Stanton commented. "The town's in a dangerous mood. Mr. McLaren, in case you didn't know it, sir, happens to be a churchwarden, so, like a true Christian, he continues to goad press and populace into apprehending young Burnham."

"I'm truly grieved to hear this." Doctor Townsend's thin, black-clad figure hunched over his desk, much like a tired old crow on a dead limb. "Poor misguided lad. God knows what's become of him."

"We seem to be deuced unchancy in our nominees,

sir," Doctor Blanchard remarked. "First Peabody disappoints us, then Burnham plays the fool, so we are no better off than we were three days back."

"Aye, and Captain Stanton must return to his post tomorrow without fail—what do you suggest?"

Doctor Townsend rubbed a perplexed hand across his brow. "I presume we had better consider young Lucius Devoe. In some ways I'd venture he is the most intelligent of the three I certificated last week."

" 'In some ways'?" repeated Stanton. "Why put it that way? Is there anything wrong with this fellow Devoe?"

Doctor Townsend's white wig shook vigorously, twice. "He is poor and proud and therefore difficult to understand, gentlemen, moreover he is a foreigner. There, that is all there is against him—and it adds up to nothing. On the other hand, Mister Devoe is industrious, uncommonly so, intelligent and singularly able in diagnosis. His medical skill is not to be questioned. I am convinced he will discharge his duties faithfully and capably."

"Mister Devoe it shall be, then," Stanton agreed. "To tell the truth I've been rather taken with him, myself. He has a rare charm of manner."

Doctor Blanchard began to pull on fine, dogskin gloves. "So, all in one week, Boston stands to lose three promising young physicians. How do your new apprentices appear?"

Doctor Townsend frowned. "No telling. Six months or more must pass ere I can decide whether an apprentice is worthy of teaching. Would God we had in America a few such medical colleges as they maintain in Scotland, Italy and Holland. Our method of apprenticeship is outmoded and most uneven in its application. I am sure you will agree, Blanchard?"

Blanchard nodded from the doorway. "Can you imagine it, Stanton? Some of our fellow practitioners dare certify their apprentices after a mere six months of instruction. God pity such poor wretches as fall into the hands of such ignoramuses."

That evening, young Doctor Devoe, radiantly happy and self-confident in appearing well-dressed, made almost bold use of Mr. Stanton's knocker. To the Jamaican's dismay, he was shown into a salon overflowing with friends calling to bid Captain Joshua Stanton God-speed; they had come to fetch packets of letters destined for relatives serving in far-off Pennsylvania, New Jersey and New York. Official correspondence, too, had filled an oiled silk sack on the hall table. Even as Lucius slipped off his dark blue riding cloak, a wind-nipped courier appeared from General Heath's headquarters to deliver a fat, important-looking packet secured by a gaudy vermilion seal.

Some of Lucius' self-confidence deserted him on hearing himself announced. Confound it, why did the sight of many lights, fine furniture and the atmosphere of gentility render him so uncomfortably conscious of his hands? They seemed nowhere comfortable, only played nervously at a row of red glass buttons decorating his new, claret-hued waistcoat.

He entered the big room unobtrusively. Better listen a bit and not appear too eager to find Sabra.

"Pray God our French allies soon break old Graves' blockade and open the sea to us," old Mr. Stanton was remarking. "Communications with Europe must be reopened and in this year—else we'll suffer ruin."

A big gentleman in dark green made an angry gesture. "How different 'twould all have been had that incredible ass Saltonstall not botched our Penobscot expedition."

A brief silence followed. Not in many a long year would the young nation—Massachusetts more particularly—forget that series of blunders which had permitted nineteen well-armed and well-manned warships and transports—the mightiest fleet America had ever produced—to be trapped by an inferior British force and sent sailing, panic-stricken, up the Penobscot to burn and destroy itself.

"For sure," Samuel Stanton allowed, "we may see as dark days again before this infernal contest ends, but we'll never see a blacker. I'll never forget how we felt at the exchange when those reports were listed. Above a thousand Massachusetts troops, as I remember, marched off under old General Sol Lovell. A heavy bill that, three fourteen-gun brigs of our Massachusetts navy, three fine Continental warships, the *Warren*, *Diligent*, and *Providence* burnt or captured. Lost an eighteen-gun New Hampshire sloop, too, and I guess it was all of twelve privateers we insured and equipped for the expedition to

Bagaduce. And Saltonstall let every last one be captured or burnt!"

As everyone knew, pious old Commodore Dudley Saltonstall owned many friends and they had tried hard to clear their champion's name—but they'd never quite succeeded. As usual, the army commanders had blamed the disaster on the Navy, and vice-versa. Again, the privateer captains had sworn the expedition would have succeeded but for the high-handed arrogance and short-sightedness of the Continental naval commanders.

True, Dudley Saltonstall's subsequent court-martial and dismissal from the Service had brought a measure of satisfaction to some; but such satisfaction failed to restore the lost ships and men. Nor did it remove that British flag from the strategic island of Bagaduce.

It was only after the Penobscot failure that the New Englanders gave up hope of maintaining a navy. Why, right now, only three Continental men-of-war flew the Stars and Stripes—and they lay in heavily blockaded harbors.

An occasional State naval vessel still was able to cruise furtively along the coast of Georgia and the Carolinas, but that didn't benefit the trade of merchants in Boston, Providence or New Haven by one jot or tittle.

As everyone knew, such traffic as persisted could be attributed to the skill and initiative of an ever-increasing swarm of private-armed vessels. Favored by superior speed and an intimate knowledge of local waters, they could and did, taunt with comparative impunity the majestic three and four deckers of His Britannic Majesty's Navy.

Lucius looked about eagerly, but not ostentatiously, bowed to Mrs. Stanton, to Phoebe, and, a little less formally, to gay Theodosia. Where could Sabra be? To his surprise Lucius experienced an agonizing pang of jealousy. Suppose he came upon her coquetting with some rich young merchant of the town who ought to be serving the Army? Only very recently had Lucius come to notice such unpatriotically inclined young men, and to disapprove of them.

Sabra wasn't. She was directing the preparation of a huge urn of that priceless and almost forgotten beverage known as coffee. At the moment she was employing a small silver hammer to chip bits of sugar free from a tall and glistening yellow-white cone.

Her flashing smile in a twinkle dispelled his mood of sombre uncertainties. "Why, Lucius! What a surprise! Why are you here?" She noted his riding garb. "Are you going somewhere?"

"You—you didn't know?"

"Know what?"

A wave of color crept across Lucius' thin cheeks. So Joshua Stanton hadn't deemed his succession to the appointment important enough to mention? Well, one day Captain Stanton—who had never, even for a day, earned his own keep in civil life—would be bloody glad to take notice of what Lucius Devoe said or did.

"Why—I'm to succeed Asa Peabody and Burnham to that post—that surgeon's-mate appointment."

Her blank expression was real. "You amaze me. I knew Peter Burnham was not going, but I had not heard of your succession to his post."

Lucius went redder. It was really too humiliating to have to explain that he had become successor to the much coveted post simply by default. He managed a taut smile. "Your brother can explain and no doubt he will."

"The appointment seems to bring nothing but disappointments." Her eyes wavered. "Poor Asa—" She meant that. Joshua's explanation of the Machias man's abrupt departure had been curt and most unsatisfactory. Why should Asa have lingered in her thoughts? Even yet she could not decide why she had bestowed on him that little volume. And most of all, she debated why had he not penned her a note of farewell. She laughed quickly, remembering that it was the Jamaican who stood there, not Asa.

"Oh, Lucius, this is a surprise and a fine one! So you're to go to West Point? What really happened to Doctor Burnham? No one will tell me."

"He—he got into very serious trouble with the watch," Lucius told her unhappily. "I fear he is, at this moment, a fugitive from the law. Alas, I am unfamiliar with details of the affair. All I know is that Burnham has disappeared and that I'm to take his place.

"Oh, Sabra! Sabra! Wish me well," he begged and his handsome dark eyes pled even more eloquently. "With your encouragement I shall indeed perform prodigies."

"Eben, the coffee is ready. You may fetch it into the salon."

"Come, Mr. Devoe." She led the way to that same

small library in which she and Asa had exchanged fare-wells. La! At Lucius' ecstatic smile and tender look her heart began pounding. Nonetheless, she was determined to be more reserved, more discreet than she'd been at Mrs. Fletcher's.

"La, sir, it would appear that you are Fortune's foster child," she remarked gravely. "Three days ago who would have dreamt that you would go riding south with Josh—my brother Joshua." Yes. She was wise to commence a return towards formality. The intensity of his expression advised it.

"Rather it should have been Asa or Peter, do you think?" Lucius demanded after an unhappy pause.

There were moments when he felt wretchedly contrite concerning Burnham and his ruined career, but who ever could have imagined such a pitch of murderous fury? Certainly he hadn't. What could have become of his luck-less colleague? It was all too conceivable that, after his fearful beating, Peter might have crawled off to some obscure hiding place, there to perish miserably of wounds and cold. Resolutely, he put aside conjecture, directed his attention to the present.

Never had Sabra appeared so delectable, so utterly desirable as now as she stood before him in a gown of turquoise blue, gold necklace and ear bobs; her shiny chestnut hair had been dressed into triple ringlets to either side of her face.

"Why so thoughtful?" he demanded while ever so carelessly pushing-to the library's door of glistening maplewood.

"I can't help dwelling on how dreadful it is for Doctor Burnham to have ruined his career—Uncle Will deemed him extra clever."

"Please, Sabra—don't grieve so," Lucius burst out. "What Peter did was intended for the best service of humanity. That Moore rascal must have lied to him. He swore he had purchased that cadaver outright, from—from—"

Aware of the fixed regard of Sabra's gray eyes, Lucius, fell abruptly silent.

She stared in puzzlement. "Why, Lucius! Just now you said you were completely ignorant of the affair."

"Why—" Lucius rallied quickly. "So I did. I didn't feel it loyal to remark that Peter had mentioned some-

thing to me of a plan to secure a female corpse. I attempted to dissuade him, and having failed,'' he sighed, studied the floor, ''I—well I presume I'm partly to blame.''

''No. You mustn't feel responsible,'' she said placing
an impulsive hand on his arm. ''But why have you kept
so still?''

''The better to track down that villain who so basely
deceived Peter, but I fear Murdo Moore has gotten safely
away. Imagine swearing that poor, respectable Jennie
McLaren's corpse was that of a bawd!''

''A bawd? What's a bawd?''

''Er—a—a common sort of female; rather like a
draught animal among racehorses.''

''Oh.'' Sabra lost interest, wandered over to a bowl of
nuts, selected a walnut meat and commenced delicately
to nibble it between strong white teeth.

''La! How much can happen in a week. Just one week
ago all of us were together at Doctor Townsend's, and
now we're scattered, perhaps never to meet again.

''Oh, by the bye, Mrs. Fletcher declares herself much
improved. She dotes on Doctor Saxnay and you for
fetching him to her.''

''It is you who are to be thanked,'' Lucius bowed
slightly.

From the drawing room came sounds of renewed con-
versation. Somebody was booming, ''Well, good riding,
Joshua, watch out for these German mercenaries.
They're devils incarnate.''

''Sabra!'' Lucius took her gently by the hands. ''Sabra, ere I depart—perhaps 'tis forever—will you not give
me a recollection to treasure during dark hours? There
will be many, you know.''

Mischievousness entered Sabra's expression. ''From
others, perhaps, this may not signify much, Lucius, but
from me 'tis a good deal.'' The perfume of potpourri
sweetened the air as, featherlight, her lips brushed his
dark cheek. It was indeed but a pale imitation of those
kisses he'd enjoyed at Mrs. Fletcher's.

Delighted all the same, Lucius took her hands, peered
anxiously into her face. ''Oh, Sabra, Sabra! Will you believe in me? I am about to accomplish great things.'' He
drew her closer, essayed once more to slip an arm about
the slender pillar of her waist, but she swayed easily out
of his grasp.

"La, sir, you are too earnest—too precipitate. Have patience, my sweet Lucius, a little patience."

"Aye, that I will," he burst out. "But in another year all Boston will know my name." Meantime the realization dawned on him that something, or someone, had altered her previous attitude. What? Who? Asa, of course. Well, he was prepared for that.

Laughing, Sabra turned to rearrange a log slipping off cast-iron fire dogs fashioned, and gaily painted, to represent a pair of marching grenadiers.

"I feel that all of your predictions will come true." She treated him to a slow, steady look. "That I am more than a little fond of you, you have learned ere now. Because you are leaving for the wars. I'll not promise myself to another—"

"Oh, Sabra!"

"—without first affording you opportunity further to press your attentions." Of course, it was silly to talk so; they both knew it, but convention demanded it.

"I will be content with that promise." He kissed her hand, straightened to find her regarding him curiously.

"Have you heard aught from Asa?"

The Jamaican shook his narrow head. "What a tragedy! Imagine Asa wasting his talents upon a parcel of savages and superstitious bumpkins up in the Eastern District."

"I venture he will not soon break away," the girl sighed.

So Asa *was* the retarding element.

"Tell me," he inquired smoothly, "are you fond of Asa?"

Sabra's chin rose a little. "Yes, but that is all. Why look so concerned?"

Lucius' cheeks were burning. What he was about to do was risky; one never could tell how a female would react to a shock; even less a lovely, cultured and well-to-do girl. He turned aside, fetched a deep sigh. "Ah, Sabra, would that I were at liberty to disclose to you the true cause of Asa's quick departure."

"True cause, Lucius? I know it. There was truly desperate sickness in his family."

The Jamaican gave her a level look. "Jupiter! He certainly cozened you all with that fable, and no mistake."

"Fable?" Sabra drew herself to her full five feet. "Lucius, just what do you mean by that?"

Lucius frowned, snapped his fingers. "Plague take it! I always talk too much."

"Mister Devoe, if there is something concerning Asa that I should know, why pray speak out. He is a great and good friend of mine. I feel I have the right to know why you imply him to be a liar."

The Jamaican's snuff-colored figure took a short turn across the room. Lord! but she looked handsome in her indignation. "I cannot bring myself to cause you grief. Oh, *why* did I ever say anything?"

"If you do not tell me what this is you know," Sabra told him in a brittle voice, "you need address me no further attentions."

Lucius was clever about managing a reluctance which a shrewder person than Sabra would have found convincing. In the end he produced, most reluctantly, a crumpled sheet of paper. "When I went to Asa's lodgings to collect a book which the dear fellow gave me I—well, I discovered this note tucked into it."

The snapping of the library fire sounded very loud. The letter, Sabra perceived, was scrawled on coarse paper by someone who certainly could boast little education. Its message was plain enough, however.

20 December 1779

Asa, my Beluvd promised Husband:
   Papa threats to force I to marry Will Dobson who owns a tannery, a bote, has two cows, and can support a WIFE, Papa says. Asa, you must return at wunce if I am ever to be yr WIFE as I want to so much. You have been gone much to long. I cannot longer endoor ye present situation. Flea to me, my luver. Despite much urges I remained trew to you All these yeres, as I am Sure you remained trew to me.
              Thy ever adooring and impatient
              WIFE to be,
                   Jessie

Sabra's hand commenced to shake; the writing lost shape. Never in all her eighteen years had she felt herself so deceived, so miserably confused. Who would have dreamed of Asa's playing such a contemptible course? Here he was avoiding service with the Army, lying to her uncle, Joshua and the rest. Of course, this explained why she had not heard from him.

With a calmness surprising to herself, she folded the letter into neat little squares.

"Let me burn it," Lucius offered; she had started to give it to him when the door stirred. Instead she tucked the note into her bodice.

"You understand my reluctance—"

"Oh, yes, Lucius, I do. It—it was splendid of you so to shield him—and me. I will never cease to be grateful."

She wouldn't forget in a hurry any detail of the young physician's appearance. Straight, alert and vital, Lucius had paused beneath great Grandpa's frowning portrait. Right now his eyes were a-gleam, his dark hair touched by the golden candlelight. La! He was as handsome as he was fascinating.

The door swung back, admitted Joshua Stanton's blue-and-scarlet-clad figure. A trifle impatiently he cried, "Come along, Devoe, we've a deal of packing. Horses are ordered at six."

XXIV. KINDNESS OF CAPTAIN ELDRIDGE

FOR HILDE MENTION to learn anything definite concerning the destination and probable sailing dates of such vessels as were tied up along the waterfront proved to be next to impossible. Had she been free to come and go—which she wasn't—she might have studied the notices of ship movements posted in a dozen taverns.

As it was, she had had to dodge furtively about the waterfront. Having loosened the green shawl, she held it high about her face. Even so, she'd experienced a close call when a shipper's agent had half recognized her and had called out her name. Hilde remembered the fellow all too well. On Ship Street they had met, face to face, but even as the brute caught his breath to call out, an eddy of the busy crowd had intervened, permitting her to dodge aside and find refuge in a near-by mercer's shop.

Weary, and on the verge of desperation, Hilde decided, now that the afternoon was far advanced, to venture out along a series of wharves jutting into the slate-gray waters of Boston Harbor.

Surely among all those ships out there there must be some vessel clearing for Nova Scotia? Yes, she would pretend to be entrusted with a message for a Mr. Jones, a gentleman sailing for Nova Scotia aboard some vessel the name of which she had forgotten.

Though promising, Hilde's plan had failed—or would have, after she had questioned this last vessel, a neat little topsail schooner bearing the name *Louisa* painted across her stern in bright red letters.

"*Dieu de Dieu,*" she thought. "There is no indication of her home port." Hugging the shawl closer and trying to control the chattering of her teeth because the sun was low and the air growing more piercing, she approached a lacy tangle of riggings showing above the wharf.

From the minute Hilde's eyes came to rest upon a comfortable figure smoking placidly beside the schooner's helm she guessed that here, at last, was someone who might be trusted.

The officer—from his position on the quarterdeck he must be such—showed a broad and shiny red face, square of design as the end of a packing case. Contrary to the current mode, this seafarer wore a full, but neat, gray beard. It matched in color a pair of enormous bushy eyebrows.

"How de do, Ma'am," he greeted on looking up and beholding the girl gazing timidly down upon the *Louisa*'s spotless deck. "How can Captain Jonadab Eldridge be of service?"

After a bit Captain Eldridge admitted, between puffs on his pipe, that he intended risking a voyage to a port called Liverpool; aye, it lay on the lower tip of Nova Scotia. Liverpool? Hilde's hopes soared, for all that this port lay many frozen miles to the southwest of Lunenburg, and was a long, long way from Wejek's village.

That what she was contemplating constituted a near-to-impossible venture, never occurred to Hilde. She needed to regain the only spot in this world where she was sure she belonged—to a people she loved and who understood her. While lying comfortably in Mrs. Southeby's bed, she'd considered the whole problem countless times; she had even conducted long conversations with herself in Mic-Mac. It had proved at once pleasing, and surprising, to find how readily the simple words and phrases returned.

From her own race Hilde had gained nothing but what she would gladly forget—with the shining exception of Doctor Peabody. Never, ever, could she forget any detail of his attractively homely features, the reddish tints emphasizing the bold line of his cheekbones and the clear brown kindness of his eyes. Whenever she remembered Doctor Peabody, her lips tingled. Yes, she still felt all fresh and clean whenever she recalled how he had kissed her full on the mouth, though well aware that she'd been a fancy-Nancy.

Timorously, Hilde advanced to the edge of Colonel Hancock's wharf. Judging by a small mound of merchandise yet awaiting storage, the *Louisa* was lading rum, ironware and manufactured goods.

"Well, Mistress—'pears like we're in for a spell o' weather come dawn." Captain Eldridge waved a well-gnawed pipe stem towards the pale yellow sun at that instant sinking beyond a pair of hills dominating Charles Town Neck. If one looked carefully, one could still discern on Breed's Hill traces of those trenches and redoubts which had witnessed the first, and bloodiest, battle of the present conflict.

Bushy brows elevated, Captain Eldridge considered the diminutive, wind-whipped figure standing on the dock above his vessel. That his visitor's gaze flickered nervously back over her shoulder from time to time did not escape his attention. So? A runaway, no doubt of it, Captain Eldridge deduced—and a pretty one, for all she looked as if even half a breeze would blow her clear over to Egg Island.

"'Tis pretty pert up yonder—even airish, ye might say. Whyn't you come aboard?" he invited.

Summoning an uncertain smile, Hilde accepted the aid of a hand lumpy with calluses, and scrambled down on deck.

"Glory be, Mistress, ye look almighty peaked and cold. Hadn't realized it. Come below and warm up."

Anxiously, Hilde studied the sea captain's face for any of those indications she had come to mistrust, but read nothing beyond a cheery kindliness and bluff good-humor. To her increasing relief she noticed the skipper was gentleman enough to allow her to precede him in descending a short ladder leading to the cabin. A blessed warmth enveloped her, emanating from a very small iron stove.

"Well, Mistress, 'tain't fer me to be cur'ous but what brought you out on old Hancock's pier on a bitter eve like this? Yer no doxy, that I can tell with half an eye."

"No more I am, sir." She cast him a look of profound

gratitude. "No. I—I seek a passage to Nova Scotia. Only, I haven't much money, sir, only sixteen shillings—Rhode Island."

"So?" Captain Eldridge's blunt fingers combed his whiskers whilst he settled back in a big, sag-bottomed chair bolted to the deck. "Sixteen shillings ain't much. Is it now?" He cocked a dubious eye at the rough-hewn deck beams above. "Ye'll admit that ain't exactly a fancy price fer such a long v'yage. Dear, dear, 'twouldn't pay for your victuals."

Hilde's wind-colored features crumpled as, in appeal, she extended a slender-fingered hand. "I—I know it, Captain, sir; but perhaps I could prove myself useful. I can cook pretty well and sew. Folks claim a sailor's clothes need a deal of mending."

Captain Eldridge broke into a bellowing laugh that set his cabin to reverberating. "Right you are, Miss! Only the *Louisa* ain't big. There'd be no place fer you to sleep. While my foremast hands are nice enough lads, they sometime get a mite rough. I'm not risking a mutiny on my ship—not even for the sake of a pair of pretty eyes."

Hilde's hopeful expression faded and her gaze sought the sanded decking beneath her feet.

"Of course you are right, sir," and the starch went out of her back. Slowly, she turned away and put foot to the companionway ladder.

The captain's big voice checked her. "Belay there, Mistress, there's more ways'n one o' skinning a cat. Let me see, now." From under shaggy brows Eldridge considered the childish figure; all the time his bearded jaws kept working at a quid of tobacco. "Now I aim to help ye, Mistress," his eyes twinkled, "account of ye put me in the mind o' my daughter, Nancy; poor child, she's gone to her reward this past year." He nodded solemnly. "Well, mebbe I will grant ye passage." In an abrupt motion, he levelled a horny forefinger. "Mind now, ye'll have to abide below 'til I grant you leave to go on deck; besides, ye'll have to bunk behind a tarpaulin slung afore yonder sea chest. Think that'll do?"

"Oh, God bless you, sir." Joy sparkled in the girl's weary eyes.

" 'Twill be no featherbed, that chest—"

"Oh, it will be wonderful and I'll cook—I'll mend all your things."

"Oh, come now—I've no intent to work ye to the bone," he reassured in his deep and kindly tones. "Then 'tis agreed—sixteen shillings and a fair day's work till we fetch Liverpool. Now, Missy, go fetch yer things and, above all, keep yer mouth shut when ye go ashore. Less I know about you, or why ye're here, the easier I can rightly claim that I don't know. Well, get going," he prompted when Hilde remained standing before the stove.

"I—I haven't any thing; not now, sir."

"Oh. What's yer name?"

"Hildegard Mention, sir."

Um. This young'un was for sure a runaway, Captain Eldridge nodded to himself. Didn't wonder but there'd be a substantial reward posted somewhere about town for Mistress Mention's arrest. Presently he heaved himself to big, thick-booted feet.

"Ye'll find a morsel o' bread and cold meat in the cuddy yonder. Help yourself to all ye can hold."

"Oh-h, Captain, you are so good." Hilde's eyes filled. "I—I can't bear it."

"Stuff and nonsense, child. 'Tis only Christian kindness."

Maybe this wasn't such an evil world after all? First Doctor Peabody and now Captain Eldridge had proved ready to befriend a helpless girl.

Battered lynx cap brushing his cabin's ceiling, the *Louisa*'s master patted her shoulder with one hand while buttoning a salt-bleached blue pea jacket with the other.

"There, there, Missy, have a good cry an' ye've a mind to. But keep my stove going. I'll be back after a spell."

Thick body half through the companionway hatch, Captain Eldridge paused, his bearded features boldly framed against a yellow and gray sunset.

"Mark this peg?" She nodded. "Well, when I slide-to the hatch, just you push it through this hasp ring and don't open lest you hear a knock like this." He tapped softly once, then three times in rapid succession. The hatch scraped shut, whereupon the cabin became plunged in a darkness relieved only by a glow from the stove and wintry twilight beating in through a pair of tiny stern ports.

Tears of relief still lingered on Hilde's cheeks when, from the cupboard, she took a sizeable loaf and a ragged joint of mutton. She ate ravenously.

Happy to feel her stomach stop aching, Hilde laid herself down on Captain Eldridge's sea chest. Thank goodness, the four or five layers of sail cloth she had arranged upon it satisfactorily relieved the hardness of its bare wood. Surprised by her boldness, she then arranged as a covering a coarse but warm Dutch blanket discovered in a locker beneath the captain's own painfully tidy bunk.

There. Now she'd sleep warmer than a muffin in an oven. Sleep was what she needed most.

Where was Doctor Peabody tonight? Dear Asa Peabody. Maybe it was because she felt so warm and tender about Asa Peabody that she felt prompted to wash her face and hands. Hilde didn't really try to explain why she did it—the water in a wooden bucket was terribly chill and her hair kept falling over her forehead and shoulders. Why was it so unruly? Hilde wondered, then recalled her gift of the new yellow ribbon to "Sir" Asa Peabody, her knight *sans peur et sans reproche*.

Would she ever see her knight again? Her soul craved another, just one more meeting with him—though it didn't seem at all likely, not with him adopting the Army in New York and her sailing in the opposite direction. But perhaps, possibly, the Lord in His infinite mercy would make their reunion possible?

"Oh dear," she thought, "I—I must be in love with Doctor Peabody—for all it's a hopeless business. He, a fine physician, and me a—a—trollop—but I'm not. I—I never went willingly. Never, *Never*, NEVER. He knows that."

Once she had loosened her stays she scratched her ribs along the vertical red streaks across them. How wonderfully white her skin shone. For that, too, Hilde was grateful to Asa Peabody. Never again would she allow more than a week to pass without washing herself from brow to heel.

Following a momentary indecision Hilde balled her shawl into a kind of pillow, then slipped out of her skirt and one of her two petticoats—more were only for the very comfortably off—then, with shift and the other petticoat clinging to her she slid under the woollen blanket

and lay flat on her back, happily gazing at the deck
beams. How very fortunate she was.

Pleasantly aware of her body's heat circulating under
this woollen covering, Hilde relaxed and presently dozed
off.

The noise of some of the *Louisa*'s crew returning
aboard awoke Hilde. Cursing loudly, they were jumping
down from the wharf and stumbling about the deck.

In shivering alarm she guessed that one sailor must
have slipped on an icy portion of decking to go sprawling
with a crash which made the entire little craft tremble and
rock. Deep-throated laughter became mingled with the
profanity of the victim. Mercy! Was one of the roisterers
making his way aft? Where had Captain Eldridge betaken
himself? Hilde commenced to quiver in great violence.
The seaman halted amidships, however, and presently
the hollow *clump, clump* of his sea boots diminished in
the direction of the bow. Voices faded. Silence again prevailed aboard the *Louisa*. Hilde smiled a tremulous smile
of relief.

How wonderful to find herself, warm and secure, under the protection of a kindly, fatherly sort of man like
Captain Eldridge. Perhaps one of her grandfathers had
resembled Captain Eldridge? Who *could* they have been?

Surely the affairs of Hilde Mention had taken a turn for
the better? Come morning, the first page of a new chapter
in the book of her life would be turned, and she'd find a
new white page.

The soft *slap-slap* of wavelets rippling against the
Louisa's hull played a drowsy obbligato. She dreamed a
little of Doctor Peabody, then drew her knees up under
her and presently her small body lay curled in a tight ball,
like that made by a tired kitten in its basket. . . .

"Ah—that's it, lass—that's it. Softly now." Jonadab
Eldridge had worked deftly for, when Hilde awoke, she
sat well nigh mother naked.

"Don't fight now," he panted. "God above, ye'll make
a rare sweet morsel!"

Hilde's slim white limbs flashed to her frenzied struggles. Half-smothered, she fell victim to an insensate terror, struggled still more wildly until, on the verge of faint-
ing, she sank her teeth so viciously deep into his lip that
they met. The pain Eldridge experienced must have been

excruciating for his arm jerked away and, howling like a trapped wolf, he clapped both hands to his lacerated mouth.

Cotton shift billowing and hair flying, Hilde made for the companion ladder. On quivering legs she clambered upwards, sensed, rather than saw, her captor rise and come lunging forward. He'd have caught her only he stumbled over his own cowhide boots and was thrown off balance.

"Come back ye little bitch!" Eldridge snarled, "else ye'll go to jail."

He recovered in time to make a snatch at the hem of Hilde's shift at the very moment she gained the deck. The fabric was worn and so tore readily. Though a big piece came away in Eldridge's hand she pulled free and, in blind terror, went slipping and blundering across gear littering the *Louisa's* icy deck.

It chanced that the tide was high so the wharf's edge loomed only a foot above the *Louisa's* rail and Hilde found no trouble in scrambling up onto the wharf to head, in blind panic, for the shore line.

Ha! As she glimpsed the dim outlines of some men advancing along the wharf she screamed, "*Secours! Pour l'amour de Dieu! Au secours!*"

Her cry achieved an instant effect upon the group of men. "*Qui ca?* Who is that?" challenged a deep voice. "*Qui crie?*"

Gasping and half naked, Hilde ran up to the foremost of the strangers, a big fellow in a wide boat cloak blowing free in the night wind. She clung to him. "*Aide! Aidez-moi!*"

"*Nom de Dieu!* Why do you cry in French?" he demanded in that language.

Hilde was too scared to reply, could only cling to the stranger.

Eldridge came pelting up, hot and yelling furious obscenities, but when a parcel of foreigners wearing heavy brass-hilted hangers at their sides moved to block his progress he brought himself up all standing. Damnation!

Antoine Fougère, *lieutenant de vaisseau* in the navy of His Most Christian Majesty, Louis XVI of France, flipped his big boat cloak about the hysterical girl, spoke words of reassurance and put an arm around her.

A gaunt captain of marines strode up grinning. "*Alors,*

monsieur le Lieutenant, you seem to have snared a very pretty pigeon. What will you do with her?''

Fougère hesitated, then broke into a light laugh. ''One esteems, my friend, that, whatever chances, she may be better off aboard *L'Ecureuil.* In the morning she can be set ashore.''

XXV. BAD LITTLE FALLS

MORNING BROKE icy cold, blue and clear, revealing reefs spouting off Foster Island and the familiar, pine-dotted outlines of Starboard, Stone and Ram Islands at the southward entrance to Machias Bay. These islands appeared so sharply detailed that they might have been executed by the brush of a miniaturist. Stretches of water, separating the wave crests, shone a very clear blue; it was so dark that it verged on black.

As Asa might have expected, the wind blew bitter cold and he yearned to swing his arms for a space but, standing his trick at tiller, he couldn't. Poised in a half-crouch, he braced his feet hard against a series of cleats as, expertly, he permitted his body to yield to the pink's vicious pitching and tossing.

The wind, Asa judged, was blowing smartish out of the northwest; anyway, it was sufficiently strong to snatch wisps of foam from the wave tops and to hurl them high enough to sheathe, in glittering ice, the pink's rail, rigging and lower canvas.

Every now and then a sheet of spray would whip, singing, over the pink's bow to add a fraction of an inch to those icicles already formed on the lee shrouds. In a little while, Asa figured, they'd have to heave to long enough for the chilled blue-lipped crew to chop ice from her bows, forecastle hatch and forward bulwarks. She was becoming sluggish under the accumulating weight.

All the same Asa guessed he'd let Ben Mead—his stepmother's cousin—young Morgan, and two half-breed Passamaquoddy deckhands sleep a mite longer.

He allowed the pink to fall two points off the wind and found she didn't pound so hard, though the heavy oaken tiller gouged more fiercely at his side. Why hadn't Ben Mead found gumption enough to rig a whipstaff, or some kind of tackle to this infernal tiller handle? It tired a man mightily to attempt, by sheer bull strength, to control the plunges of such a heavy little vessel.

Pretty soon he steered the pink past Jasper Head and the foaming reefs of Seashore Ledge. God only knew what he would find awaiting him in Machias. So much could have chanced since Morgan, junior, had set out from Machias to find him.

An hour dragged by, during which time the wind and waves decreased, especially when the pink entered the lee of Bare and Yellow Islands. While scudding past the entrance to Buck's Harbor, Asa studied the little bay with lively interest. 'Twas there Sir George Collier's ships, the *Rainbow* 44, the *Blonde* 44, and the *Mermaid* 28 had lain at anchor. Young Morgan claimed that nowadays a patriotic patrol ship, the *Neshquoit* sheltered there, too.

"Mornin', Asey." Ben Mead was never one to waste words. "Ye recall how to con a vessel into the river?" He still looked sleepy and red-eyed.

"Aye, but ye'd best call the men. Ice's thicker'n a schoolboy's head. British sure enough wasted shot on Salt Island if all they gained was to blow down so few houses."

"Aye. They waren't extry smart. Keep her headed for Indian Head, will ye? I'll go rout out the crew."

Turning his face from the bite of the wind Asa attempted to analyze his emotions at the prospect of rejoining his family. With the exception of Prudence and Morgan, all his full brothers and sisters were either married or dead. His own mother, Charity, had dutifully given birth to seven children before lapsing, perhaps gladly, into eternal surcease from the grinding toil befalling a frontier wife. None of the second brood sired by Morgan Peabody's leathery body would he have recognized in a strange village.

Of course, Prudence, the spinster, would be on hand to greet him. Poor, plain, patient Prudence, a second mother first to Ma's younger children, and then to Ruth Peabody's progeny. Sister Freelove, two years his junior, had died in the full bloom of youth during that terrible pox epidemic which, in 1777, in the wintertime descended to desolate so many lonely cabins and hamlets. Esther, Morgan explained, had married Sylvanus Snow last summer and now was rounder than a net kettle with her first baby.

While studying the set of the foresail Asa wondered whether it had been wise for Pa to marry a woman so much younger than himself? Probably he'd needed someone to run his house and mind the children for all that Ruth Hindman of Ipswich hadn't quite measured up to Peabody standards.

All the same, no one could claim that Pa's second wife hadn't striven hard to fill the family gap left by that narrow grave behind the church marked by a plain pine slab. For years Asa had known the inscription on it by heart:

Here Lieth all that is Mortal of
Charity
God Fearing and Dutiful Spouse of Morgan Peabody,
Esq.
b. 1720—d. 1764
R.I.P.

Right away, of course, Ruth had started a family of her own. Lionel, Purity, and Constance were around by way of proof.

These half-brothers and -sisters filled even the ample double cabin, but Ruth Peabody probably would have managed quite happily had not a churn handle slipped one day to deal her a sharp blow on the bosom.

Nobody had paid the accident much heed; indeed, once the swelling had disappeared, she'd forgotten all about it herself. Something over a year elapsed before, timidly, she spoke of a lump forming in her right breast. That was just after he, Asa, had taken ship for Boston and a medical career.

From that time on their stepmother had commenced to fail, so Morgan said, and went into a decay of breast; so the management of Morgan Peabody's home had devolved increasingly, if imperceptibly, upon Prudence.

Keeping a wary eye on that white smother marking the existence of a reef, Asa calculated further. Um. Purity would be about twelve, practically a young lady, and Constance should be nine. Lionel, at ten, was still too light to help with heavy chores; his efforts would be confined to woodcutting, trapping, fishing for the pantry and milking the family cow.

Young Morgan, Asa long since deduced, had struggled to play the man's part. Since Pa fell sick abed Lord alone knew how Morgan Peabody's impoverished family could have made out without him. Silent by nature, Asa's youngest full brother was thoughtful beyond his years and uncommon handy about a sailing vessel; some day he'd make an excellent ship master.

Gradually the wind was shifting to the eastward, driving Ben Mead's pink straight towards the mouth of the river where the patriotic schooner *Neshquoit,* ten guns, maintained her patrol against hostile vessels.

The shore now showed up in such detail that Asa found no difficulty in recognizing gun ports in Fort Foster on the east bank, and Fort O'Brien on the west shore near Machias Port. Plain earthworks, they'd been thrown up in a hurry during the summer of 1777 against the threat of Sir George Collier's expedition.

Despite his dark mood Asa found the sight of ranks of stately pines marching down through snow drifts to the ice-jammed shore a welcome one. This primitive wildness held a subtle charm, he found: those brief stretches of sandy beach festooned in kelp flung far above the tide mark; angry winter waves lashing at a shore line cruel as an untactful truth. And yonder, the Picture Rocks flung their enigma bold against the sky.

Home would be in sight as the pink rounded Day's Head.

XXVI. MACHIAS REVISITED

NOTHING AT FIRST seemed to be changed during Asa's near three years' absence. Ben Mead ordered all sails down save a foretopsail and a single jib; they would serve to send the pink bowling through an opening in the heavy, log boom protecting Machias.

Yonder loomed the weather-rounded and barnacled rocks from which he'd done so much of the family's pantry fishing. Yonder a small buoy, flying a frayed blue flag, marked the position of someone's net or trawl. Ah, yes, those blue and white circles about the buoy were those of

Edward Carlton; that white- and red-bodied marker further on would belong to Philip Fogg.

Amazing, how his recollection of such details came flying back. It had been in yonder cove that, as a lad, he'd set his first lobster pots. Further over was where he'd near frozen to death, one late November day, because while fishing he'd lost an oar and so got carried out on the tide.

'Twas over on the Rim, one fine spring day, he'd first become aware that girls were important; not just weak and giggling nuisances. Vaguely, he wondered what had become of tomboyish Martha Libby, soft-eyed Kitty O'Brien, and that irrepressible hoyden, Jerusha Buck.

Only when Ben Mead's vessel rounded the river bend opposite the old 'Quoddy Indian camp ground did Machias come into view as a sizeable scattering of houses and cabins clustering against a dark wall of evergreens.

Most of the wharves and piers still thrust their length into the powerful tides. On them drowsed the usual number of gray-white harbor gulls with, here and there, a big, black-backed emperor gull standing about in regal aloofness. The river narrowed rapidly so, presently, the pink set a few eider ducks and old squaws to squattering reluctantly away.

Quickly Asa checked the shore line for familiar structures and soon recognized the substantial frame houses of Colonel Benjamin Foster, Judge Stephen Jones, Ben Foss and Sylvanus Scott. There were, however, quite a number of new buildings under construction, mostly of the old, and easy-to-build, log cabin type.

Yonder was Pa's big, double log cabin in which Asa had first beheld the light of day; its gray shingled roof was located off to the left of the main settlement, down by the shore, and pretty much by itself.

Gradually the familiar sights, smells and sounds kindled a small and quite unexpected feeling of warmth. After all, this was home. Here, a tow-headed youngster, going barefoot from early spring until snow fall, he'd watched the alewives swarm up yonder creek in seemingly endless columns of glistening silver. Over there, just beyond old Job Burnham's tavern, stood the schoolhouse in which his backside had smarted more than once under Mr. Thaxter's ready birch rod.

Asa derived a deal of comfort in making sure that Pa's pier and the little fish house near its end still stood on its low and sandy point below Machias. He noted, however, that the forest had been allowed to invade a hay field beyond Pa's low, earth-roofed barn; moreover, a whole section of snake fencing was down.

Drawn up on the beach above the tide mark lay three fishing smacks, all unseaworthy because of the big holes punched through the bottoms.

Pa had stove them in himself, Morgan explained, during a lively alarm; didn't want the Lobsterbacks to sail them away. Pa, not knowing he was to be took abed so soon, had calculated 'twould be far easier to repair his boats than to build new ones. The usual mound of fish traps and lobster pots were stacked above tide water, but their gray, unused look aroused qualms.

In the old days two or three snug little fishing schooners would have been tied up to Pa's wharf. Sometimes there had been as many as four—the *Eliza*, Pa's big, well-built snow; and his second craft, a topsail schooner; Uzziel's pink and Sylvanus Snow's little shallop.

'Twas Sylvanus who'd married Esther, Asa's youngest full sister. Only the weight of public opinion, young Morgan allowed, had at last driven him to soldiering in the backwoods along of Colonel Eddy who still was clinging to his lofty dream of driving King George's men out of Nova Scotia.

At a sign from Ben Mead two Passamaquoddy seamen ran forward to strike the jib; Asa and Morgan lowered the topsail, then prepared to make fast to Pa's pier. Gradually, the pink lost way and Mead steered an easy course among the pitiful handful of vessels anchored off Machias Town, presently bringing his vessel smoothly alongside the gull-splashed pilings of Peabody's pier.

Thin outcries penetrated the screaming raised by the dislodged harbor gulls, as down from the long low cabin raced a boy and an even smaller girl. Scarves flying and cavorting like calves in a pasture, they came leaping down towards the water's edge through snow which had not been shoveled since the last storm.

"Huzza! Huzza!" they piped, waving red-mittened hands. "Asey's back!"

Employing the back of his hand, Ben Mead wiped a drop from the sharp red end of his nose. "Wal, Asey, I allow ye'll want to see yer folks," he observed. "Go on up to the house; I'll fetch yer dunnage across this afternoon."

At this moment Asa sharply regretted that time in Boston had not permitted the purchase of a few gifts, no matter how trivial. Eager expectancy was written large on the faces of the children, now wading out onto the wharf.

"Ye brought us a present from Boston, Asey? Ye did, didn't ye?" they panted even as they flung themselves into his eager arms.

"To be sure," he lied, simply unable to write disappointment across these lively, bright-eyed faces, "but ye'll have to be patient 'til I unpack."

Morgan appeared from the forecastle, sea bag on shoulder, and called in the deepest voice he could manage, "Hi, there, Connie! Li, lend a hand with my ditty bag, will you?" His tone drew a smile to Asa's well-chapped lips.

Asa picked up Constance, brushed snow first from her little homespun coat and skirt, then from heavy wool stockings nearly as thick as her own thin legs. "How's Papa?"

"Mighty poorly," chirped the little girl. "Doctor Falconer don't rightly know what ails him."

Lionel agreed, all the while owlishly surveying his big half-brother. "Ever since frost set in he's been sufferin'—not that he says so," he added, loyally.

Constance's eyes, brown and clear, sought upwards with the uncompromising intentness of childhood. "You'll make Pa well, Brother Asey? You will, won't you?"

"I'll do my best."

"You *are* a—a physician now, ain't you?"

"Yes, Connie, I expect I am." Aye. But to what purpose? Where now to test, to study and so enlarge his good but modest field of medical knowledge? He had a vision of himself a few years hence, just another underpaid, overworked frontier doctor. In setting Constance down, Asa expelled a slow, and deeply troubled, sigh.

Anyhow, this was home; the community from whence he had sprung. Icicles had formed on the two whales' jawbones which formed an arch over the yard gate; the worn-out dory his pretty young stepmother had converted years ago into a flower bed, now lay all but concealed under a drift. In July and August yellow and red nasturtiums had used to glow there.

By now Asa, Morgan, Lionel and Connie were tramping, single file, up to the far end of Morgan Peabody's house, where a woodshed created an L-shaped barrier against the frigid winds from the west.

Mechanically, Asa checked the supply of firewood stacked in the woodshed. Around Machias firewood constituted the infallible measure of a man's gumption; never would a self-respecting man allow his woodshed to be seen less than half filled. Pa *must* have been sick a long while. Why, there wasn't even half a cord in there; under normal conditions the woodshed protected never less than four or five well-dried and seasoned cords of birch.

Another bad sign was the way the front yard gate hung askew. Slowly, like a malodorous and sickening tide, alarm rose in Asa's soul. The whole house appeared weary, poor, ill-kept and that plume of smoke twisting from the kitchen chimney looked thin and acrid.

Prudence, wearing a shapeless gown of linsey-woolsey, materialized in the doorway and, arms outstretched, ran to meet him.

"Oh, Asa, Asa! My brother." As she clung to him she began to weep. "God bless you and reward you for coming home," she sobbed. "We need you so terribly."

Book Two ★ *The Sea*

PART I—THE BRIG *GRAND TURK III*— TWELVE GUNS

1. A BROOM AT THE MASTHEAD

SEATED IN the stern sheets of Captain Ashton's own gig, Peter Burnham surveyed the outline of that brig which, in all probability, he would call home for the next six months—perhaps longer. Like a dainty woman drawing aloof from a jostling crowd, the *Grand Turk III* lay at anchor on the fringes of the rest of the shipping. Seven or eight other privateers swung to moorings along the gig's course; a small ship, three brigs, three schooners and a snow or two completed the tally of private men-of-war. Carpenters were hard at work on a big, black-painted schooner, mending ominous-looking shot holes in her bulwarks, or, nearer her water line, replacing with seasoned planking temporary coverings of sheet-lead or green hide.

The *Grand Turk's* gig sped smoothly over the slate-hued waves of Boston Harbor, her oarsmen bending to their oars in rhythm to a chant raised by the coxswain.

The more Peter considered Captain Ashton's brig, the more he understood why the Virginian's admiration for his vessel verged on love. An amateur sailor, whose nautical knowledge was confined to a few pleasure cruises in Long Island Sound, Peter could not have begun to explain why the brig's lines appeared so unusually harmonious; come to think of it, Captain Ashton once had said that originally, she had been French.

The *Grand Turk* was somewhat smaller than he had expected, not ninety feet in length—she was actually eighty-three at the water line—and quite narrow—about twenty feet in the beam. Though of but two hundred tons burthen, she looked larger, perhaps because her two topmasts rose some ten feet taller than would be the rule in a vessel of her dimensions.

Even Peter could tell, when the gig rowed closer, that her figurehead was not the original one. While the turbaned and bearded Turk, who, clutching a scimitar, stared fiercely out over the water, was not badly done, the workmanship was infinitely inferior to the execution of the delicate scrollwork streaming so gracefully aft from the bows.

His convictions on that point presently became stronger because decorations about the brig's stern revealed so much imagination and well-considered design. For instance, her three stern ports, though harmoniously proportioned, were yet large enough to permit a medium-sized carriage gun to be fired through them.

Above these ports Peter recognized a handsomely carved reproduction of Jove, the old Pagan Greek god in the form of a bull. He bore on his back the unhappy maiden Europa; for such had the brig originally been christened. Ashton had been in a great hurry to alter that name; anyone able to distinguish a marline spike from a belaying pin knew that nothing in the world could be un-luckier than to christen a ship after a continent or an ocean.

When subconsciously Peter essayed to flex his injured hand a wave of bitterness engulfed him. Hell's roaring bells. Muscles in the third and fourth fingers simply would not obey, despite patient massage. They were growing red, shiny and quite rigid; eventually they would atrophy.

No use cursing the inevitable, so, resolutely, Peter returned his attention to the privateer. Her sides were of a blue so dark as to approach black; but her water line was indicated by a band of sky-blue and her streak, pierced on each side by six light-blue-painted gun ports, shone a rich red-yellow.

Yellow, too, was the color of the privateer's bowsprit, her three small boats, and the trimming of her lovely stern. Gold leaf, captured in some prize, adorned the Muslim figurehead as well as the lettering setting forth the brig's name. In graceful silhouette this brig thrust spars and rigging against the bright blue sky.

"What's that pendant?" Peter inquired of the coxswain.

He shifted his quid, looked a bit contemptuous, but replied politely enough. " 'Tis a vieft, sir, flying to summon the crew aboard—gives the bastards occasion to sober up."

As the gig pulled up, Captain Ashton's brig lay sedately swinging to her anchors and gently breasting an invisible current. From her jack fluttered a large American flag which was really too large to be in good proportion; still 'twas in the current style.

A broom lashed to her foretop advetised to the port that the *Grand Turk* was soon due to up anchor and stand out—a practice honored by all reputable shippers desiring to pay their debts. Doubtless this explained why a swarm of bumboats, selling every imaginable kind of food, clothing and hardware, was jostling and bumping under the brig's counter.

Because the *Grand Turk* boasted a fine tally of prizes, the majority of her crew were old hands who knew their way about; far less sailing day confusion was evident on her deck than one might have expected.

Today would be the first of February, Peter mused. Even the wisest of men could predict so little of their destiny. Who, on New Year's Eve, possibly could have foretold that he, Peter Burnham, would this February day be signing on as surgeon aboard a Virginia gentleman's privateer? It was to laugh—bitterly, perchance—but still to laugh. A fitting fate for one who had dared dedicate himself to the relief of female suffering.

A chill wind came beating up the harbor, caused Peter to gather his boat cloak closer. The debilitating effects of his fever were still upon him. How fortunate he'd been not to lose his left hand under the laborious ministration of that same earnest but ignorant physician who, during the blank period of his own delirium, without necessity— Peter was convinced of that point—had amputated Susan's arm, just as it was promising to heal. In a way, learning about that amputation was the hardest blow with which he'd had to cope. "Catastrophe" might be the only word adequate to describe the shock he'd suffered when, weak and struggling to regain strength, he'd learned how Doctor Chase had preyed upon the fears of Susan's distracted parents until they'd consented, most reluctantly, to an amputation of the little girl's arm.

Peter stared at the lid of the medical chest reposing between his knees. Crimanently! Susan's arm *would* have healed in time. Under close questioning, Mrs. Ashton— no hysterical flibbertigibbet at any time—admitted that the swelling of the fractured arm had commenced to subside.

Ironically, it was only because of his own high fever and suppurating wounds that Mrs. Ashton had insisted on summoning to her house myopic and jovial Doctor Chase. Peter had heard Doctor Townsend mention Chase as a practitioner belonging to the old school, completely unimaginative, and wedded to methods approved some fifty years earlier. 'Twas said that Doctor Chase would bleed a canary to death in trying to cure the bird of an earache.

Peter roused from this miserable reverie to hear the coxswain yell a string of warning curses at bumboats clustered about the foot of the *Grand Turk's* ladder. Reluctantly, they rowed out of the way.

"''Way enough. Easy all! Hup!'' As one, the gig's crew tossed their oars to the perpendicular, sat grinning on their benches. Precious few privateer crews had been taught this trick, so they were ratted proud of their accomplishment. Rob Ashton was no hard-a-weather skipper, but always he demanded smartness and discipline of his crews—and got it. Maybe that was why he was so successful? Maybe not.

"Deck there! Officer coming aboard!" bawled the coxswain steering the gig bobbing into the *Grand Turk's* lee. A member of the watch caught the painter expertly flung by the Number One oarsman.

Because of his injured hand—it seemed to have no strength at all nowadays—Peter only clumsily swarmed up a rope ladder dangling over the brig's blue side just forward of the quarterdeck's break. A flush of shame clouded his expression because two deckhands were forced to catch him by the armpits and assist him across the rail. A lean officer with the face of a heart-broken horse came running up and looking quite unhappy.

"I'm the surgeon; my name—"

"Devil take your name. Goddam' it, sir, the quarterdeck; salute the quarterdeck!"

"Beg pardon?"

The deck officer's long face went scarlet. "Salute the quarterdeck, you dunderhead. 'Tis the custom aboard men-o'-war."

Though he couldn't perceive the least sense in it, Peter raised his black tricorne in the general direction of the stern.

"Who in tunket are you?" snapped the officer, a human bean pole of a fellow garbed in a greasy blue and brown uniform which bore but a single epaulette of tarnished gold lace.

"Mr. Burnham, surgeon for this cruise, so ye'd best mend your manners," Peter advised.

"Why?"

"Suppose I were called to take off your arm?"

The horse-faced officer stared, then smiled sourly and offered his hand. "Damme, mebbe you'll do. Anyways, I'm Pickering—first officer aboard, and don't you ever forget it."

So this was Gideon Pickering, hailing from Groton in the State of Connecticut? As Rob Ashton had said, he looked it.

"So you're signing on as Sawbones?" The first officer's yellowish and bony features betrayed no emotion.

"Yes."

"You'll address your superiors as 'sir' aboard this vessel," Pickering snapped. He beckoned a tall young lad of perhaps fourteen years. "Boy! Show Mr. Burnham to the cockpit."

"Aye, aye, sir. This way, sir." The boy, a fresh-faced, cheery looking youth, led the way below. Followed by a seaman lugging his instrument case under one arm and his clothes chest under the other, Peter descended the companionway.

"Good God above, what's this?"

Peter found himself confronted, to his considerable dismay, by a tiny cubicle hardly twice as large as the bunk which occupied one full side of it. Save for the light of a bull's-eye lantern suspended above piles of stores stacked helter-skelter to all sides the place was quite dark.

"Your quarters, sir," the boy announced in malicious satisfaction. "Most Pull-Guts don't fare nigh so well. 'Tis a break-bones hammock for most."

"The Devil you say!" Peter managed to reply. Abruptly he grew aware that the impact of waves alongside the privateer now sounded above his head.

"Where'll ye have these, sir?" grunted the seaman, a small hairy fellow afflicted by a violent squint.

"Stow the medical chest beneath my bunk," Peter directed. Damned if he'd be put upon. "About the clothes chest—I well, I will have to see." Obviously, there was no space for it in this dim and malodorous hutch.

"Anything else, sir?" demanded the boy.

"No."

He and the seaman clumped off, their wooden sea-boot soles reverberating along the deck.

While the air was not quite noxious, the atmosphere of the cockpit certainly was lifeless and reeked of bilges but a few feet below Peter's bunk.

Was he actually expected to exist in such a fetid hole?

Quite discouraged, the new ship's surgeon seated himself upon the clothes chest. Damnation! Since childhood he'd abominated confined spaces. Oh God, why had he ever listened to Murdo Moore's lying tongue? A plague on Jenny McLaren's remains! Miserably, Peter peered about, aware that his head was beginning to throb because of the bad air. Still, as the boy had pointed out, he had at least space to himself, whereas in a larger man-of-war he'd most likely have to put up with some midshipman. Probably a surgeon's mate would be there also to plague and crowd the cockpit. Yes. Despite everything he was well off. Ashton had taken pains to explain that in a regular vessel of war a ship's doctor ranked just above the schoolmaster and therefore rated near the lowest of the afterguard. They must expect to take leavings by way of accommodation.

Quite vividly Peter recalled Uncle Paul—he had sailed as a surgeon in the Royal Navy—and his tales of the gloom, the stenches and the lack of privacy afloat. How well he remembered Uncle Paul's repeated observation. " 'Tis aboard ship that you come across the very dregs of the medical profession. No physician in his right wits would sign articles lest he'd no other choice."

Since it served no useful purpose to gloom on like this he'd better look alive and learn what was what. A row of wooden pegs driven into the wall opposite the bunk seemed designed to suspend his garments, so he unlocked his chest and was lifting out a coat when the boy came pounding below.

"Doctor Burnham! Doctor Burnham, sir," he panted, "Mr. Pickering's compliments, sir, and would you report on the quarterdeck immediate-like?"

Mr. Pickering was awaiting him by the foot of the mainmast, a dour expression contracting his hatchet-thin features.

"Has it occurred to you, Mr. Burnham, that ye ain't settin' forth on a pleasure cruise?"

A pleasure cruise? A bitter smile curved Burnham's lips.

"What prompts that inquiry?"

"Sir—!"

"—Sir."

No use getting resentful. Peter noticed that, with the exception of two uniformed men stationed at the ladder head—he took them to be marines—the entire crew had been mustered on the forecastle and about the base of the brig's foremast.

"It appears," observed Mr. Pickering caustically, "ye don't yet know the first thing about the duties o' a ship's Sawbones."

"Your perspicacity astounds me," Peter snapped. "I will be glad to discharge my duties if you'll be good enough to instruct me. Unfortunately, I am not a mind reader."

Pickering's lean jaws worked a little. "Just so you're a competent pill-roller, that's enough. Now go examine yonder rascals and certify 'em fit for duty, free of vermin and sound of wind and limb. After that ye'll examine our medical stores. I can tell ye one thing, though it's not my business—it's the store master's—we've already plenty o' scurvy remedies aboard, spruce beer, pickled cabbage, apples and cider. Cap'n Ashton's pertickler on that score."

"The drinking water?"

"Fresh. And we've plenty o' cream of tartar to sweeten it if it goes bad."

"Har-rump!" Peter turned to observe another of the *Grand Turk's* officers; he differed from Mr. Pickering as sharply as a man could. "This our new Pull-Guts?"

"Doctor Burnham, Mr. Doane—second officer."

Abel Doane's body seemed constructed in a series of super-imposed ellipses; he walked on thick, bowed legs and carried a sizeable paunch; his perfectly round head seemed to be supported by no neck at all. Mr. Doane's eyes shone a lively brown and his cheeks were the color of Winesap apples. All in all, he put Peter in mind of a robin after a rain, when the worms were plentiful and easy to get.

"How are you?" Uneven teeth gleamed in the afternoon sunlight when Mr. Doane offered a thick red hand. "Welcome aboard the *Grand Turk,* Doctor Burnham.

Let's hope you'll enjoy this cruise, and return from it gunnel deep with your share.''

Pickering jerked a nod, stalked over to the rail to superintend the hoisting aboard of bags of round shot.

"You're about to inspect the crew, hey?'' Doane remarked. "Well, best get cracking—Skipper'll be aboard by six bells o' the afternoon watch. Parkins!'' he roared, "Parkins! Fetch Mr. Burnham a table and stool, and step lively about it.''

"Don't mind old Pick, he's always ornier than a spring bear on sailing day,'' Doane advised. He led the way forward between a double row of dully gleaming carriage guns; eight were visible in the open waist of the brig. Because Peter knew the *Grand Turk* mounted twelve guns he deduced that the other four must be located in a short gun deck below the poop.

The cannons created a fascinating geometrical pattern; four cast-iron pieces to a side, they rested their trunnions securely on heavy oaken carriages. Each gun was equipped with four very small and solid wooden wheels tired in wrought iron. The breechings and training tackles, Peter noted, were brand-new.

Because of stores still not stowed away and because the guns had been drawn on board to permit the ports through which they were fired to be battened down, progress along the gun deck wasn't easy.

"Avast, you men!'' The boatswain, a big burly fellow wearing a brown furze coat, began herding the men into loose ranks which must have included roughly a hundred men—a very considerable number for so small a man-of-war, thought Peter.

The *Grand Turk's* crew displayed a heterogeneous variety of sea clothes; some wore brogans; some stood in heavy, wooden-soled boots; a few even went about in rope-soled shoes; most wore leathern breeches or petticoat-breeches of stained white canvas. Some few had adopted bits and pieces of blue or brown uniform apparently at random and indulging the individual's fancy. Here and there shone a gold hoop, though the style for earrings was waning. In only one respect was there any uniformity. All the men wore their hair clubbed and secured in an eelskin or by a bit of ribbon.

On the whole they impressed Peter as able and healthy-appearing. Obviously the pick of the port had elected to cruise aboard this privateer. Wasn't Rob Ashton known to be an all-fired able captain? And lucky too? Whoever sailed along of him stood good chances of returning to port with a tidy sum knotted in his handkerchief.

Among the men staring curiously at the two officers approaching them were half a dozen Negroes and at least twice as many full-blooded Indians; more numerous still were half-breeds. Impassively, their opaque, obsidian-bright black eyes followed the efforts of Parkins to arrange Doctor Burnham's table.

Soon Peter ascertained that, although the heft of the crew was American, almost every seafaring nation in Europe was represented. There were French, Swedes, Dutch, Danes, even a slant-eyed Finn with the palest imaginable blue eyes, and a trio of dark-skinned fellows out of some petty Italian kingdom. His greatest surprise came when a baker's dozen of the able seamen answered his questions in accents characteristic of Devon, Cornwall, Lincoln and Dundee.

In an aside, Doane informed him that these, for the most part, were deserters from the Royal Navy, good hands all, because they sailed with a halter about their necks and hated the King's service with a passion. Doane said the British were particularly adept at sailmaking and carpentry while Americans made superior topmen and gunners; the Indians and Negroes rated highest in their ability to board and, in hand-to-hand fighting, to sweep clean an enemy deck.

Looking sheepish, the men commenced to shuffle by. Peter told them to open their mouths—he wanted no toothless men aboard—peered down their throats, felt their abdomens for rupture and peered inside their shirts for evidences of the dread *lues venera*, or French pox.

Whoever had signed on this crew must have known what he was about; Peter felt justified in refusing not one of the *Grand Turk*'s company—nor in ordering all heads to be shaved and clothes to be boiled. Of course two or three seamen had bad colds and a few, he suspected, would become afflicted with *lues venera*, but there was no being sure of it. It went without saying that, once the brig was out to sea, all manner of minor ailments would, all at once, be brought to his attention.

During the course of his examination he learned there

were aboard four younkers or powder monkeys; lads of thirteen and fourteen years, all orphans with one exception. A boy called Larry Lord appeared to be their senior.

The medical inspection was drawing to a close when, just after the ship's bell had sounded six resonant notes, the watch sang out, "Cap'n's gig in sight!" Immediately the *Grand Turk* company was cast into a ferment of activity.

"Second comin' of Christ ain't a patch on the Cap'n's comin' aboard," grunted the boatswain driving his men to carry below the scattered stores.

Peter could see Captain Ashton's gig laboring out, right in the teeth of a moderate breeze, her bow chopping at the waves and flinging white splinters of water to either side.

Crew members off duty disappeared below helter-skelter as perhaps a dozen uniformed figures appeared on deck, still securing the flat yellow buttons of their green and white tunics.

"What are those?" Peter wanted to know.

"Them's our marines," Doane returned pridefully. "Crack shots every one; most of 'em hev been aboard at least three cruises. We'd best go aft, Burnham."

A drum commenced to roll, evidently summoning the marines to line up in a double rank facing that point where the brig's ladder was swung over the rail.

"Your place is on my left," Doane warned. "The commander of marines really ranks you, but he's a Dutchman so don't care. Ha! Here he is."

Cornet Jan Vanderhyde appeared, still struggling with the buckle of a heavy, brass-hilted cutlass.

"This is our doctor," Doane explained.

The marine held out a big hairy hand. "Goot, goot. I hope I von't need you dis cruise." He turned away.

Pickering was shouting, "Boys and marines tend the side. All hands man the rail!"

The boatswain's silver pipe commenced to twitter. Peter decided that it resembled a long flat S topped by a silver ball.

From a ship anchored near by rose derisive outcries. "Yah! Spit-and-polish swabs! My, my, dearie, ain't they real Macaronis?"

Faces grew dark as the taunting clamor floated downwards from the *Dauntless* brigantine. She, too, was making ready to depart; bumboats were pulling away from her just as they recently had from the *Grand Turk*.

Dauntless? Why did the name sound so familiar? Peter recalled the brawl at the Red Lion—God above, it had happened just a month ago. Now he recognized that black-browed marine sergeant yonder as Luke Tarbell who'd started the free-for-all.

"Yon's another lucky ship," Doan grunted. "Our worst rival."

To the measured shrilling of the boatswain's pipe, the four younkers lined up, ready to steady the ladder during the captain's ascent, were it necessary. Lieutenant Pickering barked a command; Cornet Vanderhyde ordered his dozen marines to present arms and the drummer beat his instrument louder than ever. Everyone stiffened and Pickering and the rest of the officers saluted when the head and shoulders of Captain Ashton appeared over the rail.

Peter, a stark black figure among the uniformed officers, didn't know what to do, so remained motionless. His face brown and immobile as if carved out of saddle leather, the Virginian swung over the rail of his vessel, then faced the quarterdeck and gravely saluted it. After that he moved along the line of marines, narrowly inspected the equipment of each.

"Ain't one privateer in fifty fusses with such discipline," Doane muttered. "Skipper found out, though, such fumadiddles somehow pays out when the goin' gets bad—and I've seen it that way, too."

Moving with short jerky strides, Captain Ashton came swinging aft, acknowledged Mr. Pickering's salute before running an expressionless eye over the little group of officers lined up before the helm.

"Mr. Pickering."

"Aye, aye, sir?"

"We will weigh anchor at seven bells, sharp."

II. "SHAPE A COURSE FOR THE INDIES"

THE WIND had been rising all afternoon, so the *Grand Turk*, though still at anchor, stirred enough to cause her gun carriages to creak and to strain a little at their tackles. Everyone aboard felt mighty fine once the decking commenced to lift and fall under their feet, and to hear wind thrumming softly among the shrouds and halyards. By now both the brig's whaler and long boat had been hoisted in and stowed in their cradles while the captain's gig had been snugged upon davits placed above the stern ports. Even as the broom was sent down from the fore-top the watch set a smoke sail abaft the foremast to protect it from sparks flying out of the galley's smoke-stack.

Indians in the crew claimed to smell a promise of snow in the air; sure enough, towards sunset the sky took on an ominous tan-gray hue. Peter Burnham stood among the brig's afterguard and watched the *Dauntless* crew begin heaving up her anchor. Aside from himself and the lieutenants the afterguard included the first and second prize masters, Cornet Vanderhyde and the captain's clerk.

Captain Ashton stood at the break of his quarterdeck, reading to the assembled company the "Articles of Agreement":

"Article the Fourth:" he was droning, "Prizes taken, after condemnation and other necessary charges are paid, shall be divided into two equal parts or moities. One moitie for the use and benefit of the owner, the other moitie for the use of the captain, officers, and seamen to the brig, *Grand Turk III.*

"Article the Fifth: The moitie or half part belonging to the Captain and Company of the sloop shall be divided into so many shares or parts as the share of the said captain, officers, seamen and others, shall amount to with the addition of deserving shares and shall be divided as hereafter mentioned."

There were twenty-seven articles in all. They provided that the captain should have eight shares, the first lieutenant six, the sailing master and second lieutenant four each, and the first prize master and the captain's clerk three each. Two and a half shares went to the second prize master and two each to the master's mate, doctor, carpenter, boatswain and gunner. The gunner's-mate and the boatswain's-mate had one and a half each, and the cook one and a quarter. The seamen and others on board would have a single share each, "except boys who shall be rewarded as the Committee . . . shall think proper to allow them." The committee would consist of the captain, second lieutenant and masters, and they would divide the "deserving shares" mentioned in Article the Fifth. For instance, the man who first discovered a sail, provided the ship proved to be a prize, would have an extra half-share. The man who first boarded a vessel in an engagement would be similarly rewarded. The remainder of "the deserving shares" would go to "the most deserving of the Company."

Whoever died on the cruise or lost his life in an engagement would have his share or shares paid over to his heirs—provided he had made the proper assignment. One hundred dollars would be paid to any man who lost a limb, and recompense would also be made to those maimed or disabled. But there were penalties as well. Whoever bred mutiny or disturbance on board would forfeit his shares to the company; and similarly with one guilty of the second offense of stealing.

The reading ended with the binding of all parties "for the true performance of the above Articles of Agreement."

The leaves fluttered wildly between Captain Ashton's fingers until he handed them to his clerk who rolled them into a compact cylinder and secured it.

Ashton meanwhile glanced up at the Stars and Stripes whipping from the main gaff. Through his speaking trumpet he said: "Lads, today we set sail on the seventh cruise of this vessel," he smiled "—and seven's the lucky number." Cheers. "Those among you who have sailed before aboard this vessel are aware that I require obedience, both prompt and implicit, maintaining as I do discipline comparable to that obtaining in a public vessel-of-war." No cheers. "Any well-found complaint will be considered, when presented through appropriate channels; anyone making ill-found grumble will repent it. And now let's have three rousing cheers for the flag of our country!"

He whipped off his tricorne and swung it to measure the cheers which were raised with hearty good will.

"Mr. Pickering will take over and make sail."

The first lieutenant saluted, pulled a brass-mouthed speaking trumpet from under his arm. "Up a hand! Loose foresail from the top. Present cable to the capstan and heave up your anchor walking handsomely."

Like partridges frightened by the approach of a hawk

the crew scattered to their stations and appointed tasks.
In high good spirits topmen went swarming up the ratlines. Others of the crew laced canvas covers over the
twelve, dully gleaming six pounders composing the
Grand Turk's battery.

In an amazingly short space of time the capstan pawls
set up a rhythmic *clack! clack!*—then the big cable began
to crawl on board like an endless, dripping brown serpent
to the panted verses of "Skillialee." At length a petty
officer swinging in the forechains bawled, "Anchor's
apeak, sir!"

Watched all the while by Captain Ashton, very stiff in
his blue uniform, yellow waistcoat and thick red stockings, Gideon Pickering drew a deep breath, shouted,
"Loose the fores'l in the brails, heave out your fores'l;
heave out the main tops'l; haul home the tops'l sheets!"

The petty officer in the bow yelled back, "Anchor's
aweigh, sir."

Instantly, Pickering replied, "Then walk away handsomely. Let fall your fores'l. Hoist your foretops'l."

The sails, a spanking new suit, began to gleam in the
cold afternoon light, then rattled and slapped; suddenly
they filled and the brig heeled gently to starboard. A shrill
shot through Peter's being when, slowly at first, then
faster and faster the *Grand Turk* commenced to slip
through the harbor water, with her enormous ensign
snapping bravely in the offshore breeze.

Pickering kept his gaze on the tops and the men clambering out on the yards. "Hoist up yer main tops'l there,
loose the mains'l and set it! Bring your foretack to the
cathead, and trim the sails quartering."

The anchor, all fouled by blue-black mud was permitted to dangle until the bow waves could wash it clean—
only then was it catted into its permanent position alongside.

A stiff smile creasing his broad features, Captain Ashton crossed the quarterdeck to where Peter stood staring
at Boston and the snowy hills of the surrounding country.

"Well, Doctor, we're off on another cruise. For you I
suspect this is all damned difficult and strange."

"Aye, sir," Peter said heavily. "'Tis a new life, indeed. I'm wondering whither it will lead me."

"God and Neptune willing, to the Lesser Antilles."

"Lesser Antilles?" Peter's brows climbed a trifle.

"Yonder lies Eustatius—'tis a Dutch island of the Leeward group and lying to the southeastwards of Puerto Rico. Because it's a long way off, I reckon the British cruisers won't be so thick thereabouts. Report to my cabin at two bells of the first dog watch."

With that the *Grand Turk*'s captain turned on his heel and tramped over to the lee rail there to fix a thoughtful eye upon the *Dauntless*.

"She's slovenly handled," he thought, "for all her reputation. Jonas Dawes' gear's all over the place and her gig ain't been hoisted in, even yet." But for all that, Dawes was considered the smartest sailing master out of Boston, able to coax the last bit of foot from any vessel he mastered. Privately, Rob Ashton wished he possessed at least part of his fellow captain's aptitude in that direction.

How this putting to sea differed from his first uncertain blundering out of Norfolk back in '75! He hadn't known "come here" from "sic 'em" about seamanship in those days; small wonder he'd piled his first command, the weary old *Desdemona* onto a mess of reefs off Somerset Island in the Bermudas. Then he'd been only a raw merchant, but he'd learned fast; nobody could say that the *Grand Turk III* hadn't been handled with caution, imagination and considerable skill, else how'd he been able to build, bit by bit, the fortune he intended some day to invest in vessels for the wonderfully lucrative China trade.

Basically, Rob knew he hadn't changed a whit from the merchant he'd been to begin with. For all the *Grand Turk III*'s naval trappings and his notions concerning discipline, what he really wanted most was to be able to trade—to rebuild the once-proud Ashton name. Yes, to buy and sell American goods in the far ports of the world and to watch his family grow up constituted the acme of his ambition.

Why couldn't he rid himself of an unusual and unprecedented sense of depression? Probably because Susan remained in the back of his mind. His strong jaw tightened. He reckoned he'd not soon forget the poor child's efforts to use an arm which no longer existed. Should he and Andrea have yielded to Doctor Chase's persuasions? Certainly, Susan's broken arm had looked to be corrupted—swollen and gone a frightening dark red. And yet, on recovering his wits Burnham certainly had been aghast at their decision, though he'd tried not to show it.

No use rehearsing that tragedy, so Rob Ashton directed his attention to the mainsail—the watch was swaying its peak into efficient tautness. Up there the reef points were tapping like raindrops against a windowpane. Now the brig heeled way over and commenced footing through the waters of Boston Harbor like the uncommonly handy vessel she was. So much spray came soaring over the forecastle that, presently, Mr. Doane, as officer of the watch, for protection ordered a "jimmy-green" or sprits'l rigged to the bowsprit.

III. OFFSHORE BREEZE

SAILS STRAINING, the *Grand Turk* bowled briskly along Nantasket roads on her course for the open sea. Most of the crew had remained on deck viewing the receding outlines of Boston Town, but a few directed their attention to the *Dauntless* steering a similar course about half a mile ahead.

Abel Doane was officer of the watch, his rotund body swathed in a comfortably thick greatcoat. Every now and then he would turn to give an order to the two quartermaster's mates handling the *Grand Turk's* helm to which preventer tackles had not yet been rigged—only much larger vessels in that day boasted the complicated gear of a steering wheel. The helmsmen swayed with feet braced against the cleats of a grating arranged for that purpose.

Otherwise alone on the quarterdeck, Peter Burnham found he still could count ten church steeples; four to the left, and six to the right of that great parade ground upon which the scarlet tunics of King George's troops used to parade. The light was fading and the brig sailed so fast that, presently, the town became lost to sight.

Slowly he beat a mittened hand on the rail; astern lay the cold ashes of that brilliant career he had planned. By the sunset he recognized Apple Island, sliding by off to port.

Come to think of it, Asa must have sailed this way, too, and not over a fortnight ago. Big, forthright, clever Asa; had he reached in safety the bleak coasts of the Maine District which the British, with typical arrogance, now were attempting to rechristen New Ireland? What of Lucius, ambitious, lonely and extremely able Lucius? Had he become in some way embroiled in the matter of Jenny McLaren's body? Probably not; if he'd followed instructions he must have remained safely at the Widow Southeby's, wondering why the cart failed to appear. Where would Lucius fetch up? Certainly at the top of the heap, if he kept on his present course.

Subconsciously, Peter's right hand rubbed his crippled left and he groaned. What lay ahead for himself? No telling. Privateering was a risky business; he entertained no illusions on that score. A man might return from a cruise to bank a small fortune, and he might, just as readily, leave his bones in the care of Davey Jones or perish of disease on some unknown island. He consigned to hell those brutal, superstitious oafs who'd damaged his operating skill, perhaps irreparably. What monumental stupidity! As if he'd intended to hurt them, or anybody for that matter; yet they'd torn at him like savage dogs.

His body yielded to the increased pitching of the *Grand Turk;* though it was growing very cold he wanted to postpone to the last moment a return to those malodorous quarters in the cockpit.

Suddenly he perceived new horizons. Suppose this cruise proved as successful as the brig's previous ones? And why shouldn't it? Why, then he'd become wealthy in an humble sort of way. He'd quit seafaring once the war ended, and what was there to discourage his setting up practice perhaps in Wilmington or Charles Town down in the Carolinas?

Aye. And if the fortunes of war favored him sufficiently why not continue his studies in Europe? Over there John Hunter, Percival Pott and the master of British midwifery, William Smellie, all were teaching. In Pavia there was Antonio Scorpa, and Deminco Cottengo in Naples.

Why not? With determination and a bit of luck, everything was possible. As ship's doctor he was entitled to two shares.

Down in steerage young Spurgeon Grannis crouched dejectedly on his sea bag with lower lip clamped tight between buck teeth. To restrain a spasmodic plucking manifesting itself in the vicinity of his belly-button was hard work, but he'd resolved not to give way to tears. If only he could forget that, with each passing moment, home, and all the things grown so sweetly familiar during his thirteen years, lay further behind. No, he wouldn't cry. The bosun's-mate had warned that powder monkeys weren't allowed to betray any feelings. All the same he wished that Tom Laughry, the same age but half a head taller, would break down and bawl like a hungry bull calf. But Tom didn't weep. Like two other younkers he was an orphan and was leaving nothing sweet and tender behind.

Oh, how Spurgeon ached for the feel of Ma's hand on the back of his neck and the sound of her voice. Right now, ever so clear, he could hear her say, "Spurgie, that red heifer's freshing and is likely to act fractious. Make sure you treat her gentle."

Rocking there in the semi-darkness, Spurgeon tried to recall every detail of that crude log cabin built among the hills not far north of Portsmouth in New Hampshire. 'Twasn't much, but it was home. When the eleventh child arrived he'd been able to tell, as quick as Twin Brother John, that there was no longer room for them.

And now there was only the dreary *slap-slapping* of waves against the hull, strange sights, strange smells and that odd tugging at the pit of his stomach. The Grannises had never asked favors of anyone, poverty-poor though they might be in this generation. Why couldn't Larry Lord, who, in a regular man-o'-war would have been called senior midshipman, tell a fellow what was expected of him without cuffs and dreadful-sounding curses? Most likely Larry wasn't really mean; only he'd been served that way in his green days and now proposed to enjoy his turn at bullying.

In an effort to rally his sinking spirits, Spurgeon groped in his sea bag until he found the nearly new sheath knife Pa had given him as a going-away present. Next he located the pennyroyal bag Ma warned he must wear about his neck whenever fevers were abroad. A lumpy and shapeless muffler that Sister Liza, aged eleven, had knitted for him was there, too.

Feet sounded on the ladder and he flinched at the sound of Larry Lord's voice, sat in rigid misery, waiting.

"Yep, Bub, first mistake ye make old Pickle-face Pickering will tick you off," Larry was telling a quaking junior. "Second, you'll taste a rope's end. Third—" the boy dropped onto his sea chest and warned in ghoulish and sepulchral tones, "they'll *keelhaul* you."

The powder monkey gave a frightened wriggle. "K-keel-haul, what's that?"

Employing a dramatic delivery worthy of an experienced actor, Larry explained. "They ties lines to yer hands and feet, pass 'em under the vessel's keel, then haul yer naked as a young jay clean under the ship; yep, down one side, across the keel and up 'tother so's the barnacles cut stripes in you, prettier'n ye see on a yaller perch. Of course, in tropic waters you don't never come up alive 'count o' the sharks—" he amplified.

"Sharks?" quavered Spurgeon, his throat closing. "They wouldn't do that, would they?"

"Wouldn't they?" Larry grinned ferociously, pulled out his dirk and commenced to trim a fingernail which certainly needed attention. "Why, only last cruise we lost one and a half younkers through keel-haulin'." Larry stared from one to the other of his three companions gravely. A muscovy lantern swinging from a hook in the steerage drew brief yellow flashes from his thick blond hair.

"And—and—a *half?*" squeaked Tom Laughry, eyes grown as big as tea sassers.

The senior powder monkey drew a deep breath and in a chilling voice, said, "Aye. When they drew that boy out o' the water only half of him was left."

Severe tingling broke out along Spurgeon's legs. "He—was dead?"

"Sure. You ought to seen 'im, *his guts was hangin' out*—"

Spurgeon gagged; then, tacking with each heave of the brig, went over to a slop bucket. "Ma!" he gasped between spasms of retching. "Oh Ma, please, I don't want to go to sea!"

Larry roared with laughter, glared at Tom and a quiet boy named Charlie. "Look! Look at the fancy-Nancy, who's got a spare di'per?" Tom Laughry rushed for a slop bucket.

Just then the boatswain's-mate appeared at the head of the ladder. "Rout out o' there, ye little barstards!" he bawled. "All boys on deck!"

"I—I can't," Spurgeon blubbered. His legs felt weak as rainwater.

"Oh, you can't, can't you? Well, we'll see about that." The boatswain's-mate clambered below, a short length of rope in his grasp.

Larry chuckled. "Spurgie, you were raised on a farm but I bet you never saw a colt like this before. Yep, that's a colt." He grinned at his pun.

"Don't you touch me!" Spurgeon gurgled, wiping his chin, "I—I'll go." Lurching against the *Grand Turk's* violent motion he made for the steerage ladder a stride behind Larry and Charles Prescott.

Though the boatswain's-mate's colt made sharp cracking noises over his back, Tom Laughry still clung to the slop bucket.

iv. The Duty Frigate

CAPTAIN ASHTON had calculated for his brig to gain the wide water of Massachusetts Bay just about twilight; she still sailed a half-mile astern of the *Dauntless*—not that the *Grand Turk* couldn't sail rings around the brigantine in any wind. Therefore it would be dark when he weathered the dune-crowned tip of Cape Cod. A dangerous region that—British cruisers were maintaining an especially rigorous blockade of the American coast betwixt Cape Ann and Nantucket Island.

Uneasiness pervaded the Virginian when the wind commenced to slacken and the night to turn cold and clear. Worse still, northern lights chose this, of all nights, to present a distressingly brilliant display. The whole northern horizon rippled with red, green and yellow flashes. Lord, it was almost as brilliant as daylight.

Sure enough, when dawn became more than a presentiment above the pale dunes above Province Town, the topmasts of a tall ship could be seen cruising beyond the headland.

"She's a bulldog, sir," Pickering agreed. "Ain't a mite of doubt about it."

What was sly old Jonas Dawes going to do, turn back or match courses? The answer came quickly; the brigantine shortened her canvas, waited for the *Grand Turk* to come up, which suited Rob Ashton fine.

If yonder blockade vessel proved too small her skipper would very likely steer clear of two such obviously handy and well-armed privateers. Ashton rubbed a mittened hand over features growing copper-red in the biting wind. The minute the duty vessel, a light frigate, spied them she hauled her wind and steered to intercept. Those of the crew who were on deck commenced excitedly to speculate among themselves.

"Mr. Savage, pray heave the log," Ashton snapped at the first prize master who appeared, yawning, in a blue and red Dutch blanket coat.

Promptly log, reel and chip were fetched from their locker by the quartermaster. Meanwhile, Mr. Savage, a silent humorless Long Islander of about forty, removed from its casing a handsome Spanish-made hour glass. The quartermaster, his assistant, fitted the log reel into sprockets built into the stern rail, and stood ready.

"Heave!" grunted Savage. Whereupon the quartermaster dropped overboard the chip—a triangle of wood secured by a curious bridle. Immediately the tug of the water snapped taut the log line, created little geysers of spray and set the log reel a-humming.

At the same instant the prize master started his hour glass. Fathom after fathom of the log line, marked at intervals by small white leather counters, called Knots, went hissing over a series of scars left in the stern rail by previous tests.

When the glass had run a full minute Savage barked, "Check!" and the quartermaster sharply applied a brake to the log reel which stopped its revolutions, caused a sudden tension on the line and thus jerked free an ivory peg which, until this moment, held the log chip vertical in the sea. Instantly, the chip commenced to bob free over the water.

"She's doing ten knots, sir," Savage announced. "Mebee a leetle more."

Robert Ashton merely nodded, his attention being directed to his vessel's spars and yards. Braces and canvas looked rigid as iron under the wind's steady pressure. Next his gaze sought the sinister outlines of the British man-of-war. Not until he formed a better estimate of the duty frigate's speed could he judge whether she would be able to intercept.

His heart began to quicken and, as always at such times, a faint tingling manifested itself in his cheeks.

The *Dauntless* now was sailing to starboard almost a-beam and to windward. No doubt that Dawes' vessel was bigger, but the brigantine's armament, he knew, wasn't comparable; only ten guns, miserable little four pounders at that. No wonder Captain Dawes had waited for his better-trained rival to join company.

Um. The enemy, despite a press of canvas, wasn't making good time. Probably her bottom was foul.

"If this breeze don't freshen any further," Ashton muttered, "we'll be safe as in church."

No use taking chances, though.

"Turn out all hands, Mr. Pickering, and have the gun covers cast loose."

Feet, pounding along the deck just above his head, aroused Peter from uneasy slumber. The bunk had proved uncomfortably short for a man of his inches; the accommodations, such as they were, had been designed for average men of about five feet five or six; not of five feet nine.

On deck the wind tore at his fox fur cap, drew copious tears from his eyes. Everyone was peering to starboard, for, above a mile yonder, the blockade ship was bearing down, a bone between her teeth and her white ensign was standing out stiff and rigid. As Doane pointed out, the presence of reefs taken in her courses and topsails suggested that her captain respected this ever-stronger northwest wind.

The *Dauntless* stood nearer the stranger. Presently, Dawes must have reached the same conclusion as the *Grand Turk's* master—that the frigate was a slow sailer, for sail on sail blossomed into existence along the brigantine's yards.

"Damn old Dawes to hell and back," grunted Pickering. "He figgers to run and leave us fending for ourselves."

And there, Peter perceived, lay the inherent weakness of the privateer system in which every man cared only for himself, and let the Devil drown the hindermost.

Quckly, the area of wind-whipped waves separating the two privateers increased.

Captain Ashton's jaw went out. "Mr. Pickering, you may beat to quarters. I hazard our British friend will be more inclined to chase a vessel that won't show fight against one that does."

The marines' drum barely commenced to rattle before the crew, largely veterans, were on their way to battle stations, cursing and driving the green hands before them. At the cost of an occasional wave top sluicing over the deck, the starboard gun ports were triced up and the *Grand Turk's* guns run out. Battle flags were hoisted to the main and fore tops to accompanying cheers.

Ashton, meanwhile, narrowly studied the British man-of-war.

"Shall I prepare to receive wounded?" Peter felt it necessary to inquire, but the Virginian made no reply, only kept a brass, leather-bound spyglass fixed on the enemy, his chunky figure yielding pendulum-like to the motion of the vessel.

The *Dauntless* by now was fairly flying on a northeasterly course, though she must, of necessity, pass closer by the frigate.

"Damn! The Britisher won't square away in pursuit," Mr. Savage growled. "'Pears like our luck's running out."

And so it seemed. The British ship continued on her original effort to intercept both vessels; everyone could see great sheets of spray flying over her bows and her brown and yellow sides glistening with wet.

Quite calmly, Rob Ashton ordered the *Grand Turk* brought five points nearer the wind; if he were forced to beat back into Massachusetts Bay, it wouldn't be too late.

"Fly seven signal flags!"

"Which ones, sir?"

"Makes no odds, only do it quickly."

Then, through his speaking trumpet, he hailed the gunner standing expectantly amidships.

"Have Number One gun fire one round!"

"—But the range, sir?" Pickering protested.

"The range don't matter," Ashton replied equably. "I aim to cozen the Britisher into imagining he's being lured into a deadfall."

A puff of gray-white smoke sprang from the brig's bow, was instantly swept off to leeward. A minute, then another passed, and the line of Ashton's jaw hardened; the frigate seemed determined to continue her course.

"Ah-h—" A sigh of relief arose from the brig's quarterdeck. Perhaps fearful of an agreed plan of battle arranged between the two privateers, the master of the little frigate altered course and trimmed sail in hot pursuit of the *Dauntless.*

Once Rob Ashton became convinced that the frigate

was chasing Dawes in dead earnest, he altered his brig's course across the Britisher's wake. Twenty minutes later pursuer and pursued were hull-down on the horizon and, in half an hour, only the white glimmer of their tops showed above the sea.

Ashton smiled, wrung the wet from a green and brown muffler, and, in high good-humor, clapped Peter on the shoulder.

"At times, suh, you will observe, a bold front serves better than caution. I expect that's true in medicine, too. Will you join me in a mug of hot tea?"

v. The First Prize

THREE DAYS of westerly gales harried the *Grand Turk* far out to sea, flung stinging clouds of snow across her deck, making life a frozen misery for lookouts and helmsmen. However, once the brig traversed the thirty-sixth degree, latitude, the weather grew fairer; seasick men, Peter among them, emerged to revel in the sunlight.

Thus far the brig's surgeon had found little call for his art and therefore he devoted himself to learning, as quickly as possible, pertinent facts concerning the *Grand Turk's* rigging, design and armament. Soon he commenced really to understand the reasons necessitating the intricate routine of life aboard a well-handled man-of-war.

Once his brig was indisputably clear of the blockade, Captain Ashton relaxed his stiff and curt manner—though he never did unbend as he had when ashore—and took to chatting. One fine morning he ordered the *Grand Turk* to cruise under easy canvas and beckoned his surgeon to share his privileged position by the lee rail.

"I'm coming to appreciate what a really lovely vessel you have, sir."

"Aye. That she is, Doctor. She's a love. To sail a moderately well-found ship in peacetime is fine, suh, but come war, the best ain't any too good."

He nodded to the guns constituting his starboard battery. "Now you take those cannons, for instance; they look pretty much like any others, don't they? They ain't, though. Those lilies on their breeches proves they're, every damned one of 'em, French-made of fine bell metal."

''Why bell metal?''

''In a hot engagement guns get heated so a crew either has to cease fire, or cool 'em down with sea water. Plain iron guns will crack and burst if you douse 'em when hot. These guns *won't;* therefore we can maintain our rate of fire whilst the enemy's slackens. Aye, the French cast the best ordnance in all Creation. 'Tis sheer murder to send men to sea with half the guns we are casting in America right now.''

''Of what weight is your broadside?''

''Books on ordnance would classify 'em as minions, or sakers. They're minions if the solid ball they throw weighs between five and six pounds; sakers throw balls of six to eight. These, I bought for sakers.''

Aware that Peter really was interested, not just making conversation, Rob Ashton continued, ''Now a landsman would mention the length of the barrel, but your gunner calls it the chase. These, you can see, have a chase of about seven foot, and will weigh near fourteen hundred pounds a piece—free of carriage.''

Peter next put questions concerning a variety of instruments secured in racks to the bulwarks next to each gun port.

Ashton explained, ''They're the tools with which a piece is charged. You'll note yonder ladles are of copper? That's to prevent iron from striking iron and so causing a spark in the bore which might blow a gunner's hands clean off. Sponges are for swabbing out the bore after each discharge; those augur-like contrivances are called 'worms'; a gunner uses them to withdraw, or replace, wads and charges. See that long rod? That's a rammer, used to drive home wads and to seat cannon balls like those.'' He indicated racks in which rows of dull black spheres clinked gently to the brig's rhythmic heave and roll.

Peter indicated a hole let into the rail beside him; that it was lined with iron piqued his curiosity.

''A swivel mount, that's what it is.''

''What is a swivel, sir?''

''A short, bell-mouthed gun of brass. They are mounted in an iron fork to permit their being swung in all directions; folks ashore often call 'em blunderbusses. They're useful for short-range work such as clearing an enemy's deck, beating off a boat attack or suppressing a mutiny.

There's something mighty convincing about a double handful of musket balls in your face. We mount ten swivels on a side.''

Among other things, Peter learned that the *Grand Turk* was, indeed, French built, that Captain Ashton had bought and fitted her out down in the French Island of Saint Domingue. However, he'd replaced her spars with stout New Hampshire fir; unlike some owners—as greedy as they were unwise—the Virginian replaced any item of the brig's gear upon first indications of wear.

"In peacetimes you wouldn't find half so many men aboard," Ashton remarked, dark brown eyes continuing to sweep the horizon.

"I was wondering on that. Why so big a crew?"

"Should we take prizes I'll have to supply crews to sail 'em home."

Gradually, Peter adapted his life to the routine, proved himself ready to learn; and, recognizing his capabilities, the afterguard lent him every assistance.

Nor did Peter neglect his medicine; hour after hour he studied, queried and made notes. Especially useful in the light of his present assignment was Doctor John Jones' *Practical Remarks on Wounds & Fractures,* a standard book on military medicine. The more he digested the opinions of that eminent Welsh surgeon the more he concurred. Particularly apt was his opening paragraph.

As every Operation is, of necessity, attended with a certain Degree of Bodily Pain, as well as terrible Apprehension to the patient's mind, a good Chirurgeon will be, in the first place, well Assured of the necessity of an Operation before he proceeds to perform it.

How true. Nowadays, most surgeons were all too prone to whack off a limb, given the least provocation; but for such a blunder by Doctor Chase little Susan's arm might still be hers; he was morally certain of that. What a terrible thing had been done to that bright and winning youngster.

Lips compressed, Peter read on.

Secondly, he ought to Consider whether the Patient will, in all probability, be the Better for it or whether he may not be the Worst. In all Operations of Delicacy and Difficulty he

should Act with great Deliberation and never affect great
Expedition by which very capital and even fatal Errors
have been Committed. The maximum of *Festina lenta* is, in
no cases more Applicable, than in these. It is of no small
Importance to Support the patient's Spirits with a Chearful
appearance of Success, and the Appearance of such a Degree of modest Comfort as may serve to Inspire him with
the End but not the Means, to avoid Terrifying him with the
Appearance of the Apparatus or a Vain and Ridiculous parade of any kind.

Peter's gaze swung astern, past seamen holystoning
the deck and working over the gun tackles.

Certainly the handsomest bodied members of the crew
were the Negroes. Years of toil had moulded their back
and shoulders into an anatomical perfection. By comparison white sailors looked shorter but sturdier; their torsos
varied from pale brown to a dead-white. Undoubtedly
some sad cases of sunburn would demand his attention
before long. The Indians were perhaps deceptively frail-
looking, their chests and legs woefully thin by comparison with the others.

Thus far, the *Grand Turk* had proved to be a happy
ship and a healthy one, because Peter had devoted himself to his duties with more than customary earnestness.

The sea these days had assumed tints of a deep, glowing blue across which the privateer sketched a graceful,
lacy wake.

Such a sharp pain went shooting through his crippled
hand that he studied that member, all crisscrossed as it
was by dull red scars. The pang, of course, meant some
severed nerve was trying to heal. Every night since sailing, he had devoted an hour, in his malodorous hutch, to
flexing, patiently bending those stiff fingers, though they
hurt like fury. By now, he no longer deluded himself that
the third and fourth fingers of that hand would ever again
become articulate. Question: Could he train the other
three still obedient digits to perform the work of their
senseless fellows?

Poor Pa! News of his son's disgrace would strike hard
at an old man whose trade was well-nigh ruined. But suppose that the *Grand Turk* took an enemy with a hold full
of hardware and cutlery of that quality which only the
forges of Birmingham and Sheffield seemed able to turn
out? Such a prize sale would put Pa right back on his feet

again. Dan Burnham still had money, though he'd nothing to sell.

Peter quitted the rail to take a short turn amidships, then debated whether he should climb, to join, for a while, the lookout braced inside a hoop secured to the foretop. He could see the seaman, a full-bred Penobscot, standing with stubby brown legs braced inside that hoop which kept him from plunging below. The Indian's head was turning in slow circles so that the wind whipped his long black hair over first one shoulder and then the other.

Sharp against the lighter blue of the sky shone the Indian's blue-and-white striped jersey, and sunlight, reflected from the sea, drew coppery flashes from his face and arms.

The lookout's attention was casual only because the *Grand Turk* was standing southwards and out of the customary trade routes. In these latitudes nobody really expected anything to happen.

Peter had barely put foot to the fore' ratlines when the lookout suddenly sang out, "Sail ho!"

If the ship had struck a reef, more activity could not have ensued.

"Where away?" Pickering's acid voice demanded.

"T'ree point off de starboard bow, sar. Two spars, sar."

"What course does she sail?"

"No can tell yet."

To watch Captain Ashton, his officers and crew under these circumstances was a revelation; there was no excitement which was not sternly subdued, no rushing around. Events followed in an orderly sequence. The solidly built Virginian remained infinitely calm, but alertly so, because he detected any fault or omission. He never raised his voice, nor did he curse.

The almost complete absence of profanity aboard had surprised Peter until he learned that the use of profane language was punishable by stiff fines. Martin Jameson, the captain's clerk, a pallid, red-haired youth with big brown freckles splotching his features and hands, came running on deck and duly noted the name of him who had spied the stranger; George Black Beaver would thereby stand to gain a quarter-share under the Articles of Agreement.

After a bit, Captain Ashton himself ascended the main

shrouds, carrying his spyglass with him; Doane swarmed up to join the lookout in the fore' crosstrees. Though the call to quarters had not been beaten the brig's gun crews formed about their pieces, expectant, and watching their captain focus his heavy glass.

Presently, Captain Ashton closed the cover of his telescope lens, tucked it under one arm and returned on deck. Mr. Doane followed suit.

To Gideon Pickering's unspoken query, the *Grand Turk's* master stated, "She's a brigantine, old-fashioned English or Dutch designed. Been through a storm, too, because she's juried to her fore and mizzen. From the slack way her sails are trimmed, I'll wager she's short-handed to boot.

"Mr. Pickering, beat the men to quarters," Ashton directed. "If she proves a privateer, she'll carry heavier metal than us, for all her sorry state."

Not yet hoisting her huge battle ensigns, the *Grand Turk* stood boldly towards this slovenly, brown-painted brigantine wallowing along to leeward. So far she was showing no colors whatsoever. From her master's failure to make sail it was judged that he was resigned to the hopelessness of his position.

Signal halyards in hand, stood Eldad Greenleaf, the brig's quartermaster. He kept eyes fixed on Ashton's gently swaying blue-and-scarlet-clad figure and his mahogany-hued features screwed themselves into an expectant expression.

Greenleaf, Peter had discovered to be an odd character—always drunk when ashore—though an excellent officer afloat. He was one of the very few men aboard who had gone privateering during the old French war—which had ended so successfully in '63. From the start, Greenleaf had been noticeable because of his huge gold earrings and the fact that he wore his hair clubbed into an old-fashioned pigtail so thickened with tar that it stood out behind, stiff as any club.

Shading his eyes against the glare of the morning sun, Captain Ashton remained clinging to the lee shrouds and evidently estimating his chances. Presently, the Virginian came to a decision.

"Bend on, and hoist, Dutch colors," he instructed Greenleaf.

The deckhands alternately were studying this old-style

vessel and casting curious eyes at their own quarterdeck, while the gun crews stood at stations, ready but not tense. Apparently no one expected a fight, and, indeed, none developed. When the *Grand Turk* bore steadily down until her maximum range of two hundred yards was reached the stranger ran up British colors.

A Britisher! That meant a prize certain-sure. A yell of delight burst from the privateer's men.

Easily as a hare circles a cow, the *Grand Turk* steered boldly across the stranger's bows and could have raked her cruelly. Peter cast Ashton a quick look just as the privateer captain nodded. Mr. Pickering caught up his speaking trumpet.

"Hoist our colors! Up gun ports!" he roared.

Even as the Dutch flag sank, fluttering, to the deck, three huge Stars and Stripes shot skywards, flinging defiance.

Not even a warning gun was required to send the stranger up into the wind, to lie wallowing helplessly and losing steerageway. Peter guessed he'd always remember this bright sunlight, the two vessels lying not over two hundred yards apart in this great and empty dark blue ocean.

Making not a single hostile gesture, the stranger brought his ensign jerkily downwards. Then, and only then, did the *Grand Turk* also come into the wind, taking position slightly ahead of the brown brigantine.

To an accompanying trill of the boatswain's pipe the privateer's long boat went smacking down alongside.

Brown features imperturbable, Ashton beckoned Peter. "Mr. Burnham, prepare to accompany the boarding company. I'm minded that something is confounded wrong aboard yonder vessel; might have plague aboard." This seemed more than likely, ominously few heads were visible along the stranger's rail.

"Aye, aye, sir." After dashing below for his medicine case, Peter none too adroitly followed Mr. Doane into the brig's long boat now bobbing in her lee. Despite everything, no precautions were being spared; a swivel gun was mounted on the long boat's bow and her crew were armed with cutlasses and boarding pistols.

"What ship is that?" Doane yelled through cupped hands, once the long boat had pulled over under the stranger's stern.

"Ship *Hammond*," came an answering hail, "forty-three days out of London for Tortola."

That the *Hammond* had suffered severely from the elements there could be no mistaking. Jagged gaps in her bullwarks had not yet been mended and short jury masts rising to the stumps of her fore and mizzen had been but clumsily rigged.

"Ahoy! Look alive and heave us a line," Doane directed, once the long boat was rowed expertly into the lee of the wallowing brigantine.

"You—you'll not torture us?" cried the spokesman, a fat, stupid-looking fellow wearing three days' beard. "You'll spare our lives?"

"We ain't pirates, damn your ugly eyes," Doane snapped. "Don't ye know an American flag when you see one?"

"Begging your pardon, sir." The officer on the quarter-deck still looked scared half to death. "I ain't never seen such afore, sir."

A line came snaking down to be caught by a seaman poised in the long boat's bow, then a rope ladder was lowered over the *Hammond's* rail, and Doane, still cursing angrily, went scrambling up it. Yes, the *Hammond* was indeed ancient; foul, too, with sea wrack; long green streamers of weed rippled all along her water line. A round dozen of the *Grand Turk's* men went swarming up the side.

"Now, Mr. Sawbones, up with you!" Peter clutched the wildly swaying ladder and, hampered by his crippled hand, struggled upwards.

At a glance he could tell that the crew of this prize was expecting the worst. Sullen and empty-handed, they stood awaiting their fate at the foot of the foremast—there weren't more than twelve or fifteen of them. No wonder the old hooker had made no effort in self-defense—her battery consisted of but six pitifully small cannon, three pounders.

Plump shoulders tight under the fabric of his blue uniform, Doane went clumping up the high, old-fashioned quarterdeck where stood the officer who had answered Doane's hail.

"I—I crave your mercy, kind sir," babbled the Englishman, hands a-flutter. Peter noted that this unkempt fellow's eyes were ringed with sleeplessness, that his fingers trembled. "There's a parcel o' women and babies below. You—you'll not allow your men to maltreat 'em?"

"What do you take us for?" Doane snapped. "Now then, my lad, are you captain of this relic?"

"Oh, no sir, he's dead, washed overboard along with our first officer in a terrible tempest which dismasted us come a fortnight tomorrow."

"Who in hell are you?" Doane was still angry over the fellow's cowardice.

"I'm Brandon, sir, second mate."

"Huh! Mr. Brandon, you can trot out your manifest, and no nonsense. Doctor Burnham, have the kindness to learn whether there is sickness aboard. Damned few cargoes are worth chancing sickness aboard the brig."

Accompanied by a brace of the *Grand Turk's* men, Peter followed an aged Irishman down into the main hold. There, he was informed, were quartered a party of women and children on their way out to Antigua, Tortola and adjacent islands.

"Spare us!" "For the love of God, spare our lives!" "Have mercy, kind sirs!" "Don't kill us!" Frightened cries reverberated from an area subdividing the passengers from the cargo. Some ten women, and nearly twice as many children of all ages, clinging together and holding out hands clasped in piteous supplication, were collected in a group. Most of the children wept in an access of terror, but a few were attempting to conceal themselves among the cargo and baggage. A few of the younger women were kneeling, clutching Bibles to their breasts and moaning pleas for mercy.

One figure dominated the entire scene; that of a tall young woman who, alone, stood bolt upright.

"Be quiet! No harm will be done you," Peter called as he strode forward, the two seamen at his heels. "Now, Madame—"

"Stop where you are!" The central figure cried sharply and the muzzle of a small pocket pistol was swung steadily in line with Peter's chest. "Halt, or I fire!"

It was not fear of the girl's pistol that checked Peter's progress, but her extraordinary beauty. Even in this dim place her hair shone bright as a halo. Paler in hue than any tresses he had ever beheld, her hair had been clubbed hastily, but effectively, between her shoulders and secured with a length of blue ribbon. Standing there in her gown of canary silk, this tall girl suggested a bright bird imprisoned in a gloomy cage.

"What shall I do, sir?" demanded a seaman at Peter's elbow.

"Nothing." For an instant longer the young doctor continued to stare on the amazing loveliness of this figure so fearlessly confronting him.

"You will go back, sir," the young woman instructed him in clear English which, nonetheless, betrayed a trace of foreign accent, "at once."

"That I cannot do. I am a physician, here to conduct an examination," Peter informed her evenly. At the same time he became, indefinably, aware of standing face to face with one who would loom large in his life.

"No. You are all pirates! Go at once," she insisted. "I mean to shoot."

A slow smile curved Peter's lips as he resumed his advance. "You cannot fire your pistol; its flint is too loose. See for yourself."

In the instant that her eyes wavered, Peter sprang forward, seized the weapon and forced its muzzle upwards. She squeezed the trigger all right, but when its hammer fell, his hand had intercepted its course to the frizzen.

"Lord help us!" The women screamed their despair while the children squalled like so many scalded kittens.

To Peter's surprise this lithe young woman grappled and set him reeling to one side. Never had he suspected to find such strength in a female. He recovered himself, passed the pistol to one of his companions; then, as the young woman, her pale hair streaming, gathered for another assault, he smiled, made her a leg.

"Really, Ma'am, you have nothing to fear. We are in truth no pirates, but privateersmen obedient to the laws of war."

"Bah!" her bosom lifted convulsively. "Between a pirate and a Yankee privateer there is not even a small difference."

"Your pardon, ma'am. I fear you have read too many lying English gazettes. Look." He pulled out his medicine case. "I am in truth a physician."

"These are lies!" The young woman's eyes of blue-green hardened. "You—you can kill me, but shall not force me."

"Oh, stop playing the fool, I tell you I'm Peter Burnham, surgeon aboard the private armed brig out yonder." Peter sucked at a cut the flint had dealt his right hand. "And who, Ma'am are you, may I inquire?"

The lovely, silver-blue head rose proudly. "I am the Baroness Katrina Varsaa, lady-in-waiting at the Court of Köbenhavn."

"Your servant, Ma'am."

Gradually, the Baroness Varsaa's taut attitude relaxed; lips, etched like symmetric crimson scars across the pallor of her features, formed an uncertain smile. "You are indeed a doctor? Good. Here, there is much need of your art."

VI. BARONESS VARSAA

ONCE PETER BURNHAM could vouch that no pox, cholera, or any other plague was aboard the *Hammond*, a signal was made to that effect; good news promptly acknowledged by the brig. Now captor and prize were cruising under light canvas separated by less than a quarter of a mile of water. Presently, the captain's gig was lowered, came pulling over to the old brigantine.

There could be no doubt that she constituted a true prize; both owners and registry were British. Had not the *Hammond's* company included so many women and children, Captain Ashton probably would have removed her cargo and scuttled this weary old hooker. Leaking badly, a fact attested by the continual suck and creak of her pumps and otherwise ill-found, she'd not fetch much of a price at a prize sale.

"'Tiz a pity to waste a prize master on a tub like this," the Virginian observed, "but her cargo's confounded bulky—and it'd never do to cruise with all those females aboard the *Grand Turk*. There'd be knifings in no time." Again, though he didn't mention it, women weren't considered lucky aboard ship—almost as unchancy as ministers and rabbits.

"Right you are, sir," Mr. Doane nodded owlishly. "When women come aboard, harmony takes to the maintop, and that's a fact."

"Well, I reckon she's just about worth taking over and sending her in."

"Where, sir?"

"Have to think on that," Ashton said.

One of the privateersmen having bent an American ensign to the signal yard and hoisted it above the *Hammond's* faded British ensign, a cheer came ringing over from the *Grand Turk*. In this bright sunlight the privateer looked trim and graceful as a print fresh from an engraver's shop.

Eventually, Ashton decided to send aboard his quartermaster's mate for prize master, along with five able seamen; they should be sufficient to fetch the vessel into a friendly port.

"She'll never reach Boston nor Charles Town this time of year—and in this state," Ashton was thinking. "She's so damned slow she'd never slip through old Arbuthnot's blockade. The French Islands? Maybe."

Ashton had remained undecided when, up from below, appeared the straight-backed figure of Baroness Varsaa, and unbidden, stalked in regal composure up to the table over which the *Grand Turk's* officers sat scanning the *Hammond's* invoices and bills of lading. She wore a pert straw bonnet secured by long blue ribbons below her chin and carried a bulging pocket.

"I will go at once aboard your ship," she informed Captain Ashton, quite serenely. "This dreadful vessel is all smells and sails so very slow. Send one of your men to bring my trunk from below."

The Virginian arose, bowed, then reseated himself, his gold epaulettes a-twinkle. "I vow 'twould be a rare pleasure to indulge you, Ma'am—"

"—Get to your feet." The young woman's bright blue eyes flashed in the shade of her wide-brimmed bonnet. "I am not accustomed to being addressed by a seated man." Her trace of foreign accent became more marked in her excitement.

In perfect good nature Rob Ashton smiled, but remained seated. Said he mildly, "This ain't a royal levee, Ma'am, nor do you, or anyone else, give orders aboard a prize of mine." He was at pains to be patient in amplifying his position. "Account of this is wartime and we're likely to be in action time and again, I can't have you aboard my brig. You are going to stay aboard this vessel."

The baroness stamped a slim, well-slippered foot. "I

will not stay! I detest this stinking old tub of a ship and those dreadful common women below." The tall young woman's manner then underwent a change; she spoke very sweetly now, hands in their black lace mitts gently kneading at her pocket. "Besides, I am a neutral and no ordinary person. My father is chamberlain to His Majesty Christian VII, King of Denmark and Norway."

"Is this true?" Ashton demanded of the *Hammond's* anxious and thoroughly discouraged second officer.

Before that beefy individual could make reply, the girl in blue and yellow swung her pocket across Ashton's face. "Boor! Savage! How dare you question the word of a Varsaa? Why I'll—I'll—"

The Virginian arose and, rubbing his cheek, promised in a flat even voice, "Any similar nonsense, Mistress, and I'll surely turn you over my knee and spank you right in front of everybody. Now you can clear out. You've wasted too much of my time as it is. Benson!" He beckoned his quartermaster's-mate. "Escort this lady to her cabin and return immediately."

"Oh-h. I am most regretful." The Baroness Varsaa concealed her face behind slim, very white fingers and commenced to weep. "How am I ever going to arrive at Annaberg?"

"Who the hell might be Anna Berg?" Doane grinned. "Mebbe yer granny, eh Sissy?"

"Imbecile! Pig of an American! It is a place on the Island of Saint Jan."

"Oh, thanks. Never was much good at jography," Doane grinned, stood ready to evade a further swing of the Danish girl's pocket, but, her whitish blue blonde hair shimmering, she turned to Peter; he was engaged in dressing the ulcerated hand of a prisoner.

"*Monsieur,* you have some pretensions of gentility. I appeal to you." Her teeth glimmered white in a really dazzling smile. "Will you not intercede for me?"

Peter smiled over his shoulder. "I'm only the ship's doctor; my say on such matters don't amount to a hill of beans."

"But I must get to Annaberg—*soon.* Can you not understand?" She seemed on the verge of desperation.

Peter's gaze wandered from her ringless hands to her breast, to her waist, and then up to the exquisite pink and white oval of her face. She deduced his train of thought and flushed.

"Please come aside just for a little. I—I have to talk with you, *Herr Doktor.*"

"You still have time and to spare," were his first words.

"Oh, but it is not that. I am—I am to be wedded—my marriage must not be delayed."

Peter wanted to comment, "Obviously," but didn't.

"Where is Annaberg?"

"As I have said, on our island of Saint Jan in the Danish West Indies."

"Is it far?"

"Not very, Mr. Brandon says."

Peter looked at her narrowly. "That'll be a neutral port, isn't it?"

"We are not at war, sir," she replied, obviously puzzled by his ignorance.

Peter went up to Captain Ashton on the quarterdeck.

"You said, sir, this vessel ain't fit to make the run for America?"

"I did. What of that?"

"So she'll have to try for a Frnech, or a neutral port? Then, sir," Peter suggested evenly, "is there any good reason why this vessel can't be sent into the Danish Islands? They're fairly near to hand and, being neutral, won't be patrolled by the Lobsterbacks."

The privateer captain frowned, sucked his lower lip between his teeth a moment, then shrugged. "That's not a bad idea, Doctor. Fact, 'tis a very sound suggestion, suh. Aye. We can touch there and pick up our prize crew on the way home."

Peter hesitated, then demanded boldly, "Can the lady be dropped at Saint Jan? She was distraught just now, and is most contrite."

"She's a pretty piece," the Virginian remarked. "Well, if Benson runs no risk at it, I suppose he may."

Captain Ashton and Doane returned to their work of checking off the prize's manifest; of minor importance it soon appeared. Her cargo of Osnaburgs, Holland cloth, Irish linen and duck cloth wouldn't bring any princely sum—even in a neutral port.

The baroness was radiant over his success. "Oh, bless

you! *Herr Doktor*, may the good God reward you. Now, I shall not have to lose time changing ships at Tortola and so shall gain two full weeks.'' She beamed on the privateer officers and suddenly clapped her hands, called in Danish, ''Magda! Where are you? Magda! Fetch my wine case.''

A frightened, flat-faced woman who had been hesitating at the entrance to the companionway, curtseyed and presently was back carrying by curious bronze handles a square case of jade-green Russian leather. In rising curiosity, Peter noted a most elegant crest stamped not only on the leather covering of the little chest, but worked into the lid of richly inlaid satin wood.

Crimanently! So this tall girl was of the Danish nobility? He felt a little excited; never had met anyone bearing a title before.

From her petticoat pocket the baroness produced a tiny bronze key with which she unlocked the chest; as its lid was raised some clever interior mechanism simultaneously elevated a tray. Upon it, and held in place by frames of gilt metal, stood four dainty decanters and easily a dozen tiny glasses, all etched with the same crest.

''Say now, ain't that a mighty pretty thing?''

Abel Doane came clumping below on some errand, paused and stared. ''What kin you do with glasses that size? Rinse yer eyeballs? Say, guess mebbe the Captain'd admire to see that.''

''Indeed? We shall see.'' The baroness nodded, and followed by her servant, sought the quarterdeck. ''Sir, I wish to express my thanks. I have here some cordials,'' she explained in her slightly accented English. ''Some excellent cognac, some very old aquavit. However,'' she smiled pleasantly on Rob Ashton sitting very solid and resplendent in his blue uniform, ''you may prefer some of this rum; it was made on the estate of Stephan Frydendahl, my future husband. It has been twice-distilled and is over fifty years old.''

''Thank you, Mistress,'' Ashton nodded, but returned his attention to the pile of papers before him; clearly, he was impatient to conclude this business and to get under way.

''And you, *Herr Doktor*, what do you prefer?''

''Whatever you drink?''

''The cognac, I prefer,'' she said. ''Magda, pour two

of the cognac and one of the rum. One suspects yonder gentleman finds these glasses not to his liking." She stared hard at Doane.

Doane laughed good-naturedly and winked. "Right you are, Pretty Sissy. That much liquor'd not even tickle my little toe."

"To His Royal Majesty, the King," Baroness Varsaa cried in a clear rich tone. "May the Regency end soon!"

Gravely, Peter raised his glass in a second toast. "To his Excellency, General Washington."

"Washington? Washington?" The Baroness raised slim brows. "Oh yes, he is the rebel leader, but I will drink his health!"

Presently, Trina Varsaa turned aside, embarrassment in her manner. "*Herr Doktor,* what must I do? Sometimes my ankles swell and hurt. Is that because of—?"

They were standing beside the weather rail watching a long boat shove off from the *Grand Turk.* It had the prize crew and their sea chests aboard.

"Yes. When possible eat fresh fruit."

The very depths of sea-blue eyes were visible in her troubled look. "You are most kind. You will not tell the others of what you know?"

"No. The matter is your concern, not theirs."

Her hand went out, rested on his. "*Herr Doktor,* what is your name? Always I shall want to remember it. Most grateful I am for what you have accomplished for the Varsaas."

He gave her his name. Her eyes commenced to fill again.

"But you are so good, so *sympatico;* you understand, I think, how terrible it is to be in love with one man and yet be forced—" She turned her gleaming head sharply aside. "I know I shall hate such a miserable little island as Saint Jan." Her clear eyes filled. "God have mercy on me, I do not know this man I am to marry. I have seen not even his miniature."

Peter felt a deep compassion he could no way express. "Perhaps he may not turn out to be—be, well as unkind as you fear."

The Baroness Varsaa straightened her shoulders in a forlorn sort of courage. "How could Stephan Frydendahl be anything save an ignorant brute of a planter? He has not visited Denmark since he was a boy. Ah, to think that

København I will never again see. My friends, the life I knew and loved, and my family.''

This time she bent her head and really sobbed. She was the only woman Peter ever had beheld weeping who could also remain beautiful.

Peter beckoned the peasant woman. ''You'd best conduct your mistress below.''

''Magda speaks no English,'' explained the baroness through her tears, ''but I will do as you say. Now I am no longer afraid.'' She offered both hands. ''Perhaps when your brig comes to Saint Jan to pick up the prize crew you will call? My name then will be—''

''Frydendahl. I will never forget it—or you,'' Peter declared. Of that he was quite convinced.

VII. FORTUNES OF WAR

ALMOST AS QUICKLY as the *Hammond's* tops had disappeared below a sapphire horizon, the routine of life aboard the *Grand Turk* reasserted itself. In the cool of the morning gun drills were held, for all that the crew grumbled and cursed at the seeming stupidity of such fruitless exercises. As a non-participant, Peter Burnham quite easily could perceive the ever-increasing speed and smoothness of these preparations for going into action.

Whereas to begin with, near half an hour had been required to put the brig in fighting trim, now this complicated procedure could be accomplished in half that time.

The men had nearly mutinied when, on two successive nights, Ashton, inflexible and unsmiling, had ordered ''clear for action.'' Only the Virginian's reputation for success persuaded his crew to obedience. Typical of Captain Ashton's philosophy, much expensive powder was burned at target practice every other day. On such occasions a pair of water puncheons were dropped over side; first the starboard guns and then the larboard battery were given opportunity to fire.

To Peter it remained a never-ending surprise that the kindly, genial, and sensitive *pater familias* he had met in Boston could become so completely transformed into a brusque and hard-eyed sea captain.

For instance, the *Grand Turk's* master hadn't blinked

an instant at condemning to death an Indian who, in a quarrel over cards—gaming was strictly forbidden by the Articles—had stabbed a Negro shipmate. He had ordered the *Grand Turk* brought into the wind just long enough to permit the stoically silent murderer, lashed firmly to the body of his victim, to be dropped overside. Those along the rail could see two dark figures, the one rigid, the other futilely struggling, scale downwards, further and further into the deep blue depths, their erratic course marked by a diminishing comet's trail of bubbles.

No sooner had this execution taken place than, in icy tones, Rob Ashton ordered the *Grand Turk* put back on her course towards that point where the sixty-eighth degree, longitude, crossed the twenty-fourth degree, latitude. 'Twas through this area that a bulk of commerce originating in Cuba, Panama, Jamaica and Spanish Central American colonies, went funnelling out through the Windward and Mona Channels towards the ports of Europe.

The further the brig footed southwards through ever greener water where great yellow Sargasso weed created huge freckles on the surface of the sea, the deeper she entered upon dangerous waters; accordingly, lookouts were doubled and the discipline tightened.

Flying fish were noticed just three weeks to the day after the brig had cleared Cape Cod. To Peter they constituted a wonder of speed, grace and fragility.

The nights now had become marvels of beauty such as Peter had never suspected to exist. Instead of black, the heavens, even at midnight, shone a dark, but vital, purple; and ever so many more stars of new and unfamiliar constellations went parading above the brig's topmasts— far more than one ever saw in New England.

At night Peter suffered his greatest unrest. Though it was not in any way reasonable or sensible, visions of Katrina Varsaa haunted his imagination at the most unlikely moments. Sometimes he beheld the pallid perfection of her features in the depths of the sea; sometimes an impression of her vivid lips obscured the pages of Giovanni Morgagni's interminable *De Sedibus et Causis Morborum*. Again her tall and graceful likeness hovered, wraith-like, beyond the *Grand Turk's* slender bowsprit.

There was no explaining this emotion. Why, he hadn't

been in her presence above two hours. Yet the Danish
girl's every gesture, details of her figure and face remained as vivid as if he had known her a lifetime. Odd,
he could even recall the effect of that faint pigmentation
in her pale and translucent skin which had warned him
that, come another five months, she would give birth to a
child.

Often, while lying hot and uncomfortable on his narrow bunk, Peter attempted to imagine those circumstances which had sent young Baroness Varsaa, sorrow-
fully and lonely, into exile and what appeared to be a
loveless marriage with a man named Frydendahl.

Contrary to his expectations, he found, as the days
sped by, that her memory recurred with increasing, instead of diminishing, frequency. What kind of husband
would she find awaiting at Annaberg? At best a broad-
shouldered young Dane seeking to build a fortune; perhaps he'd be the younger son of some impoverished noble. Or would he prove to be a gross, elderly fellow
stepped with rum and brutalized by those vices peculiar
to the Indies? The Danes, Pickering and the rest claimed,
were very like the Dutch and severer on their slaves than
either the Spanish or Portuguese. Could this be true?

Listening, one smothering-hot night to the monotonous
creak-creaking of the *Grand Turk's* fabric, he found himself conjecturing on how Trina Varsaa would react to
such a primitive existence. Proud, sensitive, and none
too robust, she was going to have a hard time with that
first child. Despite the voluminous petticoats she had
worn, he could tell that her pelvic area looked narrow,
dangerously so.

Damnation! There probably would be no physician
worthy of the name on an island so unimportant that it remained unnamed on half the charts in Captain Ashton's
locker. Staring up into the blackness, listening to the
whine of yards being braced about and to the vicious
squeals of battling rats, he felt immeasurably depressed.

Although gradually he had accustomed himself to the
gloom and to bilge odors, he found in the increasing heat
no end of discomfort; for one thing, it seemed to encourage that dull throbbing in his left hand.

Trina. Trina Varsaa. He would find her. He *must* find
her. There could be no doubt that he had fallen in love,

earnestly and probably hopelessly. The etched brilliance of her lips continued to curve and uncurve tantalizingly before his mind's eye.

The *Grand Turk*'s surgeon had not long enjoyed sleep before her boatswain's whistle shrilled insistently. The first light of dawn was revealing topsails on the horizon. Barefooted, both watches were sent tumbling aloft and out along the yards. Then the privateer cracked on sail on sail with such speed that, as the sun came slipping redly above the sea, she had brought under her guns a trig schooner of perhaps a hundred tons burthen.

Although new, the *Soldier's Endeavour* was not fast; the shipwrights of Bangor had constructed her along traditional British lines, sacrificing speed for more ample hold room. Mightily, the privateer's crew rejoiced. The prize proved to be a military supply ship, deep in the water with stores which now would never reach His Britannic Majesty's garrisons in Jamaica.

Gallantly, if unwisely, the schooner had fired a couple of guns and so earned a broadside from the *Grand Turk* which sent her foretop crashing overboard.

A rich prize this, Ashton smiled, one which should prove very welcome among supply officers of those threadbare regiments defending Charles Town against Lord Cornwallis' well-drilled regiments. All stores Ashton left as they were, but ordered two chests of military specie sent aboard his brig. Huzzas arose when the privateer captain, always understanding of human nature, had opened the treasure chests that one and all might feast their eyes and hopes on rich, red-gold coins, all new-minted and stamped with the well-hated effigy of ''German George,'' by the Grace of God, King of England, Ireland, Scotland, and France.

The schooner's crew were also brought aboard—with the exception of six black Galway Irishmen who proved quite ready to turn their coats against whatever wind that blew.

With a crew of four, Captain Ashton sent Quistion Savage aboard as prize master over the *Soldier's Endeavour* and gave orders to sail this prize into Boston, or New London, which ever seemed to offer the greater chance of success.

On the *Grand Turk*'s forecastle and quarterdeck broad smiles showed that day; everybody aboard already was counting this cruise to be another lucky one.

That night a Portuguese mandoline tinkled on the forecastle and the ship's boys—except Larry—blushed and laughed unhappily at lurid chanteys such as:

> "Once I had a Nigger girl and she was fat and lazy
> Then I had a Spanish girl, she nearly druv me crazy
> 'Way, Haul A-way, We'll haul away the bowlin—"

Then the men sang "Nancy Dawson" and other ditties popular among the stews and taverns of a hundred waterfronts.

These were moments when the Negro members of the crew came into their own. Often, by tacit understanding, other singers fell silent to listen to these big black boys raise liquid mellow voices to the stars or chant mightily over this great empty ocean.

Three days later they fell in with the brigantine *Hope*, a Maryland vessel prized by the *Hussar*, privateer out of Liverpool. Again this proved a lucky capture, in that she retained aboard her original crew, and so no member of the *Grand Turk*'s company was required to man her. All the same her sale would bring full shares to the *Grand Turk*'s crew. Five members of the British prize crew were added to prisoners populating the brig's forehold.

With each passing day—it was not late February—the weather grew increasingly warm and the seawrack thicker. Just across the twenty-first degree parallel of latitude, the privateer's lookouts sighted and, at the conclusion of a mighty brisk two days' chase, overhauled the *Jolly Tar*, a big privateer captained by one James Hannah.

She mounted twelve guns and wanted to fight, but her ordnance must have been extra cheap and imperfect, for during her second broadside, the Number Five gun blew up and made mincemeat not only of its own crew, but of those of the adjoining cannons. The resultant carnage cost Peter Burnham two sleepless days and nights, and opportunity further to test the usefulness of Doctor Jones' *Treatise on Wounds and Fractures*.

The *Jolly Tar*, the victors learned, was sailing a course for New York and charged with a very rich cargo of Spanish and Oporto wines, some medicines and, most valuable of all, surgical instruments and many cases of fine Birmingham cutlery.

So big a ship—she was all of two hundred and fifty tons—justified an experienced prize master and a crew to match. Unfortunately, the *Jolly Tar's* company consisted solely of stubborn, and dangerously resentful, Englishmen; never a foreigner or an Irishman was found aboard. Accordingly, Rob Ashton detailed no less than eighteen of the *Grand Turk's* crew to bring this, the richest prize to date, into a friendly port. The *Jolly Tar's* fifty-man crew were secured below the forehold hatch gratings only at pike points.

Although Rob Ashton hated to part with his jovial second officer, he put Abel Doane in command of the captured privateer. For all his easy-going ways, Doane was a clever seaman; if anybody could fetch this prize into port it would be he. The detaching of an officer and four men to each of the *Hammond* and the *Soldier's Endeavour* had somewhat diminished the *Grand Turk's* company, but the departure of eighteen more meant a reduction evident in more ways than one; the watches commenced to grumble at extra work.

After the *Jolly Tar* had swung her bowsprit northnortheast and disappeared, only Ashton, Gideon Pickering and Peter Burnham gathered at the captain's table. In a brig of this size there was no wardroom.

Peter was dining on a kid-full of salt pork and beans when Ashton, in one of his more approachable moods, observed, "You put me in mind of a cat that's been at the skimming dishes, Doctor."

"I was but dwelling on the fact that you're an uncommon lucky skipper, sir."

"You think it's all luck?"

"Lord, no. You've discipline and you take no foolish risks. But none can blink the fact that the *Grand Turk's* taken four prizes and shows not so much as a musket ball in her rail in payment for them."

"Aye." Ashton's eyes twinkled. "I have been chancy. Give me two more prizes this cruise and, well, I reckon I'll sail for home and hang up my spyglass." He swallowed a gulp of fine tea, fresh out of the *Jolly Tar*.

"Hang up your spyglass?" snorted Pickering. "Stuff and nonsense, sir. Yer the luckiest skipper afloat."

VIII. REVERIE

THE WIND having quite died out at sundown, the *Hammond* brigantine lay aimlessly rattling her standing rigging under the impulse of an endless series of glass-smooth swells. Once her steerageway was lost, the ancient vessel fell into the trough of the seas and commenced a monotonous rolling which, in short order, rendered seasick nearly all the women and children on board. To make matters worse, a humid, near-to-suffocating heat closed in.

Baroness Varsaa decided no longer to respect the prize master's order that, after dark, all save his prize crew and two of the Irishmen must remain below decks. Not very many arch glances were required to persuade Quartermaster's-mate Benson to relax his injunction.

"Well, then, ye may come on deck after dark, Ma'am, and ye'll find a bench waiting nigh the main shrouds."

Trina thanked the prize master and heaved a vast sigh of relief. Of course, Magda *would* fall seasick again, leaving her no choice but to comb out her own hair. Stroke. Stroke. Why did the servant class invariably surrender so readily to assaults by the elements—and get drunk so easily?

Poor, stupid, devoted Magda, Trina reflected, must be yearning for Papa's trim little estate at Hornbaeck on the west coast of Sjaelland Island. Like herself, the wretched girl would likely give her all for a view of red-sailed fishing smacks working the shallow waters of Öre Sound, or of trading vessels on their way to Sweden, scarcely five miles distant.

Trina was deciding that she never fell seasick because, for generations unnumbered, the Varsaas had followed the sea. Papa, in his early days, had risen to Vice-Admiral of the Royal Navy, and at this very moment Brother Antoine commanded a stumpy little corvette. She needed no spyglass to help her distinguish a bugalet from one of those clumsy howkers which came plowing northwards from the Netherlands. Ketches in their various forms were commonplace, as were Norwegian cats, recognizable by stumpy masts and huge, high bows. Once or twice she recalled sighting a patache, far from its native Mediterranean waters.

Stroke. Stroke. Repeatedly Trina's comb slipped through the gossamer-like texture of her hair; the soft rushing sound it made went far towards soothing an inward turmoil. *Dieu!* How very lifeless was the atmosphere becoming. She blessed this friendly dark which permitted her to loosen her bodice strings; latterly, she had kept them laced much too tight in an effort to preserve a secret which, so far, only that Yankee physician had penetrated.

Trina's hand carried the comb into her lap. Delighted at the freshness of the air pouring over the full globes of her bared breasts, she watched the stars a while. *Herr Doktor* Peter Burnham indeed had presented a handsome figure. Clearly she recalled the way his red hair gleamed, bright as a burnished copper plate left out in the sun. Why had he rearoused emotions she had hoped would lie forever dead?

Far above her head, the sails slatted so uselessly against the spars and stays that a fierce impatience gripped her. God alone knew what awaited her at Annaberg.

Of His Danish Majesty's Indies horrific tales were current. Every child at home knew of a slave insurrection on this same Saint Jan's Island. Back in '33 the blacks had revolted and, during a three-day reign of terror, had massacred seventy-six of the hundred and ten white residents inhabiting that island.

An officer of the Royal West India Company had described it all to Papa one night over pipes and many glasses of fiery schnapps. The colonial was drunk enough to omit none of the ghastly details of tortures inflicted, first on the whites, then on the re-enslaved blacks.

The Lesser Antilles, Kapitan Tornquist declared with conviction, were a sink of bestial cruelty, a hell of blasting heat, and a gehenna of soul-crushing boredom. A few planters made a prodigious profit out of the sugar cane their windmills ground and the rum distilled by their cauldrons, but the rest of the colonials worked—and drank—themselves into early graves.

Trina Varsaa became aware that, for all her déshabille and the night air, she was perspiring heavily. Her fine pale hair began sticking about her forehead and to her neck. If it was like this at night on Saint Jan, she knew she couldn't stand it long.

After loosely securing her bodice strings Trina crossed the deck and seated herself on one of the futile little cannon with which the *Hammond* pretended to defend herself. An American privateersman on duty at the break of the quarterdeck saw her and signalled an obscene invitation. She turned her back and felt so low in her spirits that, when he moved away, she produced from her petticoat pocket a small flask of very fine cognac and, half defiantly, took a swallow. The liquor was so warm it set her to coughing.

"A fine thing, Katrina Varsaa, you have become," she thought, "and with what a lovely future!" Banished, an exile. Why? Her disgrace, with its tragic shattering of Count Varsaa's hopes for a brilliant marriage, had not been suffered for the sake of love. Nor for intrigue, although there was plenty of that about; nor yet disloyalty. No. She had only Prince Karl to thank for this disaster— and what could Papa accomplish against a prince of the Royal House?

A powerful, red-faced brute was Prince Karl. For a long time she'd known he had his eye on her, but, from the first time, as a frightened girl of twenty, she had beheld His Royal Highness' pale little blue pig's eyes, bottle-veined nose and dreadfully pock-marked face, she had conceived for him more than a sharp dislike. Everyone despised Prince Karl for a disgraceful drunkard and there was not a brothel near the capital or over in Stockholm which did not enjoy his lavish patronage. A brawler and an insensate gambler, Karl must long since have sunk into a dishonored grave save that his dim-witted brother, Christian VII, was King of Denmark, Norway, Greenland, Iceland, and the Faroes. Alas, that her duties as lady-in-waiting to the Queen-Regent had brought him much into contact with her.

Trina drew a slow breath, listened to the bickering of some crew members at dice on the forecastle; their incredibly foul curses rang loud beneath the idle, slatting canvas. Utterly alone and forlorn, she bent her head in the crook of her arm and wept bitterly, but silently.

Wearily, Trina's mind tramped back over that oft-travelled path to the moment of her downfall. Ever so clearly she could revisualize the candlelit card room of the palace; the brilliant velvets, satins, silks and brocades; the odors of beeswax, pomatum and French scent

strong because of huge fires kindled against the bite of a
November gale screaming about the battlements of
Kronberg Castle.

There she was, herself, gay as never before and so
lovely in a new ball gown of celestial blue that all the gentlemen had stared, forgetting, for the moment, to make
their court bows. For such a state occasion as the King's
birthday ball she had worn her necklace of tiny pearls
and Aunt Klara had lent some magnificent sapphire ear
bobs.

What had rendered her especially radiant was the re-
ceipt of glorious news. Mathias was returning home from
duty in Iceland! To think that, in a few days, big bold Major Baron Mathias Lynge would take her in his arms and
crush her into blissful breathlessness.

Perhaps anticipation of this reunion had caused her not
to count the glasses of cool champagne she accepted.
Still, the Varsaas of both sexes were renowned for their
capacity in the matter of drink.

The more she thought on the subject the more likely it
appeared that Prince Karl must have added a liberal measure of brandy to that champagne bubbling in the heavy
silver goblet he'd fetched while she stood watching some
scarlet-coated Royal Guard officers playing the English
game of Hazard.

Yes, she must have been a bit tiddily; otherwise His
Majesty's brother would not, for once, have appeared
uncommonly attractive when, a moment later, he muttered, "This afternoon a ship made port from our West
Indies. Her captain brought one lovely bird, all bright
blue, green and gold. *Gott!* It is nearly as beautiful as
you."

"You flatter me, Your Highness."

"Come and view the bird; no one else has seen it, or
will. It shall be yours."

Like a silly idiot she had followed her Prince down the
long, draughty corridor leading to a small and sel-
dom-used music room. Sure enough, there was such a
bird, an adorable, dainty little thing. When she whistled
to it the finch cocked a glistening black eye.

She was turning to admire it when, in an avalanche of
lust, Prince Karl flung himself upon her, thrusting her,
terrified and furious, backwards onto a French settee.
When she attempted to scream, his hand, moist and reek-

ing of tobacco, clamped down over her mouth, half smothering her.

On one thing she could look back with satisfaction; she had struggled a long time, and had drawn great bloody scratches across the roughness of his cheeks. At length she lay, pinned beneath Karl's tremendous weight, her garments in wild disorder. Just then the door banged open and there, her heavily powdered face a quivering mask of outrage, stood Her Majesty Julianne-Marie, the Dowager-Queen.

Even now, aboard this miserable vessel Trina couldn't bear to remember the vile terms laid upon her by this royal termagant; she had used language such as charwomen shrill at each other in rage.

In the pink-gray of the following dawn a coach, its windows heavily curtained conveyed her back to Count Varsaa's crumbling castle at Hornbaeck and to the frightened stares of her mother. Count Olav Varsaa, impoverished and sensing the utter ruin of high hopes built upon her future, had turned a lean back, pushed her aside, and had refused to listen to a word. Poor Mamma, browbeaten, and timid as a mouse, had listened and understood. What mostly concerned her was that no tangible consequences of the rape should ensue.

Mamma's prayers had been to no avail; by January it had become certain that Karl's seed had taken root.

Listening now to the dull *slap-slap* of tired-sounding waves, Trina recalled Mathias' frenzied letters—smuggled in by the loyal Magda. There was nothing to be done. Papa, a veteran campaigner, knew how to keep guard.

Then, late in January, a grim court courier had ridden up to the trim little estate on Öre Sound. It was His Majesty's pleasure that Katrina Varsaa repair immediately aboard a ship destined for the Royal Colonies in the Danish West Indies; there she would remain indefinitely.

Only in mounting irritation did Trina endure the heavy rolling of the ship. Prize master Benson now appeared on deck with his shirt open all the way down to his belt. He went forward to inspect a guard posted on the forecastle. The prize master, she'd noticed, was taking no chances, despite the professed disloyalty of the eight Irishmen. Among Captain Ashton's parting injunctions was a reminder that the King's ministers were offering sizeable rewards to seamen who, pretending to desert, should re-take from the Americans a captured vessel.

Like rain drumming fitfully on a thin roof, reef points on the topsails rattled against the idle canvas.

Trina Varsaa shifted her position to a seat on a folded sail; then under cover of darkness pulled up her skirts. Even so, she remained miserably hot. Her hand crept down to test a swelling barely noticeable at the summit of her smooth and gently rounded abdomen.

During the past two months her breasts all but imperceptibly, had increased in size and in sensitivity; the pale pink of their nipples was altering to a deeper but lovely hue of rose.

How she hated this foreign thing within her, conceived as it was in loveless violence and shame. God perish Karl the Satyr! Perhaps this horrid little thing might be born dead? Trina stared out into the black expanse of ocean. What woman could be faced with a more undeserved tragedy? Giving life should be an honor, a delight, a—a—well, a pride peculiar to her sex.

So she would marry Stephan Frydendahl. As nearly as she could tell, he would be a man of about forty, so her father had said. Word already had gone forward, announcing her arrival and her predicament; the Dowager-Queen, thorough and essentially practical, had indicated that, in due course, Stephan Frydendahl might hope for a court appointment as reward for relieving a more than embarrassing situation. The Varsaas, moreover, were well connected and of ancient lineage.

Trina continued to stare into the dark, trying to visualize Stephan Frydendahl. But what she saw was Peter Burnham, stalwart and bronzed-looking in a yellow shirt, blue coat and gray breeches.

How strange that this savage of an American should so cling to her thoughts. Yes, it was surprising and disturbing, the way his plain, good-natured features kept invading her mind like some gallant entering her boudoir unbidden.

Were Frydendahl anything like *Doktor* Burnham, some little happiness might emerge from the wreck of her dreams.

If only Mathias Lynge had returned a few days earlier. Poor dear. Scarcely had he set foot on his native soil than an Admiralty order sent him sailing off again—away to the Faroes. Her Majesty, the Dowager-Queen, was leaving nothing to chance. She wanted a whole ocean between Trina and her wretched son. And no chance of revenge from the gallant Lynge.

IX. LOVELY AGNES

FROM THE *Conde de Estremadura,* Spanish brig-of-war, was learned a bit of bad news. Don Eduardo de Elizalde y Capistrano, her captain, declared that a British fleet under Sir George Rodney had, near Cape Vincent, inflicted a shattering defeat upon the fleet of His Most Catholic Majesty of Spain.

Um. Captain Ashton reckoned that quite a long time must pass before the Dons could again assemble an armada fit to challenge English maritime supremacy. This was indeed ill news. The victory of Cape Vincent would permit the British Admiralty to detach more men-of-war for convoy duty—and more cruisers to snatch up those troublesome Yankee privateers.

By way of recompense, Don Eduardo had other intelligence. Recently he had prized a heavy, slow-sailing British merchantman, short of water and for a week separated from her convoy. Said convoy, Don Eduardo reported—to accompanying expressive gestures—was guarded by a heavy frigate and destined for Saint Lucia, Saint Kitts and other British outposts in the Carribbean.

Dipping ensigns in salute, the two vessels parted; the *Conde* for her home port of Cadiz, the *Grand Turk* maintaining her southerly course.

Even boys aboard the brig were certain-sure what Captain Ashton was up to. If one merchantman had strayed from the Winter Convoy, why might not others?

Others had. The British brigantine, *Germaine* was sighted and as quickly allowed to proceed, once Peter Burnham discovered her to be rotten with smallpox.

The very next day Ashton's lookouts descried topsails on the horizon, those of a full-rigged ship of near two hundred tons burthen. She gave the privateer a real chase of two days' duration and, in the end, resistance of a sort. In fact, her first and only broadside knocked quite a jagged hole in the *Grand Turk's* port bulwarks, but miraculously, resultant splinters flew upwards and not a man of the privateer's company was harmed. Really, this was the luckiest cruise ever.

The prize proved to be the *Lovely Agnes,* out of Bristol for Antigua, and by far the most valuable capture to date being deep-laden with ordnance—fine long guns fit to set any privateer captain's heart a-dancing—chests of tea, lockers of spices, bolts of callicut cloth and other costly East India goods.

Loud rose the cheers of the brig's company when they beheld bales of striped seersucker, gay calimanco cloth and filmy, soft shawls from the Vale of Cashmere. The shouts rang louder when on deck were tossed bale on bale of fine Italian silks originally destined for the wives of planters on the great sugar estates of Jamaica.

What especially delighted Peter was an inventory of Birmingham and Sheffield hardware. Those heavy chests of cutlery should go a long way towards replenishing Papa's exhausted stocks. Crimanently! Old Daniel Burnham would rejoice at the sight of so many axe heads, adzes, hinges, chains, spades and knives of various sorts.

The *Lovely Agnes,* like the *Soldier's Endeavour,* was far too valuable to risk sending home under less than a full prize crew, so again twenty of the *Grand Turk's* men lugged their sea bags aboard her.

Gideon Pickering, looking as if he'd been weaned on sour pickles—so Spurgeon Grannis said—went aboard as prize master.

"I will fetch her in, sir," the Connecticuter promised Ashton in his rasping nasal voice. "You may lay to it. Aye, I'll take this vessel into Boston if I hev to sail clean around Sable Island and fly a British flag down to Portsmouth."

"Pray God you will. She ought to fetch eighty thousand pounds sterling, at the very least." Ashton smiled and wrung Pickering's bony hand. "We'll try for one more prize, then I'll hoist the 'homeward bound' signal."

x. THE COCKPIT

AT LONG LAST the weather, which had proved fair beyond all expectations, commenced to harden. The glass in Captain Ashton's cabin wavered, dropped lower and lower. Though by now definitely shorthanded, the

Grand Turk's master remained in excellent spirits. Well he should! To date the brig had suffered but insignificant damage and not a man of the original company had been lost—saving the murderer and his victim.

One more prize would be about enough, he reckoned, and then, come hell or high water, he'd accede to Andrea Ashton's plea and stay ashore, set up as a merchant ship owner and trader—just as he had wanted to do back in '75, before he had learned that, on occasion, a merchant has to fight for the privilege of doing business. He was sick of privateering, a profession he'd never rightly enjoyed.

During the next twenty-four hours the weather worsened until the *Grand Turk* was plunging southwards along the sixty-fifth degree parallel, longitude, under double-reefed topsails and a single storm jib. Following seas caused the privateer to pitch heavily, a treatment to which her fabric protested; a couple of minor leaks were sprung.

On the second day the wind increased to a full gale which sent spindrift flying up the crosstrees and caused the Muslin figurehead to douse his forked beard deep into the backs of an endless succession of gray-green rollers. It was then that a stay parted during the night and catapulted a seaman into a roaring and lightless turmoil. A cry, like that of a tern lost in a fog, rang out; then all was wind and flying spray again; to put out a boat was impossible. Gloom settled over the brig's company.

On the fourth day, the gale diminished somewhat, but the seas remained mountainous.

A lookout, clambering into the crow's nest, had barely settled into place than he shouted through cupped hands, "Sail ho!"

Just arrived on deck to draw a breath of fresh air, Peter glanced at his heavy silver watch—landsman-like he still reckoned time by hours and not by bells. It was, he noticed, exactly nine-thirty on the morning of February the twenty-first, 1780. So long as he lived, Peter Burnham would never forget that date.

"Summon the skipper," bawled the officer of the deck, Eldad Greenleaf. Regularly he served as the *Grand Turk's* quartermaster but, in Pickering's absence, he had been promoted to acting first officer. Everybody knew that, had Eldad been less prone to viewing a bottle through its small end, he long since would have been commanding a ship of his own.

Captain Ashton, red-eyed and fresh from his bunk, clumped upon deck carrying a brown, leather-bound brass telescope tucked under one arm. He took up a post near the binnacle. The only other occupant of the brig's tiny quarterdeck was Jan Vanderhyde, the Dutch gunner and marine officer, his flat red face intent. Above the roar and crash of the seas, Ashton hailed the masthead through his speaking trumpet.

"How does she sail?"

"Standing north'ards, sir, wi' a half-starboard tack," came the wind-distorted reply.

"How wind you aloft?"

Three tries were required before the lookout could make himself heard. "Due west, sir."

Watched by Peter, the gunner, and Eldad Greenleaf, Ashton nodded to himself.

"Clear for action, sir?" Greenleaf demanded.

"No, not yet. There is time and to spare, but order some hands aft. The ship will steer better. Masthead there! Can you tell her rig?"

"Looks like a full-rigged ship, sir," bawled the lookout, his face very red against the bright blue sky.

"Look like a bulldog?"

"No, sir, she's sailing slovenly-like."

"Well, there's our last prize, sir—a big one," grinned Greenleaf. "What a main fine cruise this has been, sir."

Ashton nodded. Should this action come off, as he intended, well, the *Grand Turk* would take the prize in convoy and steer for home.

The minutes ticked by. Seas thundered alongside and licked at the lead-lined edges of the gun ports. Peter, clinging to a backstay, watched the stranger's dark hull materialize gradually above the horizon. The ocean now was turning blue-green in sunlight suddenly released by a rift in the clouds. There could be no doubt that the weather was clearing, yet the seas remained formidable and the trim little privateer pitched and bucked over them like a colt under his first saddle.

"Ja, *iss a pig vun*," muttered Vanderhyde, fingering the blond stubble standing out on his chin. "I vunder how many cannons carries dot sheep?"

Considerable effort was required of Ashton to steady

his glass sufficiently to survey the strange vessel which, under topsails and a reefed forecourse, appeared to be coming directly on.

Some kind of flag was flying from the ship's signal peak but, at this distance, there was no recognizing it. All that could be learned at present was that the other vessel's hull was painted dull brown and that her sails were far from well trimmed.

Another quarter-hour found the two vessels perhaps a mile apart but steadily closing in on one another; the *Grand Turk* was standing due south; the stranger, a big sloop, sailing to the north-northeast.

"Yonder's a merchantman," Greenleaf grunted to Peter. "You'd never find a ship o' the Royal Navy so badly braced and a-towing a long boat."

"Hoist Swedish colors," directed the *Grand Turk's* master.

For the first time this cruise, his seventh and therefore lucky one, Robert Ashton wavered on the brink of indecision. A fine, new-built ship such as this one bearing down on him should fetch a *very* pretty penny at prize court, yet an indefinable uneasiness was pervading him. Why? Maybe yonder sloop was too big?

Were she but a simple merchantman she'd prove an easy nut to crack, but a privateer of that size might bring on a pretty stiff action. Of course his gunnery and superior discipline couldn't leave the issue in doubt overlong. And yet, and yet— After all this time he'd no desire to increase the already overcrowded ranks of the widows and orphans back home.

He glanced at Vanderhyde. The Dutchman was literally licking his lips, already translating this impending victory into tall flagons of ale and big, white-bottomed women.

Ashton did, for him, an unusual thing. He asked of his acting first officer, "What do you make of her?"

"She's a mite large, sir," Greenleaf replied. "But I allow we can take her measure in jig time."

Peter thought, "If we take this vessel my share will amount to more than enough to send me abroad." Flexing his stiff fingers, the physician drew a deep breath. Just one more action and then, well, maybe he could piece together a future.

Captain Ashton faced sharply about, his brown features set in taut and unfamiliar lines. "Mr. Greenleaf, we will clear for action."

Even as he spoke the stranger, as if belatedly sensing her danger, suddenly wore onto the starboard tack and, turning, ran almost dead before the stiff westerly wind.

A small sigh escaped Peter. The stranger yonder *must* be a merchantman—no man-of-war, regular or private-owned, would run from so much smaller a vessel.

Whooping in delight, the *Grand Turk's* reduced crew, they numbered now just fifty men, ran to battle stations, or tried to. So violent was the motion that some fell and most went reeling crazily among the guns. Under this condition it was impossible to adopt the usual precautions of rigging fine chains to supplement the principal stays and braces. Up, down; up, down. The brig lurched in a mad caracol of pursuit.

Rob Ashton's brows merged in a worried line once he noted that the forward guns would be seriously hampered by continual sheets of spray shooting over the bows; so long as he kept the brig on this course it would be impossible to fire them.

Already the gun crews, reeling like drunken men, were removing their sponges and rammers from the racks. The four younkers appeared laboring from below, thin shoulders stooped under the weight of leathern powder buckets.

"We'll turn a pretty sixpence out o' this one," predicted Larry Lord, swinging past Tom Laughry on his way to the magazine.

The older powder boy grinned. "Bet yer sweet life—if Cap'n feels generous we ought to make near a hundred Spanish dollars, or I'm a monkey's uncle. Shake a leg there, Spurgeon! We're overhaulin' the chase, hand-over-fist."

The Grannis boy nodded, already his face and arms were bright with perspiration. "Gorry," he was thinking. "A hundred dollars out of this one ship! Mr. Greenleaf says already we've near three hundred comin' if the other prizes make port. Jimminy! How Ma's eyes will shine. I'll buy her a pair of real silver shoe buckles, and Pa a new ox to replace old Brindle."

His mind ran ahead towards that wonderful moment

when he'd set foot on the path leading up to the weather-
beaten old cabin. How the neighbors would flock in to listen and admire. Maybe Lillian Bock would come?

When Spurgeon got on deck the chase was plunging
along about two cable lengths in the lead, her bows lost in
a continual welter of spray.

The *Grand Turk's* marines, unable to go aloft, contented themselves by mounting heavy brass swivels along the
rail and cursing for fear that the spray would dampen the
priming.

Once the "clear for action" order was shouted, Peter
went below, followed by his two assistants: a wizened
fellow named Larkin who had once attempted to study
pharmacy, and a gangling, but very strong Negro youth
named Frye. Peter suddenly found himself thinking it unfortunate, perhaps, that the *Grand Turk* had thus far
cruised unscathed. Despite patient and very tedious drill-
ing on Peter's part, his assistants remained miserably
inexpert and uncertain of their duties.

Once they got the great lantern alight—after many failures due to the brig's frenzied pitching—they folded a
pair of old staysails and a tarpaulin across two empty
arms chests, then lashed their crude operating platform
fast to eyebolts let into the deck.

"I want sand, plenty of sand," Peter told Larkin.
"With this motion, spilt blood will prove slippery as
grease. Yes, and you'd best rig some lifelines or we'll
crack our skulls if ever the brig falls into the trough."

They strung ropes for hand holds, then tied into place a
pair of tubs; otherwise, these essential receptacles would
have gone rolling madly about. The more Peter considered the next-to-impossible conditions under which he
must operate, the more he prayed that the impending engagement might prove brief. Why, he didn't even dare to
lay out his knives, saws and other instruments, but
stacked them as best he could in a wooden box lashed to
the head of his operating table.

It was the crazily wavering and hopelessly inadequate
lantern light which caused his sharpest misgivings. The
lantern, at best a dim affair, now responded wildly to
each violent pitch of the *Grand Turk*. Finally, for the
benefit of possible wounded, Peter ordered broken out a
keg of rum and set his assistants to rigging a loose pallet
of old sails to serve as receiving point for the injured.

To indulge his usual fancy concerning the efficacy of hot water was impossible, for, as was customary, the galley fires had been put out after the first call to quarters. Should he order ignited the iron brazier reserved for heating searing irons? Reluctantly he did so, though he hated the prospect of employing such crude methods.

It grew so terribly close below that Peter stripped off his shirt before tying on a white apron. There might be no time once the first shot was fired. After all, he owned but two sets of clothes and the removal of blood spots was a slow and unsatisfactory business.

Nervously he inspected the contents of his surgeon's chest. Damn! The privateer's motion was becoming increasingly violent. It was the very devil, this, not to be able to lay things out. Um. Peter checked his preparations. The water, the sponges, unguent basil, elemental gum were ready to hand. So were swabs to dry the operating platform, a small barrel of splints of various sizes, compresses and tapes for securing the splints. To occupy the time he set his assistants to smearing yellow basilicon on pledgets of tow.

From the grim and alert expressions of those men whose duties carried them below, the surgeon and his assistants could deduce that the size of the chase now was causing lively apprehensions.

As a last precaution Peter rigged a length of rope through an eyebolt above his head and made its bight fast about his waist. If the *Grand Turk's* plunging gave place to rolling, this alone would enable him to remain upright.

Frye began rolling yellowish eyes. "Laws, Mistro Bur'nham, dis air ain't no good." And, indeed, the motion had multiplied the always lively bilge stenches until the atmosphere was well-nigh insufferable. "Ah feels pow'ful mizzabul. Ah dunno if—" He lurched towards one of the waiting tubs but suddenly spewed all over the deck, thus earning a furious tirade from Peter.

"Boy! Fetch me a bucket of sand," the physician yelled at Tom Laughry pattering by on bare feet with his hair blowing wild over his face. "This lubber has greased the deck for fair."

At length everything was in readiness—so far as might be. Again Peter consulted his watch; five minutes after ten—half an hour gone since the stranger's tops had been raised. What would the next half-hour bring? There now remained nothing to do but to wait, so he seated himself on his operating platform, listening to Frye being sick, to the voices bawling on deck and to the ominous rumble of a loose cannon ball rolling about the *Grand Turk's* deck.

XI. THE WHIRLWIND OF DESTRUCTION

"DOWN THAT Swedish flag!" Captain Robert Ashton commanded. "Break out our battle ensigns and let's see what their colors are."

A deep, defiant cheer arose from the *Grand Turk's* streaming decks as, to the fore signal yard and the main gaff, climbed the Stars and Stripes, instantly to flatten in the wind as if they had been cut out of sheet metal.

Still the chase refused to show her colors, only kept up the losing bid for escape.

The carpenter waited in lee of the foc's'le head, together with his hammer, nails and sheets of lead ready to nail over shot holes. Long since, all hammocks had been stowed and the brig's two long boats cast adrift. Should a shot have struck them the resultant hail of splinters could wipe out a dozen men.

A slight commotion drew Rob Ashton's attention. The captain of the Number Four gun had jumped suddenly down from the bulwarks on which he had been studying the chase and had slipped on the wet deck to stun himself against the carriage of Number Six gun. Two of his gun crew dragged him, semi-conscious, to a hatch grating and left him there, dazed and gasping.

From the start of this chase Captain Ashton had been aware that hardly enough hands remained aboard his brig to handle her sails in such a blow and also to man her batteries. When it became apparent that the starboard broadside would become engaged, he directed that only those guns be readied.

Having set topgallants and all jibs, the *Grand Turk* now was closing in more rapidly. Acting-Lieutenant Eldad Greenleaf kept his full attention on the set of the sails.

"Haul the foresheet close aft!" he bellowed through his speaking trumpet. "Set in them lee braces. Haul tight yer bowlines. Quartermaster, keep the chase open under our lee."

The stranger, every detail of which now became visible, was wallowing along barely one hundred yards ahead and slightly to leeward. Ashton felt about ready to order his Number Four gun into action, when, all at once, a great cheer came beating over from this tall stranger.

In frozen dismay the privateersmen watched the progress skywards of a White Ensign—it meant that the chase was a regular man-of-war of the Royal Navy! Magically, those badly adjusted sails were trimmed and the warship wore smartly to port, disclosing gun ports already triced up. Rob Ashton felt as if a fist had landed at the base of his skull: his adversary was displaying a broadside of eight heavy-looking cannon!

As if to clinch this terrible disillusionment, the stunned gun captain roused up on the hatch long enough to bellow, "For God's sake, sir, turn aside. I was a-comin' to warn ye. Yonder's H.B.M.S. *Albany*, sloop-o'-war, sixteen guns. Saw her up at Penobscot."

To avoid being raked, Captain Ashton instantly ordered his helm put down hard. The brig responded handsomely and, as she veered off to port, her guns were run out to an accompanying rattle and a whine of tackles. Now the privateer's gun captains blew hard on their matches, watched all the while their crews who had hard work to avoid sliding all over the deck.

"Fire!" shouted Ashton, hopeful of getting in a perhaps demoralizing first blow. At that precise instant, however, the *Albany* let fly a broadside. Fearful screeching sounds preluded a noise such as a whole crew of lumbermen might make in splitting kindling. Magically, a great gap appeared in the privateer's starboard and bulwarks, and splinters flew hissing upwards to slash the lower canvas. Causing sharp reports, half a dozen taut stays parted, one of them unfortunately was that of the forecourse sheet.

"Fire!" repeated the Virginian, broad features drained of color. "Aim at her spars, men. Load chain or bar shot! Fast, fast for your lives!"

It was well enough to call for rapid fire, but, so violent was the rolling of the brig, that her gun crews, already hampered by severed ropes, kept dropping their instruments and went reeling wildly off balance. A roundshot, escaping from the grip of a Number Two man, went thundering along the deck and smashed into a bloody pulp the ankle of a gun pointer on Number Four gun.

Splinters occasioned by that first enemy broadside had not only damaged the rigging but also had stretched several figures on the *Grand Turk's* deck. Bright crimson streams spurted from them tracing zigzagging patterns over the well-holystoned decking.

One after another the brig's starboard battery went into action and two of her guns scored hits; it was easy to see the effect of her gunnery because the wind instantly snatched from the muzzles of the cannon clouds of rotten-smelling, gray-brown smoke. Although the privateers were habituated to easy victories, discipline, long implanted, asserted itself a moment later. The brig's cannon re-commenced their desperate efforts at defense.

As the *Grand Turk* paid off and swung her bowsprit northwards the brig's rolling became more pronounced.

"God above!" Ashton groaned, "why can't those men keep their feet?"

Number Four gun, he noticed, had become dismounted from its shattered carriage and was sliding in murderous caprice about the foredeck.

Vanderhyde, spouting strange Dutch oaths, went along the deck indicating those lockers containing langrage and chain shot. In these missiles lay the *Grand Turk's* sole hope of escape. Chain shot, two small iron spheres connected by a length of chain, was very useful in wrecking an enemy's rigging. Langrage consisted of scrap iron and glass enclosed in a cloth bag—it, too, in a twinkle could reduce a sail to useless ribbons. With such a sea running if enough stays and shrouds could be severed—well, the enemy's masts just might go by the board.

Keeping his eyes on the big sloop-of-war, Rob Ashton strove desperately to keep his head. In all his five years of privateering no comparable calamity had ever struck his vessel. No doubt that he was as badly out-gunned as he had been outwitted. Who could have imagined a British man-of-war's skipper capable of daubing his vessel's sides so sorry a shade of barnyard brown?

Provided the *Grand Turk's* rigging remained standing, he figured he might outsail the *Albany* in a fight to windward—on the other hand, His British Majesty's sloop seemed a fast sailer and she might blow him out of the water long before he could beat out of range.

Another course suggested itself; he mght be able to

lose speed suddenly enough to pass under the Britisher's stern and so run before the wind. By jettisoning cannon, anchors and by starting his water casks he might win free.

Accordingly, Ashton ordered his brig headed across the wind and, despite her damage, the *Grand Turk* commenced promptly to swing onto the port tack. The *Albany* fired again, hulling the luckless privateer and decimating the crews of Number Two and Number Four guns. The privateersmen commenced to falter in the service of their pieces; they weren't accustomed to seeing their fellows lying about the deck as shattered, shapeless masses of gory flesh and broken bones.

Ashton bellowed as he had not during all his seafaring career. "Fire on upward roll! *Only on upward roll!*"

More shot went screaming over the ocean at the British sloop.

In a frenzy of anxiety, Ashton glanced over the starboard quarter, saw the *Albany* had been disconcerted by the *Grand Turk's* unexpected and quick maneuver of rounding up into the wind. As in a dream, he watched the Britisher's guns reappear at the gun ports and braced himself. In an instant another devastating broadside would be loosed; one which might, if well aimed, reduce this once-graceful privateer to a shattered, smoking hulk.

Praise God! The *Albany's* gunners fired high, doubtless deceived by a sudden rolling of the gun deck.

Ashton ordered canvas made—sent the topmen scampering aloft. One was shaken from his hold and disappeared in the stormy sea.

Survivors of the two forward gun crews were lugging horribly shrieking messmates below; time and again the *Grand Turk's* violent motion threw these bearers off balance, and the injured, perforce, were dropped to create great scarlet splotches on the deck.

Somehow Vanderhyde got his gun crews back under control and three of his guns managed to anticipate the next British broadside. Once those great gray mushrooms of smoke belched from the *Grand Turk's* cannon a curious, whirring sound—such as might be made by a covey of gigantic partridges—filled the air. Double charges of chain shot were shrieking across some seventy-five yards of wind-whipped water.

"Ha-a-a!" yelled the privateer's gunners when, in magical suddenness, the British cruiser's foresail split into furiously flapping shreds. Simultaneously, two of the *Albany's* jibs vanished as if snatched away by an invisible hand.

Vanderhyde himself trained the remaining Number Six gun and touched it off—a fraction of an instant before the sloop fired her fourth broadside of the engagement.

The concerted impact of her enemy's heavy roundshot caused the *Grand Turk* to heel 'way over and, at the same moment, a great flash of blinding light shone in Rob Ashton's eyes. An instant later he crumpled, inert, onto his quarterdeck.

Not two minutes passed following the disastrous effect of the *Albany's* initial broadside than a wounded man was brought below—that gun pointer whose ankle had been shattered by a loose cannon ball.

"Put him on the platform, you two, and hold him down," Peter directed.

"Oh-h, Mr. Burnham, don't take off my foot. I just can't bear being crippled like Pa. Honest I—I'll be all right." The wounded man forced a grin. "It's just a graze, you kin see for yourself."

A quick look revealed no justification for any attempt to save this shattered extremity—its foot and ankle bones had been mashed into a shapeless mush of scarlet, pink and white slivers which dangled at a grotesque angle from the rest of the leg.

"Take courage," Peter told the heavily sweating patient. "I shall have to amputate." He caught the man who'd carried this patient below. "You stay and help hold—"

Peter got no further for, at that moment, the *Albany's* second broadside struck and the *Grand Turk's* hull resounded like an empty cask struck by a heavy hammer. Frye and Larkin cowered, shielding their heads. The wounded man vented a terrified shriek and would have slipped off the platform had not Peter, clutching the steadying rope above his head, kept him from doing so. A chorus of unearthly screams and howls upon deck set hairs to rising and twitching on Peter's neck. Then followed a distinctive *thump-thump* of blocks and rigging falling to the *Grand Turk's* deck. The physician rallied and tried to steady himself against the brig's frantic motion.

"You, Larkin! Grab hold of his good ankle. Frye, pin his shoulders after he's had a drink of this." Peter held out a rum bottle. "Drink plenty, you—your foot must come off."

The fellow's eyes grew round. Apparently he couldn't yet realize what was about to happen. "Off? No, no! Oh, God, no! Leave me be. I'll—"

"—There's the gag. Pick it up, you fool," Peter snapped to Frye who jammed the leather gag into the patient's mouth.

"Yassuh, yassuh. I'se doin' the best I kin, but Ah cain't hardly stand."

"Damn your eyes, hold him tight!" A slash of Peter's knife slit the sodden canvas of the fellow's trouser leg. Peter knew he'd have to work fast. More wounded were being lugged below.

The wildly swinging lantern was creating a dizzying kaleidoscope of light by which Peter attempted a selection of knives and a saw.

For all his gag, the injured seaman screamed and writhed, as, timing his motion, Peter cut down to the bone some six inches above the ankle. Once he had tied off the great artery, his blood-slippery hand delved into the box beside him in search of a saw. At the first bite of this cold steel the patient emitted one ear-piercing cry then lapsed into a merciful unconsciousness. The screw tourniquet, loosened by an especially violent plunge of the vessel, slipped and at once blood from minor arteries sprayed bright scarlet over the tarpaulin and onto Peter's apron. Although debating the use of searing irons, he tied off those blood vessels.

When other injured wretches were helped below, he paid them no heed. His saw rasped on and on until, at last, the foot needed only a slash of a knife to send it plopping into a tub ready beside the platform. Expertly he cut the flap, snatched a threaded needle from his apron.

"Larkin!" he shouted over the thundering of the guns. "Retighten that tourniquet." He had commenced to sew the flap into place when the *Grand Turk's* motion changed and gave a violent lurch, mingled the ministrants and their inert patient into a heap at the foot of the improvised operating table.

"Get him back in place. Quick! Quick!"

With the help of a round-eyed deckhand, the patient was replaced on the gory tarpaulin and held steady long enough to finish sewing the flap in place. Only then did the surgeon look up and perceive the magnitude of the task before him.

Half a dozen wounded men lay rolling helplessly on the pallet, draining blood all over their neighbors and themselves. Their cries were terrible to hear, their pleas for treatment heartrending. The already thick air became further tainted by a cloying reek of fresh blood and to retain self-control became a formidable task. Where to begin? Which stood most in need of attention? Which patients might be saved? Who were surely doomed?

"What'll we do with him?" Two men were dragging forward an Indian sailor from whose right side projected a long oaken splinter; blood was dripping copiously from its jagged tip.

A glance told Peter that nothing could be done. "Lay him beyond those casks," he directed. "I'll get to him soon's I can."

Again came an enemy broadside, but, praise God, it seemed to have flown high. All the same, six wounded already lay in a bloody wallow and more were struggling below. Two men, lying face down on the trampled sand, partially blocked that narrow passage to the operating platform. Over these struggled the newer cases.

Peter found another figure stretched before him on the scarlet-stained tarpaulin and, by applying forceps, drew an iron bolt from its position deep in the back of a German lad of eighteen; hurriedly Peter stuffed the hole with lint and despite the anguished screams of the patient knotted a pledget into place.

The dimly lit cockpit degenerated into a bedlam of outrageous sounds; groans, whimperings, screams and odd, lowing sounds like those made by thirsty cattle. One topman, whose whole right side had been crushed, kept on screeching until one of the walking wounded snatched up a caulking mallet and cracked him on the top of the head.

When the *Grand Turk* changed course, the rolling became so violent that not even four men could keep a patient on that ghastly scarlet tarpaulin.

"More sand! Swab off the platform!" Peter kept shouting. "Damn it, I can't operate from across the hold. Steady her, someone!"

The knife in Peter's hand began to turn, to lose its sureness; so drenched with blood was he that he could no longer find a sure grip on his instruments. Continually, he tried to dry his hands on a towel tied to his belt but that, too, got soaked—a replacement as well. By now his face, arms, and apron were a hideous pattern of crimson and bright scarlet arterial blood.

Soon, a long file of wounded were piled indiscriminately on the pallets. An Irishman, suffering from a dreadful abdominal wound, was trying to keep pinkish-gray entrails in place; but the privateer's wild rolling sent him rolling over and over and trailing his intestines across the legs of the wretches beside him.

Surely hell could be no worse than this, Peter thought. He realized he was helpless for the present. He grabbed at the wrist of a powder monkey who had just lugged below a shattered marine. "Pass immediate word to the Captain; I can't operate till this rolling abates."

"Aye, aye, sir." It was young Prescott, his smooth young face gone whiter than that of any living being Peter had ever beheld. The boy's eyes were twin pools of horror.

When the *Albany's* third broadside struck the whole cockpit reverberated to the deafening crash of a cannon ball penetrating the hull; it pierced the far side as well, let in air and daylight.

"Oh, Jesus! Jesus save me!" screamed a voice.

Like a vision seen by lightning Peter beheld the Prescott boy still standing; but his head was not there. Gushing fountains of blood spouted upwards, then the slight figure collapsed like a wet rope.

"Why don't old Bob surrender?" screamed one of those waiting his turn. "We don't stand a bloody chance. This here's naught but butchery."

One of the Negro seamen, having gulped a tremendous swig of rum, became delirious and raised a guttural chant in his native tongue. Both of his legs had been broken below the knee by a falling spar.

If Captain Ashton entertained any notion of surrendering it wasn't visible. The rumble of gun carriages being run in for reloading continued to sound on deck. Peter, locking his teeth, crawled on hands and knees along the row of wounded, worked as best he might.

XII. MR. ELDAD GREENLEAF

ELDAD GREENLEAF straightened from a hurried inspection of Captain Ashton's unconscious figure and cast a critical eye aft to where a brace of barefooted helmsmen heaved at the *Grand Turk's* tiller.

The *Albany* now was forging ahead with the obvious intention of raking her cruelly mauled adversary. With the master dead or nearly so, with the brig's gun deck a shambles—only three guns remained in firing condition—there remained only one sensible course.

"God curse the luck!" Greenleaf snarled. "We'll have to strike." He felt a chill strike the pit of his stomach. All too well he knew what would follow surrender: imprisonment in a stifling and noisome forehold, kicks, blows, and swill for food, eventual internment in some heatless British prison.

There was no longer any hope of exchange, either. Since last year, His Majesty's ministers had come to appreciate that in the revolted colonies there were none-too-many seamen, but press gangs could always round out the crew of a Royal man-of-war.

"Strike the Colors!"

But when the seaman ran towards the signal halyard, he slipped on blood issuing from Captain Ashton's sagging jaw, and fell heavily.

Greenleaf, sensing the imminence of a fourth broadside, started for the halyard himself. In doing so he cast a last despairing glance at H.B.M.S. *Albany*. To his amazement the sloop appeared to be losing way. Why? Then he noticed how many severed stays and halyards streamed from her tops.

"By God! Look! Look, sir!" One of the helmsmen was leveling a blunt forefinger at a crack opening above a shot hole showing halfway up the *Albany's* mainmast. Even as Greenleaf watched the crack expanded and, clearly visible against the sloop's brown paintwork, ran like lightning towards the deck.

Then it happened. The Royal cruiser's mainmast snapped just below its crosstrees and, to a violent threshing of yards and wild flapping of canvas, the spar went crashing over her starboard rail. Water was flung high into the air and the sloop heeled over until her port strakes showed.

Bowlines and stays leading to the foremast held a brief instant bending that spar like a bow; then the lines parted under the terrific strain. The foremast recovered but, creating a grinding, crackling roar, the mizzenmast tottered and, dragged by the dead weight of the sodden maintop, followed the mainmast over the lee rail. The *Albany* was halted just as effectively as if she had struck a reef.

The man-of-war's dismasting took place so very quickly that neither Greenleaf nor the *Grand Turk's* crew could credit their eyesight. Many fell on their knees to gasp a prayer of thanksgiving. Greenleaf found time to cry, "Almighty God, I thank Thee," before ordering the mangled privateer before the wind and preparing to run for dear life.

Almost as quickly as the single remaining mast of H.B.M.S. *Albany* became lost to sight, the wind and the sea commenced to moderate. Mr. Greenleaf shaped a course southeast; it seemed the part of wisdom to run before the wind until some of the damage aloft could be repaired.

As soon as occasion permitted Eldad Greenleaf got out a pencil and did a mite of reckoning. Of the six officers and one hundred men who had sailed the *Grand Turk* out of Boston Harbor, forty-three men and three officers had gone into the various prizes prior to her engagement with H.B.M.S. *Albany*. The murdered man and his slayer must also be subtracted. That had left aboard the brig fifty-three men and three officers with which to sail and fight.

Of those fifty-three men the *Albany's* two effective broadsides and desultory fire had slain fourteen outright, and eighteen more seamen were so severely wounded that at least two-thirds of them must perish before the brig could make port. One man had been lost overboard

during the chase and six hands, though still on their feet,
were incapable of duty.

Um. Total casualties numbered thirty-nine! A pretty
grim tally. Greenleaf licked his pencil point. Let's see.
Thirty-nine out of fifty-three leaves seventeen able-bodied men to sail a badly mauled brig of two hundred tons
burthen. His heart sank.

Eldad Greenleaf knew that he, alone of the ship's company, was qualified to navigate unless Captain Ashton recovered—which seemed mighty unlikely right now.
Um-m. To try for home in this condition wasn't practica-
ble, not by any remote stretch of the imagination. So few
hands couldn't be expected to handle sail in those late
winter winds prevailing along the American coast at this
season.

Sundown. The crew was tired out, exhausted physically and emotionally. It had seemed callous to dump the
dead overboard with never a prayer said over them nor a
hammock to swing them down to Davy Jones. He'd no
choice, though. The *Grand Turk* had suffered four shot
holes between wind and water which were admitting such
quantities of sea water that, despite the carpenter's best
efforts, the pumps had to be kept going and that required
the continual efforts of four men.

What bothered the acting captain worst of all was that
Captain Ashton still lay on his bunk, ashen-faced and unconscious from a terrific blow which seemed to have
crushed most of the ribs along his right side. Greenleaf
deduced that a huge splinter ripped from the taffrail, had
struck the Virginian broadside on; though not piercing his
body it had ruptured many blood vessels.

He felt right bad about Cap'n Ashton's taking so heavy
a wound, did Eldad Greenleaf; during three cruises he'd
come to hold this stocky, soft-spoken Virginian in great
respect. Never did a master better understand his crews
or make the most of his officers' abilities and the least of
their failings. Though it required a supreme effort,
Greenleaf silently vowed that, out of respect, he wasn't
going to touch a drop of spirit 'til the *Grand Turk* made
home or fetched up safe in some neutral port.

The brig must seek shelter promptly; Greenleaf
blinked nervously when he thought on how much temporary planking and sheet lead was in use to keep the *Grand
Turk* above water. Such stop-gap measures would suffice

only so long as the weather remained fine and the ocean smooth. Where to head? Where? Lord, Lord. The only other officer surviving was Doctor Burnham and he knew mighty little concerning navigation or the management of a vessel.

Eldad tried to figure things out just as if he were younger and hadn't consumed so plagued-many gallons and gallons of rum. Well he knew that those gallons had done little to whet his once lively intelligence. A long time went by before he came to the conclusion that the best thing was to head for Saint Jan. If all went well he'd pick up there Benson and the four men who'd sailed away in charge of the *Hammond*.

Yessiree. The more Greenleaf turned the matter over in his mind, the more he figgered that this was the proper ticket. He'd lay a course for Saint Jan. The Danes, smarting under an arrogant application of the British embargo, very likely would give even a stricken American privateer a handsome reception.

Once safe in the shallow and neutral waters of Coral Bay in Saint Jan's, the brig could be careened and her not inconsiderable water-line damage repaired. Greenleaf figgered on sending down the main topmast; a chance shot from the enemy's second broadside had cut it nigh on a third through. Tomorrow he'd have it fished; that spar would never survive a stiff breeze.

Yes, sir. No more drink for Eldad Greenleaf. He'd a whole bag full of worries to shoulder and for Cap'n Ashton's sake he hoped to make a respectable showing. Walking extra straight and steady. Greenleaf sought the captain's chart locker and there employed compass and parallel rulers to lay out a course.

Um-m. Mebbe in a week, if the weather stayed favorable, they'd raise Camel's Back Mountain and the low green hills of Saint Jan. Good thing he'd put in there, though 'twas years ago—during the old French war. Why, he could recall the entrance to Coral Bay clear as a bell.

On returning to the quarterdeck the acting captain felt his self-confidence rising; a genuine ring of authority was in his tone when he gave a new course to the helmsman, a smart young fellow out of Portsmouth in the State of New Hampshire—like himself. His name was Whittier, David Whittier and he acted bright above the average.

Sunrise, the day after the engagement, was uncommonly lovely. The air was balmy and the sea easy. If only the wounded would stop their infernal groaning! During the day, Greenleaf restored at least a semblance of order on the gun deck.

The gaunt and overworked seventeen uninjured men cleared away wreckage and ruined cannon by simply pushing them overboard through all-too-accommodating gaps in the bulwarks. Broken yards and loose equipment had become knitted by the hard weather into a vast hurrah's nest at which the men sawed and chopped and swore and sweated until, at length, the mess was cleared away.

Greenleaf, his sense of seamanship returning, saw that essential stays, halyards and bowlines were replaced or re-reeved in order of importance.

Watching the sun lift its bronze-gold disc over the horizon, Greenleaf came to appreciate how mighty smart Cap'n Ashton had been in ordering that fire at the enemy's rigging. Had he done otherwise, Greenleaf and the balance of the *Grand Turk's* crew would be lying manacled below decks by this time and pondering their fate.

A curse out of Tophet on being so short-handed! Of the seventeen sound men, four must always be at the pumps and three in the cockpit tending the wounded. Two more were required to manage the helm, which left but eight dog-tired hands free to make sail, assist the carpenter at his desperate efforts to stop the leaks, to bend on new canvas and to repair the rigging.

For a long time to come there'd be precious little sound sleep for anybody aboard. Greenleaf ran his eye about the horizon while speculating on how soon some of the more lightly wounded hands might be returned to duty. Only one man could settle that question. Accordingly, the acting master made his way down to the cockpit.

Though veteran of nigh on two dozen sea battles the weatherbeaten New Hampshire man was unprepared for the scene he encountered below decks. Halfway down to the cockpit Greenleaf paused, buffeted by a ghastly and poisonous stench. Only by holding a handkerchief dipped in vinegar to his nose could the acting captain enter that region where, under swaying lanterns, the ship's surgeon was still toiling; his movements now very slow but certain. Thanks to a flattening of the seas, the wounded were no longer tossed about, and now lay silent or semi-conscious in a long row, their complexions gone a greasy cheese-yellow. Under the light of the lanterns their bandages shone amber-splotched with red-brown.

From Burnham, Greenleaf learned that if all went well, four of the lightly wounded might be available for light duty; as for the rest—God only knew when they'd be fit.

"Bad, eh, Burnham?"

The red-haired surgeon nodded leadenly. He had changed his apron and washed, but fatigue had sketched deep lines about his mouth and eyes—fatigue, and a sense of helplessness mingled with anger.

Until late the preceding night he had worked, drawing on every bit of knowledge and skill that was his—he had been forced to use butcher's tactics—the wounded were so many. Imagine sawing off a leg, then searing its stump with a red-hot iron dipped in tar—imagine having to dress a wound with tow smeared with more tar.

He might have made out better if his Negro assistant, Frye, hadn't all at once become so crazed by the horrors that he could only sit staring at a tub overflowing with mangled arms and legs and muttering gibberish.

For all that, Peter felt he'd accomplished quite a bit. Hemorrhages had generally been checked in time, wounds had been closed and broken limbs somehow set and packed in scraped linen lint stiffened with wheat flour.

By the afternoon following the engagement, he'd got a canvas ventilator rigged which, while not really efficient, nonetheless directed a little fresh air into the cockpit. So far he'd not been able to prepare a report list for the captain—twenty-four wounded men required a deal of attention. He told Greenleaf so.

Said he, "Don't bother about that list—Cap'n won't be wanting it."

Burnham's red head jerked up and his hollowed eyes narrowed. "He's hurt?"

"Aye, sir, and badly."

"Why wasn't I told?"

"He wouldn't let me. Insisted you had enough to do for the others."

"I'll examine him the minute I finish this job."

Peter had been devoting his attention to one of the Indians who had suffered a deep splinter gash across his shoulders. The 'Quoddy went pale under his dark skin and bit hard on a folded blanket thrust between his jaws when Peter's needle and thread tugged together the lips of his wound. He made no outcry, but his knuckles crackled and his whole body trembled.

Greenleaf was desperately glad to return on deck and gulp deep breaths of the salt air. Phew! The stench of stale blood and burst entrails was clinging, not easily disposed of. How could anybody tolerate such odors for nigh on twenty-four hours?

So exhausted that his every motion required a distinct effort, Peter Burnham made his way over debris still littering the companionway and climbed on deck. Like Greenleaf, the first thing he did was to draw a dozen deep breaths then pause blinking at the pure blue of the sky. Just how many ages ago had he made his way below, blissfully unwitting of the horrors in store?

"God Almighty!" One of the crew flinched at the sight of him. Then Peter realized that, from his shoes to the crown of his head, he was spattered and spotted with fresh and dried blood. His new apron resembled that of a butcher at the end of a long day's work. Wouldn't do to appear before the skipper like this—especially if Ashton was hurt as badly as Greenleaf had implied.

Stumbling over an overturned gun carriage and pieces of broken spar Peter went limping up to the scuttlebutt at the base of the foremast. There he untied his sodden apron and flung it into scuppers yet choked with pinkish water. At the scuttlebutt he drank several deep drafts from a gourd dipper secured to it; a trifle revived, he then splashed water over his face, arms and hands, and rubbed hard to wash away those ghastly stains.

Following an old custom when weary, he rubbed vigorously the nape of his neck and immediately felt his head begin to clear. On his way aft he inspected his hands, found dark red crescents under his nails. He decided not to bother about them. Only two considerations were of importance—that everything be done to alleviate the sufferings of mangled wretches below, and that Captain Ashton receive his most considered care.

Moving on lead-heavy feet, Peter Burnham descended into that small but elegantly appointed cabin in which he had enjoyed so many cheerful repasts. It suggested an island miraculously spared by a hurricane; a haven of normality in the midst of a ravaged archipelago.

Except for a litter of charts scattered during Greenleaf's efforts to locate those he needed, Captain Ashton's cabin seemed about as always.

Peter was brought up sharp, though, by his first sight of Robert Ashton. He lay asleep at the moment—or was he unconscious? In any case the *Grand Turk's* master lay very flat, breathing hoarsely on the neatly folded blankets of his bunk.

On hurrying over, Peter realized that Ashton had gone a gray-white and his usually carefully clubbed dark brown hair was streaming loose over his pillow. What caused Peter's liveliest concern was that, from either nostril, thin threads of blood had sketched irregular streaks over the stubble on the captain's cheeks to drip onto the pillowcase.

God above! Robert Ashton was in bad case, indeed—one had only to listen to his breathing.

When Peter tried to think, attempted to flog his weary wits back to duty, he failed. That wouldn't do at all. Ashton needed him as he had needed Ashton that terrible night last January.

He sought a familiar, built-in cabinet; in it Captain Ashton kept his liquor. At random Peter selected a bottle, up-ended it and swallowed a huge mouthful. When the alcohol reached his stomach he felt strength warming his extremities and that insistent plucking at his eyelids was eased.

Eyes narrowed in speculation, Peter bent over the unconscious privateersman. Um. The sound of his shallow wheezing wasn't one little bit reassuring, and about his lips had gathered an almost imperceptible deposit of pinkish froth. A test of the pulse proved it to be soft and slow. The Virginian did not rouse when, as gently as he might, Peter undid the shirt and stripped it aside.

Damn that fool Greenleaf for not calling him sooner! A most cursory examination revealed that, from the coastal to the captain's eleventh rib, his whole side was fractured. The blow he'd suffered must have been terrific thus to crack or break every rib on the right side of his chest.

"He'll get the lung fever for sure," Peter assured himself, well aware that precious little could be done beyond cupping and bleeding.

Further examination revealed a big, discolored lump on the back of Ashton's head above the paretical bone; it

was no doubt this which had induced that commotion
which was at present holding the patient in an unconscious state. How ironic that this type of injury admitted
of practically no treatment, beyond keeping this ghastly
pale patient motionless and as warm as possible.

Using every care, Peter removed the Virginian's garments, then wrapped his cruelly bruised body in a soft
wool blanket. Luckily, the weather was growing hotter
so there'd be no necessity of piling bedclothes across that
injured chest. Eyes burning with sleeplessness, Peter
Burnham fetched a basin and pulled out the mechanical
lancet he bought when he'd thought he was going to
adopt the Army. It was a very neat French invention.
One had only to press a little trigger to release a sharp
blade which, with a deft flick, would open a vein as neat
as you pleased. Um. He figured to draw off about ten
ounces.

Until this moment, Peter had not realized how very
great was the depth of affection he felt for this quiet Virginia gentleman. Memories of that serene, quietly elegant
home back in Boston arose to plague him. For the sake of
lovely and spirited Andrea Ashton and her children, he
would do all in his power to save the *Grand Turk's* master. Perhaps he could? The Virginian's fibre was tough
and he was young—a little over thirty at the most.

XIII. Latitude 29° 5′, Longitude 13° 3′

Of the gravely wounded, three died in delirium within
twenty-four hours following the action. Peter Burnham
all along had expected the abdominal cases to prove
hopeless—head injuries would go next, if trepanning
proved ineffective. Vanderhyde, the *Grand Turk's* excellent gunner and marine commander, died quietly only an
hour after Peter removed a steel splinter from the base of
his brain. Next perished a Negro whose left leg, from the
hip downwards, had been carried away by a cannon ball;
had he not been extra powerful he would have expired a
long time earlier.

Next to die was the captain of Number Four gun; the
top of his skull had been crushed by a falling yard. Everyone was glad because, for hours, his breath had al-

most ceased, only to resume in a most disconcerting fashion.

These more recent dead were more respectfully treated than their predecessors. The sailmaker, though grumbling a lot, sewed the five cadavers into hammocks, each with a piece of stone ballast lashed to his feet.

Eldad Greenleaf, sober and hourly growing in stature under the pressure of his responsibility, bared his bald head and because he could not come across Captain Ashton's Bible, recited the Lord's Prayer before hard-eyed seamen pushed the rigid bodies out of a hole shot through the bulwarks; all to the eternal *swish-clank, swish-clank* of the hard-worked pumps.

Though Peter cupped and bled and purged and glystered his patients in efforts to reduce their fever, four more of the crew succumbed to distempers induced by their wounds. Now that nine—half of the dangerously wounded—had gone to their rewards, Peter and his assistants were able to give the survivors better care; to wash them, change their dressings and administer febrifuges and purges.

The cockpit, by now, had been cleansed with vinegar, saltpetre and water, and the nine remaining wounded were installed in cradles contrived from the hammocks of men killed during the action with H.B.M.S. *Albany.*

Peter wished it were possible to move his gravely injured on deck. Long since, he had ordered the lesser cases aloft, there to enjoy the warm sunlight from which they derived such benefit.

The brig's spars and rigging had been spliced, re-reeved and otherwise restored. Propelled by a new suit of sails the *Grand Turk* slipped quickly, smoothly southward until she entered a latitude in which the sun beat down with savage intensity, heating the 'tween decks to suffocation.

No more of the injured died until the fifth day; then gas gangrene, bloating its wretched victims to grotesque proportions, claimed three more lives. Presently but five patients were lying inert and resigned in the *Grand Turk's* stifling cockpit. Once the sun went down, it grew cooler and the wounded commenced to revive.

"How yer feelin', Otis," demanded John Wampee's Carolina accents. "Still aimin' to cheat the Devil o' his due?"

"Aye." Otis Rockwell nodded, stared fiercely at the deck beams above. Despite everything, he intended to survive; hour after hour he kept on reassuring himself that he'd once more roam the magnificent mountains, forests and valleys of the Hampshire Grants. He always thought of home under that name; "the State of New Hampshire" seemed foreign.

Of course, a one-armed man mightn't be of much use about a farm, but if the *Grand Turk* got home all right he'd be rich enough, by Crickey, to hire him a couple o' them big German fellows who'd deserted the Brunswick Army after Bennington. Folks claimed they understood farming and really liked to work.

Funny, lying here like this and listening to the soft patter of bare feet moving about the deck over head, Otis somehow couldn't credit that his right arm really was off above the elbow. Why, he could swear on a stack of Bibles so high, that he was able to make his fingers obey, like always.

At other times the Hampshireman knew the arm was gone, but he surely had to admire the 'cute and gentle way Sawbones had taken it off; no searing, no wrenching, no hot tar.

Well, he aimed to go on living and, in good time, arrive back to White Marsh. Whether he'd marry Helen Blacklock depended, of course, on whether she would consider splicing up with a cripple. She loved him all right—or said she did. Of course he'd fetch home a little bag of gold and that might clinch the matter; Pa Blacklock had a mighty keen ear for the clink of one coin against its neighbor. Otis guessed likely Helen would oblige, provided her old man set a tune in his favor.

A sudden barb of pain transfixed his shoulder almost before Otis could lock his teeth on it; he was ready to blister in brimstone afore he'd yelp like Nat Fanning, yonder. Last night he kept everyone awake for hours with his whimperings for a measure of laudanum. On turning to look at Fanning, Otis realized that his neighbor was emerging from a drugged slumber.

The more Nat Fanning regained consciousness, the deeper grew his sense of bitterness. Why hadn't those bragging, swaggering bastards at the Red Lion tavern warned him a feller could get hurt so bad? Wasn't right any created being should have to suffer as he had, with his broken arm and a crushed left foot. Though Doctor Burnham opined that he might save his foot, Nat Fanning knew better; today, it had become gangrenous and hideously painful, which meant he must go back onto the dreadful operating platform once again.

Well, he wasn't going to. Not Nat Fanning. It would be better to die. Nobody would care much what became of him, not with Brother Lem killed at Brandywine and Pa become a stumbling, red-eyed drunkard. Oh-h God, how his foot hurt! The fierce, unending pain drove breath from his lungs. Christ, how he hated his shipmates, the officers, himself, everything. Struggling up onto his elbow Fanning glared furiously about, then commenced to scream and rave.

"We're jus' murderers and thieves! Jus' gallows fruit, that's what we are!" he gibbered. "That's why God in his jus' wrath has smited us— 'S no lie! Guardian angel jus' told me so. We're a-goin' to burn in hell, forever!"

"Shut up, you goddam', zany-pated loon," Zaddock Fish, who hadn't been able to move his lower limbs since a sudden lurch of the brig had pinned him shrieking in agony between a loose gun carriage and the bulwarks, reached for a calking maul. "One more yip out of ye, ye snivelling coward, and I'll bash your head in," he snarled. "Ain't none of us livin' on silk."

Zaddock Fish spoke so threateningly because of a terrible fear rising within him. What if Fanning was right? Were he and the rest murderers? The *Grand Turk's* broadsides in the past had slain many and many a poor seaman. Fear for himself was overpowering. How weird to feel not the least sensation in his feet or legs, not even when Doctor Burnham pricked them with a sail-maker's needle.

God above! What would become of Hannah and the kids? Even if he survived this business, he would be naught but an intolerable burden to them—for all that Nancy was bright and clever and young Zaddock mighty strong for a lad of seven; a good thing he and Hannah hadn't other issue.

All at once a wonderful idea occurred to Fanning; it seized and feasted on his imagination.

"Hi, there, Wampee! What did that dunder-headed gunner's mate claim our casualties was?"

"Seems to me 'twas we lost fourteen killed outright

durin' the battle," Wampee spoke slowly, scratched gray bristles covering his jaw. "Since, there's been ten—no nine—o' us dragged outter here ter feed the sharks. And that won't be all, either."

"Oh, stow it! Stow it!" whimpered Fanning. "How dast you talk like that when we all walk in the Valley of the Shadow?"

The Carolinian gave the interruption no heed, rubbed his chin again and winked at the paralyzed seaman propped on his mattress across the cockpit. "Reckon I see what you're drivin' at, friend. Twenty-two dead men means twenty-two shares that mebbe hain't been assigned and will be re-divided."

"Whuffer you-all care 'bout that? Effen a couple o' prizes makes port we be plenty rich." For the first time in hours Jupiter Blake, the Negro spoke. He lay at Nat Fanning's left, but because of his sable color one barely noticed him in the persistent gloom of the sick bay.

"Some o' them dead men's shares will have been assigned," Otis pointed out. "Don't go counting chicks before they've hatched out, Fan."

"But most of 'em ain't been," Fanning insisted. "Yessiree, I'll lay a wager not about five hands made assignment of their share. Sailors is superstitious 'bout assignments and you know it. Did you assign yours, fer example?"

"No. I ain't axing for trouble."

Cunningly, Fanning drew out the rest and learned that his guess was a good one. Only the boy, Spurgeon Grannis, Rockwell and himself had made share assignments.

Grinning to himself Fanning lay back. The more deaths, the greater the value of shares held by survivors. Hopefully, he considered the other eight figures, shadowy and misshapen under their bedclothes.

One of the Indians, Standing Bear, who had lost a leg, was almost sure to die because he didn't want to live. George Black Beaver wasn't any too hale, either; not with such a big splinter hole in his back. There was much morbid activity in the wound and proud flesh was swelling mightily.

Almost happily, Fanning eyed the lad called Spurgeon Grannis. Being young and hale, he might survive—for all that his right arm had been carried away by one of the few musket balls to take effect aboard the privateer. The younger, he knew, had damn'-near bled to death before the Sawbones got to him just in time. Fanning conceived a sudden dislike of Doctor Burnham. But for him and his art there'd have been a lot more weighted hammocks splashing overboard.

During an ensuing period of silence George Black Beaver of the Heron Clan among the Oneida people stared blankly at the ever-swinging lantern.

"When I return to the Long House and show to the Sachem and the old men these honorable scars of battle against white men—the craftiest and most treacherous of foes—will they grant me my man's name?"

Black Beaver blinked. But for that single groan he'd emitted during the second day of tests for the young men, he'd have been accepted as a warrior, and need never have gone to sea. Even now, as he stared at the deck beams above him, he heard the surprised grunts of the elder warriors, could read the withering contempt in the eyes of Ska-mon-da-ga.

"A woman's heart," observed the Grand Sachem of the Oneidas, "has entered this lodge of men. Let it be driven forth!"

Pelted with stones and beaten by the whole town, Black Beaver was harried out into the forest; pine slivers they had stuck into his shoulders during the test were still a-smoulder.

How many lonely hours of hunger, cold and bitter shame at himself had he endured? Now, however, he had borne this even more exquisite torture without so much as a quick-drawn breath to betray his anguish. No one save the red-haired medicine man could have suspected the depth of his pain.

He knew now he must live to return and cast at the feet of Ska-mon-da-ga a banner taken from the hated French. That in this war the French happened to be allies of the Thirteen Fires did not bother Black Beaver. Since first the White Man had come to America the children of the French king and their allies, the Hurons, had been the bitterest, most relentless enemies of the Six Nations.

The Oneida's liquid black eyes sought the small form beside him. This youth possessed a rare courage and had wept far less than his grown companions. Sometime, during the night Black Beaver's hand, all rough from application to rope and holystone, crept, crab-wise, across

the blankets, to close on that of the youth and lend him
courage.

Curious, how often Pa's counsellings occurred to
Spurgeon. "Grannis men, my lad, ain't given to whimpering." A trite warning, no doubt, it had yet remained
lodged in his memory.

Eventually silence ruled in the sick bay; it emphasized
the stertorous breathing of Standing Bear. The Indian
was sure 'nough going to die, thought Nat Fanning, and
grinned in the darkness.

xiv. Fast Run The Sands

Only reluctantly did Peter Burnham respond to a
continued shaking of his naked shoulder.

"Wha—wha's matter?" he mumbled and roused up on
that bunk which had been occupied by Abel Doane ere
he'd gone aboard the *Jolly Tar* as prize master.

It was Tom Laughry, the only remaining boy of the
ship's company. "Doctor Burnham, sir, wake up! Wake
up, sir!"

Peter swung his feet to the deck but, ashamed to be
found stark naked beneath a single sheet, hugged the
covering to him. It had been so infernally hot in Doane's
cabin that he couldn't bear the thought of a long nightgown.

"What's amiss?" he asked. "Speak up, boy."

"Sir, Cap'n's come-to; he's askin' fer you. Wants you
should come to him right away."

Captain Robert Ashton, of Norfolk in Virginia, lay on
his berth breathing shallowly. When he forgot and attempted to draw a deep breath, a dozen red-hot pike
points seemed to pierce the right side of his chest. By
now he was becoming resigned to this hateful and overwhelming weakness.

Ashton didn't know quite what to think. Since boyhood he had been ever hale; never a sick bed had been his
lot. Yet, somehow, he knew his vitality was near spent.
The Angel of Death, whose wings he had heard many and
many a time during a hard-fought action, was about to lay
chill fingers on his brow and say, "Come with me."

Robert Ashton knew for sure he was about to die,
though he couldn't tell why. Lying there hot and so very

weary, he regretted that, never again, would his hands caress the wonderful cool warmth of his wife's white shoulders. Never again in all this world would he be privileged to watch the delicate deviltry of her eyes, the tenderly mocking twist of lips that still spelt Heaven.

Why didn't the surgeon come? Time was growing short. His feet, his hands, felt chill as the water of that ice pond back home when winter set in. Another breath—oh, God how his side hurt. He thought of his first wife Peggy, poor sweet, cleverly foolish Peggy, dying much like this aboard the *Desdemona*. Had such reflections troubled her last moments?

All considered, he was luckier than most men who, during this war, had embarked on the Great Adventure. Five full years of happiness had been his; years enriched with Andrea's love and blessed with comfort and their children.

It was something, Rob Ashton felt, to know that he'd done what he could, in a quiet and unspectacular way towards serving his country. Aye. He'd risked death time and again to keep alive that trade which was the very life blood of the new nation. Come to think on it, during the seven cruises on which he had embarked, the *Grand Turk II* and *Grand Turk III* had prized some twenty British vessels.

It came as a relief to realize that never once during his maritime career had he ever been needlessly harsh to prisoners fallen into his power, nor had he handled his crews with anything but fairness and generosity. How many other privateer owners could say the same?

Why didn't Doctor Burnham appear? Time was wasting—nothing could hold back this inexorable running out of life's sands.

To think that only five years had elapsed since he and Andrea had, in Philadelphia, commenced to rebuild the wreckage of his earlier life. Rob thought again of his first wife; how he'd loved her, for all she was the daughter of Major Fleming, a stern and uncompromising Loyalist. How very young they both had been back in '75. Later, he might have understood how to handle so high-spirited a girl.

At this late hour he found that he could recall every detail of that humble log cabin on Plume's Creek near Norfolk in which they had set up housekeeping. Clear as day,

Rob Ashton could recall the bold lines on which he'd built the original *Grand Turk*. Poor *Grand Turk*, burnt by a patriot mob before even she could spread her sails to an ocean breeze. It had required her loss to teach him that, in a struggle like this, no one successfully could tread the middle ground.

Then the captain's mind ran for a while on the *Desdemona's* long, tortured voyage which, on some reefs off Somerset Island in the Bermudas, had ended in disaster.

A thin smiled curved Ashton's fever-dried lips. Well, if anything the rector said was true, before long he'd see Peggy and David—that beloved and baffling brother who'd caused him so much grief. David would be awaiting him where he was headed.

In a way Rob wasn't sorry that the end was at hand; at bottom, he'd never been a man of violence. Always he had yearned for peace, but had found none during this endless, senseless war.

Briefly the *Grand Turk's* master recalled the great moments of his career—the time he'd beaten Sir Lovell Dandy and Colonel Andrus at *vingt-et-un,* his capture of General Sir Henry Clinton's pay ship off the Carolinas, his anxiety the day the twins had been born and those sweltering summer days before little David had arrived to assure a future to the Ashton name. An anxiety over Susan's future came to plague him; the poor crippled child would have need of wealth. Curious, since he and Andrea Granville had married, Susan's accident had been the only ill chance to mar their life together.

Damn that Laughry boy. Where had he got to? Why didn't Peter Burnham appear? Rob wanted to talk—needed to. That deadly chill now had mounted until it was numbing his thighs and elbows. Relentlessly it kept creeping up, up his body.

To have clasped the children, Harriet, Susan, David and tiny Robert just once more would be wonderful. Oh, to run fingers over the incredibly soft base of David's neck. Rob wondered how his elder son would turn out. Probably well enough, because Andrea, English to her fingertips, entertained firm ideas about discipline and the obligations of gentility.

The children, Rob reckoned, would make out all right; but what of the United States? Bankrupt and near exhaustion after five long years of strife, could the new nation survive? What a vast pity he wouldn't be privileged to learn what would chance.

The familiar noises of his ship under way proved soothing. From where he lay he could see most of this comfortable, familiar little cabin, a fact which reassured him.

Where had he made his first error concerning the *Albany*? Her very size should have prompted greater caution. Had his guns exacted a compensating toll of the enemy? He'd noticed right many splinters flying. Oh, well. No use conjecturing, he was so weary. Rob closed his eyes and only roused when he heard a footstep, felt someone's hand testing his pulse. He couldn't see very well, so he asked, "That you, Burnham?"

"Yes, Captain." Peter Burnham's voice now sounded nearly as soft and gentle as Andrea's.

Peter replaced Ashton's icy hand on the counterpane miserably aware that not even the greatest physician in Europe long could avert death.

Rob Ashton's voice was little more than a whisper. "I am going, ain't I?"

"Yes, there's no use lying, sir. And very soon, I fear." He had hard work to blink back hot, most unprofessional tears.

"My thanks for your honesty, Peter. Always cling to that integrity. And now—you'll undertake to see the shares fairly divided?"

"Aye, sir."

"You're to divide half of my prize money among the wounded for 'twas my stupidity—" The dying man's eyes closed momentarily and he sighed. "Take my hand, Peter, I—I feel so lonely in this half-light. There, that's better."

"Yes, sir?"

"Pray present my tenderest compliments," he employed the old, genteel phrase, "and ever enduring affections to—to—" he faltered, licked lips turning blue-lavender, "to my darling Andrea."

"As quickly as I return to Boston sir. Never doubt it."

"And pray inform Peggy—" his breathing grew shorter and more labored.

"Peggy? Who, may I ask is she?"

"Peggy Fleming, my first wife, dead the last six years. I fear, through ignorance, I used her ill."

Peter's fingers tightened on the cold hand under them. "I am certain you didn't willingly do so. Is there any special commission you wish to charge me with?"

But Robert Ashton was wavering on the threshold of Eternity. He lay silent and so motionless that Peter pressed his ear over Ashton's heart.

"He's gone—" Peter muttered, but he was wrong.

Ashton's voice sounded quite clearly amid the darkness. "Andrea, beloved." Then, indeed, the *Grand Turk*'s master fell forever silent.

xv. Requiescat in Pace

A few minutes after sunrise, Eldad Greenleaf ordered the *Grand Turk III* brought into the wind and she lay pitching gently, her canvas idle, her stays slack. Never, thought Peter Burnham, would he behold more beautiful a morning—so cool, so rosy blue, so peaceful was the ocean. The acting-captain's voice sounded thick and uncertain when he ordered the crew to attention, not only because, like all aboard, he entertained a deep, if inarticulate, affection for him whose body was about to be consigned to the depths, but also because of certain invisible demons tearing at his parched throat.

Not in many years had Eldad Greenleaf existed so long lacking the solace of rum. Yet he'd not drink, no matter what the excuse; it had come upon him that the Almighty, in His infinite wisdom, was offering Eldad Greenleaf one final opportunity of redemption. Every incentive was his.

This fine, tall brig and every man in her, would survive—or perish—through his abilities or lack of them. Main hard work, this rolling back the fogs of alcohol. To make assurance doubly sure he'd, an hour ago, tossed overboard the key to Captain Ashton's liquor locker. By the Lord Harry, he *would* prove that Eldad Greenleaf still could sail a vessel anywhere on God's green oceans he took the notion to. Amazing, how rapidly facts and instincts had commenced to return.

Now, yards creaking and topsails slatting, the *Grand Turk* was headed dead into the wind's eye. He warned the helmsman to look lively lest the brig be taken aback. Every man of the crew who could be on deck stood in two double ranks just forward of the mainmast. In unison their bodies yielded to the *Grand Turk's* motion. Their black, bronze and brown faces were taut, almighty solemn of expression.

Fingers trembling, Greenleaf opened the Book of Common Prayer to a marker, cleared his voice once, twice, then commenced: "I am the Resurrection and the Life—"

There wasn't much more could be said; Eldad figgered the Burial Service seemed to cover the whole of it, but he felt he ought to say something for his own part, so he drew a very deep breath, squared his shoulders and gazed at those brown and homely faces ranged in even ranks to either side of a mess table upon which lay the body of Robert Ashton, shrouded and sewed into a new white hammock.

"Guess everyone of ye knows I'd like mightily to deliver a first-rate speech of farewell to—to our Captain. Most likely you're all right now taking leave of him—private-like—just between him and yourselves. And, oh, hell, you'll do it a sight better than I can. So for us all I say to a fine captain, a rare gentleman and a true patriot—rest in peace."

Using the heel of his hand, Greenleaf smeared a stream of tears across his cheek, rasped, "Drummer, sound off!"

When young Tom Laughry's drum began beating the long roll the brig's ensign sank from half-mast to the quarterdeck. Many of the men openly and unashamed wept as two of the oldest seamen aboard heaved up one end of the mess table. Easily, the weighted hammock slipped overside and, creating hardly any splash at all, became lost to sight in the sea.

At a sign from Greenleaf young Laughry beat a quickstep. The bare-headed men broke ranks as the Stars and Stripes soared up to the main gaff. Simultaneously, the helm went down, the sails hesitated, then filled; smoothly, silently, the *Grand Turk* resumed her course, leaving in her wake a twisting spiral of silvery bubbles.

XVI. MARIGOT ISLAND

AS THE *Grand Turk III* continued on her southerly course Eldad Greenleaf's nerves grew tauter. Never, during his

existence, had he experienced a similar torture. Every
day the acting-captain consumed gallons of tea "strong
enough to float an axe head," so the cook declared.
Greenleaf, however, had more than his burning throat to
worry over. The lightly wounded, one by one, had returned to duty, but the brig remained dangerously under-
manned for all that. Worse still, the leaks were gaining
steadily despite ceaseless toil at the pumps.

"In this state we'll never fetch Saint Jan," the Hampshireman warned Peter Burnham over an unappetizing
supper. "Water in the forrad well's gainin' nigh half a
foot a day. Do you notice how sluggish we ride?"

Peter sat back in his chair, wiped his sweat-spangled
forehead with an already sodden handkerchief. "Yes, I
had noticed it. What's to be done?"

Greenleaf went over to stand staring out of the stern
ports at the sunset's afterglow; tonight the whole sky
seemed to be aflame.

The Hampshireman, turning, said, "Damned bulldog's
shot must have started such a mort o' sheathing below
our water line we must careen very soon. With so few
men, 't won't be easy; but if we're ever to sight Cape Cod
again, it'll have to be done."

"Where do you figure on careening?"

Greenleaf went to the chart locker, searched a moment, then brought forth a chart of the West Indies.
"Once, years ago, durin' the old French war, we got the
scurvy aboard—needed fresh meat and vegetables. Do
you see this here lady's kerchief of an island?"

"The one marked Marigot?"

"Aye, it belongs to the Frenchies. We went turtle hun-
tin' on it and came across a fine lagoon where the water
stays deep right close into the shore."

" 'Tis inhabited?"

"No—not that time, leastways. Mebbe we can repair
our damages there without molestation."

Long after Greenleaf had returned to the quarterdeck
Peter remained staring at the chart. "Marigot is a pretty
name," he thought, "but nowhere near so pretty as Trina. Isn't it absurd I should think so much on a girl I've
not known longer than a couple of hours?" There was no
sense in this infatuation, he knew. Trina was Danish and
the arrogant product of a foreign civilization. No doubt
she'd been crammed to her pretty ears with nonsense

about privilege. Her father, being a Danish nobleman, no doubt was fat and bigoted; the very antithesis of Pa and his stolid merchant background. But despite all logic Baroness Varsaa's dainty, pale blonde beauty continued to haunt him.

How was she faring? What had been the fate awaiting her on Saint Jan? As soon as the *Grand Turk* reached Coral-haven he'd make inquiries; discreet inquiries of course.

Amid the hot and mephitic darkness of the sick bay, Otis Rockwell lay trying to ignore pangs shooting from the stump of his right arm and had succeeded fairly well since becoming convinced that he would recover. The Sawbones had been almost jovial tonight while changing his dressings.

"There'll be a stump you and I can be proud of," Doctor Burnham had chuckled. "The flap's healing in first-rate shape and your ligatures will come free in a few days."

Now Otis, staring wide-eyed into the darkness, all at once became aware that the lad beside was breathing very slowly indeed. He counted one—two—three——— —nine, ten, eleven.

"Spurgeon!" he called softly. "Spurge, are you ailing?"

No answer. Otis tested the other's blanket; suddenly his hand recoiled because its fingers had come in contact with a warm and sticky puddle. He knew instantly what was amiss.

"Watch! Watch!" he shouted; cursing, the other wounded awoke.

"What's amiss?"

"Watch!"

"Ahoy, below! Coming."

A clatter of feet sounded on the companion; then a lantern's amber light grew, created grostesque shadows.

Awkwardly, Otis Rockwell struggled to a sitting position, peered at the figure beside him. God above! Where had been the bandages to his wound showed only a hideous area of mangled flesh and the rhythmic pumping of a diminishing stream of arterial blood.

"He done pulled 'em off," gasped Jupiter. "He daid—"

XVII. OFF SAINT JAN

ON THE FIRST of May the privateer lay to her anchor,
dainty and proud of being, once more, a whole ship. Only
a lack of paint betrayed neat patches in her planking and
bulwarks.

For Peter Burnham the period required to careen had
proved of inestimable value. There could be no doubt but
that his injured fingers were somewhat more obedient
than they had been, though they would never regain full
flexibility. Best of all, he had shaken off his sense of outrage, his sullen futile resentment against that which had
been done to him.

Lighter in weight, but more sinewy than ever, Peter's
body from the waist up had become burnt to a deep gold-
en brown hue which made his eyes appear an even bright-
er blue. Curiously enough, his red hair had become
bleached near its ends, infusing yellow highlights among
the copper-red tones.

This was to be the privateer's last night at Marigot Island. All day long the crew had been heaving aboard
freshly charged water casks, firewood and great sacks of
wild fruits. Helpless on their backs a dozen sea turtles
thumped and sighed dolefully between the guns.

By invitation, Peter joined Eldad Greenleaf on the
quarterdeck in order to enjoy the sunset while smoking a
quiet pipe. The hands, dog-tired and digesting their supper, lay about the deck, talking or sleeping.

"Wal," Greenleaf drawled, the glow of his pipe half
revealing his bushy brows and deep set eyes, "tomorrow
it's back to the wars for the old *Grand Turk.* God send
we'll meet with no more bulldogs."

"You've done a mighty fine job of refitting," Peter told
him simply. "Captain Ashton would be pleased if he
knew."

"Maybe he does. Who knows?" Greenleaf held up a
hand. "If ye don't object, Doctor, let's not talk of the
Cap'n—I—I was mighty fond o' him. We'll fetch home
all right." Greenleaf continued looking fixedly at the first
timid stars showing above the royal yard. "Count o' the
Captain's Missus, when the time comes I'll make a quick
run into Massachusetts Bay."

"And then?"

"I'll bank my shares and wait for this God-damned war to end. Figger I've had a belly full o' privateerin'. Come peace times I'll buy me a pair o' fifty-ton schooners and engage in the rice trade from the Carolinas; there's a mart o' profit in it, I hear tell."

The moon began to achieve brilliance, sent its rays to dancing and skipping over the mirrored calm of Marigot lagoon until her glow silvered the brig's spars and etched the delicate tracery of her rigging against the sky.

"Doctor, what'll you aim to do?"

"I expect I'll continue my studies," Peter replied.

"But yer almighty artful right now—never have seen such a handy Sawbones. The men swear by you."

"My thanks, Captain. This cruise has taught me, among other things, how little—how very small is the sum of my skill. I intend to journey abroad—to Holland, France and Italy." He turned, abruptly facing his companion. "How much do you suppose my share will amount to—at the very least?"

"Only Lady Luck and the prize courts can answer you that, Doctor. God granting that a couple o' the prizes make port I'd say ye can figger on fifteen hundred pounds, sterling." He arose.

"Well, sir, I'm to bed; we'll begin raising anchor afore dawn. Goodnight, Doctor."

Peter made no move to go below; it was balmy and cool on deck; besides his mind had begun to run again on Trina Varsaa.

Peter thought, "Right now Trina must be settling her new home down yonder on Saint Jan. How will she make out? Maybe that fellow Frydendahl—that was his name, wasn't it? Yes, Stephan Frydendahl—might take agreeably to the notion of receiving a readymade heir for a wedding present; foreigners are funny about such matters." All he knew was that Danes were something like Swedes, speaking different dialects of the same tongue.

Greenleaf, too, knew little about Denmark save that it turned out some pretty able mariners and was a small but rich kingdom on the very northern rim of Europe. Also he claimed the Danes could drink like porpoises and maintained large interests in the slave trade.

It was the last day of May. Bits of greenery and an occasional coconut went floating by; numbers of gloriously colored dolphins appeared to play about under the brig's cutwater and flying fish became so common that no one paid them the least heed.

Now tiny thrushes, warblers and finches, blown out on the sea, settled, exhausted and forlorn in the rigging; once an exquisite little hummingbird fell onto the deck. None of these castaways lived long; quite early the crew wrung the necks of the larger birds and tossed them into a stew pot.

What with the fine food and benevolent weather, the spirits of the crew ran higher than at any time since the *Albany* had showed her White Ensign. They sang "Polly in Town" with a lusty good-will.

But finally, when the *Grand Turk's* lookouts sighted to starboard numerous reefs and cays, all hands grew anxious. Had Old Man Greenleaf's navigation been up to snuff? In any case, the brig was stepping handsomely along a course laid to the south-southeast of Puerto Rico, before winds variable but favorable. Next day, larger islands were raised and quantities of sea birds appeared to circle, screaming over the wake streaming after the dainty brig like a bride's train of lace.

Eldad Greenleaf ordered the brig's canvas reduced.

"I aim to raise Saint Jan just about daylight," he explained to Peter while bent over a fine new Admiralty chart.

"By which channel do you aim to approach, sir?" inquired the acting mate, a half-breed Wiscassett from Cape Cod. "Drake's Channel, mayhap?"

Greenleaf sucked his lower lip in between his teeth and slowly shook his head. "Nay. I'm minded to sail down King's Channel, but presently I'll veer into Saint James Passage and then bear sharp to starboard and stand in to Saint Jan from the south'ard. That should allow us wide berth of any cruisers on patrol off Tortola; figger those British bastards might keep a bulldog or two stationed in Sir Francis Drake's Bay. Again, by putting into Coral Bay from the south'ard we'd find plenty o' room should need arise to run for it past Saint Croix and so out into the Carib Sea."

To attempt this passage, Peter deduced, required not only uncommon courage but sterling seamanship. On even the Admiralty's most recent charts, reefs and shoals were more often uncharted than noted.

Under reduced canvas the refitted brig still sailed so well that Greenleaf put her into the wind for half a day and used the interval to overhaul his cannon, a ridiculous proceeding since but two full gun crews remained aboard. If it came to a fight they could accomplish but little.

After dark on the second of June, Eldad Greenleaf ordered the brig's yards braced to catch a gentle breeze out of the west. His jaws working on an enormous cud of Orançock tobacco, Greenleaf remained beside the tiller, but maintained constant communication with the lookouts at both mastheads. Once the brig entered King's Channel her crew lined the rail and anxiously peered into the dark. Well they might. Let the *Grand Turk* run aground on any of the numerous reefs hereabouts, then all that they might have won would, to all practical purpose, become lost.

The land smell momentarily was growing more pronounced—so said the older hands. Though no moon shone, the stars were so brilliant that a sharp-eyed man might discern a cay half a mile distant.

Silently the *Grand Turk* maintained her course, until both lookouts at the same moment called, "Land ho!"

"What do you see?"

"Two cays off the starboard bow." Then almost immediately, "There's three islands of the larboard bow, sir, big ones and dead ahead."

Greenleaf clambered stiffly up into the shrouds, and stood levelling his night glass in obvious uncertainty. Presently, he uttered a short cry of satisfaction.

"Ha! Yonder looks like Thatch Cay. Come half an hour, we should raise Saint Thomas to starboard."

Minutes dragged by. Water whispered along the privateer's sleek sides.

Again came a faint hail from the foretop. "Land ho! A big island, sir; with a mountain raising in its middle."

"Lookout, there! Is it a pointed mountain or a round one?"

"Round, sir, kind o' like Blue Hill outside o' Boston."

"Spang on the nose, by God!" Greenleaf emitted a cackling laugh and slapped his thigh. "That'll be the Camel's Back. 'Pears like Dad Greenleaf ain't forgot much about navigatin'."

Because the Saint James Channel was so tricky,

Greenleaf ordered sail reduced to jibs, topsails and gallants; even so, the brig seemed to move dangerously fast. Presently, the indistinct mass of an island loomed to starboard—an island so large there could be no doubt it was Saint Thomas. Realization that the *Grand Turk* now sailed in neutral waters drew sighs of relief.

A faint sheen of starlight picking out her canvas, the brig entered Sundet Sound; that was what Greenleaf called it.

"Yonder Camel's Back marks Saint Jan's Island," the master explained, studying his chart by the light of a dark lantern. "Beyond lie Big Dog and Little Dog Rocks. Yessiree, provided this breeze holds, we'll drop anchor safe and sound in Coral Bay come sunup."

"My sincere compliments on a magnificent example of navigation." Peter was eager and glad to praise the old officer. "Pray God, some day I'll become equally clever with my instruments."

Greenleaf was immensely pleased. "Why, why, Doctor, that's—why, that's mighty handsome of you. But we ain't yet made port."

Before long the brig emerged from Sundet Sound and sailed boldly out into the Caribbean, now showing faintly gray by a false dawn. At once the *Grand Turk* commenced to parallel the southern coast of Saint Jan.

Here and there gleamed an occasional shore light and, up in the foothills, reddish campfires flickered.

After a bit, Greenleaf anxiously commenced to study his topsails—ordered mainsail and forecourse set. "Dag nab it! Pesky wind's a-fadin' out," he grunted. "Was afraid it might. Often does in these latitudes, just about daybreak."

His fears proved justified. The waves alongside lost their crisp sound and the sails no longer tugged strongly at their braces and sheets. The mainsail would fill, only to sag and then fill again.

To the eastward appeared a faint glow; gradually it threw into bolder profile the extensive mountains on Saint Jan, and erased the lesser stars. The smell of land grew much stronger and soon Peter detected a faint sour-sweet odor.

"That'll come from some sugar-grindin' mills," one of the deckhands informed him.

" 'Tis chancy we're so deep in neutral water," Greenleaf presently remarked. "Afore we fetch the Ram's Head it'll be broad daylight."

"Ram's Head?"

"'Tis a headland we must weather before we can stand into Coral Bay and cast anchor at Coralhaven."

The acting-captain's prediction proved entirely accurate; dawn found the *Grand Turk* still cruising parallel to the southern shore of Saint Jan and so close in that her company could easily discern a short line of jagged corals and countless softly green canefields geometrically arranged beyond them. Now and then the white outlines of plantation buildings and boiling houses dotted the mountainsides.

The sun was well clear of the horizon when the Ram's Head, a bold massive rock formation, appeared to port.

"Mebbe I'd better take a squint and learn what's what in the harbor."

Still pleased over Peter's praise, Greenleaf beckoned the physician; then sought the main crosstrees.

Because the Caribbean was so calm, Peter found little difficulty in surveying a big, well-protected bay, lying beyond the Ram's Head.

"Right smart lot o' craft in port," Greenleaf remarked. "Looks like two of 'em are making sail."

Peter made no reply; through the glass he was studying the details of Coralhaven. He saw the square towers of two stone churches, the governor's mansion on a height dominating the harbor itself and the glacis of a small fort flying the red and white flag of Denmark. Already sunlight was glancing off the dew-wetted roofs of some seventy-five or a hundred white or yellow houses clustering in disorderly fashion about the further end of the harbor.

At anchor in the harbor there must have been easily thirty vessels of all rigs and tonnages. Already, small boats were busy, plying between them and shore.

What immediately captured Peter's attention was the presence of a tall ship-of-the-line—she looked like a third-rater of maybe sixty guns, but towered over the rest of the shipping as a giant oak rises above underbrush. His brown nut of a face screwed into a knot behind the eyepiece of his telescope, Greenleaf was watching her crew shake loose sale after sail.

"My eyes ain't so good as they once was," Greenleaf muttered. "Can you make out her flags?"

"Aye, she flies a red flag bearing a white cross from each of the tops."

"Are they cut swallow-tailed?"

"Yes."

"Then, she'll be Danish, praise God. 'Twouldn't do fer us to git caught by an enemy liner in a flat ca'm like this."

The Danish man-of-war must be benefiting by some light offshore breeze, for her great press of canvas filled and she came bowling majestically out to sea with the sun glancing and dancing off the rich gold leaf decorating her bows. But where the privateer lay, the wind had practically died out and again there sounded aloft a futile rattling of reef points against lifeless canvas. The brig's huge American ensign barely stirred under the lightest imaginable of airs.

"We'll be a long while fetchin' the last half-league into the harbor," Greenleaf complained as they swung down to the quarterdeck.

Tall and still taller loomed the Danish third-rater; those aboard the *Grand Turk* judged her foc's'l must rise easy thirty feet above her cutwater. No doubt because the day promised to be sultry, the Danish ship was sailing with gun ports triced up and, as she drew nearer, the *Grand Turk*'s company even distinguished sailors and a few red-coated marines idling about her deck.

"Ain't sailin' far, sir," remarked the Wiscasset half-breed at Greenleaf's elbow.

"Aye, she'll run just over to Charlotte Amalie or mebbe go to careen at Saint Thomas. Will you look at that sea-goin' hay field she's trailing?" The stranger certainly must have been at sea a very long while, so fouled with weed was her water line.

The privateersmen lined their rail to watch the third-rater's slow, almost sluggish approach. There could be no mistaking now the identity of those flags flying from her tops—they were Danish, all right. If she held her present course she must pass within seventy-five yards of the becalmed privateer.

The privateersmen fell to waving their caps and cheering the foreigner, now sailing almost abeam of the *Grand Turk.* Everyone aboard the brig started when, aboard the liner, a bugle started to sound a discordant series of calls. At the same time a loud rumbling reverberated across the placid sea as through the liner's ports were run the muz-

zles of perhaps twenty-five cannons, their red-painted
ends glaring at the lesser vessel like so many angry eyes.

To a sharp whirring noise the Danish flags shot down
and up rose the flag of a rear-admiral of the Blue Squadron in His Britannic Majesty's Navy.

Silence, characteristic of complete and shattering surprise, pervaded the *Grand Turk's* men—in horrified
astonishment they watched appear on the quarterdeck a
number of figures in blue and white. Only fifty yards distant, a great red-faced fellow wearing an enormous
cocked hat bellowed, "Surrender, ye rebel dogs!"

Eldad Greenleaf recovered, shouted right back,
"These are neutral waters. Ye've no right to attack us."

"Tosh. Make but a single move and I'll blow your tub
out o' the sea. Haul down that rag ye fly."

There could be no doubt but that the Britisher meant to
carry out his threat, no matter how outrageous, how illegal was its basis; so, spouting blasphemies, Eldad Greenleaf ordered the privateer's colors lowered, then cast one
long baleful glance at the man-of-war before turning on
his heel. He fairly ran below as the Stars and Stripes
floated down.

In despairing helplessness the *Grand Turk's* company
watched a pair of long boats lowered by the *Raisonable*—
everyone could read her name done in flourishing gold
script beneath the liner's elaborate stern gilding—
watched red-coated marines and seamen in striped blue
and white jerseys go tumbling into them, their weapons
brightly flashing.

Peter, appalled at this sudden turn of fortune, half
heard from below a noise like that of splintering wood.

By the time the third-rater's boats came bobbing under
the *Grand Turk's* counter, Eldad Greenleaf already was
drunker than a fiddler's bitch.

Ensued for Peter a miserable interval; as the only regularly commissioned officer aboard, he recognized his responsibility and waited, icily calm, on the *Grand Turk's*
quarterdeck, but his stomach went tight at beholding the
United States flag lie, limp and dishonored, below the
taffrail. Most of the experienced hands had already gone
below; wisely they were seizing this opportunity to collect their most valued possessions.

"How far off shore are we?" Peter demanded of the
Wiscasset.

"Not more'n the half of a mile sir," grunted the Indian.

"Then, we're in Danish territorial water?"

"Aye, sir. By two and a half miles."

"What vessel is this?" hailed a hungry-looking lieutenant from the *Raisonable's* long boat.

"The United States' Privateer Brig, *Grand Turk,* sir. It appears I must remind you that we sail in neutral waters. You've no right—"

"Stow that guff, you rebel dog," rasped the Britisher, long, blue-and-white-clad body swaying to the small boat's motion. "My right is sixty-six carriage guns. Lower me a ladder, you Yankee lubbers, and look smart about it."

PART II—ANNABERG

XVIII. The Master

LYING A-BED and waiting for daylight, Stephan Borgardus Frydendahl, Friherre of Annaberg Station, felt in more than usual ill-humor. All night long a pain, stabbing in his back, had kept him sweating and squirming on sodden sheets. Hour after hour, he'd been listening to a voracious humming of insects flitting outside that gauze mosquito bar which protected his great, four-poster bed. Though the netting kept such pests at a distance, its fabric also effectively cut off any breath of air straying in from the sea. What a dog's life this was, even though one grew rich at it.

By now Frydendahl felt convinced that he was afflicted by the Stone. A weakness in that direction seemed to be the lot of all the Frydendahls. His father had died of a kidney stone. The big toe of his left foot also pained him, gave promise of gout. To imagine that great ass of a physician, Cornelis Bodger, telling him to modify his eating and drinking. *Gott!* What a fool! Suppose one cut out eating and drinking what would be left? Only the black girls and, in this climate, only so many of them might be enjoyed each week.

Frydendahl noted light peering in through the lattices across his room and, thankfully, got up.

What really had robbed him of his sleep was a sharp resentment of the trick the Varsaas had attempted to play upon him. While his toes groped for his straw slippers, he wondered for the hundredth time: had Her Majesty's ministers really sent a letter hinting at his prospective bride's condition?

Sometimes Stephan felt this to be so—else why had he been offered, next year, the post of Sub-Inspector General of the Royal Custom Houses? A fine post to be sure; but would it remain open after another ten months? A Varsaa trick? His small soul suspected this to be the case.

Stephan parted his mosquito bar, paused, half out of

the bed. If Katrina had been a trifle less haughty on arrival—no, surely this was just another attempt to make
game of the Frydendahls. The Varsaas would never forget that the Frydendahls for generations had paid them
homage.

So? What effrontery to wish an embarrassing bastard
brat on him. Well, Count Varsaa was to learn that things
had changed; the Frydendahls would tolerate no further
humiliations.

A red and yellow banyan whipping about his plump
and hairy thighs, Stephan seated himself on a terrace
overlooking the Atlantic. He was attempting to eat a light
breakfast of hard-boiled seabird eggs, goat chops, custard apples, cold plantains, and a platter of crab meat
fried to a light gold-brown. A jug of fragrant black coffee
waited, untasted, at his elbow.

Stephan Frydendahl's watery blue eyes considered the
landscape, wandered over his cane flats near the coast,
then shifted to a quartet of windmills which, situated on a
series of hilltops, ground his sugar cane.

He levelled a telescope, through which he studied various gangs of slaves already hard at work in his cane
fields. Klaas, the young Dutchman in charge of Number
Three gang, must be reprimanded; he wasn't driving
those surly black brutes of Mandingoes half hard enough.

Ach! A pang from the vicinity of his kidneys dealt Stephan a twinge sharp enough to evoke a groan and to half
close his eyes. He couldn't stand such torture much longer. Sweat broke out along the Dane's broad forehead.
Craving a drink of cold water, Stephan Frydendahl used
a heavy walking stick to pound angrily on the flagstones
beside him.

"Trina!" he bellowed, picking up a cane of supple
bamboo. "Blast your lazy soul, Trina, you blonde bitch,
rouse out and fetch your lord a jar of cold water!"

Between powerful brown hands he flexed the terrible
cane.

Out from the shadows of a short colonnade appeared
Trina Frydendahl, his wife. Her eyes, because of the
crescents beneath them, appeared more huge than they
really were. In dank, colorless strands her fair hair dangled low, as if to hide, in an ashamed way, the single garment of coarse gray cloth covering a body swelling into
an ungainly convexity.

Wearily, Trina inquired, "You called?"

"My lord husband!" Stephan prompted, staring at her over the bamboo stick ominously bowed between his hands. "God blast your treacherous eyes, must I teach you respect all over again?"

"No, lord husband; very well you have taught me how to respect you." Trina Varsaa Frydendahl swallowed convulsively and her hand tested the purple-blue weals climbing up her forearm. "How may I be of service?"

"Have you no ears, you sweet-scented amateur whore? Water, I told you. Fetch me cold drinking water."

If only she weren't so utterly weary—and exhausted. Somewhere, Trina felt, she retained enough courage to plunge a pair of scissors or a knife into that thick red crease across the back of her husband's neck. Weeks ago, she'd selected her exact target—right at the base of his close-shaven head. 'Twould prove an easy matter, since Stephan's heavy-body seldom was covered by anything heavier than a filthy and food-spotted banyan.

Fighting down her disgust, Trina managed a curtsey rather than endure a slash of that dreadful bamboo stick and started off. To his sharp "Come back here!" she checked herself.

What would he do now? Trina's bare toes curled in an agony of suspense. God, how that cane could sting through her single garment!

"Yes, my lord?"

"Don't go slinking off like a mongrel cur. Run, damn you. When I give you an order. *Run!*"

Heat, already rising from the flagstones, had a dizzying effect but Trina managed to mumble, "Yes, lord husband, I will try to remember." Then she fled, leaving her husband to scowl over his fields at the distant ocean.

A pair of house servants watched her in anxious bewilderment. For sure, the *Baas* must be losing his wits to beat and berate so pretty a lady! All the servants at Annaberg trod extra warily these days.

Trina's dirty bare feet—she was allowed no bathing privileges—whispered away into the house. Once inside, she moved more slowly; it was becoming increasingly hard to ignore the unsupported drag of breasts grown heavy and tender. A black woman, risking a shy smile of sympathy, passed Trina a long stone bottle.

Mechanically, Trina tested a damp film on its outside

attesting the fact that evaporation had cooled the water within. Feeling desperately short of breath, she paused; it was time to remind herself that, after all, she was a Varsaa.

Even yet she found herself still unable fully to appreciate the enormity of this situation into which she had become trapped. No doubt now that the promised explanatory letter had never been forwarded by the Court of Köbenhavn. Who could have failed her? Probably one of the Dowager-Queen's sycophants.

She could not have been more astonished than that her casual reference to the approaching birth of Prince Karl's child should have constituted Frydendahl's first inkling of her condition. She'd never forget how Stephan's flattered pride and ponderous gallantry had, all in a minute, switched to snarling contempt, from that to studied insult and finally to sheer brutality.

Under the circumstances, Trina could not deny that Stephan had cause for complaint; and the old, unspoken grudge between their families made a devil of him. To Stephan it must mean much that, for the first time in two hundred years, a Frydendahl—scion of common peasants reeking of manure—held the advantage over a Varsaa.

A realization of the completeness of her helplessness contributed to Trina's mounting desperation. On the Island of Saint Thomas something might have been done to alarm her family concerning her fate, but on Saint Jan Stephan Frydendahl was all-powerful. Was he not one of the wealthiest planters on the island? There were not many such landlords, only fifty or sixty pale reefs dotting a restless black ocean of near five thousand slaves.

Never, since the week following her wedding, had Trina been granted opportunity to address another white woman. At Annaberg, the servants had been warned, under pain of the most dreadful punishments, to disregard her existence. One of Stephan's first acts was to dismiss good, faithful Magda. Now she was caring for the numerous children of one Nichlos Ditlof, a crony of his. God, how she needed Magda; her time, Trina calculated, was but a scant two months distant.

In the cool of the colonnade she lingered precarious moments. Her image, seen in a tiny pool, was frightening. Gone was her rose-leaf complexion, the sun having lashed her fine pale skin, browned it and toughened it out of all recognition. Dull blue bruises betrayed that, in drunken moments, her dear lord husband was prone to be free with his bamboo cane.

In the distance the sound of a bell, jangling loudly, startled her. That would be that *Herr Doktor* Bodger, whose principal claim to distinction lay in his boast of having sired well over a hundred mulatto brats.

"Trina! Bring my water."

The flagstones burnt the soles of her feet; not yet were they toughened sufficiently to endure such a heat. Toes flinching, Trina carried her water jar across to Frydendahl's gross, half-naked figure lolling on a wicker chair facing on Leinster Bay. She had bent to serve him when his stick dealt her a stinging cut across the thigh.

"Kneel!" he roared. "Kneel when you serve me, you disgraceful trollop."

Eyes filling, Trina sucked the linings of her mouth between her teeth to keep from weeping. There was nothing to do but obey; there was nothing to be gained by offering resistance.

What particularly enraged Trina was her present clumsy shapelessness. Those small proud breasts, of which she had always been so vain, were now become painfully distended globes; her once trim ankles were slender no longer, but thick and puffy.

"I'll have fresh sheets on my bed," Stephan told her, thick lips suddenly buckling with pain. "For the sake of your hide see that tonight the wind sail is properly adjusted outside my window. Last night I nearly smothered. After that, get to your room and await my orders."

Trina forced herself to bend her head and mutter, "Yes, lord husband," before waddling back to the welcome blue-white shadows of the collonade. She was finding it most difficult to walk barefoot. Stephan had forbidden her high-heeled slippers—shoes of any sort, for that matter. As a result the great tendons along the backs of her legs ached from an unaccustomed tension.

Once Trina gained the miserable, yet welcome, shelter of that narrow cubicle into which Stephan Frydendahl locked her most of the time, she collapsed onto a rough blanket on her cot. Softly, the unhappy young woman commenced to weep. Why did Stephan have to be so hateful?

Oh, what heaven it would be to find herself magically transplanted back to the coast of Sjaelland and safely home in Varsaa manor.

At a slight sound from the direction of her door Trina started up violently. Was Stephan coming to taunt and curse and maybe beat her again? No. It was Mamma Bellona who slipped past the heavy, iron-bound portal. The old colored woman advanced with a finger held tight against great, purplish, clam-like lips. She carried a small stone jar—Trina knew what it contained—a salve rich in coconut oil.

Obediently, Trina pulled up her single unlovely garment and lay down so that Mamma Bellona might anoint the distended skin of her abdomen and so, perhaps, she might avoid those *striae* often enduring long after childbirth.

"Sweet little dove. Jus' yo' lie still. Mamma Bellona rub away de hurt."

The old creature dropped onto bony knees beside the cot, and, catching up Trina's roughened and unfragrant hand, kissed it, though she'd stood to earn herself twenty strokes with the flapper should anyone witness this act of homage.

Long held a slave in Jamaica, Mamma Bellona spoke English far better than Danish. Besides, it seemed safer to converse in the first language. None of the other Negroes understood anything but Danish or Dutch.

"Missy, two days gone by in Coralhaven young buckra gemmun speak yo' name."

"A buckra?" Out of a semi-stupor induced by her misery Trina struggled to understand. Buckra? Oh yes, that usually was applied to Englishmen and, more recently, to Americans. "He spoke my name?" Trina's heart gave a sudden leap and her eyes flew wide open.

"Yessum. Fo' true." Mamma Bellona was far from stupid.

To win Mis' Trina's gratitude—and the possibility of eventual freedom—she risked at most twenty lashes. Friherre would never set her free. Half a century ago, among certain sour-smelling jungles fringing the Niger, one of the tribal story tellers had recounted a fable—that of the bandicoot. It appeared that the little bandicoot had gnawed through a tether imprisoning his friend, the King of the Jungle. Because of that small and kindly act, the bandicoot lived long and only died of overeating at My Lord the Elephant's table.

"A—stranger?" Trina sat up on her cot. "His hair—?"

"Lak de sunset, Missy."

"Oh-h, go on. For the love of God, go on!"

"De buckra gemmun come ober fum Tortola, two, t'ree days gone. At Frederick Five Tavern gemmun he ask if young princess come from the White Country. He ask an' ask agin. When no one tell he ask, 'Whar gone de Baroness Varsaa?'"

Despite the humid heat gathering in her cell-like room, Trina grabbed Mamma Bellona's skinny shoulders.

"What did he look like, Mamma?" Suddenly, it seemed not at all strange to call this withered, gray-blue hag "mother."

"He tall, fo' true, tall lak R'yal palm, lak Coromantee warrior."

Trina's naked breasts lifted to a very deep breath; for the first time in many weeks she smiled. "You are sure this gentlemen had hair like the sunset?"

"Fo' true, Missy—not many such."

Trina's spirits revived. No longer did she feel so completely alone; but of Doctor Burnham—how well she recalled his name—how much help had she any right to expect?

Trina lay back again breathing quickly, her skin softly gleaming amid the humid gloom. The old Negress nodded to herself as she recommenced her massage. So this was how the breeze blew? Chaw! Things might happen at Annaberg ere long.

It came about, two days later, that Hostie Bronsted, landlord of the King Frederick V Tavern, dispatched a Negro boy up to Annaberg.

Perhaps Friherre Frydendahl would be interested to learn that, among the guests in his tavern, was an American, a physician? He seemed intelligent and schooled in the best medical methods of North America; therefore, mindful of Friherre Frydendahl's need for treatment he, Bronsted, made bold to mention this Doctor Burnham's presence on the island.

Down a miserable, rain-gullied road leading to Coralhaven from Annaberg rode Frydendahl's steward bearing gold and an urgent invitation to the American doctor to visit Stephan Frydendahl on professional matters.

Late the next day therefore a two-wheeled *volante* deposited at the massive door to Annaberg a red-haired individual garbed in a faded blue coat, wrinkled white duck trousers, and a cocked hat, the gold braid of which sea water had clouded with verdigris. The visitor's luggage was unimpressive. It consisted merely of a small sea chest, a medicine case, and a carefully fashioned wooden case measuring perhaps two feet by a foot.

Standing before the entrance to Stephan Frydendahl's imposing estate, Peter Burnham mopped the sweat from his forehead, though it was much cooler up here than at sea level in Coralhaven. Now he understood why the local planters, though risking damage from frequent hurricanes, built their homes on hilltops and mountainsides.

In the act of reaching for the bell-pull, Peter hesitated. In half a glance he deduced that Annaberg was no ordinary plantation house; this vast yellow mansion and its grounds were far better kept up than any he had seen on Tortola or in the vicinity of Coral Bay.

So this was the property of which Trina Varsaa had become mistress? In Coralhaven folks still spoke of the fine, elaborate and expensive wedding of Stephan Frydendahl and the lovely Baroness Varsaa. Peter found it remarkable, however, that the new mistress of Annaberg had not since been seen in Coralhaven. Why? Though unfamiliar with island customs he found it curious that even a Danish bride should not, during ten long weeks, at some time have emerged from her domain.

The blazing sun beat hard at Peter's face while the rasp of the *volante's* iron tires diminished beyond a hedge of oleanders fringing the driveway. To a covert noise from behind this hedge Peter wheeled and was amazed to behold a young male slave gazing on him in round-eyed curiosity.

That this Negro used a crutch was not odd since, in the Leeward Islands, the usual penalty for a second attempted escape was the amputation of a foot. But this unfortunate, Peter realized, was suffering from a different punishment. A heavy and shiny iron ring had been riveted about his neck and down the culprit's back from this ring ran a length of chain so short as to draw high up behind him the Negro's fettered right ankle.

Peter guessed that, during the early days of his punishment, this unhappy wretch must have suffered agonies; involuntary motions of the cramped leg must have caused a near-to-strangling pressure on his throat.

Peter swallowed hard and looked away, for all that during his captivity on Tortola he had grown somewhat accustomed to that brutality which, born of fear, ruled these little empires reared on slave labor.

The fettered black grinned foolishly; then, catching the sounds of voices from within the plantation house wheeled and went hopping away with remarkable agility; his woolly head was jerking backwards to each stride.

Depressed and apprehensive, Peter remained an instant longer viewing this long, red-roofed house. It looked at once handsome and comfortable, sheltered under clumps of palms and by a liberal growth of vines of various sorts. Yet for all its decoration Annaberg had been constructed with a fortress-like solidity.

As he stood on the drive listening to the *volante* follow the circling road downwards to distant Coralhaven, Peter recognized that the windows of Frydendahl's residence were so aligned as to permit defenders to enfilade the entrance; also, though cunningly disguised, embrasures had been designed at each corner of the house to permit musketeers to fire downwards with a minimum of exposure. Peter was soon to learn that since the fearful slave revolt of 1733, nearly all plantation houses were constructed along these lines.

So this was the home Trina had come to? How would she greet him? How would he be able to bear himself—right now his heart was thudding like an Iroquois tom-tom.

"In any case I'll see her very soon," Peter thought, then tugged at a brass bell handle. Somewhere in the depths of Annaberg a bell jangled and a big dog brayed furiously until a deep voice could be heard roaring something in Danish—a language of which Peter understood less than nothing.

Presently a series of bolts *click-clucked*, then an elderly, light-colored Negro, barefoot and shirtless, but wearing a green livery coat and pantaloons, pulled back a mas-

sive front door liberally strengthened with iron bands and
fairly studded with great nail heads.

"You de Doctuh gemmun, *Baas*?" He inquired after
bowing nearly to the ground.

"Yes, I am Doctor Burnham."

The barefoot butler again bowed double, then clapped
his hands. At once a pair of footmen wearing clean blue
and white seersucker garments ran to catch up the new
arrival's medicine case and sea chest. Peter carried his
instrument case himself, looked curiously about.

"*Entrez.* Come dis way, please, *Baas.*"

Baas? A Dutch word, it had been a never-ending
source of interest to Peter how thoroughly in the Antilles
French, Dutch, Danish and English had become blended
into a species of Caribbean *lingua franca*.

Inside Annaberg the air was cooler by ten degrees. Immediately Peter encountered evidences of comfort so
lavish that it bordered on luxury. The floors beneath the
New Englander's clumsy, brass-buckled shoes were of
gleaming mahogany and the hall furniture a hodgepodge
of good English, Dutch and Danish pieces which had
been arranged with no imagination whatsoever. Woven
grass mats of African origin and heavy Persian rugs lay
side by side; rattan chairs from the East Indies flanked a
Spanish refectory table and ponderous silver vases and
bowls supported a garish profusion of odorless tropic
blooms.

Presently a couple of little black and white monkeys
came gambolling out of a passageway to grab at Peter's
coat skirts. Chittering, they then leaped up onto the
shoulders of Peter's guide.

The little procession after a considerable progress
along a series of empty corridors finally halted in a huge
sleeping chamber, the ceilings of which stood a good ten
feet in height. The bed, Peter perceived to be a massive
affair of carved mahogany set on a sort of dais and hung
with a net of fine gauze; each of its legs stood immersed
in a copper water pot. This precaution, he had learned,
was designed to discourage the approach of creeping insects.

Two very tall windows, heavily barred, afforded a
magnificent view of the ocean and of a small harbor lying
perhaps two hundred feet below. From them one could
see for miles and miles away out to where a number of

palm-crowned cays gleamed green and white in the sometimes sapphire blue, sometimes emerald, sea.

"De Marster, *Baas*, say please when freshed to come
out on de piazza," the butler said, bowing for a third
time. Hesitantly, he raised liquid brown eyes. "My name
Wulf, *Baas*, yo' humble obedient slave; bell you ring,
Wulf come."

Peter, in considerable curiosity, surveyed these comfortable, clean and airy quarters. Certainly, they constituted a vast improvement on the wretched accommodations he'd occupied aboard H.B.M.S. *Raisonable*
and those ashore at Tortola.

So this was where Trina lived? That she had not appeared to welcome him was disappointing. Probably having grown large with child she only appeared at brief intervals. A fierce impatience to behold her set him to un-
packing, hanging his few garments in a tall armoire. Had
his memory tricked him or was her hair silver-blonde and
not gold-blonde?

It was a relief to strip off coat and shirt and, at an elaborate brass and mahogany washstand, to sponge himself
from poll to waist with fresh cool water.

"I'm acting the fool," he reflected. "I never should
have come over to Saint Jan. Trina would be a colossal
idiot even to consider leaving all this for a penniless, dis-
graced physician."

Aye, he was penniless, all right; the *Hammond* had
fallen into British hands once more off Tortola and her
prize crew was on their way to England. So, unless, by
great good fortune, some of the *Grand Turk's* more important prizes had won passage through that screen of
enemy cruisers prowling from Georgia to Nova Scotia,
he was no better off than he'd been back in January.

Standing there, blotting himself dry with a great fluffy
towel, Peter took a firm resolution; no matter what
chanced here at Annaberg, he wasn't going to betray by
so much as a quiver of an eyelid, his hapless devotion for
Trina Frydendahl. Very likely it was all imagination on
his part that she, also, had undergone a mutual, if indefinable, attraction. Besides, he had his obligations as a physician to discharge.

What could be wrong with Friherre Frydendahl? Peter
hesitated in the act of drying his coppery curls—he needed a haircut and no mistake—pray God Trina's new hus-

band wasn't afflicted with the dreaded *lues venera*, or French pox, so prevalent in these torrid latitudes.

Still naked to the waist, he unlocked the medicine chest and inspected his drug supply. Of tincture of cinnamon, elixir of paregoric, *ol Ricini* and traumatic balsam there was plenty; of sal ammonium, liquid laudanum, pulverized ipecac, Peruvian bark but a moderate supply; vials which should have contained white camphor, *Elixir Bolus cum opium*, corrosive sublimate and precipitated rhubarb were empty. Fortunately, he could do without all of these last.

Next, Peter opened his instrument case and, after testing his plaister knives, lancets and scalpels, produced a small oilstone in order to sharpen certain of them. Seating himself he set to work and ended by polishing his needles, drug scales, tenaculum, scissors, clamps, probes, directors and spatulae.

Luck had favored him in one direction at least; when herded up onto the deck of H.B.M.S. *Raisonable* Peter had not for a minute supposed that his captors would permit him to retain his medicine and instrument chests, nor that Rear-Admiral Sir George Collier would respect his claim of being a non-combatant and therefore exempt from imprisonment. All the same Sir George *had* listened and finally had agreed to set him at large—a surprising decision, considering his recent and brazen violation of Danish neutrality.

After laying away his gear, Peter clubbed his hair with a length of dark blue ribbon presented by Doctor Robert Tunney, Surgeon-General to the Royal Colony of Tortola. Tunny had proved a decent sort, going out of his way to befriend, and advise, a luckless colleague. During many a long hour he and the Surgeon-General had bickered over various points of physick and surgery and so had come to conceive a mutual respect and admiration. If ever this blighting war came to an end Peter Burnham was immediately to seek out Robert Tunney, M.D., at Surgeon's Hall in Windmill Street in London. But all that lay in the far future.

He had been lucky, once more, in coming across that little coasting sloop which, some four days earlier, had set him ashore on Coralhaven's busy waterfront. Peter had found considerable interest in exploring this tiny, neat and very foreign-appearing town—so different from its counterparts on Tortola.

On the third day after his arrival he had climbed up to wander, quite unchallenged and unmolested, about that toy fort which, situated on a bluff, commanded the entrance to Coral Bay. Fort Frederick proved to be a picturesque, but militarily ridiculous, affair of antiquated masonry and obsolescent artillery guarded by a drowsy and rather slovenly garrison. Down in Coralhaven, however, the white cross-belts of the Danish king's soldiers looked quite imposing when they wandered through the vari-colored crowd.

To Peter, the harbor presented a never-monotonous vista of ships arriving and clearing at frequent intervals; some came to refit, some to recruit crews depleted by battle or disease, some to charge fresh food and water.

One of the sights most intriguing to Peter was that of a British privateer which, having become thoroughly infected with yellow jack, or *coup-de-bar,* was being cleansed by heroic measures. Deliberately sunk in shallow water, she would for three days lie there with decks barely awash. As a result it was expected that the currents would scour away all trace of the disease. Later she would be raised.

"Will that really de-contaminate her?" Peter asked himself and doubted it, though an old Dutch shipyard master declared that soaking for fever was an ancient and well-proved precaution.

Almost always something of interest was to be seen or heard at the King Frederick V Tavern; for instance, there was a renegade Turk who, in a scarlet turban, wandered about town carrying a pair of small gray African parrots on a stick. For a very modest sum he would blow on a penny whistle, whereupon the birds would waltz gravely around and around to the delight of seamen and swarms of half-naked black children.

Some mighty depressing news was brought into Coralhaven by a British Army victualler blown off her course to Barbadoes. In no time at all news circulated that, on the twelfth of May last, some three thousand Continental and South Carolina troops and seamen, under the command of General Benjamin Lincoln had allowed themselves to become penned up in Charles Town and, being

cut off from relief, had been forced to surrender at discretion.

The war, British sea captains boasted along the waterfront, couldn't last much longer now. Why, the only major port left in Rebel hands was Boston, where all the
trouble had begun.

Loudly they toasted King and Country and declared it
was fine to have captured Charles Town at last; its surrender would go far towards obliterating the humiliation
of Sir Peter Parker's previous failure to reduce that stubborn core of Southern disloyalty.

That evening Peter had felt so down-hearted he could
hardly swallow his green-turtle soup. How would Asa
Peabody, Doctor Townsend and Lucius accept the defeat? Added to Admiral Rodney's smashing victory over
the Spanish fleet at Cape Vincent in January, this disaster
must, to foreign eyes, make the American cause appear
desperate.

Very likely Louis XVI of France and his ministers
would think twice before further re-enforcing their
forces in America. What use to stiffen an already broken
reed?

Gripped by a sombre mood, Peter donned his last fresh
shirt, then moodily brushed a heavy powdering of white
coral dust from his coat. At length he stood considering
himself in the glass; it was a very changed Peter Burnham
he beheld. By ten years he looked older, and weighed a
stone less than he had in Boston. He rang for Wulf. Silent
as a cat, the butler opened his door, bowed double.

"You may show me to Friherre Frydendahl—and his
lady."

An opaque quality dimmed Wulf's eyes. "Lady, *Baas*?
Ain't no lady in Annaberg, *Baas*."

XIX. Diagnosis

Seated in a most comfortable wicker chair Peter studied
Friherre Stephan Borgardus Frydendahl—and could
think only of a fox. Crimanently! This gentleman's florid
coloring, his small, tawny eyes set so close to a long and
roseate nose, suggested Renard grown tremendously.
Frydendahl's every gesture, the way he handled his eyes,

were essentially vulpine, and the Dane's whole bearing suggested wariness, unrelenting and perpetual.

In honor of his new physician's visit, the master of Annaberg had donned a Paisley-design green banyan, Turkish slippers and a turban of some light yellow material; following the local custom—probably a wise one—Frydendahl's head had been completely shorn of natural hair. Judging by the stubble visible above his ears it would have been yellow.

The Dane put down a lithe bamboo stock equipped at one end with a horsehair fly whisk and got ponderously to his feet.

"Velcome, Doctor Burnham, velcome to Annaberg," he boomed in tolerable English. "You haff your bedroom found?"

"I regret the necessity of keeping you waiting," Peter smiled as they shook hands. "I was so very travel-stained I needed a wash and there was so much road dust on my coat—"

"Vhat!" Frydendahl stiffened upright. "Teh! You needed yourself to clean your coat? What goes on in diss house? Wulf!" he bawled. While the unhappy mulatto wrung yellow hands and shivered Frydendahl exploded into Danish.

"Fetch me some bombo!" he yelled in conclusion.

Frydendahl shrugged, his bloodshot pale yellow eyes good-humored once more. "Dot lazy *kerl,* Piet, should haff attend you. A dozen vith the rattan vill teach him better."

"But," Peter protested, "I didn't call for him."

"It iss no matter," Stephan Frydendahl grunted. "A dozen stripes neffer does harm to a nigger."

"Where did you learn such excellent English, Mr. Frydendahl?"

Trina's husband explained that, years ago, he had studied ship construction in a British yard. Besides, every year he did extensive business with the English on nearby Tortola, Jamaica and other islands of the British West Indies.

While the sun sank, quantities of insects commenced to sing and chirp as the two men sat on the piazza, sipped their drinks and, smoking long, very thin cigars, conversed quite amicably. All the time Peter kept an ear cocked for the whisper of a woman's petticoats—for the rich sound of Trina Varsaa's voice. At dusk great, wide-winged bats commenced to swoop about a double rank of papaya trees lining a walk leading down into an elaborate garden. Still no mention was made of a mistress of Annaberg. It was very strange, thought Peter.

"And now, sir," he ground out his cigar stump, "regarding this ill health of yours—?"

"Can you tell anything by simple observation?" Frydendahl wanted to know.

The American shrugged. "I'd hazard that you suffer from the Stone. During the last hour I have seen you wince a dozen times."

"*Ja!* Dot iss it," the Dane grunted. "God, how I haff suffered."

Further description of symptoms left no doubt in Peter's mind that his big red-faced host suffered from a chronic mortification of the urethra and a stone in his bladder.

"What treatment have you taken?"

"Oh, dot old fool Bodger has made me drink *aqua animalis.*"

Peter glanced up in surprise. Not in many years had that concoction been prescribed back home. "It relieved your pains?"

"No, though it tasted bad enough to."

"I'm not surprised," Peter told him. "Do you know of what this *aqua animalis* is made?"

"No—be good enough to tell me."

Peter delved into his pocket, brought out a copy of William Salmon's *Pharmacopoeia Bateana* he'd come across in Coralhaven. He read:

> "*Aqua Animalis,* The Animal Water of Horsedung. *Bate.)* Take of Horse-turds newly dropped, add of White-wine a Gallon; Sweet Fennelseeds, Parslyseeds, avis Grocers Treacle, or: Polypode of the Oak, Butchers Broom, Liver-wort, ana MIj.: Ginger: mix and distill according to Art, with a gentle Fire.*"

Double chins rippling against the hair of his great chest, the planter watched his new physician's clear blue eyes flicker back and forth as he read. An intelligent sort, this hungry-looking Yankee and different from any other

physician he had ever encountered. About this young
man there was no mystery, no bluster, no air of patronage. He spoke as if he considered every word before pro-
nouncing it.

"Well, sir," demanded Peter, "do you wonder you
have made no progress?"

Momentarily, he forgot one of Doctor Townsend's favorite admonitions: "Never criticize the work of your
fellows, lest they unjustifiably criticize you."

Frydendahl's thick neck swelled. "So? It is medicine
from a hundred years ago dot stinking Bodger gave me?"
He spat furiously onto the flagstones. "No vonder I get
no better. Vell, *Doktor* Burnham, vhat haff you to advise?"

This time Peter remembered another of Doctor Townsend's saws: "Be not hasty about diagnosis."

"While I have no doubt but that you are afflicted with
the Stone, sir, I must understand your diet, observe the
balance of your humours and your way of life before deciding what should be done."

Frydendahl suddenly flew into a temper. "I vill not
vait. I suffer too much. Damn your soul! Are you a physician or a fortune teller?"

"Pray calm yourself, Mr. Frydendahl. During a few
days I must make observations on your condition."

The Dane glowered a moment but ended by subsiding.
"And so?"

"You will save your night water in a clean jar. You will
eat no spiced food nor drink anything stronger than tea."

Frydendahl's big hands jerked apart. "Impossible!!
Vithout good food, vines and liquors I cannot live or vant
to."

"You delude yourself, sir." A smile curved Peter's
lips and his brows climbed a little. "However, if you
prefer to continue suffering, that is entirely your affair
and I shall leave at once." He intended to stay, however,
at least until he had seen Trina.

Frydendahl drained a cup of bombo, then vigorously
fanned himself with a palm leaf fan before forcing an
apologetic grin to his full lips.

"Forgiff me, *Doktor*, I spoke in haste yust now; in my
back is lodged like a white-hot pitchfork."

"Then, I take it, you agree to follow my directions?"

"*Ja.*"

"You also understand that, at the end of that time, I may decide to operate, again I may not?"

Craftiness re-entered Frydendahl's pale, red-rimmed eyes. "Und vhat do you expect by vay of fee?" Silently, the planter seemed to add. "You know I am vealthy and think I can pay any sum—but I am not going to."

For the first time in his medical career Peter had occasion to meet such a query. "What have you been paying this Doctor Bodger—or your previous doctors?"

Frydendahl thought fast; halved Bodger's actual fee. "Vun hundred rix dalers the visit."

Being New England-bred Peter allowed for the deduction. "If I remove your Stone, my services will cost you five hundred rix dalers."

As if jabbed by a fish spear, Frydendahl's ungainly, but still powerful, figure stiffened. "Damnation, that is not a cheap price."

"I had the impression your life is valuable to you."

"Quite so. But how do I know you vill not kill me?"

A few days later, Peter had occasion to recall that remark by this big Dane—his exact wording, too.

"The success of a Stone operation cannot be guaranteed by any reputable surgeon. Well, Friherre Frydendahl, you have my price, which you are quite at liberty to refuse; should you agree to it, I shall expect five hundred rix dalers paid in advance and in gold."

"You think I might die, heh?" Stephan leaned forward, bare elbows on knees.

"You might. Your mode of living, so far as I can observe, is far from healthy. The sanguinous humours in your body, I deem to be seriously over-balanced. On the other hand you certainly will perish of a languor of the spirits and in considerable pain should your Stone remain where it is. You have, no doubt, noticed recently an increase of turbidities in your urine?"

"*Ja.*" Frydendahl's lips pursed themselves and he sat heavily back in his great rattan chair; fright was written all over his round and florid features. Suddenly he held out his hand. "Good, it iss a bargain—five hundred golden rix dalers." He shrugged, lit a fresh cheroot from a small brass lamp burning on a coffee table. "After all, such a sum is nothings to escape from this hell of pain." His yellowish eyes came to rest on Peter's face. "I know not why, *Doktor* Burnham, but I feel you can be trusted. Yes, I know not so many peoples I vould trust so far."

After an enormous supper of rabbits stewed in onions, roast pork, goose stuffed with truffles, two kinds of fish, papayas, custard, bananas, coffee and four varieties of wines, Peter puffed uncomfortably on his yard-of-clay pipe. "I will require, during the cutting for your Stone, the assistance of two intelligent white men," he informed his host. "Can you find such?"

Frydendahl frowned, passed a hand over his turbaned pate. "So? That iss not easy; you vould not vish for Doctor Bodger?"

"No. I prefer two gentlemen with little or no medical training."

"Ha, you are afraid they might observe your method?"

Peter treated his host to an irritated glance.

"Since you appear to lack confidence in my ability, sir, I venture you had best call on someone else." He spoke sharply. He was beginning to find out that, like most bullies, Frydendahl failed to respond to politeness.

Frydendahl heaved himself to his feet, laughing uproariously. "I should not haff said dot, perhaps. No, no, I trust you very vell, *Doktor* Burnham. Vell, let me see. Maybe dot Carleby, Carolus Carleby of Carolina plantation; he is anxious of buying some timberland of me. Yes, he vill come. And Ditlev Reverdil, my cousin. Vhen you vish them here?"

"Only the day before I operate. And now, sir, please listen to my instructions."

When Peter had concluded, the master of Annaberg made a flatulent noise with his lips, then spat noisily. "So you vill allow me no drink but beer?"

"Exactly," Peter replied trying to recall Doctor Townsend's discourse on the subject. "You will consume nothing but fruit, milk, and soft foods—no meats at all."

Frydendahl glared. "I think you must be trying to kill me before that—that business. I vill not—" Frydendahl just then must have suffered a pang for his face writhed. He groaned. "It shall be as you say. It has never been vorse than today. Now I shall go and sleep." He beat the flagstones with his stick, roaring for his servants.

"In the cool of the morning I will come bleed you," Peter warned and said nothing of the clyster he proposed to throw up.

"This house is yours, *Doktor*, except for the vest ving," the planter announced. "If you vish to amuse yourself with fishing or shooting, tell Klaus; he iss my gamekeeper. If you are fool enough to vish to risk riding in this *verdammt* climate, Leon vill find you a saddle horse. Good night.'' And the big fellow went shuffling off.

Peter sought a big portico which ran across the whole front of Annaberg facing the ocean, and sat listening to the musical dripping of a porous stone water jar; evaporation kept the drinking water within cool.

Yes, two or three days should afford ample opportunity of learning what had become of Trina Varsaa. To his growing surprise and uneasiness, neither Frydendahl's house nor its furnishings betrayed any trace of feminine influence; nor were there about Annaberg evidences suggestive of a white woman's occupancy, no sewing, no dainty handkerchiefs, no female garments.

Why should there be no sign of Trina? Had he not heard in Coralhaven those accounts of a wedding taking place at Annaberg he might well consider himself in error. Surely, any normal man would have been uncommon proud of having wedded so very beautiful a girl.

Certainly Frydendahl had no possible means of learning that he, Peter Burnham, was aware of Baroness Varsaa's existence and, even less, that the child she must be carrying was not his. Why? Why, then, this complete denial of her very existence?

Peter settled back in his armchair, considering the wondrous brilliance of the stars.

Um. Even before this operation took place, he would have touched a tidy sum. If his work proved a success he guessed he'd be in the way of earning a small fortune in these Virgin Islands. If only he had available a text of William Chelsenden's treatise on *High Operation for the Stone*. Along with William Smellie, Percivall Pott and that great Quaker, John Coakley Lettsom, Chelsenden had been one of Doctor Townsend's principal heroes. Peter couldn't help chuckling when he recalled a little jingle current in medical circles:

> The patients sick to me apply
> I physicks, bleeds, and sweats 'em
> If, after that, they choose to die,
> What's that to me?
>   I. Lettsom.

Peter ran a finger around the inside of his shirt collar. Lord, even after dark, the heat was something one must experience to understand. A little guiltily, he slipped his feet out of their ponderous pumps and happily wriggled his toes while running over in his mind the most approved procedures for the removal of a Stone—or Stones—from a patient's bladder.

Speed, in operation, he knew to be essential. Chelsenden was reliably reported to have removed a Stone in something under one minute and a half; Doctor Townsend attributed that surgeon's high percentage of success to his swiftness with his knife and an attendant lack of shock suffered by the patient.

How would Asa Peabody have approached a similar problem? Peter yearned briefly for a measure of Asa's skill with surgical instruments. Poor devil! Imagine such a potentially great physician immured in a smelly little fishing village.

Gently working his crippled fingers, Peter again wondered what might have chanced with Lucius Devoe. Lucius, he guessed, would be getting along all right.

Next morning, Peter drew off ten full ounces of Frydendahl's blood, administered a mild purge of jalop and left the planter cursing, but going over his accounts, nonetheless. He had the reputation in Coralhaven of being a very sharp trader.

Humid heat beat against Peter in waves, warning that a hot day was commencing; presently a slave appeared carrying a goatskin of water with which he commenced to spray the flagstones of the portico. Peter guessed his most sensible course of action would be to retire to his room and doze until the late afternoon.

At present, he could not detect a sign of activity anywhere. Even the watchdogs which roamed the ground floor of Annaberg slept, panting.

Right now, he told himself, might be a propitious time to undertake certain reconnoiterings? Donning the wide straw hat produced by Wulf, Peter casually circled the one area denied him and found that the west wing was in reality but a spur off the main body of Frydendahl's great, yellow-tinted plantation house.

Simulating an absorbed interest in those varied and brilliant flowers which, in regular beds, paralleled the foundations, Peter explored the west wing. At the same time he whistled, very softly, a series of old English tunes.

He had nearly reached the end of a row of windows ranged along the south face of the west wing when a flash of something white falling among the flowers shone in the corner of his eye. The physician took care to betray no surprise, only treated his immediate surroundings to a more thorough inspection. Only after a long interval did he work over towards a bed of nasturtiums, glowing like a floral brazier in the cruel sunlight. Under pretense of examining some particularly gorgeous blossoms, he was able to find and to palm a short strip of cotton before continuing his leisurely inspection of the flower bed.

Not to hurry at once to his quarters proved difficult, but Peter forced himself to survey, in the main hall, the mold-speckled portraits of several long-dead Frydendahls.

A brindle mastiff blinked baleful yellow eyes, rose from a cool corner and, in friendly fashion, came over to sniff at Peter's ankles. Such canine guardians roamed every plantation house on Saint Jan and, saving those who fed and cared for them, would attack any black on sight.

Reassured, the dog snuffled, then returned to his corner and flopped down, muzzle on paws, but kept amber-hued eyes open and alert.

Peter told himself, "Um. This evening I think I shall do a bit of wild pigeon shooting? 'Twould be handy to know where Frydendahl's guns are kept."

Once in his quarters, he locked the door before inspecting a strip of cloth which appeared to have been ripped from the hem of a petticoat. Written upon it in rust-colored letters were the words:

> Doktor, Help me for the love of God.
> K. Varsaa.

For a long time Peter remained seated on the edge of his great bed staring at this irrefutable evidence of disaster.

Why was Trina Varsaa being held prisoner? The explanation presented itself at once. Men far less ill-tempered and selfish than Stephan Frydendahl would become anything but agreeable over the prospect of supporting another man's bastard.

Um. Just what was Frydendahl doing to his bride? One fact stood out in sharp relief—Trina must be reached in all speed. Knowledge warned that, being so far advanced in pregnancy and quite unacclimated to this blasting heat, she stood in desperate need of medical attention. Whatever course he followed, he must proceed with the greatest of caution. At Annaberg Stephen Frydendahl was a law unto himself and on Saint Jan's Island, also, for that matter.

xx. Preparations

Deprived of liquor and his accustomed foods, Frydendahl grew increasingly irritable and surly. Conversation between him and Peter became labored, and chiefly centered on problems attendant to making the sugar crop. Rats had appeared on the island in unprecedented numbers and were wreaking havoc with the ratoon cane. Frydendahl had sent to the neighboring islands for advice but, so far, no replies had been received.

Discouraging, also, were rumors of unrest among some warlike Senegals held in slavery at Maho Plantation on Caneel Bay of evil memory. It was there that, in 1733, the terrible slave insurrection had broken out, an uprising which remained, even now, very live in the minds of all colonists.

They were returning from the sour reek and infernal temperature of the sugar house when Frydendahl grunted, "Messengers I haff sent for Carolus Carleby and Cousin Reverdil. Tomorrow they should be here. At vhat time do you expect to—" the Dane used his fly whisk to slash viciously at a black and yellow butterfly,—"to operate?"

"Late in the afternoon when the air is growing cooler but while the light remains strong," Peter replied. "I wish you to find as much rest subsequent as possible."

"How long shall I be kept to my bed?" Fine blue veining showed up sharply in the copper-red of Frydendahl's sweaty features.

"That is impossible to predict; if all goes as it should, you can hope to walk about a little at the end of a week."

"God in Heaven!" roared Frydendahl. "You don't intend I'm to spend seffen days in a suffocating furnace of a bed?''

"Mayhap longer," the American informed him. "You will be lucky if it isn't twice as long."

"We shall see about that!"

Recalling Doctor Townsend's oft-repeated axioms about not alarming a prospective patient Peter said, "You are not to worry, Mr. Frydendahl. Although a lithotomy may sound like a grave matter, actually cutting for the Stone is the least hazardous of any major operation. Besides, it is done with very quickly."

Frydendahl brightened. "How long shall you require?"

"Depending upon the cleverness of my assistants, not above two and one half minutes," Peter replied, but prayed silently that this optimism might prove well-founded. Alas, that so many months had passed since his last lithotomy. Would two assistants be sufficient? Frydendahl was very strong and, if he got to threshing around—Suddenly, Peter perceived a valid excuse for putting the question he had been burning to ask these last three days.

He drew a deep breath and essayed to speak non-committally. "In Coralhaven the pastor of the Lutheran Church told me you are married. Is that so?"

"Vhat concern is it of yours?"

"Only that we physicians have learned that, during convalescence, it is best for the patient to be nursed by his wife."

Frydendahl's heavy head swung sharply under its enormous palm fibre hat and his eyes stabbed at Peter's bland expression. "*Ja.* I vass married two, three months ago. My vife is avay, visiting Fra Holmstrup over on Saint Thomas Island."

As always when he underwent sharp excitement, a faint buzzing manifested itself at Peter's fingertips. Well, here was a baldfaced lie—proof-positive that Trina was in serious trouble.

To maintain his casual air was difficult when Frydendahl demanded, "And vhat else did those noddles in Coralhaven say about my wife?"

"Nothing more. They spoke only of your fine wedding."

"Bah! Addle-pated gossips, the pack of them. *Doktor,*

if those fellows vould spend more time at their vork and less in babbling, they might some day own properties like this Annaberg of mine."

Frydendahl, as they strode along up to the long yellow house lying, heat-hazed, on its hilltop, launched forth into a long description of how, twenty years ago, he had landed on Saint Jan as a penniless subaltern of infantry in a second rate regiment. He had, he told his companion, resigned his commission to act as overseer for M. de Argenlieu, an old French Huguenot; the original cornerstone of his fortune had been assured by a successful voyage to Bonny on the Slave Coast of Africa. He spoke of incredible hardships and dangers of the slave trade— and its rich rewards.

"And all the time I built," he rumbled. "I dreamed of a son—many children—to follow after me." Suddenly Trina's husband began to laugh, a harsh mirthless laugh that was ominous to hear.

Cautiously, Peter inquired, "But surely, Friherre Stephan, now that you have a wife, does it not seen reasonable to hope that—"

Frydendahl halted, purple-face he exploded. "Silence! Ve vill not speak of her again. You understand?"

xxi. The Whip

THAT SHALLOW SLEEP into which Peter Burnham eventually lapsed became penetrated by a sad sound—something like a muffled scream. He sat bolt upright. Crimanently! There it was again. Now he heard somewhere, and not far away, a sound as of blows; came another muffled cry, indescribably suggestive of suffering.

Slipping shoes onto his bare feet, Peter threw about him a banyan, then caught up the heavy brass candlestick from beside his bed. He was well out into the darkened hallway in short order.

A deep-throated growl struck his ear. Yonder crouched the mastiff with lips writhing back from his fangs and the hairs lifting about his shoulders and nape. He bounded forward. Peter spoke softly, remembered to remain motionless until the brute could sniff him. Reassured, the watchdog sank back on his haunches, but kept an ear cocked at a heavy door to Peter's left.

From the west wing the sound of blows was continuing, then a particularly anguished wail stung Peter to action; at the same time instinct counselled the use of self-control.

The west wing door proving locked, Peter kicked and hammered at it until the sound of blows ceased, allowing him to hear what he took to be gasping pleas for mercy.

"Open! Damn you, open up!" Peter yelled. "What in Hell's going on in there?"

Suddenly bolts went slamming back, then Stephan Frydendahl appeared, his heavy features crimson. "Vhat you doing here? How dare you?"

Through the half-opened door, Peter was able to get a glimpse of the room beyond. From whence he achieved enough strength of character to fight down an outraged impulse, he could not have told, for yonder, lashed to the footboard of her bed, Trina Varsaa lay half slumped onto the floor. Her silver-blonde hair was streaming in wild disarray over slim shoulders streaked with scarlet weals.

That was all Peter saw before the door blew shut and Frydendahl raised his dog whip. Peter ducked in and imprisoned Frydendahl's wrist; threatened to break it in a shrewd hold. The planter's whip thudded onto the floor as, bellowing in pain, he reeled aside.

"What the Hell were you up to?"

On Frydendahl's suddenly grayed features Peter could read a doubt as to whether his guest had seen into the west wing. "To explain my actions there iss no need," he growled still rubbing his wrist. Then he added, "I vass beating an impudent slave."

Furiously, Peter struggled against an impulse to beat this obese brute into insensibility; such action would not rescue Trina. Better to pretend having been deceived.

Frydendahl was breathing heavily, his lips set in an ugly straight line. "Now, *Doktor,* you vill return to your room and mind your own affairs."

Peter shook his red head and, stooping, appropriated the whip before he confronted his host.

"Now listen to me, you damned great bully. Whether you've a legal right to torture your slaves, I don't care a Continental, but whilst I'm in this house there will be no such goings on. D'you understand me? Any more whipping then you and your bloody bladder Stone can go hang."

The Dane stood glowering, massive shoulders rising and falling rapidly under the frilled nightshirt he had tucked into a pair of pantaloons. At last his gaze wavered aside. "Perhaps this iss not the best hour to administer justice."

From his pocket he drew a heavy brass key, locked the door to Trina's room; then, without another word, went waddling off down the corridor towards his quarters.

XXII. MAMMA BELLONA

To TRINA FRYDENDAHL it seemed that she must be wavering on the verge of insanity. Nothing made sense—her thoughts were hopelessly disjointed and confused. Suddenly she wondered whether she had not died back there in Kronberg Castle and now was being introduced to Hell.

Oh God! God! How her back and shoulders ached; what hurt most were the stripes he'd delt her across her thighs. Where he had used his whip handle across her buttocks great, horribly sensitive ridges were rising. Stephan had whipped her twice before, but on neither occasion had he worked himself into such a frenzy as that which had animated him tonight. She lay moaning gently, limbs twitching and shivering; the pain in her fearfully distended breasts was almost intolerable.

Even in this extremity the conviction lay deep within her soul that she was a Varsaa, descended from an ancient and noble lineage, while Stephen Frydendahl was but a common churl. She heard footsteps.

"Dear Jesus, save me," she prayed. "He is back." Small whimpering noises rose in her throat. This time, she would provoke Stephan by calling him a lowborn peasant swine; then he'd surely kill her and put an end to her torments.

"Po' lil silver bird." All at once pressure on her tightly bound hands became eased. Just in time to preserve her reason, Trina recognized Mamma Bellona's sibilant voice. "It bad plenty fo' my people suffer so, but we strong and accustomed." Angry words in her native Mandingo escaped the old woman when she commenced to rub oil onto that cruel pattern of ridges raised by the Master's whip.

''God bless—Mamma,'' whispered Trina. ''—Yankee still here?''

''*Tchaw!* Better now he know what—Master man do with you. Him warn Master never touch you again; him knew you when he look in.''

Aware of a terrible pain in her abdomen, the girl shifted onto her side. Only one fact emerged, rock-like, from the mad whirl of her consciousness, a fact to which she could cling. Doctor Peter Burnham was here and he knew something of her predicament.

Her too familiar sensation of helplessness diminished; it had been terrifying to be so utterly alone, without a single friend and as much a prisoner as if she had been plunged into one of those dungeons beneath Kronberg Castle where they had taken Doctor Struensee, the ex-prime minister who had lost first his right hand and then his head for making illicit love to unhappy Queen Caroline-Matilda.

The old Negress, her massaging completed, crouched on the floor beside Trina's cot and commenced to sing, very, very softly a curious refrain; its very monotony proved strangely soothing.

The child within Trina stirred, but less violently than in the past. Mamma Bellona sang on and on, her knobby fingers busy with a lump of beeswax; now and again she replaced wet cloths covering Trina's hurts.

Presently, the African song grew so faint Trina could hear it no longer because, at last, she had dropped off to sleep.

Once she was sure that Mistress was for sure asleep, Mamma Bellona went to the window bars and stared out on to the moon a while from wise, coffee-colored eyes. Near to unbearable had been the experience of this white mist'ss, as noble in her tribe as the kings of the Mandingo country. Mamma Bellona understood these things because she, herself, had been a chieftain's daughter.

Softly, Mamma Bellona chattered her teeth; not much longer would that red-faced boar trample this little white dove.

From her hair Mamma Bellona produced a long pin, laid it before the little beeswax figure which to her mind, at least, represented the ungainly, taurine figure of Stephan Borgardus Frydendahl.

''Where shall it be, O great Umballa?'' Then, obeying

an impulse Mamma Bellona drove her pin deep into the figurine's head at a point equidistant between its eyes. The crone's withered, purplish lips curved into a fierce smile. She knew that, sure as she breathed, something was about to happen to Frydendahl's head. It would prove fatal.

XXIII. LITHOTOMY

WITH THE HOUR for the operation on Stephan Frydendahl drawing close Peter was annoyed to detect traces of anxiety in himself. This was odd, because he had made up his mind about each step to be followed and knew exactly what he was to do. Perhaps his uneasiness stemmed from a realization that the merest flick of certain muscles of his right hand, guiding a razor-sharp edge, could set Stephan Frydendahl's blood to spurting in such uncontrollable jets that no power on earth could check them.

Back and forth the physician paced his bedroom; he guessed he had planned pretty well, too, concerning the problem presented by Stephan's wife. For at least a week after the removal of his Stone Frydendahl would be kept in bed; a week during which Peter's plans for Trina would be put into effect.

Twice Peter encountered in the great hall a withered old colored woman who always affected a bright blue bandanna turban. She pottered restlessly about, and once had been on the point of speaking but another servant had appeared and she'd scuttled quickly and lightly away, like a dried leaf blown across a polished floor.

Wulf said the crone was called Mamma Bellona and was the oldest slave at Annaberg. The respect evident in the black butler's voice was surprising and a bit strange; but, thought Peter, almost everything about this beautiful, wildly fertile and heat-smothered island was, for a New Englander, hard to understand.

Lost in thought, the physician stood staring out between the sturdy bars of his bedroom window and absently massaging the stiff fingers of his left hand. By now he had become convinced that never would he fully regain their use; those tendons, severed by the glass on that wall top in faraway Boston, would not mend. Though a surgeon's left hand, he knew played an important role in cutting for the Stone, he figured his handicap wouldn't hamper him to any serious degree.

As to his assistants, they were barely adequate: one was a big, slow-witted fellow who had to be rehearsed in his part again and again. Carolus Carleby, Peter decided, would only be useful because of his ox-like strength. Ditlev Reverdil, on the other hand, was quick to learn and clever. Above fifty years of age, he was nervous as a cat, surly and quite as suspicious in his manner as Frydendahl.

The shadows of palms sheltering the garden were growing long and sharp; it was nearly time. Peter turned back into the room to inspect his preparations. Because Frydendahl had seemed to expect it, he would wear for the occasion a ruffled shirt and his blue coat, into the lapels of which he thrust a trio of curved needles already threaded with silk.

A taut smile on his mouth, Peter picked up his case of instruments and strode along the great hall towards his operating room—a small bedroom located, for the sake of a possible breeze, on the northeast corner of the house.

After considerable debate with himself, Peter had decided upon a single bed with four posts that would do for tying down the patient should he grow fractious.

Within Annaberg a curious stillness prevailed. Of course, all the house servants and very probably every field hand knew what impended, were well aware that their future would be very intimately affected by the success or failure of this Yankee doctor. Were the master of Annaberg to die they would be sold, and that meant the break-up of families, the parting of lovers and probably a harsh new discipline to be learned.

Finding his operating room empty, Peter tested yet again those linen bands with which Frydendahl's hands would be secured to the bed posts. Across the center of the bed was waiting a firm bolster in a yellow silk cover. Peter felt it, made sure it would be firm enough for his purpose. Praise God! His self-assurance was returning during the familiar preparations.

Waiting on a marble-topped side table was a copper bleeding basin and a second wash-basin for cleansing his hands of blood. Next the New England laid on his instrument table—a pretty gilded wood and majolica affair—a sounding staff. Slim and bearing a groove in its blunt end, it was nearly a foot long. From a jar of goose grease he dipped some fat and with it rubbed the whole length of the staff. Then he arranged the scalpels he intended to use—they were sharp as an unkind look—beside a gorget and a pair of blunt forceps.

Peter next occupied himself by selecting bandages and bundles of lint from his medicine chest, then dropped some ligatures into the wash basin to soften.

Why the devil didn't Frydendahl and his friends appear? With every passing minute his nervousness grew. It was difficult not to think of Trina and a temptation soon to be faced.

At length Reverdil appeared, clad in linen knee breeches and a sweat-stained shirt; his brown nut of a face was screwed into an expression of lively apprehension.

"Efferding is ready?" he demanded.

"Certainly. Bring the patient promptly, the light soon will fail."

Peter pulled back the cuffs of his blue coat clear up above his elbows, then secured the white linen of his sleeves through buttonholes in the coat's cuffs.

With Carleby towering beside him Frydendahl came in clad in a billowing, lace-trimmed nightgown; about his head was fastened a bandage designed to keep the sweat from pouring down into his face. He was pale and sweating in apprehension.

"You have nothing to fear," Peter reassured him. "If you give me no trouble, five minutes will see the matter concluded."

Reverdil closed the door and locked it as Carleby, from a waistcoat of orange-tinted linen, transferred into his breeches pocket a short-barreled pistol. At the same time he treated Peter to a black look which made it quite clear that, if the patient failed to survive this operation, said pistol would be used.

"Get onto the bed," Peter instructed Trina's husband; then, more because it was expected than for therapeutic reasons, he produced his lancet and bled the Dane a scant six ounces. Next he pulled out a pulse watch and gravely counted the patient's heart beats.

Peter readjusted his turned-back sleeves, then snapped, "Sit on the bolster, then lie back."

Once Frydendahl had obeyed, Peter employed a pair of broad linen bands to tie the patient so that his knees were raised but secured well apart. Though Frydendahl grumbled and the other Danes scowled, Peter bound the planter's hands to the bed posts.

Trembling the least bit, Peter gave Reverdil the sound staff. "Introduce this—slowly and gently, as I have told you."

"Damn it, keep his legs steady," Peter flung at Carleby. "Under no conditions let go until I say so."

Peter felt sweat breaking out on his forehead when he felt the scalpel's cool ivory handle beneath his fingers. He drew a deep breath, bent and seizing his lower lip between his teeth, drove the knife deep through the first skin, then a layer of fat and deep into the taut flesh; ridiculous, how easily this incision could be made. Swiftly and surely, Peter drew his instrument downwards then outwards; and immediately he introduced the first two fingers of his left hand into the wound he had created well to the left of the mid-line of the patient's perineum.

Frydendahl emitted a bubbling screech, then commenced cursing in Danish.

"Hold that staff steady!" Peter growled at Reverdil. Employing the forefinger of his right hand, he groped until he located, through the hot tissues, that lump which identified the tip of the staff. His scalpel cut towards it in such a fashion that a second incision had been made upwards from below.

It was the work of an instant for Peter to pass his gorget down the groove in the rod. At the same time he passed the blunt forceps through the wound and into the bladder where it came into contact with the staff and gorget. Quickly he moved the forceps deeper into the incision. Ah— Now they came in contact with a hard object. Unluckily Frydendahl chose that moment to give a spasmodic heave so the forceps closed on nothing, and blood coursed ever more freely from the incision.

"God blast your soul, Carleby!" Peter panted. "Hold him tight! Tight! You let him wriggle like a speared eel!"

Again he manipulated the forceps' jaws until he felt them meet and grip the stone, then carefully he worked his forceps slowly outwards until he could withdraw them. Sweat was stinging Peter's eyes, yet he saw, clearly enough, that his blood-stained forceps were gripping a large chalk-white stone.

"It's out—steady now. Steady everybody. You may withdraw the staff, Reverdil!"

"Wonderful," panted Carleby; the giant was white-faced while emitting a small gasp of satisfaction.

Peter dropped stone and forceps into the water basin then, in almost the same motion, he jerked a needle from his lapel and passed it beneath the spurting veins until its point pricked the fingers of his left hand held in such a position as to protect the intestines.

Peter guessed even Asa Peabody, a perfectionist in such matters, would have admired the dexterity with which he tied the ligatures and then stitched up the wound. As a last step, he bound over the wound a pair of lint pledgets well soaked with blood. He straightened and went to wash his hands.

"Get on vith it," gurgled Frydendahl, eyes rolling wildly. "Vhat kind of a butcher are you?"

Peter held the Stone where his patient could see it. "There, sir, is your Stone. The operation has been completed."

XXIV. THE PLAGUE ROOM

THANKS TO PETER'S skill the master of Annaberg developed no fever and commenced to mend so rapidly that, towards the end of the second day, Carleby and then Reverdil made excuses to depart. Manifestly, they were bored by their neighbor's unreasonable ill-temper and those long, gloomy silences pervading the big plantation house.

A moment before he entered his carriage, Reverdil warmly shook Peter's hand. "What a marvel—your art—next to magic. If mine own eyes had not seen, I would not have dreamed such skill to be possible. *Ja, Ja!* Stay in these islands only a few years and you become rich, very rich."

"Indeed?"

"*Ja.* Next week a journey to Fort Christian on Cruz Bay will pay you well. A planter friend, Per Drotten, has bad gout; his foot commences to turn brown." Reverdil winked. "He is not poor."

"My thanks," Peter smiled. "I can use money."

To what purpose to point out his intention of not spending his life in these islands? There was a suffocating quality to that fear which, like a sword of Damocles, remained suspended over every planter and his family. Never could they forget that, some night, they might awake to behold torches flaming at their windows and hear the fiendish shouting of revolted slaves.

Carleby, on parting, was genial in the manner of a friendly bear. "Far you vill go, mine friend," he boomed, throwing an arm about the New Englander. "So glad I am there was no need to shoot so—so great a surgeon." The big fellow's blue eyes softened. "Mine oldest boy has a trouble with his speech. A Scotch doctor called him tied of the tongue. To set mine son right many good rix dalers I could pay."

Peter ended by promising to visit Maho plantation, once the master of Annaberg should be up and about. The two Danes had hardly gone driving away surrounded by outriders, when Peter made his way to Frydendahl's room. Right now the planter had cause for fidgeting; the humid heat was truly smothering.

"I cannot sleep," he complained. "Vhy do you not give me a draught?"

"Because I believe drugs should be reserved for necessity." He laid a hand on the Dane's forehead. "You suffer a touch of fever." Dispassionately he measured out a dose of Jesuit's bark in laudanum, mixed it with water and himself raised the Dane's hairless head.

"Ah—it goes better," he sighed. "Vhy are you so good? I haff not been a very good host. I know that."

"You have been ill." Peter thought fast, decided on a new tack. "Besides, you kept your side of our bargain."

An hour before the operation Frydendahl's clerk had brought into Peter's quarters a canvas sack containing the agreed five hundred golden rix dalers.

The patient winked. "It iss because I am rich, heh?"

"No. It is because you are my patient. I do my best to give all patients the same consideration."

"Vhat! You vould use the same art on a—a *kerl* as on me?"

"I don't expect you would understand; however, that happens to be the case."

The planter settled back against the bolsters, his florid hands and countenance creating vivid splashes against the pillow slips.

The laudanum began to take effect and, shortly, Frydendahl slept, making little bubbling noises through his lips.

Long since, the physician had taken two precautions: to make fast friends of the mastiffs, Krakadil and Löke, and to gain access to the armory of Annaberg. In this connection, he had gone so far as to try wing-shooting some of those huge green doves which inhabited a patch of woods down near the ocean—and the plantation's tidy little fishing harbor off Leinster Bay.

Peter sent Frydendahl's valet to fetch a pitcher of flip, an errand he estimated would require five minutes to discharge. Keeping one eye on the bed, the physician undertook a systematic search; suddenly he realized that the brass key he sought was not likely to be found in Frydendahl's temporary bedroom.

Quickly changing the scene of his activities, he discovered shortly afterwards that which he sought in a not-so-secret drawer of the Dane's writing cabinet.

From the armory Peter appropriated a light flask of powder, a handful of balls suitable to be fired from the small, but effective, French pocket pistol he had taken to carrying—a fine example of compactness and exquisite workmanship.

At ten of the second night following Frydendahl's operation, Peter strolled out of his room and down that great hall in which night lights drew dim flashes from the armor and antique weapons arranged in panoplies along its walls.

Immediately the dog Löke arose, came gravely forward, his toenails clicking loudly on the mahogany flooring. Peter patted him two or three times, then Löke sighed and clicked back to his mat.

For a long five minutes Peter waited outside of Trina's prison, every faculty keyed to observation. Finally he felt positive he was not being observed.

The instant his key slipped into the lock he heard, on the far side of the door, a scurrying sound; therefore he took the precaution of pushing open the door before entering. It was well he did so for, crouched in the half-light like a wild animal ready to spring and levelling a wicked length of steel, was the wrinkled old black woman known as Mamma Bellona.

"Ah. Doctuh!" While he was closing and locking the door behind, she concealed her knife, then shuffled forward to drop on her knees and kiss his hand.

The old creature's eyes reminded Peter of a cat's, yellow, with intense black centers. He followed her bent figure into that same room in which he first had glimpsed Trina Varsaa.

The old woman clung to his hand. "Is good you come to Mist'ess. Evil spirits work 'gainst her. Me do all me know; she fin' no rest."

Stephan Frydendahl's wife lay on her back, her swollen abdomen mountainous beneath a stained and heat-rumpled sheet. Her eyes opened to the sound of his tread and, when she beheld that big figure almost filling the door frame, a glorious look of hope brightened her delicate features.

"Trina!" he cried hoarsely, "Trina! Oh, to find you again."

"Oh, *Doktor* Peter—at last! Peter."

When she struggled to raise herself on one elbow he gently forced her back; so she contented herself by pressing his hands to her cheek; by the Phoebe lamp's dim rays he saw two large tears well from beneath her lowered eyelids and go slipping over the wasted contour of her cheek.

Trina emitted a smothered little sound. "Peter, Peter! Never will you leave me again?"

"No," he promised in a thick voice, "not ever again, as long as I shall live." When, very gently, he kissed her brow Trina put an arm about his neck and drew his lips down on hers.

"*Mon chevalier*," she sighed, and smiled in a pathetic attempt at gaiety.

Among the shadows lurked Mamma Bellona, her blue bandanna glowing in the lamplight. He noticed that surreptitiously she was hiding in her skirt pocket a curious collection of objects: a tuft of scarlet wool, the shrivelled foot of some bird and a number of what Peter instantly recognized to be human knucklebones.

Dropping on his knees beside Trina's cot, he studied her moist and colorless features while trying her pulse only to determine that she was suffering a not inconsiderable fever.

"Do you feel much pain?"

"Yes, Peter. Very much it hurts down there."

"Is this pain constant, or does it come and then go?"

"It is not a great pain," she replied smiling up into his eyes, "but it is always there—each day a little worse."

Frowning in apprehension, Peter from his pockets produced those drugs and powders he had anticipated might prove to be of use. Beckoning the old woman, he told her how they were to be administered.

"My dear, you will have to lie very still," he whispered. "Under no conditions are you to arise—to disobey will be to risk your infant."

A tortured smile marred Trina's expression. "You may be sure that I will, if *he* stays away. I want this child, who will be a boy, to be called 'Gustavus'—after my grandfather, the great general. Some day, he will grow to remind this low swine of a Frydendahl that a Varsaa is not to be beaten like a fallen horse."

The room, Peter realized, was bare except for the cot, a rough table and a wooden stool. Apparently food could be passed through a sliding panel let into a wall opposite to a barred window, so small that very little air could find its way inside the shaft.

This chamber, he deduced, had been designed as a pest room for Annaberg. Nearly every house of any size had such a chamber where sufferers were taken stricken with any of the many diseases, so prevalent in the tropics; such as black plague, *coup de bar,* leprosy, marsh sickness and the dread smallpox. There they might be isolated.

Mamma Bellona, apparently, slept in a tiny cubicle built parallel to the sick room. Nothing whatsoever had been provided for the prisoner by way of medicines; only a jar of stale rain water and a few rags to act as towels could be construed as comforts.

After administering an opiate Peter sat for a while beside his love, stroking her fingers and seeking to re-instill hope and courage. He intended, he told her, to take her away from Annaberg in two days' time. Did Mamma Bellona know of some nearby cay where they might find refuge? The old woman thought a moment then, her eyes round as ever, nodded slowly.

"Of Saint Jan and the near-by islands Mamma Bellona knows everything," Trina replied drowsily. "Dear Peter, you will surely take me away?"

"As I hope for God's mercy. The important thing, my dear, is that you rest until then and recruit your strength. He—" he nodded towards the other end of the house, "will be unable to quit his bed for another three days at least. I believe I have frightened him beyond danger of disobedience."

Sitting among the shadows, Peter spoke as if every detail of their flight were ready planned. Could she find strength enough to walk half a mile down to the fishing port?

Now Trina's eyes closed themselves, her long lashes resting peacefully against the pallor of her cheeks; her breathing slowed. He thought, "God above, how beautiful, how incredibly delicately she is made. Why, her hair's so fine it makes cobwebs seem like cables." The presence of a purplish brown bruise on her chin filled him with a murderous rage.

At length Trina sank into a profound sleep; only then did Peter rise from beside her cot. All this time Mamma Bellona remained on the stool, rocking her body. Her lips moved, emitted no sound.

"You come if your Mistress needs me. Don't delay. Come, and let no one stay you. Understand?"

"Yes, Marster, me come. No servant stop Mamma Bellona. She priestess Obeaha—they frighten'."

"Good. I return soon."

With the stolen pistol dragging at his pantaloon leg, Peter sought the dining room and there made a selection of fruits and fowl, then chose a bottle of Madeira from the sideboard.

When he returned, he fixed his gaze on the crone's wrinkled grayish features and unwinking tawny eyes. He guessed that she must have attended nigh countless childbeds and that knowledge went somewhat towards reassuring him.

"If," he told her, "birthing pains begin, you will fetch me at once?"

"Yes, Marster, but what of the boar?"

"I will handle that matter," he promised in a grim monotone.

Lying on his bed, a little later, Peter watched patterns of blue-white stars move from one square to another across a checkerboard formed by the window bars. He thought and thought; tested, then rejected one plan after another.

Granted enough time, the most desirable course would be to sail around to Coral Bay, then to take refuge aboard one of the neutral vessels at anchor in Coralhaven. The trick, of course, would be to find a vessel bound northwards and due to sail almost as quickly as he brought Trina aboard. Intelligence on that score, alas, could only be obtained by asking questions and Stephan Frydendahl was too influential on Saint Jan to make that safe.

The more Peter dwelt on the matter, the surer he became the best chance for a successful flight would come within the next forty-eight hours.

XXV. GUSTAVUS VARSAA

BY THE AFTERNOON of the third day after the operation on Frydendahl, Peter's plans were formed, but were characterized by an essential flexibility. He now knew where a fishing boat well suited to his purpose customarily was moored. It looked to be fast and sturdy and was equipped with an easily managed lanteen sail. Many and many a summer off New London he had handled a very similar rig.

Peter had halted in the shade of some trees, for though the sun was sinking beyond the summit of Camel's Back Mountain the day remained so confoundedly hot he was debating a plunge in a near-by stream when a sound of running feet drew his attention. Presently there appeared on the path a Negro boy of perhaps twelve years, who was running as if all the Seven Devils were hot on his trail.

Recognizing him, the runner halted, gasped out, *"Baas! Baas!* Mamma Bellona say—"

Peter waited to hear no more of the message but started pelting, full-tilt, up the path leading to Annaberg.

Once indoors, Peter immediately noted that the plague room door was open and that a scared-looking girl was lugging in a copper pot of steaming water. One glance into Trina's room told him everything—and that he was too late. From the cot over which Mamma Bellona bent sounded a feeble moaning. Splashes of blood had marked walls, sheets and floor and on a grimy pillow lay something swathed in a roll of rags.

Peter brushed the old woman aside, parted the sodden rags and made a rapid examination. It was encouraging to find Trina's pulse stronger than he had expected, nor could he detect any abnormal condition—though his practical experience had been dreadfully scant.

The girl's eyes slid slowly open. "Peter—Oh, Peter." His name was called so softly as to be barely audible. But when he pressed his lips to hers she managed a drawn smile.

"Everything will be well," he promised. "Everything. Now, you are to rest."

She lapsed into Danish; Peter glanced sharply at Mamma Bellona. "She want to see baby."

That so minute a human creature could live seemed incredible; the infant resembled nothing so much as a badly skinned rabbit.

"He man child," the Negress informed.

With infinite gentleness, Peter carried this tiny bit of humanity over to the cot, bent and, for a brief instant, exposed its wrinkled, plum-hued features.

"Gustavus," breathed Trina. "Gustavus Varsaa. I am content." Then she sank into an exhausted slumber from which Peter made no effort to arouse her.

Shaking his red head Peter returned the child to Mamma Bellona. In this climate few white infants of full development stood much chance of survival, perhaps one in five. For a premature baby less than no hope existed. Why, the infant's mouth was far too tiny even to accept a nipple. This child would die—a martyr to Stephan Frydendahl's hatred.

Nonetheless he bound and trimmed the umbilical cord, directed that stone hot-water bottles be placed to either side of the mewling mite, then redirected his attention to Trina.

To be sure, she had lost quite a lot of blood, but hardly more than was normal. All the same, he refused to allow her to remain in this breathless, ill-ventilated hole.

When he ordered her transferred to a room on the north side of Annaberg, Mamma Bellona went gray with fright. "The Marster—kill all who help—"

"He will not," snapped the New Englander. "I will deal with him. Go, summon Klaus and Wulf at once."

In a clean sheet the two black men carried their unconscious burden as easily as if she had been a truss of straw. But for all that they were round-eyed and shaking with fright. Once they had deposited the patient on a wide soft bed, Peter left Mamma Bellona in charge.

Once he had closed the door, the old Negress searched
a goatskin bag slung between her withered dugs until she
found the little beeswax figure of Stephan Frydendahl.
Viciously, she urged her needle still deeper into the mani-
kin's head.

XXVI. The French Pistol

Two days more elapsed, two days during which Stephan Frydendahl's strength became so greatly restored
that all of Peter's persuasion was required to keep the
master of Annaberg in bed. But that must be done. Certainly, in not less that four days could Trina have recovered sufficiently from the double shock of the miscarriage
and the loss of her infant to undertake a trip down to the
fishing harbor.

Stephan, meanwhile, was becoming steadily less
amenable to control.

"Pah! You vould make a baby of me," he complained.
"I am near as strong as ever, and feel vell. I should be
up; a thousand details demand my attention. My overseer
tells of rats destroying my young cane in the Emmaus
Valley."

"Nevertheless," Peter insisted, "your stitches are not
ready for removal. You wouldn't want the incision to
open, would you?"

"No, that I vould not."

"Every day you remain in bed, the sooner you will regain full strength and health."

Frydendahl's eyes, now a clear amber, narrowed.
"You haff no other reason for keeping me in bed?"

Peter paused in .measuring out an elixir of poppy
leaves, ginger powder and oil of cloves. "Are you finding
fault with the results of my operation?"

"No, that I cannot," Stephan protested in a hurry.
"My friend, you are vun great surgeon. You vill make a.
huge fortune." Bald head a-gleam he sank back on the
pillows. "Send Wulf to me. Now I vill rest."

Although Peter could not analyze his apprehension,
something in Frydendahl's manner had been vaguely disquieting. Maybe he was imagining it. Trina was mending
rapidly. She had abundant natural strength and her hu-
moural balance appeared to have been restored, despite

the weeks of bad food and mistreatment; yet it would be so easy to induce another hemorrhage.

Stripped to the waist, he sat sweltering in his room, the inevitable halo of flies buzzing about his head. He drew out the French pocket pistol and fell to admiring its wickedly slim outlines; the hammer had been worked into the shape of a dolphin and a grinning little lion's head decorated the boss of that set-screw which, with the help of a bit of fine flannel, held the flint in place. Every day, he changed the weapon's priming; his sweat, added to the humidity of the climate, made such a precaution necessary. Fine 4F priming powder fairly drank up moisture and might misfire.

He ate a solitary supper in the great reverberating dining room with only Krakadil for company; the mastiff had become definitely attached to him.

Time now to visit his second patient, to take her pulse, to change dressings and to administer tonics both medicinal and mental.

He found her sitting propped up, and looking lovely again beyond all description. A pair of pale blue bows had drawn the lustrous silver-blonde tresses to either side of her face. For the first time a trace of rosiness had reappeared along her cheekbones. To watch instinctive fear vanish from her eyes as he quickly closed the door behind him was thrilling beyond description.

"How do you feel?" he demanded taking her pulse.

"So much stronger, Peter. It is wonderful. And now most of the bruises have disappeared."

Um. Her pulse beat normally, but was not overly strong. Accordingly, Peter knelt beside her bed, turned down the covers and placed an ear over her heart. A thrill of relief invaded him. The soft *thud-thudding* was markedly stronger than it had been even twenty-four hours ago.

Meanwhile her fingers played with his coppery hair. "Peter, do you understand what my heart is saying?"

Peter was drawing breath to reply when, suddenly, he felt Trina's fingers go rigid; he whirled aside, facing the entrance. Yonder the door had swung silently open and there, his face an empurpled mask, towered Stephan Frydendahl. Snarling noises escaped him.

In surprising agility the Dane sprang aside, aimed at the kneeling Peter a murderous blow with a ponderous

walking stick nearly six feet long and topped with a
heavy knob of ivory.

Simply because Peter was quick did the weapon fail to
cave in his skull and only caused a glancing, but agonizing blow to land on his shoulder. Frantically, the physician rolled onto his back, at the same time wrenching for
the French pistol. Damn! It was hung up in his pantaloon
pocket.

"So? So?" roared Frydendahl. Having lost the element of surprise he dropped the stick and, from under his
banyan produced a heavy, short-barrelled pistol. Trina
screamed, flung her pillow at Frydendahl and so caused
him to dodge. With death but a split second postponed
and the Dane's gleaming barrel levelled on him, Peter
fired from the floor.

Trina screamed again. Peter scrambled crab-wise to
gain his feet, but anticipated that second explosion which
would snuff out his life.

No pistol bellowed, but some heavy object clattered
onto the floor. Through the eddying fumes of acrid
smoke he glimpsed Frydendahl standing as before, except that a bluish-red dot had appeared in the exact center of his forehead. Almost immediately Frydendahl
crashed forward, his body pinning down Peter's legs.

xxvii. Exodus

It was well that Peter's medical training had taught him
to think uncommon clear during a crisis. Even while the
reek of burnt gunpowder still stung his nose, Peter Burnham wasted not a moment in mental flounderings, but
jerked himself from under Frydendahl's semi-nude body.

Trina also had recovered promptly and was sitting up,
her night rail fallen so low that the heavy bandages with
which he had secured her abdomen were quite visible.
Calmly, she looked down upon the insensible, noisily
breathing body of her husband. No hate animated her expression, only loathing and disdain.

Presently she asked, "You are sure that this peasant
swine will not awaken?"

"No—not for a long time."

If anyone ever had recovered consciousness after receiving a pistol ball through the front of his brain, Peter

had yet to hear of it. To make assurance doubly sure, he knelt alongside the unconscious master of Annaberg and learned that his bullet had penetrated the cerebrum between its two lobes, completely wrecking the tissue, but drawing scarcely any blood at all.

The ball, which had just failed to break through the top of Frydendahl's scalp, made quite a lump. The master of Annaberg lay uglily sprawled on his face and breathing stertorously. Now and again the hairy pillars of his legs shuddered spasmodically and his stubby fingers kept opening and closing.

Peter delayed no longer, but ran down the hall towards his room, bellowing, "Wulf! Klaus!" Everything depended on whether Sverdrup, the overseer, in his house a quarter of a mile distant, had heard the shot.

Wulf appeared in trembling anxiety. *"Baas?"*

"Fetch Klaus and carry Friherre Frydendahl to his room," Peter told him. "There has been an accident; he is not badly hurt."

The only two men servants tolerated inside of Annaberg by Krakadil and Löke quickly obeyed Peter's succinct commands and soon had the planter back in his room.

"Stay with your master, you two, and bathe him with cold water while I summon help." He scowled. "If either of you sets foot outside this room 'til I return I'll see your backs sliced to ribbons."

Klaus and Wulf nodded. Though laboring under a terrible uncertainty, they respected the authority in his voice; besides the *Baas'* wound was very small and little blood was in evidence. It never occurred to them that their master would die in a few days' time; running down gradually, like a clock someone has forgotten to wind.

When Peter returned, Mamma Bellona was in attendance on Trina. Already tied into a bundle were her clothes and other odds and ends. Peter wound a soft blanket about Trina Varsaa, handed her his instrument case and then slung the medicine chest by a strap to his back. Then he picked her up and carried her out into the growing darkness. A penetrating silence prevailed over Annaberg, if any of the house servants had taken alarm, there was no way of telling so.

Mamma Bellona paused only long enough triumphantly to shove the little, steel-pierced, beeswax figure be-

neath her mistress' bed, then ran after the tall Yankee.
Already he was trotting down that path which led to
where the fishing boats swung lazily to their moorings.

XXVIII. CONGO CAY

THROUGH EYES NARROWED against a sparkling sea, Trina
and Peter watched an outrigger canoe come tacking in
from that faint blue smudge on the horizon made by Saint
Jan's Island. Side by side they lay on the warm white
sand, happily considering those changes which the past
two months had wrought in their lives.

When Trina arose and walked out to the end of a small
sandspit extending into the infinitely clear, blue-green
water he noted how the sunshine had darkened her fair
skin to a delicate and fascinatingly light bronze. While
she stood outlined against the sunset her hair, as so often
happened, escaped once more from the crude pins she
used to secure it, and floated free from under a crown of
scarlet blossoms encircling the small, proud head. The
single, blue cotton garment she wore concealed little of
Trina's magnificent figure as its fabric eddied lazily under
the offshore breeze. He clenched eager hands, trembling
to caress again the incredible, maddening softness of her
smooth body. Lord, but it was wonderful to lie here, like
some pagan demi-god caressed by a fragrant and balmy
wind, plunged deep in the magnificent adventure of a
great love bestowed and perfectly returned. How little
was understood, back in staid old Connecticut, about the
magnificent splendor of love in its various facets.

At the base of a wind-twisted palm, he rolled onto his
back and lay staring at the gentle motion of the bright
green fronds and whispered, "Yonder stands my wife,
Mrs. Peter Burnham."

The very thought made his now mahogany-colored
chest lift. Aye, he's see that she'd be made proud of the
name he'd given her. Come what might, before many
years passed she'd become known as the wife of that famous surgeon, Peter Burnham, well and favorably regarded from Charles Town in South Carolina clear up to
Boston. One doubt occurred; would much time be required to render her happy among his people?

Peter guessed most folks back home wouldn't set

much store by their marriage rites, performed by Hippolyte Cohû, patriarch of the village. His service would remain unrecognized by the Church of England or the Lutheran Church, though, for nearly a hundred years, his simple Creole-French phrases had served to bind in well-respected wedlock the black, brown, and yellow young people of Congo Cay.

How beautiful Trina had looked that day in her white gown and necklace of blue and yellow seashells; bracelets and a tiara to match, had completed her wedding regalia. "They are just as lovely," she'd told Ti Annette, "as the jewels of our Royal Family."

Sand fell from Peter's shoulders when he sat up to view the distant outrigger and, for the first time in many days, a dart of disquiet pricked his peace of mind. Yonder came not only Alphonse Crenier, but also contact with that world lying beyond surf-ringed Congo Cay.

A curious community this, consisting of the Greniers, the Cohûs, the Ottards and the Boissons of various ages—relics of the nearly forgotten French occupation of Saint Croix.

Yonder triangular brown sail advised that, after an absence of four days, Alphonse was returning home. How would his return affect Trina and himself?

How he despised to see that canoe sailing steadily closer, bearing down like a chill and evil wind on this islet wandered from the Hesperides. Of course, neither he nor Trina had deluded themselves into believing that this exquisite interlude could continue without end.

The lowering sun flung impudent rays off the sea to strike through Trina's dress and so project into perfect silhouette the proportions of her slenderly magnificent figure. As so often before, she remained there letting the wavelets curl about her ankles and revelling in the intimate and gentle caress of the wind.

A small V formed between Trina Burnham's brows. A plague on that canoe! In all probability, Alphonse's return would condemn her to the use of horribly uncomfortable stays and voluminous garments that had always to be washed and repaired. Even now she was resenting the obligation of wearing even this shapeless blue gown. On that beach which she and Peter had come to consider their own and about their hut, she had become accus-

tomed during the hot hours to wander about as unclothed
and unashamed as Nature herself.

Going nude, somehow, nourished her impression of
having been re-created, of commencing a new life devoid
of ties with the past. That old life belonged to Köbenhavn—and Annaberg. The Trina Varsaa who had flirted,
curtseyed and gossiped about the court of Frederick VII,
had been cast aside like a worn-out garment. Furthering
her concept of a new individuality was Peter's forthright
simplicity, the refreshing freedom of his thinking.

Her Peter was both shrewd and far-sighted. Not many
men would have thought to set adrift so fine a boat as that
in which they had escaped in order that prevailing winds
might drive it derelict onto the north coast of Saint Jan's
Island.

So long as the villagers of Congo Cay kept their
mouths shut, all should be well, but Peter was worried.
Although the black folks dearly loved a secret, they enjoyed, still more, hinting about their knowledge of one.

By now the outrigger canoe's brown sail, patched with
strips of yellow canvas, and water breaking in brief
spurts of white over her blunt bow, was plainly to be
seen. It was Alphonse, allright.

Bronzed features lighting, Peter arose when he saw
Trina walking back along the beach and laughing to see
the little sandcrabs go scuttling out of her path.

She thought, "How like a fine statue he looks in those
brief canvas breeches. When he holds out his arms to me
the brilliance of his blue eyes will blot out all the rest of
the world."

After they had kissed she pressed the yielding firmness
of her breasts hard against him. "Oh, Peter, I don't know
why, yet I am frightened. You don't think anything ill
will happen?"

"Of course not." Fingers roughened by fishing and
wood cutting played clumsily at her chaplet of flowers.

Almost convulsively, she clung a moment longer.
When their kiss had dissolved into memory, he sobered,
nodded at the canoe.

"We must meet Alphonse at the landing and hear his
news before it becomes distorted."

As soon as he politely could, Peter led Alphonse out to
the palm-leaf hut shared by Trina and himself in the

depths of a grove of coconut palms. Eyes rolling and
hands busy, the Negro fairly erupted information.

Yes. The authorities appeared satisfied that all the occ-
pants of the stolen fishing boat had perished, especially
following a half-hearted search for bodies among those
cays lying closer to Saint Jan.

"What of Friherre Frydendahl?" Trina spoke in a
toneless voice, and her hand closed convulsively on Peter's. "Is he?"

Alphonse's wooly head ducked. *"Oui*, Madame. He
mort. Four days in dying."

Mamma Bellona put a number of questions in her Mandingo dialect and through her efforts Peter and his bride
learned that, awaiting the arrival of heirs from Denmark,
the Governor had assigned a superintendent to preside
over Annaberg, Coralhaven Harbor was yet full to overflowing with the ships of all nations; alas, there were
nowadays very few Yankee vessels.

Trina said, "Please, Mamma, ask Alphonse, has he arranged to send us a messenger in case of danger?"

Mamma Bellona explained that this precaution had
been attended to. A trustworthy Negro of Coralhaven
was to sail immediately should a visit to Congo Cay be
contemplated by the colonial authorities.

For this service Alphonse had promised the black a
pair of silver dollars; an arrangement Mamma Bellona
thought far from wise. To the inhabitants of those hovels
composing the free village of Coralhaven a silver dollar
represented a veritable fortune. Peter saw the point; silently resolved to anticipate a more than likely piece of
treachery.

He and Trina must soon leave Congo Cay; too soon,
possibly. Although Trina had regained her strength it was
curious—and discouraging—to see how very slow she
was to learn even the rudiments about caring for herself,
for all that she yearned to become self-sufficient, *à
l'Américaine*. Since childhood, servants must have attended the young noblewoman at every turn. She had
never dressed her own hair, for instance, and knew absolutely nothing concerning the preparation of foods or
beverages. She was sweetly, but infuriatingly, ignorant
of such practical considerations as making a bed or cutting a garment.

Trina's pathetic efforts at mending his last, precious pair of white thread stockings had been so ineffectual that, a bit sobered, he took them away and gave them to Mamma Bellona to mend—thereby earning one of the few hurt looks his bride had ever bestowed upon him.

The temptation to make sail for some not-too-distant French islands, such as Martinique and there comfortably to turn his back upon the sorrow, privation and misery prevailing in war-weary America was great.

Trina could not comprehend his determination to return. She asked, was not the American currency utterly worthless? Were not the leaders of the new Republic at constant odds with one another? Were not the British forces coming and going as they pleased up and down the coasts of the Thirteen States? Peter had to admit that even if this war were brought to a successful conclusion, chances were that the various states would form several confederations, each activated by a different set of interests.

Practical, but short-sighted men, would undertake that New England states should form one nation; New York, Pennsylvania, Delaware and Maryland a second; Virginia, the Carolinas and Georgia a third. Three independent, but feeble little republics—that was what they would be. Trina agreed that such an arrangement would merely serve to perpetuate the age-old ills and weaknesses afflicting the Baltic kingdoms.

But it proved difficult indeed to dwell for long on such grim topics—with his head on Trina's lap, and peering up into the violet-hued skies, he struggled with that bane of easy living—a New England conscience.

Tonight Trina wore a simple white dress made by Mamma Bellona and calculated to reveal, rather than to conceal, the charms of her mistress. The soft lap-lapping of the waves came almost as soothing as the touch of her fingers along his temples.

Trina inquired suddenly, "How much longer are we to linger here, my darling?"

"How long would you like to stay?"

"At least a millennium," she replied laughing gently, "and that would not be quite long enough." Cheek pressed against his shoulder, she looked steadily out over the ocean. "Save with you, there is for me no real happiness on earth. But you have much to do and I must help you."

When Trina started, he looked up quickly into her face.

"See? Out there, a vessel is passing."

"What of that—many sail by."

"But, Peterkin, this one, she is so beautiful; her sails look all silvery by this light. Get up, my lazy lover, and look."

Peter permitted a handful of sand to trickle through his fingers before heaving himself up on an elbow. Sure enough, there was a vessel—a brig—bowling out of the Tortola Straits. Her skipper must be ignorant, or running needless risks, by steering so close to Carval Klippe and the treacherous reefs off Congo Cay.

All of a sudden Peter thrilled on recognizing the *Grand Turk;* no mistaking the sweet fluidity of her lines and the perfect proportions of her top hamper. Because she was headed north, he guessed she might be headed for an American port or, more likely still, for Nova Scotia. A strange restlessness flooded his being as he inquired, "Recognize her?"

"Why, no. Oh yes, I do. Peter! that is your ship! I remember her now, so dainty and like a huge toy. What a shame the enemy should own her."

Trina, like most Danes, entertained small affection for the British who, as she explained, ever since the start of this war had callously seized and condemned the cargoes of such helpless maritime neutrals as Russia, Sweden and Denmark.

Peter spoke slowly and in an unaccustomed tone. "I wonder how long the *Grand Turk* will remain under the British flag?"

"Who can tell?"

He laughed embarrassedly. "Maybe I talk like a fool, but, somehow, I feel Captain Ashton's spirit will see that she don't remain long a captive."

Trina's hand slipped over his, its slim fingers exerting a pressure at once reassuring and tender.

They sat quite silent until the brig wore and bore away to the northward, followed by a wake brilliant with yellow-red phosphorescence and tragic but gallant memories.

XXIX. La Frégate Royale, La Duchesse
de Marennes

AN EXCITED NEGRO appeared on Congo Cay one crystal clear morning. He had come sailing out of Coralhaven, making good time before a strong southeast breeze. If the truth was in him, a government sloop would depart the following day with intent of surveying the hardwood stand on Congo Cay. The colonial surveyors, so the messenger declared, would examine every foot of this long, low-lying cay. Mamma Bellona sniffed, told Trina that the fellow was lying; once two silver Spanish dollars had clinked into the messenger's pink palm, a great deal of his agitation had evaporated. And yet—there was no being sure, Peter reflected. Neither he nor his wife understood Negro nature.

To risk capture and imprisonment in a filthy dungeon would be assinine—as unforgivably stupid as it would be disastrous. Justice in Charlotte-Amalie on Saint Thomas, capital of the Danish West Indies, would be neither swift nor impartial.

Repeatedly, Trina reminded herself that Baroness Katrina Astrid Maria Varsaa, Danish noblewoman, had perished in order that Mrs. Peter Burnham, American citizen, might exist. When alone she drilled herself to correct her accent. Again and again, she tried to reproduce, for the benefit of the stone crabs and pretty little parakeets, Peter's pronunciation of certain words difficult for her. Yes, she must forget those too-correct sentence structures, such as always identify a person who has learned English by rule.

Particularly, Trina committed to memory various New Englandisms. She would, come what might, fit into her husband's world. The very size and majesty of the continent he made alive to her was thrilling; Denmark was so very little—but lovely.

"It is no use taking a risk that this baboon is lying. We must leave, my Peterkin."

Thus it came about that, at sunset of the next day, a small lugger, bought with three of Stephan Frydendahl's golden rix dalers put out to sea and left astern the friendly fires of Congo Cay.

The French islands of Marigot and Saint Martin's, Peter knew, lay to the south-southeast and in their direction he determined to shape his course. Principally, he wished to avoid Tortola, the vicinity of Jamaica, and the British Antilles to the northwest of the Virgin group. By setting sail near midnight, he calculated to have left traffic plying the Tortola Strait safely astern before sun-up.

Glancing forward, he noted that Mamma Bellona now lay motionless, and all but concealed, beneath a pile of ragged blankets. Despite their half-hearted arguments the old woman steadfastly had refused to remain on Congo Cay. Clearly, she had become devoted to the tall, pale girl of whose sorrows she had been witness—and Trina was equally attached to her who had, in effect, saved her life on two occasions. Yes, he was very glad to have the old Negress aboard. Trina, even yet, could not fully care for herself. It would require more than a few weeks to overcome habits and deficiencies acquired during a lifetime.

Silently, Peter once more checked the contents of his craft; she had been the long boat of some vessel wrecked, years ago, off Congo Cay. Though long unpainted and deprived of expert caulking, she was proving handy enough. If worse came to worst, they could always shelter among any number of cays and islands.

Between his feet his brass-bound medicine chest lay in company with a good-sized keg of water and a mound of coconuts which would supply both food and drink in addition to their regular supply. Yes, supplies would be ample for a cruise of at least ten days—and long before that time they should sight one of the French Islands.

Fortunately the weather continued fair—almost too fair, since only a breath of wind drove them past the enemy isles of Sombrero and Anguilla, lying pale blue on the horizon. The water supply, once so ample seeming, commenced to shrink with a terrifying rapidity.

Mamma Bellona remained wooden-faced, barely moving at all except to swallow her daily portion of dried fish and fruits. These last were spoiling under the blasting heat; despite all precautions, a whole basket-full of papayas had to be tossed overside. Soon the mangoes were becoming dangerously soft.

If only the wind would freshen!

During the third night after leaving Congo Cay, anyone could have predicted a storm to be making up. The air became charged with tension and an eerie stillness settled over the sea. It became so glassily calm that, when Trina tossed a bit of orange peel overboard, ripples caused by it could be seen moving yards out from the becalmed long boat.

The nearest island, Peter estimated, now lay some ten miles to the southwards. He had no idea of its identiy but, when the wind rose, he intended to steer for it with all speed because, with daylight, tremendous buttresses of cumulous clouds commenced rolling up from the southwest. Presently, an unearthly yellowish green hue corrupted the usual clear emerald of the waves and sea birds and flying fish ceased to disport themselves.

Not to betray his rising apprehensions proved difficult for Peter. To disperse them he considered getting out the oars, but promptly abandoned his idea. Any progress he might have made would have been negligible—the boat was far too heavy for a lone oarsman to move very far.

Trina, who had taken to wetting her lips from time to time with a bit of rag dipped into half a coconut shell of water, turned her head and, for the hundredth time, tried to smile encouragement though her face had become cruelly swollen and bloody cracks showed in her lips. Because, the night before she had talked a little feverishly, he paid no immediate attention when she cried, "Look Peter—a sail!"

"Really?"

"Look! Can't you see it?" Her arm, flaming with sunburn, indicated the southern horizon. "Really, Peter, look! See if I'm not right!"

He peered in the direction she indicated. He straightened up with a jerk.

"By God, you are right!"

Sure enough, there was a sail; but what might be her nationality? There were not far from Marigot and Saint Martin's—of that he was positive; all the same, two British vessels sailed these waters for every friendly one.

A sickening possibility occurred. Did those topsails belong to one of those small and murderous buccaneers swarming about the Antilles in ever-increasing boldness? God forbid! No inhabitant of maritime America had failed to hear accounts of unspeakable atrocities committed by such buccaneers. To what deviltries would the silvery beauty of Trina not tempt them?

Soon it became evident that the strange vessel—a two master—had caught some slant of wind as yet unfelt in that glassy area in which drifted the long boat. As, gradually, the stranger's hull came up over the horizon, the sky took on an ominous yellow-gray tinge.

"She will be friendly," Trina kept repeating to herself. "She *must* prove friendly."

"Friendly or not," Peter observed solemnly, "we must go aboard her." No need yet to mention the possibility that this stranger might be sailing under the Jolly Roger.

Yes. They must beg assistance. Amateur seaman though he was, Peter knew that they didn't stand a chance in the world of beating to windward in the teeth of such a gale as was brewing—and all the Atlantic stretched away to leewards.

Should the stranger prove a picaroon, he would have time to use the two shots at his disposal. Not the slightest doubt lingered in his mind that this was the only course. Perish the thought of Trina, dragged from one brothel to another, in one of those semi-piratical ports strung along the southern coast of Cuba.

An eternity seemed to drag by before, at last, a breeze arose and commenced to chase itself in playful cats-paws across the water. Meantime, the stranger, a foreign-looking brigantine, appeared to be bearing directly down upon them.

As the long boat's lug sail commenced to fill, Peter peered anxiously at the stranger. Damnation! As near as he could tell, no flag was flying from her signal yard.

He put an arm about his wife, looked steadily into her eyes. "Trina, my love, have you realized that yonder vessel may be a picaroon?"

Steadily, her gaze returned his. "Yes. Whatever you tell me I shall do."

Now the wind blew in fierce, unreasonable gusts which set the long boat heeling so far over that Mamma Bellona, under her coverings, began to chirp like a bat frightened in its cave.

The strange brigantine was but half a mile away when he instructed Trina to stand up, to wave one of her petticoats—a red one. Would this craft heave to? She had better. In this storm making up to windward, their ancient long boat could not long remain afloat.

The brigantine sailed so close they could make out the gilding about her bows and figurehead, a long row of black and white ports and even a knot of officers standing about on the quarterdeck.

Peter commenced to feel reassured. A pirate craft hardly would present so trim an appearance. Nearer towered the brigantine's masts and straining canvas. If she kept sailing as she was, she must pass not fifty yards to windward.

In dramatic suddenness a shifting of the wind revealed her ensign a great white flag dotted with golden lilies. Peter's heart gave a great glad leap. "French! By God, that's what she is! French!"

An officer in a gold-laced blue tunic picked up a speaking funnel and, as the brigantine shot by, he bellowed, *"Désirez-vous le secours?"*

Frantically, Trina waved the signal cloth. *"Oui, monsieur. Au secours! Pour l'amour de Dieu!"*

Peter braced the tiller with his knee, cupped his hands and yelled, "Pray pick us up, sir; we can pay our way!"

The Frenchman glanced at the onrushing storm, then at his tops. Some order was given which sent topmen to scrambling up the ratlines. At the distance of near half a mile, the brigantine finally rounded into the wind and lay there with canvas furiously slatting and presenting her broad, heavily ornamented stern to the long boat.

Immediately Peter loosed his sheet and steered to run into the Frenchman's lee. It was then that he and Trina learned her identity. The name, *La Duchesse de Marennes*, was written in graceful script above her very elaborately carved stern ports.

xxx. The Expeditionary Force

During two interminable days and nights the *Duchesse de Marennes* fled for her life before a gale of near-hurricane intensity. Peter could not recall such seas even during that storm in which the *Grand Turk* had engaged H.B.M.S. *Albany*.

Trina fell immediately seasick—as was only to be expected after her illness and exposure to the sun—and lay silent and supine on a bunk gallantly surrendered by a junior infantry officer of the Bourbonnais Regiment. Mamma Bellona, like a withered creature from another world, remained unaffected by environment and weather. The hairy and lusty French sailors promptly christened her "*La Ouistiti.*" There could be no denying the aptness of her nickname; with her small shrivelled hands and bright yellow-black eyes set in patches blacker than the rest of her face, Mamma Bellona did, in fact, resemble those little monkeys which the sailors of His Most Christian Majesty were forever bringing up from Brazil and the Presidency of Nicaragua.

As for Peter, he found it most difficult to make himself understood; very few of the sloop's officers understood even a few words of English. But the captain, M. Jacques de la Chapelle, made him extra welcome—perhaps because the brigantine's crew was rotten with scruvy—induced, no doubt, by an undue absorption of air-borne sea salt into their blood streams. During the course of the storm several seamen suffered fractured limbs when a carronade broke from its lashings and rampaged, like a maddened minotaur, along the *Marennes*' gun deck. Peter was glad to take charge of them—they were so pathetically grateful for any attention whatsoever.

The brigantine, he learned from Captain de la Chapelle, a lieutenant in the regular naval establishment of His Most Christian Majesty Louis XVI, had become separated during a dense fog from the balance of a vast armada which, under the command of Admiral de Ternay, had sailed for America from Brest on the sixth of May—over two months ago!

Even while the little ship plunged like a spirited young horse, Peter learned that, at long last, the French king had dispatched an army to fight in America. One composed of the finest troops in France and commanded by a renowned and redoubtable veteran general—Jean Baptiste Donatien de Vimeur, Comte de Rochambeau. The comte, so said the officers of the Bourbonnais Regiment, was irascible and a martinet of martinets, but eminently fair in the application of discipline. After a week aboard the *Duchesse de Marennes*, Peter entertained no doubts that the flower of the French army indeed had been devoted to this campaign.

Also aboard were elements of the famous royal Deux-

Ponts Regiment; and a battalion of Soissonsais which, since 1598, had boasted of a brilliant record.

Other units were represented among the officers aboard; for example, the Saintonge Regiment was entering this campaign under command of Rochambeau's own son. Miserably seasick were a couple of cavalry officers of the Legion of Lauzum. The regulars aboard held no high opinion of them. The Duc de Lauzum was little more than an irresponsible adventurer, fire-eater and *beau sabreur*; no good would come of him.

Some little time was required for Peter to understand why certain senior officers, grizzled veterans of many a hard-fought campaign, should remain painfully polite to some very youthful cornets, ensigns and lieutenants under their command.

"They are sprigs of certain families great in France. *Par exemple*, yonder cheese-complexioned lieutenant," de la Chapelle sniffed, "is the Comte de Montclos—a natural grandson of the father of our present monarch— whom God preserve."

"Can he fight?"

An inexpressibly Gallic shrug was all that Peter obtained by way of reply.

To observe how this ship was managed by contrast to the methods employed aboard the *Grand Turk* was fascinating. To Peter's vast surprise the crew, Bretons and Basques for the most part, were skilled seamen and their officers were far quicker than the British to sense a change in the weather.

If the chasm dividing British Commissioned Officers from the Other Ranks was wide, that in the service of Louis XVI was abysmal. Whereas a British captain might treat his crew with brutal indifference, enlisted men aboard the *Duchesse de Marennes* received far less consideration than those fowls and pigs, which were kept for the benefit of the captain's mess in the brigantine's small boats.

To his dying day, Peter would never forget his first visit to the brigantine's berth deck. Well accustomed though he was to all manners of mephitic odors, he all but gagged. No bedding whatsoever had been issued to the troops; their food was vile; issued but twice a day from a vast malodorous cauldron rigged aft of the foremast. One man of each ten troops brought up to the galley a slimy wooden bucket into which a communal ration was dumped. The unshaven and long-unwashed infantrymen then fed with their hands from the common bucket, the strong elbowing aside the weak. It was horrible; no eating implements other than those provided by the men themselves were in evidence.

Stowed deep in the transport's hold lay bales of those gay uniforms in which survivors would disembark on Rhode Island, but, aboard ship, they went about in the filthiest of imaginable rags and tatters. No water was issued them for any purpose but drinking. Ulcers, festering cuts, fevers and ugly bruises received not the least attention from an army surgeon aboard until the poor wretch was in immediate danger of death.

"Fresh food? Washing water? *Mais non*, such scum would not understand better treatment," explained Colonel Dosterre, a one-eyed veteran of the Seven Years' War. He was the senior army officer aboard, also far gone with *lues venera*. "Such *canaille* are little better than the brutes; fit only to obey orders and die without question."

The *Duchesse de Marennes* herself was kept clean—not in the British style which required that every inch of deck be white with holystoning—but where cleanliness served a definite purpose. Brass was polished only where it showed, or was in use. Deck drills were conducted in the most casual of fashions. At the same time, the rigging of Captain de la Chapelle's command was subject to continual and critical inspection; those blocks and tackles by which the ship's guns were trained continued to be oiled. The brigantine's gun crews knew their drill.

To Peter, it was amazing how very neat the officers managed to keep themselves. Always their linen remained sparkling white; their wigs well powdered and the gold lace adorning their white tunics bright as sunlight. For a long time the New Englander wondered by what miracle such neatness was maintained until he discovered that the Lieutenant Comte de Montclos, Louis Fifteenth's bastard grandson, alone, had brought aboard six great coffers of personal clothing, food and equipment.

What the colonels and majors might have fetched along by way of baggage Peter could not even imagine. The unending formality and strict protocol obtaining

aboard even this medium-sized transport was amazing.
If, at the simplest repast, less than a dozen toasts were
proposed and drunk it must indeed be rough.

During those first days aboard, Trina remained miserably seasick, but, on the afternoon of the third day, she
began to believe that she wouldn't be far better off dead,
and so to accept food and various gruels patiently
fetched by Mamma Bellona.

A prodigious boon to her spirits was the presentation,
with compliments and humble admiration, by Comte de
Montclos, of a choice of silks, brocades, laces and ribbons. When Mamma Bellona brought them in, every yellowed, snaggled tooth visible, Trina almost wept with delight, so long it had been since she had experienced the
sensuous feel of silk against her skin—and the spiritual
satisfaction of such lovely colors.

Immediately she begged Mamma Bellona to begin preparations for a costume suitable for a formal banquet
planned in her honor by Captain de la Chapelle and Colonel Dosterre. She intended to make Peter proud of his
clever young wife.

What a shame that such exquisite materials must be
left to the mercy of the willing, but inept, fingers of the
old Negress; Trina guessed the crone could sew a straight
and sturdy seam in cotton cloth, but seldom, if ever, had
touched such fine silk, which was proving so slippery between inexperienced fingers. Ah well, she would have the
costume made over, once they reached land, and so the
gorgeous stuffs would not be wasted.

The first thing, she decided, was to contrive a substitute for stays. What would she not have given for her
cherry-colored set with their white kid welts and silver
lace edging! There was small use in bemoaning what she
had not, so, at her direction, Mamma Bellona fetched in a
piece of fine duck—it had been used for a gun cover—
and had it scrubbed clean. This they fitted about her tiny
waist, then up to support her breasts. They laced up the
contraption by means of holes punched by an awl; for
laces she employed sailor's thread doubled on itself. By
what she considered no less than a miracle, Trina hit
upon the marvelous idea of shaping the make-shift stays
by the use of seams which were to be large at the waist
and tapered toward the top and bottom.

Next Mamma Bellona cut lengths of cobalt blue satin to reach from her mistress' waist to her ankles and sewed them together in a straight seam.

For the bodice Peter's wife settled upon an exquisite blue, pink and yellow brocade laced up its front with pink ribbons. This proved much more of a challenge to the amateur dressmakers. After much heated debate they cut a straight garment, again shaped with those curved seams Trina was so proud of inventing, and coming to a point at the waist front. The neckline they cut low and round and edged it with lace.

But the sleeves—oh, those infernal sleeves—they just wouldn't come out right. After many tries Mamma Bellona grumbled and became nigh mutinous, so Trina decided to leave them as they were, though they remained inexplicably bunchy under her arms.

Some silver lace lent a brave effect at their elbows and a fine gauze kerchief could be made to cover them if they remained too unsightly.

Draping and basting paniers with the same exquisite brocade proved not too difficult.

On the night of the banquet she found herself all of a-twitter while adding a few finishing touches.

Dinner was not to be served until nine—after the blazing sun had dropped and tables could be set up upon the quarterdeck—so, at six of the evening Trina felt not at all pressed for time when she commenced dressing.

Because Peter swore he preferred it that way, she had, for weeks, worn her hair clubbed simply enough over the nape of her neck. To gather courage Trina brushed her tresses a long while before cutting short the side hair.

Once Trina began trying to roll and to secure curls to each side of her face, the hair kept slipping out of her fingers. A pox on such fine and silky stuff! Finally, she remembered the use of pomatum and applied it liberally. This stiffening proved so helpful that not only did she succeed in forming three rolls to each side of her face but also of anchoring them in place.

Now for the front. From Peter's medicine chest she borrowed a fat woollen pledget—it would serve admirably as a cushion and, surely, he wouldn't object if she returned it promptly.

Earnestly the exasperated girl strove to comb her front hair evenly up over the cushion—a good thing she hadn't snipped that short, too! The cushion continued to elude her until, in a fit of desperation, she anchored the pledget with pins and only after many unsuccessful attempts, managed to conceal it with her hair.

Long before her coiffure was completed Trina's arms were aching and she felt close to hysteria while she contemplated bows of pale pink ribbon to be arranged above her side curls.

Triumphant at last, she sat down quickly, feeling flushed and a little dizzy with her exertions. Well, *messieurs les français* could have something to look at to-night. Not that they hadn't always been admiring to the point of embarrassment.

When she had made her appearance on deck, the routine of the officers' mess increased in formality and almost court courtesy became the mode. The officers, from scarred and grizzled campaigners to soft-handed knights, became her devoted champions. Even her husband, plebeian physician though he was, gained respect.

To the delight of all, the beauteous Madame Burnham, being court-trained, spoke fluent, if sometimes inaccurate, French.

The banquet was a grand success, but when the officers collected in the brigantine's small wardroom, Peter felt dun as a cowbird in a company of bluejays and tanagers. His worn peajacket boasted no bright buttons, not a single decoration twinkled on his chest and his ordinary linen shirt, clumsy pumps and none-too-spotless breeches afforded but dingy competition in such company. Naval officers wore gold and blue; officers of the Soissonsais had white tunics with rose lapels and wore fine lace at throat and wrists; those of the Saintonge sported revers and cuffs of a glowing, jade-green velvet; all the silver and gold buttons were something to see by candlelight.

All the same, Peter was well liked, nay, admired and respected, on his own account. Captain de la Chapelle swore that never in his career had he seen such medical art applied to common soldiers and sailors; impressively few of the ship's overcrowded company nowadays were being pitched overboard.

Thanks to favoring winds, the transport made such good time in her voyage to the north that, on the first day of July, a hail came ringing down from the masthead, "*Voilà, la flotte! La flotte!*"

The news spread instantly throughout the transport, interrupting a game of hazard under way in the wardroom. Madame Burnham, assisted by Colonel Dosterre on one side, and the young Comte de Montclos on the other, gained the quarterdeck in time to see the first of many topsails glimmer on the horizon.

There were three, then ten, then, all at once, the whole Atlantic appeared to be covered by great, white-sailed French men-of-war and transports. They all cruised steadily northeast—towards America.

PART III—THE HUDSON

XXXI. LETTER TO WEST POINT

BEHIND HER Mistress Sabra Stanton closed the door to
her room. A small sigh of relief escaped her. Mercy! If it
could grow so dratted hot in Boston, how terrible must be
those temperatures prevailing further south. Thrusting
forward her under lip Sabara blew damp hair free of her
forehead.

Just inside the door she paused, peering about, as
might a stranger, on the familiar aspect of this bedroom
she had occupied ever since she could remember. Soon
she would leave behind this comfortable, homely scene.
She wanted to be able to recall its every detail, the long-
disused doll house, her pretty little fireplace which never
would draw when the wind blew southeast, her first sampler—a pretty poor one—executed at Miss Pringle's
Seminary for Young Females of Gentle Birth.

Sabra thought, while advancing towards the center of
her room, "La! I'm getting near to becoming an old
maid—why, I'm nineteen and going on twenty."

The sun must be beating harder than ever at the brick
walls; the lifeless hot air of her room seemed so smothering that she undid the limp cambric kerchief clinging to
her neck, flung it carelessly onto a chair. Then, mechanically her fingers untied a series of apple-green bows securing the front of her pale yellow lawn bodice.

Heavens to Betsy; it was a mercy to be out of that
dress. A wicked, unlady-like impulse occurred—sent delicious, if shameful, currents to mounting from her loins
to her shoulders. To release her stay cover required less
than a moment. Then, flushed and breathing quickly, she
undid the ties securing her five muslin petticoats, let them
ripple to the floor in rapid succession.

What gave her the greatest joy was to cast loose her
stays, cruel hickory-splinted affairs which restricted her
waist like the inexorable and unyielding claws of a demon. Ah-h-h. To feel the air commencing to cool her skin
was a subtle sort of ecstasy. Only her perspiration-damp-

351

ened shift remained as clothing. Sabra hesitated. What she was about to do undoubtedly was wanton, but she didn't care—the impulse was too great to be resisted.

Her cheeks went hot and her rounded breasts began to tingle at the idea of completely disrobing while not preparing for bed. In a defiant twist of her lithe young body Sabra rid herself of the shift; stood nude save for shoes and neatly gartered stockings. Her fingers rubbed hard at the vertical dark pink indentations caused by her stays. Air evaporated perspiration, dewed her skin and caused goose-flesh to rise on it. La! it was wonderfully stimulating to stand like this, permitting a faint breeze to cool her body. For all that Sister Phoebe had, once or twice, passed her a grudging compliment, never had it occurred to Samuel Stanton's second daughter that she might be uncommonly well built.

She cast a guilty glance over her shoulder and was reassured that a heavy brass bolt securing her door was shot. Of course, in all modesty, she now should don a negligée or at least a nightrail, but it was much too hot and—and it was exciting for once to go about naked, like this. The chair cushion felt pleasantly warm on her buttocks when she seated herself before that desk at which she'd learned her girlhood lessons and opened a writing case.

Sabra's fingers trembled a little as they selected a goose quill with a nice sharp point. Brows joined in concentration Sabra wrote in a pretty, quite formless, hand:

Boston, ye 30th of August 1780.
Dear my Heart's Beloved:

Yr two *precious* Letters arrived by ye stage yesterday. I am Transported with Joy to learn how well You fair. Bro. Joshua hath wrote several Times to Papa. He spoke of yr quick Success which he says surprizes everyone—saving me! O, my darling, yr Sabra is so *vastly* Proud of yr Advancement and ye Promise of that Fine new Post at Hartford.

By this time you must have received Papa's letter granting his Consent—I yet can scarce credit that he did. Oh, my Darling, I near swoon with Delight when I consider that our nuptials are but one short month removed. Another thirty Days then I shall, O so Truly, pledge you my Troth and become MISTRESS LUCIUS DEVOE! What a career we shall build for you. All my Heart and Head will Labour towards yr advancement. You may rely upon it. You will soar to Fame's pedestle. I know it as surely as I sit here—

Sabra blushed a trifle, though it was just as well that Lucius could not see her sitting as she was.

Papa hath no doubt made clear to You that Sister Phoebe and I will commence our Travels—O happy hour—to West Point on ye 19th of next month—unless the accidents of war forbid. Would cruel Father Time could dissolve his hours and already I could sense yr very dear arms about your loving Sabra. We shall journey under ye protection of a Friend of Papa—one Major Amos Clark. Cured of Grievus Wounds he is about to Rejoin his Regiment serving under dear General Washington.

Oh, Dear Heart, could you but behold ye many beautiful things Mamma and her Friends have bestowed for my bridle Chest. Ere many days You shall admire them, each and every One.

Among other Things my aunt Matilda hath presented me with a cannistre of cone sugar and most wonderful of all a pound of Mocha coffee which Mamma intimates she did Acquire three Years agone, when near a hundred Indignant Boston Dames invaded ye warehouse of an unpatriotick Merchant, and so took Possession of his stock of Sugar and Coffee, the which he refused to sell for less than Six shillings ye pound.

You failed of a missive from me last Month, because Mamma, Phoebe and I Voyaged to New Port in Rhode Island, there to Visit Aunt Abigail who hath suffered severely from an attack of Megrims. By a most fortunate Accident we witnessed ye arrival of a great French Fleet and an Army.

Oh, Lucius, be of good Chear! With such powerful Allies we cannot fail to win this War! I hear You asking, how many Men are in this Foreign Army? It is an *Immense Array*—near six Thousand of the French King's best troops.

It was a sad gray day on which they came ashore and, through some Mischance, no proper Welcome was in readiness. Yet the French commander—he hath some outlandish name like Rockyambo—was tolerably agreeable none-the-less. Next Day ye Matter was Mended. O, ye salutes that were fired by our gallant Batteries! Ye fire works! Ye cannonades by Seven great Line of Battle Ships, five frigates and many Transports, all fired their big guns. How Terrifying was Tumult they made! No one who witnessed ye Arrival of our Allies will ever forget it.

Sabra sighed, straightened and lifted the hair tumbling, so hot and clinging, down her bare back. La! That *had* been a day to remember!

The writer paused, listening absently to the cry of a tinker who, ringing a bell, was stumping along the alley below with mending gear slung over his shoulder.

You say we are for a pace to have Quarters at ye Fort? How many Chambers are there? Shall we have a Man Servant? Major Clark says probably. I am learning simple Modes of coiffing my hair, though it will be a Difficult to do without a Hairdresser. What will the other Wives be like? Are they young like Me, or old and Shrewish?

Until we reach King's Ferry, my Love, where I shall once more delight my lips with yours—

A sound of steps on the stairs sent Sabra flying to snatch a pale green negligée from her wardrobe. She thought to recognize Sister Phoebe's quick step.

Flushing at having so nearly been trapped in such immodest, if lovely, nudity, Sabra hurriedly snatched the pile of her clothes from the floor and flung them onto a chair before unlatching her door.

It came as a relief to perceive that, like herself, Phoebe had put aside her normal house garments and looked prim yet comfortable in a yellow and violet robe of sprigged voile.

Phoebe treated her sister to an irritatingly superior smile when Sabra hurriedly sanded Lucius' letter, turned it face down.

"—And, my Poppet, how many thousand kisses have you dispatched the gallant surgeon?"

"Not one—" Sabra burst out, "yet—"

"Oh, you needn't be ashamed," Phoebe said a little sadly. "When Ned Hitchcock was alive I used to post him whole pages covered with what I called 'kiss crosses.'"

Phoebe emitting a little sigh, caught up the turkey wing fan and, seating herself commenced gently to make use of it. "Has Alice Blodgett finished your gown yet?"

"Not yet, but I'm sure it'll be vastly modish. Do you think these will be fitting for a formal banquet? Mrs. Harrington—she was in from Southborough to see Mamma—says General Arnold is most hospitable and there is much

entertaining by his staff. And, I—well, I must not put him
to shame, must I?"

Robe billowed about her, as Sabra hurried to the new
travelling coffer—a present from Uncle Will; it contained
her growing collection of bridal finery.

"So you make progress towards—underthings?"
Phoebe was smiling, but Sabra blushed.

XXXII. PRACTICALITIES

THAT MOMENT at which Samuel Stanton could remove
his wig was the pleasantest of any hot summer's day.
Eben placed the dreadfully expensive, carefully curled
affair of horsehair on its block within a powdering closet
to the right of the entrance. After a narrow inspection for
chance vermin, Eben combed the chop wig and expertly
reset one of the ivory pins securing its side curls in position.

Another wonderful comfort Sabra's father found was
in shedding his snuff-brown gabardine coat and waistcoat
of yellow silk. Absently, he noted that perspiration had
stained the coat's armholes.

"That third button is loose," Stanton grunted. "Remind Juno to see about it."

"Yassuh, Misto' Stanton." Hastily Eben's eyes travelled over the study. Was everything as it should be? A
pitcher of cool lemon water waited beside Master's lad-
derback armchair; he preferred it in summertime because
of its greater coolness. Yessuh. Misto' Stanton's heavy-
lensed reading glasses lay ready to hand. The Negro
stooped and eased off the merchant's heavy, silver-buckled pumps, substituted red morocco slippers. As always,
Mitso' Stanton wriggled his foot until Eben pulled free
the creases made by the white cotton stockings between
his toes.

"Big day, suh?"

"Not so big as it couldn't be a deal better, Eben. Trade
is slow, confounded slow these days." Stanton jerked a
kerchief from his breeches pocket and mopped the close-
cropped contour of his skull, then vented a gentle sigh.
Thankfully, he sank onto the woven rush seat of his lad-
derback.

Down at his counting house, the day had been stifling;

because there was so little to do time had dragged on and on. Using precise, efficient gestures the merchant undid his stock, after making sure that his banyan lay ready to hand in case of callers. As a last gesture he pulled forward his ruffled shirt front and blew noisily down inside of it.

"Well, well," he remarked, as always, when Eben poured out a glass of lemon water Stanton slipped onto his nose a pair of heavy, steel-rimmed spectacles then hesitated between perusal of the *Boston Gazette & Country Journal* and the *Massachusetts Weekly News Letter*.

Deciding on the latter, he shook out its folds and starting on the back page of that single, once-folded sheet; immediately he became absorbed. Merchant-like, he left the news to the last, and studied the shipping news with great alertness.

"Entered inwards, Schooner *Neptune* from Falmouth; Ship *Peggy* from Philadelphia." Lips pursed, he ran on down the list. "Prizes of War." His interest sharpened. "Arrived this day, the Ship, *Lovely Agnes*, prize to the Massachusetts privateer Brig, *Grand Turk III*; Gideon Pickering, prize master."

God above! This *Grand Turk's* luck was as infallible as ever. Why, only a fortnight ago, her prize the *Jolly Tar*, a fine new brig had made port under command of one Abel Doane.

Between sips of lemon water—and mighty refreshing it was, too—Stanton viewed the usual advertisements: a public vendue of captured goods at Colonel Hancock's Wharf—"Colonel John's making a pretty thing out of this war, and no mistake," Stanton thought, not without envy. "Um."

"A woman with a Young breast of Milk to Hire out as wet Nurse. Inquire of printer."

"The Sheriff hath taken up one Henry George Talbot on Suspicion of being a Servant. He was found Riding a mare of Thirteen Hands bearing no brand, in Possession of a Silver Watch and was riding a half worn Hogskin Saddle."

"Doctor Jonathan Begg wishes to Acquaint the Publick that he Inoculates for the Smallpox at his Hospital at Sewall's Point in Brooklyn. Patients may lodge at the Sign of the Punch Bowl."

Bah! The same old tripe. What really counted was the

nearly complete lack of advertisements of merchandise—especially such goods as might interest Samuel Stanton, Esquire.

Stanton reversed his newspaper. Um. It would appear that the Hessian General Knyphausen had been attempting to invade New Jersey. The correspondent claimed that this mercenary's purpose was to test the effect of the surrender of Charles Town upon the American public. Good old Nathanael Greene, however, had checked Knyphausen in a smart little battle fought at Springfield in New Jersey and the Hessians had been sent plodding back into their defenses near New York.

Another item informed the reader that a strong British fleet yet cruised off Point Judith, effectively blockading in Newport Admiral De Guichen's French squadron.

Disturbing news had been received from upper New York. Incredible though it might seem, the Tory General Sir John Johnson and Chief Joseph Brant of the Six Nations, once again had closed upon some settlements in the Mohawk Valley the horrors of Indian warfare. Sam Stanton's jaw tightened. What could the Royal Tyrant hope to gain loosing such red hellions on his former subjects? Nothing but an undying hatred.

Stanton sighed, set down his lemon water. God above, would this war *ever* end? It seemed as if the country never had been at peace. Though a little ashamed, Sabra's father found himself wishing that the Congress had not been quite so hasty about spurning those offers of conciliation, advanced last year by King George's ministers.

Stanton tossed aside the *Weekly News Letter* and shifted in his chair before commencing to read the *Gazette*, in hopes of more encouraging news. He found none at all; quite the contrary.

That ineffable Horatio Gates, leading an army to the relief of the Carolinas, had permitted himself to be surprised, by inferior forces, and roundly trounced on the nineteenth of August before a place called Camden, in South Carolina. General Gates, it was reported, had retreated with precipitation some eighty miles to escape pursuit by Lord Cornwallis.

The account continued:

This mortifying disaster following that at Charles Town gives a severe shock to our Army. It must be Productive of the most important & Serious Consequences as respects the welfare of the Southern States. The Continental troops display'd their usual Courage and Bravery, but at the first on-set of the Enemy the whole Body of the Militia became panic struck, were completely routed & ran like a Torrent, leaving the Continentals to oppose the whole force of the Enemy.

This Defeat was not without Loss on the part of the Foe, they having upwards of Five Hundred Men with Officers in proportion kill'd & wounded. The whole number of Continental officers killed & wounded & missing is forty eight. Among our slain is Baron de Kalb, Major General. While leading on the Maryland & Delaware Troops he was pierc'd with Eleven Wounds and soon after Expired. He was a German by birth, a brave and meritorious Officer and a Brigadier-General in the Armies of France; serv'd three years of High Reputation in the American Army.

Stanton's gaze wandered from the smudged and poorly printed page—the paper was execrable. Obviously, the correspondent was attempting to dress up this miserable affair as well as he might. He, Sam Stanton, stood ready to bet a fine beaver hat the American losses were triple, and the British half, of what he'd reported. More bad news. Incredible though it seemed, food prices had risen once again. Victuallers were actually daring to ask forty shillings for a barrel of flour. Salt fish of the common sort went for *thirty* shillings the hundred weight!

The editor invited Patriotic citizens to send corn and cattle for the feeding of the troops. Stanton wondered how much longer the troops would continue to serve without their pay? Surely, not even in the black year of the Three Sevens, had the outlook appeared so hopeless.

True, a French army under Count de Rochambeau *had* arrived, but it was small and blockaded in Newport; the French king's Second Division was reported to be rotting in Brest while waiting for a break in the British blockade.

Yes. The new nation's military and financial situation was desperate, all right. Joshua's letters, very explicit concerning the general aspects of strategy, had made it so clear that even a child could foretell what would follow, should Sir John Johnson and his painted Indian devils succeed in descending the Mohawk Valley towards New York and should General Clinton march north to effect a junction. Only the fort at West Point could prevent such a fatal meeting.

A fly, droning steadily around and around Sam Stanton's comparatively cool library made a comfortable, homey sound. Feeling utterly discouraged, Stanton pushed the spectacles up onto his forehead, settled back in his chair, let the newspaper slip to the floor and commenced to doze.

XXXIII. NEWS FROM MAJOR STANTON

"PRAISE THE LORD," mused Sam Stanton, with his eyes tight closed, "for having thus far, guarded my only son through four pitched battles and a lot of skirmishes which could have killed him just as dead." Odd, thanks to this war, he hardly knew anything of his son's way of mind; his ideals or ambitions. Josh seemed so old for his age and hard as nails, mentally as well as physically. So many parents nowadays were finding their sons grown into unfathomable strangers. Would Josh wish to carry on the once-thriving business done by S. Stanton & Company?

He could find no answer. Yes, he hardly knew his own son any more. But a stripling of nineteen when the first skirmishes had taken place out towards Concord and Lexington, Joshua was now a fine large fellow. If only he returned safe from the war! So many very promising sons would not. The old man sighed again, tried not to worry on that score.

What if Joshua got back, all right, but refused to marry and so failed to produce issue? Then the Stanton name would die out; a name held honorable around the Massachusetts Bay for nigh on one hundred fifty years.

The old man experienced an extra fierce impatience with the small-souled squabblings of Congress and the ruinous jealous bickerings of so many generals. Could the country ever again regain the tranquility of those good old days when, provided a man feared God, cherished his family and remained reasonably honest, he could feel confident of a secure old age?

Stanton settled deeper into his chair.

Stanton finally went to sleep and roused only when Eben knocked and entered, his shiny black face grinning above his white stock. The butler's fat, gray-black hands trembled a little as, on a silver salver, he offered an envelope secured by a red paper wafer.

Eben couldn't read a word, but for all that, he knew

this letter came from the young major, and hoped he might be allowed to stay. Sometimes old Master would read aloud a few lines. Alas, Misto' Stanton's head made a short motion towards the door.

After eagerly breaking the seal, Samuel Stanton readjusted his glasses, then read:

> At Headquarters
> Tappans, New York
> Ye 1st Aug. 1780.

Um, the letter must have travelled express to have arrived so very promptly.

Respected Sir:

Pray make my duty to my Mother and Sisters.

Of late we have seen much activity; seeming endless marching and countermarching because the Enemy have brought Vessels, so our spies inform, to launch a great Attack against the French new-arrived in New Port. At this Intelligence Gen'l Washington set our Army in Motion at once across the Hudson River and moved in threatening array upon the Island of Manhattan, the which caused our Enemies to think Better of sailing northwards.

News of the arrival of the French Troops hath done much to mitigate our Army's Discomfiture over poor Gen'l Gates' Shameful and total rout at Camden. Indeed our Troops had begun to melt away near as fast as last Spring. Only on the Continentals can we count. The Militia—a plague on 'em all—are as chancy as a young girl's whims.

I am glad, most Respected Sir, you share my opinion that young Mr. Devoe would make an excellent Husband for our Sabra. Since we rode out together January last, I have had considerable Opportunity to study him under the Various Rigors and Conditions peculiar to Field Service, and can truthfully vouchsafe that the Promise he offered at the Beginning hath been Sustained. This young Physician is a tireless worker but enjoying an inventive turn of mind which hath earned the earnest Commendation not only of Doctor James Craik, his immediate Superior, but even that of the Director-Gen'l of the Medical Department, Doctor William Shippen.

For the moment quiet prevails in New Jersey and New York & it is well that this is so. The Discipline in our Forces is very low indeed; mere Children of fifteen and sixteen are being paid Fifteen Hundred Dollars for Nine Months service in order to fill the ranks.

As for myself, I confess considerable concern in securing *Absolutely Necessary* supplies for my Battalion. I have drawn no Pay since February the last, and the Merchants hereabouts dun me without let. Respected Sir, I hesitate once more to Trespass on your Generosity, but if you can alleviate me to some Extent I shall be Ever Appreciative. All too many of us Field Officers find ourselves, through no fault of our doing, in my Predicament. We cannot fathom why the Congress does not take Steps to Pay us in currency of some value.

I trust Mamma endures the Summer's heat agreeably and that her Rheumaticks are no Worse.

Permit me, Sir, to offer my filial homage. I hope to obtain Leave again this Autumn that I may once more clasp you by the Hand and embrace Mamma and my Sisters.

> Y'r Most respectful, obedient son,
> Joshua

XXXIV. THE INVITATION

DOCTOR JOHN FLETCHER of Nottingham, Maryland, yawned a prodigious yawn and gazed through the window of that small cottage he shared with Lucius Devoe. For some moments he watched the Hudson, flowing so smoothly and clearly under a heavy log boom and great chain barring progress upstream from West Point. They formed mighty effective obstructions, Fletcher reckoned, blocking the channel as they did all the way across to Constitution Island. An enemy vessel, attempting to pass the boom, inevitably would be delayed long enough to permit her being sunk or disabled by heavy guns firing from the Chain Battery or from Fort Arnold, above.

From where he stood, the Marylander couldn't see Fort Arnold—the principal fortification among a dozen lesser forts and batteries—since it stood some distance back on heights dominating this narrow bend in the lordly Hudson. But he could make out a cluster of houses dotting a small plain between it and the river landing.

Victim to supreme boredom, Fletcher yawned again. For nigh on a year now he'd served at West Point as junior physician to the garrison which, at this moment, numbered just above three thousand milita and a handful of three hundred regulars. Because this was late summer, even the militia remained healthy, despite the fact that country boys—such as most of them were—proved almost eager to come down with every known malady, the moment they were ordered into cantonments.

The brazen, ill-tempered voice of a drill sergeant putting his awkward squad through various evolutions, floated in through the window, accompanied by dust and a generous assortment of flies. It was warm, but not hot, on this eighth day of September—and nowhere near as humid as it would have been along the lovely, lazy Patuxent River.

Fletcher turned, yelled, "Jennings! Goddamit, Jennings! Where in hell are you?"

"Coming, sir." The orderly appeared, rubbing heavy eyes.

"Good God, Jennings! Can you do nothing but sleep?"

"Yessir." He stifled not very effectively a yawn. "But there's nawthin' else to do."

"Is Doctor Devoe back from across the river?"

"Nawsir. But I allow he will be soon. Thorne rode for 'e landing with a saddle hoss near a hour ago."

Hesitantly, John Fletcher passed a hand over a humorous-appearing brown face. Short, he lent the impression of being taller, perhaps because his head was so narrow and his shoulders not even ordinarily wide.

"Apprize me as soon as Doctor Devoe returns," he instructed, then swung over to his desk and commenced drafting a requisition for a pair of cupping cups—the type he needed were brass-mounted glass, equipped with a membrane valve which could be used to control the flow of blood.

Just why he bothered to make out a requisition John Fletcher couldn't have explained, since almost never were pleas for even the most urgent medical supplies granted the least attention. Yet he completed the form and impaled it on a hook ready for the call of a medical messenger.

The beating of a drum indicated that the garrison was being summoned to stand Retreat. Fletcher smiled his satisfaction. An almighty change for the better had characterized discipline at West Point since Major-General Benedict Arnold had assumed command. Genial, easygoing General MacDougall had been content to let disciplinary matters follow the line of least resistance.

Amazing, how quickly a commanding officer's personality could find itself reflected in almost any army post.

Now, when guard details turned out, their buttons and metal work shone bright and spotless and sentries walked their posts smartly, like real soldiers. At the end of each tour they executed the "about-face" neatly, no longer shuffling along like the dispirited militia they once had been.

It was encouraging for one and all to hear that the works would soon be repaired and strengthened. General Arnold himself had conducted a penetrating, and sometimes embarrassing, inspection of stores accumulated in various souterraines and magazines.

Rumor had it that Arnold was extra anxious to improve his command because, last spring, he had so narrowly escaped being cashiered for peculation. But for the intercession of his Commander-in-Chief, Arnold would have been dismissed—everybody was aware of that.

Fletcher watched a platoon of Colonel Sheldon's dragoons regiment clatter by and noted that the black horsehair crests of their heavy leather helmets were combed and that their dark blue, yellow-edged saddle cloths were clean.

In deep satisfaction, Fletcher rubbed his hands. Goddamit! It was fine to be serving once more under a real commander—his first since duty at Nathanael Greene's headquarters. Yessir, old Arnold, gimpy leg and all, certainly had set the militia colonels to dancing a lively tune. Colonel Wills and Colonel Livingston were reported harassed to the point of an official protest.

What was the sense of all this spit and polish, all these exercises, they wanted to know? Hadn't Clinton been driven back into New York. He wasn't likely to come out again until—well, until next spring, anyhow.

Doctor Fletcher felt so well he returned to his desk and signed and sanded a requisition for six plaister knives, two dozen screw torniquets, a set of scales and weight and two and a half fluid drams of spirits of lavender compound. Of course, he badly needed some syringes, a silver probe and at least half a thousand pins, but on such luxuries there was absolutely no point in wasting paper or ink. These days the Medical Committee of Congress was tighter than the bark on a tree.

Something of an amateur artist, Fletcher fetched from his field trunk a piece of drawing paper and pencil and, moving out onto the porch, fell to sketching those craggy heights across the river. Yonder, eagles nested in the spring, and all manner of birds and beasts took their rest.

Beyond the heights, and perhaps half a mile down stream on the east bank, was situated the Beverly Robinson house which, successively, had served as headquarters for General Washington, then Heath, then Mac-Dougall, and now Benedict Arnold. First chance he got, John Fletcher intended going over to make a drawing of that handsome little farmhouse.

Raising eyes from his drawing he noticed that the military ferry was on its way back. Right now, the little craft's stained sail was hanging limp, but the oars of the bateau men kept it moving. Their long ash sweeps were raising little showers as they pulled for the landing.

As a ferry yonder craft wasn't much; nowhere near as elegant as the commanding officer's barge which, nowadays, was continually plying the river. Some days General Arnold's barge descended the Hudson as far as Verplancks' Ferry and Stony Point. The King's Ferry-Stony Point crossings were, by far, the most useful remaining in American hands and by them passed all land communication between New England, New York and Southern States.

Fletcher's pencil quickly filled in those bold headlands looming beyond the Lantern Battery which guarded the main boat landing for Fort Arnold.

Why had Devoe been summoned so peremptorily to General Arnold's quarters? Maybe it was because the general's wife, a Philadelphia beauty of great spirit and charm, had just arrived, together with the general's little son.

Rumor had it that Mrs. General Arnold had not travelled well from Pennsylvania and declared herself, in fact, exhausted.

A little enviously, Fletcher recalled Devoe's undeniable success in treating ailments of various officers' ladies. Especially odd was the young Jamaican's equal attention to the needs of the post washer-women and the wives of common soldiers. How tireless, how burningly ambitious was this curious, dark-skinned Jamaican.

Returning to his drawing, Fletcher sketched on the margin a trio of bateau men engaged in throwing a hunting knife at a peg driven into the ground and became so intent on his art that he became aware of his roommate's

presence only when a shadow fell across his sketch book.
Devoe was grinning as he tossed his riding gloves onto a
settle on the porch, patted a sagging pocket.

"Compliments of his sublime and unpredictable majesty, our commanding officer. Tonight, we will drink Arnold's health in Canary."

For all he must have had a tiresome journey across the
Hudson, down to the Robinson house and back, Lucius
was in high good spirits.

"Well, John, what do you think has chanced?"

"At headquarters you plucked a few more soft plumes
to feather your nest."

"No, no; seriously."

"You're to act as physician to General Arnold and
family?" the Marylander ventured.

"Yes, that's it. My fee will be a mere twenty pounds
monthly." Lucius stripped off his coat and yelled for Jennings to bring a wet towel. "Lord, John, you should see
in what elegance he lives! What silver, what fine linen—
and the general's lady."

In ecstasy the Jamaican rolled dark eyes towards the
fly-brown ceiling of their porch while casting loose the
new glass buttons of a long waistcoat. "Lord, John, Mrs.
Arnold's a raving beauty; her hands are tiny and each little nail glistens like mica."

Fletcher failed to respond to his companion's enthusiasm. "You didn't notice any Union Jacks embroidered
on her petticoats, did you? The whole Shippen family she
springs from are known to be red-hot Tories."

"No, I wouldn't care a fig if I did. John, here's the really good news. You and I are bidden to take supper at
headquarters next Friday!"

"Not really? Damned decent of you, Lucius, to get me
invited, too."

"Stuff. Then will be the time to mention your desire
for a posting to Yellow Springs Hospital. Confidentially,
John, I have learned that old Bodo Otto is growing weary, and yearns for relief."

Smiling broadly, Lucius clapped his friend on the
shoulder. "If I can accomplish aught to further your ambition, John, I will do it. You, Jimmy Thatcher and I will
inject a measure of vigor and imagination into the Medical Department—chance what may."

Their orderly uncorked the dark green bottle Devoe

had brought and looked about for glasses until he came across two of varying design. Into them he poured the clear yellow wine.

Fletcher, smilingly, offered a fold of paper. "And now it's my turn with good news. Thanks to Doctor Thatcher, you have been bid to mess at the quarters of His Excellency, Major-General Frederick von Steuben."

Lucius' gaze steadied itself on the Marylander's narrow features. "Not really!"

"Aye, one of his Dutchmen came clanking in this morning and made inquiry for you."

Lucius, laughing, tossed the unopened invitation onto a table—a gesture which pleased him enormously—as if a summons to General von Steuben's mess weren't a matter of great concern. It was, though. While serving on the staff of Frederick the Great, the old Prussian had learned how to set a most excellent table, even in the midst of a very bleak campaign.

Devoe recalled their orderly. "Look to my uniform, Jennings, and mind you burnish its buttons better than you did the last time. I shall want it tomorrow night."

Though Lucius spoke carelessly, Fletcher laughed. Very few medical officers had elected to bear the expense of purchasing a uniform; yet it was entirely in keeping with Devoe's character.

"I learned something at headquarters today," Devoe remarked suddenly. "Did you know that Dr. Shippen has been cleared of the charges brought against him by Rush and Morgan—his predecessors?"

"—And well he should have been," Fletcher declared stoutly.

Lucius dropped onto a stool, sat staring into his wine glass. "Of course, and yet—"

Quickly Fletcher glanced at his roommate. "You don't doubt our chief was blameless?"

"No. He's honest, practical and hard working—but lacking in tact. He has so very many enemies I begin to wonder if—"

"—You may wonder all you wish," Fletcher observed, "but for my money, William Shippen is a great surgeon and has accomplished more in the interests of the Medical Department than Morgan, Rush and all the rest of them put together. Dammit, Lucius, any strong man is bound to be criticized."

Lucius listened with but half an ear, thought back to talk circulating at Arnold's headquarters. Politics, politics! Some group, or some state, was forever pushing forward its candidate.

Um. How much longer could Director-General Shippen cling to his position? So far, the Congress always had supported that irascible but capable individual but, somewhere, somehow, Shippen must have antagonized the Commander-in-Chief. Moreover, down in Philadelphia— once more become the national capital—Morgan and Rush owned hosts of friends. They, too, were graduates of Edinburgh University and, unlike the Shippens, were untainted by Toryism.

In a sunburnt, none-too-clean hand, the orderly again offered the general's wine.

Lucius smiled his singularly captivating smile. "Well, Johnny, here's to your appointment to Yellow Springs."

"—And to you, Deputy-Director of the Middle Department!"

In their bare and uncomfortable quarters the two physicians solemnly raised glasses and drank.

Devoe remarked, "Once I reach Hartford, John, I'll set about building more of those Indian Long House hospitals. The churches and barns we have employed so far are miserably devoid of convenience and ventilation."

xxxv. Major-General von Steuben Entertains

Because the evening proved fine and a breeze off the Hudson had carried away such mosquitoes as had survived an uncommonly early frost, General von Steuben's aides decided that dinner should be served beneath a wide fly rigged before the general's quarters. Although out in the open odors of cooking were not inescapable, and besides a fine prospect of the Hudson formed a magnificent background for the banquet. In a little backwater, formed by the river, bullfrogs kept on calling "jug o' rum, jug o' rum" and the gruff call of late bittern rose softly.

Heavy-bodied and long-nosed, the old Prussian occupied the head of his table, his wig crisp and snowy and his dark blue and white regimentals spotless by the glare of the candelabra. Diamonds in decoration—the star of

Pour le Merité glowed and glistened on the lower left side
of von Steuben's tunic.

As at no other mess, big wooden-faced orderlies waited ram-rod-straight, one behind each chair. They remained quite expressionless and kept their eyes fixed
straight ahead. Despite everything, the Prussian touch
could be felt even across the Atlantic.

Never had Lucius watched guards present arms with
such an automatic and uniform precision, seen sentries
stand so very erect in uniforms evincing such painstaking
care. No wonder that the Commander-in-Chief's personal bodyguard were, almost without exception, of German
origin. Only these docile foreigners would surrender
enough individuality to follow instructions to the letter,
to drill like so many obedient children. No American
could, or would, tolerate such discipline, such a loss of
personal self-expression. All the same, General Washington's own bodyguard was the object of wonder and admiration of all who saw it on duty.

The Inspector-General's long, linen-draped table was
literally heaped with food; hams, cold ducks, great roasts
of beef hemmed in a centerpiece consisting of an enormous golden pumpkin which appeared to erupt grapes,
apples, persimmons and other fruits. The von Steuben
coat-of-arms adorned a profusion of silver vessels gleaming frostily all the length of the dinner table.

By Prussian standards this was neither a large, nor an
elaborate supper; not more than twenty officers and as
many ladies seated themselves on chairs brought out
from the general's headquarters. On a rude sideboard behind General von Steuben, many dusty bottles ranged in
orderly array, awaiting use.

For Lucius the occasion afforded one thrill after another. Why, tonight the guest of honor was Major-General
Greene, spoken of throughout the Army as the Commander-in-Chief's *alter ego*.

What a strange character was Quartermaster-General
Nathanael Greene. At the outbreak of the war a simple
blacksmith, one of whose legs was a full inch and a half
shorter than its fellow, he had through sheer ability and a
very intimate understanding of the military principles
embodied in Caesar's *Commentaries*, risen from a humble subaltern in the Rhode Island Militia to a reputation

second only to that of George Washington—in the eyes
of the fighting men.

True, there were also Anthony Wayne—capable but
impetuous; and Henry Knox, dependable, but quiet and
impassive as any of those oxen which drew his trains of
artillery through one long campaign to the next—but they
had their limitations, and Greene hadn't.

Looking down the table, Lucius immediately noticed
the blue and white uniform and glittering gold lace worn
by Major L'Enfant, who had laid out the original defenses of West Point. The majority of the male guests
wore blue turned up in scarlet for the artillery, light blue
for the infantry, yellow for the cavalry and so on.

Toasts galore were offered to His Excellency the
Commander-in-Chief, to the Congress, to His Most
Christian Majesty of France, to Count Rochambeau, to
General this and General that, until Lucius' eyes were
swimming. Director-General Shippen wore black and sat
three places nearer the head of the table than Lucius; his
angular and slightly mottled face red by the candlelight.

It annoyed Lucius that, for once, he had failed to catch
more than a couple of the ladies' names. Firmly, he reminded himself he must have no more to drink—though
he would pretend to.

Jupiter! It annoyed him to find memory beginning to
play tricks because, once the diners arose and the ladies
withdrew, he intended addressing himself to the Director-General. William Shippen, Jr., might be on his way
out of favor but he was still supreme commander in the
Medical Service; right now, his nod or frown might make
all the difference to the career of one Lucius Devoe.

Struggling to rally his wits, the Jamaican settled back
and listened attentively to the table talk. Come to think
on it, already he had progressed quite a way from that
poverty-stricken hovel near Kingston.

If only his several brothers and sisters could behold
him now, sitting in the company of great noblemen, famous generals, and even a statesman or two of the first
importance! The best of it was that he had come this far
thanks to no one but himself. Silently, he reminded himself, "This is only the beginning." Yes. A far-sighted fellow might achieve almost any goal during the social
upheaval now taking place in America.

Take General Washington's favorite aide, Major Alexander Hamilton; everyone knew him to be the illegitimate sprig of a Nevis Islander—one of the least important West Indies. It made no odds that Hamilton was a bastard; his opinion was held in high importance by the Commander-in-Chief, who listened to Hamilton as to few others.

After the war what great estates might not be carved out of that rich wilderness reported to lie to the northwest? If, a few generations earlier, the Schuylers, Phillipses, the van Rensselaers and the van Wycks had been able to fashion baronies for themselves, why should a Devoe not be able to do the same?

The two goblets of malaga he had consumed continued to warm Lucius' innards, to titillate his imagination. Jupiter! Why, in time, should there not be a Devoe township, nay, a Devoe County? It seemed possible, entirely possible.

Gradually, almost imperceptibly, the Jamaican became aware of someone's regard. Drawing a deep breath, he looked up and saw, seated almost directly opposite, a handsome young woman of about his own age. She was richly clad in a gown of dark blue velvet trimmed in crimson and wore, at the division of her breast, an enormous brooch of gold set with pearls. Inexplicably, his breath quickened as he summoned a shy smile and his fingertips buzzed.

A long instant this raven-haired young woman's intense and dark blue eyes met his—then swung away. She sat straight as any ruler, listening, or pretending to listen, to the ponderous gallantries of a young German sapper major at her left. How white was the skin of her arms, her throat.

As he hoped, her eyes, vibrant and well formed, returned to meet his. Yes. They *were* dark blue; but by the candlelight they approached black. She possessed, he realized, a small and beautifully formed mouth which perfectly assumed a succession of gracious expressions as if in obedience to the commands of a drill master. One couldn't say that she seemed to be in the least out of place, yet somehow her bearing seemed foreign to that of the American ladies.

"Of course, Major," he overheard her say to her companion, "the defeat in South Carolina was most dis-

couraging; yet our army has suffered far worse reverses
at Quebec and Long Island.''

Lucius became lost to all other considerations; equally
he neglected the plump young woman to his left, and the
bird-faced wife of Colonel Birchard to his right.

This dark-haired girl's voice fascinated him; by no
means strident, it yet carried clearly across the table. Although continuing to address her companion, she seemed
to study Lucius. Heart hammering, he risked the faintest
imaginable smile and nod. To his delighted astonishment
she acknowledged his attention with a slow and gracious
smile which revealed even, white, very white, teeth and
the hitherto unsuspected existence of a dimple in the rosy
curve of her left cheek. Then she looked away.

''Studied!'' was the one word adequately to describe
her. Her every motion, her coiffure, the care with which
her quietly elegant clothing had been selected, suggested
considerable reflection. It occurred to Lucius that the
dark young lady opposite him seldom would act on impulse.

Of Mrs. Birchard, the tired-looking, elderly and plainly
dressed lady to his right he inquired, ''I confess to being
very awkward about names. Can you give me that of the
young lady in blue who sits directly across the table?''

Mrs. Birchard smiled faintly before directing a quick
glance across the table. Said she evenly, ''You must
mean Mrs. Wynkoop?''

''Ah, yes. Mrs. Wynkoop.'' Lucius lingered on the
name, converted it into a question.

''Emma Wynkoop, for your further information, is a
widow, I believe, of a year's standing.'' Mrs. Birchard's
manner suggested disapproval that the young widow no
longer wore weeds—even had tucked a few wild gentians
in luxuriant black hair. ''She owns an estate up the river
and is very rich, I am told.''

Wise enough to let the matter drop, Lucius put forward
a question concerning a picnic projected for the following week, yet, try as he would to keep his gaze from
Emma Wynkoop's roundish white face and its large,
navy blue eyes, he couldn't.

Jupiter! This Mrs. Wynkoop was the handsomest bru-
nette he'd beheld since leaving Cuba behind and a certain
Señorita Paquita de Gutierrez y Castro. To find his usual
obedient emotions plunging, rearing like a pair of badly

trained carriage horses, was to Lucius a novel and a disquieting sensation.

When candles guttered and this well-nigh interminable banquet came to an end, the ladies amid a rising gale of voices, withdrew into Major-General von Steuben's quarters. Quite without appearing to, Lucius ascertained in the meantime, that his vis-a-vis' full name was Emma Ten Broeck Wynkoop and that her property was situated up river near a place called Kaaterskill. Curiously enough, few of his informants seemed prepared to dwell on the subject of Emma Wynkoop and, in short order, changed the topic of conversation.

The necessity of manufacturing diplomatic and possibly fruitful conversation with Doctor Shippen presently removed Mrs. Wynkoop from Lucius' thoughts. When, an hour later, the ladies emerged to rejoin the gentlemen gravely sipping port under the fly, he wasn't in the least surprised that Emma Wynkoop, in masterly casualness, came sauntering almost directly up to him, dark eyes alight and friendly.

"You," she began, "must be the clever and very promising Doctor Devoe we have heard so much about?"

Unaccountably, Lucius stammered, "Why, Mrs. Wynkoop, Ma'am, I—I do protest, I deserve—no—such fine description."

"But was it not you who caused the construction of a flying hospital built along the design of an Iroquois Long House?"

"Why yes," he admitted blushing to his ear tips. "I presume I was responsible." He needed to display a becoming modesty and so indulged in a rare bit of frankness. "The idea, however, was not mine to begin with, only its application here at West Point. 'Twas devised by Doctor Tilton. Last winter he employed it in New Jersey with much success."

She moved nearer to where he stood just outside the perimeter of tawny light cast by a new supply of candles brought by the general's stalwart, wooden-faced orderlies.

"Do you care to inform me further concerning these hospitals of yours?" She looked eagerly up into his face and moved so close he became aware of a nerve-tingling French scent afloat in the still air. "I am not just making small talk," she added and laughed softly. "During this war I have cared, from time to time, for many wounded men."

Sombre eyes riveted to the face so eagerly lifted, Lucius burst into explanation. "In my type of hospital, you see, our heating fire is built in the exact center of a ward on an open hearth and is served by no chimney at all."

"But, Doctor Devoe, what of the smoke?"

"If the ward room doors are the right size," he made brief gestures with his hands, "the smoke circulates high up and passes off through an opening about four inches wide let into the ridge of the roof and takes the poisonous exhalations of wounds with it. The draught thus insured maintains a continual supply of fresh air so often lacking in sick rooms.

"I place my patients with their heads next to the wall and their feet turned towards the fire all round the ward room. Further," he lowered his voice, aware that several of the guests were regarding them, "I may point out that smoke combats contagion, but without giving the least offense to the patients." His voice rang once more with enthusiasm. "In this way, dear lady, I am able to accommodate, with impunity, double the number of patients possible in any other ward of comparable size."

"Why, this is amazing!" Mrs. Wynkoop clapped hands in gentle enthusiasm. "Were I to send some victuals for your sick, will you sometime show me your flying hospital?"

"I would be charmed," he burst out. "But these days victuals are plagued hard to come by, as we are here at the Fort know only too well."

Emma Wynkoop's long, but strong and capable-appearing, hands deliberately smoothed the rich texture of her skirt. "Within the week I will send to your hospital a full wagon load of provender from my estate." Though the young widow spoke carelessly, Lucius recognized an underlying pride. Her gaze intensified itself. "You were not aware that I—well, I have inherited the great—or so people deem it—Ramsdorp estate in Kaaterskill?"

"Why no," he assured her, then wrinkled his brow. "Wynkoop is a Dutch name, is it not? Holland Dutch, I mean."

She looked out over the darkly flowing river. "Yes. My people emigrated to New Amsterdam nearly a century and a half ago."

"Then you must be one of what they call—" he struggled for the word—"patroons?"

A momentary hesitation marked her reply. "Why, why I—I suppose so."

Of course, Emma knew she wasn't, and so did all the great landowners of Dutch origin. Nicholas Ten Broeck had been no patroon. In fact, but newly arrived from Veendam a generation ago, he had made his way upstream from Staten Island carrying all his earthly belongings in a bandanna handkerchief and lacking shoes to cover his sturdy brown feet.

Old-timers about Kaaterskill could recall other things about Nicholas Ten Broeck; that he had served Klaus Wynkoop long and faithfully, toiling while that hulking patroon and Jan, his ninnyhammer of a son, travelled in Europe, eating and drinking more than five ordinary men.

The van Rensselaers, the De Witts, the van Wycks and the Myers proved quite as ready to criticize old Nick Ten Broeck for gradually plunging his employer into debt—to himself—as they were to praise the industry and skill with which Emma's father maintained the broad fields and fine flocks of Ramsdorp. Emma, rendered motherless at birth, soon had come to writhe under patroon contempt for a mere overseer's daughter. They had modified their tune only a little when Klaus, to avoid financial disaster, had affianced his only son to Nick Ten Broeck's handsome and extremely capable daughter.

While she accepted a massive silver goblet of flip Emma was thinking, "Of course Doctor Devoe will hear about my husband's death and that it was my dare which provoked Jan, dead drunk, into trying to ride such a wild two-year stallion. Like all the rest, he will wonder about it."

Maybe sometime Doctor Devoe could be made to understand how bitterly she'd hated and disdained Jan Wynkoop, that lazy, arrogant and useless waster of opportunity, money and time.

Tonight, though, Emma refused to concern herself on the subject. This young Jamaican, too, she judged to be something of an outsider in society. He'd prove a clever, shrewd young fellow, or she had made the poorest guess of her life.

"Mrs. Wynkoop, my poor patients will relish fresh meat, eggs, and vegetables more than I can say. I—I can't tell you how very sensible I am of your generosity." Lucius beamed then, on impulse, bent to kiss Emma's hand.

A thrill of excitement quickened Lucius' pulses. By God, things *were* going well! Hadn't the great Doctor Shippen promised to inspect his Long House hospital at the first opportunity? Yes, ever since adopting the Army his star steadily had risen.

As a group of other guests bore down towards them, Emma Wynkoop murmured, "Though I hesitate to suggest so long a ride in hot weather, perhaps, Doctor, you would care to make a selection of the supplies yourself?"

Instantly, he replied, "I would be charmed to do so. When?"

Without any greater hesitation, she said, "Come next week, the tenth—if Mrs. Arnold can spare you. Anybody in Kaaterskill village can tell you how to reach my estate." She manufactured a bright laugh and turned. "Good evening, Captain!" She acknowledged the deep bow of William North, one of Arnold's favorite aides. "You have been neglecting me most shamefully. What a very modish wig!"

The aide started to talk but fell silent because the Baron von Steuben's guttural bass was booming out. "Duels! *Pfui!* To them must come an end. Vot nonsense, this murdering of goot officers. Haff you heard, *Herr* General Greene?" The Inspector-General breathed heavily through a long and pointed nose, while offering a well-polished silver snuff box.

Greene said he hadn't heard. "Another duel?"

"*Ja wohl*, on the twenty-ninth vas another such affair between a *Leutnant* Offut and Mr. *Herr* Parr of Colonel Maryland's dragoons regiment. Vot follows? *Leutnant* Offut kills *Herr* Parr and iss himself gravely wounded in the thigh. Vot stupidity! Vot criminal nonsense! *Ach!* His Excellency should do like His Majesty Frederich, *Koenig von Preussen.*" Von Steuben passed a hand over a sharply receding forehead, then inserted a finger under his heavy, old-fashioned wig and scratched vigorously.

Someone inquired about the solution arrived at by the Prussian king.

While Greene, his small eyes narrowed, slapped a mosquito from his chin, von Steuben laughed harshly. "His Royal Majesty had ordered no more duels—so, when two *offiziere* disobeyed and exchanged challenges, he commanded they should meet in his presence at a place and time set by him. Ven dese fine fire-eaters came to duel, *Mein Gott!* the whole Prussian Army vas there to vitness!''

The scarlet revers of von Steuben's cuff flamed to the short gesture he made. "And do you know vhat else was on the Field of Honor? A gallows! Ho! Ho! Ho!'' He clapped Greene on his enormous epaulette. "*Ja, mein Freund,* a gallows, a rope and two coffins. *Der Koenig* he order those two *offiziere* before him. 'Now go ahead and duel,' says he, 'shoot straight, because any survivor vill hang, so soon your duel is ended.' ''

Von Steuben laughed again, wiped his nose on a lace-trimmed handkerchief. "*Ja,* I was there and saw it all. Ho! Ho! Vot did do dose two bloodthirsty fellows? They fell on their knees and prayed His Royal Majesty's forgiffness. For a long time there vas no more duelling.''

He nodded several times. "*Ja,* and that is vot should happen here, in our Army. Of goot officers have ve too few, that they should kill each other instead of the *verdammt* English.''

XXXVI. March and Countermarch

In spite of special care and every treatment Doctors Thatcher and Craik could devise, Brigadier-General Poor of the New Hampshire Troops, succumbed to putrid fever. Lucius thanked his stars for having been summoned to consultation only at the very last moment. No one could rightly state that he had lost so distinguished a patient.

The weather having turned unseasonably warm, there could be no delay concerning a funeral. Lucius never forgot that sad ceremony because it served as the first occasion to observe, at close range, the American Army's well-beloved Commander-in-Chief.

Long campaigns probably had done less than ceaseless bickering with the Congress to etch careworn lines in General Washington's powerful features. Everybody moved warily since His Excellency's temper was mighty short, these days. Jimmy Thatcher claimed it was because his false teeth fitted so badly—for all that no less an expert than Paul Revere had fashioned them out of the finest quality of Indian elephant ivory.

Lucius welcomed the excuse to share a tent with Thatcher, that indefatigable note-taker and diarist, and to remain at Paramus for General Poor's obsequies.

Because General Poor had a fine military record and had fought from the beginning, quantities of notables came riding into the camp. Major Lee, whose troops of light horsemen were the pride of the command, cursed and raged until every trooper was turned out in almost Prussian smartness.

When at length the good gray warrior had been laid to rest Doctor James Thatcher retired to his writing desk.

Lucius watched his colleague writing about General Poor's funeral, at the same time wondering why Providence should have elected to strike down so well-beloved and so capable an officer. Why should Poor have been spared during so many battles and skirmishes, only to fall victim to a loathsome disease?

Thatcher locked his writing case and, looking up, sighed, "Well, that is that. God rest the poor gentleman's bones." He helped himself to a pinch of snuff. "Have you determined on going up to Kaaterskill?"

"I scarce know," Lucius smiled. "Why?"

"Were I you, I'd accept. Breedon visited at Ramsdorp last spring and claims it to be one of the very finest estates along the entire Hudson Valley." Thatcher winked. "She's a handsome young lady is Mrs. Wynkoop; and owning a fortune of near ninety thousand pounds shouldn't make her look any plainer, either."

Lucius stared. "Ninety thousand pounds! *Sterling?*"

"Aye," nodded the Massachusetter. "They say her pa, old Nick Ten Broeck, willed her some of the finest timberlands in this part of the country. She owns God alone knows how many slaves and farms. Emma's origins may not be so *haut ton* as those of the Schuylers and Phillipses, but I warrant her money bags clink quite as musically." He stretched lesiurely. "By the bye, what were you and Emma Wynkoop talking about the other night at von Steuben's?"

Lucius' pointed features contracted a trifle. "Chiefly about the Indian hut hospital and such matters. Why?"

James Thatcher, Jr. showed irregular teeth in a grin. "You were always a shy speaker, Lucius, yet you sat

aside with her nigh on an hour, instead of getting decent-
ly drunk with the rest of us. Phew! That old Prussian's
brandy must be distilled in Hell. How I wished for a lid to
the top of my head next morning. You've heard, I presume, that His Excellency will be riding north in a week's
time?''

Lucius was annoyed that so significant an item of information had not sooner reached him. ''He's to meet the
French commander?''

''Aye, that's it. We're all praying that General Washington succeeds in coaxing a bit of hard cash out of our
gallant allies.'' Thatcher looked mighty serious all at
once. ''God knows what will chance should he fail. Last
week there were two near-mutinies, but the paymaster
grandly handed a few Line regiments pay due since last
January.''

''During His Excellency's absence who's to succeed in
command of the Army?''

''Nat Greene, of course. Who else?''

The Jamaican bent, commenced packing saddle bags
for his return to West Point. ''Why not Arnold, he's senior?''

Thatcher cast his friend a sharp look. ''But for the
Commander-in-Chief's good offices, your friend Benedict would have been dismissed the Service, last summer.''

''What a miserable and sordid business!'' Lucius broke
out—he'd come to like, and to admire, the Commandant
of West Point. ''The charges never were proved. I can't
understand why he suffers such ingratitude from Congress, and the envious hatred of so many officers. Precious few of 'em have fought so long or have suffered so
much for our Cause. Well,'' he held out his hand, ''I'm
off. I hope you'll attend my wedding.''

''The thirtieth, isn't it? Yes, I'll be there to buss the
bride.''

On the long and dusty ride back to West Point Lucius,
for once, failed to take note of his surroundings. No need
to; his saddle horse, a gangling, shaggy beast, knew the
road.

Thank fortune, Sabra was due to arrive at the Fort
within another fortnight. He'd make a valuable friend of
Emma Wynkoop for the two of them.

Jupiter! What a pother was in prospect. News of the

Devoe-Stanton engagement had circulated far and wide—chiefly because Major Joshua Stanton was so universally known and well liked. Lieutenant-General Knox, Chief of Artillery, was swearing that, during the next campaign he'd make young Stanton a colonel, come what might.

Body swinging to his animal's slow trot, Lucius schooled himself. It was Sabra he loved. Yes. He loved her very deeply indeed. From a pocket he produced her miniature and rode quite a distance peering intently upon Sabra Stanton's cheerful, lovely and innocent features. He'd no doubt whatever but that she'd make him an excellent wife, for all that she'd a mind of her own—and probably a temper to boot.

Once he'd returned the miniature to its place he fell, for the hundredth time, to conjecturing on how much old Sam Stanton might be worth. Certainly before the war he had been one of the very wealthiest merchants of Boston, worth probably more than ninety thousand pounds—sterling.

The six-year spell of interrupted trade, however, must have cost him dear; again, there were three other children to share in his estate. That would—impatient with himself, Lucius broke off this line of thought. He had asked to marry Sabra Stanton and had been accepted. Nothing remained to be said or done on that subject.

Suppose he accepted Mrs. Wynkoop's invitation to visit Ramsdorp? Gossip would travel many a dusty lane, faster than a swallow's flight—conjecture would enter the officers' mess at the Fort. Let the idle tongues wag! He wasn't going, really, to see Emma Wynkoop, but to procure support and supplies badly needed for his patients—and always there seemed to be more. Nowadays, hardly ever did a seasoned veteran turn up among replacements for the garrison.

Generally the recruits proved to be gangling, utterly confused country lads who never before had ranged more than a few miles from their birthplaces.

In barracks these bumpkins inevitably fell easy prey to any one of many diseases. Absently, Lucius watched a small flurry of golden yellow birch leaves go scurrying across the dirt road before him, under the propulsion of a brisk breeze.

When he got to Hartford, by God, he'd see that enough

sentries were provided at his hospitals to enforce the orders of his physicians and surgeons. Infected men wandered freely about most military hospitals because there was no one to restrain them—inevitably, diseases spread and spread.

He was thinking about other changes he intended to make when thoughts of Emma Wynkoop again obtruded themselves.

There was something subtly stimulating and tremendously vital about the widow. Had she been a male, certainly she would have risen high in the Army. Hers was the quiet self-assurance and force of a born commander; yet all the same, she remained softly feminine. In Emma he recognized much of his own restless nature and desire for accomplishment—a need for justification in the eyes of contemporaries.

What a pity they could not have met but a few months earlier! As no other female, Emma Wynkoop commanded his attention and respect. He remembered her low crisp voice and direct reasoning complicated by no feminine circumlocutions.

Irritably, Lucius beat his heels against the nag's furry sides. Damnation! With Sabra to become his wife in so short a time he'd no right to be even thinking of Emma Wynkoop whose only relatives now dwelt in New York and were fire-eating Tories. Who could blame them? Patriot forces in the fighting around New York back in '76, had burnt and plundered their property without mercy.

Definitely, he decided against a visit to Kaaterskill.

xxxvii. Cannon Fire Downstream

To Doctor Devoe's vast astonishment a note, regretting, in the most polite of terms, his inability of making a visit to Ramsdorp resulted in the arrival, at West Point, of three oxcarts, heavy with choice supplies for his hospital. Carts, oxen and all, had been sailed down the river aboard Mrs. Wynkoop's own flatboat.

Soldiers off-duty at the Fort gathered by the dozen beside the landing enviously to watch the great, two-wheeled carts come creaking ashore freighted high with vegetables, salted meat, bacon and hams. Later inspection revealed also numerous heavy Dutch blankets and a box of linen shirts; these last could not have been more highly esteemed had they been of pure cloth of gold.

The arrival of this magnificent gift elevated Lucius in the esteem—and envy—of his fellow officers because Hans Hodenpuyl, the broad-faced Dutchman in charge, loudly announced that the shipment must be receipted for by Senior Surgeon Lucius Devoe, and no one else.

Hodenpuyl brought from Emma Wynkoop a curious letter; one which implied that she understood his reasons for failing to visit Ramsdorp and respected him accordingly. She had, Emma wrote, thought over his remarks concerning those stringent problems confronting the Medical Service. Possibly they would find opportunity to discuss them further since it chanced that she had been bidden to make a visit to her old friend Mrs. General Arnold whom she had met in Philadelphia.

"I shall be their guest," Emma wrote, "during four days, beginning the twenty-third of September. Perchance your official duties will bring you to Robinson house at least once during that period?"

The twenty-third? Lucius passed a hand over his jaw. Um. If all went as planned, Sabra should reach King's Ferry not later than the twenty-fifth. Again, he congratulated himself on his decision to avoid visiting Kaaterskill. The impact of Emma Wynkoop's charm and personality on his imagination, somehow, was terrifying.

"How," he asked himself, "can I reconcile Sabra to a friendship with Mrs. Wynkoop? Surely, she will be able to perceive how valuable Mrs. Wynkoop's friendship can be to my advancement."

As nearly as he could determine, this sprightly young widow seemed to be acquainted with almost everybody who was anybody—or was likely to become important.

He pulled a wry face, hoped Sabra wouldn't prove of a jealous disposition.

The following week proved a busy one for Lucius. Aside from his routine duties which demanded periodic visits to a number of other fortifications guarding the Hudson, it was necessary to make preparations for the wedding. To his delight Mrs. Arnold promised that her distinguished husband would, indeed, give the bride in marriage. The ceremony, moreover, was to be performed by the Reverend Doctor Hitchcock in General Arnold's own quarters; because of this, certainly no less than three general officers were likely to attend and any quantity of colonels.

Essential repairs were under way on the tiny cottage the newly married couple would occupy, but Lucius fretted no end because the work was behind schedule.

What with the war raging, Lucius had found it desperately difficult to come across even the most indispensable items of furniture. Had not a farmer's heirs, in a great hurry to dispose of his property, offered for sale a huge double bed and mattress the young physician would have been hard put to provide even that fundamental of all households. As it was, he experienced a thrill of real pride when the rather handsome old cherrywood four-poster was unloaded from an oxcart, together with three applewood chairs, a couple of clothes chests and a well-made table. For the present they'd do, but would not compare to what the Devoes would some day enjoy.

Yes, in the not very remote future, Sabra Devoe might expect to preside over a handsome brick mansion, brave with white columns and tall windows; its rooms would have high ceilings, elaborately carved wainscotting and no end of rich draperies. Eventually, he intended to import some Italian marble. Statues, standing about a mansion, lent a mighty refined atmosphere and constituted a hallmark of gentility. Smiling confidently, he dreamed of the day when he would suggest oh, so casually, that Sabra import some Italian or Frenchman to lay out a formal garden as big as she wished.

Major Joshua Stanton stopped in on the way to Paramus from his post at Fort Ticonderoga. He was sunburnt, hearty and full of enthusiasm over the task of remounting on limbers a number of fine old French cannon he'd discovered there. Characteristically, he had scoured the countryside until he'd located some wheelwrights and now they and a crew of carpenters were turning out an impressive number of caissons and limbers.

"I've near enough to equip a whole regiment," he exulted to the senior officers' mess at Fort Arnold. "By God, you can't beat the Dancing Masters when it comes to casting fine guns. For all they're sixty years old, they're the best I have ever seen."

On arrival at Lucius' quarters, Sabra's brother flung his hat onto the settle and stood using a hazel switch he had cut somewhere on the way down, to slap the dust from his sweat-whitened riding boots.

"Well, well. The great day draws nigh, eh, Lucius?" He grinned. "Who'll you have to tie the knot?"

"The Reverend Doctor Enos Hitchcock, Josh. He's chaplain to General Patterson's brigade."

"A good man," Joshua agreed. "Hails from Beverly, I think, back home." Joshua tramped indoors in search of drinking water. There he cocked a curious eye at Lucius' uniform, hanging, brand-new and brave with gold lace, in a wardrobe. "So they've slapped you Pull-Guts in uniform at last? It's a good thing, makes you seem really a part of the Service."

Lucius smiled and flushed a little. "What do you think of our new cockade?" He indicated his hat.

"Why's the damn' thing black and white? Ought to be blue."

"'Tis so ordered in honor of the French Alliance—the white that is. By the bye, I presume you've heard that blue is now the only official color for American Army uniform?"

"Yes."

"You've a set of regimentals fit for the wedding?"

A good-natured smile rippled all over the artillery officer's broad brown features. "I'll be the macaroni of the occasion. Yes. I've a whole new uniform—found enough cloth up in Newburgh. Is Pa coming down?"

Lucius frowned. "Sorry to say he ain't. Sabra hinted his affairs are too tangled to admit of so long an absence. Of course, Mrs. Stanton is—" he broke off.

"Poor Mother; she'll grieve over missing Sabra's nuptials. However, we'll do a bang-up job for her, won't we?"

"I have tried to foresee all contingencies, Joshua," Lucius told him quietly. "With General Arnold, and maybe Baron von Steuben and their staffs in attendance, I fancy your lady mother will be satisfied with the brilliance of our wedding ceremony. Mrs. Arnold and her friends have engaged to decorate the headquarters with autumn leaves and flowers; they'll relish the excitement as an escape from *ennui*."

The big artillery man sank onto a chair, thrust brass-spurred boots far out before him. "You're a clever hand at understanding womenfolks. I'm sure you'll have a first-rate wedding, so make the most of your last week of single blessedness."

Lucius looked hard at Joshua's big, travel-stained figure. Could an idle tongue have mentioned Emma Wynkoop? No, he was only spoofing.

Joshua winked. "I allow you've been leading an exemplary life hereabouts, no temptations, eh?"

Said the Jamaican stiffly, "Had I been on duty in the heart of Paris, I still would have remained celibate."

Joshua pretended to misunderstand, spoke good-humoredly, "Um. I see—wouldn't want anything to spoil your new posting to Hartford. Of course not, Lucius." He tramped over to a table and plucked up an apple from a very choice selection presented by Mrs. Wynkoop. "Hope you enjoy these fleshpots. We've nothing like this at Ticonderoga. Up there—"

Joshua Stanton checked the apple halfway to his mouth. Somewhere, far to the south sounded the unmistakable *boom!* of a field piece. Faintly, the report reverberated along that deep trough through which the Hudson flows at West Point. Glancing off first one rock wall, then another, it sounded like a giant's game of ninepins in progress.

Joshua flung his companion a quick look. "What the deuce does that firing mean?"

"I've no idea, unless some battery is at practice."

Their conversation resumed and had continued but a few minutes before it was interrupted by a second report, then a third.

"How long can you stay here?" Lucius hoped it would be long. The sight of Joshua restored, freshened his image of Sabra, reinforced his always deep affections for her.

"Overnight. I'm off to scare up some ammunition and cannon balls at Paramus." He clapped the physician's rusty black shoulder. "Don't worry, I'll be back in plenty of time for the wedding. When are you expecting Sabra and Phoebe?"

"They're due in King's Ferry on or about the afternoon of the twenty-fifth, so even if they're delayed, there will still remain a decent interval for preparations."

The *clip-clopping* of a horse trotting slowly up that road which led down to the river sounded progressively louder.

The rider proved to be a bandy-legged sergeant of dragoons. Perspiring heavily, this cavalryman dismounted, read the names painted on a shingle nailed to the door frame; then, with his sabre's ferrule sketching a furrow in the dust, he rapped.

"Doctor Devoe, sir?" He gave Lucius a smart salute.

"Yes. What can I do for you?"

"I've a message for you from headquarters, sir."

The note proved to be brief. Mrs. Arnold, it appeared, had become so indisposed as to require immediate medical attention. Doctor Devoe would please attend her with all speed?

"So you're personal physician to the Commanding General's wife." Joshua whistled briefly. "Is there no height to which you can't fly? Well, keep it up. I'm off to the ordnance officer." Again he clapped his future brother-in-law's slight shoulder, then his big, well-knit figure went swinging off across the scant, dusty brown grass covering Fort Arnold's parade ground.

XXXVIII. MARGARET SHIPPEN ARNOLD

ONCE THE MILITARY ferry had deposited Doctor Devoe on the Hudson's east bank and his saddle horse had been led dancing, snorting in fright, out onto the muddied landing, the afternoon was well advanced. By the time the physician had covered some two and a half miles, separating Major-General Arnold's quarters from the landing place, he arrived to discover the pleasant smell of evening mess strong in the air.

How typical that, about Benedict Arnold's headquarters, the sentries were smartly turned out in blue tunics boasting white lapels and cuffs; their breeches were brown and their gaiters black. Cross-belts supporting bayonets and cartouche boxes shone white as snow and, when they presented arms, their hands slapped smartly on well-oiled stocks and barrels. Not even at Paramus had Lucius been so frequently and promptly challenged, required to give the watchword.

Grass before the Robinson house proved to be unusually green, and as even as the cropping of half a dozen sheep could keep it. Stones marking the course of a wide driveway glistened with fresh whitewash.

Lucius had barely drawn rein before the Beverly Robinson house than an orderly ran forward from a guard tent and led away his horse just as an infantry officer hurried up, looking very anxious.

"Doctor Devoe? I am Major Franks, special aide to Mrs. Arnold. Kindly follow me."

This short, dark-featured officer then conducted Lucius up the three steps leading into Arnold's quarters. Considerably larger than was the rule, this fine farmhouse had been built in three sections of white-painted clapboards—the one added on behind the other; all were shuttered in dark blue.

On a narrow porch extending the length of this two-storey structure sat various members of the staff, some writing, some merely idling. Most of them glanced curiously at Lucius' wiry black-clad figure when he passed carrying his silver-bound tricorne in one hand and a pair of black saddle bags containing his medicines in the other.

At the foot of a staircase leading above, Major Franks advised in a low voice. "Best be extra civil. The General's in a curs'd foul mood. He's just returned from down river and is weary out of all conscience."

Lucius nodded, waited quietly.

Presently a small brown and white spaniel appeared and after considering the physician from sombre brown eyes, thrust a moist and cold nose against his palm. Carelessly flung across a delicate settee must be one of the general's coats; because of its extra rich blue and buff cloth, heavy gold epaulettes and the two big silver stars winking on each shoulder, it could belong to no one else. On a low table close by rested the general's hat, and a brandy bottle flanked by some empty glasses.

Somewhere upstairs a man was talking angrily.

Looking acutely unhappy, Major Franks beckoned sharply from the head of the stairs. "This way, Doctor, I'll show you your quarters. There you may prepare presently to attend Mrs. Arnold."

The second-floor room to which Lucius was conducted proved to be both small and stuffy.

"You'll have to make out here," Franks explained. "I'll summon you, directly Mrs. Arnold is ready."

To Lucius' surprise an earthenware jar, skilfully arranged with gentians and wild asters, decorated the plain pine chest-of-drawers. His bed was clean, but proved, when he prodded it, to be none too soft.

While bathing his face and hands he wondered what could be ailing Mrs. Arnold. A touch of dysentery most likely; it was very prevalent hereabouts. God forbid that she should be afflicted with the cholera morbus!

"Whew, it's damnation hot in here!" In an attempt to secure some cross-ventilation, he opened his door. Someone else must have been activated by a similar impulse for, across the hall and slightly to his left, another door opened.

"Good evening, Doctor," smiled Emma Wynkoop and curtseyed. This evening she was most effectively gowned in dark green, and cherry-red ribbons secured her dark brown hair.

For a long moment neither moved; the widow's gaze remained fixed on his; gradually, the lids parted until her great dark eyes were narrowly, but completely, ringed by white. It was a curious effect, one which held Lucius in delighted fascination.

Yes, seen thus by the vivid sunset glare Emma Wynkoop presented a memorable image, lower arms and bosom a-gleam above her Lincoln green bodice, teeth glinting behind slightly parted dark red lips.

"Why—why—" Lucius stammered, then recalled his manners enough to make as elegant a leg as was possible in the cramped space of the hallway. "I am overwhelmed, Ma'am. The gods of chance have been uncommon kind."

When Emma held out a hand his lips lingered in contact with its fragrant softness.

"There is so much to thank you for, dear lady," he declared. "We shall never forget your generous gesture towards my hospital."

Emma's tone became crisp. "Nonsense. 'Twas nothing, if 'twill advance your undertakings." Her handsome eyes flickered sidewise. Then more softly she added, "That you accomplish your ambitions, Lucius, is not without importance. Oh, bother!"

A serving girl wearing a striped blue and white petticoat and a neat white shawl was advancing timidly along the hallway.

"Mrs. Wynkoop, Ma'am. Please fetch in the doctor. Mistress Arnold is ready."

The Jamaican drew a deep breath and made a successful effort to assume his professional manner; grave, dignified and yet displaying a profound concern over his patient's symptoms.

Lucius followed the maidservant along a winding corridor towards the opposite end of the house.

Emma Wynkoop had preceded him and was saying, "There, there, Peg, my poppet—Doctor Devoe is here; I am positive your malady will prove nothing grave."

"I pray you are correct," a man's deep voice interrupted. "Where's that ratted sawbones?"

The serving maid curtseyed, and, turning a brilliantly shined brass knob, opened a door to disclose a wide mahogany bed, a pink satin coverlet and an extraordinarily handsome young woman under it.

The invalid's bosom was smothered beneath a veritable cascade of lace and her face was partially veiled by a mob-cap trimmed with a small pink bow. Mrs. Arnold's blonde, faintly reddish hair fell in attractive ringlets about sharply sloping shoulders. Lucius received an impression of gay blue eyes, a pointed little nose and a mouth just a touch too small to be in perfect proportion.

On the opposite side of the room lingered Major-General Benedict Arnold wearing definitely informal attire. He yet retained the white riding breeches he must have worn on his trip downstream, and wore in addition blue morocco slippers and a ruffled shirt. Obviously, he had been keeping on with his drinking. A toddy glass was in his left hand.

There could be no denying that Benedict Arnold presented one of the handsomest figures Lucius had ever beheld. The general's florid profile was strong and dominated by a very long, straight nose jutting out over a bold, well-rounded jaw which was growing fleshy. The slender black brows were straight, but rose sharply at their inner ends. The commanding officer's neck emerged as a heavy red pillar from the ruffles of his stock.

Quite easily Lucius could understand why Benedict Arnold, when seen in profile, was said to resemble his great good friend, George Washington.

When Arnold moved towards the foot of his wife's bed he limped a little as a result of that musket ball which had disabled him at Freeman's Farm.

Lucius bowed stiffly. "Sir, Senior Surgeon Devoe has the honor to report himself."

The commandant drank thirstily of his toddy. "Mrs. Arnold complains of pains in—ahen—the digestive region. Damme, Emma, don't you ever again permit her to drink iced water! I vow that has been the cause of her undoing." He shuffled over towards the door. "I'll see you at mess, Devoe. You're to sit at my table."

"Oh, no, Benedict," Peggy Arnold raised a protesting white hand. "I have ordered a tray for Doctor Devoe sent upstairs. There are many things I need to discuss with him. You will not desert me, will you, Doctor?"

"It's as you command, Ma'am," was all that seemed tactful to say.

"Very well. I fancy Emma and Doctor Devoe can give you proper care. My service, darling!" From the doorway General Arnold cast his wife a glance eloquent of real devotion to this small China doll of a woman. He paused. "And how is our lad?"

"Doing splendidly, sir," Emma Wynkoop told him. "He teased the cat this afternoon and got well scratched for his pains."

XXXIX. A DOOR IN THE NIGHT

WHEN LUCIUS CLOSED the door to his bedroom it was tilting pleasantly, not sickeningly, about his head. Lord above! General Arnold's sack had seemed mild and fragrant as a spring breeze in the lee of an apple orchard. No, it couldn't have been that which had set his tongue to clacking, to fancying himself the very soul of wit? Probably it was the sherry? Or was it the applejack he'd sampled last of all? Had he appeared as monstrous clever as he'd imagined?

At any rate Mrs. Shippen and Emma Wynkoop had laughed so heartily over his anecdotes that, finally, General Arnold came stamping up; he'd been cross at first, but later joined in their merriment. In almost unreal eagerness he'd guffawed and kept the aides, Lieutenant Allen, a big-boned youth with a too-easy smile, and Major Franks travelling downstairs to fetch up glasses and still more bottles.

Lucius seated himself on the edge of his bed and, grasping its coverlet, essayed to recover complete control of his equilibrium. Jupiter! How Mrs. Wynkoop's dark beauty had shone forth! Why, right now, he could ever so clearly visualize her smile flashing in the candlelight. Praise God, the general's lady was suffering from nothing more serious than a touch of Summer Complaint which the bismuth and paregoric he'd administered should relieve in short order.

Seated in the dark, Lucius wondered whether he was correct about a curious impression that, for all his outward gaiety, General Arnold's manner had remained restless and constrained. All evening long, he had kept glancing out of the windows. Perhaps his uneasiness stemmed from the approach of a rainstorm which now was rolling down from the north?

Like salvoes fired by a whole brigade of heavy artillery, thunder began to reverberate along those natural battlements ranging the Hudson all the way from Kingston down to Verplanck's Ferry.

Ha! Lucius felt steadier once the air commenced to freshen. Through his window he could see branches beginning to be thrown into sharp relief by lightning and their tired autumn leaves beginning to stir and toss.

"Damned roads will be sopping tomorrow," Arnold had grunted.

Downstairs could be heard the footsteps of orderlies hurrying to secure shutters; then followed the gentle *thump* of dropped window sashes.

Um. What could have caused the general's face to flame so suddenly when Lieutenant Allen asked, "Considering this weather, sir, do you still wish wood-cutting details sent out tomorrow?"

"—And why not, sirrah?" Arnold had barked. "Are my troops a parcel of females afraid to muddy their feet? And make note that I want the Sixth Massachusetts to forage around Cornwall. Nearer, they'll find not near enough hay."

The lieutenant had blinked, amazed at the violence of the commandant's speech. "Yes, General. Of course, sir."

"See, also, that Colonel Lamb dispatches all fatigue details on the point of the hour. Draw an order to send those Connecticut sluggards out on maneuvers; they ain't fit to fight a soft pillow! A few nights in the open won't do 'em a speck of harm.''

"Yes, sir. Where will you wish them to proceed?''

"Oh, to, to—'' Arnold had hesitated a moment. "Oh, to Greycourt.''

"But, sir, have you forgot? That's distant by three days' march and would leave the Fort—''

"Stab me!'' Arnold had roared his visage purpling. "Are you issuing orders, sirrah, or taking them?''

Only after Mrs. Arnold had raised up to place a hand on his arm, had the Commandant of West Point calmed himself. "Lieutenant Allen is merely attempting to interpret your wishes,'' was all she'd said, but General Arnold had quieted himself.

After that, the commandant had retailed anecdotes of his heroic, if disastrous, campaign against Quebec. To all that went on, Emma Wynkoop, like himself, had listened and ventured nothing. But her attention had flickered from one to the other of the speakers.

Still dressed, Lucius sank back onto his bed; though he hated to admit the fact, he remained a bit too dizzy to contemplate disrobing.

"Mus' think of Sabra—sweet li'l Sabra,'' he reminded himself. "Goin' to be my wife. I love her. Not Emma. Gen'leman can't go back on his word, and I'm a gen'leman. Mus'n' think about Emma.''

Aye, that was the only wise and honorable course. Yet to follow this course was not easy. Across the hallway, not ten feet away Emma Wynkoop must be preparing her warm, deliciously smooth body for bed. Emma. The curve of her breasts under the thin linen of her bodice— the lazy, all but feline play of her eyelashes—the, the, *female* aura of her person.

Jupiter! All he had to do was to open his door, cross the corridor and try her latch. Oh, to try the warm fragrance of those lips, dark and luscious-looking as oxblood cherries.

"No! Mus'n' think of Emma—only Sabra—Sabra—Sabra,'' he whispered.

Christ, but he was drunk! Never had been so drunk before.

"Now le's concentrate an' sober up,'' he advised himself. "Never'll I get so slopped again—Gener'l or no Gener'l. No, sir.'' It came as a sobering realization that, in another three days, Sabra would be clasped in his arms, the smoothness of her cheek cool under his lips, the fragrance of her hair in his nostrils. Sabra! To have forgotten his affianced wife so completely this evening was downright disgraceful.

But Emma was only a dozen yards away. Emma was rich; Emma was ambitious; Emma was experienced, too, no doubt of that.

He imagined that rain was falling, but it proved to be only the wind rustling in a giant poplar beyond his window. The sash rattled, roused him from a half-doze. Then a brilliant flash of lightning lit his room in its every detail; the stained section of plaster above his wash bowl, his travelling cloak and hat hung to pegs behind the door.

Lucius felt better when he kept his eyes open.

Was he drunk? No, not really. Couldn't he think? Couldn't he move in perfect balance? Of course; then he wasn't jingled—intelligent men never let themselves become befuddled. Once Peter Burnham had got that way—what had chanced with Peter Burnham? Strange, not a word had been heard of him in Boston, or anywhere else, after that frosty night back last January.

Lucius squirmed on the hard and narrow bed. He'd not intended for anything untoward to happen to Peter; really, he hadn't planned for such a tragedy. Only it had seemed so *very* necessary for Lucius Devoe to receive that junior surgeon's commission. Hadn't he proved his superior fitness? Plague take it! Lucius Devoe had accomplished a lot during these past eight months. Neither Asa Peabody nor Peter Burnham could have worked harder. Would either of them have become senior surgeon in so short a time? No. Would either of them have been nominated for Deputy Directorship of the whole Middle District? Not likely!

A door kept banging softly; so far not loud enough to warrant an investigation. But now the storm closed in, and, raising an eldritch shriek, swooped down upon the Hudson River Valley. Under its assault little branches were torn loose and hurled against the roof of Colonel Beverly Robinson's house. At the same time the lightning fired a *feu de joie* and the rain lashed so wildly at his open window that Lucius roused himself and dropped the sash. More violently still raged the storm, pounding in baffled fury on the windowpanes.

The banging of that door down the hall grew more insistent. Lucius thought, "It'll disturb my patient." Yet he lay still a full five minutes before, finally, he swung stocking feet to the floor and got up.

Good. Standing up, he didn't sway any more. Where *was* that cursed door? The corridor proved dark save when a flash of lightning illumined a series of bedroom doors. Ah! The trouble-making door was opposite his, almost. A ray of dancing candlelight sprang across the bare boards and was instantly eclipsed.

Again the door swung open, flung a golden carpet down the hallway.

Breathing with unaccustomed rapidity, Lucius left his room, closing his door after him. Again a furious draught of air flung open Emma Wynkoop's door. Looking inside the physician saw a modest chamber done in nail-rust red and a single figure bent over the washstand and apparently oblivious to his presence. Emma Wynkoop, hair unbound and in her night shift, was measuring something into a tumbler.

Only when a particularly violent crash of thunder shook the house, did Emma Wynkoop see him standing on the threshold. Three things leaped to her attention, the vivid black of his eyes, his unbound hair streaming free and the tense curve of his mouth.

"Your door—I heard it slamming. What are you about?" he inquired in a strained voice.

"Why, why, the storm upset my stomach—" Emma straightened, turned and held up a small bottle. "I thought perhaps an elixir—" Even by this uncertain light he could tell that her nightrail was of light, very fine lawn. No other fabric save silk could fall so lightly loose from her shoulders. How white the cloth shone under the dark torrents of her hair.

"What is that stuff?"

"Why—'tis an elixir," she explained, added quickly, "don't be a ninny for Heaven's sake. Either leave or come in and shut that wretched door; its latch seems to be broken."

Lucius looked about and presently located a cloth-covered door stop which silenced the banging all in a moment.

"Aren't you clever? I never thought of that," Emma said with a half-smile. "Isn't this storm terrifying?"

Lucius agreed, but directed his attention to the elixir bottle. "That stuff serves no useful purpose. Allow me to fetch you a draught of elecampane. 'Tis capital for an upset digestion."

"Oh, no! Pray don't disturb yourself."

But he darted out; reappeared a moment later, a vial in his hand.

"Thank you. I was beginning to fear that I had contracted Mrs. Arnold's complaint," Emma said. "I feel much better, now."

"Pray get into bed," he ordered, keeping his eyes on the tumbler. "I will mix your draught, myself."

Emma Wynkoop turned back the sheets and slipped in between them with a sinuous twist of her body that whirled the nightrail's hem well up towards her knees. "Am I not obedient? The model patient?" she demanded, rearranging the ruffles about her throat.

Presently she sat propped against three great pillows, her eyes become as large and luminous as those of a night-hunting cat.

He would have answered her, but several peals of near-by thunder rendered speech impossible. He saw Emma's hands tighten on the sheet and expected her, female-like, to shriek and to hide her head under the pillows, yet she did not—only stared at him from those dark and intense eyes of hers.

Protected by its storm glass, the candle by the head of her bed created a pool of white amid the shadows of the bedroom.

"Here," Lucius said, holding out the glass. "Drink this."

She took the glass, but made no motion to obey.

In a suffocated tone, he told her, "It won't hurt you. Please drink it."

"As soon as the thunder and lightning lessens. Now, I am too agitated."

"I must leave. Suppose someone came here?"

"Let them. Please stay with me a little longer. The other evening at General von Steuben's you spoke concerning a balance of humours. What is your theory on the subject?"

Sweating, trying to control tremors inexplicably agitating his hands, Lucius sank onto the foot of her bed and plunged into an explanation of his doubts concerning the validity of the four humour theory. "—It don't make sense," he declared, "for all 'tis a well-accepted principle."

"Humours?" Emma Wynkoop demanded. "Exactly what are 'humours'?"

To ignore the rise and fall of those pale shadows created by her nipples under the fine lawn was difficult—and he succeeded only partially.

"All physicians, Ma'am, nowadays are instructed that four elements or humours are present in every human." He hesitated, swallowed hard on nothing. "I do not wish to be indelicate—"

"Pray continue," Emma urged, all the while smoothing the bedclothes until they outlined, all too effectively, the graceful outlines of her legs and thighs.

"For near a hundred years the best scholars of Europe have believed that four humours exist in every human."

"—And they are?"

"Blood, phlegm, black and yellow bile," Lucius explained hurriedly. "Other schools describe these humours as 'sanguine, phlegmatic, bilious or choleric, and melancholy.' We are told that when one humour overbalances its fellows, illness ensues. To restore health the volume of that excessive humour must be reduced."

Fingering a lock of her hair, Emma frowned in thought. "So if too much blood accumulated in a body, the excess sanguinous humour must be drawn off? Like poor papa when he had the gout?"

"Aye, Ma'am," Lucius replied. Jupiter! He would, he *must*, remain the grave, considered physician for had she not, in a tacit fashion, become his patient?

"Very adroitly you grasp the principle. My belief contends that this theorem is false. Were it logical, surely Nature would have provided means of allowing such an excess of blood to escape. The body of a healthy man, killed by accident, disclosed no elements indicating the presence of what might be called black or yellow bile."

He leaned forward, spoke earnestly. "Ma'am, 'tis my belief that these so-called humours—if they exist at all—are abnormal and the product of disease."

Emma Wynkoop's slim form sank further back on the pillows and her gaze sought the candle's flame. "Oh, Lucius, to think that you have formed this theorem without instruction in Scotland or at the Hôtel Dieu! Surely, some day you will become known as the most celebrated physician of our century! Oh, but had I a brother—or a son—to dream such dreams—and that I might advance them." She laughed quietly. "What a paradox. Here am I, possessed of a great fortune, yet able to accomplish—what? Nothing. Ah, Lucius, Lucius."

From his seated position at the foot of the bed the Jamaican shifted to occupy a chair nearer its head. Though he seated himself on some of her intimate garments, Emma offered no protest.

Although it seemed impossible for the rain to sluice down any harder—it did so; the kettle drums of thunder, however, now were thudding further down the Hudson and nearer to New York.

All at once Lucius was astonished to find himself speaking of Jamaica, confessing his humble origin and the desperate poverty of his family. In vivid detail he described his adventures at sea; his fixed ambition to study medicine and to win greater than local acclaim. He spoke even of Sabra, of being affianced to her—but nothing of his impending nuptials. Most likely, she knew of them through her intimacy with Peggy Arnold. No point in dwelling on the matter.

Emma's fingers closed over his in a friendly and sympathetic manner. All the same, they were quivering ever so lightly. "It must have been a lonely and miserable childhood you suffered. You must be very proud to have risen so far without the aid of friends or family. Oh—how I admire determination, ability—and ambition."

"Do you? Do you, really?" Lucius bent toward her. "Then you understand what it means to be snubbed, despised, patronized? Yes! By God, you do! I can read it in your lovely face. Though why—"

"—Never mind," Emma sat up, eyes enormous by the dying candle's flame. "Lucius—tell me, will you swear before God, one thing?"

His face loomed nearer, sensitive, hungry, avid of approval. "What shall I say? Emma, what?"

Her nightrail fell open, unnoticed, exposing magnificent pale brown-capped breasts. Fresh, intoxicating auras eddied below the canopy, as almost fiercely, Emma demanded, "You will never be content with less than being first, nay supreme, in whatever you undertake?"

The Jamaican laughed in exultation. Here at last was

one who penetrated the unannounced, undetected secrets of his mind. "Oh, my dear—Success and Fame—have I not all my life adored those twin goddesses? Like any pious pagan, I would sacrifice anything in their honor. Do you understand?"

"I—I want so much of this world, Lucius." Emma's warmed and vital features were scant inches distant. "I'll see the stupid queens of society feel privileged to curtsey, to fawn and to beg favors of Nick Ten Broeck's daughter! You'll help me?" Emma was breathing now like a peasant woman fresh finished with her churning.

"By Jupiter! lass, that I will! You *must* believe in me. 'Fore God, Emma, betwixt us nothing is impossible. Have I not proved my capacity? Aye, you know it. Moreover, till now, I've gone it alone, but with you—" Unconsciously cruel, his fingernails dented the widow's forearm, but she winced not at all, only curved crimson lips back from even teeth gone golden white in the candlelight.

Her nearness and a scent of lavender had a magical and an unprecedented effect upon him as wine fumes, suddenly rising again, clouded Lucius' mind. Her candle commenced flickering towards the end of its life, reminding him of an old lady he had once attended on her deathbed. She had still been lovely for all her failing vitality.

He was describing the scene to Emma Wynkoop when the wick fell over, and in her bedroom existed only the faintest kind of light cast by a fire cheering some guard detail. Ineffective and faintly red firelight came slanting in the shutters' slats to create weirdly dancing streaks of light.

It seemed as if a gale, far more overwhelming than that still roaring outside, were pressing him forward until, at length, he lay beside her with heated features pressed to the intoxicating softness of her breast.

XL. An Express from Colonel Jameson

NEXT DAY, storm clouds had vanished from the sky and a warm September sun beat down, emphasizing the coppery brilliance of the autumnal leaves. Tempest winds still beat, however, at Lucius Devoe's peace of mind. To perceive how thoroughly fascinated and dominated he had become by dark-eyed Emma Wynkoop's mental and bodily appeal, was appalling.

In vain, Lucius attempted to reason with himself—to thresh the matter out in all its implications. He, hard-headed Lucius Devoe, could not possibly have become so senselessly infatuated. Senselessly? Um—maybe not. He began to suspect that cold, if subconscious, logic rather than physical passion had, from the start, attracted him to Emma Wynkoop.

From every practical point of view, the widow promised to make a more useful and socially adroit wife for an ambitious young surgeon than refined, but inexperienced and insular Sabra Stanton. Above all, he judged he could understand a woman of Emma's type far more thoroughly than a girl like Sabra.

Barring those Tory cousins in New York Town, Emma possessed practically no relatives who might attempt interference in his family affairs. No, there'd be no attempts at dictation by in-laws. Again, if he married Emma, it would not be long before he'd have the bulk of her property in his possession. Aye, had he but the courage and the wit to grasp it, a fortune lay ready to hand. Ninety thousand pounds wisely invested could, and would, be made to multiply and to flourish like the green bay tree of Holy Writ.

Lucius thought, "Speaking of property, old Sam Stanton is still damnably hale and hearty; why, the old codger might live for years. God knows to what size his estate's shrunk by this time. Um. Wonder what a fourth share— there are Josh, Phoebe and Theodosia to be considered— would amount to? Not much, come to think of it."

And yet, and yet, Lucius, somehow, could not bring himself so cruelly to hurt Sabra—his affianced wife, even now travelling happily southwards. To wound her forth-right, true and tender love, would be sheerest wicked-ness. No doubt existed in his mind that, loving him pro-foundly, she would remain true through thick and thin.

Another point. How would his brother officers, his su-periors, judge a fellow who broke his solemn pledge to a sweet and trusting young girl? For one thing, Joshua Stanton could be dangerous, once his New England calm was shaken. No, sir. Josh would not suffer, passively, such a mortal affront to his sister—particularly, since he had encouraged their match.

On Sunday, religious services were conducted at headquarters by the chaplain, so together with the rest of Major-General Benedict Arnold's official family, Lucius attended and joined quite heartily in the hymns. Despite resolutions not to, he seated himself at Emma's side and, in the afternoon took her strolling down to that ferry landing which served the Robinson estate.

This called for a generous good half-mile walk, but the day was fine and the woods a-flame with color. From the rim of heights above the Hudson they could watch any number of pleasure craft sailing about. A party of soldiers, off duty, were fishing and loafing about that landing to which General Arnold's gaudy blue and gold barge lay moored; its crew, always ready for service, were lounging under the trees, playing cards and drinking spruce beer.

At first, neither Emma nor her escort talked much, but once they had gained a copse of yellow-leaved white birches halfway back up to the Robinson house, Emma suddenly turned and put her arms quickly about his neck. Closing her eyes, she murmured, "Oh, my love—my own sweet Lucius." He kissed her fiercely, hungrily, again and again; then in silence they resumed their ascent to headquarters.

Mrs. Arnold felt so much restored that she appeared for supper, and partook heartily of the cold fowl, ham and sausage and sipped the General's Canary wine with eagerness. After the repast Mrs. Wynkoop suggested a few hands of whist, but General Arnold declined in a nervous, preoccupied way; in Lucius' opinion he appeared to be uncommon ill at ease. Accordingly, the ladies played picquet.

Lucius was terribly aware of Emma's proximity, of the smooth arc formed by her neck, the fullness of those curves beneath a fichu smothering her bosom. In desperation, he pled the necessity of perusing a book on medicine by one Ambrose Paré and hunted up the headquarters' adjutant to report his intention of returning to Fort Arnold early in the next morning. Resolutely retaining an official manner, he then bid the ladies good night.

The morning of Monday, September twenty-fifth, 1780, proved so sparklingly beautiful that Lucius felt moved to whistle while lathering in preparation to shaving. During the night he had reached a final and irrevoca-

ble decision; come what might, he would keep his word
and marry Sabra Stanton. Now he felt at peace with the
world.

Probably, over at West Point, he'd discover a message
announcing the arrival at King's Ferry of Sabra and
Phoebe. Aye. Almost certainly within twenty-four hours
he would clasp her in his arms.

It facilitated matters that Mrs. Wynkoop was not present at the breakfast table; nor were any of the other officers' ladies. When Lucius entered, General Arnold
glanced up quickly, then nodded and went on eating,
hugely, as usual. Captain North, his personal aide, had
reappeared from delivering troop movement orders to
Colonel Lamb commanding at Fort Arnold, and was
leafing through documents destined for the general's attention.

Other officers on duty at headquarters lounged about,
drawing on after-breakfast pipes and scanning newspa-
pers, for all that the bulk of them were quite young.

Conversation then ran on local problems and events.

Someone asked, "Suppose you all heard that can-
nonading Saturday afternoon?"

"Yes. What the Devil was it?" demanded Major
Franks.

"Odd thing; a British man-o'-war, a sloop called the
Vulture, came sailing upstream, bold as brass, and
dropped anchor off King's Ferry. Stayed there, too, until
some of our artillery got into battery and peppered at her
till she dropped down to Teller's Point where the river is
wide enough for her to escape our shot."

On seating himself, Lucius immediately became aware
not only of an unaccustomed activity but the presence of
two strange officers: a big burly major and a gentleman
dressed in the usual black garb of a physician. They
were, he learned, Doctor McHenry and Major Shaw,
both aides to General George Washington, who had ridden in expressing regrets that the Commander-in-Chief,
unexpectedly, had decided to inspect the North and Middle redoubts on the Hudson's east bank, and therefore
would not arrive in time for breakfast.

This, of course, accounted for that extra neatness of
uniform about the mess. Everyone was speculating on
what might have transpired as a result of the recent inter-

view at Wethersfield between General Washington and Count Rochambeau, the French commander.

"Judson, fetch me some more eggs. I seem to have a prodigious—" Arnold broke off and his big head swung sharply towards the window, watching the headlong approach of a horse and rider. Without awaiting instructions, Lieutenant Allen bolted out onto the porch.

By craning his neck, Lucius glimpsed a red-faced officer wearing a lieutenant's single epaulette, hurling himself from the saddle of a foam-lathered horse.

"For General Arnold's personal attention!" Everybody could hear the messenger's breathless cry.

Allen reappeared with the heavily breathing officer at his heels. "It is for your hand alone, sir," he explained.

"Where are you from?" Arnold demanded.

"—From Colonel Jameson's command, sir, at Westchester." The courier stood very straight and held out a sweat-marked letter.

Major General Arnold's black brows joined. In a harsh monotone he demanded, "Do you know the nature of this dispatch?"

"Only that it deals with a matter of the first importance, sir."

The clinking of a dish, set on the table by an orderly, sounded very loud in the penetrating silence. Every eye in the room watched Arnold score the seal with his thumbnail. As the general's bold black eyes flickered over the dispatch Lucius noted a muscle begin to twitch in the fullness of Arnold's cheek while gentle perspiration commenced to spangle his forehead just below the wig line.

"Gentlemen, pray excuse me. This matter requires my immediate personal attention over at the Fort," he announced, shoving back his chair. "You will continue your breakfasts, gentlemen, and carry out such orders as you have already received to prepare West Point for General Washington's inspection."

Heavy epaulettes of gold bullion surmounted by their twin stars of silver flashed in the bright sunlight when Arnold got to his feet. All over the mess room gilt buttons began winking as the various officers turned to see what was going on. Lucius noted that General Arnold's lower lip had become gripped between his teeth. Almost hurriedly, the general's big figure limped out through the door. Lucius heard him snap,

"Captain North, see that I have a horse immediately."

"Any particular charger, sir?"

"Blazes no! Get me a horse, I said. I'm in a tearing hurry; even a farm horse will do. And you—" he flung at Allen, "gallop down to the landing and have James Lowery get my bateau men turned out on the double and ready to row."

Various officers stared at each other in bewildered conjecture. "What the devil can he be up?"

"What's amiss?"

"'Fore God, I've never seen the old boy in such a swivet!"

Those on the ground floor heard Arnold's limping tread on the staircase, heard the door to his wife's room bang shut.

"We'd best get cracking, gentlemen," advised a red-faced colonel. "With His Excellency due any minute and Arnold on a rampage, well, I'm going to secure for squalls, as they say back home."

Struck by the wisdom of this observation, staff members also pushed back their chairs and, dispersing to their duties, made such a considerable racket that Lucius, afterwards, could not be quite certain of hearing a stifled scream sound upstairs.

"Where's my mount?" Arnold roared from the head of the staircase. "Goddamit! Why am I kept waiting? North! North!"

Pulling on his boat cloak the general came *clump-clumping* back down the stairs, his black eyes strangely bright against the leaden background of his features. Pausing only long enough to snap at Lucius, "Attend my wife, she has been taken ill again," he hurried out of the Robinson house and, spouting curses, he struggled into the saddle of a common trooper's mount led up by Captain North himself.

"Shall I come with you, sir?" the aide demanded anxiously. "Is there aught gone wrong?"

Arnold gathered the reins, shook his head. "No. Wait here to greet His Excellency. I—I'll see him on the other shore."

Without further ceremony Arnold jabbed spurs into the bony gelding he bestrode and wrenched its head about. Together with half the staff, Lucius watched their commander go galloping off, cloak a-flying, then, soberly, the physician made his way upstairs to find Mrs. Arnold sprawled in a dead faint on the floor. A terrified chambermaid was bent over her, rubbing her wrists.

"Oh, dear God—'tis a lie! No! 'Tis not possible," were the first words Peggy Shippen Arnold choked out once Lucius' sal ammoniac had returned her to consciousness. The distracted creature's great blue eyes rolled wildly, her fingers clenched and unclenched themselves and her diaphragm heaved convulsively.

"He's made to say such things! Benedict would never do such a thing!"

Major Franks, the aide detailed to Mrs. Arnold's service, came running in. "Pay no heed to her words, Doctor! She is undergoing a phrenzy and knows nothing of what she speaks."

Lucius nodded. It was well known about the post that Mrs. Arnold was subject to fits of what was properly called "phrenzy."

"He is *not* a traitor!" Mrs. Arnold screamed at the top of her lungs. "He is not! Not for all the gold in England!"

Lucius pressed a cold cloth over the congested features, managed in a measure to muffle her outcries.

"I'll kill myself—where's my child? I'll kill him, too, rather than he should live in shame. Kill me, Doctor—I—I can't support this disgrace."

"Pray calm yourself, Ma'am," Major Franks implored, hastily shutting the door behind him. He shot Lucius a desperate look. "Quiet her, for God's sake, or we are all undone."

XLI. "WHOM CAN WE TRUST NOW?"

LUCIUS DEVOE'S patient had scarcely lapsed into a drugged slumber than voices outside began bawling, "Turn out the guard! Turn out the guard for the Commander-in-Chief."

Bugles sounded flourishes, guard details came pelting up on the double. Then one could hear the trampling of many horses advancing along the driveway.

"Atten—shun! Present—harms!" rasped the officer of the day. Out of the window Lucius could see two platoons of smart-looking infantry drawn up and presenting their pieces as General Washington, accompanied by Generals Lafayette and Knox, chief of artillery, and a small staff came riding up to the porch and there acknowledged the adjutant's salute.

A hasty breakfast was provided, then the Commander-in-Chief and all of his staff, with the exception of Major Alexander Hamilton remounted and descended to the landing for transportation to West Point.

Doctor Craik, in a tone that brooked no argument, said, "Doctor Devoe, you will accompany me across the Hudson. His Excellency has expressed a lively interest in your Indian Long House hospital."

"Yes, sir. I'll go for my saddle bags immediately."

Upstairs he beat at Emma Wynkoop's door and found, to his amazement, that she was just then rousing from sleep.

"Why, Lucius—what's afoot?" she yawned.

"More than I can explain in a moment. Pray attend Mrs. Arnold when she wakes," he begged. "I'm ordered immediately across the river."

"Oh, Lucius. You—you will return?" she demanded, dark eyes burning into his. "Come, kiss me, my darling."

"As quickly as I may, dearest." His manner was convincing, despite his determination not to meet Emma Wynkoop again until Sabra Stanton had assumed his name.

He kissed her hard, then ran downstairs, saddle bags a-swing in his hand. Five minutes later he was swallowing dust at the rear of a cavalcade trotting down to Beverly Robinson's landing.

Arnold's barge, of course, was nowhere to be seen, so while the Commander-in-Chief was waiting for another barge to be readied, he observed to Knox:

" 'Twill be a pleasure to inspect West Point once again. I expect our indefatigable Arnold has put things to rights, and will be burning to display his accomplishments." The general, Lucius thought, showed the effect of his long ride up into Connecticut; but not so much as his staff. "It is one of the sorrows of war," Washington continued, "that old companions-in-arms so often become separated. During the early days of this war, what a pack of troubles did we not meet and overcome as best we could. Arnold was, indeed, as the shade of a rock in a weary land back in 'seventy-six and 'seventy-seven."

General Knox blinked his little blue eyes; otherwise his heavy inverted egg-shaped face reamined impassive. Lafayette's delicate, cameo-like profile contracted—it was well known he had small use for Arnold—two such spirited leaders were bound to clash.

To the growing surprise and vexation of the Commander-in-Chief—ever expectant and appreciative of the courtesies of war—no guard detail was waiting, drawn up on the landing platform of Fort Arnold. No cannon thundered salutes.

In fact, surprisingly few soldiers of any description were to be seen anywhere and these were occupied with usual and commonplace duties. Nor was there any sign of Major General Arnold's barge—a fact commented upon by Doctor McHenry.

Eventually Colonel Lamb, in immediate command of Fort Arnold came galloping down from the fort, very red-faced. He declared himself mortified and, noting the angry lines about Washington's mouth, stammered apologies for not having been warned of his distinguished visitor's approach.

The staff commenced exchanging glances as General Washington demanded sharply, "How is that possible, sir? Did not General Arnold cross over to this Fort not two hours ago?"

Colonel Lamb looked dumbfounded. "General Arnold, sir? There—there must be some error, sir." The unhappy colonel spread his hands. "We have not seen General Arnold in a week's time."

Washington drew himself up, mouth clamped into a tight line. "This is a most extraordinary and irregular situation. I shall expect a written explanation. Colonel Lamb, dispatch messengers in search of General Arnold; pray present him my compliments and instruct him to report to me at once. In the meanwhile I will inspect your works."

The inspection proved so brief and perfunctory that, to Lucius' bitter disappointment, no visit was made to his hospital.

"Oh, curse the luck!" His chagrin became acute while watching His Excellency's party return to the landing. Presently, the Commander-in-Chief's barge reappeared from under the shore and pulled hard for the east bank.

Ever a philosopher concerning disappointments, Lucius set about discharging such duties as had accumulated during the past three days. Presently his spirits rose. At his quarters he discovered a note in Sabra's clear, unformed hand:

At Haverstraw, N.Y.

My Beloved:

A Gentleman riding by hath volunteered to leave this Note at yr Fort. Know, that we have suffered a slight Delay due to ye breakdown of ye Coach, but we are certain to Arrive at King's Ferry during ye day of ye 27th. My darling one, I count each *lagging* Instant until yr dear Arms shall close once more about me.

Yr. Devoted and Obedient Wife-to-be,
Sabra.

Lucius was laying out a series of saw blades preparatory to sharpening them—there would be some amputations that afternoon—when, from their emplacements in the fort above, a cannon boomed, then in rapid succession a whole series of reports.

"The general alarm signal, by God!" Like hornets from a disturbed nest, the handful of troops remaining in garrison in and about West Point ran to man their posts. Only then did it become apparent how very destitute of troops was Fort Arnold. What with the absence of woodcutting and foraging parties and troops away on maneuver, not one gun in five could be manned.

Speculating wildly on what could have chanced, Lucius ran for his post at the hospital and thus came across John Fletcher. He was talking to a wildly excited courier.

"Yessir. Y' should ha' seen Gen'r'l Washington's expression when Major Hamilton handed him them papers. They wuz forwarded by Major Tallmadge down to White Plains. There's no doubt—"

"—They concerned General Arnold?" Lucius broke in.

The courier spat and caught up his cap now that Fletcher had applied sticking plaster to a branch slash across his nose. "By God, that they did, sir," growled the rider. "Proved fer a fact old Arnold was plotting to sell this here post to the British; lock, stock and barr'l."

"Well, I'm damned," gasped the Jamaican as all manner of minor incidents fell into a pattern terrible in its implications.

"You were there?"

"Yessir. You should ha' seen His Excellency's expression when he finished reading. 'Arnold has betrayed us,' he sez and tears were runnin' down his cheeks. Then he says to Gen'r'l Knox in a choked-up kind o' voice, he says, 'Whom can we trust now?'"

XLII. THE WISEST COURSE

TENSION, engendered of Arnold's plot with Lieutenant-General Sir Henry Clinton, Commander of all His Majesty's Forces in North America, reigned over West Point. On the twenty-seventh of September two regiments of the Pennsylvania Line arrived after forced marches up from the Continental Army's encampment at Tappan's.

Fort Arnold, hastily re-christened Fort Clinton, in honor of General George Clinton—there were four general officers of that name in this war—was readied against attack. All leaves granted the officers were cancelled, no passes were issued and, as quickly as possible, those garrison troops, so treacherously dispersed by Arnold, were recalled.

Vigilance became the order of the day; every person entering or leaving West Point was subjected to the severest scrutiny. Of course, wild rumors burgeoned. The British were reported marching up the Hudson to attack the all but betrayed fortress. Arnold had been apprehended and shot on the spot. This and that officer had been implicated in the plot and was being held under close arrest. Executions by the dozen were bound to follow. All these tales were, of course, nonsense, and pretty soon, the facts came out. Arnold had been quite alone in his treason.

Alas, that his opposite number, now held for espionage proceedings at Tappan's should have been the gay, clever and amazingly handsome Major André, adjutant-general to Sir Henry Clinton, and the scion of a distinguished English family.

Poor fellow, he was doomed, even before trial. Beyond any question of doubt he had been captured down in Westchester, wearing not his regimentals, but civilian clothes lent him by one Joshua Hett Smith, now sharing Major André's captivity. He was bound to meet the same tragic fate as Captain Nathan Hale of Connecticut, who also had been detected in disguise.

There were stormy scenes at the Commander-in-Chief's headquarters; persistent questioning of everyone belonging to the traitor's staff. Lucius was forced to endure a savage inquisition conducted by a gimlet-eyed major of the Judge-Advocate General's office.

Aye. He'd never forget the nasty turn it gave him when a pair of tough Pennsylvania Continentals came tramping into his hospital bearing an order for him to accompany them to the Robinson house. It had availed him not at all to protest that his intended wife was, at that moment, waiting downstream.

"Let her wait," snapped the grim major. "You've some questions to answer."

In the end, Lucius Devoe was acquitted of active complicity, at least; but was directed to remain in the immediate vicinity of Fort Clinton. No member of Arnold's official family was yet fully freed of suspicion so any attempt to leave the post would be construed as a confession of complicity.

Just when he became aware of Emma Wynkoop's continued presence at the Robinson house, Lucius could never be sure. Probably, it had been the evening of that memorable day when Major André had been conducted up from Fishkill, calm and dignified, but, in his borrowed clothes, much resembling a broken-down country squire. He saw her then, peering out from the window of that room in which Mrs. Arnold lay prostrated.

After a dinner rendered constrained by the presence of so many hard-bitten and weather-browned officers, it was only natural that Emma and he should take a stroll. Presently they were occupying a bench so arranged as to overlook the Hudson.

"Oh, Lucius! Thank God you've returned! It's been so—so dreadful. Poor Peggy Arnold."

Despite everything, when she raised her face and offered those dark red lips of hers, he caught her close and kissed her so wildly that her chip hat went tumbling to earth.

"Surely, by this time, my precious, you must have perceived the wisest course? This little girl from Boston—what can she accomplish in your interest? You know that I, and all I possess, is yours for the asking."

Spasmodically, Lucius' fingers closed over hers. His gaze sought the distant lights of Fort Clinton. The wisest course? How easy to say but how hard to recognize! Here was another major turning point in his life. He tried to think clearly, dispassionately. If only Joshua hadn't mentioned old Sam Stanton's many mercantile reverses. Marriage was a mighty serious affair and, well, divorce was practically unknown.

"I have only one lifetime," he thought. "Instinct, I've never acknowledged as a true force, but perhaps now I had better respect it. Sabra's pretty and sweet, but Emma's handsome, too. Best of all, I know what I'll get by way of a bedfellow if I marry Emma. Sabra might prove difficult, cold as a fish. Think on it! Emma owns outright a vast fortune and is far more intelligent than Sabra.

"Of course, if I marry Emma there'll ensue a scandal, but now Arnold's disgrace and treasons are filling all minds, folks won't heed such a small matter. Stands to reason Joshua and his folks will be pretty mad, but such things blow over. After all, I have done Sabra not the least harm, while I owe Emma loyalty for—for the other night. Some would declare that I'm constrained to marry her."

Emma started to draw away her hand; in the semi-darkness he could read in her eyes a pained expression.

On the seat he turned abruptly and took her into his arms. "Oh, Emma, Emma dearest," he cried, "I want you to be my wife and as quickly as possible."

"Oh, yes, yes, yes, yes!" After a little, she straightened, smoothed her hair. "The Reverend Doctor Carver is still at the Robinson house, I believe. Since the betrayal, I have been dwelling in the overseer's house."

"What of the banns? They're required to be posted a fortnight."

"A pox on the silly custom," Emma laughed softly. "Have you never learned that a pair of golden sovereigns can erase time as easily as a chalk mark?"

A little before midnight that night, Emma Wynkoop and Lucius Devoe in the overseer's house joined hands before the Reverend Doctor Carver. Piously, the minister raised his eyes and commenced to recite: "Dearly beloved, we are gathered here—"

Peggy Arnold's chambermaid deemed it all very romantic, and said so. The other witness, a raffish sergeant of dragoons Lucius had encountered on the road, grinned as five silver doubloons fell into his broad hand.

"Well, Doctor, here's wishin' you and yer lady the best o' luck. I'll get me well bedded and royal drunk come Saturday."

Spurs jingling softly, he strode off into the dark, leaving Doctor and Mrs. Devoe to stare upon each other in sudden curiosity.

XLIII. Reflections by Firelight

THREE OR FOUR years earlier, Major Joshua Stanton, in all probability, would not have bothered to slap Doctor Lucius Devoe's face before the whole mess; nor would he have dispatched young Captain Calvert of Colonel Smallwood's Maryland Dragoons to convey a challenge. He would merely have seized an opportune moment to beat the lights and liver out of the scoundrel.

As it was, the practice of duelling—imported by Southern officers—had become so thoroughly accepted in the Army, that no other course occurred to Joshua Stanton.

Lucius decided that in his estimate of Joshua's probable reactions he had erred grievously, nay, had made the first major miscalculation of his life and one which promised to be his last.

Seated alone and miserable in his quarters, Lucius realized that he stood every chance of losing his life. Of sword play he knew nothing at all and it came as thin consolation that Sabra's brother was reputed to possess only a field soldier's skill with pistols. A shiver mounted his back. He knew that Joshua Stanton was going to kill him; the conviction became rooted in his soul.

To his dying moment he would never forget the cold, contemptuous light in the New Englander's hazel eyes as his open hand had landed a resounding slap.

How amazing was this change in status. From a self-assured and well-liked member of the staff, he now was treated with a frigid formality little preferable to open contempt. Head burrowing between clenched fists, Lucius cursed his stupidity.

Even now Major David Page's icy tones beat at his memory. "Second you? Never. I'd sooner second the Devil himself than a rascal so lost to all sense of honor."

Captain Carl Schmidt had grunted in his best Pennsylvania Dutch accent. "*Nein*. Only for gentlemans do I act. Excoose me."

As a last resort Lucius had had to fall back on the services of one Captain Gustave Delacroix, a none-too-savory appendage of the Marquis de Lafayette's headquarters. This saturnine individual had agreed to act, frankly admitting that his participation was prompted by a certain penchant for duels—and for no other reason.

A long pull of hard cider did little to ease the physician's self-accusations. What a great, lop-eared jackass he'd been to blunder out of his depth like this! Emma, his wife, had appeared utterly amazed at his failure to foresee this duel as the inevitable result of a flagrant affront to the sister of a respected and popular veteran of the Commander-in-Chief's own family. When he'd told Emma about the challenge, the soft lines of her face had faded.

"What else did you expect, you ninny? A fine pickle you've let us in for," she'd snapped. "Why didn't you tell me your Boston wench was on her way down to marry you?"

"But I thought you knew—" and he was sure this was so—"why, talk about our wedding was all over the post."

"Nonsense! Can you be so purblind as not to perceive that there's a world of difference twixt breaking off an engagement at long distance, and marrying another woman under your affianced's very nose?"

The shadows deepened but still Lucius sat bent over his desk, trying to find some way out of this disaster. He couldn't. No matter what chanced in this duel, his career stood in the gravest jeopardy. Suppose that, by some miracle, he killed or disabled Joshua Stanton? A judicious use of Emma's money and influence might serve to reestablish him at some later date. Possibly. Human memory paled before the glitter of gold.

"Judging by Doctor Craik's stony silence this morning my Deputy Commissioner's appointment had better be forgotten," he warned himself. "He'll probably order me to some damned little blockhouse out in the wilderness."

Consumed by that acid rage which afflicts a shrewd man who has out-maneuvered himself, Lucius stared at scarlet-gray embers dying in the fireplace.

One other man, he guessed, must also feel pretty badly

tonight. On the morrow, October the second, Major John
André, courageous and almost too truthful, adjutant-general of His Majesty's Army, would be conducted to a
place of execution and, at high noon, hanged by his neck
until dead. Poor André. He, at least, would die with honor, and in the service of his King.

If only there were someone to converse with. In scornful silence John Fletcher had sent an orderly to remove
his possessions to cramped quarters in the post hospital.
The thought became unbearable that, never again, would
he be able to make his rounds of the wards or watch the
progress of various treatments.

As if in answer to his necessity, someone rapped softly.

He started up, called, "Come in."

To his vast astonishment Emma entered. She was
muffled in a dark cape, its hood drawn low about her features. Her cool lips merely submitted to a quick kiss.

"May the good God bless you, my darling, for coming
just now."

"I deemed it advisable to seek you. Throw some sticks
on the fire please. There is a cold wind on the river."

Mrs. Devoe threw back her hood, then mechanically
smoothed black hair arranged about her head in unmodish but becoming tight plaits.

"I take it you have been having a bad time?"

"Beastly! No one will even address me. Even the enlisted men are rude."

"I am sorry for that, Lucius," Emma said, drawing her
skirts against the back of her legs in order to let the heat
filter through. "Have you no cheer to offer your wife?"

"Beg pardon—" he almost said "Ma'am"—"I am forgetful."

He crossed to a cabinet, hurriedly produced a bottle of
burgundy and a pair of glasses. Wryly, he recalled that
this wine had formed part of a shipment sent by her while
he was Senior Surgeon at Fort Arnold, and destined for
unusual honors.

Emma accepted her ruby-tinted glass in silence, seated
herself and said thoughtfully. "I presume you realize
that, through your inept conduct, we have suffered a serious setback?"

"Yes, Emma, I perceive that." God! How it went
against his grain to admit failure.

Emma Devoe took a slow sip of her wine, kept her gaze on the now brilliantly snapping fire as she observed, "Still, this silly business may not redound wholly to our disadvantage."

In amazed wonderment, Lucius considered his wife. That any advantage might be derived from this catastrophe had escaped his imagination.

"I have always deemed you remarkable, my dear," he smiled uncertainly. Damn! She had him on the hip now and didn't intend to over-look that fact. Across the room their eyes engaged, not tenderly, not hostilely. They were just two people re-estimating one another.

"I suppose I am," she admitted. "You, too, are remarkable, Lucius, but not quite so remarkable as I had esteemed you."

"Then you have never misjudged a problem?"

"Yes. But not so gravely as you have this one."

"You mentioned some advantage?" he reminded.

"How well are you acquainted with the present desperate situation of the Colonies—the States—I mean?"

"Passably. The future is not encouraging, particularly after General Arnold's attempted defection."

"It goes deeper than that, Lucius. Our armies have been defeated again in the South; Georgia and the Carolinas are lost beyond recall," the dark-haired girl asserted. "At this moment Cornwallis, Lord Rawdon and the rest ravage and burn at will."

She moved away from the roaring blaze. "Next spring Cornwallis is expected to march north, desolating all Virginia and Maryland." Emma spoke softly as if fearful of eavesdropping.

"Do you know that the Royal Navy has regained control of the sea? And what have our dear French allies accomplished since last July? Nothing! Absolutely. The Dancing Masters are quite content to linger in Newport, playing *écarté* and teaching our country girls the minuet.

"You have just witnessed the rottenness of our high command." Emma lifted her face. "Oh Lucius. Think! Reason! But for an accident, West Point would have fallen to the enemy. Do you see?"

The physician recoiled a little. "I see, Ma'am, that you believe our American cause to be lost."

"Don't adopt that tone with me, Lucius!" Emma warned. "I am but attempting to forestall the future.

How can the Independence movement fail to collapse? No currency worthy of the name is in circulation. Countrymen and merchants will not sell to the Army—and it goes so hungry and naked that, despite endless floggings and executions, desertions increase each week.''

Before putting his thoughts into speech, Lucius swallowed the whole of his wine. ''Are you suggesting that—that we should turn our coats?''

In sharp impatience his wife's dark eyes again sought his face. ''How *can* you be so dull? Never suggest such a thing! That would be stupid. Think back, my dear husband, on how many times the American cause has seemed at its last gasp?''

''Yes. All seemed lost, many a time.''

''True, and then the patriots manage to stumble on, long after they should, in all reason, have admitted defeat. No logic explains their stubbornness,'' Emma observed. ''Despite everything, they may persist until Parliament is unwilling to continue. No, Lucius, to turn Tory would not be intelligent.''

His quick mind perceived what Emma was driving at. A hard smile creased his lips and he looked on her in admiration mixed with trepidation. ''I believe I understand your intent, my dear. You wish to back the winners, whoever they may be, without risking confiscation of your property?''

''Naturally.'' Emma arose, set down her wine glass, then standing in an almost masculine attitude, confronted him. ''Attend what I say, Lucius. Despite your evident fears, I have no intention of abandoning you in your difficulties. I am very fond of you and believe in your ultimate success. I am only resentful that you were so maladroit as to embroil yourself in an unpopular duel.''

Jupiter! How could she be so dispassionate over the possibility that a pistol ball might sear his brain or bowels—come another ten hours?

His laugh was hard. ''Would it not solve everything for you if I were killed tomorrow morning?''

''Oh, no, not at all. Like you, I detest admitting to having made a mistake.''

More narrowly he studied his wife's face by the leaping firelight. What lay back of this sudden softening?

''So you still need—'' he almost said ''want''—''me?''

''Yes. I have become convinced that I am to have a child.''

"What! In so short a space? 'Twas scarce a week ago that we—"

Suspicion leaped into the Jamaican's mind. A child? Whose? No wonder she'd been so headlong to accept his name! Hold hard, though. As a physician, he knew she might not be prevaricating. Where lay the truth?

"God knows," Emma was saying, "a child will need its father in the years to come."

"Oh—oh Emma!" The possibility that the child might really be his proved unexpectedly unnerving.

She smiled up at him. "You see, dear, why it would not suit me to have Major Stanton kill you? Not in the least. I shall pray God to spare you—and am confident that you will survive."

"Would that I shared your confidence, my dear," he sighed.

Emma sighed, treated him to a bleak look. "You know, of course, that your career with *this* Army is at an end?"

"All day I have been reminded of that fact. 'Tis reported that General Greene will depart soon to take command of the Southern Army. He has always regarded me favorably and, being above all things practical, asks nothing of his officers beyond that they know their duties and will work loyally. He knows that I——"

A sharp gesture of Emma's hand cut him short. "Fiddlesticks! Lucius, Greene's will be a subordinate staff. For all I'm a weak and stupid female I have observed much concerning military matters; once in disfavor, an officer seldom, if ever, rises again to his original position."

He drew a slow breath, so much it stung him to concede the accuracy of her logic.

The fire drew dark red tints from her sultry-looking mouth. "I believe you've the wit, after your duel, to decide on the only sensible course—"

"You suggest that I should go down to New York?" His voice was hushed at the very audacity of her suggestion.

"Yes," came the imperturbed reply. "At the same time I will return to Kaaterskill and look after my—our—property. Yes, you will travel to New York and set up a practice; you will succeed because I have many connections there and will advise them of your arrival. Physicians are much in demand there, I hear."

Emma arose, poured herself another glass of burgundy. "You need not actually adopt the British Army; you need only to insinuate yourself sufficiently into their favor to protect our interests should the Crown prevail in this miserable war. Do you comprehend my intent?"

Lucius said that he did, but felt his agreement to be of no consequence. Tomorrow he would be killed in a duel.

XLIV. Sunrise Above the Hudson

A BLANKET of silvery mist was yet concealing the river when Joshua Stanton and Captain Paul Calvert reined in at the edge of a small and level clearing situated a good half-mile upstream from the Shelburne Battery, most northerly of the defenses at West Point. To their surprise, three saddle horses already were tethered in a clump of birches near the middle of the clearing.

Although Joshua didn't know Doctor Fletcher well, he nonetheless recognized Lucius' former roommate; he wore a black coat and, very politely, lifted his silver-bound tricorne hat. Waiting beside the physician stood he who had agreed to act as president of the meeting, a Lieutenant-Colonel Dickson from the Cape Fear Region in North Carolina.

Captain Calvert looked mighty easy in his saddle as he circled the clearing to appraise its peculiarities, if any. He saw that fairly long hay stubble covered that stretch of even ground on which the duellists would meet; also that the rising sun would, within a quarter of an hour, strike directly sidewise across the proposed positions and favor neither antagonist. Calvert nodded. Colonel Dickson, an old hand in affairs of honor, had chosen well.

As he rode up to dismount he heard the Carolinian say, "'Tain't spo'tin' fo' Devoe to insist on such close range—fifteen paces don't call fo' pretty shootin'."

Joshua shook his head. "Probably doesn't know any better." Dickson frowned, took a pinch of snuff. "Sho'-ly, his second should have insisted on a decent interval."

Fletcher said, "Captain Delacroix, they say, doesn't care a damn so long as somebody gets killed."

"Strange," Joshua was thinking, "that I should find myself here about to kill, or be killed, in a duel. How war changes us all. Logically, 'twill prove nothing if I kill that

Jamaican rascal; 'twon't make poor Sabra feel one whit better—probably worse, if anything. Maybe I'm a coward to fight like this, just because the staff expects it of me? Of course, Lucius may kill me."

He looked at the heights of Constitution Island opposite, noticed a hawk circling busily above a bare brown ledge.

"For sure, this is a senseless way to settle a quarrel. Here am I, Pa's only son, risking death and without the opportunity of taking some damned Lobsterback along to balance the account. If it's in any way possible, I am going to kill that little rat simply because I don't want him to drill me. Mamma surely will die of a broken heart if I get slain in a duel."

Major Stanton had stood in mortal danger far too many times to feel rattled or jumpy—as he had that long-gone day up on Boston Neck. Lord, he'd shivered then like a sick dog and his hand had been so unsteady he'd scarce been able to reprime his musket.

What chiefly surprised him was that he experienced, about this business, none of the exhilaration he had come to associate with going into battle. In this quiet clearing sounded no banging of muskets or thundering of cannon; lacking was the inspiring rattle of drums or screaming of fifes. There was no thrill to be found in the fact that, on this morning of October second, 1780, polite murder was about to be committed.

Joshua decided suddenly, "To hell with this business! I won't be such a fool," and opened his mouth to say so. But there stood Calvert, Francis Apley, Captain of A Battery, and two other witnesses—all close friends, all looking mighty serious and a trifle pale. He remained silent.

Hoofbeats sounded on that trail which led up from Fort Clinton. The foremost figure proved not to be Doctor Devoe, but a thin, waspish individual wearing a very sharp-pointed mustache. Despite the fact that Delacroix wore an American light cavalry uniform, he suggested nothing other than the French cavalryman he was. A few paces behind Captain Delacroix rode the man Joshua Stanton had come here to kill. Right now, the physician looked scared half to death and ridiculously small astride his bony white nag.

Somberly, Joshua watched the Frenchman dismount,

gather the reins over his left arm and smartly salute first the president, and then witnesses. Apparently, Lucius had received some coaching in the niceties, for he raised his hat to the officials.

In some amusement Joshua noticed that Lucius wasn't wearing his uniform today—just his old black costume.

Colonel Dickson beckoned the seconds to conference, so Joshua turned aside watching a string of wild ducks— they looked like black mallards—go winging swiftly downstream. Somewhere, in the chestnut woods behind him, a jay screamed, then a squirrel raised an outraged chattering. It would, Joshua judged, prove a beautiful day; a few high clouds now were turning from deep rose to gold.

Captain Calvert was back at his elbow, his handsome, fine-boned features taut. "Pray remove your coat, sir." Then he added, "Take your time, Josh. He's shaking like an aspen and can't help missing."

Joshua nodded, slowly cast loose the flat yellow buttons securing his tunic; chill air struck sharply through the cambric of his ruffled shirt.

Captain Delacroix drew near, his boots bright with dew and making a soft *whiss-whiss* through the hay stubble. "*Messieurs*, you pairmeet I ex-amen?" Joshua underwent a perfunctory inspection; of course his opened shirt concealed no illegal protection, only skin growing pink and pimply with the sharp air. Captain Calvert then stalked over to examine the other principal.

Now the seconds were standing to rigid attention before Colonel Dickson, listening to the president's final instructions. Beneath a scarlet-leaved sumach, John Fletcher was laying out instruments and dressings, and, in his nervousness, kept swallowing on nothing at all. Meanwhile, while the seconds, from a covered wicker basket, drew carefully primed and loaded pistols for instant use on either principal who committed a breach of the rules.

A coin was spun and Delacroix called the turn. As a result the president walked over to Lucius Devoe, offering a second basket. His was first choice of two pistols, the butts of which protruded uglily from beneath a clean white napkin.

Joshua watched Devoe, gone very pallid beneath his dark skin, draw forth a weapon and stand curiously considering it. Now the remaining pistol was being brought over to him.

A faint singing noise commenced to sound in Joshua's ears when the president, his long gray cloak stirring gently in a sudden breeze off the Hudson, moved to a point mid-way between the two parties. Colonel Dickson placed a handkerchief between boots glowing with polish, then, watched by everyone, stepped off fifteen even strides. Again he bent and placed a handkerchief between his boot toes before walking back to his post a few feet opposite the mid-point.

"You have all in readiness, Doctor Fletcher?"

"Yes, sir."

"Doctor Devoe, are you ready to fire?"

Lucius must have answered, but his voice was so faint Joshua could not hear it. He warranted the Jamaican must be terrified. That was well; wouldn't do for the last male Stanton to die here.

"Major Stanton, are you ready to fire?"

"Yes, Colonel, whenever you wish."

Colonel Dickson's big voice rang out so loud that the tethered horses pricked their ears. "You will advance to your marks, gentlemen, and turn your backs to one another. I shall count three; once you hear the word 'three'—and not an instant before—you will turn and exchange shots at will. Seconds will shoot either gentleman who anticipates my count of three."

While he advanced to that white splash made by the handkerchief against the hay stubble, the singing noise sounded louder in Joshua's ears but he felt calm as a mill pond. The pistol he held was a long, wickedly delicate French weapon designed for just this purpose.

Arriving at his mark Joshua turned, facing a clump of yellow birch leaves at the far end of the clearing.

Captain Calvert cocked his pistol, quite ready to fire should Devoe, in terror, or by mischance, disobey the rules. Joshua watched the white revers of Calvert's blue uniform glow suddenly pink. The sun must just have climbed above those heights across the Hudson. He watched the Marylander's eyes narrow until all sight of their blue pupils became lost. No doubt the Frenchman, Delacroix, was equally ready, his vice-sharpened features tight and his hand steady.

"Ready yourselves, gentlemen!"

Colonel Dickson's voice rang out, sharp and clear. Maybe the voice of God announcing the arrival of Judgment Day would sound like that?

In the depths of the birch woods that jay now was fairly shrieking at his squirrel enemy.

"One!"

Joshua recalled the first deer he ever shot—

"Two!"

—A grenadier of the British Forty-Second rushing at him once more, with bayonet levelled.

"Three!"

Joshua bent his right knee and, as Calvert had taught him, pivoted his whole body until there rushed into his scope of vision a black and white figure. Levelling his pistol with care, Major Stanton fired, but at that same, precise instant something struck him so violently that it spun him about. Off-balance, Joshua fell onto his back and saw the treetops go wheeling crazily about; nothing more.

Book Three ★ *The River*

PART I—EASTERN DISTRICT

1. SUNDAY-GO-TO-MEETING

"THANK HEAVENS," sighed Prudence Peabody, "spring's come, 'twon't be so perishing cold in here." The spinster's sharp black eyes considered a series of large and small figures uncomfortably occupying benches ranged the length of Machias' only church.

With most of these people Prudence had been intimately familiar since childhood; yes, she knew them all—the Samuel Scotts, the Ben Fosters and the Japhet Hills. Yonder slumped Daniel Merserve, bored and restless, no doubt because he was fresh returned from service with the Massachusetts Army; in the old days he'd sat quiet enough. Beyond him sat the O'Briens, Morris, Jeremiah and John, sons of the veteran old John O'Brien. Well disciplined, their progeny also sat erect and kept their eyes dutifully fixed on Pastor James Lion. Perhaps because he hailed from the distant state of New Jersey he commanded their attention.

Everyone had rejoiced when back in 1772, the Reverend Mr. Lion had settled in Machias. Nobody had expected so gifted a divine would be content with an agreed salary of eighty-four pounds a year, plus a hundred dollar settlement, but 'most everyone in Machias agreed the Reverend Mr. Lion had made a first-rate preacher, capable of throwing a fear of God into the most hardened sinner. When he got going, the pastor could make a body fair smell those sulphurous fires awaiting the ungodly.

Beneath her packed-thread and hickory-splint stays Prudence's thin body ached as she looked sidewise to make sure that Lionel, Purity and Constance were retaining miens becoming of the moment.

Her toe impacted against Purity's ankle. Mercy! The child was attempting to pick her nose and Mrs. Pine was glaring at her from across the Meeting House. A fine thing! Purity should have been heeding the Reverend Mr. Lion's prescription for salvation. Suddenly it came home that she, too, might be listening. Prudence returned her attention.

"I come now," the minister was saying, big bony hands locked above the pure white birch bark adorning his pulpit, "to a warning sent us by Providence on May the nineteenth of last year."

A muffled groan resounded in this shadowy House of Worship. Nobody present could ever forget that awful day. Even the smallest children could recall the extraordinary and unprecedented phenomenon characterized by a great darkness. Huge black billows had closed over the sky so thoroughly that, at noonday the fowls had raised their night cries and gone to roost; the oxen had lain down and not even coarse print could be read in the open. Great had been the tribulation along the entire eastern seaboard of New England. Trembling families gathered about Bibles from which elders sought words of encouragement. Hour after hour the unnatural gloom had persisted. Many sinners—to their later embarrassment—had rushed about attempting to pay off debts and confessing to sharp practices. Others had literally rent their clothing and torn their hair out by the roots.

"You will recall that He sent a great darkness to blacken His heavens, lo, from mid-day until sunset. Surely, this was His reproof against the lustfulness, the worldliness so prevalent in our community." The minister's deep-set and penetrating gray eyes travelled along the double row of benches until they came to rest upon seats occupied by soldiers from the garrisons manning Forts Foster and O'Brien. Already hot and uncomfortable in their best fragments of uniform, they flushed, stared hard at the splintery floor.

"Let it never be stated that our Lord hath been unduly impatient with sinners. Did He not proclaim in the Book of Joel, Chapter Three, fifteenth verse, 'The sun and the moon shall be darkened and the stars shall withdraw their shining'? Doubt not, that should human wickedness persist, He will cause such a darkness to prevail forever and ever."

Again a soft groan arose from the congregation and children grabbed for their parents' hands.

The Reverend Mr. Lion leaned 'way out of his pulpit and in a deep voice cried, "I charge you, my flock, therefore, to repent your wickedness and to recall the words of Daniel, Chapter Twelve, the twelfth verse which saith, 'Blessed is he that waiteth, and cometh to the thousand three hundred and five and thirty days.' "

For the life of her, Prudence couldn't make much sense out of it, nor, she suspected, did Asa nor Ahab, sitting there with his peg-leg stuck out straight before him. As always when she failed to understand the preaching, Prudence closed her eyes, pretended to be drinking in the Reverend Mr. Lion's words of wisdom. Actually, she was conjecturing over whether the cow would throw a bull or a heifer calf—she had prayed so hard for a heifer. By the time Divine Service was over she might learn.

Asa's gaze wandered moodily along the lines of familiar countenances and lingered a brief moment on the acid features of the one certain enemy he owned in Machias. The most charitable thing he could say about Doctor William Falconer was, that in a curious, crabbed way, he meant well. Aye. Falconer was well meaning, like a dog that would chase a rat across a shelf loaded with a family's best china.

Doctor Falconer had not welcomed his return to Machias. In a twinkle the old man sensed that Morgan Peabody's third son, young as he was, already had forgotten more than he, Will Falconer, would ever understand about the practice of physick and surgery.

A couple of sea captains were dozing comfortably, chin on chest. Where was Doctor Clark Parker? Absent again. Most likely he had gone fishing; but Mrs. Parker was in attendance. She was a homey, determinedly cheerful little body, anxiously ruling her five small children. Even as he smiled at her the baby she held set up a querulous mewing. Nobody paid attention.

Colonel John Allen, commander of the garrison defending Machias, and commissioner from the State of Massachusetts, maintained his usual grave and thoughtful appearance; a bluff hearty figure in a blue uniform turned up in red. What a tower of strength this man had proved throughout the war.

Asa's throat contracted when, at long last, the Reverend Mr. Lion concluded his hour-long sermon and prepared—as was the custom—to read aloud various items of news.

"Intelligence hath been received," the minister announced, "that God has prospered our fortunes in the

South—albeit moderately. General Greene hath met the enemy in a better than drawn battle, at the place called Guilford Court House and hath sent Lord Cornwallis retreating to a place called Wilmington in North Carolina. Lord Rawdon's forces, when last seen, were retiring on Charles Town.''

Even better news was the report of a great naval engagement—ending in victory—fought off the mouth of Chesapeake Bay. The Machias people glanced quizzically at each other. Where might one find Chesapeake Bay? Most of them had no idea; but, one and all, they rejoiced to learn that, for once, a French squadron, under a certain Admiral Chevalier Charles René Destouches, had thumped old Marriott Arbuthnot whom all Americans knew only too well, capturing the H.B.M.S. *Romulus*, man-of-war, and dealing the enemy a mighty smart kick in the steerage.

"So much for news of national import." The minister removed square, steel-rimmed spectacles and drew himself up. Asa's heart lurched. Well, the news would be out in a few minutes now—news which would set all Machias tongues a-wagging sixty to the minute.

"My friends, according to custom," the minister announced gravely, "I shall, at the conclusion of this Service, post banns stating the intention of certain members of this congregation to exchange the vows of Holy Matrimony. Should any among you be aware of any just cause or impediment against the wedding of these people—" he paused, lent special emphasis to his next words—"I do charge you, as true Christians, not to bruit your knowledge abroad but to confide such knowledge in me. Remember, Satan thrives on scandal, gossip and idle talk."

The Reverend Mr. Lion's manner was so earnest that even the youngsters stared in anticipation of what was to come. Asa stole an uneasy glance at his elder sister. Ahab, when he learned what was intended, might bellow like a bull calf for a spell, but then he'd very likely fall in and be loyal.

Eventually the two-hour service came to an end as, in discordant unison, the congregation raised the Doxology—they sang heartily, because it meant an escape into the open air and sunshine.

The children already were wriggling in anticipation. As if in need of support of some hand, Asa took that of little Constance, ten now, and, as the villagers said, growing like a weed.

Prudence, the physician prayed, would hurry home to see about the expected calf; but she didn't. Like everybody else, she intended to linger until old Paul Gideon, the sexton, shuffled out, taking a deliberate time of it, to post those banns.

"Oh, look! Flowers!" Constance pointed to the graveyard where a few hepaticas and violets had begun timidly to show their blossoms. Child-like, she brushed carelessly past a long row of raw wooden headboards. There would be stone markers later on, but a lot of people had died last winter—quite the most severe in years.

Asa paused, suddenly saddened. How well he knew one of the headboards; he himself had carved the inscription upon it.

Here Lieth ye Mortal Remains of
Morgan Peabody, Esq.
b. 1718 d. 1780
A kind Husband, a loving Father and a true Patriot.

To one side of that simple slab arose the weatherbeaten headstone of Charity Morgan, his own mother. The dead grass on it stood long and brown, but earth forming a mound above his step-mother's grave still was raw.

Poor Ruth Peabody, his step-mother, what a hideous death had been hers! Her whole breast had been eaten out by a form of decay of which even the most learned physicians of Europe understood nothing. To watch the gentle creature's agony, and find himself unable to do more than to bleed and to administer laudanum, had been most depressing.

Pa had died shortly afterwards, not once rising from the bed on which hip gout had laid him a month before Asa's return. That old French and Indian War wound had reopened with a vengeance.

Over his shoulder Asa realized that, sure enough, half the town was waiting about a notice board affixed to the church's log wall to the right of the entrance. Precious few people would approve, and even fewer still understand, his decision to marry Jenny Starbird. The minute those banns were posted he figured to lose several dozen so-called friends and patients.

Asa remained where he was, watched the bent old sexton come shuffling out, snaggle teeth yellow in the bright June sunlight.

Paul Gideon's hammer posted a sheet announcing that Benjamin Tappan, bachelor, and Josephine McNeil, maid, proposed to become joined in marriage. Tap! Tap! Now the Machias folk learned Arthur Jones, bachelor, had sought and won the hand of little Ellen Libby. High time too!

A curious sense of unreality possessed Asa when the sexton plucked from his sagging, half-ripped pocket a third square of paper. Tap! Tap! Now the secret was out. Asa Peabody, bachelor, intended marriage with Jenny Starbird, widow!

The babble of the crowd swelled; people pressed forward, craning their necks clear out of their Sunday stocks and scarves. Children squirmed, eel-like, between the legs of their elders to get a look at this last set of banns.

Would it have helped matters to have had Jenny here? No. As a communicant of the Church of England, she had never been welcomed into such a solidly Dissenting congregation.

Disjointed sentences reached his ears. "Well, I never!" "And him so downright respectable." "For shame." "And to think a Peabody'd marry Jenny Starbird." "Why, she's at least half a Tory and, my dear, those clothes! No *honest* woman—" The conversation impinged on his ears like the hum of angry bees.

Now the throng commenced to disperse. People strode by, either looking stonily ahead or casting him brief reproachful looks.

All at once he was aware of Colonel Allen's broad, blue-clad figure striding towards him. He offered his hand. "No doubt you've good and valid reasons for taking this step, so here's wishing you the best of luck, Peabody." He spoke louder than was necessary, treated the crowd to a level look, then moved on, the tarnished brass buttons of his uniform glinting.

Now Brother Ahab stumped forward, the peg of his wooden leg and his walking stick sinking deep in the soft black mould beneath those pines which shaded the

House of God. His gray eyes were hard and his neck thick and red as always when he got mad.

"Have you gone daft?" he snorted. "What of our good name? God's teeth, man, you don't have to *marry*—"

"Ahab!" Asa's voice was as incisive as one of his own surgical instruments. "Pray remember that Mistress Starbird has become my affianced wife."

Ahab choked off an ugly word in mid-pronunciation. "But, but, why did it have to be *her*? I sure dread Elizabeth's having her say—let alone her folks. Oh, Asa, Asa! Must you do this? We Peabodys have always kept ourselves decent, honest—"

"—And so we will continue," Asa snapped. "Good day, sir!" How dismaying to learn that Ahab objected to this decision so much more seriously than he had anticipated; probably he was afraid of the attitude his own affianced wife would adopt.

Sister Prudence forbore to address him at all; only stalked past, stiffnecked as any crane and shepherding the younger Peabodys before her. Several soldiers of the garrison, however, swung up to shake him by the hand and wish him well, but these were shiftless lads with no particular status in the town. The only woman who spoke to him was little Mrs. Parker. Followed by her round-eyed brood, she came bobbing up, cheerful as a robin at sunup.

"You have done well," she assured him warmly. "What we need here in Machias are more people of imaggination and intelligence."

Helen Parker had been born in New York Town, Asa recalled, and had proved to be the only female in Machias willing to attend Jenny Starbird through a low fever she'd suffered last fall.

The Reverend Mr. Lion broke away from the last knot of his parishioners and very quietly said, "Always remember, Brother Asa, that you have a friend in me."

It would have helped had he said so, earlier and louder. Still, the assurance was no end comforting.

Grimly, resolutely, Asa lingered before the church until every last member of the congregation had departed, eager for gossip and Sunday dinner. Only then did he set his jaw and put foot to that familiar track leading out of the town and towards Jenny Starbird's comfortable dwelling.

II. RIVER ROAD

ASA, tramping along that wagon track which paralleled
the south bank of the Machias River, experienced a burning resentment. Godfreys! Who'd have dreamed Christian folk would take on like that? Why, if Jenny'd been
branded felon, a public woman or a witch, they couldn't
have acted more hostile. Jenny Starbird, of course, never
had been popular with the women of Machias because
she kept a servant, wore hats, owned at least four gowns
and was well educated. Most of all, they resented the fact
that she was really lovely and gay as a catbird on a pump
handle.

He guessed people would get used to the idea after a
while; perhaps, on his account, they'd prove kinder to
Jenny. After last winter, precious few families in
Machias weren't in his material or moral debt. Judas
Maccabaeus! He couldn't count the times he'd rooted
himself out of bed to tramp or row miles through screaming blizzards to attend some stricken member of the community. Surely, they'd recall those visits and the good
care they'd received?

Asa decided it was lucky that Phil Starbird had decided
to construct his sawmill 'way out on the furthest edge of
town—near a mile from Burnham's Tavern. Burnham.
What could have chanced with big, genial Peter?

Even though he'd be late for Jenny's Sunday dinner,
Asa guessed maybe he had better look in on the Widow
McNeil's boy who was suffering from a mortification on
the ankle. What particularly worried Asa was that the
gash was deep and had been sustained in Mrs. McNeil's
stableyard.

For a hundredth time, the physician pondered an elu-
sive connection between deep cuts, the presence of
horses and a subsequent appearance of lockjaw. Why
should horses appear to encourage this universally fatal
malady? Maybe in Europe they were finding out?

An impatient sigh escaped him. What had he to show
for this year and three months, except an exposure of
Doctor Falconer's dangerous ignorance and archaic
methods? Little, precious little; save experience with
fractures, amputations and some baffling experiences
with lung fever and the screws.

In this case of Mrs. McNeil's boy he felt a special interest and a sense of obligation—the widow's husband had been slain during the capture of the Royal cutter *Margaretta*, nearly five years back. Asa took the boy's improved condition as a good omen. He seemed less feverish and the lad's pale white diaphragm revealed no ominous tensity.

"Walter's coming on fine," Mrs. McNeil declared, wiping floured hands on her apron. Like most of the Machias folk, her respect for the Sabbath did not preclude the cooking of food nor the lighting of fires—practices frowned upon in many a frontier village further south.

After drawing a couple of pails of water for the widow's convenience, Asa resumed his progress along the river road.

Not far below Mrs. McNeil's house he encountered a party of militia men coming to town. They were stationed at a battery built on the river's edge at Stillman's farm—one of several fortifications designed to guard a wooden boom rigged across the Machias River at a strategically narrow point.

Swinging down the road, loose-kneed and easy, Asa noticed several columns of smoke rising from the far shore of this dark, brown river. The presence of the many smoke pillars he had seen earlier in the week must mean that more savages had appeared on those traditional camping grounds where, each spring and fall, the 'Quoddies met to trade and talk policy. So many and so high were the clam shells it looked in mid-summer as if a snow bank persisted on the far shore.

Right now, Asa couldn't see the Indian camp, but from Jenny Starbird's home he knew he'd see rows and rows of birch bark canoes dawn up along the beach. He hoped not to count too many canoes over there. Colonel Allen was meeting with considerable trouble, this spring, in keeping the Red Men neutral. For a fact, last year Allen had been forced to send as tacit hostages his young sons to visit certain Passamaquoddy chiefs. Only a few days ago the lads had been returned because, for a miracle, the British at Bagaduce were remaining quiescent. Apparently, they did not intend to follow up their crashing victory over Dudley Saltonstall and General Lovell on the Penobscot.

He looked back over his shoulder and considered the
scattered houses composing Machias. Under this warm
spring sunlight they looked very homey and far more
comfortable than they really were. Built of logs, with one
or two exceptions, they sheltered some eighty families
and above a hundred single men. Like a tall ship at anchor in a small harbor, Burnham's Tavern loomed above
the rest of the buildings yonder.

Strange, that unearthly calm which descended over a
town on a Sabbath. No hog reeves were herding swine
among the oaks down by the river, no cowherds guiding
their precious charges down to feed on those succulent
grasses growing along the fringes of the marsh.

More soldiers appeared, faces fiery red from their first
contact with a hot sun.

"Any news, Doctor?"

"General Greene handed the British a mild beating
down in Carolina."

"Did he? Did he really now? Well, now that's good."

Four privates, each clad in a variety of garments came
striding up, all curiosity. "Say, sounds like mebbe we're
gettin' somewhere, at last. That feller Greene must know
his business. Huh? When d' you think the war will be
over? Soon, eh, Doc? Me, I'm sick of playin' sojer, all I
want is to get back to timberin'."

Presently they moved off towards Machias, coats slung
over their arms and talking now about Greene's victory
and the chances of demobilization. One of them turned,
called over his shoulder. "Hi, Doc! Heard tell the Injuns
aim to raise a phullabaloo tomorrey night. Might pay you
to paddle over; they's some right pert squaws among
them wigwams. Saw 'em myself."

Smiling, Asa called his thanks. Pretty soon he could
recognize, through the trees, the low, pearl-gray outlines
of Jenny Starbird's home.

Because Jenny had espoused a sawyer, her house was
one of three private residences constructed of clapboards—another point which irked the ladies of Machias.
Now its boards had weathered to a pretty silver-gray.
Unlike most of the local housewifes, Jenny had bothered
to lay out a small flower garden.

Poor, pretty little Jenny! Again Asa wondered whether
he was marrying her for love, or because he felt so over-
whelmingly sorry for this gay, bright young thing so

hopelessly imprisoned on the edge of a dark wilderness. Nobody had any idea how far west the forests stretched from these rocky shores.

Would it be a sound idea to take his wife into the woods for their honeymoon? In clement months of the year, such as this, a prospective bridegroom more often than not hunted out some pretty dell and there constructed a lean-to. Such accommodation might prove crude, but at least it afforded a privacy lacking in most of the over-crowded cabins.

Although Jenny's house really wasn't large, she had scandalized all Machias by hiring a half-breed Indian girl from a settlement on Chandler's River to keep it clean.

A faint frown appeared on Asa's broad red-brown forehead. Either Philip Starbird had possessed, at the time of his death considerably more of the world's goods than anybody suspected, or else, these last years, Jenny had been living 'way beyond her means. In fact, he'd heard rumors of Jenny's borrowing quite a tidy sum from Sylvanus Snow, Sister Esther's husband. If so, she had been ill advised to borrow from such a skinflint. She had arranged loans with certain others of the townsmen, smiling sweetly all the while, as if she'd some private idea back of those transactions, a fact which made the lenders' home life none too pleasant, once their wives found out about it.

Abruptly, Asa checked his stride and still outside the range of vision of Jenny's house, he seated himself beneath a tree. Why shouldn't he have a home of his own? Hadn't he earned one? What with Morgan, now a big and steady young man, and doing mighty well as carpenter's assistant at Jeremiah O'Brien's shipyard, what with Ahab back and earning more than moderate bread as a full-fledged shipwright, he reckoned Prue and his young half-brothers and sisters should be well taken care of, especially if he continued to supply them with a modest contribution. After all, had he not a right to live his own life?

What if Sabra had answered any one of the three letters he'd dispatched to Boston? For a long while he'd read, every night from *Evelina* until its pages were worn and tattered—just because Sabra had favored it.

He drew a deep breath. Well, best forget about Sabra Stanton. Um. He brightened on a sudden possibility.

Maybe Jenny could be persuaded to sell out? Certainly, she'd small cause to love Machias. Good. Perhaps, in a few months' time, they could sail south, perhaps 'way down to Pennsylvania? The best physicians in America were supposed to be practicing there.

Heaving himself to his feet Asa smiled while beating sandy dust from his Sunday breeches. How cheering it was to know that, in a very few moments, Jenny's light laughter would be brightening him. What a fundamentally good-natured creature she was—so cheerful and generous to all and sundry—even to the ragged, verminous savages who appeared at her door, hungry but too proud to beg. They doted on the Widow Starbird.

These past three years must have proved a terrible trial, what with her husband dead, and she a stranger. Had Jenny possessed a little more resolution, she must have packed up and sailed southwards, long since. But Jenny wasn't like that. The pretty little New Yorker was too easy-going, too indolent and disinclined to bother over practicalities, until they stared her right in the face.

While setting foot to a pathway leading up to her door Asa wondered, for a last ime, whether there could be any foundation to the whispers that, more than once, her house on the edge of town had sheltered an escaped British prisoner, or a Nova Scotian Tory working his painful way up towards Bagaduce and Halifax? He reckoned not. Hadn't Phil Starbird been killed during the boarding of H.B.M.S. *Margaretta*?

Under Jenny's easy-going manner he had discovered a serious streak deep in her nature. Though he'd never broached the subject, he deduced that she might prove quite as satisfied as anybody in North America if the King's cause prevailed. For that, she couldn't entirely be blamed. As all Machias knew, Jenny's father right now was serving as colonel in a Loyalist corps campaigning down in Virginia under that damned traitor Benedict Arnold.

Thank goodness that the Reverend Mr. Lion had remained first of all a minister of the Gospel. While he disapproved of Jenny Starbird's uncertain loyalties and Anglican ties, he had not hesitated when Asa inquired whether he would officiate.

"So long as you truly love one another, and are free to marry, I would indeed derelict in my duty to refuse my services," was all he had said.

Only fifteen more days, and then, and then—well, for the first time in his life, he'd have a home of his own.

Jenny, he knew, would suit him fine. He suspected she concealed a deal of intelligence under those yellow curls which were the envy of all the women and girls because when it rained her locks only grew curlier and more lustrous.

The sun's warmth, the liquid warbling of some blackbirds nestbuilding in a patch of reeds bordering the river, filled him with a rare sense of peace. Even the raucous cries of a number of great, gray and white gulls wheeling over the Machias River did not seem discordant.

Summoning a wide smile, Asa knocked at Jenny's small house; by comparison to the big mill just beyond and its dripping, slowly creaking water wheel, it seemed tiny.

In a dress of sprigged blue muslin Jenny flung open the door; her naturally pink cheeks were flushed and her clear gray eyes very bright.

"Oh, Asa, Asa, my beloved!" Jenny clung convulsively to him, very much like a child fearful of being deprived of a holiday. "I thought some patient might keep you from me!"

Immediately, he became aware of the scent of potpourri; always she sprinkled her wardrobe with it. Only when she pressed herself fervently to him did he become aware—and with very mingled reactions—that Jenny was not wearing stays. Well, why should she! God certainly hadn't created womankind sheathed in a carapace like some miserable tortoise—He had meant them to be soft and yielding.

When he kissed her, she surged up to him, clung with lovely eyes all but closed and pink lips parted. She made little whispering noises, even darted the warm and moist tip of her tongue along the rim of his ear.

"Really, my dear, I discover you to be quite the perfect pagan," he laughed uncomfortably.

"Oh, bother! Admit you like being kissed in the ear—I do." Her breath fanned his cheek. "It makes little shivers run along my back."

Jenny retreated indoors, swept him a graceful curtsey, then moved in a series of light dancing steps across her minute living room, her skirts whirling up until her knees displayed their rounded perfection.

"Oh, Asa! So wonderful a day—'tis glorious to be living—I declare I despaired of feeling the sun again during that eternal winter. Oh, Asa, Asa! How can I ever come to love such a grim and forbidding country?''

"There are those who like it," he reminded, and brought a delighted flush to her features when he added, "but I am not one."

Soberly, he placed his tricorne on one of the two rush-seated armchairs. Jenny ran out to fetch a pitcher of elderberry wine—she was clever about its manufacture. Maybe she was not such a lax housekeeper after all?

Across a mantelpiece of smoke-stained oak, a row of pewter dishes glowed bluish white, bright as patient scouring with horsetail rushes could render them. Silently, he went to admire a blue glass vase in a far corner from which sprang three jewel-bright feathers fetched from India. They, so the sea captains said, had been plucked from the tail of a wonderful bird known as the peacock. Like three eyes, the vibrant blue-green spots on them shone iridescent in a chance sunbeam.

"And how did the good townsfolk of Machias greet our banns?''

Crimson, Asa struggled to belittle their lack of enthusiasm, and deceived her not at all.

"A fig for them—everyone!" she laughed. "I am accustomed to their jealousy—their enviousness. Darling, that's all it is, just enviousness. Come let us dine. I have sacrificed one of the geese.''

Asa was aghast. "Surely, you didn't kill a goose—not with the hatching season just coming on?''

Jenny laughed, wrinkled her short and faintly upturned nose at him. "Oh, what difference? Isn't this a very especial occasion? Not every day do we become affianced before God—and Machias!''

Asa sighed. How typical. This goose Jenny had caused to be killed might, in all expectations, have hatched out a dozen goslings, each worth up to six shillings, hard money.

"The best of everything I have is yours, my sweet sobersides." She kissed him lightly then ran to fetch out their goose, brown and fragrant, from behind an iron door securing a big oven let into the left-hand side of an uncommonly fine brick chimney place.

She plumped herself down onto his lap, put an arm around his neck and hugged him. The warm pressure of her buttocks against his lap sent the blood singing through his body. "We had best get into practice, had we not?"

Despite himself, Asa couldn't help noticing, in a shamed sort of way, the pallid perfection of breasts riding high beneath her thin muslin bodice. Why, the pale oval outline of her nipples was distinctly to be discerned and the perfume of potpourri was fascinating.

Their repast proved delightful—beyond a doubt Jenny could cook if she wanted to—and excellently since wonderful and unfamiliar spices flavored the dressing. He was glad also to commend her on the johnny-cake.

"Oh, that was Wateka's doing," she confessed in disarming candor. "I bake only passable." Eyes suddenly full, and yellow hair a-flying, Jenny ran over to fling her arms about his neck. "You do love me, Asa, don't you? Honestly and truly?" An odd undertone was present in Jenny's voice.

"How can you doubt it, you great sweet silly." To reassure her—and for his own secret pleasure—Asa swung her onto his lap and became deluged with expertly delivered kisses and caresses, so intimate he would have taken alarm but for the fact that she was a widow.

The meal was rendered further memorable by a stone bottle of perry—a faintly bitter, but definitely warming, wine made of green pears.

Before he knew it, Asa had his coat off and was eating more hungrily than ever he did at a table set by Sister Prudence. Chuckling like a naughty school boy, he all the while feasted his eyes on Jenny's pert prettiness, or her rare fine figure and the most shapely ankles of any grown female in the community.

Despite everything, his well-developed powers of observation sensed, rather than noticed, a certain watchfulness on her part. It was as if Jenny were studying the effect upon him of everything she said or did. The impression that some idea obsessed her, grew steadily stronger.

"To Mrs. Peabody!" she lifted one of those tiny pewter cups unique in the Eastern District. Her light manner vanished as she pressed her cheek against his. "I will do my best to make you happy. I'll be a good wife, Asa—a true one."

"I am sure of that."

'Thank you. I—I needed you to say that. Asa—?''

''Yes, Jenny.''

''Have you ever heard of what is called a 'shift wedding'?''

''The old English custom?''

''Yes.''

''They aren't common in America, but their validity is recognized. Why do you ask?''

''A chapman stopped in here a day ago and spoke of the custom.'' She blushed prettily. ''He said that if—if, when I marry you, I stand just as—as bare as when I came into the world—then I would bring no debts to our marriage.''

Asa stared at her. ''Why, why, yes—I guess that's what a 'shift' marriage means.''

What in the world could be reminding her that, from time immemorial, common law admitted that if a widow were married a second time, she must be forgiven all debts were she willing to be married quite nude—more recently a loose shift were permitted her—while standing on the King's Highway.

Such ceremonies, for the sake of modesty, were usually performed at night. In some localities the bride might conceal herself behind a curtain or in a closet. At any rate, were she willing to submit to such embarrassment, a widow couldn't be sued for debt and her new husband was permitted the full enjoyment of her property.

Asa couldn't restrain the surge of a crimson tide into his face. ''What an idea! No, I won't have it.''

''Bah!'' She flared up. ''Let people talk; they have enough, already. We'll have to think twice on the idea. You see, Asa, my debts amount to,'' she hesitated, ''to a hundred and fifty pounds, sterling.''

He gaped at her. ''A hundred and fifty pounds! Why—that's a small fortune up here.''

''Full well I know it,'' she sighed.

Sterling meant hard money. Judas Maccabaeus! Phil Starbird's mill would fetch little more than that. Suppose Jenny's creditors chose to foreclose? The mill then would have to be sold on their terms. Breathing hard, Asa stared at a bed of embers slowly paling in the chimney.

Her fingers ruffled the dark brown of his hair. ''You could not hope to pay my debts in years—and there's no reason you should. Believe me, beloved, what I have suggested is only sensible.''

"But Jenny, for you to marry me all unclothed—why, it's not decent.''

Cornflower-blue bows and bright yellow curls bobbed to a vigorous shake of her head. "Fiddlesticks! We'll not have much of a wedding in any case—I doubt a dozen persons would attend. Besides, this chapman told me that, because no King's Highway passes near Machias, we could be wedded right here in this house.'' She laughed and kissed him fondly. "All I must do is to stand disrobed behind a curtain through which I must thrust only my hand.''

Unhappily, Asa recalled well-known instances of this curious rite. Certainly, Jenny's already difficult position in Machias would become intolerable after such a proceeding. They must expect from her creditors, Sylvanus Snow and the rest, only open hostility.

It was a little shocking to him to perceive how completely unabashed Jenny was at the prospect of such a rite; she might have displayed at least a modicum of modest embarrassment.

How would Sabra Stanton have contemplated such an ordeal? He arrived at no conclusion because Jenny's soft, pinkish white arms went about his neck and once more he tasted a magical sweetness and tenderness well-nigh forgotten since long, long ago Charity Peabody had been laid to rest in the churchyard.

An ineffable sense of peace filled him as he sat in this cheery, bright little room, with Jenny's yellow and fragrant head resting against his shoulder as, through the open doorway, they watched early butterflies flit above the new grass. The widow's three remaining geese were moving about out there grazing and snapping up grubs; every now and then one of them would cackle at a curious gull that came wheeling over from the river.

Suddenly he asked, "Tell me, dearest, when the *Margaretta's* crew was taken prisoner, did you not welcome here certain of her officers?''

She reminded him quietly, "We were not at war then.''

"Did a Mr. Midshipman Moore visit frequently?''

She stirred and he heard her breathing quicken. "Why, why yes. I was but newly widowed then. I needed the companionship denied me by the ladies of Machias.''

He wished he dared ask her whether she had ever sheltered Tory fugitives and so set at rest a lingering doubt, but the moment was too perfect, too beautiful, to risk spoiling. He settled back, gazed into her face and thought he had never been so happy.

Of course he missed certain items of furniture usual in a frontier home. There was no carding board in evidence, no spinning wheel, not even a candle mould. On the other hand, there were two shelves loaded with books and a book was a rare sight here on the rim of the wilderness. Instead of the usual basket-full of clothing waiting to be patched or mended, a little tambour frame lay on a table with a design in petit-point all but completed.

Reluctantly he guessed that Prudence had been right when she'd snapped, "Now take that Starbird woman; why she's as improvident as a butterfly and as helpless as a turtle on its back."

Asa thought, "If I'm patient, Jenny can be taught a deal of useful accomplishments," but now with his hand on the softness of her breast, the prospect did not seem to alarm him. Presently she sighed, gave him a peck of a kiss on the forehead and, arising, commenced to clear away the dinner dishes. Asa, meanwhile, strolled over to the bookshelves.

Um. They supported perhaps three dozen volumes, probably more books than one could discover in the combined collections of Reverend Mr. Lion, Colonel Allen and maybe Captain John O'Brien. Idly he inspected their titles; besides a book of Common Prayer and Bible, he noticed Fielding's *Tom Jones*, which struck him as a trifle bold for even a widow's perusal. The newest-looking book, he noticed, was one called *A Sentimental Journey*.

Interested, he plucked it out while Jenny bustled about, transferring the remains of their feast into a tiny pantry. Behind the rank of calfskin and vellum bindings he noticed a bit of fur and plucked out a pair of large and well-worn rabbit-fur mittens.

Raising a semi-humorous brow he turned, "Ah ha! Now I perceive your secret."

"Secret?" Her voice sounded sharp and breathless.

"Aye. How you keep your hands so soft."

"Wha—what do you mean?"

"In performing manual labor you wear your gloves."

"Why, yes, that's true," she laughed. "I—I'm so ashamed to do outdoor work, I hide them."

"Why did you get 'em so large?"

Her gaze flickered sidewise an instant, just the barest hint of a motion. "Why, they were all I could get. I bought them from an Indian."

Carelessly he tossed them aside, and picked up *A Sentimental Journey.*

"Where did you get so new a book?"

"Oh, that chapman I spoke of gave it to me in exchange for a night's lodging in the mill house."

That chapman, eh? How odd that a peddler would carry in his pack a book he couldn't hope to sell in one out of a hundred frontier homes. Usually such roving merchants were much more practical. His suspicion returned. If that visitor had been a real chapman then Asa Peabody was an Italian sculptor! Well, once they were married all such nonsense would cease.

"Come, darling," she called brightly, "Let's go walk along the river before the sun lowers."

The first chance she got, Jenny slipped those rabbit-skin mittens back behind the books.

III. FAMILY CONCLAVE

THE MINUTE Asa set foot to that walk of bleached and well-crushed clamshells leading up to Pals long low house, he knew he was in for a bad half-hour. Voices, raised in heated dispute, died away when he lifted the whittled white pine latch and stepped indoors.

All the grown-ups of the family and their kin were present, even Esther. He wondered how she had ever managed to get here being so big with child and so pinched of feature. How small and tired she looked crouched beside her burly, Psalm-shouting husband, Sylvanus Snow.

Ahab looked wooden-faced, much resembling the weather-beaten figurehead of a ship; at his elbow his waspish affianced bride, Elizabeth Shannon, was sitting, straight as any poker. Morgan, Junior, alone smiled at him.

As he shut the door behind him Prudence's hands tightened in her lap and she called out, "Purity! Just you take Lionel and Constance out to the woods and cut me some bundles of broom twigs. You'll come across plenty of birch in the back lot. Now git!"

That the children were loathe to depart was plain; full well they sensed that a drama of some sort was about to take place.

In studied deliberation Asa hung his hat to its customary peg, pulled out the cuffs of his Sunday shirt and turned to face the tight-jawed semi-circle occupying the other half of the room.

"Have all of you come to meddle in my affairs?"

"They are not just your affairs," Ahab spoke up. "As the eldest male member and present head o' this family, I'm here to call you to account."

This, Asa noted, was the first time Ahab had ever claimed to head up the Peabody clan. Good. By this declaration, he had removed a load of responsibility from his younger brother.

"Oh Asey, how *could* you take up with Jenny Starbird?" Prudence demanded in a flat, acid tone. " 'Tain't as if they ain't plenty of eligible maidens in this town. Why did you do it?"

Asa moved over to a rude sideboard and rested his hand lightly on it. "For the best of reasons, Prudence. I love Jenny Starbird and I'll have her for my wife."

Sylvanus Snow got suddenly to his feet. He was every bit as big as Asa and probably a few pounds heavier. "Beware. Profane love is against God's order. We cannot stand idly by while you introduce into our decent family this—this Jezebel!"

Asa's broad features grew so tight his cheekbones stood out in sharp relief. Esther uttered a little choked cry. "Oh, Sylvanus, you mustn't say such things. Asa has a—"

"—Peace, woman! It is a wife's part to be meek."

Asa's eyes commenced to sparkle. " 'Vanus, if you weren't Esther's husband I'd take an almighty pleasure in knocking that lie back down your throat. I warn you to watch your tongue."

Sylvanus snarled, "I'll say what I please, you son of Belial, so long's it's the truth."

Prudence got up hurriedly, ran between the two angry

men and Esther heaved her enormously swollen figure to its feet and went to cling to her husband's arm.

"What kind of talk is this on the Sabbath?" Prudence fluttered.

"Well may you inqure," Asa flung at her.

Ahab remained seated, looking downright unhappy. Probably he'd have said nothing if Lizzie Shannon hadn't prodded him with a rapier-like glance.

"But, Asey," he rumbled, "ain't you forgot? This woman's pa is a colonel over a Tory regiment that's fightin' and killin' us right this minnit?"

"I'm not marrying Colonel Ludlow, nor his politics, either. Jenny's no Tory."

"Isn't she?" William Shannon spoke for the first time. "Mebbe you can explain, Doctor, why near every strange man who comes here and dodges our town makes a beeline for her house? Most of 'em talk mighty British, 'tis said."

"Mrs. Starbird's house is the last on the wagon track leading north." Asa knew the explanation sounded weak. "She is known to be charitably disposed."

"In more ways than one," sneered Sylvanus Snow.

"Amen to that," snapped Elizabeth Shannon.

Because he despised people who failed to control their tempers, Asa fought to restrain the fury boiling within him. "Now listen, every one of you—the Peabodys in particular. For one year and a half I have toiled night and day to put food into your mouths, to keep whole this roof above your heads." He let his gaze bore into Prudence's flint-hard eyes.

"On you, and on this community, I have bestowed my best skill, giving far more than I have received by way of recompense. Should you, which I begin to doubt, possess a shred of gratitude, or a trace of Christian tolerance, you'll go quietly about your business. I intend to marry Jenny Starbird; that is the way 'tis and there isn't any 'tiser." In his agitation, Asa dropped into the handy phrases of his youth.

He wheeled to face Ahab. "Just now you proclaimed yourself head of this family. Very well, I concede you the responsibility. Since you are now become a success-ful shipbuilder—I'll now accord you the privilege of maintaining Prudence and our stepmother's children."

Ahab went red, hurriedly cleared his throat, "Now, Asey, don't git all 'riled up and go foamin' over. Mebbe I was a mite hasty—"

Syvanus Snow, who had no axe to grind in this matter, seized the opportunity to cry, "Stand steady, Ahab. There can be no compromise with evil. Remember that Righteousness and Lust cannot share the same roof-tree."

Asa smiled thinly. Why, the fellow was working himself up into a phrenzy. "Keep that up, 'Vanus, and you will come down with a fit of the strangury."

"Strangury? Bah!" Sylvanus Snow choked, his face red with passion.

"Oh, dear, oh, dear." Esther had slumped into a chair, and covered both her eyes with her hands. "'Vanus don't be so hard."

"Peace, woman! Too often has this proud-stomached fellow, arrogant in his pretended wisdom, violated the Holy Ordinances. Rest assured, Asa Peabody, that God's justice will level your pride, strike you a swift and a shrewd blow."

All at once Asa was comforted to realize that he could rise above such a puerile welter of malice, envy and petti-ness. Quite calmly he heard Sylvanus ranting, "The Dev-il will take you and your high-flung notions! A pox on your fancy cures and pagan violation of decency and modesty. Do you know"—Esther's husband whirled, facing the wide-eyed semi-circle—"that, under the cloak of professional necessity, this fellow would have caused Mrs. Whipple to expose her breast? Aye, he commanded that decent, God-fearing woman to lay naked her body that he might feed his lecherous gaze upon it!"

"That will do!" Asa's fists tightened by his side. "Your venomous and stupid self-righteousness I can tol-erate, but when you attack the ethics of my profession, Sylvanus Snow, you'd better clear out of here ere I lose my temper."

Morgan rose, and dark eyes a-gleam, moved to stand beside Asa. "That's telling him!" he panted. "Far's us Peabodys can see, 'Vanus Snow, yer just a damned snot-nosed old froze-spit!"

"Why, you damned insolent puppy!" Sylvanus rasped, but he made no overt move.

Esther's sobbing grew louder.

"I said, jest you git out o' this house, Snow," Asa repeated. "Esther, don't you go lest you've the mind."

"Now! Now!" Ahab arose hastily, his wooden peg thumping loud on the rough board flooring. "I allow mebbe we've all been too free-spoken. Let us speak of this matter another time. Come, Lizzie." He offered his arm. "Such proceedings are too unseemly for your tender ears." In frozen dignity Elizabeth Shannon arose and gathered her cloak about her.

"Yes, Ahab, I will go," she said. "But not before I've said my say. Listen to me, Asa Peabody. Whatever you may think, Jenny Starbird is a lazy, disloyal, cozening and unchaste female. Don't you dast ever bring her to this house after I move in."

No fool, Sylvanus Snow seized his opportunity to backtrack and turned away from the Peabody brothers. "Get your cape, Esther; 'tis time we got back for evening prayers." He raised a hand and rolled his eyes ceilingwards. "May God take pity on you, Asa Peabody, as a poor soul laboring in error." His manner was so damned sanctimonious that Asa laughed right aloud.

"Whilst you're praying, 'Vanus," he chuckled, "why don't you ask the Lord to let a mite l' Christian kindness seep into that pickle vat you call your soul?"

Presently only the brothers and their elder sister, Prudence, remained in the bare, sunset-lit room. The voices of the young children floated in through an open window together with the querulous mooing of the milch cow—she had not yet dropped her calf.

Prue sat, patched shoes held close together, head bent and eyes on the big, work-blunted hands limp in her lap. She looked terribly tired, plain and forlorn.

Asa squeezed Morgan's arm. "My thanks. Never will I forget your—your loyalty. Now, d'you mind taking the youngsters to evensong? Prue and I will join you later."

When Morgan went out, Prudence's neat white cap gleamed as she raised her head. In his sister's clear brown eyes he read anguish, yes, and contrition. "Oh, Asa, forgive me for what I said, especially before Sylvanus and the Shannons. I was un-Christian." Her lips were trembling and she looked so sad his anger melted.

"There, there Prue—don't take on so."

"I—I can't help it," she sobbed. "W-why must you remain so blind?"

He rested a hand on her thin shoulder. "I know what you mean, Prue—the gossip and all that. Perhaps more than you imagine. Still, my Jenny is a warm, kindly and very human girl. She must have been terribly lonely all these years."

"There might be plenty in what you say, but, Asey, she's not been as lonely as you allow." Prudence's lips once more became colorless slashes across her face. "Say what you will, she's still a Tory. The way she carried on with the *Margaretta*'s crew was a scandal. Why, old Jones' first officer was to her house night after night! When the British attacked us back in 'seventy-eight everybody heard her singing."

Asa said, "Jenny sings all the time. It's her way."

"Not like that. Oh Lord! Lord! It don't seem right." Prudence unseeingly stared at the floor. "Account of Pa was a widower and ailing, all these years I have scrimped and slaved and nursed Pa's children."

"So you have," Asa admitted softly. "God, in His high Heaven, knows no woman could have been less self-seeking, more tender and dutiful than you, Prudence."

Features rigid as those of a tragic mask, Prudence clung to his arm, sobbing gently. "Oh, Asey, my brother," she wailed, "why is it that some women, no matter how good they try to be, never find favor with men? Oh, it ain't just, it ain't right!" Her tears fell, spattered his hand.

"I've been virtuous all my life and never a soul has even come courtin' me. Then there's those, like that Starbird vixen, who thinks of nothin' but clothing, vanity and pleasure and—and now she's to have *two* good men! Oh why wasn't I granted just a little measure of Jenny's looks?"

Slowly Prudence's hand beat her flat breast. "Mebbe if only she weren't so pretty, I wouldn't feel so bad. But, oh, Jenny's so cheery, so pretty and so, so—" The spinster broke into a wild fit of weeping, sobbed out her despair, hunger and loneliness.

IV. THE NIGHT OF THE BIG RAIN

THE DISCOVERY CAME to Doctor Peabody as a mighty pleasant surprise that once the shock caused by the posting of his banns was over, Machias folk, for the most part, wiped off their sour expressions and came up to wish him well. The men, especially, found friendly things to say and quite a few of the womenfolk allowed as how, maybe, Jenny Starbird had never been granted much of a chance to win public approval. Was it really her fault that she had money *and a servant?* No. Just the same, everybody knew this New York girl hadn't sense enough to avoid boiling potatoes in an iron pot.

The true explanation of this sudden friendliness never occurred to Asa until, one afternoon, he wandered over to Doctor Clark Parker's cabin. In Parker's absence he had attended one of that physician's patients; following Doctor Townsend's advice he made it a point, under such conditions, invariably to stop by and explain what treatment he had adopted. Naturally, he returned such a patient to his colleague's care.

Answering Asa's gentle knock, Helen Parker appeared, smiling and cheery, for all that, at the back of the house, two of her babies were squalling like scalded tomcats.

"Well, I declare, Asa 'tis fine to lay eyes on you again. Come in and set a spell. Maybe there's a mite of cider left, but I fear there ain't. Clark—" she smiled apologetically—"he kinda took to the jug last night. You know how he is."

Asa nodded, stepped inside and accepted a cup of sweet milk instead.

"Clark! Dunno when he'll be back. He got took with another attack of 'ichthyosis' this morning." They both laughed at the joke, as always. "Ichthyosis" was what Doctor Clark Parker had christened a disease which prompted him to go fishing when he should have been tending his patients.

"Yes, just this morning Clark and I were talking about how fine it is you're fixing to marry and settle down right here in Machias. Lord knows, you have been a true friend to Clark and me." Helen dropped her big humid eyes. "Clark might have amounted to something like you saving for, well—" She nodded towards the empty stone jug. "But the Lord's ways are inscrutable, say I. Well, like I was sayin', the whole town's might pleased. They were afeared Mis' Starbird just *might* talk you into movin' away."

So *that* was why people were being so nice all of a sudden? He was pleased, all the same, that they valued his services so highly.

"Even poor Toby Blakiston—" he was the village idiot—"knows that there'd been above a dozen more graves in our church yard, but for you. Even that old thornback, Doc Falconer, has to admit it."

"My thanks, Helen, for saying it, even if 'tain't so. Will you and Clark come to my wedding?"

"Of course, if I can find somebody to mind the children."

" 'Drink to me-e-e only with thine eyes.' " Uncertain carolling sounded from the edge of the forest, then down the path wandering across a field in which were tethered the two Parker cows, appeared Helen's husband. Apparently, she had been mistaken as to the nature of his sport for he carried a fowling piece, not a fishing pole, across his shoulder.

He dropped his song and waved a disreputable hat, "Greetings and salutations, O gentle stranger within my gate!"

"Get any ducks?" Asa shouted.

"No. Didn't kill a thing," Parker chuckled wiping a round, very red face.

"Ye'd have averaged better if you'd stayed to home," his wife gibed, then they both broke into peals of laughter.

They seated themselves in the bare single room composing the cabin's lower storey but only after Parker had up-ended and shaken the jug to no avail.

"I am concerned over my sister," Asa announced when Helen shuffled off to separate two of her children doing battle in the backyard.

Parker's bloodshot eyes steadied, then narrowed.

"You've cause to worry. I've been meaning to have a confab with you over Esther. It's a crying shame old Falconer's tending—or should I say neglecting her? That pompous old donkey ain't fit to practice." He looked at Asa squarely. "For one thing, I s'pose you've noted Esther's baby ain't being carried naturally—any squaw could tell it. For another, Esther's such a little mite of a creature and that infant's near two weeks over-due by Helen's reckoning, and getting big as a cub bear. If she'd not had one child already, I'd be almighty fearful."

"I am fearful and I love little Esther best of all our women," Asa grunted, "but Sylvanus Snow hates me, always has. He is one of those Bible-pounding ignoramuses who believe only a woman can, with modesty, deliver an infant. Won't even hear of a modesty sheet." His unhappy gaze probed Parker's reddened features.

"All Falconer will do is purge, physick and bleed her nigh to death," Parker sighed. "If ever the word of God has been perverted, it is that nonsense they find in Genesis which suggests, that, because old Mother Eve fell from grace, children must ever afterwards be birthed in sorrow and pain. I'll talk to Sylvanus," Parker promised, "though I dunno as it'll accomplish much."

"Thank you. Esther's a fine woman and deserves better care." Asa nodded, reached for his hat. "Well, I'd best be gettin' along home. Looks like there'll be a right smart tempest striking out of the west before long. Saw fishermen scudding for home on my way up here."

Helen Parker reappeared. "Mercy! I hope it don't lightning enough to sour my cream. There's three big pans a-cooling downstairs. Clark, just you go and fetch in them cows. 'Twouldn't do for 'em to get struck by lightning. They're about the valuablest things we own."

"Plenty of time," her spouse rumbled, "Plenty of time. Sorry, Asey, I can't offer you a noggin but—"

Asa smiled; the reek of hard cider was still on Doctor Parker's breath. "Let me know if there's aught I can do for Esther." He lingered beside the greasy marks of many hands on the door frame.

"You can rely on it. I'll send over Hepzibah—the best midwife I know of—to look the patient over. Shall I instruct her to let you know if matters get too bad?"

Asa nodded. "Yes, tell her to warn me," he said, and went tramping off down a sandy track leading to that straggling cluster of homes which composed Machias.

"Better make tracks," he advised himself when he saw how tall the orange, white and black thunderheads were piling up to the westward. The birds stopped singing and everywhere people were hurrying to secure their livestock and to close their windows and doors against the storm.

At first Asa figured his bedroom window's shutter had fetched loose. No wonder if it had, the wind was howling and screaming louder than ever through those tall firs beyond Pals well-built log house. Godfreys! This was a more than ordinary tempest. Why, lying there in bed he could hear waves beating a furious tempo against the river harbor's edges.

Then something about the cadence of that banging made him rouse up. Always a light sleeper, his profession further had trained him to arouse at the slightest alarm.

He knew now that the shutter wasn't loose; someone was knocking, pounding desperately on its solid white-pine panels. First thing he did was toss a huge scroll of birch bark on the ashes of the fire, then, barefoot and with long nightshirt flapping about his ankles, he ran to raise the window sash.

The birch bark, flaring, illumined a wild, rain-streaked face just outside; it was that of a gray-haired woman with a shawl pulled tight over her head. A sickening pang of apprehension shot through Asa when he recognized Granny Hepzibah, reputedly the cleverest "wise woman" in the Eastern District.

"Oh, Doctor," she quavered over the rush of the wind, "you got to come. Quick, quick! I done the best I could but—she's near gone."

Even before she'd done talking, Asa was stuffing the nightshirt's tails into a pair of pantaloons, and, while Granny Hepzibah sheltered her head behind the blind he pulled on a seacoat, and crammed bare feet into a pair of sturdy brogans. As always, his medicine chest and instrument case lay ready to hand.

Barely a minute elapsed before Asa let himself out into the gale-driven rain. Good, the old creature already was struggling off towards town, her body bent against the blast and skirts fluttering like mad.

Lord, how black and wild was the night. He gasped for breath, had to shield his eyes against the invisible raindrops. Overtaking Hepzibah Devens, he took her arm and fairly dragged her off her feet in his hurry to round the line of the cove. A smell of brackish water was strong. All the houses they passed were uniformly dark and not even a watchdog or a sentry goose—these fowls, as everyone knew, made the best lookouts—raised a clamor.

Only after they struggled, drenched and breathless, past Burnham's Tavern did a faint light become visible.

What time it could be, Asa had no idea, but some sixth sense informed him that, under normal conditions, day would not be long in breaking. Just outside Sylvanus Snow's house he put his mouth to Granny Devens' ear.

"What about 'Vanus?"

"Useless, all of a scatter," she snapped. "When that pious whistle-belly ain't been raisin' ructions, he's been down on his hambones praying like mad ever since yer pore little sister took the pains."

A dreadful doubt shook Asa. "How long since she went into labor?"

"Oh, 'twere round six of the evening, but Snow and that old fraud Doctor Falconer," she sniffed her contempt, "didn't summon me till near midnight."

"Is Falconer in there?" Asa demanded dashing the wet from his eyes.

"No, he declared her a hopeless case, and went home sayin' God's will would be done, and that was all there was to it."

Asa said thickly, "What God intends is yet to be proved. Granny you go in the back door. Get ready a bucket of cold water, another of hot water and every blessed piece of cloth you can lay hands on."

"There ain't no cloths," the midwife cried, her face a pale blur in the gloom. "When I left the pore little soul been bleeding like a stuck shoat for all I could do for her."

Asa gave the old creature a shove towards the rear of Snow's big frame house. "Then tear up bedsheets—I must have pledgets and bandages."

Without knocking, he pushed open Sylvanus Snow's front door and paused on the threshold, face streaked with rain, hair hanging in lank strands and medicine bag dripping.

For a moment the figure outlined against a far wall made no move. Sylvanus Snow was kneeling, staring at an open Bible propped on a chair before him. His hands were clasped and his eyes riveted on a page illumined by a beef-tallow candle, the rank stench of which filled the cheerless interior.

The door blew wider open and the candle flame nearly failed. Stiffly, Sylvanus got to his feet growling, "What do you want? No Pharisee or lechers are welcome here."

"Stow that guff. Where's my sister?" Asa used his

buttocks to close the door, shifted the instrument case to under his left arm. Never, thought Asa, had he read such malignant hatred written across a man's face. At the same time a deadly sense of outrage was clouding his brain.

"Answer me, you great blundering idiot." Three long strides carried Asa into the center of the room. "Every second is of importance. *Where* is Esther?"

"You shall not defile her body with your pagan, indecent hands and eyes. I forbid you. Get out of my house!"

"A plague out of Egypt on you!" Asa snapped. "Stand aside."

Sylvanus clenched his fists and gathered himself. "You shall not approach my wife! God hath decreed that a female body is for the eyes of her husband, alone."

Asa said slowly and distinctly, "Get out of my way, Sylvanus Snow. I am going to my sister."

"I'll have the law on you! How dare you break in like a thief in the night?" Sylvanus Snow's eyes were round as those of a night-prowling cat. Jaw muscles swelling, he aimed a savage blow at his brother-in-law.

Barely in time Asa avoided the blow, then, spinning on the balls of his feet, he tossed the medicine bag onto a chair. Squaring off, he smashed at his enemy's throat. The blow wasn't effective because Sylvanus Snow was leaping back when it fell.

As Asa had hoped, Esther's husband came charging, in a blind fury of flailing fists. The physician easily evaded the lunge and succeeded in driving a fist hard against his brother-in-law's ear. Though it rattled Sylvanus, he returned to the attack in savage determination and twice his fists found a mark.

One punch landed on the side of Asa's head and sent a handful of white-hot sparks to flying before his eyes. Then the bigot's other fist landed just above Asa's groin. It hurt like fury.

Asa, however, was solving his problem, felt his fist go *splat!* against Sylvanus' nose and snap his head back, hard—then his shirt bosom suddenly was stained dark. Pressing his vantage, Asa rained hard punches at his adversary until Sylvanus went down, smashing a chair beneath him.

Panting, Asa gave his enemy an intent look, undecided as to whether he should linger. No. Sylvanus lay semiconscious and precious instants were ticking by with inexorable rapidity, so, wheezing for breath, Asa ran over to retrieve his medicine bag then bounded into the bedroom. Here he paused just long enough to drop into place a heavy oaken bar. Dragging a sodden shirtsleeve across his forehead he then turned to estimate the situation.

By the light of half a dozen guttering candles, Granny Devens could be seen fluttering helplessly beside that bed upon which lay Esther.

In one gesture Asa Peabody ripped off his seacoat and ran to the bedside. Breath halted in his throat when he perceived how hideously, incredibly prominent was her abdomen. He snatched up her wrist. Damn! His own heart was pounding so hard it was impossible to detect a pulsation.

"Feel her pulse, Hepzibah—I am too shaken. Can you get it? Can you get it? I can't feel anything."

Granny Devens obeyed but cast him a despairing look. "Ain't been no pulse I could feel since I got back. She's still a-breathin' a mite, though."

Sick with alarm, Asa lifted his sister's eyelids and was shocked to find the eyeballs had rolled back in her head; still, Granny Devens was right! There remained the faintest sort of respiration. Esther's color was a greasy yellow, her parted lips shone purple-pink but flecked with the blood she had drawn in biting them during climaxes of her travail. When he flung back the patchwork quilt he gasped. The impact of his realizations were horrifying. There remained only hope now of saving the child, and that was to attempt the nearly impossible.

As he ripped open his instrument case and selected a scalpel, he half-heard bumping sounds in the other room. Asa paid no attention; all the world was lost save this bed and the motionless form upon it. He was slashing apart his sister's dreadfully sodden night shirt when a pounding commenced on the door connecting with the living room. He ignored it. Granny Devens screeched, averted her face, when his knife slit the strained, faintly mottled skin containing the arc of the patient's abdomen. What little blood the poor woman had left in her body welled quickly out of the incision, warm and terribly slippery on his chilled hands.

Despite everything, Asa remembered what he must do. Where does the placenta attach itself to the wall of the womb? As he worked, magically, the severed muscles drew apart wider and wider. The blue-white steel blade became lost to sight, but his fingers guided it and faltered not at all.

Oh God! Esther's child was the same dreadful purple color as Tom Duneen, when cut down from the gallows tree. Granny Devens, gray hair flying, was terrified; only crouched in a corner, apron over head, and wailed.

A new sound impacted on the bedroom door. That murdering fool Sylvanus was using an axe! He must have become crazed or he'd have remembered that he could have entered through a window, or the back door, for that matter. The umbilical cord was twisted, anchored by the dark red mass of the placenta.

"C'mere," he snarled at the midwife. 'Sever the cord and tie it, or, by the living God, I'll cut your throat. Do as I say! Tie that cord!''

"Oh, no! No!'' Granny Devens emitted a whimper, but scuttled over to the mantelpiece and grabbed a short length of cod line she'd left there for the purpose.

A moment later the still purplish and inert infant was freed from the placenta. Hurriedly, Asa gripped the infant by its ankles, struck it a sharp blow across the buttocks. The empurpled little creature moved, but only gave a convulsive jerk. Must do something.

Good, Hepzibah had obeyed his instructions and the two buckets were ready. He plunged the tiny figure first into the pail of warm water, then, after a momentary pause, into the cold, then back into the warm water. Three times he did this before he again struck the tiny buttocks a sharp blow. No sound. What was wrong? Then he remembered and the tip of his forefinger curved into that tiny mouth. Ha! He fetched out a lump of mucous. One more blow, then a thin, mewing sound rose above the crashing blows of Sylvanus' axe.

"Here, keep him warm."

'"Her,'" the midwife corrected. "More's the pity."

Asa turned to busy himself again, but abruptly checked his movement. There could be no doubt that Esther, his sister, now was dead.

v. THE MEETING HOUSE

FROM THE VERY start of this war, the Machias' Committee of Public Safety and Correspondence had constituted about the only local government over the community. Sylvanus Snow therefore took his grievance before the committee the very next day after Esther's frail, mutilated body had been laid to rest. Hollow-eyed and consumed with grief, Asa answered the sheriff's summons to present himself at the Meeting House.

Built just before the war, the Meeting House still smelt of fresh pine, and pitch still wept from cracks along the skinned logs inside.

Despite that all logic was on his side, Asa didn't deceive himself that, for him, this was not a mighty critical moment.

Sylvanus Snow was nowhere to be seen. It turned out that, after having sworn out an arrest warrant charging one Asa Peabody, B.M., with trespass, assault, obscene conduct and, of all things, murder—he'd departed in a hurry.

While listening to a reading of the charges against him, Asa's sombre brown gaze examined the committeemen; present were Deacon Joe Libby, Colonel John Allen, Stephen Smith, and Colonel Benjamin Foster, still in the old hunting shirt he had worn coming from the forts down river. Also in attendance were Jeremiah O'Brien, and Ahab's father-in-law-to-be, old Jimmie Shannon.

The only non-member committeeman was Captain Ephraim Chase, master of the *Neshquoit*, that locally armed and supported sloop-of-war which defended access to the Machias River from Birch Point to just off Scott's farm. Scott's burnt-down tanyard was all Admiral Sir George Collier could show to justify his four months' blockade maintained with no less than two Royal frigates, a sloop and a cutter.

The morning was still so young that the robins and thrushes had just quit singing and, at the foot of a lane, the town cowherd's horn was braying, warning people to turn loose their cattle. All day these would feed in the fresh water meadows under the warden's watchful eyes, and within range of his old Tower musket.

After Deacon Libby had read Sylvanus' charges, Asa remained silent, just stood rubbing one blunt brown hand against the other. In a few minutes now he guessed he'd learn whether Maine folks were any different from the pickle-faced, narrow-minded folk inhabiting the coast further south. Right from the time they'd settled in this wilderness, Maine folks always had prided themselves on their common sense and liberal way of looking at things. For instance, they held it no sin for a man to adorn his house with graceful moldings; they even liked to laugh and to live as comfortably as might be.

"Gentlemen, all I ask is that you put yourselves in the position I found myself on the night of the big rain," Asa invited the committee in his precise, grave tones. "I am a physician and, as such, am sworn to save human life under any and all conditions. What would you each have done, had you learned that your sister was perishing, needlessly dying for want of proper medical care?"

He felt their eyes coming to rest upon him, some in hostility, some in sympathy. There was no doubt that old man Shannon's voice would be raised against him.

"That Esther Snow was my dearly beloved sister, makes no difference. I'll follow the same course and run the same risks to relieve any woman of this settlement. So, if you aim to jail me on that account, you better go ahead."

Colonel Allen, his second-best militia uniform looking sadly faded in this bright light, said quietly, "Doctor, pray allow us to judge your conduct. You may continue."

"I expect you all are aware that Sylvanus Snow forbade my attending his wife, my sister, and offered me bodily harm when I insisted on attempting to relieve her agonies."

"Did 'Vanus strike the first blow?" Deacon Libby's eyes narrowed themselves behind his square-lensed spectacles.

"Yes. He caught me a clip on the jaw."

"You fought him?" asked Stephen Smith.

"Only wanted to get by—I didn't want to fight him. As it was, my hands were shaking so badly that—"

"—You bungled the operation, and killed your sister?" suggested James Shannon.

The physician's eyes swung slowly. "I expect you've been listening to Doctor Falconer. Well, all I have to say to that is—Falconer went off and left Esther and her infant to die, because he hadn't sufficient art to save either."

"Easy now," cautioned Jerry O'Brien. "Doc Falconer has been here a sight longer than you."

"Does that make him a better physician?" Asa's voice

deepened. "I say Falconer was derelict in his duty when he went home, leaving my sister to die, because he was afraid to defy Sylvanus' obscene objections against allowing a physician to examine his wife."

"Let's get back to the main question," Colonel Allen suggested. "Was Esther Snow alive when you arrived?"

Asa hesitated. For the life of him he couldn't swear whether he had heard Esther's breath or no.

Sturdy old Jeremiah O'Brien shook his silvery head. "Damnation, Allen, we all heard the midwife swear Esther was dead. Me, I say Asa here performed a shining miracle in saving that infant for this community." He glowered at James Shannon.

"That ain't the point," Shannon insisted. "We're here to uphold the law which says a man has the say over his wife; and Peabody, here, downright defied Esther's lawful husband and beat him up. Is Machias a law-abiding community, or ain't it?"

Colonel Allen picked at a smear of pitch defacing the pale blue cuff of his tunic. "Personally," he observed, "perhaps illogically, my friends, I have always felt that the law's one thing; common sense is different and of superior worth. Therefore, it's my bounden conviction," his fine big voice filled and resounded throughout the otherwise empty Meeting House, "that, law or no law, Sylvanus Snow weren't privileged to condemn his wife to painful death through a *nasty*—" he emphasized the word and looked hard at Jim Shannon—"interpretation of the Scriptures. Right now, I'll lay any taker that Parson Lion can quote you a dozen texts from the Holy Bible that makes nonsense out of what Sylvanus Snow preaches."

Silence prevailed in the Meeting House until Captain Ephraim Chase drawled, "'Pears like Allen's right as rain. Where's the use in settin' a young feller a-studyin' how to doctor folks and then deny him the right to use that there knowledge?" Warming to his theme, Captain Chase pounded the table. "I'm a-tellin' you, Asa Peabody here hez preserved more lives in one year than that old poop, Falconer, has in five.

"Puttin' this matter in a religious way, can any of you name a better Christian in Machias than Asa Peabody? Why, time out o' mind he's physicked folk so poverty-poor they couldn't pay him a copper penny—and he knowing it all along. Colonel Allen, ain't he cared fer yer garrisons nigh on a year 'thout axing a stiver? He's doctored my crews, month in and month out, and won't accept pay.''

Allen jumped right up. "Right you are, Eph, and I'm ashamed that this here committee has to be reminded of Doc Peabody's patriotism. Deacon, I claim we're wasting Doctor Peabody's time. Me, I moved down here from Nova Scotia account of I heard Machias people were tolerant—and so they are, mostly. Some of you, like Steve Smith, and you, Joe Libby, are original settlers. Jerry O'Brien, if your pa was alive I'll warrant he wouldn't stand seeing a fine and able physician gravelled by a dirty-minded crackpot like Sylvanus Snow."

'Twas a mighty fine feeling warmed Asa's soul when the committee showed hands to sustain or reject Sylvanus' complaint. Eph Chase, being no committeeman, had no official voice but he cheered louder than any when, with only one dissenting vote, Sylvanus Snow's charges were dismissed.

vi. Shift Wedding

Because he owned only two suits of clothes, four linen shirts and a few smallclothes, Asa's sea chest wasn't exactly a heavy burden when he dumped it onto the tail of Elmer Foster's oxcart. His medical books, laboriously collected, and his medicine chest weighed far more.

In view of the family's attitude it was only sensible that he move into his future wife's comfortable little house.

Sadly, his half-brother and sisters watched him lug his belongings along the clamshell walk to where Elmer Foster's big brown ox stood solemnly chewing its cud. Unnecessarily prolonging her baking, Prudence remained in the kitchen. Morgan was working down at Jeremiah O'Brien's shipyard along with Ahab; there were two new schooners on the ways.

Yes, sir, Lionel, Purity and Constance looked real downcast. Who could whittle a prettier doll's head, or a tidier toy sailboat than he?

Now that the oxcart was loaded, the Foster boy wiped away the last crumbs of a mid-day snack and picked up his ox goad. At that the children began to whimper.

Asa said, "Don't take on so, Connie. Why, I ain't leaving for the West Indies. I'm only moving down the road a piece. You and Lionel and Purity will be coming over all the time. Get on the cart; you can ride 'round the cove."

In the kitchen, he found Prudence, sleeves rolled up to the elbows and kneading her dough.

"I am leaving now, Frue—"

"Are you?" his sister said without looking up. "Well, I hope *you* will look in on us sometime." Her fingers worked at the dough with such needless energy that the white substance came surging up between her bony fingers.

"Prue, won't you wish me well?" He marvelled that hate and envy could so spoil an otherwise unselfish and gentle disposition.

"Asey, you should know better than to ask that of me." Quite deliberately, she looked at her younger brother. "What I say is, in a short while you'll be back. I'm so sure of it I'm keeping your room ready. Always remember, Asa, you are welcome here."

Asa tried to sound light-hearted. "By the same token, Prue, you'll always find a welcome at our home."

"Don't say 'our' like that!" she burst out. "I—I can't stand it."

In a rare demonstration of feeling, he went over to kiss her thin and leathery cheek.

"I wish mightily you'd attend my wedding tonight. Won't you come over?"

When Prudence jerked her head away two drops sketched dark spots on the well-floured bread board. In a thick voice, she advised, "You better go, Asey, before I say something I might be sorry for."

The children tagged out to the road where now the dust lay soft, thick and yellow under their bare feet.

After rolling down his sleeves Asa hugged the children briefly, then swung up onto the cart's tail. Young Elmer Foster raised his goad. "Hup! You Tiger! Hup!" Obediently, the ox put his weight into the collar and the axles commenced to screech like twenty cat fights.

Elmer's gap teeth showed dark in the sunburnt expanse of his face when presently he observed. "Say, Doctor Peabody, it must be quite sumpin' to be gettin' married."

"It certainly is quite sumpin'. Can't we move a little faster?"

"Git along, Tiger!" the boy yelled and used his nail-pointed goad until the cart's solid wooden wheels began to *clunk* more rapidly over stones studding the rutted track at frequent intervals.

A mercy, too, his route to Jenny's did not require passing through town.

"Well, well," Asa reflected, "on this twentieth day of June in the year of Our Lord 1781 I'm going to be married. Hope Jenny don't really come down with a cold—" She had suffered from a watering of her eyes and nose, and yesterday she'd complained of an uncommon sore throat.

All at once he found himself wondering, "Is Sabra Stanton married, too? Must be. She was a sight too pretty to remain single." Odd, he could remember the different ways she had dressed her hair, the clear, dark gray of her eyes, the merry curve which so seldom deserted her lips. Um, she'd be all of twenty years.

Of course she'd married. Curious, her giving him that book and talking so sweet that last night in Boston—and then not answering any one of three letters. Lord, women were unfathomable as the flight of birds. Almost guiltily, he realized that *Evelina* lay at the bottom of his book chest—a fragile strand attaching him to the past.

Seated on his clothes chest, Asa watched the roadside slip by as the cart rocked lazily along the sandy road. If only Peter Burnham could have attended the ceremony—and odd but witty Lucius Devoe! Their presence at the wedding supper would make it a merrier occasion than it promised to be; too bad that he had not the vaguest notion where either of them might be living.

Still and all, Asa was feeling almighty set up. The action of the Committee of Safety, added to the friendliness of a majority of the townsfolk, was fine to dwell on.

Because the afternoon had grown downright warm, Elmer paused to breathe his ox in the shade of a grove of sugar maples through which was drifting a stratum of blue-gray smoke. Seized by uneasiness, Asa jumped down from the cart to investigate, though the woods weren't really dry enough to take fire.

In a minute he found Hilkiah Fenlason busy burning charcoal with which to supply the new smithy he had set up between Burnham's Tavern and the Meeting House. He was quite an old man, folks said, to have dreamed up such a venture—really too old—for charcoal-burning wasn't exactly a holiday.

Yesterday Lionel had told how the old fellow stood quite heavy logs up on end with their ends touching—like an Indian teepee—four and five feet long they were at the core of this wooden cone, but much shorter around the edges. Asa studied Fenlason's just completed oven with interest and saw that, inside the stack, there were a lot of sticks taller than the blacksmith himself. As Asa trampled up through the woods he judged this charcoal stack must be near twelve feet across its base.

Fenlason had built sods up to cover the whole cone until it looked, for all the world, like an earthen pyramid mound, topped by a small smoky flue. Further, it might be entered by a short tunnel leading into its center. The smith must just recently have lit a fire at the end of this entrance.

"Howdy, Hilkiah; how're things going?"

The old man's frown relaxed when he recognized the physician. "Wal, I allow I hev made a fair start. If you want good charcoal, cookin' it ain't no short affair."

Asa noticed a lean-to. "Do you aim to stay out all night?"

"Yep. If your fire flares up, you hev to choke her down else the hull stack will go up in a blaze of glory, and ye won't hev nowt left but ashes."

Old Fenlason puttered around to press a sod over a chink from which a spiral of blue smoke had commenced to creep. "Aye, Mr. Peabody, 'coal-makin's a mighty lonesome business; if ye've of a mind this evenin', stop by. There's somethin' in yonder jug which ain't exactly spring water."

"My thanks," Asa laughed, "but I can't accept—I'm marrying the Widow Starbird in about two hours time."

"Now dew tell! Well, when you git around to needin' a rest you kin come to this lean-to. I'll let you sleep and plague you nary a bit." Baring his few remaining yellowed teeth, Fenlason leered and emitted a cackling, high-pitched laugh. "You're sure a lucky young fellow; you've got yerself a neat arm full of female to warm yer bed—and no mistake."

About four of the afternoon, Colonel John Allen, first of the wedding guests arrived, lugging a big black bottle and a pair of brass candlesticks in his arms. Asa let him in.

"The bottle," Allen announced, grinning broadly and tossing his hat onto a settle, "is for you, and the candlesticks a present for your lady. Came out o' a Dutch vessel wrecked up near Bagaduce.''

"Godfreys! these are *mighty* handsome,'' Asa declared admiringly. ''Jenny will be tickled pink with them.''

With care he set the candlesticks among a small collection of wedding presents scattered about the living room table. He showed the colonel a pretty little tinder pistol left by Captain Chase on his way down to the boat landing.

Then, there was a niddy-noddy for reeling homespun, sent by the Widow McNeil. When it appeared, Asa felt a plucking at his throat because he knew that niddy-noddy was from Mrs. McNeil's own spinning wheel and that she could ill afford to part with it. There was also a cheese press, a draining board, and a nest of cherrywood bowls from various patients.

Probably the most valuable of all the gifts was a handsomely engraved Spanish boarding pistol Jeremiah O'Brien had sent. Mounted with what looked like real gold, it was half the weight of those clumsy weapons most officers were forced to jam into their breeches tops. 'Twould come in handy on some of those long night rides a physician must expect to take.

Morgan had whittled some mighty tasty cracker stamps out of applewood. The initials ''J.P.'' on them were done as neat as any engraver in Boston could have cut them.

The other guests put in an appearance and, pretty soon, Jenny, invisible behind the sheet barring her bedroom door, began to call out, ''Isn't the minister here yet?''

The Reverend Mr. Lion arrived just at sunset, its light touching his thick silvery hair with fire.

In Mrs. Starbird's little living room there had gathered Doctor and Mrs. Clark Parker, Colonel John Allen and young Morgan Peabody, looking mighty serious and more like his father every minute; Mrs. McNeil clutched a ragged shawl to her breast and looked ready to burst into tears of happiness. Poor soul, all too well, she knew what being a widow meant.

Wateka, the half-breed Abenaki who worked for Jenny, cast Asa a shy silent question.

"Yes. We are all quite ready.''

Pretty soon the door to Jenny's bedroom opened.

By the light of two sperm-oil candles—which gave nice clear light and didn't smell up the living room—the Reverend Mr. Lion for once appeared embarrassed. If, in the past he had performed a shift wedding, it must have been long ago; for he went red as fire when he inquired of Wateka, "Your—er mistress is, er—prepared according—er—to custom?"

Wateka nodded, dodged back behind the sheet.

The Reverend Mr. Lion turned to Asa, beckoned the witnesses closer and, from a side pocket, produced a prayer book. Mrs. McNeil commenced to sniffle softly.

"Mistress Starbird?" he called. Came a soft rustling noise, then pink feet and a shapely length of bare limbs become visible below the sheet. Young Morgan was staring open-mouthed.

"Thrust your hand through this sheet."

Asa swallowed hard when, promptly enough, the pink-tipped hand of Jenny Starbird appeared through a hole cut in the fabric.

"Jenny Starbird, do you swear before God that you bring to this ceremony nothing of this world's goods; er—that you stand—er—just as the Lord created you?"

"I do." Jenny's voice sounded small and rather frightened.

The minister turned to the witnesses. "I call on you to bear witness that, to her marriage with Asa Peabody, Jenny Starbird brings naught but herself. Therefore, no man truthfully may claim that she hath endowed Asa Peabody with any of this world's goods."

"So, on becoming the wife of Asa Peabody you bring nothing material, neither do you bring any debts."

Doctor Parker grinned broadly, murmured to his wife, "Won't 'Vanus Snow be tickled over that?"

"Asa Peabody join this woman's hand with yours," the minister directed, then drew a deep breath, and commenced to recite the marriage ceremony.

VII. NADIR

HOW GRAND to have the house to themselves, now that jollifications, however modest, were over. Only a few minutes ago, Mrs. Parker, assisted by Colonel Allen, had led her most amusing but well-jingled spouse off in the direction of Machias. Even before that, Morgan had bade the newly wedded pair a shy good night. One thing was clear; nothing that Asa could ever think or do would be wrong in the eyes of this sturdy, black-browed lad. Leaving, he'd whistled defiantly at a screech owl hunting in an orchard new-planted across the river road.

Now all was still save for a faint *thud-thudding* of Indian drums in the encampment across the river; the Abenakis 'Quoddies and Mic-Macs were raising a phullabaloo.

Jenny Peabody sat happily beside her new husband with her head on his shoulder, snug within the assurance provided by his arm. Right now, she felt she had begun a new life. Where it would end, and how, there was no telling. She tried not to cough and hoped he wouldn't notice the dry and feverish condition of her skin.

It went without saying that they'd have children. She'd always wanted some and she'd never been able to figure why she and Philip had never been so blessed.

On Asa's lap she stirred, hunted for her kerchief. Why, tonight of all nights, should she be coming down with an influenza? Asa, all the same, thought his bride looked all-fired pretty by the firelight, with her piquant profile picked out in warm rose tones, with her yellow hair snaring any number of faint golden tints.

How becoming was her gown; he'd never seen it before, nor her daintily contrived blue satin slippers, for that matter. Jenny looked so young, so fresh, so virginal it seemed well-nigh incredible that she'd known three years of married life. He found the full sweep of her bosom more entrancing than ever. Thank fortune she'd arranged a modest piece of lace much higher than it was her custom. Why?

Perhaps she feared exposure. Only this afternoon she had admitted, carelessly enough, that her sore throat was no better. For it he gave her a decoction of milk and honey, containing a dash of Peruvian bark.

Eagerly, tenderly, his arm slipped about his wife's tiny waist. Judas Maccabaeus! She was his now; his to love and strive for.

When his lips brushed hers he was disconcerted to recognize a faint mephitic aura. All the same he ignored it when she turned, and covered his eyes, mouth and face with kisses—her manner ardent and indescribably provocative.

"Asa, Asa, my husband, I suppose you've heard talk that I haven't always been wise or clever, that I've even been, well, indiscreet on occasion. At this moment I wish to tell you—"

He laid silencing, imperative fingers across her lips. "Sweeting, recall only one thing. When you married me you left behind debts of all sorts. I have no interest in them."

"Oh, bless you, Asa, bless you, my husband." To his surprise Jenny wept a little while, but quickly dried her eyes.

A log in the fireplace fell, raised a handful of jewel-bright sparks to swirl up the clay chimney. She gave him a swift kiss, then jumped up, diminutive body outlined against the firelight.

"Shall we share a noggin of Colonel Allen's cordial, before—?" Her light gray eyes swung towards the bedroom door from which the curtain long since had been removed.

They drank with a recklessness which took Asa's breath away. Gorry! Even in Boston, people weren't so handy with their liquor.

"What do you think of your wife?" Jenny demanded, dancing and whirling before him. "Look, darling, has your wife pretty legs?"

When, laughing, Jenny flipped up her petticoats high enough to expose trim legs gartered in blue ribbon, Asa felt his whole body grow hot.

"Jenny, for pity's sake—take pity on me."

Picking up her glass, she ran towards him. "To our happiness here, and beyond. Oh, Asa! What an innocent you are. Really, 'tis a good thing you've married a widow." Again she dropped onto his lap, put a finger under his chin. "Confession is good for the soul. Tell me, Asa, have you known other—girls?"

Scarlet to his hair line he mumpled, "Boston's a big town—I—well, it wasn't exactly pleasant. Besides I'm physician enough to fear—to be frightened."

A sudden stillness immobilized Jenny's features. "Frightened? Why? What of?"

"Many things. You wouldn't know it, Jenny, but such

waterfront doxies know many men and from them contract certain hideous distempers—'' He broke off, looked
shy and shamefaced. ''What a fine thing to be talking
about on our wedding night!''

''Yes, aren't we the great sillies?'' Passionately she
kissed him, then arose. ''Bank the fire, my dearest; by
the time you've done it I will be awaiting—oh, so tenderly.''

On light feet Jenny vanished through her bedroom
door, fingers already tearing at a series of salmon-colored
bows which secured her bodice.

The cordial warmed Asa, made him feel so fine he
crossed over and poured out a second noggin. When he'd
downed it he went over to the hearth and, very seriously
indeed, raked log ends together before employing a gourd
to cover them with ashes.

He straightened, smiled to himself; Godfreys! He'd
found a wife—a mother for his seed. What a beautiful,
what a dainty thing Jenny was! No man in the Eastern
District could boast of a lovelier helpmeet.

When he heard her summons he stripped off his coat
and hung it, employing absurd care, to a chair, then he
sought the bedroom to find Jenny seated on the edge of
their bed and busily tying up her gleaming hair. Beside
the big four-poster a single candle created a limited radi-
ance.

''Jenny!'' he cried hoarsely. ''My Jenny!''

Even as he took her into his arms and the loose fabric
of the muslin gown billowed beneath his touch, Jenny
smothered a little cough and cleared her throat. Asa
slowly straightened, his gaze shifting from Jenny's parted lips to the base of her throat. What he discerned by the
candlelight was so appalling that had a club been brought
down upon his head he would have felt less stunned.

''Oh, God!'' he thought and reeled aside. ''Oh, merciful Jesus! Deny me this!''

But there could be no denying that evidence.

Unaware of the fact that her husband was trembling,
shaking like a colt which scents a bear, Jenny still re-
clined against the pillows.

''Lover,'' she whispered. ''Come to me, my husband.''

Because he remained rigid, unresponsive, Jenny

stirred and opened her eyes and when she saw his expression, she sat suddenly upright, hurriedly closed her shift.

"Oh, Asa, isn't this a nuisance? I fear I have taken the scarlet fever. I should have told you, I know, but, Asa, dear, I couldn't bear to delay our wedding." The timbre of her voice soared. "Asa! What's wrong? Don't look at me like this—what's wrong with me?"

Once he commenced to back away Jenny scrambled out of bed; he flung out a fending arm. "Oh, no, Jenny! *NO!*"

Weeping, bewildered and terrified, Jenny collapsed on the floor. She raised stricken eyes. "Asa. Tell me truly. I—I have the French pox?"

"Aye, and damned well advanced."

Asa paused only long enough to put on his shoes before picking up his coat and running out of doors. With the jerky motions of a mechanical contrivance he set his feet to the river road. Somewhere, perhaps half a mile away was the blacksmith's charcoal fire.

VIII. A SHALLOP IN MID-STREAM

HILKIAH FINLASON was so sound asleep he failed to rouse when Asa hailed softly, so the physician was able to seat himself, without explanations, upon a log before the lean-to. For hours he remained so, peering miserably, unseeingly at a fierce red circle showing at the base of Finlason's charcoal cone. Under the stress of his grief, Asa's big hands tightened until their knuckles cracked.

A maelstrom of fears and impulses whirled about his brain, defying all attempts to re-align emotions and to recover reasoning power. Gradually, his sense of outrage subsided, permitting his tortured mind to commence functioning more rationally.

It could not be denied that here was a young woman stricken with a terrible, and generally fatal, malady. Accordingly, when the first gray streaks of dawn commenced to cast the maples' and chestnuts' tops into silhouettes, Asa arose quietly. The blacksmith still lay snoring mightily with shaggy head pillowed on his leather breeches.

To Asa's mild surprise, the door to his new home was

standing open, just as he might have left it when bursting out. Once he entered the house he stood listening, but hearing no sound, concluded that Jenny had dropped off to sleep. Stooping, he righted that chair from which he had snatched his coat; then, walking very softly, he sought his medicine chest and selected ingredients for Doctor Cullen's decoction. One of those new cherry-wood bowls would substitute excellently for a mortar, he thought, and set to work.

Presently, the faintest imaginable sound attracted Asa's attention. Concluding that Jenny must be awake and washing, he pushed open the bedroom door.

Forcing a smile he began, "Jenny, you must take treatment. I—"

The words died on his lips while his body immobilized itself. From a cord inexpertly knotted about one of the roof beams, Jenny Peabody's body hung suspended directly above an overturned footstool.

Gripped by complete paralysis of the will power, he remained an indeterminable time staring upon the suicide. The gown, trailing to the floor, and the lowness of the ceiling created an impression that Jenny must be standing there in her night shift.

A subconscious force sent tears to blurring Asa's eyes. He dropped onto his knees and, covering his face with his hands, prayed forgiveness from the Heavenly Father for Jenny, that she had taken her life; for himself, that he had hurt her so.

After that, the physician stumbled outdoors, frightening away a few robins worm-hunting in Jenny's flower garden. He studied a patch of sandy soil between two half-grown apple trees which yet retained a few pink and white blossoms.

In the woodshed he came across a spade, and fell furiously to work. Because the ground was sandy and he encountered very few stones Jenny's grave was dug before the sun lifted over the forest.

Precise and dispassionate as if performing a major operation, Asa cut down his wife's slight body, arranged its stiffening limbs. Tight-lipped, he swathed Jenny in a brand-new linen sheet and found no small trouble in keeping her shining hair from escaping her improvised shroud.

Only when the grave was refilled and a low mound of

fresh earth had risen between the apple trees, did he pause for breath. He had to. All the world was spinning about his head.

On a plain pine board he carved Jenny's name, and the date, then planted it as a headboard.

After that he went indoors methodically to replace the unused medicines in his chest. Since he had not yet removed his clothes from the sea chest, it proved quite a simple matter to prepare to leave. His medical kits made quite a wheelbarrow load, but he reckoned he could manage them.

From Jenny's writing case Asa selected a goosequill, ink and a new sheet of foolscap. Seating himself he wrote:

Certification of Death

21 June 1781.

This will certify that the woman known as Jenny Starbird Peabody died of Strangulation by her own Hand during the Night of June the twentieth, A.D. 1781. Her mortal remains lie interred in the orchard beside this house.

Attest: A. Peabody, B.M.

He then wrote a second message:

Deed of Gift

On my true and Loyal brother, Morgan Peabody, Jur., I do bestow this Dwelling, Mill, Land and all appurtenances thereunto, without condition or reservation, and forever.

Asa Peabody, B.M.

Done this twenty-first day of June A.D. 1781.

The two documents he weighted with a book, which by chance proved to be *A Sentimental Journey*. It came as no surprise that the rabbit-fur mittens had disappeared from their hiding place.

Before long a shallop, propelled by a stained and well-patched leg-of-mutton sail appeared on the river. Asa recognized the craft almost immediately as that tender which, twice a week, conveyed provisions to the militiamen manning the forts downstream, and to the *Neshquoit*, man-of-war. His first wave and hail were enough to bring the shallop pushing her blunt nose onto a sand spit below Phil Starbird's mill.

IX. REPRISE

FOR ALL THAT Asa Peabody could tell, Boston had
changed very little during the past year and a half. Surely, it must have been longer ago than that he had followed
young Morgan to board the *Sally*? Late summer, he noted, had robbed the lawns and gardens of greenness, and
yellow patches marred the leaves of elms fringing the
Common. Children and ordinary folk still went barefoot,
and under this late August sun goats, chickens and pigs
scavenged, happily and numerously, along Boston's
streets.

All the same, by the time Asa set foot to a strip of
brown cobbles running down the center of Bennett Street
he'd come to appreciate a subtle difference in the atmosphere of the town. The people here appeared less well
dressed and more worried of mien. That hard times were
at hand was evinced by the number of windows which,
after being broken, had been paned with sheep's bladder
or oiled fishskin in place of glass. Nowhere did fresh
paint conceal the weathering of the past six years.

The sound of his footfalls conjured up the past; how
many times had he not tramped along these same sea-
smoothed cobbles towards Doctor Townsend's? Perhaps
the old master might be able to advise him—if Townsend
still wasn't angry about his returning to Machias.

Machias. Weeks ago, he had closed a mental door on
that phase of his past. Even so, for the thousandth time,
he explored with the tip of his tongue the inside of his
mouth, anxious lest it reveal the presence of a blister
which would warn that he had taken the *lues venera*.

On rising and retiring, he had taken the habit of closely
examining his body, fearful of discovering a fateful rash.
How long would it be, he wondered, while swinging
along, before he could consider himself safe?

What he needed, Asa knew, was work, plenty of work;
only then, might he really dismiss that horrible picture so
deeply etched into his memory.

Ah! Up the street had materialized the pale pink brick
of Doctor Townsend's house and, almost opposite, the
façade of Mr. Samuel Stanton's fine residence. When he
walked a bit closer he noticed that both residences could
do with some paint.

Was Sabra within—was she now less than a hundred feet distant? Why hadn't she answered those letters? Too flighty, he guessed.

While diminishing the interval to William Townsend's front door Asa found time to wonder how Joshua's military career was shaping up. The exciting possibility presented itself that Lucius or Peter might be in Boston! How good it would be to see either of them. Strangely enough, he recalled his first patient—that dark, sickly and big-eyed wench. What had been her name? Helen? No. Then he remembered; Hilde, Hilde Mention, that was it!

What a strange, unhappy little creature, yet sweet and gentle, despite all she had experienced. Most likely, she'd be dead by now. Girls in her profession, who weren't extra robust, ended around the high-tide mark in short order.

While reaching for Doctor Townsend's bell handle, he found time to wonder also about Wallace Blanchard. There was a fine physician for you. Maybe he could find employment at the Drydock?

The silver plate affixed to Doctor Townsend's door remained bright as ever and the same old colored woman responded to his knock. She threw upwards her hands.

"Fo' de good Lawd's sake! Ef it hain't Misto' Peabodeh!"

"Afternoon, Sophie. Is Doctor Townsend in?"

"Yassuh, an' he'll sho' be pleased to see yo'. Come right in, suh, jes' come right in." Sophie stepped back into the house, began calling, "Doctuh Townsend, suh! Oh, Doctuh Townsend! Please come down di-rectly, suh. Yo' is in fo' one mighty nice surprise."

Asa made bold to tramp down the short hallway while snuffing the familiar odors of camphor, nitre and the other drugs.

"Good afternoon, sir!" he called. "May I have a little of your time?"

"Eh? Who's that?" Doctor Townsend appeared at the head of the staircase.

"Mister Peabody, sir."

The old physician halted momentarily, blinking in his incredulity, then, to Sophie's giggles of delight, he pattered down to the ground floor. "Asa! My boy!"

To the younger man's surprise Doctor Townsend not

only wrung his hand but put both hands on his shoulders, held him at arms' length and studied his face.

"As God's my life! 'Tis really you. I've hoped, nay prayed, that you might return to use, and to improve, your skill. Come in, come into the consultation room."

To Asa's embarrassment, Doctor Townsend waved his guest to that worn, shiny-seated armchair he himself usually occupied, and took a stiff-backed chair reserved for apprentices.

"Now tell me, lad, what's chanced with you while Sophie fetches us some rum—no more fine brandies or wines these days, alas."

In terse sentences Asa accounted for the past, admitted he'd become a new widower, but otherwise said nothing of Jenny Starbird and her tragedy.

"So there you have it, sir," he concluded. "To your health."

"And yours, Asa—"

"Tell me, sir, what do you hear of my friends Burnham and Devoe?"

Most of all he wanted to inquire concerning Sabra but, somehow, he couldn't bring himself to, right away—needed to brace himself against the almost certain disclosure of her marriage.

"Now about Burnham, let me see, let me see—" Doctor Townsend removed his spectacles, rubbed his one good eye and looked mighty thoughtful. "You knew that he was selected to fill that post which you—er—could not accept?"

"I hoped for as much. Pray continue. I have had no word from Boston since I departed. I'm sure he has done excellently."

"Alas, you are wrong."

"Wrong?"

As briefly as he could, the old physician described the scandal concerning Jenny McLaren's body, told of the hue and cry and of Peter's subsequent complete disappearance.

To Asa the account came as a profound shock. What a tragic ending to so promising a career.

"—And nothing since has ever been heard from him?"

"Nothing. I fear he must have died that very same night. 'Twas a great pity; young Burnham possessed courage, imagination, and a rare capacity for learning although he never could match your surgical skill, nor that Jamaican lad's gift for diagnosis.''

''—And what of Lucius?''

Doctor Townsend put down his glass and took a turn down the room. ''I fear, Asa, you were unlucky in your fellow apprentices. Devoe, after brilliant beginnings, proved a great scoundrel.''

''Scoundrel? What do you mean, sir? Has he—''

''You recall my niece, Sabra Stanton?''

A chill tide of apprehension rose within him. ''Indeed I do, sir.''

''Well, this rascal—this, this villain, played upon Sabra's sensibilities until she fell very much in love with him. Also he cozened her father and her brother—''

''—Captain Stanton?''

''He became a major upon his return to the Army. As I was saying, Sabra became affianced to this fellow.''

An icy trickle started from the base of Asa's brain and crept down his spine.

''They—they were married?''

''No.'' Red invaded the pink and white pattern of Doctor Townsend's wrinkled features. ''Almost on the day they were to become espoused, Devoe deserted Sabra for a rich woman from the Hudson River Valley. Oh, Asa, it was very shameful business and particularly painful for Sabra because near the whole Army knew of her impending wedding.'' Doctor Townsend broke off, motioned to the rum bottle. ''The instant my nephew learned what had chanced, he yielded to a natural, if represensible, impulse, and challenged Devoe to a duel.''

''Reprehensible, sir?''

''A duel, Asa, is the most mistaken mode of avenging a wrong.'' Slowly, the old physician shook his head. '' 'Twasn't like Josh to do such a thing; I am sure he must have acquired the idea from some of those corrupt Southerners. Folks say the Virginians and Carolinians will attempt to blow each other's head off over the vainest of excuses.''

''But what of Joshua?'' Asa begged. ''He killed Lucius, of course.''

''No. Through sheer bad luck—Devoe, they say, was no part of a marksman—Joshua took the rascal's pistol ball through his shoulder, where it so grazed the bone that a mortification set in."

"Joshua survived?"

"Aye. Though he lay at death's door for weeks, and would have perished but for the care his sisters bestowed upon him. My nephew is yet serving with our Army, but it is known that he will never regain the full use of his right arm."

"—And Lucius?"

"The rogue escaped unhurt." Doctor Townsend sniffed his disgust. "The Devil cared for his own that morning."

"What of Sabra? How is she? Where is she?"

The old man's single eye surveyed his caller with renewed interest. "You *were* fond of her, Asa, weren't you?"

"Yes, sir, far more than she ever realized; far more than I did, for that matter."

"Then why did you two quarrel the night you started back for the Eastern District?"

Asa started violently. "Quarrel, sir? We didn't quarrel. To the contrary, we parted on the very friendliest of terms."

Now it became Doctor Townsend's turn to appear confused. "Are you sure, my boy, that you may not have forgotten saying, or doing, something which you may rightly have deemed to be of no importance, but in which a young girl might find cause for resentment?"

"Lord, no! Why, that evening Sabra even made me the compliment of a book of romance. Later, I wrote to her three times, but she never answered."

"How odd. How very odd." Townsend seemed to be speaking to himself. "How well I recall an evening when her mother spoke of you; Sabra sprang up, went red as a poppy, and rushed out crying, 'Never again mention Asa Peabody's name in my hearing!'"

No amount of questioning or thinking back could supply an explanation.

"Do you suppose Mr. Stanton would know—no, damn it, sir, I will confront Sabra and ask her myself!"

"I fear you will be unable to do that," Townsend informed him. "As I told you just now, Sabra lingered long at Fort Clinton to nurse her brother. She has not yet returned to Boston, but she may be on her way home. I imagine Sam Stanton could answer that."

The old physician raised a detaining hand. "No, stay just a little longer, Asa. I have something to say."

Once Asa had reseated himself, Doctor Townsend said, "It is perhaps providential that you should have returned just now. You see, I would like to confine my activities to instruction. I fear I grow too old to go running about at all hours." He looked Asa squarely in the eyes. "Would you care to take over my practice?"

"Take over your practice!" Asa's jaw dropped. Judas Maccabaeus! William Townsend's practice was one of the richest in all Massachusetts. "Of course, sir, but having no money, I could not even begin to buy—"

"I believe I said nothing about *selling* my practice?" Townsend smiled quietly. "I possess quite enough of this world's goods to provide for the remainder of my span."

"But—but, sir. Why offer *me* this—this honor?"

"I believe that, during the course of my life, I have instructed near three hundred apprentices. Of them all I consider you to be the most promising. Tut! Tut! No protests, please. That's the plain, unvarnished truth as I see it. Well, Asa, what do you say?"

The offer was so completely unexpected Asa for a time could only smile helplessly. "I'd admire to accept, sir, and will; if you're of the same mind after this war ends. However, I conceive it to be my duty first to offer my services to the Medical Department."

Quite deliberately, Doctor Townsend refilled their glasses, made a little tinkling noise when the trembling of his hand allowed the bottle to touch against his goblet's rim.

"I respect that sentiment in you, sir. May I add that I am not surprised, only pleased. My practice will keep—and this war soon must end, one way or another, America is near exhaustion and the French are disgusted; but, also, the British people have become deeply discouraged and the Parliament grows more conciliatory every day.

"A decisive victory for one side or the other will settle the issue." Doctor Townsend arose, offered his hand. "Er—if you should need some—er—pecuniary assistance, you won't hesitate to call on me?"

"No, sir."

"Then, get along over to Sam Stanton's. I expect you'll find him in at this hour."

Mr. Stanton had aged perceptibly; those chocolate-hued liver patches freckling his neck and hands were darker. His back, however, was still straight and his voice steady.

When Asa approached the question of that outburst on Sabra's part, her father shook his head. "No man can understand what goes on in a female's mind when she's in love. I'll confess her tantrum astonished me because Sabra ain't as flighty as most maids of her age. What's more, I guess she used to set considerable store by what you thought and did."

"Sabra—is she returning home?"

"No. She remains with Joshua, for all that I've pressed her to return. Mayhap, she's fallen in love again—"

"—And Joshua?"

"His last letter declared that our Army is preparing to march on Philadelphia."

"But doesn't Sir Henry Clinton still hold New York?"

"Aye, and in force. The ways of our military minds are strange indeed."

Asa spent that night at Doctor Townsend's and, early the next morning, purchased a seat on the Wethersfield coach. Bad weather aside, he should reach White Plains, New York, within four days.

PART II—WATERS OF DESTINY

x. The Road to Annapolis

EARLY AUTUMN in Maryland was a wonderfully gay and brilliant affair, thought the French troops; the scarlet dogwood and sumac leaves, the yellow hickory trees and the fields of tired green suddenly became refreshed with bursts of goldenrod and purplish blue asters.

The country here was reminiscent of home—with its gently rolling terrain and so many broad, lazily flowing rivers such as the Patapsco, Patuxent and the Gunpowder. Somehow to one's eye, it seemed not quite so new as the lands they'd travelled further north.

How incredible, they assured one another, that this interminable march which had commenced, aeons ago it seemed, up in Newport on June the ninth, now in September was nearing its conclusion. How many stifling, dust-choked and thirsty miles did not lie behind? *Nom de Dieu!* Could one ever forget those weary leagues and the curious friendly towns marking that route, Philadelphia, Whippany, Paramus, King's Ferry, and Wethersfield.

By now, the faces and hands of the Comte de Rochambeau's men were burned quite as brown as those of any American. Being intelligent, the men of the Saint Onge, the Soissonsais, Deux-Ponts and Bourbonnais Regiments had learned, very quickly, to avoid the middle of the day as a marching time.

Although a few misanthropes grumbled, a vast majority of the rank and file had come to love this great, sprawling, and nearly empty country. The friendly openhandedness of the natives never ceased to astonish these sons of peasants accustomed, from birth, to suspect and to distrust all strangers. These Americans betrayed a flattering, and sometimes embarrassing, curiosity concerning the customs and habits of their allies.

Only the oldsters scowled on the Frenchmen; they were too steeped in a lifelong hatred of that Power which, time and again, had incited the crafty Hurons and fierce Algonquins to sudden bloody raids along the length

of the frontiers. Happily, such oldsters were scarce—few
men lived past forty, or expected to, in North America.

At nearly every crossroad and hamlet, flowers were
thrown before these bandy-legged, carefully uniformed
troops, or hung in awkward wreaths from their musket
muzzles. All the troops in the column—it marched in two
divisions of two regiments each—save the Royal Deux-
ponts, which wore light blue tunics—were uniformed in
white turned up in rose, green, blue or black as their design demanded.

Because the colonel of the Soissonsais had been pru-
dent enough to issue linen breeches to his troops, they
suffered far less of the heat. To one and all, thirst had
proved their chief affliction; however, the choking red or
yellow road dusts ran a strong second.

Though very difficult to keep clean, the white regimentals of Louis XVI's men proved cooler, by far, than the
dark blue of such American regiments as had found uniforms.

What particularly surprised and impressed the inhabitants was that, like the British, the Frenchmen always
marched arranged in precise companies, battalions and
regiments; for them there was no tramping comfortably
along in a straggling column with muskets held any which
way, and with the forage and baggage wagons God knew
where.

Their discipline, too, was a shining example. 'Twas
said that French troops would camp in an orchard full of
ripe fruit and leave without having touched a single apple, plum or peach. A far cry, this, from the ruinous depredations committed by State troops or militia.

In the rear of each contingent rolled long lines of ox-
drawn baggage and sumpter wagons; these generally
were crowded to overflowing with women who had en-
thusiastically elected to follow so generously equipped
an army. Above all, these wonderful allies paid for everything they needed in silver or gold, and thereby
brought great joy to merchants along the route.

At the head of each regiment, and just before its colors, usually rode the colonel and his staff. They made a
brave show on blooded horses, astride saddles usually
housed in leopard's skin, but sometimes with the pelts of
tiger, panther or bear's fur. To each side of their pom-
mels were slung huge horse pistols protected by gold-

mounted holsters, adorned with the owner's coat-of-arms. The Frenchmen's bridles, martingales and reins glistened with polish and all bright work shone like new.

However much dust-stained might be the rank and file, trampling along behind the regimental music, the commanders and their staffs revealed no trace of dirt on their breeches, boots or tunics—not even on the gay panaches nodding above their tricornes. The inhabitants soon discovered the reason for this discrepancy; even the least important officer had, at his disposal, at least one wagon in which he might convey his personal apparel, weapons, saddlery, table linen, silver, glassware, and hampers of choice wines and foods.

The men of the Bourbonnais and Soissonsais Regiments had proved famous for an unconquerable gaiety; always they were ready to plant a kiss or snatch a swift embrace from the brown-cheeked country girls standing, barefoot and giggling, by the roadside.

The Saint Onge Regiment, in green cuffs and green piping, for some reason appeared to be a slightly soberer lot; but for all that, they boasted the best band of music in the whole French Expeditionary Force.

It was for the Royal Deux-Ponts Regiment, however, that local inhabitants reserved their greatest enthusiasm. Perhaps this was because they, alone of the French infantry, wore light blue tunics most effectively turned up in yellow at their lapels and cuffs.

Somehow, the Maryland people, like the Pennsylvanians and the rest, interpreted this wearing of blue as a gesture of courtesy towards their American allies who, several days earlier, had travelled this same road.

There had been among these many State troops, including General Mordecai Gist's three fine, new regiments of the Maryland Line. But they had all, with the exception of the Continental Line regiments, confiscated or stolen everything that hadn't been nailed down—and a lot that was.

From a light, two-horse carriage purchased for her in Philadelphia by Hector, Chevalier de Lameth, Hilde smiled and waved happily at the population of a tiny crossroads village which was raising a cheer for the Royal Deux-Ponts Regiment. She heard it because, today, her mettlesome dappled grays were carrying her along almost among that regiment's rear guard.

Hilde Mention, politely—if a trifle inaccurately—addressed throughout the Expeditionary Army as "Madame de Lameth," had no intention of being left behind, once light transports, dispatched by the fleet of Admiral de Grâsse, took aboard these dusty troops belonging to His Most Christian Majesty.

A long-drawn command, transmitted from the van where rode Colonel Count William Deux-Ponts and his principal officers, caused the rear guard to halt. Another order sent them scattering under the trees to avoid the hot September sun—all save the musicians who, unlucky dogs, must now strike up a tune. This they presently did, and their playing of *"Les Grands Chevaux de Lorraine"* caused these simple country folk to grin in shy wonderment and approval.

Sunburnt children, clad only in homespun smocks or jumps, were the first to approach, quite round-eyed and ready to scurry back to the underbrush as quickly as quail chicks.

Because their thousand-mile-long march was very near its end, the Deux-Ponts felt in high good spirits. A few light infantrymen commenced to sing—more joined in. They even drank cheerfully of such vinegar and water as remained in their canteens and then lit their pipes. *Pardieu!* Was it not something to continue in such good condition after marching near a thousand miles over the most execrable roads in all the world?

To begin with, the infantrymen clustered around the wells of the village after tossing tiny silver coins to surprised and delighted well owners. These then worked their well sweeps as fast as they could. By the dozen, tall, dust-streaked grenadiers came running back from companies resting further up the road and carrying clusters of wooden canteens in their bronzed hands.

Hilde, undecided as to her course of action, watched a sergeant bow profoundly to a huge-bosomed housewife. "'As, Madame, perhaps a leetle *fruit?*"

"La, sir—I dunno what ye mean." She got the idea, however, when he pointed to a tree heavy with big rosy apples and held up a silver demi-piastre. "Why, sure, help yerselves, boys," she called pocketing the silver piece.

"*Oui,* eet ees dry beesness, thees marching in September." His English was very good, Hilde thought.

"Jacques," she directed in silvery French, "turn my carriage into that field. Yes, over there—near the big oak tree."

"*Oui, Madame.*" Hector's valet guided her grays off the road and into the shade of a clump of golden green pin oaks. Jacques swung down from the box and opened the door.

"Madame possibly would care to visit the tavern while I water the animals?"

Hilde nodded, though she had not the least intention of entering another of those scruffy little ordinaries which inevitably occupied a corner of nearly every crossroads in America.

Long ago, she had learned to avoid such country inns; without exception, their furniture was filthy, their parasites beyond calculation and their food miserable. Even while dismounting onto the sun-dried ground, Hilde kept an eye on the road. Unless Colonel Deux-Ponts had detained him during this customary mid-afternoon halt, Hector would soon appear, pointed dark features alight with tender anticipation.

Even while Jacques was unhitching the grays, the nearest Deux-Ponts troops bowed to this so-beautiful little lady and raised their hats. A lieutenant ran up, silver gorget a-winking in the sunlight, to inquire if he might be privileged to assist.

By now, even the dullest drummer boy serving in the Royal Deux-Ponts recognized this cheerful, dark-eyed girl who had kept house for Captain, the Chevalier de Lameth back in friendly little Newport, Rhode Island.

The *vieux moustaches* and *grognards* of the Deux-Ponts, neither knew nor cared, whether she was in fact Madame de Lameth. They loved her for her irrepressible cheer and dainty loveliness, quite as much as they valued the care she showered upon the regiment's sick and unhappy. How many times during this march, had Madame de Lameth not taken into her comfortable carriage some poor, smelly soldier rendered ill by this terrible sun of America?

No less did the men of the IIIième *Compagnie* admire their captain. *Nom d'un nom!* He was the gallant one, the Chevalier de Lameth. Though barely twenty-one years of age, the chevalier had afforded his men more than necessary proof of his courage and, amid an army in which officers maintained a studious disregard of their men, *le capitaine* was forever bribing, threatening, conniving with the commissary to procure the best possible for the Third Company. Yes. That was why every man and boy was quite willing to follow Hector de Lameth wherever he led.

In many ways Hilde would have preferred riding a-horseback; it afforded a freedom of maneuver and vision and a ready change of pace denied her by the carriage. Alas, that, below the camp at Whippany, her strength had betrayed signs of failing and Hector had made her give up riding the gentle gray gelding, Cupidon.

One eye on the orchard and the other on Jacques holding a bucket to the near horse of her pair, Hilde wandered about in a little field, picking bunches of goldenrod, brown-eyed daisies and asters. The earth looked very dry and the flowers a little tired, yet their colors remained wonderfully brilliant. Those clumps of scarlet sumac glowing, under the little oaks at the far end of the field, were quite as bright as the tunic of that captured British officer brought into Baltimore.

Over her shoulder, Hilde could see familiar patterns repeated yet once more—perhaps for the final time. The Deux-Ponts had for the most part stretched out, propped against the trees, listening to their band playing a favorite song, "The Huron March."

"*Garde à vous!*" The blue and white uniformed men beneath the trees began springing to their feet; non-commissioned officers hurriedly adjusted their buttons. From the road sounded a delicate patter of hoofs and, a second later, Hector on his golden chestnut mare, Victorine, cleared the pasture fence of split rails as easily as a gentleman could lift his hat. Delicate ears cocked and moving with the effortless grace of a wave up a beach, Victorine cantered to the carriage.

"*Ma petite fleur*—my heart!" Hector called and, swinging his leg back over the cantle, dropped from his saddle as lightly as a bluebird descending from a limb to the ground.

Whole small face radiant and transfigured with joy, Hilde pulled aside the black travelling mask with which Hector insisted she shield her complexion. He kissed her just as hungrily as if they had not frolicked nearly all the previous night on his camp bed amid the dim, horse-scented heat of his pavilion.

Reins trailing from the crook of his elbow and with the sun glaring off his golden epaulettes, Hector de Lameth kissed her again and again, in full sight of the resting infantry. Silently, they approved. *Ma foi!* What a Sevres figurine of a woman was this. At length the chevalier produced a lace-trimmed handkerchief and with it wiped from his peeling and cruelly sunburnt forehead a generous beading of sweat.

"Tomorrow, little dove," he assured her, "you will have suffered your last ride over these cursed, incredible roads."

"We near Annapolis, then, my soul?"

"But yes, I have sent Pierre riding ahead to engage us decent quarters in this village of Annapolis."

Hector was speaking in French as usual, for somehow an uncanny facility with the language had returned to Hilde. Why, she could even write French—not perfectly, of course, but at least as accurately as a majority of the officers on the staff of the Baron de Viomesnil, Commander-in-Chief during this march.

"*Dis-donc, chéri,*" she demanded, "there has been fought a great naval battle, no?"

"Yes."

"With what result?"

"So far we do not know." The Frenchman's almost too-finely modelled features fell into worried lines. "Monsieur de Viomesnil merely stated that a dispatch boat has reported a naval action of the first importance taking place at the entrance to this Chesapeake Bay."

"And where is that?" Hilde slipped an arm through his.

"What does it matter, *ma mie?*" He shrugged. "Such a huge country—it is almost terrifying. *Mon Dieu,* so very big and so empty."

"Yes; you like it?"

His lips brushed the back of her hand. "Always I shall love America because here I found you, flower of my heart. You are not too tired?"

"Oh, but no," she laughed. "Today the road has not been difficult at all and, as always, Jacques is most solicitous of my comfort."

"If he is not, I will have the skin off his back," Hector laughed. "Have we still any of the Rhine wine?"

"I think so, darling—"

Saffron-tinted skirt a-flutter, Hilde ran back to the car-

riage and opened a leather-covered travelling cellarette.
It contained two bottles and over a dozen wine glasses
secured into place by a curious mechanism. When she
raised the lid a mirror fixed inside of it reflected her pointed, rose and ivory features. They were more serene and
softly rounded than those of that Hilde Mention who, terror-stricken, had been rowed out to the *Ecureuil* that terrible winter's night over a year and a half ago. The sleek
dark hair now was skillfully coiffed, her cheeks had color
and her eyes were large and clearly blue-black.

They sat under a tree watching Victorine trail her reins
and crop at the fading grass.

Hector smacked sun-cracked lips and half-closed intense and sparkling hazel eyes, "*Bon!* 'Tis as good as
Rhine wine can be expected when warm and thousands
of leagues from Alsace. *Chérie*, one ponders—"

He broke off and shifted on the grass to view the road.
Along it from the direction of Baltimore was travelling a
two-wheeled chaise. In the warm air the hoofbeats of a
pair of dusty bay horses sounded very loud. A postillion
was a-stride the lead nag—although the word really was
too elegant a description for the sullen-faced boy who
wore a crumpled straw hat, patched boots, a linsey-woolsey shirt and leather breeches.

In the chaise sat a single figure but so effectively
masked, bonneted and gloved, that not even Hector de
Lameth's discerning eye could estimate her age or condition.

When the Royal Deux-Ponts called out greetings the
passenger waved absent-mindedly, but took no other
heed. As the chaise passed her Hilde noticed an unusually small calfskin-covered portmanteau strapped under-
neath its seat, just before the vehicle became lost to sight
beyond a dim and shifting pall of yellow golden dust.

Once the chaise had disappeared and the curiosity of
the Deux-Ponts had subsided, Hector eased a travelling
stock of white wash-leather, idly snapped his fingers at
Victorine, then tossed his hat on the grass at his knee.

"Do you know something, my darling? I am consumed
with impatience to commence the fighting."

Hilde's fingers tightened on the pale green stem of her
wine glass. "Yes, dearest, I know—since you are by tra-
dition a soldier, it is only natural." She tried to hold
steady her voice. "There is news?"

"Yes. De Custine swore this morning that we will find Milor' Cornwallis pinned against the River of York. Yes. It is planned that we shall converge on him from all directions. The American Generals de Lafayette and Greene from the southwest, *le grand* General Washington from the west, ourselves from the north, and the West Indian troops of the Marquis de Saint-Simon will advance eastward, from the direction of the River of James. *Enfin*, at last we shall roundly trounce *messieurs les anglais*."

Hilde's eyes sought the field flowers in her lap, "But will they fight hard?"

"In that direction lies the greater honor. *Mon Dieu*, the sacred English always fight their best against us. Do not doubt that many of yonder brave fellows," he indicated his troops adjusting gear by the roadside, "will remain forever in America. Am I not in a macabre mood? I wonder why?" Hector laughed shortly, then raised his glass in a characteristically gay flourish. "A toast, queen of my heart, to a hard siege and confusion to our enemies!"

Hilde's fingers came to rest on her lover's light blue sleeve, played with its texture an instant. "Hector?"

"Yes, darling?"

"Never imagine that I would wish you—an officer of the famous Deux-Ponts—to avoid any part of your duty; yet I beg you to promise that you will not seek out danger for its own sake."

Epaulettes a-twinkle, Hector twisted his shoulders until he could press her lips with his. He laughed lightly. "Ha, jealousy at last! Now there is a fine promise to exact from me! Danger! Here's to that fickle wanton. Next to you, my love, I find her the most irresistible witch in all the world."

Impulsively Hilde dropped her glass, flung a slim arm about his neck. "You will take care? Promise," she insisted. "Promise. Should anything happen to I—I would not care to live."

In some surprise de Lameth peered into her passionate features, said a shade more soberly, "What a strange, intense little creature it is here. If once he were to see you I am convinced Papa would consent to our marriage—*dot* or no *dot*."

Hilde's dark red lips curved themselves into a small, mechanical smile. "You must not delude yourself, Hector. Are you not the last bearer of a name that was al-

ready great when the English were driven out of Calais?
No, my lover, for you there must be a great marriage and
many children to restore the family. The wife of the last
Chevalier de Lameth must bring him position, domains,
and many, many *louis d'or.* Your little Hildegarde can
bring you only—''

''—The most perfect, the most priceless of all dower-
ies—true love.'' He shrugged. ''As for the rest—the domains, the monies, the titles—I shall win them with my
sword—as did my ancestors.'' His voice filled, resounded with earnestness and a complete conviction. ''But
come, *mignonne,* we become too serious for so beautiful
a September afternoon in Mary-land; this will never do.''

Somewhere, up near the head of the column and far up
the road, a drum commenced its dry, imperative rattle.

''*Voilà.* The march resumes itself.'' He jumped up,
slapping dried grass from the travel-stained white
breeches. ''Now attend what I say. You will seek, in this
Annapolis town, a tavern called the Reynold's and there I
will seek you out tonight as quickly as our camp can be
pitched.''

Onto his carefully curled and powdered hair Hector
swept his tricorne, bravely supporting a new blue, white
and yellow cockade—a panache symbolizing the alliance
of America, France and Spain. ''Until that felicitous
hour, my queen, I have the honor to bid you *au revoir.*''

Then he made Hilde as profound a bow as his thigh-
high black leather riding boots would permit, swung into
the saddle and cantered off across the goldenrod-dotted
ground.

Dust veiled the brief flash of iron horseshoes as Hector
put Victorine to the snake fence for a second time.

Soberly, Hilde recorked the bottles, returned the
glasses to their case and stood watching Jacques lead up
her carriage horses.

xi. Mistress Susan Stevens

THE ANNAPOLIS ROAD ascended another long low hill
and up it were panting the grenadiers of the Bourbonnais
Regiment—and well they might gasp for breath, swathed
as they were in tight and heavy woollen uniforms, and
carrying sixty-five-pound knapsacks. All light troops of

the Expeditionary Force, those lucky devils, had been embarked at Head of Elk and already were concentrated in the vicinity of Williamsburg.

The distinctive light blue of the Royal Deux-Ponts became visible. Possibly half a mile distant, they were bracing themselves for the climb and Hilde, leaning far out of her carriage window, thought to recognize Hector and Victorine upon that distant slope.

Hot and suddenly impatient to reach Annapolis and a change of garments, Hilde settled back on the upholstery. Because the regimental wagon train was drawn by slow-moving oxen it could not be expected to appear for quite a while, so, for the moment, her carriage had the road to itself. The only sounds were the rasp of the wheels, the creak of leather and the hollow, rhythmic impact of the grays' hoofs.

How pleasant it was here in the shade. Gratefully, she discarded her mask, being able to do so because dust, raised by the marching men had, by this time, drifted off to coat tangles of honeysuckle draping trees to either side of this twisting, sun-blasted road.

By the roadside she recognized the usual evidences of a passage of troops; here a broken canteen, there a worn-out gaiter or shoe, yonder a length of reddish brown stained bandage. Hilde settled back on the gray and yellow cushions of the coach and attempted to doze—but in vain, so through half-closed eyes, she watched the countryside slip by.

How comfortably this well-built carriage rode on its excellently designed springs! Life indeed was very kind these days, as if anxious to atone for all those miserable years of her girlhood. Looking back, Hilde saw that her luck had seemed to change with her rescue by Antoine Fougère. Although tough and blustery in appearance, Antoine had proved to be kindness itself—had the big naval officer not supported her during her recovery from her experience with Captain Eldridge? Had he not, quite unselfishly, protected her against all manner of dangers and difficulties and not once made the least effort to possess her?

Faintly, drum-and-fife music cheering on the sweating infantry drifted back along the road.

In her brief life but three men had ever treated her with a selfless kindness. What could have become of that demi-god, Doctor Peabody, back in Boston? Never, as long as she breathed, would she forget his gentleness and humanity towards a bedraggled, soiled little creature who had fainted so inconsiderately in his bedroom. Come to think of it, it was reallyAsa Peabody she must thank in the first instance for knowing the Chevalier de Lameth— and all that his love had brought.

Fougere, of course, had been more directly responsible for her encountering Hector. Dearly adored Hector! Sensitive, handsome and dangerous, as a *preux chevalier* should be. Was ever a lover more generous, more tender, more considerate? She knew she would have loved him just as well, had he been a mere orderly around the Comte de Rochambeau's headquarters—and not the wealthy young nobleman he proved to be. That his *four-gons* carried no less than three chests of clothes, laces, fans, hats and lingerie counted for nothing—but it did render life wonderfully gay and agreeable and capable of imaginative pleasures.

He had made a curious observation when they first had met. "*Ma foi, Ma'm'selle,* somewhere, sometime, I have beheld someone so very like you it appears incredible that you should be a female."

Since then, Hector more than once had beaten his forehead in trying to remember from whence the recollection had stemmed.

Almost with first sight of the Chevalier de Lameth she had fallen so hopelessly in love with him that, somehow to share his bed and the fortunes of war had seemed never less than perfectly natural.

"Oh, Hector," she thought. "Ever since then you have proved so steadfast, so gentle and very understanding."

Twice he had asked her hand in marriage, but she loved him too much, for, more or less tactfully, officers of the Royal Deux-Ponts at various times had made it entirely plain that such a step surely would ruin not only Hector's military career but precipitate a disastrous break with the old Marquis de Lameth.

By dint of patience and tact, finally she had brought him to agree that the wisest course would be to await the end of this war, then return to France and to allow the acid old Marquis to see for himself how truly, how profoundly they adored one another.

Hilde began thinking how wonderful it would be to reach Annapolis. A finger board, passed a little while ago, declared that town to lie but a dozen miles distant. Were this distance correct her carriage should arrive before the Reynold's Tavern long before darkness set in.

All at once Jacques reined in and applied his brakes as a voice called, "Oh, please stop. I—I am in such trouble."

Before Jacques could reply, Hilde donned her mask and peered out to recognize, some yards ahead, that same chaise which had rolled by during the afternoon halt. The vehicle lay crazily tilted in the weed-choked ditch with one axle resting on the thoroughly mashed remains of one of those over-slender wheels.

The two nags, traces loosed, were nibbling eagerly at dusty herbage beside the road. While, under the direction of his passenger, the surly postillion was engaged in unstrapping the portmanteau from its position at the rear of the chaise.

Hilde called, "How can I be of assistance, Ma'am?"

"Oh! A lady!" The distracted young woman in a dark blue cloak vented a small cry of astonishment. "Oh yes! You see what has chanced and I—I must continue my journey; really I *must*."

"You are for Annapolis?" Hilde demanded through the window. The stranded traveller, she judged, could be little older than herself but a bit heavier in build.

"Yes, Madame. I know 'tis a great imposition, but I wonder whether you would consider—" reaching into a petticoat pocket, she produced a not very heavy purse. "Possibly I could purchase conveyance of you?"

As the woman by the roadside removed her travelling mask Hilde received an impression of chestnut hair, of cool gray eyes and wide sweeping brows. She added anxiously, "I am on my way to Virginia, to a town called Williamsburg."

Hilde said pleasantly, "You are welcome to share my carriage—but please first put away your purse."

Hilde turned the carriage's door handle, gave Jacques rapid instruction in French which sent him leaping down to unfold the steps and then secure the stranger's portmanteau. The girl in blue hurried forward, smiling widely.

"Really, you are uncommon kindly, Madame—"

"Who are you?" Hilde demanded.

The strange girl hesitated just a moment before replying, "I am Mistress Susan Stevens of—of Hartford, Connecticut. I told that donkey of a post boy not to turn so sharp, but he would in spite of everything."

Producing some silver, Mistress Stevens pursed full red lips, then turned to confer with her postillion who immediately aided Jacques to strap her portmanteau onto the luggage rack of Hilde's carriage.

"Just now you spoke French, Madame?" Mistress Stevens inquired.

"I am Madame de Lameth, and originally I came from Nova Scotia where many people speak French," Hilde informed. "And you come from Connecticut—a fine city?"

Her guest nodded gravely, then steadied herself to a swaying of the body caused by Jacques' return to his seat. "*Allez-y!*" The carriage lurched into motion once more.

"I can't begin properly to thank you," Susan Stevens presently declared. "I really don't know what I would have done if you had not chanced along. I suppose I'd have mounted one of the chaise horses," she said more to herself than to her companion. "Or maybe one of your baggage wagons would have assisted me. Your troops are so very courteous."

"I am glad there was no need to put their gallantry to such a test."

"When I crossed over to New Jersey from New York, I did not know of this great march to the South," Mistress Stevens declared, eyes busy first with the handsome luggage, the brocade curtains, then with her companion's modish attire and tiny blue morocco shoes. "So, for days on end, I have become entangled with the troops of either our Army or of yours. Travel, you can imagine, has become most difficult, since every horse of any quality has either been bought or stolen."

The iron tires rasped out onto a ford where, presently the horses halted to drink thirstily of tawny water slipping silently over the gravel.

"Madame de Lameth, do you fancy I will meet with many difficulties in attaining Williamsburg?" Susan Stevens inquired, as, emitting a sigh, she undid the bonnet strings. For all her mask and bonnet, her pleasantly open features proved to be both sunburnt and dusty.

"Such a journey at this time will not prove easy," Hilde predicted. "There are many troops in that vicinity."

"Oh, dear! I don't know what to do and my money—well, I believe I will have just enough. Let me see—" Lost in calculations, she stared fixedly at her dusty shoe tips.

Hilde became interested. "You are perhaps to visit friends or relatives?"

The girl in the blue travelling cloak stirred and blinked several times. "No, not exactly. You see, Ma'am, I am most anxious to—to find someone who was very dear to my heart."

"I trust he is not ill—or wounded?"

"So do I, but I don't know. He serves under contract to—" Susan sat straighter—"well, to one of the enemy regiments."

In her turn, Hilde drew herself up. "Did you say he serves with an *enemy* regiment?"

"Yes, Ma'am. But don't mistake me. My—my friend is not a soldier, nor does he hold a King's commission. He is in fact, a physician dedicated to the saving of human life. Does it matter in what army he labors?"

"No. You need not explain further, Mistress Stevens." Hilde's voice softened. "I quite understand, because it chances that I owe a vast debt to a physician."

"Where does he practice?"

"In Boston," Hilde replied, "but that was long ago."

XII. MUFFS AT REYNOLD'S TAVERN

TO CLAIM THAT Annapolis, a lovely, somnolent little town happily situated at the confluence of the Severn River with Chesapeake Bay, was fairly bursting at its seams with troops and attendant visitors would have constituted an understatement. This, the capital town of Maryland, was more than a little proud of its neat brick ivy-draped homes, busy wharves and a handsome new State House set near the buildings of little King William's School. The local citizens, it soon became mighty evident, set great store by the presence of this college in their midst; though of late there had been no classes and troops were occupying dormitories designed for scholars.

Folks claimed outlying plantations in the vicinity of Annapolis were among the handsomest in America—Virginia not excepted.

Once Madame de Lameth's gay yellow and black carriage began raising dust on the far limits of the main street, it encountered herds of sheep and cows homeward bound from pasturing at the edge of town. Because so many soldiers were about, these creatures moved under heavy guard and, long since, housewives had moved their fowls, ducks and even pigs indoors.

On the outskirts of Annapolis, Hilde's carriage was overtaken by a strong detachment of cavalry which, in the vivid glare of sunset, presented such a brave sight that both she, and Susan Stevens—who had proved to be no part of a Loyalist—waved and smiled at these big, blue-jacketed fellows in black jack boots, white waistcoats and breeches.

Their helmets, Hilde noted, were of brass, sported white horsehair crests and had a band of brown bearskin bound across their fronts. For arms they carried carbines slung across their backs and beneath their left knees curved, useless-looking sabres swung downwards towards dust raised by the hoofs. These, she learned later on, were a troop of Continental dragoons.

In every vacant lot along the fringes of Annapolis, French troops were either pitching tents or engaged in cooking supper. Deeper in town, the streets and footpaths were overflowing with the military.

Once Hilde's carriage turned into College Street, the teeming traffic there forced it to proceed at a slow walk—which pleased Susan no end. Neither in Newport nor even in occupied New York, had she beheld such a galaxy of decorations, such a prodigality of gold lace and such a wonderful variety of uniforms.

A band of music—it turned out to be that of the Royal Deux-Ponts—was playing before the State House to a large and enthusiastic throng of Marylanders, many of whom had ridden many miles into town to witness this, the greatest drama of their lives.

In every public house, watermen from all over Chesa-

peake Bay were discussing the curious rig of vessels sent
up from that vast French fleet reported to be anchored off
Lynnhaven Bay. A few well-travelled seamen identified
some of these craft as *goélettes* and *saiques,* but the most
outlandish-looking craft had slender, overhanging sterns
and such a multiplicity of slender yards as to baffle the
native eye. These, the wiseacres called "polacres." Very
numerous, too, were *pataches,* distinctive because of a
mainmast consisting of but a single spar supported by
four shrouds to a side. This lone mast supported a gaff
mainsail—which lacked a boom of any description—
hubbed tight against it.

Although the bulk of the French troops were en-
camped beyond Spa Creek, little cooking fires flickered
under trees fringing the side street of Annapolis. From
them odors of saffron and garlic, unfamiliar but inviting
to native nostrils, drew crowds of onlookers to view
those large cauldrons in which was being prepared that
magnificent *soupe* which ever has proved a boon to
French armies.

Only by dint of the most skillful driving was Jacques
able, at length, to guide his carriage around Church Circle and so bring it to a triumphant halt before the Reynold's Tavern.

"*Mon Dieu!* Miss Stevens, what *can* have happened to
my husband?" Hilde, who had been looking eagerly for
Hector, asked.

"In all this crowd 'tis no wonder he is hard to discover," Susan remarked.

"But certainly he will be here. Ah-h! There! There he
goes. Hector, *chéri! Me voici!*" Hilde leaned 'way out of
the window and commenced blowing kisses and waving
her scarf. Susan watched in some astonishment. What
odd ways the French had of greeting one another.

"*Holà!*" Hector waved and began pushing through a
mob of French and American officers thronging the tavern's entrance. Even before he was halfway to the carriage, Hilde had alighted and was running up to be
clasped in his arms.

"Oh, dear. Will anyone ever rush to hold me like
that?" Susan Stevens gazed enviously on their obvious
and mutual adoration before remembering to avert her attention. Presently, the de Lameths commenced a rapid
conversation punctuated by many expressive gestures.

"To find shelter for tonight will be difficult, my girl," Susan told herself. "Aren't I the silly fool to get myself in such a pickle?"

Madame de Lameth came back almost dancing, the small oval of her face radiant. "Ma'm'selle Stevens, the Chevalier de Lameth has returned to seek the patron of this inn. He will do what he can, but, in any case, you must share my quarters. The Chevalier insists upon it."

Susan shook her dark brown head and answered softly, "I'd much sooner sleep in your carriage than to separate you from your husband."

Hilde's pale-green-gloved hands rested briefly on those of her travelling companion. "Do not worry. My Hector, like most Frenchmen, is a fine provider. He has a way with him. You will see."

Susan nodded. During those agonizing and mortifying weeks in New York she had come to learn how quickly the gleam of gold can transmute the sourest expression into a beatific smile.

Things turned out very much as Hilde had predicted. Tall and spare as a lance, the Chevalier de Lameth soon reappeared in company with a short, plump and very jolly officer of Smallwood's Maryland Cavalry.

Gravely, Hilde performed the presentation to Susan Stevens of her cavalier. It was quite something to behold that easy grace with which the Chevalier de Lameth bent to kiss Mistress Steven's dusty blue glove. In turn he waved forward this rotund, middle-aged Marylander.

"Mademoiselle Stevens, permit me the honor to present Major Joseph Ridgely of Colonel Smallwood's Horse."

Susan found herself looking into genial, ruddy features, and two of the merriest gray eyes she had ever beheld.

"Your obedient servant, M-Mistress Stevens," he boomed in a big and hearty voice. "You are most welcome t-to Maryland. Captain de Lameth"—to Hilde's surprise he pronounced the name correctly—"explained y-your situation—and m-makes it possible for me t-to indulge myself by inviting you to make use of m-my quarters."

Occupy a strange officer's room? Mercy to goodness, no! Susan flushed. "You are most kind, sir, but I could not think of putting you out."

Major Ridgely uttered such a hearty laugh that the coach horses started, then turned questioning heads. "God bless you, Ma'am, there are other beds at my disposal in Annapolis. Oh, my soul, yes!"

Before Susan could voice further protest, Hector de Lameth clapped Ridgely on the shoulder. "Ma'm'selle Stevens, one suspects, observes only the niceties in her refusal. Eh, *mon ami*? Come, shall we move in the ladies' things?"

Major Ridgely turned, yelled, "Ambrose! Trot right over heah."

"Yassuh, mos' direckly, suh." Grinning, a black lad in a smart, dark green livery sped forward

Some ten minutes later Susan Stevens found herself installed in a tiny bedroom reeking of horses, hounds and choice liquors. To one side lay a pair of distinctly odd-looking wicker panniers—she couldn't guess their use.

Thankfully, Susan poured out a basin full of water and washed the dust from her face and hands. After that, she unlocked her travelling chest and, producing comb and brush, set about removing as much dust as was detectable by the uncertain light of a single candle. Down in the street some Maryland troops were swinging along, singing:

> "Man is for woman made
> And woman made for man
> As the spur is for the jade
> As the scabbard for the blade
> So man's for woman made
> And woman made for man—"

Susan became aware of a slight scrabbling sound and whirled about, convinced that something was gazing at her.

"Land šakes alive!" Through a small aperture woven into one of the panniers protruded the head of a live cock. His fierce, sherry-red eye glared upon her in uncompromising suspicion.

"*Cuck!*" observed the bird. "*Cuck-cuck!*"

"Poor thing! This Major Ridgely must be mighty partial to chicken pie."

As if affronted, the cock cackled a fresh defiance.

"Poor fowl, so you, too, must to the wars?" Laughing,

she put down her comb as there sounded a knock at the door. "Pray enter—"

The door opened and a handsome yellow-haired young fellow wearing the white cross-belts and Lincoln green shell-jacket of Smallwood's Horse made her a hasty bow, gulped, "Beg pardon, Ma'am. I was just looking for Beau—er, Major Ridgely. I'd no idee he was entertainin'. Most truly regret this intrusion."

Susan assured him the error was of no real moment, then treated him with such a dazzling smile that this red-faced cavalryman lingered in the bedroom's doorway.

"Hi, there, T-Tom! No p-poaching my territory, you d-dog!" She had no trouble in recognizing Ridgely's voice. "Just moved over to C-Cousin Grace's for the night. Reckon we can fight our little main down to the Indian King Coffee House." He bowed on appearing at her door. "Miss Stevens, may I p-present Cap-Captain McHenry? He—he's a rascal, but handy on a fox hunt or in a tight corner. Are your F-French friends settled in yet?"

"They've the second room to the right. You—you have been most kind." She couldn't help asking. "Do you always take a rooster along—how do you cook them in the field?"

"C-cook?" Acute horror became written all over Major Ridgely's plump features. "Rooster? Oh, my soul!"

Captain McHenry laughed nervously. "Ma'am—that ain't a rooster—that's a fighting cock, and a damn' good one, too. Cut my Jupiter to frazzles last week, eh Beau?"

"Always claimed that g-gray hackle strain was-wasn't strong enough—" Major Ridgely grunted. After stroking his pet's neck and allowing it to peck at his finger he looked reassured. "If you're ready, Ma'am, let us proceed downstairs where I have arranged a table f-for us. Tom, sup-suppose you amble down and s-see that Richard places no one else at our t-table. Oh, yes, and tell Richard to f-fetch up s-some of the 'fifty-six Madeira. You know, Tom, it's the-the stuff in the very dark green bottles. I'll rouse out our F-French f-friends."

His faintly veined and roseate nose a-gleam in the candlelight, and fairly exuding good nature, Major Ridgely departed, leaving young McHenry to feast his gaze upon this grave, gray-eyed girl.

"Beau's always the soul of hospitality, Miss Stevens.

What Major Ridgely doesn't know about blood horses and fighting chickens ain't enough to write on a thimble. Do you aim to tarry long in Annapolis?"

"Oh, no, sir—I am travelling southwards to Williamsburg."

"Indeed?" The young giant looked his surprise. "Possibly you will beat us down there. We were supposed to have embarked two days ago, but our transport ain't showed yet, curse the luck! Campaign may be done before we arrive."

Susan tucked a bone pin into a rebellious lock, then turned smiling. "You have no idea where I might find passage aboard some craft bound for the James?"

"Ah, so already you have acquired a gallant?" Laughing gently, Hilde appeared in the corridor, a small bottle in hand.

"Your servant, Ma'am," McHenry bowed and beat a reluctant retreat as Hilde entered the room.

"I would be flattered, Miss Stevens, if you would accept a small measure of that Parisian scent you so admired." While she spoke, Hilde's eyes strayed to Susan Stevens' portmanteau, then widened momentarily.

Painted in clear letters across the inside of its lid was: "Sabra Stanton, Boston, Massachusetts." *Nom de Dieu!* Faint as a cry of a bird lost in a storm, came a voice saying, "Somewhere, sometime you have heard that name before now."

Delightedly, Susan accepted the perfume but, sensing an obligation to reciprocate, sought her portmanteau. After a brief search she produced a tiny silver-and-enamel bosom bottle—one of those fragile receptacle designed to keep fresh flowers alive when tucked into the front of a bodice.

Too late, she saw her name betrayed, but only casually closed the chest. A moment later she turned, smiled sweetly innocent. "I fancy I am now as ready as possible, Madame. This scent is indeed divine!"

To her who had called herself Susan Stevens, the evening proved unforgettable. Under the benign influences of the Chevalier de Lameth's Moselle and Major Beau Ridgely's Madeira, most of Sabra Stanton's doubts and sorrows seemed to melt away.

As was fully expected, the tavern dining hall was jampacked with guests and its air heavy with the smells of food, liquors, beer, pomatum, tobacco, sweaty wool and leather.

The round-bellied Marylander seemed to nod almost to every other person in the dining hall. "Hi, there, Cousin Henry—how're those warhorses shapin' up? Evening Uncle Fred! Comin' to the main tonight, Charlie?" And so on. He did so with high good humor and quick wit that fascinated Hilde and Hector.

Later he described the first families of Annapolis—the Hammonds, Chases, Carrolls, Dulaneys, Brices and a dozen more. The State House they had seen was almost brand new, completed only three years before the present war had begun. Thanks to wealth pouring from the great tobacco estates, as well as from a thriving shipping business, the social life here had been nearly as brilliant as that of Williamsburg.

Deeply absorbed, Sabra at length inquired, "Your pardon, Major, but why in the world do you keep those roo—er, fowls in your bedroom?"

Young McHenry threw back his head and roared. "Ma'am, you would liefer find Beau going around sans breeches, than without a pair of his famous Jamaica red game chickens somewhere within reach. Right, Beau?"

"Oh, my s-soul, yes! Come, let's quit th-this bedlam." And he cleaved a path through the whirling smoke up to his own quarters. "Tommy, fetch out one of th-them stags of yours; we'll put the m-muffs on them and s-show Captain de Lameth and the ladies a bit of s-sport."

"I am all anticipation," Hector declared. "By observation one learns so much. Let me offer a bottle of anisette in honor of the occasion."

"Muffs? I—I do not understand," Hilde expostulated. "Muffs are for ladies and gentlemen, not chickens?"

"Usually, but not tonight, Ma'am." McHenry grinned and hurried off.

"Shall we not use my room? It is larger."

When Ridgely accepted his suggestion, de Lameth was enchanted; thin features alight, he began pushing aside chairs and tables to clear a space. Presently, Ridgely and his companion returned, each holding under his arm a bright-eyed game bird and having undoubtedly used the small end of the anisette bottle to good effect.

"These chickens ain't trimmed, Captain," young McHenry apologized. "Only do that when they fight with gaffs. Will you muff first or shall I, Beau?"

"Go ahead, T-Tom."

From a small box the major, now redder than ever of complexion, produced little, leather-covered pads much resembling miniature boxing gloves.

"Ready, Beau?"

While McHenry held his bird's feet upwards Ridgely tied on the muffs with quick, practiced movements—then prepared the second cock.

"What about a w-wee spot to wet our w-whistles before we b-begin?" Ridgely suggested. "Ladies, please mark how deuced quick these chickens move."

Once tumblers had been filled and passed about Ridgely and his companion prepared for action.

"Old man Reynolds sure will have conniption fits when he finds feathers over his best carpet," chuckled McHenry. Now minus his tunic, he squatted onto his heels facing Ridgely.

The two cocks for a minute were held close enough to permit them to peck and glare at each other. Then, amid whoops of delight from the male onlookers and muffled squeals from the ladies the combatants were released and flared up, striking out hard with their padded spurs.

Hilde shrieked softly and gathered her skirts tight about her legs, but Sabra only stared round-eyed at the incredibly rapid motions of the fighting chickens. Because of the muffs, neither bird suffered the least hurt, but all the same the air became filled with flying feathers.

"Handle 'em!" ordered one of the gentlemen. "Look a bit winded and old Beau looks thirsty. How about a tot?"

The bottles were passed again and, after a brief respite, the birds were permitted once more to fly at each other.

"Oh, Susan," Hilde begged, "can't we take refuge in your room till they tire of this? I've seen enough—and will you look at my Hector? *Ça va, chéri?*"

"*Parfaitement.* This is a sport of supreme swiftness and delicacy."

She laughed when her lover snatched off his immaculate blue and yellow tunic and, in shirt sleeves, crouched to watch, with the perception of the excellent fencer he was, the lightning blows delivered by these feathered combatants.

The Marylanders obviously were delighted over this foreigner's genuine enthusiasm and kept offering him seegars and any number of drinks. Pretty soon, Ridgely felt called upon to lead his companions in song and, even in Sabra's room, Hilde could hear them serenading the chevalier. Presently Hector's clear tenor returned the compliment with a spirited rendition of the gay "Marie Galante."

Suddenly Hilde's expression sobered and her straight black brows crept closer together. "My dear Susan," she began, "I am not of the curious sort, perhaps because I have met with much sorrow in my life—and many difficulties. I have come to like you more than a little. Can I be of—well, of any assistance?"

Sabra's smile faded as she looked her companion full in the face. "What leads you to imagine that I stand in need of assistance?"

"As a rule young ladies do no travel towards a battle for mere pleasure alone—least of all, unescorted," Hilde pointed out.

"You see many women and girls riding both animals and the baggage wagons."

"Yes, but very few nice girls," Hilde returned quietly.

The wine perhaps had released a measure of Sabra's natural reserve. "Why do you deem me—unhappy?"

"You *are* Sabra Stanton, are you not?"

Sabra's eyes flickered over to the portmanteau. "Yes. That is my true name. I have good reason to travel under another."

"No doubt. Please say no more. I am perhaps indiscreet in having said so much."

"Oh, no," Sabra burst out. "I want to talk to you. For weeks I have been stifled for lack of conversation."

They seated themselves on the bed; Sabra leaning against its footboard, Hilde's doll-like figure propped against the bolster and pillows.

Sabra indulged in no self-palliative preambles, but spoke in disarming frankness. "You see, Hilde, last year I became affianced to a certain officer on service with our Army. I was madly in love with him."

"'Was'?" Hilde murmured.

Sabra flushed, shrugged. "It is possible that I still am. I don't know. It is that very uncertainty which plagues me, night and day. Although I have endeavored to do so, I seem unable to put him out of my mind." Her voice softened. "Lucius possesses—well, qualities which prompt me to believe that I don't fully understand the reasons back of his abominable conduct."

Hilde merely regarded her hands. "'Abominable conduct'?"

"Yes," Sabra began talking faster. "I journeyed down from Boston to King's Ferry—a place on the Hudson River. We were to be married two days later, I forgot to tell you that." Sabra sighed. "Well, you can imagine how thunderstruck I was to learn, in Kingston, that Lucius—my intended husband—had that very day espoused another woman; a very rich lady, I believe."

"I think," Hilde announced evenly, "you are most fortunate to be shut of so great a fool."

The shake of Sabra's head was instant and vigorous. "No. That is just what is wrong. Lucius is no part of a fool!" Her hands commenced closing restlessly in her lap. "Mayhap I'm a looney, yet I cannot rid myself of a notion that, somehow or other, Lucius was forced into this maneuver.

"You see, Hilde, I *know* he loved me until that time. You should have read the tenderness of his letters. Oh, they had a way of creeping into the very core of my heart. Really, I cannot have been so badly mistaken." Sabra's voice gradually had lowered itself until, in order to hear, Hilde had to lean forward.

"You have my sympathy." She was thinking of her long fruitless passion for Doctor Peabody—"And after you learned that he had betrayed you?"

"There was a duel. Lucius remained unhurt, but shot my brother through the shoulder, and very nearly killed him. Surely, if Lucius had been as guilty as it appeared, God would have punished him, and not Joshua?"

"One has yet to hear of *le bon Dieu* serving as president in an affair of honor," Hilde commented drily.

"Be that as it may, it was well that Phoebe and I were there to care for Josh. Sometimes, we feared he would never shake off that terrible fever. Eventually he did, and recovered rapidly because he is strong. It was only then that I—"

"—That you felt impelled to find this Lucius and question him face to face?"

"You are very clever, Hilde."

"Oh, no, Sabra, I am a very simple person, indeed I am. But of life I have observed a little."

"You are quite right. I can find no peace. I cannot continue my life until I see Lucius, hear his story, and judge whether any excuse exists for what he did. Then, and only then, can I banish his memory from my mind and heart. Am I so foolish?''

''Not in the least.'' Hilde's fingers closed gently on her companion's hand. ''But it is really unfortunate that you have undertaken to seek this Lucius during such terrible days and in so dangerous a region. Tell me; how did you learn of his presence—in Williamsburg?''

''Would that Lucius were there! No. I fear him to be in York Town. You see, Lord Cornwallis gave up Williamsburg some weeks ago—was driven out, rather.''

''But how can you be sure this Lucius is indeed in this York Town?''

''Because I travelled to New York in search of him. There I sold my wedding clothes, the linens I had been given to set up housekeeping. As it turned out, I arrived in New York only to learn that, a few days before, Lucius had sailed as contract surgeon to certain reinforcements being dispatched to the assistance of Lord Cornwallis.''

''Do you know with what regiment he serves?''

''Not for sure,'' Sabra replied gloomily. ''Last I heard, he was on duty with a German regiment—the Anspach. All the same, I shall find him, and then I will know whether I still love him.''

''His wife accompanied him?''

''Not she. After the scandal and the duel she retired to her estate and left Lucius to scurry away to New York.''

''I must ask yet another question,'' Hilde murmured smiling. ''Suppose that you discover this Lucius to be, indeed, the base villain he would appear?''

''I shall hate him doubly, because I have begun to think that he may have dealt me a second injury.''

''' 'A second injury'?''

''Yes. He may have cost me the love of another man. Now do you understand why I *must* find him?''

XIII. SCOUT SHIP

CAPTAIN ANDREW WARREN came to the conclusion that this evening of September the fourth, 1781, was pretty near the loveliest he could recall. Out of the north-north-east a breeze was blowing just strong enough to send his new command, the *Grand Turk III*, surging southwards at a speed thrilling to one appreciative of a vessel's sailing qualities.

Square jaw for once relaxed, captain Warren cast a glance at his quartermaster and, by the binnacle's light, made out the fellow's scarred brown face quite clearly. Good. He was minding his task. More content than in a very long time, Warren raised his gaze to the yards, and watched the brig's topmasts go swinging rhythmically back and forth, back and forth. Canvas bent onto them briefly obscured great patches of stars.

God above, what sheer luxury it was to feel a deck tilt and lift once more beneath his feet. Though Warren hated to admit it, this privateer was a damned sight handier in the wind than any of the regular naval vessels he'd ever sailed in. Watch cloak blowing free, Andrew Warren strolled across the otherwise deserted quarterdeck to its weather rail. From where he stood he could discern the black outlines of the starboard watch huddled among those long eight pounders with which this brig's original battery had been replaced.

A soft sighing of wind through the shrouds, the gentle tap-tapping of reef points against taut canvas and the steady *hiss whiss* of the waves alongside, played a familiar symphony in his ears. If only this handsome brig had been a regularly commissioned naval vessel, instead of a privateer under charter to His Excellency, Admiral de Barras, Andrew Warren's cup of happiness would have overflowed.

Jerusha! It didn't seem possible that, three short months ago, he had been hungry and freezing half to death away up there in Halifax Prison.

Surely, his wife's despairing prayers must have been answered, else he'd never have been exchanged for a British naval lieutenant who had connections at Court. Come to think on it, God had been kind about letting him find Minga so quickly in Newport for, during those two interminable years, he had heard from her but once.

Even as Warren's brooding eyes explored the ocean to windward, he experienced yet again his burning resentment against that timorous old jellyfish in naval uniform, Commodore Dudley Saltonstall.

Yes, sir. If any one man could be held responsible for the destruction of American naval power in this war, the blame must rest upon Saltonstall's sloping shoulders. A curse on that stubborn incapacity of his which had doomed a fine, well-equipped fleet to sinking and burning itself without having struck a single blow in self-defense. Outraged protests had availed not at all. Acid old Saltonstall had merely stared down his long thin nose and whined that Warren was to obey orders and destroy the *Diligent*.

Surely, that summer's day back in 'seventy-nine would live in shame so long as the American nation existed. Andrew Warren, unassigned lieutenant in the Navy of the United States, still could feel hot tides of rage rip through him whenever he recalled watching fire burst from the tops of his first—and last—naval command, the U.S.S. *Diligent*, fourteen guns.

Andrew Warren had hoped at least to preserve his crew—well-drilled naval gun crews were scarcer than scarce—by dodging away in the small boats under cover of a fog. However, they had blundered slapbang into a British flotilla.

The boats had fired a few desperate shots before surrendering, but, all too soon, the Royal Marines came closing in.

Then had followed the misery of the stockade at Halifax where, on starvation diet, freezing, ague-shaken and despairing, he'd lived weeks and months enduring a torment of anxiety over how Minga and his boy might be faring. Beyond his pay, uncertain and now all but valueless, Minga hadn't had a *sou marqué* to keep her alive.

At the sound of footsteps he swung sharply about. "Good evening, Doctor Burnham. You are up late."

"Good evening, Captain. When do you imagine we will raise land?"

"Around sunup, I expect."

"Any sign of a British squadron?"

Andrew Warren's teeth glistened amid the bold planes of his features. "I followed our Dancing Master's instructions so we sail well to the east'ard of any bulldogs. 'Tis a handy vessel you and Mrs. Ashton own, Doctor. For all her two hundred tons she handles dainty as a yacht. She's handy into the wind, yet I'll warrant she can run down-wind like a scaled cat."

"Thank you, Captain. You see, this vessel means considerably more to me than just an—an investment." Peter Burnham experienced a deep sense of satisfaction at hearing the *Grand Turk III* thus praised, especially as his present captain had proved to be a grim, hard-to-please fellow.

From the start, though, it had been clear that Captain Warren knew his duties from A to Zed. Why, in three day's time he got the brig's crew jumping about as smartly as if he yet commanded a regular man-of-war.

An odd character, this Andrew Warren. Peter Burnham thought back to that day, near a month ago, when he'd come across this lean, black-haired giant studying shipping notices affixed to an inn's notice board. Noting the anxious and bitter lines about this stranger's intelligent-looking eyes, he'd entered into conversation with him, had brought him home for dinner and for further observation because the *Grand Turk* needed a capable master.

Lord, how the poor fellow had eaten! Presently, it turned out that he was a returned prisoner, with a wife and child to support and down to his last stiver.

When first Peter had beheld a vessel which resembled the *Grand Turk* to a marked degree, she had been standing in past Beaver Tail Point towards Newport Harbor and he had refused to credit his eyesight. He could, though, when halfway out to this brig riding under the guns of the *Concorde,* frigate, with the French flag flying above a British Jack.

H.M.C.M.S. *Concorde,* later investigation revealed, had run down and recaptured the *Grand Turk* off Saint Kitts.

Captain Warren went forward to bellow a command to the watch and Peter, seeking the taffrail, peered over the stern.

What fine luck that all Ashton's prizes save the *Hammond* had reached friendly ports. "I made no mistake in buying a half-share of this brig," he told himself. "Already she's earned Mrs. Ashton and me a tidy sum. Poor woman, she'd a thousandfold rather have her husband alive and well."

When he'd announced his purchase, Trina had thrilled at the thought of his owning that vessel which had played so critical a part in her life.

The only discordant note about the present moment was the fact that Trina again was big as a house with child, so big that her infant would be born within the next two or three weeks—certain while he was absent. A comforting aspect of this situation was the fact that she'd have level-headed, and supremely capable Minga Warren on hand to serve in the dual role of friend and nurse.

Well, mused Peter Burnham, here he was, under contract as surgeon of the squadron of Admiral Vicomte Paul François Jean Nicolas de Barras, who, commanding eight lumbering ships of the line, by now must be sailing at least a day and a half astern of the fleet little *Grand Turk*.

This voyage to the Chesapeake might have required much less time had not Admiral de Barras so fully appreciated the extent of his responsibilities. Did not the transports he was convoying carry in their holds the only siege train in North America? Therefore he had elected to cruise far away from the American coast, in an effort to reach the James River without risking capture at the horny hands of Admirals Graves, Hood and Drake.

It was entirely logical that a chartered privateer, swift and handy into the wind, should have been dispatched as scout ship. No less reasonable was the idea that he, Peter Burnham, should sail aboard her that he might set up in Virginia a flying hospital ready and capable of receiving the sick and injured of de Barras' squadron.

Peter figured he'd made no mistake in picking Andrew Warren for the *Grand Turk's* new master. Rail though he could, and did, at the Marine Committee of Congress, this dark-browed ex-naval officer was a first class captain; in all likelihood he'd have commanded a frigate by now if fate, and Dudley Saltonstall, had not intervened. Yes, even more skillfully than Robert Ashton himself, this tight-lipped New Hampshireman could coax every bit of speed out of the brig.

Now she was stepping towards the Chesapeake with the speed of a lance hurled by a powerful arm. Peter felt pretty certain that this ex-naval officer was eating his heart out for fear he wouldn't be allowed to engage the enemy. Lord, how he doted on those new French eight pounders!

A falling star streaked brilliantly across the western sky and, for a wonder, Warren made comment. "Let us hope, Doctor Burnham that yonder presents an omen."

"Omen?"

"Yes. The decline of the British Navy. Would to God that the United States could play some part in its fall!"

Curiously, Peter Burnham surveyed his employee. "Is America indeed so destitute of sea power?"

Andrew Warren gripped the taffrail with both hands. "At this moment, sir, only two wounded and homeless frigates, the *Alliance* and the *Deane,* comprise our Navy. May I assure you, Doctor, but for the French fleet we would long since have been smashed."

Rapidly, his fingers commenced to drum against the scarred woodwork of the rail, damp now with sea moisture.

"Perchance matters will mend somewhat now that Mr. Robert Morris has been appointed Agent of Marine." Warren turned. "I don't envy him his task, Doctor. Up until we lost the *Trumbull* two months agone, I had fancied we still might build and sail a fleet." The wind sharpened and Warren gathered his cloak. "Now 'tis hopeless."

"Tell me, Captain Warren, why is it so extremely distasteful for you to sign aboard a privateer?"

"I'll not answer that." Warren's laugh was bitter. "Ashore they warned me, 'Be civil to your owners and you'll get ahead.'"

Peter Burnham's jaw closed with a click. "I had deemed you more intelligent, sir, than to address such a remark to me."

"Your pardon, Doctor. Very well, I will speak the truth. Had I been content to ship aboard a privateer three years ago I reckon I could have made my fortune twice over. Many less capable than I have done so." He stepped closer, hungry-looking features taut. "But damn my soul, sir, our Union can't survive without a navy and a strong one. Can't you understand? Without naval strength we are nothing and can become nothing great. Mark my words, if our Dancing Master admiral doesn't rendezvous with the French West Indian fleet and whip old Granny Graves and his bright lads, Cornwallis will be re-enforced, and this war lost for good and all!"

"I ask your pardon." In friendly fashion Peter Burnham placed a hand on the other's arm. "Knowing perhaps something of the meaning of disappointment and frustration, I can admire your constancy in persisting so long in a luckless Service—and without recognition or hope of reward.''

For some time after that the two men remained silent on the quarterdeck. Right now, it would not have surprised Peter if they never sighted land again or encountered another ship.

Summoning a wry smile, Warren abruptly offered his hand. ''Doctor, forgive my bluntness. Since I needs must serve aboard a private ship-of-war I'll quickly say I couldn't find a finer vessel. Mayhap you don't appreciate her extraordinary speed and staunchness—the man who commanded this brig must have loved her much like a mistress.''

''I venture that he did,'' Peter murmured and wondered whether Robert Ashton's spirit might not, even now, be pacing the quarterdeck of his beloved vessel.

Captain Warren still must be feeling embarrassed for he inquired, ''Your wife, sir, was she well when we sailed?''

''In fine spirit and health, thank you. With Mistress Warren in the house she will suffer few qualms when her time comes. Besides, she has your fine lad to remind her how worth while all that sorry business can be.''

''You were mighty kind to shelter Minga. She made heavy weather of it whilst I lay a prisoner. Not that she ever complained.'' He grinned suddenly. ''I fancy we could shake hands on our womenfolk.''

Once Doctor Burnham had cast a final look at sea and sky before going below, a strange restlessness pervaded Andrew Warren's being. Hourly, a conviction was growing in his imagination that tomorrow would prove a vastly significant day. Come dawn, his brig would commence to shape a course directly for Capes Henry and Charles which marked the entrance to the vast and rich waters of Chesapeake Bay. The big question was—would he sight Admiral Graves' fleet bearing down to blockade the Bay? Nobody knew where the British ships really were.

He passed the word below to summon Mounseer Aristide Loubet who, under the terms of the charter, was his first officer. Not that Warren had found grounds for complaint. Mounseer Loubet had proved both clever and imaginative; besides, he could speak to that half of the crew which spoke no English at all. M. Loubet displayed many evidences of gentle birth, for all his slipshod dress and foul language. Warren suspected that this first officer must have come to grief in the French king's Navy; cards perhaps, or an unfortunate duel.

For third in command, Warren had signed on that same Abel Doane who had sailed under Captain Ashton. Warren estimated Doane as the kind of man who would never command a ship of his own except by accident; a natural-born second mate, that's what Doane was.

The crew was the usual hodgepodge of Americans, French, Negroes and even a few English deserters, but in Newport nowadays one had to take what one could get by way of hands. Manning, his boatswain, was English, and if ever the Royal Navy had been hated by a former member of that Service, Manning was that man.

Like Aristide Loubet, George Manning, despite his ruin, retained several gentlemanly qualities, for all that, steadfastly, he denied a knowledge of navigation. Warren, nonetheless, felt certain that, should occasion arise, his boatswain could shoot the sun and navigate a vessel as handily as any officer aboard.

Presently Loubet appeared, a bandy-legged little Breton with a round red head, flat impassive features and a coppery complexion. He saluted punctiliously and thereby gained Warren's approval.

"*Bon soir, mon Capitaine.* A fine night, is it not?"

"Yes, Mr. Loubet," Warren agreed in a fluent French acquired during early visits to the Mediterranean.

Loubet drew a deep breath and, in view of Warren's own ruminations, asked a remarkable thing. "Does one scent glory in the air, sir; or maybe it is only a land scent?"

"It must be glory you sense, Loubet—there'll be no land smell on a northeast breeze," Warren smiled. "Pray order the log tossed and give me your estimate of our position. 'Twon't do to be in error once we stand in towards the Capes of Virginia."

Confident of the Breton's competence, Andrew Warren went below and, for a space, remained bent above his charts, calculating and recalculating his brig's position. That the *Grand Turk* should win through to Lynnhaven Bay was imperative; no less a personage than Admiral de Barras had emphasized the fact only the day before.

How nervous the admiral had been. No wonder. His shrift would prove short indeed should his eight line-of-battle ships become intercepted on their way to the Chesapeake by Graves' infinitely superior squadron.

Locked in Andrew Warren's personal clothes chest reposed a box carefully weighted by strips of lead. It contained most urgent dispatches destined for the immediate attention of Lieutenant-General, the Count of Rochambeau and Major-General the Marquis of Saint-Simon.

When the privateer's captain reappeared on deck it was to find Dawn painting glory in the east and flinging bright golden lances against the broken purple-blue surcoat of defeated Night.

To his surprise Abel Doane, usually a slug-a-bed, already had appeared and was bending his globular figure over the flag locker. M. Loubet, he noted, had ordered a shortening of the forecourse probably because the wind now was blowing very fresh out of the northeast.

Once again, an inexplicable premonition of impending drama gripped Andrew Warren. In a tense and mounting suspense, he and his first officer stood watching the first bright fingernail-paring rim of the sun slide over the horizon and commence to gild brisk and feathery whitecaps. But for all that, neither of them could have predicted that a most decisive day in America's War for Independence was dawning.

XIV. LA LUTTE DES TITANS

THE SUN BARELY had cleared the horizon than a lookout posted in the maintop yelled down, "Sail, ho-o-o-!"

Immediately Andrew Warren shouted through cupped hands, "Where away?"

"Broad off t' starboard bow, sir."

"What rig?"

"Can't make out yet, sir, she bein' hull down. I only caught the flash o' her sails."

'Foremast hands, crowding excitedly up on deck, noticed that the sea was changing from dark to light blue, and was losing some of its previous sparkling transparency.

"River silt," Doane grunted, pointing to an occasional streak of sand-colored water.

Warren nodded agreement and felt relieved. His vessel was off the mouth of Chesapeake Bay, all right, but far enough south and east of the Capes to avoid the attention of a chance British watch frigate, he hoped.

He picked up a leather speaking trumpet. "Masthead, there! What course does the stranger sail?"

"'Pears like she's sailin' 'bout west-southwest, sir."

Excitement mounted because, just then, the 'foremast lookout shouted suddenly, "Sail, ho! Two points off our sta'board bow and hull down, sir!"

The crew began to look anxiously at each other. This second ship must be cruising many miles distant from the first.

"How does she sail?"

"South-southeast, sir; looks like mebbe she's a frigate."

"If that first vessel is a Britisher," Doane remarked, "then I allow yonder's a French ship, cruising on lookout."

Warren's manner grew crisp and his dark eyes sparkled. Enjoying the weather gauge of both strangers he didn't feel in the least concerned.

Both lookouts sang out in unison. "Sails! Many sails, sir! Broad off our starboard beam, sir."

"Mr. Doane, take the deck. Monsieur Loubet, come with me."

With that Andrew Warren went swarming nimbly up to the main crosstrees. Loubet followed only a few ratlines below; the Breton's scarred, blunt face had assumed a wooden aspect.

Warren felt his heart quicken as, one after another, many tall ships, six, seven, eight of them, poked their tops over the horizon.

Ever the efficient officer, Warren glanced at his watch and read the time as seven o'clock. Below, the brig's whole crew had swarmed to her starboard rail, watching sail after sail flash in the morning sun. Even the least intelligent among them guessed that, beyond a shadow of doubt, yonder, sailing southwards, was an impressive number of men-of-war. Of what nationality were they?

"*Voilà la flotte Britannique,*" Loubet announced. "*Vous êtes d'accord, mon Capitaine?*"

Andrew Warren, spyglass glued to eye, nodded. "You are quite correct. By their course and position that must be Admiral Graves' squadron coming down from New York. How many tall ships do you count?"

"Fourteen for sure, *mon Capitaine*," Loubet called over the creaking of the yards and braces. "And you, Monsieur?"

"I tally sixteen heavy frigates or line-of-battle ships."

The passage of half an hour proved them both wrong. Steering a roughly parallel course, but sailing nowhere near as fast as the *Grand Turk,* cruised no less than nineteen majestic ships of the line! Perhaps as many more transports, tenders and victuallers were struggling along in the wake of the men-of-war.

What claimed Warren's closest attention were the maneuvers of a couple of fast-looking frigates cruising like watch-dogs on the flank of a herd of sheep. Damned if they weren't wearing, as if they intended to give chase to this solitary brig.

"Mr. Doane, clap on royals and studding sails," Warren called down and experienced a thrill of pride at the smart way his topmen went swarming aloft. Under this added pressure of canvas the *Grand Turk* heeled 'way over to starboard and spray commenced shooting over the bows in great sheets of silver lace. Before long, the privateer left the British far astern and had the ocean to herself again.

By that time the sea water had assumed a definite tan color and carried an increasing amount of driftwood; it therefore surprised no one that, near nine of the morning, land was sighted.

Once he became convinced that Cape Henry, southern-most of the Virginia Capes, indeed loomed ahead, the *Grand Turk's* master ordered his vessel on a course calculated to send her running straight into the six-mile-wide entrance of Chesapeake Bay. There they were. Cape Henry off the port beam and Cape Charles, blue off the starboard bow.

The day continued fine and produced a breeze still and steady enough to delight any honest sailor.

All was going almost too well, Warren mused. As if to justify his apprehension there materialized from under the land a cruiser—she looked like a big sloop-of-war of a light frigate. She was crowding on sail as if running to beat the privateer into the entrance and proved so fast that, presently, Warren determined to bear up and force the unknown vessel to make clear her intentions.

Within half an hour the stranger—she was a frigate, all

right—cruised near enough to permit observation of a predominantly white flag snapping from her signal yard.

"Might be a French flag—or a British white ensign," Doane told Peter Burnham. "Skipper's right to haul his wind and look lively. Stranger's got the metal of us and plenty to spare."

"Looks like a Frenchie to me, sir," remarked the quartermaster presently.

"Aye," Doane agreed. "Yonder'll be one of old de Grasse's watch ships streaking in to raise the alarm. He'll be barely in time. Look up yonder." Away off to the northeast had reappeared a string of white dots heralding the approach of the British squadron.

The words were hardly spoken when the watch frigate commenced firing alarm guns, then ran up to her signal yards of string of vari-colored flags. From his chosen position in the *Grand Turk's* main crosstrees, Warren, in growing anxiety watched the British ships commence to maneuver as if seeking battle position.

"God help de Barras if he comes up now," Andrew Warren muttered. "He'll blunder straight into that array." Then he levelled his speaking trumpet at the quarterdeck. "Send Manning to me!"

The ex-naval officer's deep-set eyes were a-glow now, his lips drawn hard and flat against his teeth. Because it had escaped its tie ribbon, his dark brown hair was flying.

"Will you be able to recognize any of those enemy liners to windward?" he inquired when the boatswain came up, hand-over-hand, to join him.

"Yes, sir, very likely, sir," panted Manning. He shaded his eyes. "I can be surer in a little while."

It had become apparent, meanwhile, that the British armada was even more numerous than previously estimated. All lookouts agreed that, standing majestically in towards Cape Charles, cruised nineteen liners, a fifty-gun ship, no less than six frigates and what much resembled a fire ship.

The British, without exception, were sailing the port tack and in no particular order. Apparently, Vice-Admiral Sir Samuel Graves had not as yet decided upon his order of battle.

"Must be waiting to learn what his spy ships will report," Warren reasoned. "Well, he's still got plenty of time."

Half an hour dragged by during which those aboard the *Grand Turk* watched, in mounting awe, a series of maneuvers that concluded by dividing this vast fleet into three lesser squadrons. By now, George Manning commenced to recognize certain of the enemy.

"That for'ard ship, sir," he called over the rushing of the wind, "is the *Alfred*, she's a seventy-four; behind her sails the *Belliquex*. She's only a third-rater, sixty-four guns. The third ship in line I don't recognize, but the fourth is the *Barfleur,* a first-rater, ninety guns. The red pendant to her maintop shows she's got an admiral aboard, Sir Sam Hood, most likely, and may God rot his guts!"

"What's that blue pendant showing 'way off in the third division?"

"That will belong to the admiral commanding the division, probably Rear-Admiral Sir Francis Samuel Drake."

"And where'd you calculate Admiral Graves will be showing his flag?"

Manning hesitated, shielding his eyes from the glare of the sun. "See that only other first-rater, sir, right in the center of the fleet? She's the *London*. See how she towers above the rest?"

Each passing moment sharpened a question foremost in the New Hampshireman's mind. Due to the privateer's round-about course, and to the time lost in standing away from the French spy ship, the *Grand Turk* might not be able to beat those screening British frigates in a race for the entrance.

From a close study of some excellent French charts, Andrew was aware that, although the gap separating the two capes was a good six miles in width, a shoal called the Middle Ground in reality divided the entrance into two comparatively narrow channels, of which the southernmost was the wider.

Under every stitch of canvas that would draw, the brig now was fairly flying along with her American ensign standing out, crisp and clear, against the flawless September sky.

For a while Warren felt confident he could successfully enter the Bay, but then something happened which caused him to order the helm hard down a-starboard and send his crew scrambling aloft to shorten sail.

Crowding around the dull green and sandy yellow bluffs of Cape Henry shone the canvas of another fleet, quite as great as that standing in from the Atlantic—and New York. On the privateer's deck, First Office Loubet slapped his thigh and fairly danced in his excitement as Warren slid down a back stay to resume his normal post before the binnacle.

"*Alors, voilà Monsieur de Grasse! Maintenant commence la lutte des Titans!*"

Peter Burnham, frankly, was awed by the grandeur of those two great fleets with their tall canvas, bristling guns and vari-colored sides.

"The Frenchies," Doane explained, "are fixin' to get out to sea in time to take formation before meeting the British. See, there come the lead ships of the French van." He pointed to two or three frigates, one blue, one bright green and the third dull yellow, rounding Cape Henry with battle flags flying and guns run out.

"The tide, Mr. Doane?" Andrew snapped. "How runs the tide?"

"Near the flood, sir," Doane replied. "'Twill ebb sharply soon."

The *Grand Turk* now was practically retracing her former course, but stood more to the southwards and as near to the yellow dunes of Cape Henry as Warren dared take her. It was really too risky to try for the passage when a single excited liner might make a mistake and blow his little brig to kingdom come. Ship after ship, singly and by twos and threes, the French came crowding out of both channels, all huddled together like sheep chased out of a fold.

Now signal guns commenced to bang and boom among the ships to the northwards. Like bright-colored and demented butterflies signal flags shot up, then disappeared.

Warren determined that the British admiral was ranging his squadron into a "line-ahead" formation which would place Rear-Admiral Sir Samuel Hood's division in the van, Graves himself would take the center, leaving Rear Admiral Sir Francis Drake to bring up the rear.

In bitter envy, the ex-commander of the U.S.S. *Diligent*, through his glass, watched those huge two- and three-deckers go surging into position. The screen of lighter ships, sloops and frigates promptly formed out on either flank. Far, far behind, the transports and victuallers idled, awaiting the outcome of this impending battle.

At last the French *avant-garde*, clear of the entrance at last, commenced also to assume a "line-ahead" formation. Aristide Loubet identified the leading man-of-war as the *Pluton,* seventy-four guns and commanded by d'Albert de Rions; then came the *Marseillaise,* another seventy-four. That Loubet at some time must have held a staff position, Warren now was certain; how else would he be able to reel off the names of the vessels as they fell into line? *Duc de Bourgogne,* seventy-four; *Diadème,* seventy-four; *Saint Esprit,* eighty, and so on.

"That fourth vessel in line," he was explaining in explosive French, "is the flagship of the van, commanded by Admiral de Bougainville—she is called the *Auguste* and mounts eighty guns."

Considering his orders, Warren had no choice but further to shorten his canvas, back his topsails and stand back and forth—a mere spectator of this rapidly developing clash of Titans—until an opportunity presented itself to dash through the South Channel and, with all speed, head for the James River's mouth.

Closer and closer, sailed the great French line-of-battle ships, their lofty top-gallant masts climbing dizzily high into the heavens. To Warren's experienced eye, the French van was being quite as smartly handled as Sir Sam Hood's huge vessels.

All at once—Andrew Warren and Loubet both wondered why—instead of bearing down with all his strength upon the French as they came struggling out of the entrance to Chesapeake Bay, Admiral Graves now ordered his whole fleet to wear and shape courses out to sea; why, now they were bearing approximately east-south-east!

Incredible though it seemed, the British Admiral was actually allowing the French opportunity to reorganize and to properly space their *avant-garde.* Not only that, but, with each passing moment, more of King Louis' great blue, white, and gold ships-of-the-line were running out of the South Channel and gaining the open sea.

xv. The Signals of Admiral Graves,
September 5, 1781

That stiff breeze which, since sunup, had been blowing steadily out of the north-northeast gave no indication of diminishing and, under its compulsion, both fleets went steering out to sea—the British clinging doggedly to their priceless advantage of the weather gauge.

So engrossed with the drama was the brig's polyglot crew that very few mess captains appeared to draw rations. It wasn't in every man's lifetime to behold no less than forty-three line-of-battle ships—nineteen British and twenty-four French, feinting and maneuvering for an advantage over one another. Shaping up over there, was the sort of sea battle the old gaffers were forever maundering about. Once again, the world's two greatest naval powers were squaring away for an engagement, the outcome of which was to shape the destiny of mankind for the next hundred years—if not for a millennium.

By a quarter to two of the afternoon, the last French ships had cleared Cape Henry and, with the last of the *arrière-garde* in tolerably good formation, were starting after the center and the dangerously detached *avant-garde*. All the same, this forward division remained perilously far ahead of the main fleet.

Soon the French center division began passing not a quarter-mile to windward of the impotent little *Grand Turk.* First the *Pluton,* seventy-four, then the *Caton,* sixty-four, next the *Souverain,* seventy-four, and after her the enormous *Ville de Paris.* She was the flagship of the irascible Provençal, Admiral Comte de Grasse, Loubet exulted. When her captain so decreed, her crew could run out one hundred and four guns to hurl death and destruction up on the enemies of His Most Christian Majesty.

Standing among the privateer's afterguard, Doctor Peter Burnham stood breathlessly surveying the unfolding of this drama and thinking, "Dear God, so many poor devils will soon be dead or shrieking in agony."

Beneath the exteriors of those towering hulls now so brave with gold leaf and paint, and below those proud white battle flags all spangled with little golden *fleur-de-lis,* he could reconstitute the horrors of the *Grand Turk's* cockpit—but multiplied a hundredfold.

Like a mosquito circling a battle between two huge swarms of beetles, the brig maneuvered downwind and waited her chance to run for the entrance.

Both fleets were now arranged in an orderly "line-ahead" formation—with the British sailing almost due

east, and de Grasse heading for the broad Atlantic on a
course slightly south of east.

At two-fifteen in the afternoon, a number of signal
flags appeared at the *London's* signal yard.

Doane, eyeing a broad expanse of tan water opined,
"They'll be about three miles apart. Give 'em a half-hour
and we will see what happens."

For once Andrew Warren neglected to check the disposition of his crew. Jerusha! Before his eyes was developing a major naval engagement between two closely
matched fleets—that experience dreamed about, and passionately yearned for, by every good naval officer. Right
from the start, he had perceived Graves' missed opportunity of destroying the French, piecemeal, at the entrance. Now it would appear that Graves was committing
a second blunder by advancing his line at a long, obtuse
angle towards the French, instead of closing in by divisions and fighting on a parallel line. If a sudden flurry of
flags on the *Barfluer* meant anything, Rear-Admiral Hood
wasn't being backwards about protesting these tactics.

The *Grand Turk's* master barked at Manning. "What
means that signal from the *London?*"

" 'Keep more to starboard,' sir."

Now both fleets were sailing sluggishly—liners were
never fast—but majestically away from the entrance.
Even the dullest eye could tell that the British vessels by
no means were as handy sailors as their enemies.

Time seemed to halt for those aboard the privateer—
they were watching the lead ships of the British van—
that which had been the rear, until the line reversed itself—come bearing down on the now rigidly correct formation of Rear-Admiral de Bougainville.

Loubet groaned, "*Nom de Dieu!* Had we the weather
gauge, our whole fleet might now attack." He clasped his
hands. "*Sainte Vierge!* Change the wind. Now! Now! We
can enfilade the whole *maudite* fleet of Albion."

The wind, however, remained in the north-northeast
and the British van under Drake and those of de Bougainville drew closer. More French ships sailed by, passing
the little brig not two cables' lengths distant—roughly
fourteen hundred feet.

Andrew Warren's mouth went dry and his soul burned.
Oh, curse the luck! Damn it! God damn it! Why must he
and his command be forced to stay on the outskirts of

this fight like some shy bitch watching two great hounds join battle! Yet to a naval officer, orders were orders. That his brig, with her pitiful battery of twelve eight pounders, could no more affect the outcome of this engagement than a man clapping his hands on the forecastle, never occurred to Andrew Warren.

Nearer and nearer, sailed these marine mammoths, heeling well to starboard under the northeast breeze. The *Grand Turk* sailed as close to them as Warren dared; he wanted those Frenchmen to see, if only as a token, the huge American ensign streaming at his gaff. Nobody paid the least attention.

The weather remained so fair that everyone aboard the *Grand Turk* received a clear impression of the beginning of the engagement when, all of a sudden, the British, at a cable's length, let fly a tremendous broadside at the *Réfléchi*, fifth vessel in the French column. Everyone saw gray-white smoke burst from the sides of the *Shrewsbury* and *Intrepid* then, seconds later, heard the roar of the discharge.

"*Mon Dieu!*"

"My God, look at the *Réfléchi!*"

Under an iron hail dispatched by the British guns great jagged sections of the French liner's fabric—she was the smallest in line—sailed high into the air, her masts swayed and her previously orderly canvas sagged, flopped crazily on broken yards. All the same, Captain Bondel's men fired back a reverberating, deafening defiance, then a great billow of gray-white smoke formed and briefly concealed the *Réfléchi*.

"Look! Look at that!" Manning was biting his knuckles. "See that vessel bearing down? That's the *Princessa*, Drake's own ship."

Thirty-five cannon, composing the *Princessa*'s starboard battery began spouting flame and roundshot as that tall seventy sailed straight at the seventy-four gun *Diadème*. Soon not two hundred feet of sand-colored water separated the two contestants. Every time a broadside thundered, those aboard the *Grand Turk* could see the lower sails writhe under the concussion. Deafeningly, the reports of salvoes beat out over the waters, momentarily flattening the waves.

Open-mouthed, Peter Burnham stood watching ship after ship of the two vans begin to fire, then become locked in a death struggle. Scarlet, blue, green and gold glimmered through dense, greasy-looking clouds of powder smoke.

Now the huge *Saint Esprit* came up, half of her eighty guns spouting fire.

Lying as she was to leeward of the fight, great clouds of rank, rotten-smelling smoke presently drifted down and enveloped the American brig, set her company to coughing, cursing and rubbing their eyes. For a time Peter could see nothing at all. Lord! his eardrums ached. It was as if a continuous and savage thunderstorm were raging a quarter of a mile to windward.

Once the battle smoke had drifted by, Warren shouted, "I say, Manning, what ails old Tom Graves? Why don't he bring up his rear?"

Manning laughed a little wildly. "God knows; must be something wrong sir. Ha! There's the cause. D' you spy that pendant, sir, the striped one at the *London's* yard?"

"Aye, and what of that?"

"'Tis our—their signal for 'line-ahead.' Now can you read also a red flag with the white Saint Andrew's Cross flying just below, sir?"

"Aye. I see that, too. What does it signify?"

"Yon's the signal for 'close action,'" Manning yelled. "By God, old Graves has Hood nicely fixed. The Admiral's flying contradictory orders!"

Immediately Andrew Warren's experienced eye sought the British rear division and perceived a distinct uncertainty present there.

Sir Sam Hood's division, apparently, had commenced to change course in compliance with the "close-action" signal, quite ready and eager to grapple with the nearest French ships. But now that the "line-ahead" signal had reappeared they were floundering, hesitating before returning, ever so reluctantly, to obey the flagship's orders.

Meanwhile, the French *avant-garde* and de Grasse's center was concentrating their enormous fire power on the luckless and outnumbered British van—Admiral Graves' center had not yet closed range. H.B.M.S. *Terrible* and *Ajax* must be suffering heavy damage.

Warren watched a topmast and several yards go spinning up above the smoke clouds; terrific explosions ensued. Nor were the French ships going scatheless. Gulls wheeled frantically away from sails and pieces of fabric flying high into the air as the rumbling thunder of guns set the air a-quiver and presently surpassed all description. All the sea seemed peopled by ships wearing, tacking and changing sail. Away off to the rear, some British ship was badly afire and another nearly dismasted.

During the late afternoon the wind changed, forced Admiral de Grasse to wear and sail more to the south-wards, with the British still trying to close in. The parallel fleets had become stretched across the ocean for a distance of over three miles and everywhere the sails of lesser men-of-war dotted the sea.

Now broken spars, shattered small boats and big pieces of wreckage began to drift past the *Grand Turk*. Many mangled corpses and bodies, some of them smashed beyond all recognition, appeared bobbing sullenly along the privateer's water line. Next was sighted a topmast and a yard smothered in wet canvas, then several splintered sections of bulwark. Finally, a great, elaborately carved section of stern gilding drifted by. Peter noticed a shattered scroll bearing the letters "—ERRI—" done in gold as, for the first time, a division of enemy ships loomed near.

Loubet, a wild gleam in his eye, ran up to Warren. *"Pour l'honneur, mon Capitaine, tirons un peu.* Let us fire on them a little."

"'Twould accomplish nothing," groaned the naval officer. Then something in his nature gave way and he shouted, "Monsieur Loubet beat to quarters! Clear for action with the starboard broadside."

Peter Burnham grabbed his captain's arm; this was sheer madness, yet understandable. "My God, Captain, you don't intend to attack a line-of-battle ship?"

Andrew Warren shook his head. "No. I won't hazard your vessel but, so help me God, at least one American gun is going to be fired this day!"

"C'est magnifique! Pour l'honneur du drapeau!" Loubet was beside himself with excitement while the *Grand Turk*'s gunners ran to man her starboard battery.

Although a-blaze at several points, the huge French liner *Caton* came sailing by on her way to rejoin the fleet. That the sixty-four was badly hurt, any experienced eye could testify; all her lower sails were shot through and her main topmast had been carried away; her mizzen was swaying like a drunken man on the edge of a gutter.

Three of her consorts moved to shield her from the threat presented by Admiral Hood's division, now sailing dangerously close.

Swallowing hard on nothing, Andrew Warren glanced at the privateer's gun deck and noted that his gun crews already were in position; their captains blowing on their matches. Under each roll of the brig, the whole pattern shifted a little and the guns strained at their tackles.

By the set of their sails Warren knew that these British ships were not going to come any closer, so, when a huge seventy-four—she was the *Invincible*—came surging by at near three cables' length, he snatched up his speaking trumpet.

"Guns Number Two, Four and Six, one round! Sight on that vessel." Immediately followed the familiar screeching of blocks and tackles and the dull *thump, thump* of mallets knocking loose quoins.

Warren caught a deep breath, then shouted, "Fire!"

The three guns belched smoke and flame then recoiled savagely against their breechings. When the wind carried off blinding clouds of smoke Warren bit his lips and watched his brig's three cannon balls raise quite harmless water spouts a good hundred yards short of the *Invincible*'s dull yellow beam.

Particularly galling was the fact that this liner did not deign to fire even a musket by way of reply.

"Cease fire!" A sharp stinging manifested itself in Andrew Warren's eyes as, sadly, his gaze sought the *Grand Turk*'s ensign. Surely, so beautiful a flag deserved a better showing? Well, by God and by gravy, some day he'd see that flag better served by a damned sight.

Despite the brevity of their fight with de Grasse the British had suffered serious damage; the *Terrible* and the *Ajax* appeared to be in very bad case and were limping out of line. The *Shrewsbury*—or so Manning identified her—had lost all her topmasts and the *Princessa* was trailing the fleet at greatly reduced speed. Meanwhile, both fleets had quit firing and were continuing out to sea—away from those capes looming so gray and yellow in the late afternoon.

Like men emerging from a trance the *Grand Turk*'s company shook off the spell induced by this overwhelming spectacle. Before a strong, but diminishing, stern wind the *Grand Turk* pointed her dainty bowsprit to-

wards the Middle Ground and commenced to sail straight
into a sun sinking ever lower over Chesapeake Bay.

xvi. The Circle Forms

ALREADY ANCHORED in Lynnhaven Bay were those numerous transports and supply ships which de Grasse had
conveyed up from Saint Domingue. From them had been
debarked all of the 3,100 men destined to fight under the
command of the Marquis of Saint-Simon.

From the *Grand Turk*'s quarterdeck next morning,
Doctor Peter Burnham viewed this crowded bay with a
lively interest. He noted that all the transports had
buoyed their anchor-ropes and were ready to cast loose
and run at a moment's notice. Clearly, their masters must
remain on tenterhooks until a final outcome of the fleet
action was announced.

Once Andrew Warren had delivered his dispatches he
ordered the *Grand Turk* thoroughly cleaned and her
stores and water restocked. Would de Barras, with his
eight liners and the convoy transporting that all-important siege train, manage to slip through in safety? Along
with Generals Washington, Rochambeau, Lincoln,
Saint-Simon and a few hundred others, Warren lived in a
ferment of anxiety.

Following the privateer's arrival off the mouth of the
James, Peter set about learning as much as possible concerning the disposition of the allied forces. Such knowledge was essential to determining the correct situation of
his flying hospital.

On an old chart begged from Captain Warren, the physician commenced to note the positions of ships and
troops already on the scene and, morning and night, he
corrected his map to include intelligence obtained during
the day.

He learned, for instance, that when that doughty Provençal, de Grasse, had sailed out to meet the British he
had left behind sufficient ships to maintain his blockade
of the York and James Rivers. Besides, it was known
that H.B.M.S. *Charon*, a fifty-gun ship and the frigate
Guadaloupe, thirty-two cannon and a number of smaller
men-of-war, were riding under the protection of Lord
Cornwallis' batteries at York Town.

Engaged in preventing a British retreat across the James were the *Experiment*, fifty—taken from the enemy by d'Estaing off Rhode Island—and the *Andromaque*, also of fifty guns. Escape across the lower reaches of the York were secured by the *Valliant*, sixty-four; *Glorieux*, seventy-four, and *Triton*, sixty-four—all third-class ships-of-the-line.

By degrees Peter deduced that French and American forces, while awaiting de Barras' arrival, were concentrating on the south bank of the York, slowly but surely driving the besieged British in on a hamlet grandiloquently called York or York Town.

His Lordship, Major-General Lord Charles Cornwallis, or so spies reported, was beside himself for fear that Graves had been driven away and that no reinforcements would come sailing up this broad tea-colored river.

On the afternoon of the ninth, a despatch boat came racing in from the Capes firing signal guns and flying flags informing all and sundry that de Barras' fleet had been sighted standing into the entrance. Andrew Warren, perceiving the implications of this successful passage, so far forgot himself as to dance a little jig in his cabin. Next morning the crews of all the ships at anchor lined the rails to watch the great *Duc de Bourgogne*, eighty guns; the *Neptune* of equal power and six lesser ships-of-the-line come sailing in to salvoes of welcoming salutes. They were escorted by three frigates, one of them that same *Concorde* which had recaptured the *Grand Turk III* off St. Kitts.

Even greater delight was displayed ashore when transports from Rhode Island commenced to discharge the all-important—and only—train of siege artillery. These magnificent and ponderous pieces of ordnance everyone calculated, would treat Lord Cornwallis and his troops to one of the sharpest and most unpleasant surprises recorded during this war. Not one of them dreamed that a heavy train of artillery existed in all of North America.

Endless festivities ensued aboard the *Duc de Bourgogne* and Captain Warren attended them all—Admiral de Barras being hugely pleased over the *Grand Turk's* prompt delivery of his dispatches. Perhaps the privateer's officer was included on several fêtes merely because he commanded a vessel flying the American flag— the French were most tactful in such matters.

Everyone aboard the *Grand Turk* took special pleasure when, on the tenth of September, two liners of de Grasse's returning fleet surprised a pair of British frigates attempting to cut away those anchor buoys left behind by the French fleet on the fifth of the month. The Britishers proved to be the *Iris*, thirty-two, and the *Richmond*, thirty-two. Neatly trapped and under the guns of a far superior force their captains had no choice but to grind their teeth and strike.

When, next day, the *Iris* appeared in Lynnhaven Bay showing a white and gold *fleur-de-lis* banner flying above the Union Jack, Warren clapped Loubet on the shoulder. "*Regardez-moi, ça!* A piece of poetic justice, *hein?*"

"*Comment?*"

"Take notice of that figurehead on the prize?"

"*Mais oui, Monsieur le Capitaine,* 'tis that of a man, but lacking his right hand."

"There's quite a tale concerning yon figurehead. Back in 'seventy-seven I was commissioned aboard our frigate, the *Boston*, Hector McHeil, commanding. We were sailing in company with the *Hancock* when we took H.B.M.S. *Fox* and then were chased by the *Rainbow*, forty-four, and *Victor*, eighteen, and later the *Flora*, thirty-two." Spasmodically, Andrew Warren's jaw tightened. "We escaped, but the *Hancock*—that ship—" he pointed to the captured frigate now rounding up to her anchor "—was captured, and for the reason that her figurehead was an effigy of John Hancock, the English rechristened her *Iris* and thought it clever to knock off Hancock's right hand because he'd used it to sign our Declaration of Independence."

Warren's long dark face broke into a broad smile. "She mayn't be American now, but, at least, she ain't British. God send she is never again captured."

It came as no surprise that, on being apprised of de Barras' arrival, Admiral Graves had thought hard—and then had decided to return north to refit. Much could be advanced in favor of this decision since the French fleet now numbered thirty-four ships-of-the-line against his battered eighteen—the *Terrible* having had to be burnt as unseaworthy. Moreover, wild gales inevitably attendant on the equinox, were due any day now.

So, very reluctantly, the British squadron headed back to New York, thereby abandoning Lord Cornwallis, General O'Hara and deservedly well-hated Colonel Banastre Tarleton to Fate and their own slender resources.

Two days before de Barris added his ships to this great, and still growing fleet in Virginian waters, the *Grand Turk*'s long boat sailed up to the very entrance of the York River and there set ashore Doctor Burnham, together with is precious chests of medical supplies.

Once on land, that capable physician lost no time in commandeering a house and two large hay barns which would serve, well enough, as a flying hospital—he preferred the more accurate description of "field hospital."

Whilst he stood superintending the removal of trash from his hospital-to-be, a baffling experience befell Peter. Some of the Agenais Regiment—troops of the French West Indies contingent—were marching up the York Town road, when the aspect of a young officer on a tall black charger drew Peter's attention. When Peter lifted his hat the other smiled, turned in his saddle and returned the courtesy before riding on.

Peter stared after the white-coated figure. Gorry! Where had he seen that finely chiselled and sensitive face before? In Newport? Couldn't be; these troops hailed from Saint Domingue. Then the impossible impression offered itself that the face he recalled *was that of a girl!* Impossible. And yet, yet he knew that somewhere in the past he had viewed an almost exact duplicate of that handsome young officer's oval visage. Where? Where?

Of an infantryman delayed by a broken shoelace, he asked, "Can you give me the name of your commander—that officer on the black horse?"

The soldier made immediate reply. "Monsieur, he is Major, the Marquis de Menthon. Monsieur, perhaps, has met him at Cape François?"

Peter rubbed his chin, smiled perplexedly. "That is just what puzzles me, my friend. I am sure I have never met the Marquis, yet somewhere I have encountered a person who resembles him to a marked degree. Does he perhaps own a twin brother?"

The soldier stared, then shook his head. "But no, Monsieur. We of the Agenais know the family well. Monsieur le Marquis has two brothers, both much older than he."

"A sister?"

The Frenchman shook his head. "One has not heard that Monsieur le Marquis has a sister."

Long after the infantryman had shouldered his musket to set off after his company, Peter stood where he was, mulling the puzzle over and over. By grabs, he *had* seen this marquis before—or his very spit and image. Sure enough, halfway back to the barns he remembered. So startling was the recollection that he halted and laughed right out loud. It wouldn't have seemed half so funny if he hadn't been perfectly certain of his memory. A vivid impression of the Red Lion Tavern in Boston, of that dark-haired young trollop who, on the eve of the New Year, had sung a ballad just before that famous free-for-all had commenced.

XVII. GOVERNOR'S PALACE

MOODILY, Doctor Asa Peabody, senior surgeon and commandant of the Medical Department's General Hospital in Williamsburg, Virginia, studied a sheaf of returns made by his subordinates. Plague take it, this siege was yet of a week's duration and already his slender stock of drugs, pledgets and bedclothes had run low—most discouraging of all was the lack of nurses. Frowning, Asa considered a double row of sycamore trees reluctantly shedding yellow-gold leaves beyond the broken windows of what had once been the Royal Governor's Palace.

At this time of year one shouldn't expect much sickness among the troops. Early autumn was considered to be the most salubrious of all seasons. Yet, thanks to this concentration of men not only from all over North America but from Europe and the West Indies as well, the wards, on this ninth of October, had become filled to overflowing; the smallpox, dysentery, *lues venera*, cramp-colic, mania and the putrid fever all were too well represented.

At first, he reflected, he had been able to segregate the sick from those wounded who now appeared daily and by the wagon-load from the environs of York Town. True, the allied lines gradually, inexorably were closing in on Lord Cornwallis' system of redoubts and earthworks, but the cost was mounting faster than most of the allied staff realized.

Despite the testimony of such unbiased witnesses as Ensigns Tornquist and Raab, on duty with the French fleet, Asa found it difficult to credit tales that the British and their German mercenaries had stooped to such barbarous practices as murdering pregnant women, enslaving the civilian population and inoculating fugitive slaves with smallpox before liberating them to spread the contagion among the investing troops. Still, the charges became repeated by so many and quite diverse sources they couldn't be ignored. Ensign Gustaf Tornquist, an intelligent young Swede, deposed that he, himself, had beheld the severed heads of luckless Virginians ranged like gruesome crockery on the mantelpiece of a house he had entered.

On top of these reports there was no denying that nearly every well on the York peninsula had been polluted with bodies of murdered Negroes and dead animals. The result desired by the enemy had been obtained; putrid fever was raging throughout the allied forces; a really thirsty soldier will drink, despite warnings. New wells, of course, were being dug in a hurry, but, all the same, pure water would be scarce for a long time to come.

For the first time Asa developed a sense of hatred for the Redcoats. It was revolting to behold so many fine and healthy young troops dying of disease. So far, battle casualties had been surprisingly few; about their care the senior surgeon felt reasonably reassured.

Sitting at his desk in a small rust-red chamber immediately to the head of the staircase, Asa Peabody thoughtfully leafed through his requisition lists. Where, where to replenish his supply of essential drugs and physicks? To canvass the various flying hospitals he knew would prove quite useless. Such crude installations near to the entrenchments were even more hard pressed for necessities because, more often than not, the rascally regimental surgeons in charge of them were selling precious supplies to private buyers. The best of these flying hospitals occupied barns or churches which quickly became horribly malodorous and, in his private opinion, encouraged the spread of disease.

Asa rallied his thoughts. "Let's see now, what we need most is tartar emetic, petroleum albumen, plenty of corrosive sublimate, jalap and, most of all, Peruvian bark." The bark somehow always ran short. "Guess I can get along for a bit without more tincture of myrrh and aloes, aromatic salts of ammonia, but certainly I must come across some laudanum—and in a hurry."

Wearily the senior surgeon settled back in a crude chair which, somehow, had survived five years of looting and misuse by both sides. Fixedly he regarded an obscene inscription scratched into the reddish plaster of the wall opposite. Up the stairs from that pale blue ballroom in which belles and their beaux once had danced, arose a sad undertone of voices—the male nurses must be removing those patients who had died during the afternoon. Under the broken remains of some boxwood hedges at the far end of the palace flower garden an ever-lengthening ditch had been dug to receive bodies.

A delirious wretch, bedded on straw in the once handsome old supper room, kept calling out, "Molly, Molly, Molly!"

"Ah-h, stow that caterwauling!" snarled a voice; then followed a resounding slap.

Asa started to his feet—no use to intervene for the hundredth time; his ward nurses, usually stupid incompetents detailed to the hospital by various units glad to be quit of such brutes and ineffectives, were all too few. Towards the end of a long day these dullards grew short-tempered and extra mean, due to a lack of sleep.

Alas, that most women inhabiting this rich and pleasant countryside had taken flight last spring during a series of terrible raids conducted by the traitor, Benedict Arnold. Those few females who did remain had regretted such a decision for, equally merciless, and replete with atrocities, were the much more recent depredations committed by British dragoons under Colonel Banastre Tarleton. Everyone wished that a man-to-man struggle, fought on horseback not long ago between the duc de Lauzun and "Butcher" Tarleton had not been interrupted.

To staff his hospital, Asa felt he had been lucky in the matter of surgeons and physicians—but where, oh where, could he find additional nurses? His face, when he bowed his weary head, felt uncommon hot and dry between his hands.

In a little while now, that great journalist, Doctor James Thatcher should be returning from a round of flying hospitals in the immediate vicinty of Williamsburg. During the past fortnight Asa had become mighty attached to this acid-appearing, but enormously efficient and kindly, Massachusetter. Thanks to the painstaking manner in which Thatcher maintained his journal of this campaign, future generations might learn much, and profit greatly from his accounts of army life.

Long since, Asa had decided against the employment of impressed slaves for hospital work—except as a last resort. They were so stupid, lazy and dishonest. Another appeal to regimental commanders? No. Those already harassed gentlemen would prove firm in their refusal to detach more men; they had marched too far and suffered too much to lessen their chances of winning a signal victory.

His thoughts ran on. "I'd better mount up tomorrow and visit headquarters—maybe the surgeon-general will listen. Yes, I can safely leave Jimmie Thatcher and John Fletcher in charge—they can handle the younger physicians perfectly well."

Through John Fletcher he'd learned, nearly two months back, all about the scandal attached to Lucius Devoe's marriage. Fletcher proved well informed on the matter and small wonder—he had, for some time, shared quarters with Lucius at West Point.

From Fletcher he ascertained, also, that once Sabra had nursed her brother back to health and seen him ride off to rejoin his unit—then in Philadelphia—she'd let on that she was starting back to Boston—but had gone to New York instead. Just why Sabra Stanton should have risked crossing the Neutral Ground, of infamous repute, to reach the occupied seaport of New York he, Fletcher, couldn't attempt to explain.

Quite beyond Asa's comprehension was Lucius' capacity for doing so callous a thing. How could anybody bear to hurt Sabra—sweet and trusting Sabra?

Since his talk with Fletcher, Asa perceived that he'd come to solve quite a few enigmas. It was because she'd fallen in love with Lucius, that Sabra hadn't answered those letters he'd dispatched so hopefully from Machias! Yes, there lay his explanation.

Poor, humiliated girl. Small wonder she'd gone to New York rather than face the wise expressions of folks back in Boston. Was she likely still in New York? Once this campaign came to an end he'd go there—physicians, as a rule, were passed through any and all lines.

Irritably, the senior surgeon slapped a fly from his cheek, then tilted 'way back in his chair and stared at the smoke- and water-stained ceiling. Alas, that John Fletcher knew no more of Peter Burnham's fate than did anyone else.

How long ago seemed that night when the three of them had sat on the edge of their chairs watching old Doctor Townsend write out their certificates. Aeons appeared to have elapsed since he and Peter celebrated their certification at the Red Lion.

"Molly! Molly! Where are ye, Molly?" the delirious patient began calling once more.

Heavy feet kept tramping up the battered stairs and past his door.

Ah. The Red Lion. What a night *that* had been! All at once Asa recalled that grimy young trull who had tried to entertain the guests, the cripple who'd believed that that preposterous quack, Doctor Saxnay could restore his withered leg. What had been that poor girl's name? He rubbed his forehead and grinned ruefully. Judas Maccabaeus! To think he could ever forget the name of his very first patient. No, he hadn't! Her name was Hilde, Hilde something. Of course, being in such feeble health, she must have died long since; the nature of her profession demanded a strong constitution. Poor, tragic little Hilde. How well he recalled her heart-shaped face, jet hair and great black eyes.

A knock at the door roused him from his abstraction. "Come in." That would be Doctor Thatcher in from his rounds.

To his surprise an orderly appeared. "Leddy to see ye, sir." He jerked his thumb down the corridor.

"A lady? What in God's name is a woman doing in here?"

The fellow shrugged apologetically. "Couldn't nowise stop her, sir. Says she's heard yer short o' help." He lowered his voice. "She's a mighty fancy piece, sir, dressed kind o' foreign-like."

"Is she French?" Asa demanded sharply.

"Mebbe so, sir. Leastways she's got some kind of furriner orderly to her kerriage."

"Very well, you may show her to my office."

A Frenchwoman, eh? Amazing though it seemed, not a few ladies of quality accompanied their men to war—an old custom in Europe, so it seemed. At the sound of light feet climbing the staircase he got to his feet and stood waiting behind his desk.

Sounded a whisper of petticoats then, in the doorway, appeared the diminutive, black-masked figure of a lady clad in the peak of quiet elegance. The caller's Capuchin cloak and gown were of dark green silk, her bodice of yellow, richly embroidered brocade.

In a quick movement she allowed her calash bonnet to fold back, revealing sable hair puffed and pinned into symmetric ringlets. All the while she held a black velvet mask in place by the silver mouthpiece gripped between her teeth. This left her white-gloved hands free to undo the scarlet ribbon ties securing her cloak.

"Well, Doctor Peabody, and what do you think of your patient now?" this caller demanded, a trifle uncertainly as she removed the mask.

Asa gaped like any bumpkin at a strolling juggler. "Why, why you're Hilde."

"Yes, Doctor, I am Hilde Mention—or was."

"Judas Maccabaeus! Why, only this minute I was thinking of you!"

Suddenly Hilde extended both hands over the desk; they stood silent and transfixed a long moment as their eyes met. "Doctor Peabody! How can I tell you how very glad I am to find you again?"

"And I, you, little Hilde," he smiled gravely, offered silent reassurances as to his discretion. "How are you addressed nowadays?"

"I am Madame Hector de Lameth. My husband," Hilde flushed at the technical untruth, "serves as a captain in the Royal Duex-Ponts Regiment."

"Then you are married and happily, too, I'd hazard; my sincere good wishes."

Her first hero had aged, Hilde perceived and was thinner, but his features had gained in character. Yes, Asa Peabody looked as innately distinguished as any man in all North America.

He was pushing forward a rush-bottomed chair. "Pray seat yourself."

When she had done so she said, "Only today I heard your name spoken and learned that you were—here. I came at once, as fast as my carriage could travel over from the tavern."

"Then you are—er quartered here in Williamsburg."

"Yes. I have accommodations at the Raleigh."

While the sun drew longer and longer shadows from the sycamores shading the former Royal Governor's Palace, Hilde described, quite frankly, all that had happened since she had run pell-mell out of Mrs. Southeby's house.

"—And so," she concluded smiling softly, "I am come to discharge my debt to you in offering my services and those of my companion—a young lady who shares my rooms at the Raleigh." Hilde smoothed her skirt. "For reasons best known to herself, my friend calls herself Susan Stevens, but I am not sure that really is her name because another is painted in the lid of her portmanteau. Although I have not known Susan long, she is most anxious to be of service to our Army; moreover, she has what I lack—experience in attending the sick and wounded. You will allow us to assist as best we may?"

"On one condition." Asa's manner became serious. "You shall attend only the wounded—not the sick."

"It shall be as you say," came her quiet assent. "When shall we appear?"

"At seven of tomorrow morning. It is then we commence washing the patients and changing their dressings," he told her then smiled at her modish costume. "Best wear your plainest gowns, both in your interest and that of my patients. Wouldn't do to rouse their—er—enthusiasm too quickly."

Hilde arose and picked up her mask. "I shall bring what I can by way of dressings and delicacies."

"By the bye," Asa inquired curiously, "what was the name in the lid of Susan Stevens' trunk?"

"Sabra Stanton from Boston. I wonder if you have ever heard the name up there?"

XVIII. York Town Besieged: The Second Parallel

SHELLS FIRED from mortars on those redoubts protecting Major-General Lord Cornwallis' besieged garrison, continued to arch high into the sky, trailing graceful comet's tails of white smoke. On this tenth day of the siege, the liveliest artillery duel to date was thundering towards a new crescendo. Most of the defenders' shells generally burst too high to inflict much damage on the allies but sometimes their cannon balls plunged deep into the ground before exploding with a sullen *boom!* which blew dirt high into the sky.

Desperately prodigal of ammunition, the British artillerists were firing in a fierce, but futile, attempt to halt the French from digging a second parallel begun but three hundred and sixty yards short of their own badly pounded works.

"This bombardment? *Peste!* It is but childish rage," remarked a grizzled French colonel of artillery in a dark gray coat lined in scarlet.

"*Nos amis, là-bas,* treat us to a very pretty display of fire-works, but accomplish nothing of moment." He was quite correct. Steadily, relentlessly this new parallel crept on towards the enemy redoubts and more and more yellow earth was appearing before the French and American works. An increasing number of shell holes dotted sere hay grass covering a series of flats reaching nearly all the way to York Town. Certainly, if ever a commander had found himself in a position utterly destitute of natural defenses, Lord Cornwallis was that unhappy man.

Since the first of October when the siege had commenced, the French batteries hardly ever had been completely silent. And now, emitting deep-throated bellows, the siege guns from Newport were hurling heavy cannon balls at the enemy lines or into the crumbling village beyond. Time and again, clouds of lazily climbing bluish wood smoke betrayed the fact that another of the sixty or seventy houses comprising York Town had taken fire.

These works, supporting the first allied parallel, commenced on October the sixth, now were properly ditched and palisaded. Should Generals Cornwallis and O'Hara attempt a sortie, their troops would be in for some very unhappy moments.

Happily, each passing day brought an increased mutual respect among the allies. The Americans could not wonder enough at the magnificent skill and profound knowledge evinced by the French sappers and artillerists. On the other hand, the French greatly admired the remarkable ability of their allies with small arms. The Americans could, and did, display amazing marksmanship. They were also complimentary concerning works planned by old von Steuben and constructed by eager American troops who certainly knew a lot more about the handling of a spade than about laying a siege piece.

To Major Joshua Stanton's envious eyes those great cannon of the siege train represented the ultimate, nay, the *ne plus ultra* in ordnance. Lovingly, the New Englander's eyes dwelt on these magnificent, perfectly proportioned pieces, each one of which was engraved near its breech with the lily coat-of-arms of France and the personal cipher of Louis XVI. What fine, sturdy carriages, what solid wheels skillfully tired in massive iron bands; they even had cleats welded across their treads to prevent undue recoil.

Jehosophat! What a mort of powder was required to charge one of these black-throated monsters which, slowly but surely, were knocking the British parapets, bastions and salients to bits. Fortunately, the French never seemed to be afflicted with that shortage of powder which, throughout this war, had proved the bane of General Knox's corps of artillery.

By a considerable margin these siege guns outranged the heaviest cannon mounted on the British works, mostly fetched ashore from H.B.M.S. *Charon*. Long since, she had been nearly stripped of her ordnance to reinforce Lord Cornwallis' light field pieces.

Yes, it was quite something to watch the French gun crews at work and performing their duties with clock-like precision. Once the charge, wads and projectile had been rammed home the gun captain would lay his piece employing a set of marvelously intricate sights. Quite gravely, heavily perspiring and blackened gunners would fall back to their posts and watch their gun captain cock his fancy new fling-and-steel lock.

"*Vive le Roi!*" they would yell when the gunner jerked his lanyard and the gun roared and rolled back under the recoil. The gunners swung their hats especially hard every time a shower of bricks and timber erupted from the house which was their target. On such occasion they would run around, shaking each other's hands and taunting the other gun crews.

Following a particularly well-placed shot the officer in charge, mighty fine in his clean uniform, usually would call for wine, whereat a leather jug would be passed around once, and again. After that the artillerists would shake hands all around again, and only then commence to reload with unhurried movements.

What amazing effectiveness! Mathematics, unknown to those weary, cold—and determined—batteries which had travelled the length of the American sea coast—was at the fingertips of even the humblest *sous lieutenant* in the French Service.

"I must remember," Joshua told himself. "Our future gunners must understand higher mathematics."

His envy vying with his genuine admiration, Major Stanton walked on towards his own batteries. Most of the guns they fired were also of French manufacture; a few of these pieces had been dragged all the way down from that fort which M. de Vauban had designed at Ticonderoga—hundreds of miles nearer Canada.

His American gun crews, Joshua noted, invariably seemed more intent on the business in hand. To these bronzed, inelegant men, each shot appeared as a personal affair. Whether they hit or missed was, in their way of thinking, a matter of life and death.

All the same they were ready to raise a cheer for General Washington whenever they scored a prettily placed salvo. Unlike the French, the American artillerymen stood around their piece any-which-way; each one trying to learn as much as he could about the fine points of sighting, loading and firing. These hickory-brown men drank no wine, only squirted tobacco juice upon the dusty ground. When they got hot they plunged their heads into the same wooden water buckets used for sponging the bore after every shot.

He was inspecting this same battery three days later when a dark-faced officer hurried up. "In a minnit, sir, 'soon as the Gen'ral and his guests show up we're aimin' to try to fire His Bloody Majesty's ship *Charon*. Will ye linger around, Major?"

Having participated in the plans to destroy said *Charon*, Joshua grinned. "Aye, that I will, Mr. Pitman. Is the hot shot well a-glow?"

"Allow it is, sir. We been heatin' 'em since noon."

Hopeful of creating an impression on the French, Joshua sought that great oven in which red charcoal had been built into a great, face-searing mound. Good. Linktongs with which the red-hot shot must be picked up were ready to hand. Critical of all details, Joshua next inspected a row of tubs in which many extra-thick oakum wads lay absorbing moisture against the moment of their use.

Captain Rich, a cheery fellow from the Eastern Shore of Maryland raised his hat when he noticed Major Stanton advancing, then, glancing abruptly to his left, pointed to a glittering group entering the battery from its rear. "Three cheers for General Knox!"

While the artillerymen raised a mighty yell, their officers ran to haul uniform coats over their raw-red shoulders. The afternoon was unseasonably hot. Walking behind the blue-and-red-clad figure of General Knox stalked a dozen French officers. He in the blue and white tunic and sporting all the decorations must, Joshua concluded, be Monsieur de Villefranche, chief of Count Rochambeau's engineers. Present also were de Chastellux, chief of staff of the French Forces, Maréchal de Camp General Viomesnil and the Marquis d' Andrechamps, colonel of the newly arrived Agenais Regiment. Among the American officers were General von Steuben and General Gist of the Maryland Troops.

Displaying intense interest the visitors climbed a parapet the better to witness this attempt to destroy the *Charon* and several transports swinging to their cables at either side of that tall warship. The *Guadeloupe*, luckily for her, lay out of range, 'way across the tea-colored York River, where her guns could protect Tarleton's positions on Gloucester Point and a scattering of merchantmen huddled under her guns.

At General Knox's approach Joshua Stanton drew himself up straight and saluted as smartly as his injured arm would permit. Redfaced, pot-bellied old von Steuben quite unexpectedly nodded—he wasn't much for recognizing mere field officers.

"*Ach!* So you are back, Major Stanton," he grunted, digging at the ground with a gold-headed walking stick. "Good. You are just in time for Lord Cornwallis's country dance."

This battery being from his own battalion, Stanton hoped that these rough-and-ready artillerymen would behave. They were deplorably prone to make flatulent noises, take mincing steps and kiss hands to one another whenever even the highest ranking officers of the Auxiliary Forces appeared.

Perhaps these grimy and unshaven gunners were too

tired to misbehave but, for a miracle, they stood to attention, well-muscled brown torsos a-gleam with sweat and
their greasy hair dangling any-which-way about their
ears.

Colonel de Villefranche drew General Knox aside and
commented interestedly upon the fact that these Americans, in order to diminish the recoil of their pieces, had
built a counter-slope back of their gun carriages. Further,
they had lashed bags of sand to the trail of each piece.

"You taught them this, Your Excellency?" Villefranche demanded of von Steuben.

The German puffed out his cheeks, laughed a little.
"Nein, mon Général, always these monkeys think up
new tricks. *Ja.* After four years, I haff come to egspect it.
Now let us see vot your poys can do, Captain Pitman."

From his coat-tail pocket the old Prussian produced a
small brass-mounted telescope and waddled forward to
an empty embrasure, watched all the while by the dusty
gun crews. They regarded him with no small affection.
For all that "Von" was a foreigner he had proved his
worth during many a dreary march and campaign. No,
sirree—the Inspector-General wasn't like most of these
God-damned tin soldiers from Europe who would forget
nothing of Continental tactics and learn even less about
war as it was fought in North America.

Stanton ran forward when, without looking, von
Steuben called his name. The old Prussian had climbed
up onto the embrasure and, through his telescope supported on the end of a fascine, was studying the *Charon*
as she lay, perfectly mirrored by the placid waters of the
York.

"Dot iss extreme range," he grunted. "Tell your poys
I send them vun case of Rhine *wein* if they hit dot sheep
in less than six shots."

Von Steuben, Stanton realized, understood American
psychology, all right. The crews of the four guns fairly
flew to their posts and prepared to open fire.

The French field officers watched closely. These
brown faced professional artillerists displayed no trace
of the carpet knight; their well-worn uniforms showed
patches and sweat marks and most of their blunt features
bore scars from earlier wars.

Deadly serious now, the crew of Number One gun
manhandled their long-snouted piece back from its em-

brasure. Number Two gunner selected a powder cartridge, dropped it into the bore and shoved it as far down as his arm would reach. In silence Number Three raised his rammer and, bronzed shoulder muscles bunching under the effort, shoved the charge all the way home. Captain Pitman who was in charge of the battery, hesitated, cast Joshua a questioning glance. "I'd add an extra half-charge. That's a fine strong gun and you're shooting at extreme range, you know."

Presently, Number Four came running forward back from the row of water tubs, a four-inch-thick oakum wad dripping between his hands. Water from it left a distinct trail of dark spots along the trampled sandy-yellow earth.

For a second time Number Three lifted his rammer and making a soft squishing noise shoved the dripping wad deep into the bore. Number One, the gun captain, meanwhile, had, with the aid of a handspike been traversing the piece. Now he bent and squinted through his sights, now he ordered another quoin—a hardwood wedge—to be knocked out from under the breech, now he hung a gunner's quadrant from the muzzle to check the angle elevation.

Everyone present turned to watch Numbers Five and Six men lower a pair of tongs slung from a bar into that blinding glow generated by the well-bellowsed charcoal fire. So intense was the heat that these gunners had to make three tries before the claws of their bar-tongs succeeded in closing upon a glowing cannon ball. The sphere gave off bright little sparks—it was a truly impressive projectile weighing all of twenty pounds.

The other three gun crews stood watching attentively. In a moment would come their turn and they intended to profit by any advantages or mistakes committed by their predecessors.

Von Steuben leaned hard on his tall walking stick, glared angrily around. "Captain Pitman! Vhere iss your cup?"

Joshua Stanton cursed silently. Of course, something would have to go wrong! There wasn't any cup ready to hand. Everything therefore was held up—the cup being that concave metal rammer especially designed to ease a glowing projectile out of the tongs and into the bore.

At this point, veterans among the witnesses unobtrusively sought what shelter offered itself. That wet wad, they knew, would cool the cannon and sudden heat as from a red hot iron ball had, in the past, been known to split a defective barrel upon discharge and send murderous iron shards hissing in all directions.

"Fetch a cup, you dunderheads!" roared Captain Pitman. "There's one in the magazine."

To which Numbers Five and Six added, turning aside streaming scarlet faces. "Stir your arses for Christ's sake! We're fryin' with this damn' thing."

Once the cup was brought up, they heaved the glowing ball to the lip of the bore and Number Two brought his brass cup beneath the projectile. At the command of "Ease," the tong men lowered their burden into the waiting receptacle.

When the red-hot sphere went rolling down the bore a great plume of steam gushed out and a sharp hissing noise resulted as the glowing iron came in contact with that sodden wad. At almost the same instant, Number One held out his linstock and touched his match to the priming. Instantly, a thin jet of smoke spurted vertically from the touchhole, the cannon emitted a deafening report and vomited a huge cloud of gray-white smoke while, under the recoil, its ponderous carriage backed halfway up the earthen ramp.

From their embrasure, General Knox and his guests followed the projectile's flight high, higher into the sky, saw it attain the zenith of its parabola and then rush earthwards. Raising a brief cloud of steam, it plunged into the York River some fifty yards short of the anchored man-of-war. They watched the *Charon's* deck teem into sudden activity; like ants in a disturbed hill, the tiny black figures of her crew rushed hither and yon.

When the Number Two gun took its turn, Captain Pitman, Indian-like features tense, ordered the angle of elevation increased. This time the glowing ball carried over the *Charon's* tops, but plunged into one of the transports. Very quickly flames broke out on the unlucky vessel's forecastle and sent tendrils of blue-gray smoke spiraling into a nearly windless sky.

The battery just missed sampling General von Steuben's Rhine wine, for not until their ninth shot did the gunners plump a red-hot ball smack through the *Charon's* gun deck. They cheered all the same and now that the range had been determined all four pieces commenced, at will, an increasingly accurate cannonade.

By twilight, H.B.M.S. *Charon* presented a sight to remember as, a-blaze from stem to stern, she swung to her moorings with flames soaring high above her tops and creeping out along her yards in brilliant parallels.

Panic reigned aboard the helpless merchantmen—and with reason—no breath of wind blew to assist their attempts to escape. Gripped by the ebb tide, a big sloop was carried downstream until she fouled the *Charon* and took fire herself.

Although the British artillery commenced an angry bombardment by way of retaliation, they failed to range this punishing American battery.

All along the banks of the York throngs of troops gathered to watch the *Charon's* final destruction. Now cascades of sparks swirled hundreds of feet up into the evening sky and, one after another, her guns went off·as the raging heat discharged them.

Because, in addition to the *Charon*, three merchantmen were now thoroughly a-flame, the conflagration lit the whole river, even tinted sand banks on the far shore of the York a bright pink. Loud cheers arose when the fire ascended well-tarred rigging and commenced to sketch lacy, golden red patterns against the sky. Burning sails set sections of flaming fabric to riding whirlwinds created by hot gasses.

At length flames reached the *Charon's* magazine and it blew up with a report so thunderous it was heard all the way to Williamsburg. Dazzling lances of fire stabbed hundreds of yards into the night and bits of flaming wreckage fell over in Gloucester. Bathed in flames, H.B.M.S *Charon* settled gradually at her anchorage until, amid clouds of steam, she slipped below the surface, leaving only her burning masts visible above the current.

"*Ach, du Lieber Gott!* Dot is goot shooting." Von Steuben slapped his fat thighs. "Dot *wein* you shall have all the same, poys."

Monsieur de Chastellux was of the same opinion and insisted on shaking hands with each of the gun captains. All in all, it was a mighty satisfactory evening's work.

XIX. WITHIN THE PERIMETER

WHEN ABOVE nine thousand human beings find themselves contained within an area some twelve hundred yards long by five hundred yards across, together with their animals, supplies, weapons and vehicles, not much vacant space is left. Crowded within a perimeter described by ten redoubts and sixteen batteries, lay 7,257 officers and men of the regular British Establishment, 840 seamen, several hundred refugee slaves—their lot espe-..ly was pitiable—and half a thousand horses.

.Necessarily, what one person or group of persons did, immediately affected their neighbors and in general irritated them, no matter how worthy or innocent the act might be.

On the afternoon of the eleventh of October, Doctor Lucius Devoe found himself in an especially foul humor. Every one of the few houses remaining more or less intact in York Town, was already jam-packed with sick and wounded and the sick lists were growing steadily longer.

It was terrible how this smallpox was spreading. Soldiers of half a dozen famous regiments lay dying in backyards on piles of the autumn leaves. These poor devils had only their great coats with which to shelter themselves from the still broiling sun of mid-day and the sharp chills of night. Down on the river bank, where the soil was sandy and digging easy, long trenches had been opened. Into these the dead were tumbled, twice a day, in the most perfunctory manner.

Once shells from the besieging French and American batteries had begun to range York Town itself, conditions had worsened rapidly and continually, one encountered nightmarish scenes. Men killed by bursting shells lay unburied for days at a time, until, bloated and hideous, they created such an intolerable stench that sullen Negroes, driven at the bayonet point by brutal German mercenaries out of the Seyboldt and Anspach Regiments, gingerly passed loops of ropes about the dead men's ankles and with the aid of starving horses dragged them down to the burial pits.

Largely unlisted, the dead sank into a common grave. Side by side, stalwart veterans from the elite First and Second Life Guards lay among raw replacements for the Eighteenth of the Line; men of Fraser's Eighty-second and McDonald's Seventy-sixth Highlanders, lay with their campaign-stained tartans sprawled across the blue-clad corpses of German mercenaries or the green tunics of some Loyalist who had paid his last bitter tribute to his

King. Occasionally, the bodies of seamen, landed from the sunken *Charon,* were added to this mephitic pile of human debris.

Within the perimeter, surgeons and physicians were desperately few, and consequently worked to the verge of collapse. Lucius, toiling in the solid brick house he had selected for his operating room and emergency receiving ward, found it hard to recall those early days of the siege when there had been plenty of room in this once-pleasant little town and the officers' messes were still ceremonious and well served.

Boom! Bam! That accursed French battery opposite Number Eight redoubt was reopening fire. Somewhere down the street resounded two sharp, flat-sounding explosions.

Anticipating the arrival of more shells Lucius raised hands to cover his ears. *Bam! A-r-rump!* The red-aproned surgeon bent once more over the hopeless abdominal wound he had been examining. In a moment he straightened, beckoned a pair of round-eyed bandsmen serving as orderlies.

"Carry this man out into the orchard."

"No! No!" The patient, a magnificent young grenadier of the Second Guards' Composite clutched Lucius' hand. "Don't send me out, sir. I—I don't want to die. Save me, kind sir—" Then a ghastly smile convulsed the purple-blue lips. "Or are you savin' yer art for some bleeding officer?"

Lucius paid no attention, bade the two musicians to carry him away.

Boom! Bang! Those last shells had fallen much nearer, so near in fact, that the whole house shook and bits of plaster fell from the ceiling upon wounded a-waiting their turn on the operating table.

If only they'd drag away that dead horse lying just outside the operating room window! Already a haven for countless flies, its bloated belly had burst just an hour before, poisoning the air with an indescribably noisome stench.

The next case awaiting his attention was an amputation to be performed upon a gigantic corporal from the Eighteenth of the Line. When he saw the knives being laid out, the fellow became seized by terror and screamed and struggled as hard as a man could with one of his legs, from the knee downwards, degenerated into a shapeless mass of splintered bone and crushed flesh. In vain, the musician-orderlies tried to lift him onto the operating table but cursing fearfully, he struck out with his fists and drove them off. Lucius' hollow eyes swung to his principal assistant. "Jones, pray attend the patient."

A hulking bandmaster of the Seventy-first Line Regiment promptly picked up a bung-starter and, once the orderlies succeeded in pinioning the screeching wretch, he brought his mallet down hard atop the patient's skull. Lucius hated to employ such crude methods, yet they speeded up operations and time was pressing for now a farm cart was rumbling up to his door laded with more wounded men. Presently, the corporal's crushed limb was tossed out of the window onto a blackened pile already formed.

He worked until the sweat poured down his forehead into his eyes. Certainly things could not continue as they were much longer. A pattering of musket shots sounded in a near-by field.

"They're killing o' our pore starving 'orses," grunted a patient in the uniform of Tarleton's dragoons. "They're luckier than us. At least they shoots those pore creatures and puts them out o' their misery.

"Cheer up, chum," said another. "This business carn't last much longer. We're done for."

"Aye! 'E bloody Rebels and the Dancing Masters 'ave done us in this time."

But another said, "Nah, we'll 'ang on. Mark my words, any day now old 'Arry Clinton, 'Ood and Graves will come a-sailing up this bleeding river and we'll hand the Froggies another drubbing."

A gaunt figure on a pile of straw stirred feverishly, tried to brush away flies creating a noisome halo about the soaked bandages encircling his head. "Garn! That's wot yer said three days back. 'E ain't never comin'. Not now, 'e ain't."

Lucius worked on and on, suturing, sewing, adjusting tourniquets and smearing unguents on suppurating older wounds.

"That last man spoke the truth," he thought, and smiled bitterly beneath a two days' beard and the sour sweat on his cheeks. "Clinton hates Cornwallis for intriguing at Saint James's behind his back. Besides, our noble commander *has* been outrageously insubordinate, so I wouldn't wonder if dear Sir Harry stays in New York together with all his twelve thousand men, and lets us fry in our own juice.''

At length Lucius finished operating and swayed out into the fresh morning sunlight and away from the reek of that dead horse. At a pump in the backyard he washed a measure of the dried blood and serum from his face and arms. Jupiter! Sleep he must have, and soon. His hands were shaking as if palsied.

Under the withering leaves of an apple tree he gazed about. Few of the sixty houses comprising York Town but bore marks of the bombardment. A long line of fugitive slaves, under the guard of a Loyalist company, appeared on their way to repair recent damages to Number Seven Redoubt. Damn them, anyhow; it was the blacks who had brought the smallpox.

Sheltered in holes dug in the all-too-friable earth, groups of infantrymen off duty ate their rations or lay on their backs staring blankly into the air. Their scarlet tunics, hung to near-by bushes or trees, suggested enormous and grotesque blossoms.

Across the river at Gloucester Point there sounded several fusillades; some kind of a skirmish must be taking place between Tarleton's troops and de Choisy's French Marines.

''Awa' with ye. Ye domned carrion bir-r-ds!'' A rawboned Scot glanced upwards and suddenly began to shake his fist at a number of buzzards wheeling, circling, high in the sky. Although there was too much activity in, and around York Town to encourage their settling, foul odors were attracting these unclean birds by the hundreds.

Cursing wearily, the Jamaican sought refuge in a solid-looking brick privy because, soaring up into the sky, flew another of those deadly bombs from the French mortar batteries.

Once the shell had burst, harmlessly enough, in an open field, Lucius resumed his progress and noticed that all along the street and among the shattered houses lay quantities of abandoned or ruined equipment. From the Fusilier's redoubt, away off to the right of the British position, now sounded a spiteful crackling of musketry. No peace for the weary, no rest for the—well *was* he wicked?

An orderly, on duty at the nearly deserted mess, today

could produce nothing more palatable than a slab of
horsemeat and a few water biscuits—but Lucius de-
voured them eagerly enough.

Feeling a thousand years old, he then wandered over to
a small orchard where he found a pair of Loyalist infantrymen asleep and snoring behind a wood pile. Lucius
paid them no heed, but sought a small patch of shade and
sat employing a sliver to remove tough threads of meat
from between his teeth.

Jupiter! Never had exhaustion so nearly conquered
him. His eyes ached and burned like fury and, as he
stretched out on the ground, the sound of axe blows delivered by sappers working to repair a striken battery
sounded maddeningly loud.

He closed his eyes. What would Emma be doing now?
She must be getting very large with his baby—or was it
his? Stronger than ever, doubt rankled in his mind. A
smart girl, Emma, and an exquisitely passionate bed
companion to boot. How long before his arms once more
could clasp her vibrant warm smoothness?

Certainly, Emma must have been pleased to learn
about his appointment as surgeon-in-chief to Lord Cornwallis' forces in Virginia. Yes, sir. If British arms prevailed, despite this impending disaster, he could count on
a fat appointment from the Royal Governor. Emma had
reasoned it all out extremely well. Was she not even now
supplying food for the patriot armies at very low cost?

An ant crawled onto his chin and, absently, he brushed
it away. Then an unhappy thought came to plague him.
How had Sabra weathered the dual blow he'd dealt her?
Never had he been quite able to forgive himself for his
defection and the last he'd heard, Joshua was lying at
death's door. Very probably he had died, long since.
Who'd have thought he'd come out so well in that awful
duel?

Well, despite the misadventure at West Point, he was
again forging steadily to the top. Certainly, he had out-
distanced both Peter Burnham and that big, trusting clod
of an Asa Peabody.

Cannon reports from a hitherto silent direction made
him sit upright. Jupiter!

A brand new allied battery must have opened up. Instinctively, he flung up a warding arm when a terrific
crash, like that of a big tree falling into a dry thicket, re-

verberated through the hot and lifeless air. Another, and another shell burst just beyond the orchard, made the trees shake and leaves fall. He hurried forward, then halted.

God above! A shell from this new battery must have landed square on his receiving ward. Its roof had disappeared and, even as he stared in open-mouthed horror, one of its walls collapsed inwards. Stiffly, like an old man, Lucius started running for the ruins.

xx. General Hospital

THE OLD CART'S long ungreased axles screeched loud as battling tomcats, but their plaint sounded in Asa Peabody's ears as sweet music. He still couldn't get over having secured so many supplies from the troops just in from Newport. Allowing his body to sway to the cart's lurching progress, Asa grinned from ear to ear.

At first he simply couldn't credit his eyesight, but there indeed was Peter Burnham, all-fired dignified and polite, conducting a party of French officers about the flying hospital he'd set up amid a grove of towering sweet gum trees.

At first they'd stood there like a couple of dolts, simply gaping on each other, then had followed a joyous beating of each other's shoulder blades and wringing of hands. When they'd loosed a torrent of questions, the amused gentlemen of General Viomesnil's staff had turned tactfully aside to inspect a ward they had already seen.

How utterly amazing, how wonderful to find big, redheaded Peter again! Imagine his being married to a lovely Danish noblewoman. The only sobering element about their reunion was the sight of Peter's cruelly scarred left hand but there'd been no time, then, to inquire about how he'd come by such an injury.

Dear old Peter! They had agreed to dine together as soon as one, or the other, was freed of the press of duty.

Over a dusty shoulder, Asa glanced at those neat boxes and bales stacked on the cart's floor and his heart lifted.

Another cart turned into the driveway right behind his. On it stood a big wooden barrel slopping water over its rim. Asa felt cheered for clear spring water, at this time, was near as hard to come by as fine gold.

The prospect of greeting Hilde de Lameth was definitely cheering. That diminutive young woman sparkled through the dark wards like a bright ray of sunlight and displayed a strength surprising in so fragile a figure.

It was hard to credit that nearly a week had elapsed since she and the girl who now called herself Susan Stevens appeared to work eight and sometimes ten long hours a day. No little resolution had been required to deny himself a private encounter with Sabra, but she'd failed to seek him out, as she would had her failure to answer his letters not made clear her sentiments.

He came upon Hilde sponging the feverish forehead of an old sergeant out of the Virginia militia; he'd taken a sabre slash across his shoulder.

"And where is Mistress Stevens? You usually work together, do you not?"

Hilde looked about, passed the back of her hand over her damp forehead. "I can't imagine, Doctor. She was here only a moment ago. Oh, orderly, pray fetch a jug of the fresh water."

From a wooden bucket she used a gourd to dip sweet water for her patients. In the end she herself drank thirstily, then summoned a faint smile.

"I hope, sir, you'll not object to my quitting my duties a little early tonight?" Her fringed eyelids dropped. "You see, my husband is riding over to call on me."

"Naturally not," was Asa's instant reply. "I trust to be honored in meeting so fortunate a gentleman."

In company with Doctor Fletcher, he made a round of the sick wards, then finally climbed from an octagonal hallway up to his own little office situated by the head of a sadly scarred and gritty staircase. To his vast astonishment Sabra Stanton was waiting just outside the door.

"May I—see you, Doctor?" she demanded in a low voice. "I have waited some time to find sufficient courage to address you."

Puzzled and intensely excited, Asa closed the door behind them, shut out the hospital noises. He bowed. "I had hoped you would call sooner Mistress Stevens, or should I say Mistress Stanton?"

His heart began drumming like a partridge's wings when at last he faced her squarely, regarded the well-remembered, modest loveliness of Sabra's features. Yes, she *was* beautiful in a newly grave and mature way, despite heated features, disordered hair and work-stained apron. Nervously she began to finger a pair of scissors secured by a ribbon to her waist, then drew a quick breath, much like a child preparing to recite a piece learned by rote. "Doctor Peabody—Asa, I have a single question—for me a most important one. Will you answer it quite truthfully—no matter what the cost?"

Silence widened in the chief surgeon's office. He smiled, "Of course, Sabra. What do you wish to know?"

The intensity of the expression in her large gray eyes puzzled him. "When—when you returned to Machias—" she paused dropped her gaze.

"Yes?"

"Did you marry?"

His expression tautened and his voice sounded flat when he replied, "Why, yes. You see when I—"

"—Thank you." Sabra Stanton straightened almost convulsively and blinked several times. "Thank you, Doctor, that was all I needed to know." So Lucius *had* told the truth! That note from the girl in Machias was not, as she had come more recently to suspect, other than it seemed. Her manner changed. "And now another matter. I really came to warn you that Madame de Lameth's devotion to her duties quite exceeds her strength."

"But, Sabra," Asa burst out. "Please listen. There is much I wish to ask—to—to tell you," he stammered, "about me—a—about us."

Sabra's chestnut head averted itself to gaze out of the window. "Really, we have no subject to discuss unless it is Madame de Lameth. On our way back to the inn last evening she practically swooned. Please, Doctor, forbid her to return here for a few days. I—I have met a farmer's wife—she has agreed to assist me in the wards. We can manage very well until Hilde recruits her strength."

Something further lay beneath the surface of Sabra's manner, but what, Asa could not fathom.

"Thank you for the warning," said he as she started for the door. "I shall follow your advice. And may I add that my colleagues and I are most sensible of your services? Because of you and Madame de Lameth, many of our patients still live and will recover."

Sabra dropped the big figure a stiff little curtsey. "Of

that we are very thankful, sir. May I bid you good evening?'' and, skirts whispering softly, she hurried out and down the staircase.

XXI. M. le Marquis de Menthon

Chevalier Pierre Louis Marie Phillipe de Menthon, major of the Agenais Regiment, drew rein before the long, white clapboard facade of the Raleigh Tavern.

"To you, *mon ami,* I will confess," said he to his companion, Captain de Berthelun of the Gatinais Regiment, "that I have welcomed this opportunity to visit the village of Williamsburg."

"Indeed?" de Berthelun shifted in his saddle and allowed himself to appear politely intrigued.

"Since we have landed here in Virginie a number of persons have mentioned the presence here of a young woman who is reported married—" just a trifle he emphasized the word—"to young de Lameth—you know of the family, of course." De Menthon kicked his right foot free of the stirrup preparatory to dismounting. "*Pardieu!* No less than five officers of the Deux-Ponts, that amiable red-haired American surgeon, and two American officers have observed of an incredible resemblance between this lady and myself."

"To be so closely resembled must give one an uncanny feeling, Monsieur," de Berthelun smiled, guiding his charger over to the inn's mounting block, "especially when your counterpart wears petticoats."

Once his orderly had come trotting up to take charge of the horses, de Menthon, very slim and graceful, brushed dust from a perfectly fitting white uniform faced in rose. The orderly bent, wiped more dust from the Marquis de Menthon's tall black leather boots. "The spurs, too, you idiot. Go around in the innyard and wait."

"*Oui, mon Commandant.*"

"Let us hope that we are fortunate enough to find the lady at home," de Menthon smiled, straightened his stock and, followed by his companion, entered the famous old tavern. They were exploring the Apollo Room in search of the publican when the tinkle of an overturned glass a few tables distant drew de Menthon's attention to a large, black-clad individual—a physician by his dress. As if on a phantom, this broad-featured medical man stared at him. No less startled of aspect was his companion, evidently a fellow physician.

"My God! Look, Thatcher! *Look there!* Am I deluded?" Asa Peabody passed a hand before his eyes. For a moment he thought Hilde was masquerading, perpetrating some mad prank, but as quickly realized that this undoubtedly was a man.

"Your pardon, sir," he apologized as the Marquis drew near. "Forgive my staring so, but—"

De Menthon smiled. "Ze resemblance she strikes you, too?" he inquired.

"It's, it's incredible," Thatcher agreed wiping spilt coffee from his waistcoat. "''Pon my word, sir, save in identical twins, I wouldn't have dreamed so precise a resemblance possible." His eyes narrowed. "You and Hilde ain't twins, are you?"

"Hilde?" De Menthon's manner remained unruffled. "I know no lady of zat name. You permit zat I present myself, ze Marquis de Menthon; and ze Captaine de Berthelun."

With the names "Mention" and "de Menthon" resounding in his brain, Asa pushed forward a pair of chairs and would have given an order, but the Marquis clapped his hands for the drawer. "Ez zere per'aps cognac?"

"Afraid not, sir," Thatcher supplied. "British cleaned the cellar out last winter. But our host can serve passable rum."

De Menthon's silver epaulettes rose in a resigned shrug. "*Ron! Ron!* Always ze rum. On Saint Domingue we almost drowned in it, eh, Louis? If ever again one be'olds *la belle France* nevaire will one taste a drop of ze stuff."

Captain de Berthelun produced an elaborate tortoise-shell snuff box, offered it.

De Menthon spoke carefully. *Bigre!* here was a mystery of the first rank. "It would appear, *Messieurs les Medicins,* zat you both are—how you say it?—friendly with zis Madame de Lameth?"

A host of conflicting impulses made a battlefield of

Asa's mind. Of one thing he was sure; under no circumstances was he prepared to reveal the whole sum of his knowledge concerning the past of Hilde Mention.

Thatcher's craggy features contracted. "She is really Doctor Peabody's old friend."

"Ah, eendeed?" Silver buttons winked to the Marquis' half-bow. "My felicitations. Thees *mystère* ees of ze most eenterest to me. You met—?"

"In Boston. As Mistress Hilde Mention she was a patient of mine. I attended her for several days."

Up flew the Marquis' slender black brows in an expression uncannily reminiscent of Hilde. "'Men-shun'? *Comment*—'ow did she spell her name?"

Asa told him while de Menthon wrinkled thin nostrils over a rum and water brought by a perspiring Negro.

"Since then she has become Madame de Lameth." A look flashed between the American and the Frenchmen— a look which confirmed a mutual understanding of Hilde's true status. Asa went on, "Here, she has been assisting at my hospital—too vigorously, I fear."

"*Hélas.* She 'as spoken possibly of 'er origins?"

"Very little. Hilde was orphaned at a very early age— by a shipwreck off Canada, I believe."

"'Ow, mos' *romantique.*" The Marquis sighed. "One is puzzled, very puzzled. Between ze names 'Menthon' and 'Mention' one perceives ze closest similarity, no? And yet—one 'as no seestairs, but several *cousines*—all of whom one knows. Um, per'aps *grandpère*—" He broke off, smiled quickly. "Per'aps, you weel do me ze *honneur* to present—?"

"Certainly, Major. It'll be a pleasure. I'm just as mystified about your resemblance as anyone." Asa accepted a pinch of de Berthelun's snuff. "We are waiting to see Madame de Lameth ourselves," he vouchsafed. "Unfortunately, she and her husband have gone out to take the air. They should return soon."

"One 'opes so. Soon we mus' return to ze siege and eet ees a long ride back to York Town, no?"

More drinks were brought as conversation shifted to the present campaign. All four of them felt convinced that the enemy soon must surrender. Warmed by the rum, Captain de Berthelun hinted that an attack soon would be made on those two redoubts which secured the British left.

All too soon, church bells of the town sounded nine sonorous notes.

"*Peste!*" de Menthon growled. "What a meesfortune." He checked the time against his own handsome gold chronometer and nodded to his companion. "*Hélas,* we mus' return to our duties." He arose. "Be assured, *Monsieur le Medecin,* one will return at ze first opportunity. If you please, my compliments to ze lady and to my old friend, Monsieur de Lameth."

Asa, too, was tired of waiting. Once he and Thatcher had watched the Frenchmen ride off he penned a brief note of instructions. Hilde was to repose herself and to avoid the hospital for forty-eight hours at the very least. Mistress Stevens had undertaken to see that all duties would be performed in her absence.

XXII. EVENING STAR

WARM AND CLEAN-SMELLING air drifted through that little woods where Hilde lay, weary but irrepressibly content, with her cheek pressing against Hector de Lameth's tunic. It being unbuttoned, she could feel the warmth of his skin through the fine lawn of his ruffled shirt.

"My darling, I can hear the beating of your dear heart," she murmured drowsily.

"Do you know what it is saying?" His fingers skewered one of the curls lying across her partially bared shoulder. "No? Well then, it repeats over and over again, 'I love you, I adore you; I love you, I adore you! and so it will until the end of my days."

"That is a great deal for one heart to say."

His fingers brushed her cheek, found it unusually hot. "*Mon ange,* are you quite well?"

"But, of course, Hector, why not? I am well—and, oh, so very content now that you are by me."

"At supper tonight I thought your eyes very bright and your color higher than usual."

"'Twas caused by the prospect of meeting my lover after four endless days of separation."

"*Bon.*" De Lameth settled back against the bole of a huge sycamore, vastly comfortable because his cloak lay folded beneath his shoulders.

"*Ma foi!* It grows so late. Look, do you see that eve-

ning star? Why it shone above these branches when we
came; now it it ready to set.''

''Which star?''

''That huge pure white one,'' he explained gently and
indicated it. ''See, like none of her fellows, she displays
just a touch of blue. Such a gay and pure star reminds me
of you, my sweet little nightingale.

''Hector is worried,'' Hilde told herself. ''He never
makes conversation like this unless he has concerns.''
She wriggled up into a sitting position. ''Hector, please to
look in my eyes. There will be an attack—very soon?''

Sharp profile picked out by the afterglow, Hector
watched the evening star sink towards the skyline. Said
he ever so tenderly, ''Even the longest and dullest of
campaigns end in a few battles.''

''Then there will be one tomorrow?''

Hector de Lameth suddenly swept her back into his
arms and kissed her. ''You guess well,'' he admitted.
''But remember *chérie*, the storming of a redoubt is not
like delivering charge *à la baionnete* across an open field.
Mais, non. Besides, our little business will be attended to
under cover of darkness.''

Hilde's slight body commenced to tremble gently.
''Oh, Hector, *must* you go?''

A mild surprise manifested itself in his voice. ''But
consider, my love, an office of the Royal Deux-Ponts,
and a de Lameth, could not be found anywhere but at the
head of his men—like Papa at Minden, great-Uncle
Charles at Malplaquet and Grandpapa at Blenheim.''

Her trembling became more uncontrolled. ''Mercy,''
she thought, ''Hector is right. I am coming down with an
influenza, but I mustn't let him suspect,'' she warned
herself. ''He would worry himself.''

Hector was murmuring. ''Take courage, my heart,
Milo' Cornwallis in a few days must capitulate. The British fleet has been driven back to New York and he is
quite destitute of assistance. Soon, there will be no more
fighting here in Virginie and then we shall find ourselves a
pied-à-terre until the regiment is ordered home to
France.'' Hector's voice thrilled. ''Ah, France! *France.*
That is a country you will come to love, *ma petite!* I
swear you will. You cannot escape loving the beautiful
green countryside of my land, her forests and slow

streams; her great cities, the magnificent chateaux along the Garonne. All this we shall see together."

Hilde pleaded. "Hold me tighter, my hero, then tell me more of France."

Obediently, the young officer spoke on and on. He dwelt on their future. Should Papa refuse his consent to a marriage they would return to America. True, he had not yet come to love America as well as *la patrie,* but still it was a wonderful land. So much lay waiting to be accomplished here.

"Oh, look, Hector," Hilde cried suddenly. "My star! It is ready to disappear."

Again he kissed her fondly. "As so am I. Comte Guillaume will be furious over my tardy return. Come, my lovely one—tidy yourself. We must return to the innn."

Hilde's arms swept out to clasp his neck and almost desperately, she pressed herself to him. "In trying to forget this assault of tomorrow, I shall dwell upon this most perfect of afternoons and evenings," she whispered. Her laugh was a little choked when Hector, rising, swept her off her feet and carried her a few steps on the way back to Williamsburg.

XXIII. BAYONETS IN THE DARK

BITING HIS KNUCKLES in mingled envy and anxiety, Major Joshua Stanton watched, by the starlight, two dense columns of infantry, the one dark, the other light, form upon a level field just to the rear of the first parallel. Because of shell holes, half-dug trenches and debris, they were experiencing a little difficulty in ordering their files, but presently both columns moved off in nearly perfect silence.

The Americans, thanks to their dark blue uniforms, quickly became lost amid the gloom. Yonder went picked troops: two full regiments of the Maryland and Pennsylvania Line. For a long time Joshua would remember dark and handsome Lieutenant-Colonel Alexander Hamilton listening attentively to the last-minute instructions of Major-General de Lafayette.

The worthy marquis still was sputtering, furiously angry, over a well-intended if tactless suggestion from Baron de Viomesnil that, if the American troops met with difficulties, the French storming party should come immediately to their aid.

Joshua grinned to himself. The French were forever forgetting that Marquis de Lafayette considered himself to be just what he was—an American, and not a French General. How stiffly he had replied, "We are young soldiers, *mon Général,* it is true; our tactics in this matter, however, will be to fire our fusils but once and then press on with the bayonet."

Because, of all Continental troops, Lieutenant-Colonel Gimat's battalion of light infantry had served longest in Virginia, they were selected to lead the advance on Redoubt Number Ten. The center was commanded by Lieutenant-Colonel Alexander Hamilton and the rear brought up by Lieutenant-Colonel John Laurens of South Carolina.

Sabra's brother found it far easier to follow the progress of that long column of French troops now filing off to the left, towards Redoubt Number Nine. Picked grenadiers of the famous Gatinais followed hard after a detachment of sappers and axemen. Fresh laurels for the colors of this ancient regiment—it had been organized during the reign of Henri IV—lay within reach. Most impatient for action were the stalwart Provençals and Auvergnats of the Royal Deux-Ponts who were no less anxious to come to grips and to acquit themselves well under the eye of their colonel, Comte Guillaume de Deux-Ponts.

Joshua experienced a familiar constriction of his diaphragm; he had experienced such a sensation before, at Saratoga and again at White Plains. The staff stood conversing quietly on a little knoll commanding the dimly-seen parapets of the two threatened redoubts. Beyond, could be heard the occasional *clank* of musket barrels colliding and the trampling noises caused by nearly six hundred men. General Washington himself peered intently after the two columns with fingers drumming on gloves tucked into his belt. Knox, Joshua knew, was keeping his attention to the left where lay that battery which would fire a signal for the attack to commence.

Occasional clouds briefly obscured the stars, but luckily, what breeze there was, blew from over the York and

Redoubt Number Ten at the extreme left of the British line.

The Commander-in-Chief's deep voice inquired, "Major Tilghman, what o'clock have you?"

"It lacks but ten minutes of eight, Your Excellency."

"How the time drags at moments like these," Washington observed.

A puff of the river breeze brought once more a faint sound of clinking accoutrements and the trampling of feet. Now both columns had become lost in the darkness.

Under this damp wind Joshua's crippled shoulder began to ache. Minutes dragged by. Would the British be surprised?

At the head of the second battalion of the Maryland troops Major Thomas Offutt, swinging along with bared sword ready in hand, felt his breath come faster. He reckoned this was very like putting a fast, but green young hunter at a high and very solid post and rail fence.

"So this is what a night attack is like?" he was musing while the irregular black ground slipped by. "It's all pretty confusing. Give me daylight every time." His two other battles hadn't been a bit like this. About two hundred yards, dead ahead, was a big redoubt mounting a dozen cannon and defended by a lot of hard-shooting and level-headed veterans. Over his shoulder Major Offutt could recognize little except lines of white cross-belts rising and falling behind him, that, and in indistinct blur of faces.

A captain called softly, "Lay you two to one, Tom, we carry the place in ten minutes."

"Silence there!" hissed Lieutenant-Colonel Gimat. "Quiet, for your lives."

How many of these men marching around him would remain unhurt after six bombs fired in rapid succession touched off the attack? Offutt wasn't afraid he was relieved to discover. Suppose a musket ball took him square in the chest? Most likely it wouldn't hurt—he'd just never know what had happened.

The Marylanders tightened their grip on their bayoneted muskets and, as if marching into an invisible downpour, began to bend forward a little. As their nervous tension mounted, the men began to yawn, seeming bored to extinction. All of a sudden, Colonel Gimat signalled with his sword and brought the shadowy column to a halt.

To the men about him, Offutt whispered. "We have no axemen to cut us a path and must get over those palisadoes any way we can. You'd better hoist one another over the first obstacles."

A concerted sigh of relief arose when the first of the signal bombs sailed high up into the sky. Its fuse had been cut so short that the projectile burst—creating a brief but dazzling golden-red blossom in the night sky—when at the zenith of its trajectory. By its brief red glare Offutt could see his men's faces, all shadowy eyes and stiff, motionless mouths. Briefly their shadows became sketched on the trampled earth, then the report came, loud as a giant's handclap. Another bomb hissed upwards followed by yet another.

"Lay you two to one, Tom, I'm into the redoubt before you," called the irrepressible captain. "Are you on, Tom?"

"Done."

By the time the fifth bomb had uttered its spiteful, staccato roar, the men had tightened their belts and now were examining the priming of their muskets.

The sixth and the last of the signal bombs burst directly over Redoubt Number Ten, but too high to be effective. All the same it flooded that objective in a vivid crimson light. The prospects looked encouraging; no lines of heads were visible behind the parapet.

"*En avant!*" bawled Gimat, in his excitement reverting to his native tongue. "Forward, on ze double!"

Offutt's fingers cramped themselves on the grip of his sword.

"Hark away!" he yelled. "Hark away!"

Raising a mighty yell the whole dark column surged up a slight incline, bayonet points swinging in quick arcs to their stride.

Surprisingly, from above them came no sound until a startled voice shouted, "*Wer da?*"

"Hurray fer America!" "Hurray fer Washin'ton!" The infantry at Offutt's heels were just yelling, crying nothing intelligible.

Because his legs were short, Major Offutt had to work hard to keep ahead—just a few paces behind Colonel Gimat. Now the ground beneath his feet felt softer, broken;

the ditch must lie just ahead. The rush of the column became slowed now that jets of fire spangled those dim outlines of the redoubt's parapets.

Gigantic and deadly leaden bees began humming by; the storming troops dropped into a ditch and, struggling up its far side, became entangled among those sharp-pointed stakes which formed the palisado. Projecting upwards at right angles to the earthworks, they presented a most formidable obstacle. At once broke out a mad splintering and breaking of wood.

The men caught up to Offutt and with him wrestled over the palisadoes. Colonel Hamilton's force now came up.

"Boost each other over!" the New Yorker kept shouting. "Sooner yer over the safer ye'll be!"

More shots crackled and banged when Offutt turned to haul a short infantryman up through a gap among the stout wooden spears projecting from the base of the glacis. All about him the Marylanders and Pennsylvanians were being heaved up on their comrades' shoulders. The man Offutt was helping all at once emitted a hollow grunt, then as if infinitely weary, pitched forward on his face. The men rushing up behind trampled the dead man's body and swept up and over the parapet. The uproar swelled as hand to hand fighting commenced. A scream or two rang out.

"Come on! Come on, you bastards." Shrieks, screams and panted curses beat through the smoke clouds. For the moment Major Offutt could see absolutely nothing and to keep himself from becoming spiked on a friendly bayonet though it wise to shout, "This way, Maryland, this way."

Allied batteries meanwhile were raining death and destruction on the British supporting areas, as fast as their clumsy guns could be loaded and laid.

Almost before Offutt realized it, he and a knot of his men stood swaying on the parapet. So far as he could tell not a single American had discharged his musket, but, like a sheet of steel, their bayonets now were slanting downwards.

Through choking, confusing smoke, Offutt glimpsed a number of dark figures running pell-mell across the redoubt, obviously in hurried retreat.

"Forward! They're running!"

Followed a sound of steel striking wood, grunts, screams, a few more shots, then an English voice called out, "Quarter! Quarter! For God's sake grant us quarter."

Unfortunately, most of the defenders had run through a gate to the rear of their redoubt and had escaped to fight another day. A group of perhaps thirty-five or forty men, however, had dropped their weapons and now stood holding high their hands and begging loudly for quarter.

By the light of a high-bursting shell, Offutt caught the gleam of brass on a number of those high, miter-like caps affected by the King's German mercenaries; the furry shakoes of some British grenadiers were not nearly so distinctly to be seen.

To most of the officers it came as a great and glorious realization that Redoubt Number Ten, of such enormous tactical importance, was theirs at the incredibly low price of nine men killed and twenty wounded. Someone was calling for a physician. Lieutenant-Colonel Gimat, Captain Olney, and a Major Gibbs, it appeared, were slightly wounded.

"Clear a way for our sappers," Hamilton's shrill voice was calling across the swarming redoubt. "Quickly now, man the breastworks. The enemy will be coming back."

Obediently, his Pennsylvanians and Marylanders scrambled up onto the fire step and peered through the darkness towards the British inner lines. Yonder, to the left of the captured position, a savage battle must be waging for the possession of Redoubt Number Nine. Undoubtedly, the Royal Deux-Ponts and the Gatinais were meeting a more stubborn defense.

A bit breathlessly, the new garrison challenged a small party advancing from the allied lines. It proved to be General de Lafayette and his staff. "'Amilton! 'Amilton, you 'ave secured the position?"

"Yes, sir," Hamilton hurried forward together with Lieutenant-Colonel Laurens, proudly carrying the sword of the British commander. "General, may I present Major Campbell, formerly in command here?"

Once Lafayette and the Englishman had exchanged brief salutes, the former spun on his heel. "Major Barber!"

"Yes, sir?"

"Please convey my compliments to the Baron de Viomesnil and inquire of him,'' he chuckled like a mischievous school boy, ''whether he requires any assistance. We shall be delighted to oblige.''

XXIV. REDOUBT NUMBER NINE

AMONG THE FOREMOST of his men Captain the Chevalier de Lameth crouched in the fosse before Redoubt Number Nine cursing that incredible deliberation with which the sappers were hewing down the palisadoes just ahead. With each passing minute, the British and German fire was increasing in effectiveness. Already dreadful screams and groans were rising on all sides; every so often some grenadier would collapse, kicking blindly, uselessly like a beetle impaled upon a pin.

''Fire at the parapet,'' de Lameth ordered and used the flat of his thin sword to beat back a frightened recruit who would have bolted.

Some of his men obeyed, their musket flashes revealing a squirming pattern of human figures.

He had no time to judge the results for a shout arose, ''*En avant! En avant! Vive le Roi!*''

''At last, *mon Capitaine*, we shall—'' The sergeant emitted a queer choking cry, clapped both hands to his throat and reeled crazily, knocking off balance the men nearest him. The rest of the Deux-Ponts, however, were scrambling upwards through the dense and drifting smoke, yelping like scalded dogs despite a continual blaze of musketry from above.

More shouts. Hector de Lameth, while trying to see what lay ahead, wondered if Papa had felt this way at Minden. What a superb moment! A heady exhilaration seized him. Ahead waited the ancient enemies of France.

''*En avant, les Deux-Ponts!* For honor and victory!'' And waving his sword, he struggled up the sandy, treacherous footing of the glacis. Half a dozen infantrymen withered under a sudden and murderously close volley. Like ninepins they tumbled to the ground.

Hector sensed, rather than saw, indecision seize the men of his company. ''*En avant! Pour Dieu et Saint Louis!*'' he screamed, just as had his forebears at Crécy and Agincourt.

An outstretched leg tripped him and, sobbing for

breath, Hector was just recovering his feet when something like a hot branding iron was laid across his left thigh. All the same he limped on, sword held high and yelling encouragements. Ha! Now more and more white figures had gained the parapet and were thrusting downwards at a series of white cross-belts. The Gatinais must be over the opposite parapet. Hector judged so by the changed pitch of their cries.

All at once Hector de Lameth found himself on the parapet and looking down onto a little lake of struggling men and flashing weapons. A tall British grenadier jumped up onto the berm snarling, "'Ere's for yer, ye bloody Dancing Master."

De Lameth evaded a savage thrust by the fellow's bayonet, levelled his sword and sank it deep into the grenadier's throat. Another enemy, however, had clubbed his musket and with terrible effectiveness swung it against the Chevalier de Lameth's side.

Amid a great blaze of light, and a torrent of whirling sparks, Hector de Lameth collapsed, fell miles backwards into an unbroken blackness.

XXV. CONSULTATION

THE BRITISH COMMANDER's failure to order a counterattack, coupled with the perfection of the surprise, left many beds vacant that were expected to have been filled. Not even the most optimistic of the allied tacticians had anticipated such light casualties—less than a hundred and fifty injured was indeed a cheap price for so valuable a gain. In fact, there was so little to do that Peter Burnham found himself feeling resentful and foolish at having left his own hospital in which lay the sick and disabled of de Barras's fleet.

Surgeon-Colonel Dubois and his assistants were quite able to treat and operate upon sixty-odd wounded men. Only three of the many officers participating in the assault now reposed beneath the sun-yellowed canvas of the officers' ward.

One of them immediately attracted Peter's attention. He was so slender, so young, and he was remaining so cheerful despite his serious wounds. He was attempting to determine the nature of this young captain's injuries when Colonel Dubois came up.

"Ah. He is the tough one, this Chevalier de Lameth. Imagine it! He has suffered a musket ball passing through the left thigh and a shallow sword slash of the right shoulder."

Gazing down at this patient resting on the sheets arranged across a deep pile of straw, Peter thought he noted a fleck of blood or two on the young fellow's unshaven chin.

"Your pardon, sir, but what causes those blood specks?"

The French surgeon shrugged. "In addition to his other wounds M. le Chevalier has suffered an injury to the chest. *Le bon Dieu* alone knows the extent of that hurt. Would you care to make an examination? It goes not well with the Chevalier, as already you have distinguished."

Peter, on testing the pulse, found it hard and rapid and, when he applied his ear to the pallid, nearly motionless chest, he made sure he could hear a faint sucking noise. Um. A big purple-blue bruise was located just to the left of the sternum.

"It is a pretty flower that I grow, no?" wheezed de Lameth and tried to laugh, but ended by coughing instead. A faint, rose-colored spray burst from his lips and despite everything he grimaced in agony.

"It hurts you to breathe, does it not?"

Hector de Lameth's pallid and sweat-spangled features contracted. "Most damnably," he admitted.

Surgeon-Colonel Dubois frowned, stood wiping big and hairy hands on his apron. "That Monsieur le Chevalier has sustained an injury to the chest is inescapable. Yet to open the hurt is but to court gangrene and death. You will admit that is true?"

The American surgeon's red head inclined. "In most cases. All the same, Colonel, I remember—" One day back in Boston a drover had fallen, his chest was partially crushed beneath the wheel of his own cart. "A colleague of mine was able to save him." How well he could recall Asa's sure hands identifying the extent of the damage. Of French sensibilities Peter had learned enough to word very carefully his next remarks.

"Captain de Lameth suffers great pain—would you deem me impertinent, Colonel, if I were to invite for consultation that same colleage—he commands our hospital at Williamsburg?"

Under the sun-brightened canvas Colonel Dubois'

heavy brows merged. His response was just what Peter hoped for.

"Ah! That is the Surgeon Pea-bodee? Yes, I have heard of him—good things. Of a certainty, we shall invite his opinions. One could do no less for so gallant an officer as Monsieur de Lameth. Any physician, Monsieur, whose skill even approximates your own is welcome; should he teach us anything we do not already know, he will be made doubly welcome."

Thus it came about that, on the afternoon of October fifteenth, Asa Peabody appeared at Surgeon-Colonel Dubois' hospital.

Peter appeared at the flap of the hospital tent, greeted him warmly. "I hope you weren't too occupied, but well—the problem presents peculiar aspects."

"I am fortunate in my assistants—Fletcher and Thatcher," Asa said, then lowered his voice. "Did I read your message correctly—that your patient is named de Lameth?"

"Whatever are you so dramatic about?"

"He's Hilde Mention's husband. D'you recall her?"

"Vividly. You know, there's an officer of the Agenais who—"

"—Who is her spit and image? Yes. I know. I saw him recently. 'Tis the most amazing resemblance."

The two physicians perforce fell silent, so violent became the bombardment of York Town. The second parallel having been completed, allied cannons now were emplaced less than three hundred yards distant from the inner British lines. Now that the lighter pieces could range the enemy, sweating French and American gunners were maintaining an incessant fire. They wondered how humans could endure so violent a rain of iron and fire. Yet endure the English did, and, more than that, replied as best they could from their inadequate batteries.

The sky streamed smoke and the reverberations of the guns were deafening when Peter led Asa into the officer's ward.

"Ah, Captain de Lameth. Glad to find you looking so well." Asa tried hard to appear casual.

"Ah, Pea-bodee, *mon ami.*" A faint smile curved the wounded officer's lavender-tinted lips. Asa felt a great wrench in his heart; this hollow-cheeked, sunken-eyed wretch little resembled that gay young officer who, only a few nights before, at the Raleigh had led the guests in songs and dancing.

That the patient was delighted to behold Asa's familiar face was inescapable.

After a little, Peter took Asa aside and only then gave a detailed description of de Lameth's condition. "The bullet wound in his leg is painful and deep, but so far it displays no signs of mortification. The sword cut on his shoulder is unimportant. Were these hurts all we had to consider, I would never have summoned you for consultation. As it is—only a minor miracle can preserve de Lameth's life. Since there is no time to be lost and Colonel Dubois declares himself helpless, I have arranged for your—examination to take place here."

The eyes of the two physicians, dark brown and blue, met and clung.

"You expect me to operate, Peter?"

"I think you will. You possess the skill requisite to meet such a problem. I—" he held up his crippled left hand, smiled sadly. "I, well, I haven't."

Asa put down his saddle bags, noticed that a house door lay supporting a thin mat upon a pair of saw horses. Um. So he was expected to operate, was he? Well, Peter at least had selected a favorable hour of the day; at two of the afternoon the sun was still high and its light, striking through the canvas, was strong yet diffused.

The tricorned and powdered head of a sergeant appeared at the flap. "*Vous êtes prêt, Monsieur?*"

Peter nodded and, a moment later, Hector de Lameth's litter was brought in. Surgeon-Colonel Dubois followed a few paces in its rear. Hector de Lameth lay very white, his jet eyes sunk deep into their sockets.

"*Alors,*" he whispered, managing the faintest imaginable smile. "You are about to deliver a fresh bayonet charge?" His hand, veined in blue and pallid beneath the sunburn that lent it a yellowish tinge, beckoned Asa. "And how goes it with my lady—my wife?"

"Splendidly. She is more beautiful than ever."

Asa was lying in his teeth and he knew it. Hilde had not returned to the hospital after her two-day vacation and Sabra Stanton reported her to be feverish to the point of lightheadedness. Her symptoms, Asa thought, suggested a touch of la grippe.

That evening, when he returned to Williamsburg, he intended to call and determine for himself the nature of her malady. The best tonic for Hilde he knew would be intelligence of Hector de Lameth's improved condition. Of course, some fool had had to tell her about de Lameth's having been wounded.

"Please to proceed, Messieurs—I—I fear I—" his eyelids sagged closed. "I am most impolite, but one is a trifle fatigued."

Quickly, Peter exposed de Lameth's chest and Asa's eyes widened when he noted the extent of that mottled, mulberry-hued discoloration.

Two orderlies stood awaiting instructions, their close-cropped heads bent a little forward by the slope of the canvas. As for Surgeon-Colonel Dubois, he tactfully remained silent, but attentive of what followed.

"If it hurts please cry out," he instructed de Lameth. "Do not be ashamed. Only in that way can I test the injured area and determine what is to be done."

Slowly he tapped the vicinity of the bruise. Then he said brusquely, "Give him a bullet to bite on, Peter, I can't avoid hurting him now."

Hector de Lameth's eyes widened, but nonetheless he accepted a soft lead bullet and stowed it between his molars.

Asa exerted first a gentle lateral pressure, then a horizontal one. Next his two forefingers tested the apex of the contusion; when he did so a gurgling groan escaped de Lameth and sweat appeared at his temples. When he commenced to cough, blood ran in tiny scarlet threads from the corners of his mouth.

"As you have no doubt deduced," Asa told Peter, "a severe blow has ruptured the patient's sterno-costal joint inducing a complaint known as *emphysema*. In my opinion a bone splinter has been driven inwards, piercing the vesicular part of the substance of the lungs. This has permitted air to pass into the cavity of the thorax which induces a difficulty in respiration by compressing the lobes of the lungs."

Surgeon-Colonel Dubois edged closer. An aide translated when he commented, "That has been our opinion as well, Monsieur. Yet to open the lung cavity of the patient—"

Asa's brown eyes sought the Frenchman's. "If the break is clean, I shall attempt operation of the *paracente-*

cis thoracis, or opening into the cavity of the chest. It may be possible to remove that splinter.''

"Possibly, but not probably," grunted the Frenchman. "You really intend to attempt to remove that splinter—or splinters?''

"He will die otherwise," Asa whispered. "Peter, I've always favored your tenet that instruments dipped in hot brandy promote a swifter recovery and less risk of a mortification setting in. Can that be arranged?''

Twenty minutes later, Peter his sleeves rolled back to the elbows, dipped scalpels, knives, forceps, needles and retractors into a basin of hot water heavily laced with cognac.

Asa, stripped to breeches and shirt, mopped the sweat from his brow before bending low over de Lameth's inert figure. "You must understand, Monsieur, that—well an operation of this gravity is not always successful. Have I your permission to proceed?''

The young officer spoke without opening his eyes. "There is but one condition.''

"And that is?''

"Should you fail—you will convey to Madame—my wife," he emphasized the title, "that my last thoughts were of her and of the great love she so generously gave to me.''

Intent, Peter and Dubois stood watchful and ready by the improvised operating table. There was no need to hold down the patient when Asa's knife bit into the ivory smooth skin—he was far too weak. Then, happily, de Lameth fainted.

"*Festina lente*—make haste slowly," Doctor Townsend's voice warned in Asa's memory. He forced himself to move deliberately as, cautiously, he pursued his dissection following the direction of John Jones, that admirable Scotch surgeon who had written:

This opening may be made without much difficulty or danger, by dividing the integument something better than half an inch in length, and then cautiously pursuing the dissection through the intercostal muscles and pleura, with the point of the scalpel.—There is no danger of wounding the lungs under such circumstances, as they are sufficiently compressed by the air in the chest to keep them out of the way of the knife.

At length Asa guided the forceps into the incision, gripped the splinter and worked it free, using immense patience and delicacy.

When, at length, Asa had tied the last of the bandages and straightened, Dubois offered his hand. "My most sincere compliments on your art. One would not have deemed it possible to withdraw such a large splinter without rupturing the lung case."

Peter beamed. "You're a shining wonder, Asa. Are there any further instructions?"

"Only that the patient be kept warm, and if he becomes demented a watch be kept to assure the position of his bandage. Though I'd admire to linger, I fear I must leave at once," he apologized. "It would seem that a storm is brewing."

He was quite right. Towards sundown, a shrieking, howling gale blew out of the southwest; a storm so violent that great trees went crashing down, small ships were driven ashore, and crews of the men-of-war downstream were set to putting out extra anchors.

All night long the wind raged and, in so doing, thwarted Lord Cornwallis' last and most desperate attempt to break out of the trap into which he had thrust himself. Displaying a surprising if belated, energy and hardihood, the unhappy Earl, under cover of darkness, attempted to ferry his doomed command across to Gloucester Point. From there he might have attempted a long, long retreat northwards. As it was, the river boiled like a stew pot and the carefully collected small boats were either sunk or driven ashore under the lashing of the wind.

XXVI. General O'Hara and the Sword

The siege guns and field artillery had not fired in near two full days; even so, after nearly three weeks of almost incessant bombardment neither besiegers nor besieged could quite accustom themselves to this sudden silence. For a second time during this war—and, curiously enough, on the anniversary of Burgoyne's capitulation at Saratoga—a British field army had asked permission to surrender its colors and to lay down its arms.

Those officers and men who, during six long years, had fought King George III's courageous and well-disciplined soldiers had to pinch themselves to realize that at last, at long last, the victory was theirs. Those Massachusetts soldiers who had first thrown their sights on a Redcoat in the spring of 1775—there were precious few of them left—remained especially thoughtful. Through their minds surged half-forgotten and confused recollections covering not only half a hundred raids, skirmishes and battles, but even more poignant memories of chill and miserable retreats.

Virginians, Pennsylvanians, Marylanders, and New Yorkers shared their scanty liquor supply and went round with fixed grins decorating their bronzed features. This time, the news seemed just too good to be true.

To think that Lord Charles Cornwallis, that merciless scourge of the Southern States, must soon surrender his sword. The news soon got about that, in the Articles of Capitulation, there was a specification that Cornwallis must hand his sword to that same General Benjamin Lincoln—recently exchanged—who had been forced, under humiliating conditions, to surrender his own sidearms last year in Charles Town.

The French, too, were smiling. Not often did they enjoy the sight of a British garrison marching out to surrender, for all that a few of the older officers could recall similar, if lesser, victories in the Lowlands. *Grace à Dieu*, on the morrow a whole British army—artillery, foot and dragoons—was about to dip its colors before the golden lilies of Louis XVI.

Eloquently and frequently, toasts were offered in the messes of the French gentlemen and, in their bivouacs, the rank and file also got gloriously *zig-zag* for, in an unprecedented gesture of generosity, the officers had supplied for their benefit whole hampers of wine.

Around noon of October the nineteenth, 1781, elements of the victorious armies commenced to move from their positions in order to line a two-mile route leading out from York Town to the Field of Surrender. Lazy dust clouds arose and settled on the marching men who soon commenced to sweat.

Rank on rank, regiment on regiment, wearing new or freshly cleaned uniforms and with accoutrements newly burnished, the French maneuvered to line the left-hand side of this road leading from the enemy positions. The Americans, garbed in their usual weird assortment of uni-

forms, formed up along the right. Some of their units—
the Virginia militia in particular—wore no uniform at all,
only crossbelts secured over a second-best suit of civilian
clothes.

Mighty picturesque on the other hand, were companies
of mountain men whose faces were burned to a hue almost identical with that of their fringed buckskin hunting
shirts. These sinewy fellows carried long rifles and wore
scalping knives or war hatchets at their belts. Once the
order, "stand easy," was given, everybody began to talk
sixty to the minute and to crane his neck in the direction
of York Town.

Very near to the Field of Surrender, but not adjacent
to it, rode General George Washington and a whole company of general officers. Smiling, chaffing one another,
they sat their horses, dusted their coats and reset their
stocks.

Between the Commander-in-Chief and the town were
posted that backbone of America's endeavor—the Continental regiments of the Line. In firm, erect ranks these
regulars stood just as choleric old von Steuben had
taught them, with buttons bright and their blue and buff
uniforms clean, though stained through hard campaing-
ing.

At irregular intervals were posted regimental standard
bearers, together with their guards. Lazily, these vari-
colored banners stirred in a cool wind blowing up the river from Chesapeake Bay. The day was a glorious one,
clear and crisp, but warm in the sun.

Behind their infantry the Allied Army's handful of cavalry was drawn up. Bravely, the sun glanced from the
brass helmets of the dragoons and the cheek pieces of
their horses' bridles. These troopers must have been cur-
rying since sunup because their mounts shone like newly
minted coins.

French array displayed many distinctive colors. Most
noticeable in the long line were the light blue of the Royal
Deux-Ponts and the dark blue coats of the Sayonne Regiment of those French Marines who had fought so well
across the river at Gloucester Point. Dozens of regimental ensigns, blazoned with the records of two hundred
years of warfare, stirred lazily.

The surrender hour, two o'clock, remained half an
hour distant, so accustomed to the age-old military max-

im of "Hurry up, then wait," the French and Americans commenced to call to each other across the twenty yard interval and exchange cheerful insults.

"'Allo, you Yankee son-a-beech!" greeted a towering sergeant of the Soissonsais.

"Hullo, yerself, ye sister-seducing frog-eater!" boomed an equally huge Virginia militiaman. When he kissed his hand and made the Frenchman an awkward bow, roars of laughter arose from both sides of the route.

"We feex ze Anglais good. No?"

"Damn' right, Mounseer. We'll alter 'em, too, if they don't act purty!"

More, and rougher pleasantries followed, but no one took offense. The affair of Redoubts Nine and Ten had inspired a mutual respect as genuine as it was hearty.

Because he belonged to no particular unit, Captain Andrew Warren, together with his officers Loubet and Doane, stood on a small knoll on the American side. He had sat up late at night burnishing the buttons of his old American naval uniform—never having been retired by the Marine Committee, he guessed he retained a right to wear it. No trace of verdigris stained his single epaulet, earned in such bitter disillusionment—and unswerving loyalty. Not a few curious glances were directed towards him.

He felt sure that not one man in a thousand would recognize him for a lieutenant in the Naval Service of the United States. Very likely, none would record his presence at this momentous ceremony, no matter how many pens might describe that glittering blue, gold and scarlet rank of French naval officers who, for all their importance, were joking and staring around like so many schoolboys. For them, also, this must be a rare moment.

Nearly a quarter of a mile nearer York Town, Brevet Lieutenant-Colonel Joshua Stanton chatted happily with lesser members of General Knox's official family.

Jerusha! What a memorable day this was proving! First a promotion, and now what looked like an end to this war. From his position between Colonels Nicholas Fish and Walter Stuart, Joshua found that he could enjoy a fine view of the French senior officers. Quite a few of them he knew by sight—Colonel William Deux-Ponts, for example, and the Comte de Custine, standing next to the always picturesque Duc de Lauzun who still wore

Madame de Coigny's black heron feather nodding in his hussar's busby.

He even received smiling nods from General Choizy and the Baron de Viomesnil, with whom he had had much to do of late. Yonder, mopping his face, was his old friend the Marquis de Chastellux, General Rochambeau's principal aide.

Of Colonel Fish, Joshua learned that a bandy-legged, heavy-set officer looking most uncomfortable a-horse-back was Admiral de Barras.

At the extreme end of the French array, Admiral Comte de Grasse sat his horse more comfortably while chatting gravely with Lieutenant-General, the Comte de Rochambeau—faithful, patient and able Rochambeau.

Opposite the French high command and occupying the extreme right of the American line, the Commander-in-Chief sat easily astride his fine bay charger.

No trace of haughtiness or pride manifested itself on General Washington's countenance—only serenity. To the left of his commander was General Benjamin Lincoln. Solid and red-faced, he was fully occupied in controlling a tall gray charger.

Never again, during the war, would so many famous ranking officers come together; big-nosed, red-faced von Steuben, General Trumbull, Colonel Cobb and General James Clinton of New York—no doubt happier today than his namesake on the British side—Mad Anthony Wayne, Major-General Henry Knox and shrewd, opportunistic Colonel Alexander Hamilton.

The only major architects of this victory not present were the great Nathanael Greene—he was occupied far away, retaining Lord Rawdon in Charles Town, South Carolina, and Major-General de Lafayette, who over at Gloucester Point, was preparing to receive the surrender of Colonel Banastre Tarleton's garrison.

While minute after minute dragged by, horses fidgeted, switched at flies and pawed the ground and the officers began to grow both irritable and suspicious. Weren't the British coming out after all?

Ha! A deep, muffled cry came ripping along the double ranks. Everyone tried to see down the road. There it was; a thumping of drums in the distance. *Boom-a-rattle—ta tat. Boom! Boom!* Although distant, voices of officers could be heard calling their troops to attention.

Joshua recognized the flashes of hundreds of bayonets being brought to "present arms." In gradually increasing volume, came the music of many fifes and drums beating a march, but they were yet very far and many minutes must pass before the surrendering army approached this sector.

Joshua's gaze sought the Commander-in-Chief's tall figure and saw that, calm and dignified as ever, Washington was looking skywards. Presently he turned on the leopard skin housing of his saddle and said something to Knox. Several of the French, following the direction of the Commander-in-Chief's interest, also gazed upwards and Lauzun tilted his fine head backwards so far that braids of false white hair to either side of his lean face swung to the rear. "Ah. And what kind of a bird is that?"

"He is an eagle, suh," called one of the Virginia officers. "He is what we call a bald eagle."

Lauzun laughed joyously. "Ah, *mes amis*, have we not here an omen—like the Romans of old?" His voice rose. "Gentlemen of France, look upwards and behold that eagle in the sky—an American eagle and free as the air in which he flies! Today, my friends, a new nation soars to take a sure place in God's world."

"Hurray for you, suh!" yelled a Virginia colonel. "That's right well spoken, suh."

Drums now began sounding louder and, by craning his neck a little, Joshua could distinguish a line of scarlet and gold breasting a rise nearly half a mile away. In a moment more he could make out the lift and swing of gaily painted drums as they responded to the stride of the little drummer boys; soon he recognized the flash of sunlight on their brass-mounted drumsticks.

On foot, and a few yards to the rear of the field music, a contingent of scarlet-coated officers were marching straight and stiff as so many ramrods. High behind them appeared the thick black outlines of dozens of color staffs; all British flags were cased because, at Charles Town, Sir Henry Clinton had, in his arrogance, decreed that no American —"Rebel," he'd called them—colors might be displayed.

"Where is Cornwallis?" "I don't see Cornwallis," voices cried in undertones. "Where's their commander?"

One after another, the allied units presented arms to

the defeated officers marching by at the head of a seemingly endless scarlet column flowing up between the
ranks of blue-and-white-clad infantrymen.

That singing noise commenced to play again in Joshua
Stanton's ears. "It's six years since I first saw a Redcoat
on Boston Neck," he reflected. "I was only a lad then, a
sc_ _ed little lieutenant, who didn't know his arse from his
elbow about soldiering, and now I'm seeing them
whipped at last."

Nearer and nearer tramped the field music, red in the
face from playing so long and marching so far but render-
ing "The World Turned Upside Down" tolerably well.

"That ain't Cornwallis. Where is the bastard, anyhow?"

The black and gold revers of a British general officer
had become visible through the veiling dust. Mounted,
the stranger rode between a French and an American
officer. The three tried to keep abreast but the American's horse curvetted and caricoled.

"Where's Cornwallis?" called a grizzled militia colonel, eyes glowing in hatred. "He's the one to make surrender!"

"Shamming sick," someone replied disgustedly. "Old
Charley ain't got the stomach to admit he's been licked."

Now appeared a row of blue-clad figures. Colonel Fish
muttered that this was von Saybothen of the Hessian
troops and his aides; next came a group of green-coated
Loyalists who, especially, must feel that their world was
turned upside down. Following these marched the blue
coats of a dozen naval officers, then more scarlet and
gold tunics.

Almost before Joshua realized it, General Charles
O'Hara, Cornwallis' second-in-command, was passing,
his mottled cheeks thin and his hooked nose sharp-looking as a knife.

On a signal the music halted and fell back towards
either side of the road. The surrendering troops also halted. Now that the music was silenced, everyone present
could hear General O'Hara in a choked voice inquire,
"Where is General de Rochambeau?"

The French Adjutant-General, Comte de Dumas, mis-
understanding the Englishman's intent, indicated his superior, but when O'Hara urged his mount in Rochambeau's direction, Dumas spurred ahead fast enough to

overtake O'Hara before he could draw rein before the French commander.

The Comte de Rochambeau took no notice of O'Hara's intention except to indicate General Washington sitting impassively to his right. General O'Hara of His Britannic Majesty's Coldstream Guards advanced toward the American commander, his lips drawn thin and colorless over his teeth. A deep and general sigh could be heard as O'Hara held out Lord Cornwallis' sword—he had carried it across his pommel.

Washington, quite imperturbable, despite the Englishman's attempted affront, halted O'Hara with a brief gesture. "Pray address General Lincoln."

Because Cornwallis' sword glittered so brilliantly several horses curvetted and began to snort. Benjamin Lincoln, at Washington's left, drew in his big stomach and accepted the sword. "Not from so worthy a hand," he rumbled and, reversing the weapon, he returned it hilt first to O'Hara.

"God bless my soul! You are most generous, sir." Everyone heard the Guardee's startled words, then saw tears suddenly slip down over his ruddy cheeks.

The surrendering general and his staff immediately were conducted to one side where, in tents previously erected, they refreshed their drooping spirits. Meanwhile the field music struck up again and, directed by a pair of American sergeants, the head of that long, red-coated column advanced into a field about the limits of which had gathered swarms of seamen, cooks, sutlers and camp followers.

On the trampled brown grass the British laid down their arms.

XXVII. DESCENT INTO DARKNESS

ON THE DAY AFTER the last of the enemy troops, sullenly and ill-temperedly, had stacked arms before being marched away under guard, American pickets on the Williamsburg road were astonished to see a young woman driving into battered York Town. Beside her, in a decrepit chaise, shone the scarlet coat of a paroled British officer—he had been taken prisoner during an unsuccessful sortie attempted earlier in the week.

"Aye, Madame, 'twill require small imagination on your part to comprehend our sufferings." Three golden buttons adorning his cuff glittered when he indicated shattered windows, crumbled brick fences and dozens of houses, the walls of which were pierced through and through. Loose bricks, scattered over the road, caused the chaise to bounce sharply once they turned into the village square.

"I can vouch for the fact that your people did all they could to make miserable our lives. My word, my ears still ring from a shell which burst so near as to knock me off my feet. Why I wasn't slain, Madame, I'll never understand." He grinned. "Maybe I was born to hang—Grandma always said so."

Captain Staniforth was young enough to have recovered in a large measure from the shock and humiliation of finding himself a prisoner on parole. He pointed to a house barely visible to the right of the village. "Over there is Mrs. Moore's house, where the Articles of Capitulation were drawn up. Mrs. Moore's a lucky lady to have had a home so far removed from the village."

"I'm sure she has showered Providence with thanksgivings. I know I would."

All the way from Williamsburg Sabra Stanton had been impressed by the great numbers of Negroes travelling the road. Of both sexes and all ages, they looked terribly apprehensive—and well they might—since all of them had run away from their masters to seek British protection. Most of them carried bundles or pathetic sacks of possessions as they started their slow journey back to their home plantation—and punishment. Every now and then one of the blacks would halt before American troops guarding the road and make inquiries. When Sabra's chaise drew near, these humble folk invariably removed round, woolly-looking hats and bowed deep.

During that interval in which Captain Staniforth picked a route through the captured positions, Sabra found opportunity to glimpse many British guns standing deserted in their bastions. Some were smashed, but most stood intact among low pyramids of dully gleaming cannon balls.

Once Sabra's eyes grew wide and she pinched her nose. The chaise was approaching what appeared to be an extra wide trench. Horrors! A shiver chilled her heart;

this was no trench at all, but a common grave nearly overflowing with grotesquely tumbled dead bodies.

All at once aware of her strained expression, Captain Staniforth—of the Second Life Guards and very proud on that score—said, "Even before the siege began, Doctor Devoe was well and favorably known, Ma'am. A deuced clever surgeon, if I may say so. Came down under contract to von Seybothen's Anspach troops. Would you credit it? Inside of a month he became senior corps surgeon to the Guards, and later surgeon-in-chief to our luckless little army?"

"Yes," Sabra said. "I can believe it. I am not at all surprised."

Sidewise, the Guardee regarded this remarkably handsome young woman, then ventured, "'Tis most urgent business with this Doctor Devoe brings you so promptly to York Town?"

"As you say—most urgent business."

Sabra refused to be drawn out. On attempting to understand her present sensations, she found that she simply could not. All manner of emotions and ideas were swimming about her mind like peas boiling in a pot. It was somehow frightening to know that, in a very few minutes, she and Lucius Devoe would meet again.

For the life of her, Sabra could not predict her probable course. Would she fly into his arms, forgiving everything, or would she listen coldly, allowing the rogue an opportunity to explain his faithless and mortifying conduct?

As the chaise bumped and jolted across a little square one part of her mind kept repeating, "Lucius and you were made for each other. Despite all he's done, you still love him." Another part warned, quite as often, "What you have suffered is an infatuation. From the start you have been taken in, like the silly moon-struck girl you were, back there in Boston. True love is more like that sensation you experienced when you met Asa in the Governor's Palace."

To cling to her decision to avoid Asa Peabody had been more than difficult. Always, an unaccountable warm and happy sensation seized her whenever she recognized his tall figure moving quietly, surely among the wards. No wonder the patients doted on him and followed his injunctions to a degree unprecedented with such an undisciplined lot, most of whom enjoyed taking orders for the sake of disobeying them.

Two or three times Captain Staniforth waved solemnly to fellow officers in the street. Devoid of sidearms, every one of them looked as if he had just quitted the funeral of his best friend.

"When I was captured we maintained here two principal hospitals, one under a German named Reinhoff—a really amazing fellow—the other was directed by your friend, Doctor Devoe."

"Please, let us proceed to—to Doctor Devoe's hospital." Sabra tried hard to steady her voice, but it was difficult because, in a very few minutes now, she would know for sure what course the rest of her life was to follow.

"Well, I'm damned," Staniforth reined in, looked hurriedly about. "Hullo! That house there—that was his hospital. I'm certain on it! But look—"

The roof was gone, the windows blown out and a great section of wall had collapsed into the yard. Fire had scorched the bricks.

A broad-faced Yorkshireman wearing the uniform of the Twenty-eighth of the Line nodded solemnly. "Aye, zur. Was hospital till struck by a pair o' gradely bombs, zur. Roof fell in. Moved what was left to yonder barn."

"'Tis most unchancey, Ma'am. I trust nothing's gone amiss with Doctor Devoe." Captain Staniforth dropped the reins across the beast's dusty back. "Your pardon, Ma'am, but I fancy you'd best wait here whilst I make inquiries."

Fighting down a rising nervousness, Sabra forced herself to remain on the lumpy and mouldy-smelling seat of the chaise. Half expecting to recognize Lucius' small and wiry figure emerging from the barn she tensed herself. Ah! But there appeared only the Guardee in the company of a tall, gray-eyed individual wearing an apron marked with new blood.

"May I present Doctor Reinhoff?" Staniforth said as the other bowed gravely.

"Good day, sir," Sabra murmured, "but it is Doctor Devoe I came to see."

Doctor Reinhoff gave a tired shake of his head. "I t'ink you are yet in time, *Fräulein*. In dot shed lies *mein* poor colleague."

"Lucius is—he's hurt?"

"*Nein*. He iss dying," Reinhoff shrugged. "A great loss, *Fräulein*. He most inderesting ideas hat. *Ja*. Next to me, Devoe iss der cleverest surgeon in America."

Sabra bit hard on her lip. Lucius dying? Why, it didn't seem comprehensible.

"You are sure, there is no room for hope?"

"*Nein, gnädige Fräulein*." The German looked genuinely unhappy. "An arm he lost, but his real hurt iss in der belly; it vass slight, but mortifications began und so—" Reinhoff made a circular motion about his head.

Sabra only stared. How curious that the possibility of Lucius being injured had never even occurred to her.

"I said, do you still wish to see Doctor Devoe?" gently reminded the Guardee. "I gather he ain't rational, so possibly you'd best not harrow yourself—"

"Oh, no. I must see him. I must."

"*Ach, Fräulein*, Why iss it always der *gut* men ve lose? During der siege Devoe splendid vass; his art, his courage und his energy *kolossal* were."

At the door to the shed Doctor Reinhoff excused himself saying that much remained to be done and most regimental surgeons were far from capable.

Gratefully Sabra accepted the offer of Staniforth's scarlet arm.

Only two figures occupied the woodshed; an orderly of sorts and a figure lying on an officer's cot bed. A flash of perception told Sabra that Lucius' right arm had been amputated at the elbow.

The Jamaican's dark eyes, sunk deep in his head, slid slowly open. The always sharp outline of Lucius Devoe's cheeks and chin now were more than ever pronounced beneath a black stubble covering his cheeks and chin. A blue cloak had been folded to support his head and, covering him, was some officer's greatcoat.

Captain Staniforth was tactful and turned to look out of the door as, skirts a-flutter, Sabra hurried across trampled straw covering the floor.

"'E's out o' 'is 'ead, Mum," the orderly warned.

"No, not any longer—" Lucius' voice sounded faint indeed. "I am quite sensible."

He wasn't so sure, though when he thought to behold Sabra Stanton bending above him, lips parted in a tortured smile and hands uncertainly extended. To raise his head a little he tried, but couldn't. That settled matters; as a physician he recognized the import of this deadly chill which, gradually, had been advancing inwards along his limbs—such as remained to him. Before long, that chill must reach, and silence, his heart. The possibility, somehow, didn't trouble him now. He felt tired, so very tired.

The orderly suggested, "'Ere's a bit o' rum, Mum. Shall I give it to 'im?"

"I think you had better do so."

The dying man's head, outlined against its halo of dark disordered hair, inclined ever so slightly. "Is—is that really you, Sabra?"

"Yes, Lucius," she whispered, dropping onto her knees. "It is really I. You can feel my hand." An instant she rested her fingers along his forehead.

"Thank you. Now I know that you are more than a wondrously beautiful spectre."

Staniforth cleared his throat. "Ma'am, if you don't mind, I will wait outside. And you, soldier, go fetch a mug of fresh water."

Twice the door was darkened then, for the first time in nearly two years, Sabra and Lucius were alone together.

Several moments passed as they gazed on each other and Sabra succeeded in ignoring a terrible odor pervading the shed; in Williamsburg she had become accustomed to noisome smells, but the terribly swollen condition of the stricken physician's abdomen was not lightly to be dismissed.

"Lucius," she knew, even as she spoke, that no overwhelming surge of tenderness was smoothing her voice, "Lucius, why—why did you desert me?"

"'Twas ambition," he sighed. "Ambition reinforced by circumstances. I beg you to believe one thing—I have never loved—truly—anyone—but you, Sabra."

Gently, the kneeling girl fanned away a swarm of dreadfully persistent bluebottle flies. His teeth, all at once, seemed abnormally prominent and when he spoke again his eyes remained shut.

"I confess I loved you—yet, in my ambition I have wounded you—and others who befriended me."

"You hurt others?" Sabra prompted in a small and quiet voice. "Do—do I know of them?"

"Yes." He sighed several times and his breath grew

slower. "Asa and—and Peter Burnham, I have hurt them little less cruelly than you, Sabra dear. Should you ever see—" His voice faded but, when she started to speak, he reopened his eyes. "Pray indulge me—there is very little time left—I—I know." He sighed, another of those long sighs significant of a heart weary unto death. "D'you—recall—letter I said I found—in—in Asa's room?"

Sabra's eyes filled. By instinct she sensed what he intended to confess. "Never mind—I—think—I—"

"—I forged that letter, Sabra, because—wanted you—your family's wealth—position. And—destroyed farewell letter—he left—you—"

Steady footfalls, raised by a file of troops passing down the street, beat through the shed door. "Water please—bad for abdominal wounds—but can't harm me now." When he had sipped a little of the lukewarm fluid, he spoke a bit more clearly. "Please hear me out, Sabra. Peter was my friend, yet I ruined him by spreading a rumor—which set a mob upon him and may have caused his death."

"No! No. It didn't. He got away and is doing well."

"Praise the—Lord." By a Herculean effort Lucius thrust his remaining hand from beneath the gray overcoat. "Can they ever forgive my trespasses, Sabra?"

His last conscious sensation was of her hair brushing his cheek, the faint scent of that allspice with which he had always associated her. All but imperceptible, came the cool pressure of her lips on his forehead as he traversed that horizon which divides life from eternity.

XXVIII. ASA PEABODY, B.M.: HIS JOURNAL

ALTHOUGH A DEFINITE chill pervaded Doctor Peabody's office he was patient; as soon as the sun rose high enough to warm the slates not far above his head, it would disappear. Right now his eyes felt uncommon hot and tired.

Several moments passed before he perceived, lying among the papers on his desk, an envelope heavily sealed with brilliant yellow wax. Picking it up he turned it over and noted that a coat-of-arms he did not recognize was clearly impressed upon the seal. Something of this letter's general aspect piqued his curiosity. He ripped it open, glanced at the signature and, in mounting interest, read the signature as that of the Marquis de Menthon. Odd—this name was uppermost in his mind at that moment. He unfolded the letter, smoothed it and read in the handwriting of somebody other than the Marquis:

My dear Dr. Peabody:

Fortune plays many tricks. This day a naval officer of the fleet of M. de Barras was struck by that same resemblance which has puzzled us all and approached me. An explanation of our little mystery becomes quite simple. It appears that my great granduncle, Andre, having incurred the displeasure of Madame du Barry, was exiled to the interior of Canada. For fear of a worse fate the Comte Andre de Menthon gave out that he had been slain at an Iroquois ambush. Actually he voyaged with his family to an obscure region far to the north of Quebec where he and his descendants have lived as *petits seigneurs* ever since.

The last male of that line having died, she who had married the grandson of the original refugee determined to return to France to claim the title for her infant daughter. *Hélas*, the vessel, was cast away on the coast of Nova Scotia and only those in the boat occupied by Captain de Riom, who tells me this tale, were believed to have survived.

Because of the amazing family resemblance it cannot be doubted that your maid of mystery is other than the Comtesse Adrienne de Bussac-Menthon.

At the first opportunity I shall avail myself of the pleasure of kissing my fair cousin's hand. Until then, please accept, most distinguished sir,

My respectful service.

Well, there it was. Asa put down the de Methon letter and stared for a long while at the scarred door panels opposite his desk. So Hilde of the Red Lion Tavern was in fact of noble descent. But what good could this knowledge do now?

After devoting great pains over the cutting of a perfect point on his goose quill, he laid the plume before him and, from a drawer, produced his medical journal for, since adopting the Army, he had felt it incumbent upon him to record the histories of such puzzling or outstanding cases as reached his attention.

Once peace was restored it was his intention to review

these problems. Possibly fruitful conclusions could be derived from a study of present failures and successes.

Hum. So Hector de Lameth was mending and would live to bring further distinction to his name. That at least was good news.

Slowly, Asa reviewed the past forty-eight hours while rubbing his hands together to rid them of stiffness. As if his quill weighed pounds instead of ounces, the physician dipped its point deep into a portable lead ink bottle. Carefully, he then wrote:

CASE NO. 246.
>   The matter of H.M. (dL)
>   Female
>   Aged Approx. 20 yrs.

Symptomia:
   Grippe resolving into a severe Chill followed immediately by a Fever, Pulse high, 120 to the Minute.
   Query: Why doth no truly accurate thermometer exist? Record of the exact Degree of fever would appear of First importance. Thus could Danger be recognized & prompt treatment afforded.

Asa stopped writing. There could be no doubt that he and Peter had followed the most recent and highly considered treatment for peripneumony. All the same, Hilde de Lameth had grown increasingly feverish.

It was only then, that again and quite reluctantly, they had resorted to bleeding—although neither of them held that age-old practice to be definitely beneficial. For a little while Hilde had calmed down, but then her fever soared until she had relapsed into a further hallucination.

Eyes staring and rolling wildly, the stricken girl kept crying piteously for Hector. At length she had commenced talking in a language strange to Peter, but which Asa recognized as Mic-Mac. An incoherent jumble of German, French and English phrases escaped her pallid lips.

Asa's head sagged forward onto his chest and he tasted so great a bitterness that a groan escaped him. Savagely, he reproached himself.

"Should I have bled Hilde? I don't hold with the practice and yet—" What benefit could be derived from blistering a failing patient, despite opinions held by the most learned authorities? Why should it not be possible earlier to arrest, or eliminate the formation of a purulent tumor?

"Dear God," he prayed, "grant me the courage, the intelligence to seek the truth along paths yet untravelled."

His fingers were rasping over bristles standing out along his jaw when the office door suddenly swung open, admitting a brilliant flood of clean morning sunlight. Sabra stood there, hesitant, her eyes yet inflamed by the tears she had shed. Diffidently, she advanced towards the big figure sitting so crushed and weary behind his desk.

"Asa—oh Asa." She placed a light hand on his shoulder. "I can only guess how very downcast you must feel this morning. I wish to say by way of comfort that no living physician could have struggled harder, could have done more to save poor Hilde. Please Asa—don't reproach yourself so—I—I—can't bear it." Her voice softened. "The Lord's will was being fulfilled. Think on how your art saved Captain de Lameth—your art and no one else's. You and Peter did everything possible for Hilde."

"Aye. Everything—and nothing," Asa muttered and got to his feet.

In silence, he gave to Sabra the Marquis de Methon's letter, then watched surprise briefly animate her weary features, a surprise which soon gave way to an expression of infinite sadness.

"How tragic this letter came only now," she murmured. "Poor Hilde wanted so desperately to learn who she was, and to whom she belonged." Sabra looked up, gray eyes brimming. "This intelligence, at least, will afford Hector de Lameth some consolation. He will be greatly pleased to learn she was as gently born as himself. The French are odd about such things, aren't they?"

"Yes, they set quite a store by family," Asa replied heavily.

"You are most kind to—to have come to see me, Sabra, especially when you lack even more sleep than either Peter or I."

"Asa?" A sudden intensity in Sabra's expression surprised and puzzled him.

"Yes?"

"I have something to tell you."

"Yes?"

"You know I went to York Town?"

"Yes, Sabra, I heard that you did."

"I went to seek out Lucius Devoe."

"*Lucius!*"

"Yes," Sabra explained, "I had reason to believe him to be serving with the Anspach Regiment."

Asa frowned. "You sought Lucius, after—"

"Yes. I found him, Asa, and watched over him—as—as he died."

"Poor, unhappy devil—"

"Asa," Sabra moved closer, her gray eyes luminous. "I received those letters of yours—from Machias but, because Lucius had lied to me, I never even opened them."

"Lied, how?"

"He forged a letter purporting to come from some girl in Machias and reminding that you were promised to marry her. Then, when you left Boston so very abruptly—I—well, I believed him—the more because he had destroyed your letter of explanation."

Tense in every muscle, Asa listened and, understanding so many things all in an instant, was rendered speechless.

"Do you recall when first we met here in Williamsburg, when I asked if you had married in Machias?"

"Yes. I married but 'twas near two years later," he explained gently. "And to a woman I had never met before coming to Boston."

"Peter told me that she—she died."

"Aye. She is dead. Did you really love Lucius?"

Slowly Sabra's eyes rose. "I believed that I did, Asa, but I know now that my love for Lucius was unreal as a false dawn which precedes true daybreak and, I—I—oh, Asa, try to comprehend—to—"

"Sabra! Sabra! How much happiness we have lost— but how much more lies before us."

As easily as a doe slips into a thicket, Sabra Stanton entered the stout protection of his arms.

MORE EXCITING HISTORICAL FICTION
NOW AVAILABLE FROM BERKLEY